Joint Eagles

Robert C. Hagan

Steve,

Hope you

enjoy

[signature]

Joint Eagles
Robert C. Hagan

ISBN 0-9728303-0-8

Library of Congress Control Number: 2003090296

Printed in the United States of America
by Mennonite Press, Inc., Newton KS 67114

This is a work of fiction. Names, characters, places, facilities, companies and incidents either are the product of the author's imagination or are used fictitiously, and any resemblance to actual persons, places, facilities, corporate entities or events is entirely coincidental.

INTRODUCTION

BEFORE the horrific attacks of 9-11-01, the adventure Joint Eagles was conceived, drafted and copyrighted with revisions continuing until the moment of printing. Employing my experience in the nuclear field, I envisioned a plausible nuclear terrorist threat aimed at disabling the United States; a scheme with reverberations world-wide forces old enemies to work together. Russia and the U.S. cautiously combine their best intelligence and high-tech weapons-of-war to blunt the threat.

Events in Joint Eagles engulf two American citizens, Ben and Laura Andrew, in a swirl of danger and international intrigue, during which they discover their destiny as well as a surprising ability to persevere in the face of terror.

The story rises to a crescendo in each of three parts of Joint Eagles: Conspiracy, War, Revenge. Yet the ultimate climax doesn't occur until the end, as the survival of Ben and Laura Andrew and the mysterious role of the ubiquitous Professor Dudaev remain in doubt.

In no small measure, my admiration for Russia's great writers and the courageous Soviet dissidents, many of whom overcame terrible adversity in the expression of their ideas, inspired this story. Also my desire to expose our vulnerabilities to new amorphous terrorist organizations steered this saga. The eventual triumph of the human spirit provides a dominant theme that will inspire the reader.

But they that wait upon the Lord
shall renew their strength; they
shall mount up with wings as eagles;
they shall run, and not be weary;
and they shall walk and not faint.

ISAIAH 40:31

ACKNOWLEDGEMENTS

Through their tireless editing, typing, cover design and encouragement, my supportive family made this story possible.

The literary inculcation of this engineer by Hazel Dalbom, a retired Kansas English teacher, was invaluable and *Joint Eagles* benefited greatly from her persistent labors.

Dr. Helga Scheer, a talented editor, offered brilliant suggestions that synchronized and streamlined the story, while augmenting the dimensions of the main characters.

Col. Dale Soderstrom proved to be a fountain of military information that enhanced the authenticity of the war sections.

There were many other important contributors to whom I am most grateful, but a special thanks is extended to Dr. Dean Eckhoff for his kind recommendation of *Joint Eagles*.

CONTENTS

PROLOGUE

October 23, 1970 3 P.M. National Jumping Arena Stuttgart, Germany

The baby cried and the nanny railed, "This baby is sick. Very sick! She needs help. If we do nothing, she dies."

Trying to ignore the ranting, the KGB agents hunched their shoulders as if fending off a biting Siberian wind.

The nanny though, would not be turned away. "You idiots! You better listen."

The older agent turned to his junior partner, "Tell her to shut up."

"Not me. You can if you are brave enough."

The senior agent couldn't let that challenge go, "Shut up, old woman."

"No. Our champion's baby dies, thanks to you heartless *duraks*. Not good. Shame! Shame!"

The Soviet security agents were trapped by the old woman. Their sole job was to accompany the Soviet Union's riding team to guard against defections. The Soviet competitors were doing well. Marina Tarasova, the final rider, had excelled throughout the competition and was on the verge of bringing the Soviets their first world team championship. The KGB guards knew that they dare not mess up this grand opportunity for Soviet propaganda. Yet there must be no escape.

"How revolting that Marina's baby gets sick at this awkward moment," lamented the senior agent.

Finally he found a solution. Marina Tarasova would go nowhere without her child, so he directed, "Comrade, take the bawling brat and this fussy old hen to the hospital. We will watch Marina and the rest of the team."

He and the other agents would remain on guard as Marina completed the competition. He congratulated himself on his creative solution. His superiors would be proud of him. No escape. No dead baby. Not on his watch.

After the child, the nanny, and the younger agent sped away toward the Katharinen Hospital in downtown Stuttgart, the senior Soviet agent elbowed his way through the crowd. He must be at the fence to monitor Tarasova's final jumps.

With admiration he watched as the elegant Soviet rider and her horse, Khan, performed flawlessly. The dappled-gray Tersk, bred in the northern Caucasus region, was jumping brilliantly under Tarasova's guidance. The grand horse and the slender rider, resplendent in her red habit, comprised a strikingly beautiful team.

Without hesitation, the stallion pranced toward the most difficult combination jumps. Exhibiting a ballet-like grace, he cleared the final challenging hurdles. It was accomplished. The championship belonged to the Soviet team.

Amidst the swelling ovation for the flawless performance, the unexpected happened. Absent any warning, the gray stallion veered off course and raced straight for the distant fence. The ovation abruptly subsided and the shocked crowd collectively gasped as horse and rider sailed over the far fence.

The senior agent stared aghast as the great Tersk galloped away from the arena. Tarasova and her charger headed across the adjoining field, which had earlier served as the venue for the cross-country phase of the competition. Unerringly the gray champion raced for a remote wooded corner. There was little doubt. This was no runaway, rather it must be an escape.

The agent swore in disbelief, "Damn *Merzavetz!*"

Knocking aside all in his way, he bulled through the crowd toward his nearby car. He barked orders to the driver to follow horse and rider.

Swerving around the jumping arena, the black roadster broke brazenly through the fence and sped along the soft grassy path the horse had just traveled. They were gaining. The champion rider would soon be back in communist hands, except that the car began to lose traction. The wheels spun and the heavy vehicle slowed. Inevitably, it bogged down in the middle of the soggy field. The agent was furious. He would not be defeated this easily!

He grabbed his rifle and leaped from the car. Racing on foot after the rapidly retreating pair was obviously futile. Tarasova and her horse were about to reach the safety of the woods. Yet, his standing orders were clear. No one escaped from the Soviet Union. He leveled his rifle at the fleeing animal. A series of staccato shots rang out in a profane violation of the peaceful valley. The mortally wounded champion staggered, but refused to fall. The game stallion snorted in defiance. Unsteadily, he loped on.

With horse and rider about to enter the woods, the KGB guard turned assassin. He hurriedly reloaded the rifle and took aim at Tarasova's back. Before he could squeeze the trigger, a shot from the woods found its mark. A hole materialized between his eyes. He was dead before his body struck the damp sod.

Throughout the pursuit, the German officials did not react. Only an hour earlier they had been warned by their superiors to stay out of any unexpected developments surrounding the Soviet team.

Unaware of the fate of her pursuers, Marina Tarasova, carried by her courageous jumper, reached the safety of the forest. At the edge of the dense woods, she slid from the failing horse and led him the final yards. Just as promised, a jeep and soldiers were waiting. Two heavily armed commandos met her. A third stared intently along the path she had just navigated.

The stallion, eyes ablaze with pain, sank to its knees. The two soldiers forcibly tore Marina's arms from around his neck. They carried the distraught equestrian toward the awaiting jeep. Seeing that the horse was mortally wounded and in obvious agony, the third commando, who knew and loved horses, fired one well placed shot. Khan's suffering came to an abrupt end.

While restraining the hysterical Marina, the three soldiers scrambled aboard the jeep and headed down a narrow, winding trail, which eventually opened onto the autobahn.

Looking back Marina cried, "Khan, Khan, I'm sorry Khan!"

She broke down sobbing. Yet despite her tears she realized that her baby's life and her own depended upon her thinking clearly. She must remain calm.

Taking a deep breath in an attempt to regain her composure, Marina demanded, "Is my baby safe?"

"Yes, it goes well. You will see her at the airfield."

As tears, that would not be denied, streamed down her face, Marina softly disagreed, "It goes not well. Not for my Khan. He is dead. If I had known this would happen, I would never have agreed to escape."

The commando sitting next to her was uneasy. He didn't understand women, especially when they were distraught, but he did understand horses and warriors. Khan was both rolled into one magnificent package. He could only mumble, "He was the greatest of champions."

October 23, 1970 6:15 P.M. NATO Airfield

The jeep carrying Marina and the commandos roared across the tarmac toward the Military Air Transport plane. The DC-7, with its engines throbbing, was poised for a long journey. Marina spotted her baby in the nanny's arms at the bottom of the plane's steps.

Before the jeep screeched to a stop, Marina jumped out. She raced toward her child. Tears of relief and gratitude streamed down Marina's face as she reached for her girl. In her excitement, she cradled the infant almost too tightly. "Laura, my soul. Thank God you are safe."

The leader of the commandos cut short the reunion and hustled Marina, her baby, and the nanny up the stairs. "Hurry! We must get you airborne."

He knew that the Soviets would lodge a protest and pull all strings necessary to get Marina back, except they wouldn't know to whom to protest. To maintain absolute secrecy the fugitives must be flown out immediately and subsequently vanish. All official Western organizations would deny any knowledge of the escape and indeed, although they had helped, none of them had masterminded the getaway.

Once on board, Marina continued to protectively tend her one-year-old. The thunder of the engines washed over mother and baby. The torrent of sound, though, could not drown out the haunting rifle shots which still echoed in her mind. She resolved that she must be brave. She would not remember Khan as the dying horse, but rather as the graceful jumper, who brought a championship to the country she loved. Bringing her back from the nightmare of Khan's death, the baby's nanny gushed an explanation of the events at the hospital.

She proudly reported, "I fool KGB good. The sour milk I gave the baby made her stomach cramp, so she cried. A simple pill caused a fever. That and my yelling fooled the bullies. At the hospital we went to the emergency room. There, it was almost funny. An ambulance screeched up. Women in white coats wheeled in a gurney. It rolled right past our KGB guard. Then the blankets flew off and a man with a silent gun sat up and shot our guard. He threw him on the gurney and covered him with the same blankets. Then the women and the man with the gun took us to the ambulance, which brought us here. The rest you know."

As she listened to the tale, Marina marveled at how precisely the escape was executed. Whoever conceived of this rescue left little to chance. Once the plane leveled off, the exhausted nanny fell asleep. This was Marina's chance to check on her clandestine cargo.

While cradling the slumbering baby in one arm, she pulled the baby bag from the snoring nanny's lap. She felt for the secret pocket in the bag, found the hidden zipper and slowly coaxed it open. Yes! The papers were still there.

She somewhat understood their importance. The dissident who brought them to her a month ago had partially explained things. A father, whom she had never known, had written this collection of essays, letters and poems. Due to the recent Soviet crackdown on the dissidents, the safety of the papers could no longer be assured. They must be smuggled out or they would be lost forever.

Marina was told to deliver the secret collection to a man whom she would meet upon her arrival in the U.S. Despite her relief to be free of the Soviets, a surging melancholy overcame her. Would she ever see Russia again? Were these papers' survival and her and her baby's freedom worth Khan's sacrifice and the deaths of her countrymen? Would her daughter really have a better life in the West or would danger pursue them wherever they fled? The tears flowed again as the engines droned on. Did those who arranged this desparate exodus care about her and baby Laura or only the secret papers?

The commando leader who had shepherded the entourage aboard the plane had watched as the plane rumbled down the runway and lifted into the sky. Once it had disappeared in the evening haze, he sighed in relief. Mission accomplished. He returned to a nearby NATO building, where he called his temporary boss. Proudly the soldier reported that Marina and her baby were on their way to U.S. soil.

It had been a strange mission. His select British commando unit had taken orders from an American civilian whom he had never seen and whose name he didn't even know. His Army commander had instructed him that the mystery man, who had a barely perceptible East-European accent, was his superior for the entire exercise. No questions were to be asked. Ever.

PART I
Conspiracy

CHAPTER
ONE

January 10, 2005 Washington, D. C.

Mr. Fred Bumgardner, we are preparing several videos for your family and hometown press. Enclosed is a complimentary copy for your amusement. Pictures of you and the pretty girl exploited for your extracurricular pleasures should leave nothing to the imagination of your faithful wife. Does Mrs. Bumgardner tolerate your philandering?

Let us clarify. You resign from your job immediately, with no complications, and these videos will disappear. Any wavering, Mr. Bumgardner, and things will become very uncomfortable for you!

Bumgardner's hands shook spasmodically. He dropped the note. As it fluttered to the floor, he shoved the cassette into the VCR. Suddenly, like a cheap, X-rated movie, his dalliance materialized before him. He cringed as detail after intimate detail of the now shameful episode unfolded.

Trapped, alone and hopeless, he despaired. The overwhelming depression, which had recently suffocated him, came flooding back, more debilitating than before. Walls of cold, gray stone closed upon him. Reason failed. He felt dirty. Unrelenting pain throbbed inside his head. He grasped only that he faced the loss of wife, job and reputation. Everything precious to him was gone forever. That this might be a setup, that an evil global force might have orchestrated his unfaithfulness, never crossed his mind.

He stuffed the incriminating video and the threatening note into his coat pocket and reached for his pistol. Still wearing yesterday's rumpled clothes, he moved unsteadily toward the hotel room door.

In a daze he descended the hotel's stairs and crossed the lobby. Once out of the main entrance, he collapsed into the rear seat of a waiting Yellow Cab. Slurring slightly he whispered, "Drop me at Roosevelt Memorial Park." He figured that the heavily wooded sections of that Potomac Island would suffice.

While the flat-faced Uzbek driver weaved his cab through the evening's traffic, he shook his head, marveling at what sick birds roost around the city. This bum in the back seat was either stoned or loony tunes, as the Americans said.

The disapproving immigrant adjusted his blue and orange Mets ball cap, as though gearing up for action. He had no way of knowing that his passenger's anguish started when a severe nuclear "accident" opened the door for a NuEnergy takeover of the Texas power plants.

The stale stench of tobacco seeping from the cab's upholstery gagged Bumgardner. He fumbled with the handle in an attempt to open the window. It wouldn't budge. Forced to live with the putrid fumes, he dully recalled his last hectic days as Texas Power's chief engineer. He was sure that the accident at his plant was no accident at all. The Feds never had a clue as to what really happened to his plant. The idiots wouldn't listen to him. That plant was done in on purpose. It was sabotage for sure.

He had watched in agony as his bosses fell into a trap leading straight to hell. That God-awful mess cost Texas Power billions. The whole world blamed him for the damned delays and the crushing costs. No one saw it for the sabotage it was.

NuEnergy swooped in like vultures after a road kill. They ripped off Texas Power big time. He had seen chickens plucked with more difficulty than his upper management was stripped bare by NuEnergy. Within months after the "Nuclear Accident," the NuEnergy takeover was wrapped up.

Bumgardner did not notice how aggressively his cabby was cutting in and out of traffic. He coughed. The stale tobacco fumes irritated his nose and throat. His mouth was too dry to swallow. Yet a flood of unwelcome recollections washed through his mind.

The NuEnergy bunch was crooked to the core. They would siphon off his company's wealth and after they were long gone, Texas Power would be left with three worthless plants. But, Bumgardner lamented, that was no longer his damned problem.

After several minutes of fighting through the downtown D.C. traffic, the Uzbeki sensed something was amiss. He checked his rear-view mirror again. This time he caught a black Lincoln running a red light and recklessly turning from the wrong lane. Upon further scrutiny he became convinced that the car was tailing them.

"What is this?" he puzzled.

Rousing from his profound self-pity, Bumgardner became slightly more aware of his surroundings. His watery eyes alerted him that they were nearing the Roosevelt Memorial parking lot. Thank God, the pain would end soon.

The cabby turned from George Washington Memorial Parkway into the parking lot. He hastily collected his fare, then eagerly abandoned his disoriented passenger. Not waiting to see if the stricken man could manage to shuffle from the parking lot to the island, he aimed straight for the exit. When the persistent Lincoln pulled in just as he was leaving, he gathered that something bad was about to happen. He gunned it. His tires squealed in protest as he raced back onto the highway.

Unaware of time or his surroundings, Bumgardner in his rumpled brown suit wandered aimlessly about the island. Finally, emotionally and physically exhausted, he slumped down on a remote bench.

He sunk still deeper into an abyss of guilt and hopelessness. He shoved the cold muzzle of the .357 magnum against his temple and froze in that position for what seemed an eternity. His wrist went limp. The gun fell onto the park bench. He couldn't do it. Sobbing, he bent forward and clasped his tear-stained face in his cold and trembling hands.

Chiseled in that downcast posture, he failed to see or hear the approach of the stranger. The well-dressed man was only a step away when he authoritatively announced, "Sir, handguns are illegal here. I'll take that."

Startled, Bumgardner peered upward. His blurred vision revealed a confusing, dark image of a man reaching for the gun. Before he could react the assassin thrust the magnum against his head and fired.

Bumgardner's body sagged back against the bench. His bleeding head hung askew and his arms dropped lifelessly to his sides.

The gloved executioner carefully placed the weapon in his victim's hand. After a brief search, he found and removed the incriminating video and the threatening note from the dead man's coat. Then he faded swiftly from the scene.

The black of the D.C. night waxed intense, like a play where all stage lights were extinguished and an opaque curtain descended.

CHAPTER
TWO

One Year Later January 15, 2006 9:50 A.M.
Black Bear Nuclear Plant Near Tulsa, Oklahoma

The dense fog blanketing northeastern Oklahoma deepened as the warm, moist Gulf air crept north over the cold, red earth. Resisting the weak winter sun's futile attempts to burn it away, the persistent fog bank cast a pall over the area.

Two technicians, dressed as state park officials, ferried their equipment across the Arkansas River. Carrying just enough sampling gear to support their ruse, the two posed as state biologists running a mid-winter game survey. The heavy fog, offering essential cover, fashioned an eerie river crossing. They literally couldn't see where the fog ended and the water began. The sound of the paddles dipping into the river offered reassurance that the water was still there beneath their boat. Despite their inability to see past the boat's bow, their precision Global Positioning System (GPS) receiver and compass led them unerringly to the east river bank.

A sudden beating of wings, first against water, then against air, testified to a frightened flight of surprised waterfowl.

The phony biologist snickered to his companion, "Guess ve should count them since ve on survey. Sounds like maybe ten?"

"Yep. How fitting. That bunch spooked, but our target flock still sits fat, dumb and happy," scoffed the leader

"And that's how ve vant it," responded his companion.

After beaching their boat, they hauled their gear through the knee-high corn stubble, damp from the fog and last night's rain. The iridescent yellow Fish and Game uniforms of the two imposters shone brightly enough that, despite the fog, they could make out each other.

Their GPS receiver and compass again led them precisely to the desired location, just outside of Black Bear's double security fence.

They spent the next hour busily setting up, adjusting and then readjusting their precision gear. Two tripods topped with their high-tech equipment pointed ominously in the direction of the plant. Despite being unable to see their nearby target, they located it with great accuracy. The sophisticated radar gave them a precise image of the metal pole and the protective box perched on top of it. Inside the metallic housing was the objective, a remotely operated plant surveillance camera.

12:05 P.M. Black Bear Service Road

Despite being able to see only a few yards, a lone runner pressed forward along Black Bear's gravel perimeter road. Clad in a dull green and black North Ridge warm-up suit, the lithe lunch-hour jogger reveled in his good fortune.

Good, he thought. Finally, just as the Channel Seven weatherman predicted, heavy fog, thick as vintage borscht, smothers the plant. At last, it is a go.

The plant worker, installed recently at Black Bear by NuEnergy over the strong objections of the plant's Technical Services Manager, glanced nervously at his watch. Eager to take full advantage of this rare opportunity, he carefully counted the passing fence posts, "Forty-five, forty-six..."

Following the interior service road paralleling the plant's double security fence, Helmut clogged onward. He checked his watch again and slowed his pace.

Today the nearby high-voltage power lines were invisible, as were the titanic plant structures. The hum of the unseen lines, though, attested to their presence. The buzzing overhead cables, alive with power, stretched from the plant's nearby electrical switchyard west toward Oklahoma City.

The runner and his well-rehearsed allies had thoroughly examined aerial photos of the place. Now that study paid off, for even with poor visibility, they knew precisely where everything was located.

12:06 P.M. Cornfield bordering Black Bear

Finally the wait was over. All preparations were completed and the precise second for action was at hand. From the imposters' hidden location, an intense red flash of laser light cut through the gray fog toward the targeted housing. The beam quickly seared a tiny hole in the metal box and then melted Black Bear's camera controls. The camera instantly ceased relaying images to the security control room.

Seizing the opportunity offered by the temporary blind spot in Black Bear's security perimeter, the technicians, at exactly 12:06, launched their battery-powered, computer-guided plane. With a wingspan of six feet, the stealthy phantom, fabricated of space-age composites, climbed above the motion sensors and disappeared into the fog bank. Carrying its explosive cargo, the gray ghost passed undetected a few feet away from the now defunct camera.

12:06:30 P.M. Black Bear's Service Road

Helmut, a Bulgarian immigrant, was jogging slower now and carefully counting, "ninety-two, ninety-three, ninety-four. Izz it, ninety-five."

He paused while checking the time. Perfect! Exactly 12:06:30, but where the hell was the plane?

He squinted in a futile attempt to pierce the gray fog. Frantically he scanned the nearby fence and the thick air above it. Suddenly there it was. The miniature plane soared smoothly over the barriers and descended, exactly as programmed. It landed on the gravel road no more than twenty feet in front of him.

Just as he had practiced a dozen times, he deftly detached the package from the plane, placed the payload securely in his backpack, and flipped a switch, launching the pre-programmed plane back over the fence to his partners. All of his well-rehearsed maneuvers took less than thirty seconds.

12:07 P.M. Black Bear's Security Control Room

"Lieutenant Miller, we just lost camera eight."

"Shit! On the foggiest day of the century! The backup cam is no help in this soup so there's a hole in our surveillance. It must be plugged! Who is out there?"

"Hutchens and Stuart."

"Are they on the inside?"

"Yes, sir."

"Good. Tell them to haul ass over there pronto and stay 'til told otherwise."

"Will do."

12:09 P.M. Black Bear's Service Road

As Helmut watched the retreating plane merge into the gray mist, he heard a small pickup truck racing his way. He promptly resumed his lunch-hour jog. Passing the rushing plant patrol vehicle he waved to the guards, who were accustomed to seeing him out here every noon hour. Because of the load of explosives in his pack, the balance of his workout was slightly more strenuous than normal, but far more rewarding. Now he could quit this lunch-hour running façade. He didn't like jogging. Never had.

He stored his precious package where it would not be found. His comrade, the new NuEnergy plant manager, had a locker in the executive gym, which should suffice. Soon these explosives would be put to good use. Until then he must study every detail of the switchyard.

12:10 P.M. Black Bear's Service Road

The guard, driving the truck, fussed, "This sure as hell is boring duty. Here we sit on our asses watching the fog roll in. Nothing exciting ever happens at Black Bear."

"That's not true," the other guard sarcastically disagreed. "Remember the dog, Lucky."

"Oh, yeah. The poor critter that wandered in here."

"That's the one. The idiots on night shift chased him all over."

"I remember now. They clubbed the 'security threat' to death didn't they."

"Yes, and that won't be forgotten soon. Some joker still sneaks onto the plant intercom pretending to be the dog's owner and plaintively calls, 'Here Neutron, here Neutron.'"

CHAPTER
THREE

Once again, Dr. Ben Andrew, the Technical Services Manager, was summoned to Zoglemann's office. Ben knew what faced him, but he intended to resist, even if he incurred the plant manager's wrath.

"Dr. Andrew, why haven't you done as directed? You must give the switchyard drawings to Helmut. What don't you understand about my instructions?"

Yep. Here we go again, Ben thought. This drawings spat was merely the latest in a series of disagreements between him and this NuEnergy rube.

Ben distrusted the new plant manager. As he saw it, Zoglemann was brought in as a NuEnergy stooge, who by deliberately corrupting the plant's once sound engineering, procurement, and maintenance practices, was endangering the plant. The why behind those changes could not be good. The scheme, it appeared to him, was to increase short-term profits while sacrificing the long-term health of the plant. Ben knew that shortchanging maintenance would eventually compromise the safety and viability of Black Bear.

"Dr. Andrew, give Helmut those drawings before you leave here tonight. Is that clear?"

Ben, with what he believed were good reasons, intended to defy this order. He replied, "I respectfully disagree. He has no need for them. Plus, he wasn't given an adequate security check. Give him a real screening and then we will talk about the drawings."

From the start Ben had reason to be wary of Zoglemann. Zoglemann was the same guy imposed upon the Texas plants after the NuEnergy takeover there. This Zoglemann apparently was the point man for the changes NuEnergy imposed upon their new acquisitions. The jerk had certainly made life miserable at Texas for his friend, Fred Bumgardner, and he was trying the same thing on him. Maybe Zoglemann was finding out that Ben was a different kettle of fish. Unlike the late mild-mannered Bumgardner, Ben actually relished a good fight.

Despite Helmut's not being the most qualified candidate interviewed for the engineering opening, Zoglemann had insisted that he be hired, and over Ben's objections, had forced him into the engineering organization. Zoglemann and Helmut were close, too close Ben figured.

After learning that Helmut's background check had been waived by Zoglemann, Ben had done some sleuthing. He asked a close friend, an Oklahoma highway patrolman who had served with him on the same submarine, to look into the employee's background. Word came back to Ben of Helmut's extensive criminal past in Bulgaria.

Armed with that knowledge, even under the threat of being fired, Ben was not about to turn over sensitive material to Helmut.

In the face of Ben's defiance, the red-faced Plant Manager gritted his yellowed teeth and announced, "This is unacceptable! You need to re-think your position."

"I'll think about a lot of things, including how to protect the security and safety of this plant from your unwise directions."

"Is that so! Then perhaps a change of venue is in order. Let me remind you that NuEnergy has offered you a very generous severance package. I strongly advise that you seriously re-consider it."

After that thinly veiled warning, Ben was summarily dismissed by the seething plant manager.

January 22, 2006 6:04 P.M. Black Bear Plant Manager's Office

In response to a blinking red light on his desk, Zoglemann reached into a nearby cabinet. He grabbed the hidden phone and pressed it to his ear. He proceeded to eavesdrop intently on Dr. Andrew's cell phone conversation.

"Laura, I am on my way home. I had another run-in with Zoglemann. Things are getting worse. Actually the atmosphere's downright hostile. Anyone here with an ounce of ethics is in trouble."

Zoglemann couldn't help smiling at Andrew's remark about trouble, for it was far truer than the problem manager knew.

"Oh, no! I was afraid of that," Laura said.

"I didn't mean to worry you, Laura. Maybe it's not as bad as I make out."

"It is bad, and it is time for you to get out of there, Ben. Take their severance deal. I'm worried for you."

Zoglemann chuckled to himself, "Good advice, little woman. He would do well to listen to you."

Ben had expected that counsel from Laura. He had heard it before. "I don't want to get out yet, Laura. I have too much invested in this plant to just quit."

Zoglemann slammed the phone down snorting, "You just sealed your own fate, Doctor."

He picked up the desktop phone. "He is on the road. Everything is ready. Finish it."

Zoglemann hung up. He had his fill of the obstinate Doctor. He figured that the man had chosen his own fate. Too bad that he hadn't listened to his wife.

January 22, 2006 6:15 P.M. Oklahoma State Highway 104

Eagerly placing miles between himself and Black Bear, Ben steered his forest green Blazer west along the darkened, and nearly deserted, two-lane state highway. Since the hundreds of plant workers had already left for the day, rush hour was over. Deserted was good tonight, since his preoccupation with problems at the plant diverted his attention from his driving.

Nothing made sense. Events at the plant were becoming downright ominous. The plant accident nine months ago, which, in Ben's opinion, was no accident at all, had started a string of malevolent events.

No. That's not right. It actually started a year earlier, with the coolant loss at the Texas plant. His good friend, Fred Bumgardner, God rest his soul, was convinced that one of the Texas plants had been sabotaged. Ben had always suspected that his friend had been right. Then Black Bear also went down in an odd way. He had never seen control rods respond as they did on that fateful day. They had moved out when they should have gone in. It had to be sabotage. What a coincidence that both plants suffered a similar fate. But the coincidences didn't stop there. NuEnergy rushed in to take advantage of both the Texas and the Oklahoma predicaments.

In many ways his circumstances paralleled Bumgardner's. Ben was the manager, who stood in NuEnergy's way here, just as had

Bumgardner at Texas. Ben was starting to pay for his stance. His career at Black Bear was in serious jeopardy. NuEnergy obviously wanted him out. His responsibilities were being steadily stripped away.

Reaching the crest of a hill, he spotted a farm tractor dead ahead. He slammed on the brakes. The tires screeched as he swerved to narrowly avoid a collision. Shaken by the close shave, he swore, "Damn! Why was that idiot out here at this time of night?"

Ben didn't notice that the Blazer's brake warning light lit up after the encounter. Instead he renewed his mulling over of plant events.

Everything about NuEnergy reeked of corruption. The Bulgarian turkey, Helmut, whom Zoglemann hired and forced into his Technical Services group, was one strange duck. The guy didn't take any direction from his supervisors or Ben. The weirdo and Zoglemann were thicker than thieves. This kook ran every noon hour, just like clockwork, and then suddenly this week he stopped. Said he had a cold. But as far as Ben could tell, he didn't even have a sniffle. Ben knew runners and this stocky guy was no distance runner.

Ben tried to distract himself from these troubling thoughts by focusing on his wife's birthday. She was thirty-seven years old today and more beautiful than ever. He wanted to make this birthday special because it was the first one she would celebrate without her beloved mother, who had died last year.

Before marrying Laura, he had never fathomed how close a mother and daughter could be. It was a closeness that he appreciated, for her mother had, in so many ways, nurtured the wonderfully talented woman whom he had married.

The intersection with the busy US-64 had slipped up on him. He hit the brakes hard. Nothing! He pumped the pedal. Still nothing! He jammed down the emergency brake pedal. No effect! His heart leaped into his throat. He was headed straight for the heavy cross traffic.

Reacting instinctively, he sensed only one slim chance to avoid a collision. He floored the accelerator and dodged between a narrow gap in the speeding cars. But he was still in deep trouble.

Highway 104 ended here, so after flashing across the busy federal highway, he hit the far ditch doing about eighty-five. His Blazer impacted the bottom of the ditch hard. After a couple of ferocious bounces, it careened onto its side and slid through a farm fence, where it plowed a wide furrow in a muddy milo field. Finally, covered in mud, it came to rest upside down.

Shaken and hurting, Ben hung upside down. He took inventory, realizing that his seat belt, air bag and the wonderful, red mud had just saved his life. He thanked God for the recent mid-winter thaw, which created the soggy mess. With one well-muscled arm he held enough of his weight so that the seat harness slackened. He released the seat belt and fell to the roof. Then he kicked out a window and crawled out into the cold, wet stubble.

8:15 P.M. Tulsa General Hospital's Emergency Center

After receiving a call from the Highway Patrol, Laura rushed to the Emergency Center. She was worried. She had just lost her mother and now Ben was in an accident. What else could go wrong?

Upon arriving, Laura worriedly quizzed the head nurse, "How is he? Is he okay?"

The nurse replied, "He is pretty beat-up, but will be fine. You can go on back and see for yourself."

Finding Ben, she fretted, "Your clothes are a mess. It looks like you wallowed in mud."

"That's because I did, dear."

"Are you sure you are okay?"

"They tell me I am."

After listening to Ben's description of the accident, Laura, with tears in her eyes, suggested, "You need to tell your patrolman friend to inspect the Blazer."

"I already did. I want to know just what happened to the brakes."

"And so do I. Ben, for God's sake, if they were tampered with, then that's it. No more procrastinating. You leave that place!"

"We have been through all of this before. I can't. You know that I just can't walk away."

One reason for staying remained unexpressed by Ben. They had borrowed a sizable sum to open their bookstore. He really needed the income from his job until the bookstore could stand on its own financially.

Laura had her reasons for her stance as well. Her good friend, Sally Bumgardner, had from time to time confided in her about what Fred had endured at Texas. This situation at Black Bear was looking way too familiar to her, so Laura wasn't about to give up. "Ben, you must listen to me. This accident proves it. Something profoundly evil has invaded Black Bear. Everything and everyone good will be destroyed by them."

With tears flowing, she resolutely added, "If those brakes were tampered with, I'm calling Mark Foster."

"Don't be silly. He is way too busy with important stuff. He doesn't have time for our petty problems."

"NuEnergy is a lot more than just our problem. Nothing about them is petty. There is a pattern to their actions that scares me."

"You are just borrowing trouble, Laura, based on what happened to Fred. Fred and I are different. I enjoy a fight. He wasn't like that. He really couldn't stand conflict. It made him nervous."

Laura shrugged for she still wasn't convinced. She intended to call Mark Foster if they found that Ben's car had been messed with.

On the way home, Ben reached for the birthday card he had salvaged from his wrecked car.

"Happy birthday, Laura. I'm afraid it got a little muddy." As he handed her the soiled card he apologized, "Sorry I didn't get home in time for dinner. I'll make it up to you, dear."

"I know." Laura was bombarded with conflicting emotions and suppressed a nearly overwhelming urge to cry. "It's okay, Ben. I'm just glad you are alive."

Ben knew what lay behind that poignant comment. Laura's mother's recent death had been preceded by the sudden death of their only child, Ryan, three years ago. Laura was still struggling to come to terms with those losses. If it was so important to Laura, maybe he really should re-think leaving Black Bear. After all, a job and the financial security it brought wasn't nearly as important as Laura's sense of well being.

Attempting to reassure her that all would be well, he embraced her tenderly.

CHAPTER
FOUR

Day 1 February 1, 2006 10:30 P.M. White House Lawn

"Mr. President! Mr. President!" The shouts drifted away, lost in the cold, damp wind that whistled across the frozen White House grounds.

Undeterred by the biting chill, President Grant Arthur strode briskly across the south lawn past the famous landmark fountain and away from the fruitless shouts emanating from the White House. On these raw winter evenings, Arthur observed that few, if any, tourists were either hardy or foolish enough to be out beyond the tall, black, wrought iron fence that surrounded the White House grounds. Tonight, no one was out, save his contingent of Secret Service agents joining him on his impromptu walk about the grounds. They obviously enjoyed the diversion but remained nervously alert as his safety was their singular responsibility.

President Arthur quickly discovered that his alpaca sweater and light jacket weren't up to the job of protecting his lanky frame from a biting D.C. winter wind. He would have to go shopping one of these days for a warmer coat. Catching the irony of that thought, he laughed aloud, startling the nearby agent. His carefree shopping days were history.

Suddenly, in response to the faint shouts, the nearest agent moved protectively to a more advantageous covering position

"It's okay," the President reassured the tense man. "Don't shoot. I actually need Don," he mused.

Don North sprinted across the lawn with a shortened stride brought on by the relentless stiffening of middle age and the cowboy boots that made footing uncertain on the frozen turf. Closing the distance, he breathlessly repeated, "Mr. President! Mr. President! The Russian President is on the line. He's waiting…wants to talk with you right away. Says it's important. God damn, it's hard to catch you when you get rolling."

A longtime friend, Don North had been the first of the White House team chosen by the President. President Arthur picked him as his White House Chief of Staff for his superior administrative skills, political savvy and unquestioned loyalty, attributes demonstrated as the Arizona Governor's executive assistant. Also, maybe his choice of North was a somewhat roguish move in that North's brutal bluntness and earthy language, born in the Southwest oil and gas fields, totally rankled the Washington sophisticates.

"Mr. President, you'd better start wearing more than that. We aren't in sunny Arizona anymore, Cowboy. It's colder out here than a well digger's ass."

"What's with all the panting, Don? Out of shape, old man?"

"Old man, hell! I mean hell, Mr. President, sir."

"Cut the Mr. President crap. Are you trying to annoy me?"

North laughed at Arthur's annoyance.

Arthur turned his huge strides toward the White House. "When we get back, pull up my Russian file. I want that in front of me when I'm on the phone. Did he say what the call is about?"

"He said the missiles will be here in seven minutes."

"I should give you press duty for that smart-assed answer."

Once the two comrades reached the White House, President Arthur's demeanor became abruptly more formal. "Tell the Secretary of State and Vice President Foster that I want them here pronto. I'll take Strahkov's call in the Office."

North was familiar with this sudden transition from informality to business as usual. The man played hard and worked hard. Sometimes, though, those endeavors were separated by mere seconds.

North watched as his tall friend retreated with an accompanying Secret Service detail toward the Oval Office. Arthur's highly successful terms as governor of Arizona had propelled him into the national spotlight. During his governorship, he had proven that he could deal effectively with difficult economic, political and administrative issues. His courses at the University of Arizona in economics, political science and law had provided him with a well-balanced, formal education. In addition, his experience in managing the family's ranching empire had ingrained in him a practical appreciation for the free-market enterprise system. North knew this man to be uniquely qualified to be not only a damned good President, but if circumstances permitted, a great one.

Day 1 10:40 P.M. Oval Office

President Arthur questioned the timing of Strahkov's call, since the Russian President and he were planning to meet privately in London next month after the G-Eight Economic Summit. So what was it that couldn't wait until then?

He was familiar with Alexander Strahkov's past. Strahkov had risen rapidly from relative obscurity to become mayor of the federal city of St. Petersburg. A year ago he had surprisingly won a tight three-way race for President against two strong candidates. That special race had filled the vacancy created by the sudden death of Yeltsin's immediate successor, Putin. Sudden death, hell! Murder was more like it in that rat's nest of criminality.

One candidate opposing Strahkov represented ultra nationalist military and hard-line Communist factions. The other candidate had been a handpicked Putin protégé. A resurging Russian Orthodox Church was Strahkov's most apparent backer. Their support was not primarily money or election workers, but rather a tacit approval of the man. The church apparently did carry weight with many voters. Strahkov also benefited from the younger generation's distrust of the Communists and the older's disillusionment with the Yeltsin/Putin crowd. The CIA also credited the startling Strahkov victory to an unexpected and unexplained, yet tremendously effective, grass-roots movement.

Arthur knew from intelligence briefings that by now the FSB, the successor to the KGB, would have made its peace with Alexander Strahkov and vice versa. No Russian President could wield power effectively without reaching such an accommodation with the mighty security agency. It was the only entity in Russia, other than the Mafia, that could make or break any Russian political figure, even the President.

President Arthur would have preferred to have his vice president, a man with important knowledge and insight on Russia, at his side during this call. Vice President Mark Foster, Don North and Secretary of State Norma Kohlmeier were among the few in this town whom he completely trusted. Each always gave frank advice, unconcerned over any negative personal fall out.

It was fortunate in more ways than one that he had selected a vice-presidential running mate who had vital military and foreign affairs experience. He almost didn't. His campaign advisory committee had narrowed the list of vice-presidential candidates to the stiff, impassive, former military leader, Mark Foster, and the good-looking, out-going North Carolina Senator, whose star was rising rapidly.

As Arthur had pondered his decision, he happened to read an article in the Hartford Herald. The essay, written by a most distinguished professor and foreign affairs expert, struck him hard. It advanced the theory that Foster was the ideal selection because he brought complementing foreign affairs expertise to the table and he was uniquely qualified, if circumstances required, to serve as President.

It turned out that the choice of Foster saved him. In the closing weeks of the campaign, Arthur's lack of experience in international affairs had been a glaring weakness his opponent attempted to exploit. His running mate, Foster, had boldly stepped forward to effectively debate the issues raised by Arthur's opponent. Foster had, through his brilliance in that arena, turned foreign affairs to a net advantage for their team.

Under the previous administration, Foster had served two years as Under Secretary of State, specializing in European affairs. Prior to that he had fashioned an exemplary Naval career, culminating in his chairing the Joint Chiefs of Staff. The first black man to serve as Admiral of the Navy and Joint Chiefs Chairman, he was highly respected both abroad and at home for his service as Undersecretary of State and Joint Chiefs Chairman. With his keen insight into the Russian culture, he had been instrumental in gaining the trust of the Russians, persuading them to go forward with ratification and implementation of the latest nuclear arms treaty.

Gingerly easing his lanky frame into the chair behind the desk in the Oval Office, President Arthur took a deep breath and clicked on the speakerphone.

"Hello, Mr. President. I didn't expect that we would talk before our meeting next month."

After a short delay created by signal transmission times, Strahkov responded, "Neither did I. However, some disturbing matters have come to my attention."

The newly elected Strahkov's fluent English momentarily caught Arthur off guard. Recalling, however, that Strahkov had been sent by the Russian government to study economics at Oxford, he admonished himself. But, of course! It was there that he perfected his command of the language.

Strahkov continued, "I do look forward to discussing our countries' mutual interests in London. However, I'm calling today about a special matter."

"You have my full attention. Please continue."

While the two Presidents were in the introductory phase of their conversation, North slipped in with the Russian files. He had efficiently paper-clipped the pages dealing with Strahkov.

As President Strahkov continued, Arthur paged through the briefing notes. He fully appreciated that Russia was faced with many extremely difficult problems and that their progress toward democracy, individual freedom and a free market economy had been disappointingly slow. He also grasped that from a Westerner's perspective, Russia and its people were difficult to understand. The evolution of historical events in Russia over the centuries had followed a very different course than those of the Western civilizations. This led Westerners to frequently draw erroneous conclusions about that mysterious country and its leaders. Things were not always as they seemed in Russia. That is why he had summoned Vice President Foster and Secretary Kohlmeier. He wanted informed opinions whenever Russia was the subject.

Strahkov moved directly to the point, "What we have facing us is stolen nuclear weapons."

"Oh!" President Arthur stiffened and stifled an, "Oh shit!"

"We suspect that behind this theft is a criminal conspiracy of global proportions. Highly placed operatives in both our governments may be involved. Let me give you some background. As you know, our countries have been slowly reducing nuclear armaments for years. Please excuse my bluntness, but despite those reductions, we still have enough weapons to blow each other off the face of the earth."

Blunt indeed, President Arthur observed. What brought that on? Was it just for emphasis or posturing for the next round of arms reduction talks?

"The Soviet nuclear weapons were concentrated mainly in our country and three former Soviet republics. After the Soviet breakup, each of those states inherited thousands of strategic and tactical nuclear weapons. Thus Kazakhstan, the Ukraine, and Belarus fell heir to huge stockpiles of nuclear weapons.

"The early nineties, in the aftermath of the empire's disintegration, proved dangerous. We labored to gain control of the scattered weapons and the bomb-grade material. The U.S. helped at times, but that assistance proved unpredictable as shortsighted U.S. budget cuts occasionally stopped that most important aid."

So now I have heard their rationalization for why this problem is at least partially our fault, President Arthur thought as from force of habit he stretched to a more upright posture, relieving pressure on his troublesome back. He unwrapped a stick of chewing gum. The chewing habit had always calmed him in tight golf matches and it worked for him in this job as well.

Strahkov continued, "Our previous leaders made several incomplete attempts to bring all of these weapons and nuclear materials back onto Russian soil. As it turns out, they didn't move rapidly and resolutely enough. As soon as I became President, I asked our FSB to conduct a study of all former Soviet nuclear materials. I demanded an accurate accounting.

"Let me elaborate. Many of the former weapons are in various stages of being dismantled as we progress to the smaller Russian nuclear force required by our treaty agreements. Much of the weapons-grade uranium from the dismantled weapons is being blended down below bomb-grade quality. It in turn is used as fuel for Russian nuclear power plants, as well as for your U.S. reactors. Unfortunately, this government-sanctioned process of nuclear swords-to-plowshares has been slowed by both your and our bureaucracies."

Still another not-so-subtle implication that whatever had happened, it was at least somewhat America's fault. Where was this leading? Why did Strahkov detour to take another shot? Had Arthur missed the importance of that zinger? Arthur was surprised for Strahkov still wasn't dropping the uranium subject.

"This transfer of what once was weapons-grade uranium to the U.S. as commercial fuel is a very important source of revenue for us. It's worth billions. I must assume it is just as vital to your security and economic interests. I offer that to your attention, believing it's in our common interests to remove those roadblocks to an enterprise that improves conditions for both of us."

"So are you suggesting that this swords-to-plowshares process is being deliberately sabotaged by this international conspiracy?"

"Yes, I am!"

"That's a big problem."

"You are right, but back to the stolen weapons. Mr. President, here's the bad news straight up. The investigation found that at least fifty tactical nuclear warheads and up to one hundred metric tons of weapons-grade uranium were smuggled out of the Republic of Kazakhstan."

"How much uranium?"

"Enough for hundreds, perhaps even thousands, of nuclear weapons."

President Arthur, struggling to hide his skyrocketing apprehensions, swallowed deeply before commenting. "Hundreds! Thousands! That many nuclear weapons out there, God only knows where!"

"God only knows where, pretty well sums it up. The bomb ingredients seem to have disappeared from the face of the earth."

"No idea where?"

"Nothing certain. The stuff could have been smuggled into any country as far as we know. It's baffling."

The President's sinewy hands lost all color as they clenched the edge of his desk. He was incredulous. His gum was already in shreds. "Who can afford that many nuclear weapons?"

"Good question. We know of no third-world country that could afford such a purchase. Plus, major nuclear powers, such as China, already have their own supply."

"Do you have any theories on where this stuff wound up?"

"Theories, yes. Facts, no. I have ordered our FSB to stop at nothing to find the answers. That is priority number one."

"What entities could achieve this diversion?" quizzed Arthur.

"Only one or two possibilities. Either a faction of the government of Kazakhstan or the Mafia."

"So Kazakhstan's definitely the source and the Mafia may be involved?" Grant probed.

"Yes. The Russian Mafia is a highly efficient machine. They have gained tremendous wealth by preying upon our businesses. They control fifty percent of our economy. They are everywhere. They have even more financial resources than we can explain. Make no mistake, they are a major international power."

Concerned about the strong intimation that the Mafia might be behind the uranium's disappearance, Arthur probed, "I know you campaigned against the criminality gripping your country, but can you really put a stop to them?"

"Perhaps, but it will take the equivalent of a prolonged civil war," Strahkov somberly admitted. "That fight could make the ghastly war between the red and white armies look like a picnic. The Mafia must be stopped, no matter what it takes, but first we must deal with the missing weapons. They must be found. I believe it's imperative to do so quickly, before disaster strikes. These weapons could be aimed at you or us or..."

Strahkov paused for a moment. The difficulties Russia faced threatened to overwhelm him. Seconds later, however, he calmly continued, "If the Russian Mafia is behind the smuggling, then it isn't just our problem. They have ties to rogue and terrorist countries. Thousands of these criminals have emigrated to Europe and the United States. They are your problem too. They are expert at finding the most corruptible agencies of government. Their use of a country's bureaucracies to accomplish their aims borders on the ingenious. They can and will use your society's systemic flaws to their own criminal gain."

Was that the third jab at the U.S., or was some of this possibly meant to be helpful warnings? Or could it be that Strahkov needed help badly and the bluster was just to cover that fact? President Arthur was not totally taken aback by this nuclear smuggling news. His briefing papers, classified above Top Secret, confirmed what everyone suspected, that the control of the former Soviet Union's nuclear arsenal had been very shoddy. The magnitude of the problem as described by President Strahkov, though, was greater than anything revealed in his intelligence briefings.

Strahkov broke the lengthy silence, "The danger to both of our countries of nuclear weapons in criminal hands suggests that we should work together."

"Yes, it does. I am going to turn to my foreign affairs team with these revelations. Especially I want to hear from our vice president, Mark Foster."

"We have the highest regard for Mr. Foster. Our Mr. Vasilly Kruschev, FSB Director, is in charge of our efforts to find the missing weapons. He reports directly to me. Actually he headed the investigation that uncovered this problem."

Arthur was more than a little concerned with Strahkov's picking the FSB head for his man in charge. When Kruschev's name came up, he turned immediately to the information on him. Bless good old efficient Don. He had even paper clipped the small section on Kruschev. According to those papers, Kruschev was an enigma. The trustworthiness of the Russian leaders, Strahkov and especially Kruschev, was a big question.

Obviously, it was inappropriate for him to argue with Strahkov's reliance upon Kruschev as head of the Russian investigation. Instead he offered, "Why don't we have Foster and Kruschev talk in two days.

That allows each of them time to review matters. Your man, Kruschev, is obviously starting out more informed on this problem than my vice president."

"Yes, let's leave it at that for now. I look forward to our meeting in London, Mr. President. My apologies for bringing you such disturbing news."

"No apologies necessary. The possibility of so damned many nuclear weapons in criminal hands is a nightmare."

"Since receiving the report, I have not slept well at all," admitted Strahkov.

"That's understandable."

"Goodnight, Mr. President."

"Goodnight."

Then remembering the early morning hour in Moscow, President Arthur quickly corrected himself, "Rather, good morning, Mr. President."

President Arthur pushed the off button and leaned back in his chair. His back hurt. Maybe he would have to start wearing a brace to protect his herniated disk as his doctor advised. He took a deep breath and stared at the ceiling for a few moments. Why on earth had he fought so hard to become President? No one in his right mind wanted to face problems of this magnitude.

The vice president and the secretary of state would arrive momentarily. President Arthur passed his sinewy hands through his prematurely graying hair. He couldn't overlook any facet of Strahkov's disturbing message when he briefed Kohlmeier and Foster. He told North to set up an office just down the hall. For the foreseeable future he anticipated that it would belong to Foster.

CHAPTER
FIVE

Day 2 8:15 A.M. Vice President Foster's Office White House

"Show that orotund-voiced Scotsman in. But tell his subordinates to wait."

"Yes, Mr. Vice President." North retreated from the office shaking his head and mumbling, "Orotund? Shit! Where did he dig up that damn word? He is playing with my simple mind again."

Vice President Foster was impressed that the President assigned North as his special assistant for the duration of the investigation. With that move, President Arthur clearly signaled the importance he attached to solving the mystery surrounding the missing Soviet nuclear arsenal.

Secretary of State Kohlmeier, the President and Foster had agreed it was prudent to heed President Strahkov's warnings that secrecy was essential. The possibility that U.S. agencies were infiltrated by spies implied that only a select few should be apprised of this investigation. That concept even applied to Director James Stockton's CIA.

The portly Central Intelligence Director burst through the vice president's office door as flamboyant as ever. Stockton's strong voice possessed a charming hint of a Scottish brogue. Its full resonant quality, coupled with his self-assured manner, commanded one's immediate attention. Foster never tired of listening to the musical and almost pleading quality of his Scottish dialect.

"Mr. Vice President, by golly it's good to see you. You and I have had so many spirited exchanges in the Senate that it's only fitting that we finally have a chance to work together."

"Work together we will, Senator. No, it's Director now, isn't it? Old habits are hard to break."

"They say that the older you get, the more that's a problem." Stockton then hastened to add, "Of course, I'm not implying you are old."

"How wise of you." Foster enjoyed the give and take with Stockton, who wasn't intimidated in the least by him.

"Your call posed quite a challenge. Collecting the material you asked for took what little was left of the night. But we managed. We pulled together tons of intelligence for your amazement."

"You better get used to the late nights, James. I have a hunch that there will be many more before this thing is over."

Foster, in his past role as Chairman of the Joint Chiefs of Staff, had gone before Senator Stockton's Military Affairs Committee more than once. An appreciation for each other's abilities had developed in those days. After the irrepressible Stockton chose not to run for reelection because of self-imposed term limits, President Arthur had appointed him Director of Central Intelligence. An excellent appointment, Foster had thought at the time. Considering Stockton's position as Director of Central Intelligence and his confidence in him, James was a shoe-in for membership on the select investigative team which he would be forming.

"Before we bring in your two analysts, I want your word that they can be trusted."

"They are clean. I went over every detail of their personal and professional history. I would stake my life on their loyalty."

Foster, dressed in a conventional dark blue business suit and white button-down shirt, noted with amusement Stockton's natty attire of a gray three-piece suit with crimson suspenders. Coupling his shock of red hair with his bold adornment, he was akin to a walking neon sign flashing, "Look, I am James Stockton." No undercover work for him, Foster thought to himself, trying to hide an amused smile.

Stockton elaborated on the question of security. "I sent briefs of their backgrounds to you, Mr. Vice President, so you could form your own opinion. What do you think?"

"I read them. Nothing I saw alarmed me so I am inclined to agree. Have them join us. But don't forget that I want the scope of our investigation known by as few as possible. And that includes your house. Is that clear?"

"Of course it is, Mr. Vice President. As I see it, only these two need to be deeply involved."

James introduced the CIA operatives as they entered Foster's office. "Mr. Vice President, this is Dwight Munson, our nuclear weapons expert, and Elizabeth Neiman, our Russian and Commonwealth of Independent States lead analyst. Elizabeth prefers to be called Liz. I believe Mr. Munson prefers Dwight. Is that correct?"

Both answered with an affirmative nod.

Foster had read with interest that several years ago Neiman's husband had been stabbed to death when he intervened in a mugging. He had challenged several thugs who were harassing a young woman with an infant on the D.C. Metro. What a tragedy. Foster empathized with her loss, for he, too, had lost a spouse.

"I am sure Director Stockton explained to you that absolute secrecy is essential."

Both responded again with a nod. Liz, despite being attired in a conservative brown business suit, was strikingly attractive. She was tall, nearly 5'10", blond and thin, yet athletic in appearance. Mark surmised that she could have a career as a model if the CIA didn't work out for her. Munson was the antithesis of Liz. He was older, short, and balding, with a thin face and squinting eyes nearly hidden by thick-lensed glasses, but Foster didn't give a damn what they looked like so long as they were competent and could contribute to the investigation.

"Liz, give me a brief, and I do mean brief, description of Kazakhstan. According to the Russian President, the chances are good that the nuclear weapons disappeared from there."

"Yes, sir. Kazakhstan has been independent from Russia for over a decade, yet it is closely tied economically and politically to its northern neighbor. It's half the size of the continental United States, yet its inhabitants number only nineteen million. Forty percent are native Kazakhs; forty percent ethnic Russians; and twenty percent others."

"Where is it exactly?"

"You might look at this map of Central Asia."

With obvious fervor, Liz unfurled the map on Foster's desk.

Pointing to the center of the map she said, "Kazakhstan is right here, in the very heart of Central Asia. It's generally flat, surrounded on the east by China, on the north and west by Russia, on the southwest by the Caspian Sea and on the south by three fellow CIS republics: Turkmenistan, Uzbekistan, and Kyrgyzstan."

With a twinkle in his eye, Foster asked, "Why don't they call China, Chinastan and Russia, Russiastan?"

"Are you serious?"

"Yep."

"They are not in the Central Asian club," replied Liz, also with a twinkle in her eye.

"Oh."

"Back to this ancient country of Kazakhstan. This book is a great read on their history. I will leave it for you. Today, I will touch just on the last century."

Foster nodded indicating that she should proceed in that vein. He appreciated her approach. Many bureaucrats, who were tasked with briefing him, would go to one extreme or the other. Either they would become falsely self-confident and too aggressive, or overly timid. Liz had found the middle ground of reasonable confidence coupled with a businesslike manner. He was still pondering her central Asian club response, though.

She continued, "In the 1930's, under the Soviet Regime, hundreds of thousands of Russians and Ukrainians were resettled to sparsely populated Kazakhstan. At that time, ethnic Slavs actually outnumbered the native Kazakhs.

"The fiercely independent Kazakhs, descendants of the Genghis Khan hordes that ruled the steppes centuries earlier, reacted defiantly to the flood of immigrants and the threat of Soviet Communist centralization. They slaughtered their livestock rather than see their possessions collectivized into Communist state farms. Some twenty-four million sheep and goats, five million cattle and three million horses were slain in 1933 alone."

As Liz talked, she noted that the vice president remained extremely attentive and was apparently absorbing all that she presented. Despite his stern appearance, Foster occasionally nodded to indicate he understood or otherwise encouraged her to keep going. The encouragement pleased her.

Liz followed up, "Despite such hapless resistance, the Russian migration surged into empty Kazakhstan. In the late forties, the cream of Moscow's nuclear physicists and rocket builders arrived and erected nuclear complexes and rocket launching facilities. They created closed cities whose very existence was cloaked from the outside world. Kurchatov was a closed city of seventy thousand near Semipalatinsk." Elizabeth pointed to Kurchatov and Semipalatinsk on the map in front of him.

"I see them, near the eastern border."

"Right. Fifteen years ago you would not find Kurchatov, named for the father of the Russian atomic bomb, on any map. It officially didn't exist. In a closed city like Kurchatov the citizens were not free to leave or move, except under the rarest of circumstances. Between 1948 and 1991, the Soviet scientists and technicians who lived in that city exploded more than five hundred nuclear bombs over and under the Semipalatinsk test site."

"My God! That's far more than we ever tested. We should have left them alone and they would have blown themselves out of existence."

Liz laughed at the remark. "Yes, sir, perhaps so. Regardless of courageous efforts by the dissident physicist, Sakharov, and others, the nuclear arms race prompted an 'anything goes' mentality among the Soviet leaders. They continued testing weapons and burying nuclear wastes from Soviet fuel reprocessing plants throughout the Kazakh countryside in a helter-skelter manner. The environmental damage to Kazakhstan from these and other Soviet excesses is among the worst anywhere in the world. Despite this abuse, the country retains tremendous potential wealth in its fossil fuel reserves and in its mineral deposits, including rich uranium ore reserves. The uranium and other mineral deposits are mainly near the eastern border, here in the Altai Mountains." Liz donned a pair of glasses to refer to the map.

Continuing with her most informative briefing, she added a summary of the developing oil industry in the Caspian Sea region.

After listening to that aspect of Kazakhstan, Foster directed the briefing more specifically to the nuclear mystery. "What portion of the former nuclear complex at Semipalatinsk remains today, Liz?"

Before continuing, Liz belatedly asked, "Is it all right with you if I walk about as I talk? It calms me when I'm nervous."

"Sure. Whatever you find comfortable."

How interesting, Foster thought. He did the same thing to burn nervous energy. Even though his guard was always up against any involvement with women, he felt an unwelcome twinge of interest in Liz.

Moving with an easy grace, the confident CIA agent resumed her briefing and her pacing, "Of course, the nuclear bomb tests were halted in 1991 as a result of a well organized indigenous protest. The disarmament treaties eliminated the need for the enrichment facility at Semipalatinsk, which for decades churned out enriched uranium. That product was used to fuel the Soviet nuclear weapons arsenal and the Soviet subs. Because of these post cold war treaties, the plant was mothballed in 1995.

"The uranium mining industry in Kazakhstan, though, survives and in fact thrives. Western know-how, primarily, advanced mining technology imported from Canada, infused new life into their mining operations, transforming those rich mines into economically competitive ventures."

"What happened to the nuclear scientists who worked at Semipalatinsk? By the way, what a mouthful these names are, Kurchatov and Semipalatinsk?"

Liz shrugged, "I guess I am used to them. Many scientists just melted away as their pay dwindled to nothing. Some are still there more or less as caretakers of the rusting facilities."

"Where did those that left end up?"

"Back to Russia. Into society in Kazakhstan. Many went to nuclear 'wanabe' countries, where they are probably quite wealthy now. They helped those countries develop or expand their nuclear weapons technology."

"Which countries?" asked Foster.

"Many immigrated to Iran, India and a few to Libya. North Korea, Pakistan and even China also got their share."

Foster observed, "So Pakistan is in the club, too."

Liz, caught off guard, replied, "What club?"

"Your Central Asian club."

"Oh, yes," Liz recovered quickly from being skewered by her own earlier retort.

"Who controls the reins of power now in Kazakhstan, Liz?"

Liz relished this question. The fractured power structure in Kazakhstan fascinated her. "Power is shared by many. The list is long, Mr. Vice President: criminal elements, new businesses, oil and mining interests, the churches, both Moslem and Orthodox, an extremely shrewd Kazakh President, the Kazakh security apparatus, and the Kazakh Border Guard. All of these maintain some power, but the alliances between them are continually shifting."

"Which of these powers could smuggle nuclear weapons and bomb material away from Kazakhstan?"

Liz hesitated for the first time. Hedging her response, she ventured, "It would need to be an amalgam. No one group separately could do it. Most likely it would require a joint effort of the criminal gangs, the Kazakh security apparatus, or the Kazakhstan Border Guard. But that is just a guess on my part. Also it seems to me that the brains behind such an operation would have to be someone with an extensive background in nuclear weapons."

Foster caught how closely that answer fit with the Russian President's emphasis on the dangers of the Mafia.

"Liz, help yourself to some coffee. We will give you a break while Dwight fills us in on the nuclear arms subject. Keep it simple, Dwight."

The diminutive Munson was quite intimidated by Foster, who had served years ago as Commander of the Pacific Submarine Fleet. Munson knew that he was reporting to no neophyte on the nuclear subject. In addition, Munson was on the defensive since the CIA did not know of the extensive scope of the smuggling that President Strahkov had revealed yesterday. He knew, of course, that he was not entirely to blame for the CIA's lack of information. After the budget cuts of the nineties the CIA, despite the recent emphasis on the war on terror, had yet to rebuild the extensive network of sources they had in the past. The next question, despite its predictability, served only to enhance Dwight's apprehensions.

"Dwight, is the CIA aware of the missing nuclear arms mentioned by the Russian President? If not, why not?"

A sinking feeling in the pit of Dwight's stomach nauseated the specialist. His knees were wobbly and his voice wavered as he fought an urge to vomit. "In a word, no. Ah, Mr. Vice President, if it's all right with you, I would like to address the missing nuclear bombs and the missing uranium separately."

"Sure, that's fine. Whatever makes sense."

Seeking a comfort which eluded him, Munson referred frequently to his notes. Avoiding direct eye contact with the imposing Foster, he proposed, "Let me first take the part that we know most about. We have been concerned that some tactical nuclear warheads, which were once in Kazakhstan, have disappeared. Some of them we believe have wound up in Iran and North Korea."

"Some?"

"Yes, we can only trace the movement of roughly twenty warheads."

"So where the hell are the rest?"

"Let me take that one," Stockton, familiar with the no-nonsense approach of Foster, interjected a save for his squirming nuclear weapons analyst.

"Before last night, we weren't aware that more than twenty were missing. Records in the former Soviet states are such that I don't know how anyone could be certain of the number. Taking Strahkov's statement at face value, however, it appears that the Russians believe that at least fifty are actually missing. We are working hard on the problem. I planted CIA operatives, who pose as buyers on the European and Asian black markets. If the weapons show up on those markets we will know it. Also, we increased our budgets for informants in several fledgling nuclear countries. Those initiatives were begun after I took over as director. The frustrating truth is that they need time to bear fruit."

"Well, you better shift into high gear, James. We don't have the luxury of time!"

"Yes, sir. We will." Stockton punched a difficult to achieve task into his planner.

Foster turned back to the analyst. "Dwight, how sure are you that those weapons or the weapons-grade uranium came from Kazakhstan? Why are you able to rule out Belarus or the Ukraine as the source?"

Foster's intense questioning had a purpose. He must discern why
U.S. intelligence was caught short by Strahkov's revelations. Had the
war on terror focused too narrowly on al-Qaeda, when even bigger
threats existed? Also, he was reinforcing the fact that under this
administration such inadequacies were unacceptable.

The analyst's spinning brain turned temporarily to mush under
the stress of the inquiry. "Uh, uh, I believe that question should be
addressed to General Adair. Military intelligence has the most complete information on that subject."

Foster clinched his teeth and frowned, a characteristic manner-
ism whenever he was displeased. Stockton, reading Foster's displeas-
ure, was equally disappointed but withheld a rebuke of the analyst
until a more opportune and private moment presented itself.

Stockton once again picked up the presentation, "Mr. Vice
President, let me take that one."

"Certainly." Not to his surprise Foster had confirmed that
Stockton remained the cool, capable leader even when under pressure and absent most of a night's sleep, attributes that could prove
vital later.

"When you told me that Strahkov suspected Kazakhstan might be
the source, I did some studying. Our National Security Agency's satellite information on Iran shows unexplained shipments from
Kazakhstan to Iran via Kazakh border guard patrol boats on the
Caspian Sea. We know that those shipments wound up at the Karaj
nuclear facility. Ongoing analysis of the photo bank should reveal
more."

"I know you will endeavor to narrow those possibilities over the
next few days."

"Yes, sir. Absolutely." Another major commitment was logged into
Stockton's planner.

"Iran has exchanged arms shipments with North Korea. We
know that Iran has Korea's NoDung, intermediate-range missiles.
They possibly received them as a quid pro quo for Korea's receipt of
nuclear weapons from Iran. In addition, Iran has bought missiles
from Kostova, Russia. They are capable of delivering nuclear warheads up to twelve hundred miles. This puts Israel, Saudi Arabia,
and now, ironically, even southern Russia, as well as our fleets in
the Mediterranean and the Persian Gulf, within range of these
weapons.

"Iran is building itself into a nuclear power. We believe that they
are the biggest threat to peace in that part of the world. Their rulers

are intent upon expanding their sphere of influence and they have acquired the military capability to carry out those ambitions.

"Our reading on their internal politics is not as clear as it should be. It's possible that radical elements in their command structure are giving us the impression of an overall bellicose posture. Just how much their President supports their nuclear buildup is unknown. But he has apparently done nothing to stop it.

"As I mentioned earlier, I have initiatives underway to improve intelligence there. We have recruited a source from within the Karaj Nuclear Weapons Complex, who could provide much needed intelligence. Within a week or so I hope to receive some answers as to what is going on at Karaj."

Foster caught a pause in Stockton's report and used it to reinforce his desires. "Those efforts of yours are vital, James. Do not let a lack of money stand in the way. Do whatever you must to obtain prompt results. We seem to be short on vital information, Director. That must be corrected."

With that admonishment, an increasingly concerned vice president, who had begun his customary pacing, turned once again to Dwight Munson. "Okay, Munson, let's see if we can get anywhere on the second subject. What do you know about the huge quantity of missing uranium?"

"We are really in the dark on this one," admitted Munson. "It's a large enough quantity to construct hundreds of nuclear warheads. There isn't a market anywhere in the world for that number of weapons."

Foster asked, "How could this much bomb-grade uranium wind up unaccounted for?"

Finally, upon hearing a question which he could handle, Munson stood a little straighter. "Mr. Vice President, the Russians kept records of their uranium enrichment in, of all things, rubles, rather than kilograms."

"You're kidding! The ruble is a variable, for God's sake! How on earth would they ever know what they had produced?"

"Exactly! No one can quantify from the Soviets' books alone exactly how much was actually produced. We theorize that they deliberately did this to frustrate any spying attempts. Thus it is a significant question as to how the Russian President could have achieved an accurate estimate. We would need not only each of their enrichment plants' production records, with all their attendant inaccuracies, but we would also need to actually go to each site and physically sample and analyze the uranium tails. That is probably what the FSB investigators have done."

Foster admitted, "Now you lost me, Dwight. Uranium tails?"

The analyst, growing increasingly confident, responded, "Tails is just what we call the waste or tailings left behind by an enrichment plant. Some of these Soviet plants could have been run in a clandestine mode to produce more product than the official record keeping showed. That would show up, though, in the waste piles. We have heard rumors that this extra production might have happened at the Kazakh Enrichment Plant at Semipalatinsk."

Foster found that rumor about extra production important.

With a rare grin intruding upon his normally stoic face, Foster boomed out a challenge. "So you did have an answer."

"To what?"

"To my earlier question of why we should suspect Kazakhstan as a source."

At first a puzzled look clouded Munson's face. Then the light dawned. The suspicion of clandestine over-production at the Semipalatinsk Enrichment Plant operation was what Vice President Foster meant. Wow, this guy was sharp.

"Yes, sir, I guess I should have put those pieces together myself," he sheepishly admitted.

Foster agreed silently with that self-assessment, but turned to Neiman. "I have one more question for you, Liz. Can we trust Strahkov and Kruschev?"

"The short answer is Strahkov yes, and Kruschev maybe."

"Elaborate."

"Alexander Strahkov is the best thing that could have happened to Russia as well as to the Western world. A devout Russian Orthodox Christian, he is educated in capitalist economic theory and believes fully in the free-market system's merits. His family history is fascinating. His father was banished to a Siberian camp by the Soviet Communists for his unshakeable religious beliefs and for being a disciple of one of Russia's most gifted and courageous poets of that era. Strahkov's father's health was broken while laboring in the coalmines. He died when his son, Alexander, was only ten. Alexander can't remember ever seeing his father, a father, nevertheless, whom he worships.

"Through his mother Anna's nurturing and training, he was reared with strong moral and religious beliefs. He seems to be motivated by a fervent desire to serve Russia in what he sees as its hour of need. He has acquired many of his ideas from the writings of the same poet who earlier inspired his father."

"Who is he?"

"Viktor Sumurov."

"I don't believe I have ever heard of him."

"Few outside of Russia have, but within the country, he is revered by many who prize personal and religious freedom. Some of his earlier works miraculously survived the censorship and repression of the Stalin and the post-Stalin eras. His essays on personal freedom are today given the credit for inspiring the dissidents of the sixties and the seventies, including Solzhenitsyn and Sakharov. Rumor has it that many of his most poignant works were confiscated and destroyed.

"Anyway, after the Soviet Union collapsed the young Strahkov, because of his outstanding record as a student and his promising leadership qualities, was selected by the Russian authorities to study economics in England. He achieved a brilliant scholastic record at Oxford, receiving a graduate degree in economics.

"He then returned home to St. Petersburg, the most European of Russian cities, to enter politics. He quickly rose through the political structure there to become mayor of St. Petersburg. Last year, as you know, he won a most surprising victory. Apparently with the support of staunch reformers and the Russian Orthodox Church, Alexander overcame a strong challenge from the extreme nationalist and communist candidate, who represented the forces of recidivism."

"Liz, recidivism?" Stockton could not resist the opportunity to slow her down a bit. She was good and he appreciated that, but she was putting on almost too good a show. He was accustomed to occupying center stage; however, Liz's brilliant performance had wrested the limelight from him.

"Yes, that simply means a tendency to relapse to, or attempt to return to things as they once were." Elizabeth was unmistakably miffed with Stockton's interruption.

"I see," said Stockton, stunned at the prompt, precise retort. "I only wished to ascertain whether you fully fathomed the verbiage you chose."

Liz quite understood Stockton and knew he would respect her only if she stood her ground, and stand her ground she would. "If you have discerned your answer, Director, I will resume. If necessary, I am willing to elucidate further."

Stockton just waved a hand in surrender, "It is very clear, Liz. No elucidation necessary. Plow ahead, by all means."

Foster resisted an overwhelming urge to burst out laughing. Rolling his eyes, he looked away for a few moments. Suddenly he recalled who Liz reminded him of—Laura. Laura Andrew, whom he had not seen since his Navy days, had the same steel-trap mind, quick wit, enthusiasm and courage so clearly demonstrated by Liz.

"As you probably already know, Mr. Kruschev, the head of the Russian security apparatus known as the FSB, is a much more complex animal to decipher. To understand him and the power he wields, you need to comprehend the nature of today's FSB, which, of course, is the Russian successor to the old Soviet KGB.

"Contrary to Western popular opinion, most of the totalitarian practices of the old KGB haven't been dismantled. In fact, they thrive, incorporated in the current FSB. Permit me to go into some detail, as I believe this is absolutely essential in accurately understanding Kruschev and Russia."

"That sounds reasonable. Continue, Liz."

"As I said, the Russian FSB inherited most of the old Soviet KGB organization. Only external security and the border guard were separated. The KGB split into fifteen pieces, paralleling the fifteen CIS republics. The Russian FSB, though, retained the bulk of the resources. The FSB still makes or breaks politicians. Every President from Yeltsin to Strahkov has been dependent upon the FSB's support to govern effectively. There are still hundreds of thousands of agents that spy on citizens, maintain personal files and retain police state powers to imprison whomever they perceive as undesirables. Just the sheer number of agents alone gives you some sense of their vast influence. They have ten agents to every one of our CIA and FBI agents.

"Kruschev, as the head of the Russian FSB, is the second most powerful Russian, behind only President Strahkov. Here our understanding of the individual slips slightly out of focus. He may be a staunch 'Chekist,' but we are not sure."

"What's a Chekist?"

"The Chekists were the forerunners of the KGB. In the name of the Bolshevik revolution of 1917 and under Lenin's express orders, the Chekists perpetrated a systematic campaign of repression and murder. Hordes of civilians and members of any suspected armed resistance were slaughtered. Cheka Chief Dzerzhinsky, architect of what he himself called the 'Red Terror,' marked not only individual opponents but entire classes of people for physical liquidation because of their social origin."

"Now that you remind me, I vaguely recall having heard of that SOB. Didn't Stalin establish a cult following of that butcher?"

"Yes, under Soviet Union premiers from Stalin through Gorbachev, the Chekist cult of Dzerzhinsky worship grew like a cancer within the KGB. Gorbachev inherited the evil system. Instead of marking it for reform, he insulated it from publicity during Glasnost and Perestroika. Later, under Yeltsin and Putin, the Chekist cult culture was once more allowed to thrive. Even with the breakup of the Communist Party as a control structure, the Chekists retained their domination of the security apparatus.

"Here is still another troubling aspect of the FSB. Over the past decade, certain elements of the FSB evolved more than ever into an organized criminal enterprise. They networked into business, banking, the news media, the political process and the government. Often they appear to be in open partnership with the potent Russian Mafia. Thus, at a minimum, portions of the FSB are a significant asset to the Mafia."

Foster was stunned. He knew much about Russia but had completely underestimated the FSB. "I had no idea that their security apparatus retained such police-state powers."

"Yes, I would expect that, Mr. Vice President. Very few Western leaders are aware of this."

Until Liz's enlightenment today, he had bought into the conventional wisdom that real reform in the area of human rights had occurred in Russia. So the freedom-inhibiting security apparatus of the old Soviet KGB was not merely a nightmarish memory of the past but an appalling reality still today. This required a major paradigm shift on his part.

"The FSB security machine is used by Russian politicians in a symbiotic manner to maintain their political power, and in return the political leaders allow the security structure to operate unchecked. No pun intended. This symbiosis has been a fact of life before and after the demise of the Soviet Union and Communism."

"Do you see any hope for change?" asked Foster, glancing over at Stockton to see if he was going to challenge Liz's knowledge of the word, "symbiosis."

The uncharacteristically humble look on Stockton's face said it all. It translated as, "No way am I asking her. You can if you want."

"Strahkov's election is a good sign. Also, the best hope for a change was that, as the Russian economy grew stronger and more diversified, a new economically powerful middle class would emerge and demand true reform. The rise of the Mafia has inhibited this from occurring. In essence, the criminals have taken the place of the hoped-for, honest middle class."

"The interests of the Chekists and the Mafia seem to be closely aligned."

"Correct! To truly reform Russia, both would have to be challenged."

"You're getting to Kruschev, right?"

"Of course! Vasilly Kruschev wields all of the power vested in the FSB. He appears to choose his stance on any issue based on his goal of doing what is best for 'Mother Russia.' As long as he believes it is in Russia's national interest to cooperate with you, Mr. Vice President, in the search for the missing nuclear weapons, then he will work with you. The moment he doesn't see it that way, you're in deep trouble. His God is Russia."

Foster inquired, "What if the weapons smuggling turns out to be the Mafia's handiwork? With the FSB so enmeshed in criminal activities, won't Kruschev back away from helping us?"

That was a very good question. Liz was impressed with Mark Foster's ability to absorb all that they were throwing at him so furiously and still focus on the important aspects. Exuding confidence and power that she found quite attractive, he was even more impressive than she had expected. Neiman met very few men who were not threatened by her intellect, beauty, and self-confidence. Foster was one of the rare breed who fell into that category.

"Not necessarily. I believe his decision will still hinge on what he believes to be in Russia's best interest, but honestly I can't be sure of that. He appears to us to be a practical Chekist whose true loyalty is not to the Dzerzhinsky cult but to Russia. If he were to see the Mafia as a threat to Russia, we think he might actually go after them. He is tough and courageous. Beyond that, he's an enigma to us."

After those profound insights by Neiman, the vice president ended the conference. "Thank you for an excellent briefing. Leave the information you brought. It will be part of my homework assignment. Director, you prepared well considering the very short notice I gave you. I will be in touch with you later today."

In this session, Foster had heard nothing to throw doubt on President Strahkov's revelations. His apprehensions about where this could lead had not subsided. Nuclear weapons were missing. They must be found or something far worse than the World Trade Center catastrophe was possible.

As Stockton walked down the hall with Nieman and Munson, a myriad of thoughts flooded through his mind. This had been his first chance to see them perform under pressure. Nieman had done extremely well, Munson okay at times. It was no surprise to him that the vice president was capably attacking this matter. Foster was going after his fact gathering methodically and intensely, precisely as he should.

"Liz, what is your impression of this situation?" Stockton asked.

"Reading Russia correctly is essential."

"I agree. You did a great job, but what else could be done to assure we are operating with all available expertise?"

"Ask the authority on Russia, Dr. Dudaev, to brief the vice president. Foster should avail himself of the very best."

"Yes. We could do that just for insurance. That is a great idea. I will talk with Dudaev first and based on how that goes, I could then suggest that Foster request a briefing by him?"

Pleased with Stockton's acceptance of her idea, Liz predicted, "His unique insights on Russia and its leaders will prove invaluable."

CHAPTER
SIX

Day 2 1:45 P.M. Vice President Foster's Office White House

"How long have you been with Grant?" Foster asked between mouthfuls of his ham and cheese sandwich.

"Too damned long. Look where it's got me." North settled down with his rattlesnake-skin cowboy boots propped on a chair he had pulled close.

"What do you mean?"

"This screwed-up city is the last place on earth I care to hang my hat!"

"So you don't like it here?"

"Hell no! It's full of goddamned takers sucking the Federal tit, eh. I'm here for one reason, to help my friend as much as I can. Otherwise I wouldn't even come visit this hole."

"He is lucky to have people like you around, Don. He needs a few that he can trust. You are right, there is an army of slicksters in this town. They will take him good if they spot an opening. We agree on that, but tell me more about your early days with the President."

"We met at the University of Arizona twenty-five years ago. We both tried out for the varsity golf team. He made the team and I didn't. We became friends during those tryouts and remained so ever since. I never saw anyone clobber the ball like he did. That tall frame of his gave him some tremendous leverage. I always accused him of stowing depleted uranium in his clubhead. His senior year his back started giving him trouble or he would have wound up on the pro tour.

"So he was that good?"

"Absolutely."

"You miss Arizona?"

"Yep. He is the only one who could convince me to leave that great state for this corrupt place."

"What do you think of the assignment we face?"

"The possibility that the crazies of the world have latched onto nuclear bombs scares the living hell out of me! Normal deterrents won't stop them."

"You are right on target. It scares me too, Don. It puts a heap of pressure squarely on us."

"My crystal ball says this is going to get a lot worse the more we dig in, which reminds me, I had Secret Service set up security on your office."

"Good. I appreciate your tending to those details. Boy, there is a ton of stuff to learn."

North sincerely observed, "I don't envy you your job. You know, I have a hunch that how we solve this could end up defining our President's legacy, eh."

"Don, did you ever spend time in Canada?"

"How did you guess? Was it the 'eh's?'"

"Yes."

"My oil company wildcatted up in B.C. I kind of liked the 'eh's.' It's a handy way to say 'are you listening,' 'do you agree,' or 'back at you.'"

"You picked up the damns and the other four letter epitaphs from the roustabouts, I assume."

"No, I got most of those early on, on the two hour bus ride to school in Wagon Wheel Gap, Arizona. Later, the roustabouts taught me how to use the words for maximum effect."

Foster chuckled. He liked the rough and tumble North. The guy was blunt and damned efficient. He was built like a fireplug or maybe more like a little bull with no neck. He bet North more than held his own with his oil field workers.

"I tell you what, I try like hell not to pick up any habits from this foul place. If I do just take me out and shoot me."

Foster broke into a rare smile and asked, "Explain your aversion to D.C.?"

Don's eyes lit up with that opening. "The pea-brained people around here arrogantly believe everything originates from within the Beltway."

"Pea-brained?"

"Yes. Pea-brained. Most of the bureaucrats, consultants and politicians in this town are out of touch with the true underlying greatness of this country. They strangle our enterprises with their 'red tape.' They slowly regulate away our freedoms and the creative spark that fired our country forward. Every one of them should be thrown out of here on his or her fat ass and forced to live in Texas, Idaho or Ohio, and earn a damned living."

"You might have something there. They might get a renewed sense of the ingenuity and strength the American people."

"Yes, and also, they might get a more accurate read on what they regulate with such perverted gusto.

"The army of bureaucratic piss-ants back here creates no useful product, only reams and reams of stifling rules and regulations. They don't grow the wheat or the corn, or manufacture the planes, trucks and cars, or create the vast new high-tech innovations that have fueled this country's economic boom. They take no risks. Instead, the Beltway Bandits become ever more inbred and parasitic and make life more and more difficult for the producers in this great country."

"Anything else?" asked an amused Foster.

"Yes. Hell, they can't even run the damned Aquarium back here. It's a national disgrace. That place is dilapidated. Signs are old or wrong. They label a squid a jellyfish. We have excellent municipal aquariums in the Southwest which put the national one here to shame."

"So what do you really think, Don?" Mark asked rhetorically. "That was quite a tirade. Maybe you and President Arthur can do something about all of that."

"You mean the pitiful aquarium or the pompous out-of-touch attitude permeating Washington?"

"Yes and yes."

"These entrenched assholes will beat us bloody before it's over, but with luck, we might bring the National Aquarium up to par."

Day 2 2:15 P.M. Vice President Foster's Office

"Come in Director Lang. Welcome, Agent Garrison."

Foster shook hands with the two FBI representatives as they entered his office.

With the abbreviated preliminaries out of the way he initiated the business at hand. "I want a quick summary of the history and status of Russian Mob activity in the U.S."

After Liz's references to the Mob this morning and Strahkov's warning to Arthur, Foster concluded that he must learn everything possible about the Russian Mafia and the sooner the better.

FBI Director Anthony Lang was a holdover from the previous administration. The former FBI director had resigned and was replaced with Lang. Foster had observed Lang to be a political lap dog who had not, and would not, defend the integrity of the FBI. Unimpressed with the director, Foster held out hope that the young agent, Brad Garrison, had the necessary ingredients to serve on his team. He received his first indication rather quickly when the wimpy Lang opted for silence, letting Garrison carry the ball from the opening bell.

Garrison commenced his briefing of the vice president without assistance or even a preamble from Lang. "The breadth of the influence of the Russian Mob in this country is large and expanding. We at the FBI hadn't really considered them a significant threat until about seven years ago, when we uncovered bank, stock market and credit card swindles that netted the Mob hundreds of millions of bucks. We sent several mobsters to jail in 1999 on charges of mail fraud, tax evasion, theft and forgery. Yet, this didn't seem to make a dent in their operations. After that we placed more agency resources on the job of investigating them."

Foster instantly liked the tall, affable Garrison. His unpretentious, easy-going manner was designed not to impress, but to educate. His confident bearing and smile were reassuring. So far it looked like he had found a winner.

Garrison explained, "This Russian Mafia is unlike any other criminal organization we ever faced. Many members are highly educated and intelligent. They emigrated from Russia and former Soviet republics to the U.S. They also descended on central Europe big time. They are hardened by years of resisting the old KGB in an era when the KGB had full and absolute power to deal with the criminal society, or society in general for that matter. Some of them are the most resolute criminals we ever faced."

The vice president observed, "From what I learned earlier today, I would say the power of the old KGB is not all that diminished. Worse yet, at least a portion of the FSB collaborates with the Mafia."

Garrison, confident in his knowledge of the subject, echoed Foster's thoughts, "You are right. Today the line separating the current security apparatus in Russia from the existing criminal factions there is murky at best. But let me get back to the mob's U.S. activities. If it's acceptable, I will start by giving a few examples of past Mafia leaders and their crimes. It shows just what we are up against

in this country. The sophistication, wealth and scope of their enterprises here has expanded amazingly."

"That's fine, Garrison. Just make it brief and to the point."

"Yes, sir. I'll start with Agron, who was a diminutive Russian
immigrant. The gangster moved into Brooklyn's Brighton Beach section. Despite his mild appearance, he was a natural born leader as
well as a callous SOB who had survived ten years in the harsh Soviet
prisons. He extorted money from the Brighton Beach businessmen,
making his rounds with a cattle prod that he used as a weapon on
recalcitrant victims. He extorted fifteen thousand dollars from one
Russian immigrant by threatening to kill his daughter on her wedding
day. Not surprisingly, there were several attempts to kill Agron.
Finally, two killers completed the job where others had failed. They
assassinated the gangster as he waited for the elevator in his posh
Parkway apartment complex. He was one of the pioneers for Russian-
based organized crime that sprang up in several East Coast cities."

Garrison's self-assured manner reminded Foster of himself when
he was younger, except that the young man grinned far more than he
ever did. With a nod of his head he signaled for the well-spoken agent
to continue.

"The Mafia was a loose knit assortment of thieves, extortionists,
confidence men and white-collar swindlers. These cunning criminals
sometimes referred to themselves as the 'Organizatsiya,' or simply, the
'Organization.' Most were veteran gangsters from the former Soviet
Union. Their survival in the Soviet criminal underworld meant evading
the dreaded KGB and carrying out their activities within the strict confines of a totalitarian system. The Soviet police didn't need search war-
rants to sweep through a suspect gang's headquarters. Beatings and torture were the favored interrogation techniques. By comparison, the
Russian mobsters have found the police and the justice system in this
country to be complete pushovers. We had one of these toughs in for
questioning. His leg looked like a pretzel. It had been broken in a dozen
places at the hands of the KGB. He proudly showed off his battered limb
and laughed insolently at us, 'You're going to do worse to me?'"

Foster listened intently. This aspect of organized crime was completely foreign to him. Garrison's tale was so engrossing he had nearly forgotten that Director Lang was still in the room.

The FBI agent went on to describe the ever-increasing sophistication of the U.S.-based Russian gangs. "Their development of close ties
to their counterparts in Europe, Russia, and its former republics is
most alarming to us."

Foster decided to test Director Lang. "Director, what policies have you instituted to deal with this escalating criminality?"

"Well, uh, I think Garrison can answer that. Basically I maintained the policies of my predecessor."

Foster gritted his teeth for that was as near a non-answer as he had ever heard. His low expectations of Lang were rapidly being confirmed. Turning back to Garrison, Foster directed, "Go on with your report, Garrison."

"Decades ago an elite, closely knit group of Russian criminals formed a brotherhood called the Thieves-in-Law. They recently dispatched their emissaries to Western Europe and the U.S., but by far the shrewdest and wealthiest leader yet of the Russian Mob immigrated to Switzerland. From there he systematically took over control of Russian Mafia activities worldwide. We believe that even the Thieves-in-Law chief now reports directly to him. This individual is a brilliant Russian physicist, who during the eighties and early nineties directed Soviet operations at the Semipalatinsk nuclear complex."

Foster, struck by the coincidence of Semipalatinsk coming up again, nodded. "Yes, I heard of that dismal place earlier today from CIA. This is starting to tie together. A little bit anyway." Damn! What was it Liz had said that related to this new information?

Agent Garrison replied, "I am not surprised that the CIA mentioned the place. It was basically Russia's answer to our Los Alamos, as well as the Nevada Test Site. Within the Semipalatinsk complex Russian nuclear weapons experts designed, developed and tested Russia's nuclear arsenal. Anyway, this fellow who now heads the Russian Mafia became director of those facilities in 1984 and was in that position until he immigrated to Switzerland. Under his clever direction the Mob has made tremendous strides in integrating into the legitimate international business economy and power structure."

Listening with one ear, Foster finally recalled the point Liz had made. She had said that to get the nuclear weapons out of Kazakhstan, a nuclear expert would have to direct things. For sure, this guy Garrison was describing fit that profile.

"His financial base is now within the huge conglomerate, R.M. Holding Corporation, of which he is the sole owner, as well as its chief executive officer. This vast holding company has grown from its start as a large Mob-controlled Russian banking conglomerate to become, by any standard, the world's wealthiest corporation. This newest leader of the Russian Mob seems equally at home talking to a U.S. Senator or a CEO of a business conglomerate as he is in dictating a hit on an enemy. His lieutenants, Brent Lepke and Ray Goldstein, the North American Mafia Chieftains, directly manage the thugs, con men and white-collar criminals comprising the North American branch of the Russian Mob."

Foster was stunned with the sophistication and raw economic power possessed by this criminal organization. "I want to know more about this man. Whom does he associate with here? Has he contacts with government officials? Get a complete breakdown of the R.M. Holding Corporation. By the way, what is this criminal genius's name?"

"Boris Andropov."

Day 2 5:15 P.M. Vice President Foster's Office

Foster leaned back in his chair, resting his feet on his desk in a noble, but futile, effort to relax. A good tough karate workout was way overdue, but unfortunately out of the question today. He stared at the door that had just closed behind Lang and Garrison. He had heard of this Boris Andropov somewhere before but where?

It was Fortune Magazine! That's where he had heard of this mogul. Andropov was the world's wealthiest human, leaving Bill Gates far behind.

To help decide who should be on his team as FBI representative, Foster again reviewed Garrison's personnel dossier. It confirmed his impression of the young man. He was an energetic agent knowledgeable on the organized criminal elements in this country. The only potential concern was his personal situation. He was divorced two years ago. His wife had even written the agency that she could no longer stand the pressure-cooker stress of not knowing whether, after a day's work, her husband would be coming home alive. She had gathered their two children and left for her parents' home in Seattle.

Evaluations of his performance, though, revealed no attenuation in his excellent work. Even his extremely active social life didn't seem to hinder his work. Since the discovery several years ago of traitors in their midst, the FBI had instituted far-reaching checks on every agent. Foster found the extensive personal detail to be almost embarrassing, but it helped him conclude that he would use Garrison rather than the spineless Director Lang.

Lang's ego, though, would have to be assuaged. A quick call to the director, informing him that Garrison would be assigned directly to the vice president, was next on the agenda. Garrison would be given unlimited authority within the agency, and would report directly to Foster. Foster would mollify Lang by pointing out the importance of the director's job in keeping all of the other FBI activities humming.

Day 2 6:30 P.M. FBI Director Lang's Office

Director Lang's instincts told him that he had just been "dissed" by the vice president. The phone call from Foster only moments ago telling him that Garrison was needed for a special assignment was too much. Garrison report directly to the V.P., humph. This would not stand. He summoned one of his most trusted agents to his office.

"Agent Karpenko, You are assigned to White House duty for the foreseeable future. Keep me informed on what the vice president and Garrison are up to. It will be impossible to get anything out of either of them so try to befriend those in the know there, personal secretaries, Don North, some of the Secret Service detail. Anyone like that. I want information. Do you understand?"

"Yes, sir! When do I start?"

"In one week. I don't want your appearance there to be obvious. It will be just a routine rotation where you replace the agent who is there now."

Karpenko left the director's office mumbling in amazement, "Holy shit! Is this my lucky day or what?" Obviously his new assignment pleased him far beyond the call to duty.

Day 2 11:15 P.M. Vice President Foster's Office

Sipping his hot coffee, a habit originating during his Navy days, Foster rolled his head from side to side trying to relax his neck muscles. Attempting to sort through the mountain of information laid on him today, he stared at the mug. A picture of his first submarine command, the SSN Jacksonville, graced the cup.

Nothing he had heard today reduced his assessment of the severity of the pending crisis. Indeed it seemed very possible that the Russian President's estimate of missing weapons was accurate. It also seemed plausible that a criminal mob such as the Russian Mafia, headed by Boris Andropov, could have orchestrated such a feat.

North broke into the vice president's reflections with a note that his daughter Dione had called for him. She and her twin sister, Dedra, were Mark's pride and joy. Dione and he had become very close since his wife, Elisabeth, had died of cancer. Elisabeth had been instrumental in everything that he had accomplished in his life. Not only had she nurtured their twins, Dione and Dedra, but she had also cared for the submarine wives with get-acquainted coffees and other social functions while Mark and his crew were out on extended Pacific cruises. Elisabeth had always encouraged him in his endeavors. In her quiet way she had infused him with confidence, far more than he had ever realized until he had faced losing her. The diagnosis three years ago of her inoperable lung cancer had come only months before her death.

Dione had recently completed Law school at the University of Virginia and had been hired by a prominent legal firm located in the Northern Virginia suburbs of D.C. A bright girl, she possessed the same quiet confidence and efficient manner as her mother. Dione was expecting the results of the bar exam any day and he guessed that her call was on that subject. He wasn't worried. He knew she would pass.

Dedra reacted very differently to her mother's death. Her way of dealing with her grief had been to withdraw from close involvement with the family. She plunged fully into her medical career. He had not seen or talked with Dedra for several months.

Foster had several things yet to do tonight. Calling Dione was first, after which he must study. His crucial call to Kruschev wasn't far off. He wanted a little more insight and information from his other sources before he began discussions with the formidable Russian leader.

Moments ago Stockton had called him recommending a briefing by Dr. Dudaev. Stockton strongly suggested that the meeting should occur before Foster called Kruschev. Foster remembered Dudaev as the professor who had taught a Russian history class years ago at the Naval Post-Graduate School. Foster knew that the aging historian was in high demand by the Washington think tanks. He would invite the respected professor to D.C. to share his insights on Russia.

CHAPTER
SEVEN

Day 2 6:15 P.M. Tulsa, Oklahoma

After picking up the medium pan pizza, Ben Andrew stopped at the home of his highway patrolman friend. Over the last few months, Ben had shared some of his suspicions about NuEnergy with the patrolman. At Ben's request, the officer had checked into Helmut's background and discovered his criminal past.

Today he filled Ben in on the investigation regarding the Blazer's brakes. He gave Ben a complete rundown on how the brakes had been tampered with, explaining that it would take an expert to accomplish the clever weakening of the hydraulic hose. It had been deliberately and precisely thinned so that the full pressure of a quick stop would cause it to fail.

"So," Ben observed, "I was supposed to crash into the tractor."

"That's our best guess."

"Did you find the farmer?"

"No. No one with a Deere admits to being out there last night."

"Then the tractor was part of the plot?"

"As of now, it looks that way. The tractor's tracks ended on the shoulder of the road at the top of the next hill. It was apparently loaded on a trailer and hauled away."

"So it would be hard to prove anything."

"That's about it, except I would be damn careful around that NuEnergy bunch. You seem to be crossways with some really bad dudes."

After thanking his friend for the information, Ben headed for Laura's bookstore with cold pizza, but with confirmation of his and Laura's worst fears about his car accident. He fully expected that after Laura heard the story she would renew her insistence that he get out of Black Bear and for the first time he was willing to give it serious thought.

Day 2 7:05 P.M. Laura's Bookstore Tulsa

Ben found Laura near the back of her small bookstore, intently staring at her computer terminal.

"What are you doing, Laura?"

"Oh, just counting my blessings."

"Blessings?"

"Yes, that you survived another day at that God-forsaken place."

"Yes I did, not a single attempt on my life today, if you don't count..."

"Count what?"

"The massive turbine ring they nearly dropped on me."

Laura's eyes grew big as saucers, "You're kidding?"

"What do you think?"

"I think that either way Mister, you are in a lot of trouble."

"Meaning?"

"Meaning, if you are lying, I may show them how it's done."

Ben grinned. At least Laura still had her sense of humor, and he hoped that she was just kidding.

"Are you hungry enough to eat cold pizza?"

Having returned to her computer screen, Laura absently answered, "Sure, that's fine."

Seeing that she wasn't listening, but was riveted to her terminal screen, he teased, "I got anchovy pizza, your favorite."

Not hearing the comment, Laura said, "Ben, I'm really worried about you and this NuEnergy bunch. Wait till you hear about all I uncovered."

Ben thought, then we both dug up a pot load of trouble. Trying again to distract Laura, he shoved the cold pizza under her nose. "Have some."

Bemusedly, Ben noticed that Laura hadn't taken time to change from her riding habit. The form fitting outfit revealed how appealing and fit his wife was.

She had undoubtedly ridden her jumper stallion earlier, which was her tonic, her relaxation and pleasure. He judged from the stack of papers, which she had printed out, that after riding she became so engrossed in her Internet research that she hadn't taken time to shower or change clothes. That wasn't like her at all, so she must have found something especially interesting.

Laura, finally turned away from the computer screen and searched Ben with her big inquiring eyes. She demanded, "So spill it, Ben. What did he tell you? I can see it in your eyes. It's bad news, isn't it."

"Yep, Bad news. He told me a lot, Laura. Just as we thought, the Blazer's brakes were tampered with. He is almost certain that it was done while I was at the plant."

Ben didn't bother to go into the great detail that his friend had provided about how the deed was done and how the hydraulic hose was cleverly weakened.

"That doesn't surprise me with all I found out today! Anything else?" Laura couldn't help recalling what her friend, Sally Bumgardner, had said about how Fred had felt threatened at Texas. Was she paranoid or was the same thing happening to Ben? No she wasn't exaggerating the danger.

Ben added, "They can't find any farmer in the area who admits that he was out on the highway with his tractor that night."

"So, was even the tractor part of the plot to kill you?"

"It's possible, but it's all circumstantial. There is no proof of anything, honey."

Dropping the slice of pizza before taking a bite, she again shoved the food away, exclaiming, "My appetite's gone."

Thoughtfully, Laura sank into silence before finally launching into an explanation of her discoveries.

"Here's the story Ben. I used every news search engine on the Internet for info on NuEnergy. What I found places them in very interesting company. Come look at this chart I put together."

R. M. Holding Corporation
(Boris Andropov)

	Deutsche Erste Bank	Investment Holdings	Slavic ImEx Bank	Global Pharma-ceuticals	Founders Federal Bank	NuEnergy	Joint Ventures
ASSETS	$150B	$200B	$60B	$200B	$50.0B	$1.0B	Unknown Billions
INCOME	$ 15B	$ 15B	$30B	$ 20B	$ 5B	$2.5B	Unknown Billions
LOCATION	Germany	Worldwide	Russia	England	U.S.	U.S.	Worldwide

Total Assets $661B+Joint Ventures
Total Net Income $ 98B+Joint Ventures

"So NuEnergy's owned by R.M. Holding. So what?" Ben challenged.

"NuEnergy is part of the huge conglomerate called R.M. Holding Corporation. Who was the man at the NuEnergy Board meeting who you had run-ins with?"

"Boris Andropov."

"He's the sole owner of this Holding company. I found a few articles in European papers which imply a link between Andropov, his R.M. Holding Company and the Russian Mafia."

"So that's it! I'm facing the Mafia."

"Yes, I'm convinced of it."

"I'm in more than a little bit of trouble, aren't I?"

"Yes, big time."

Ben was momentarily confused. How could all of this slip past the federal authorities who licensed NuEnergy? Then it dawned on him. NuEnergy was an American company, which didn't own the plants. It only operated them. Perhaps the supposedly distant parent holding company wasn't closely scrutinized since ownership of the plant wasn't involved. Or maybe the ultimate holding company was sufficiently obfuscated by a series of confusing corporate pyramids.

Laura had already pondered her findings and concluded what was to be done. "Ben, I couldn't be more serious. You must get out of Black Bear."

Not surprised with that admonition, Ben shrugged, "Laura, I know that is what you think and I'm coming a little closer to that opinion myself."

"Well, I am going to call Mark Foster about all of this. Something smells rotten, rotten and..."

"And what?"

And, I believe we have only scratched the surface."

Ben was convinced that Laura was right about the danger, and he couldn't disagree with her about her plea for him to leave Black Bear, but for some reason he didn't want to back out, not just yet. He had always been able to face-down anything that came his way. Why should he give up now?

"Laura, I can't quit yet. It's just not in me to cut and run."

Laura stubbornly insisted, "Then I am calling Mark Foster. Maybe he can talk some sense into you."

"Since Lis's death all we get from Mark is a Christmas Card with no personal note. Call him if it will make you feel better, but do you really think you will get through?"

"Maybe yes, maybe no. If he ever hears that I called, I believe he will respond. He needs to know that the Mafia could be involved with nuclear plants."

Laura believed that Foster was her best chance to protect Ben. If

Ben's old navy friend told him to get out of Black Bear, he would listen. She knew Ben was stalling, hoping that something would ultimately break in his favor.

"Well call him then, Laura. If he tells me to get out of there, then I guess I will have to. How about after you call let's go home, have a few beers and watch movies till we fall asleep. By the way, that riding outfit is very flattering."

Laura sighed, "After all of these problems your thoughts can turn to fun."

"My thoughts can always take that turn."

CHAPTER
EIGHT

Day 3 7:10 A.M. White House

An agitated North strode up and down the west-wing hall, anxiously awaiting the vice president's arrival. Each time he negotiated the stretch of dull gray carpet between the Oval Office and the vice president's office, he cursed the interior decorator. "What idiot picked these carpets? They are either gaudy or depressing, nothing in between. This one is damned depressing. Which past first lady perpetrated this travesty upon the tapestry in these hallowed halls?"

North confronted Foster the moment he appeared. "We need to talk! Now!"

North hustled Foster into his office and slammed the door behind them. Foster looked questioningly at North, "What has got you so riled up?"

"Late last night our surveillance cameras caught one of our miserable Undersecretaries of Commerce pushing his ugly nose where it doesn't belong."

"Who?"

"A Mr. Vince Foley. The cameras caught him trying the door."

Moving toward the DVD and the TV monitor in the office, North loaded the disk he was carrying. "Here's the nosey butt in action."

After viewing the scene, Foster reacted, "Have Garrison check the FBI files on him. Who has keys to this office?"

"You, of course. I have a set. So does the cleaning crew."

"What do you think about staffing an agent on the cleaning detail?"

"Good idea."

"Have the cleaners been in here yet?"

"Nope."

"Good, hold off on any cleaning for one more day. Let's make certain that you and I have the only combination to the files in my office. Alert the Secret Service to be on guard for any more of Foley's antics."

Trying to place the Foley event in its proper perspective, Foster stated, "Foley strikes me as a bungler, not the real deal. Be alert to any other suspicious behavior around here. There could be spies around who are not quite as amateurish as our Mr. Foley."

North, relishing the excitement, assured Foster, "I'll take care of things. By the way, don't forget to change your computer password."

As a fired-up North left, Foster reviewed the possible explanations. Was this incident just idle curiosity on the part of the Commerce official or something more sinister? After only two days, how could his investigation have raised any suspicions? Only a handful of people knew of this. Who of those did he trust the least? The easy answer was FBI Director Lang. Could he be trying to find out more about Foster's investigation through Foley and possibly others, or was he becoming paranoid and grasping at straws? In any case, he would caution Garrison to watch out for Lang.

Day 3 11 A.M. Vice President Foster's Office

Agent Garrison neared the end of his second appearance before the vice president. In the welcome absence of FBI Director Lang, the agent skillfully presented a concise and factual report.

"Mr. Vice President, let me show you this chart of the phenomenal R.M. Holding Corporation. We put it together late last night and, frankly, we were all blown away with just how mammoth this mysterious conglomerate is."

Garrison unfolded a chart onto Mark's desk. It revealed a powerful corporation of awesome wealth and vast international breadth.

"What does R.M. stand for, Garrison?"

"At the bureau, only half jokingly, we call the conglomerate the Russian Mafia Holding Corporation. The initials presumably signify something entirely different to Boris Andropov. We don't know what, although it could be *Ruskamu Myedvyedyei* for all I know."

"Which is?"

"The Russian Bear."

"It would seem Mr. Andropov has done right well for himself since 'free enterprise' came to Russia."

"No kidding. He has achieved·astounding wealth and power. He runs both the Russian Mafia and the R.M. Holding Corporation with an iron fist. Tens of billions of R.M.'s yearly earnings are suspected to be illegal gang 'takes', laundered through their 'legitimate' holdings."

"Where is this conglomerate based?"

"Zurich, but their holdings and operations are worldwide."

"I see that Germany, Russia, England and even the U.S. are homes of major subsidiaries of R.M. I also see what you mean about the earnings being large. Any other international corporation would kill for R.M.'s unbelievable earnings to asset ratio."

Garrison grinned at that observation. "They undoubtedly do kill for those profits. Probably at least fifty billion of the Corporation's annual income is derived directly from the criminal portion of Andropov's empire."

"What do you know about the joint ventures?"

"Not much yet. They are a recent addition to R.M. Holding Corporation. We believe they are an outgrowth of Western businesses cutting deals with the criminal element overseas. Those corporations were under great duress from the criminals. Apparently, in return for the Mafia's protection against the killings and sabotage aimed at them, joint ventures were formed. These shakedown deals involve various international oil giants and R.M. Holding Corporation. It's just a sanitized form of payoff to the Mob."

"I see. Through this ruse, the corporations can legally bypass the Corrupt Practices Act."

"Yep and the Mafia's future take through those joint ventures is believed to be colossal, probably tens of billions yearly."

Garrison turned to the nuclear aspects of R.M. "Now, Mr. Vice President, here's some fascinating stuff. After tracing through a series of corporate shells we found that thirty U.S. nuclear power plants and a Munich Enrichment Plant are under the control of the Mafia Chieftain Andropov."

North, who had opted to attend this meeting, became suddenly very interested and moved close enough to see Garrison's chart. Could this possibly relate to yesterday's call from the distraught Tulsa woman, who was worried about her husband?

"So this R.M. bunch, through NuEnergy, operates thirty American nuclear power plants. Does it own them, too?" questioned Foster.

"No. NuEnergy's structured as an operating company."

"Isn't that strange."

"Not necessarily," Garrison responded. "They avoid much regulatory scrutiny by not becoming owners of the plants."

Foster shook his head in confusion.

An anxious North, who rarely spoke up at the briefings, asked, "I hate to interrupt, but is one of the plants Black Bear?"

North was beginning to suspect that the call from the Oklahoma woman was more significant than he had first thought. Maybe he should have let her talk to Foster. Maybe she really was the friend she claimed.

"Yes, it is, Don. Why?"

"Never mind. You and the vice president continue."

After shooting a puzzled look at the fidgety North, Foster directed Garrison, "Tell me about the Munich Enrichment Plant."

"Not too much to tell. We know little about it. It's a uranium purification plant. Makes commercial fuel for power plants. Natural uranium is sent to the place for enriching. It is operated by NuEnergy, but owned by the Deutsche Erste Bank. With that business setup, Boris Andropov and the Mafia have absolute control of the facility."

This struck Foster as very odd. Perhaps the intricately interlocking ownership and operation of the enrichment plant by R.M. Holding Corporation were just happenstance, but he doubted it. Could R.M.'s involvement with this enrichment plant in Munich possibly have a link to the missing uranium? Boy, he was grasping at straws, but any possibility was worth checking.

"Garrison, I have what's probably a dumb question, but hear me out. Since the Mafia may have a hand in the nuclear materials theft and since they built an enrichment plant around the same time as the theft, can there be a connection?"

"Anything is possible, Mr. Vice President," answered Garrison. He was impressed with Foster's conjecture. It was an avenue he would pursue even though on its face it made no sense.

"Find out all you can about that plant. Report as soon as you discover anything at all," ordered Foster.

"Yes, sir."

Garrison, wrapping up the subject, informed Foster that R.M. had grown far faster than other international companies. "In just five years the giant has leapfrogged from thirtieth largest on the list of international corporations to the largest, and its rate of growth hasn't diminished. The latest scuttlebutt has them acquiring the largest European insurance and financing company, Voyagers. It alone is worth two hundred billion dollars. If R.M. continues at this pace of earnings, it can gobble up one large international corporation every year."

"That's not a very pleasant outlook," Foster opined.

Garrison shook his head in agreement then turned to the issue of the curious Undersecretary of Commerce. "Vince Foley, who was caught on your security camera late last night, joined the department six years ago. It was at a time when some background checks were being waived. His no-clearance appointment appears to be a political reward to a big campaign contributor. Guess who, Mr. Vice President?"

"I have no idea," Vice President Foster retorted dryly. He hated guessing games, but he was curious about Foley's connections.

"Well, Mr. Foley was recommended for the undersecretary job by Mr. Parris, the president of none other than the NuEnergy Company."

"How about that for a coincidence."

North, becoming more fidgety with each revelation, winced at that disclosure. Still he remained silent.

"If you think that's a coincidence, listen to this. Your man Foley is head of the Resource Import Division."

"Do uranium imports fall under him?"

"Yes."

After Garrison left, North returned to the table where the R.M. chart lay.

Pausing for a double take on North, who was intently studying the R.M. chart, Foster queried, "What's up Don? Why has this grabbed your interest so?"

"Have you ever heard of a Ben and Laura Andrew?"

"Sure. They were Lis's and my best friends in the Navy." Pausing he recalled, "Strange that you should bring them up. I was just thinking of Laura yesterday after I set up a meeting with Dudaev. She tutored me through Dudaev's tough Russian History class."

"She called yesterday. I intended to handle it myself, since you are so busy."

Foster leaned forward, "What did she want?"

"Her husband works at Black Bear. Apparently he is having some serious run-ins with NuEnergy. She is worried about him and says that they suspect NuEnergy of criminal activity."

Foster boomed, "Call Garrison. Tell him about this. Have his Tulsa agents get a secure phone in the Andrews' hands. Their phones could be tapped. I want to talk to them today."

Foster allowed himself a little time to reminisce about his good friends from his Navy days. He thought highly of them both. If they said there was a problem at Black Bear, then it was so.

CHAPTER
NINE

Day 3 2 P.M. White House

Foregoing lunch, Foster went through a light workout in the gym. Boy, had he needed that. A workout each day was his fix. Even though he showered, his shirt and slacks still stuck to his steaming skin. Nearly late to his next meeting, he paused for only a moment to ask North if they had gotten a secure phone to the Andrews yet.

North replied, "Garrison says give him an hour. His agents tell him that Ben is at the plant, so they can't get to him right now. They are taking one over to Laura at her bookstore."

"That works."

Foster's thoughts returned to his next guest. General Dale Adair's career was exemplary. In the latter stages of the Vietnam War, Adair had distinguished himself as one of the Army's outstanding junior officers. He was one of the cadre of bright, dedicated military officers who had labored tirelessly since their baptism in Vietnam to ensure that the armaments, strategies and training of the U.S. military were unequaled. Their overriding goal was that never again would the country experience the agony of a Vietnam. Foster shared that goal. U.S. military supremacy was beyond question from the late eighties through the nineties. Maddeningly to him, the hard-won post-Vietnam superiority had been steadily eroded by neglect, lack of mission and budget cuts up until the WTC attack. That event had prompted the start of a rebuilding and restructuring of the U.S. military.

But Third World rogue powers that once deployed second rate armies were no longer to be lightly dismissed. These countries now fielded advanced military armaments, including, in many cases, weapons of mass destruction. Mark was apprehensive that, should it ever become necessary, it would be difficult for the U.S. to confront successfully one of those armed-to-the-hilt countries.

Foster had watched the general's rising career. His Special Forces background could be handy in this situation.

North interrupted his reflections, "Mr. Vice President, General Adair has arrived."

Foster moved to the door to greet the Joint Chiefs Chairman.

Turning to his aide, General Adair instructed, "Set those briefcases down here and then you are dismissed."

The aide set the two large legal briefcases and several rolled-up charts on the table and promptly left as directed.

"General, I apologize for the sizable assignment I dumped on you. For now, though, you are the only one in the Pentagon who needs to know about this mess."

"No problem, Mr. Vice President."

After reviewing the latest on mutual military friends, Foster plunged into the briefing. "Let's get started. Bring me current on the global status of nuclear weapons. Much has changed since I had your job. In particular, I want a refresher on how many nuclear weapons there were in the Soviet Union at the peak of the cold war buildup, and how many there are now in Russia and other CIS countries."

In response to Mark's request, the general rolled out two charts. "Let me show you these, Mr. Vice President. This first chart illustrates the Soviet's strategic nuclear warheads, and the other their tactical warhead inventory. 1988 represents the time of peak Soviet nuclear power, while 1991 represents the status after the Soviet Union breakup, but during Start I implementation. Of course, this last column shows where they stand today in their nuclear weapons inventory. The grand totals have gradually dropped from over twenty thousand in 1988 to around three thousand today."

"What is the status in the three former republics who had nuclear arms?"

"It's different in each. Having already turned over their strategic warheads to Russia, the Ukraine agreed in 1994 to return the less-powerful tactical nuclear warheads to Russia for dismantlement. In exchange, the Ukraine received security assurances and financial compensation for the nuclear material in the warheads. They also received expanded Western aid. Ukraine acceded to the Non-Proliferation Treaty, NPT, and has apparently shipped and removed all former Soviet nuclear arms from its territories. Within our ability to account for the warheads, we believe this to be true.

"Belarus ratified the START treaties and acceded to the NPT as a non-nuclear weapons state. Thereby they codified their intent to become nuclear-free. The withdrawal of weapons from Belarus was completed in 1997. We believe the accountability in Belarus is reasonably accurate, although, some materials or weapons could have slipped through the cracks.

"Kazakhstan, though, is different. It did ratify the START treaties and acceded to the NPT as a non-nuclear weapons state. But progress was slow in removing the warheads from Kazakhstan soil and accountability is doubtful. The Kazakhstan President maintains that his country should be compensated for the enriched uranium in the warheads before any more are turned over for dismantlement. We don't buy that excuse. Our Intelligence agencies believe that a sizable number of tactical nuclear weapons are missing from that country. I'm sure CIA has already briefed you on that subject."

Foster nodded indicating that the general was on track and should keep going.

"Kazakhstan also had a large amount of weapons-grade uranium stockpiled at the Semipalatinsk nuclear facility. You may remember that, once in 1993, Kazakh officials informed the U.S. about a vulnerable cache of approximately six hundred kilograms of that uranium which they had found. Kazakhstan cooperated with a joint Department of Defense and Energy team in removing that relatively small amount. Sometimes I think that was more for show than anything."

Foster appreciated just how well informed Adair was on this subject. The wide range of issues under his purview made it difficult to remain fully apprised on every subject.

"I have just a few more questions for you on nuclear armaments. Just as you surmised, yesterday the CIA did provide their estimates of the number of missing warheads. They also described the difficulty in calculating how much uranium might be missing from Kazakhstan."

After pausing for a moment, Foster moved on to his next round of questions. "What other countries now have nuclear warheads or weapons material?"

General Adair pulled a file from his closest briefcase. He handed the vice president a copy and then he recited without a glance at his own copy, "China has at least 500 nuclear warheads; France, 290; Britain, 190; Israel, 100; India, 80 to 110; Iran, 12 to 25; North Korea 12 to 25; and finally Pakistan has about two dozen nuclear warheads."

"What about Iraq?"

"The War of 2003 took care of them for awhile," responded General Adair.

"So is Iran enriching uranium for nuclear weapons?"

"They are doing something in the nuclear weapons business which they don't want discovered. They won't allow IAEA inspectors in."

Foster asked, "Do they have thermonuclear devices?"

"We have no firm evidence of that yet. But I couldn't say with certainty that they don't," replied General Adair. The military had deep concern about Iran's nuclear capabilities, but he would go into it further only if Foster requested. It was his meeting.

Foster again changed the direction of his questioning. "What has happened to the 'retrieved' nuclear warheads returned to Russia by the CIS countries?"

"Those returned to Russia from the three republics fall into three categories: dismantled, being dismantled, or stored in a disarmed configuration. The material from the disassembled weapons was earmarked for blending through the U.S. enrichment plants to become commercial fuel for our power plants. The actual flow to the U.S. enrichment plants has slowed lately. Frustrating bureaucratic roadblocks, primarily in Commerce and Energy, have reduced the Russian uranium flow to a trickle."

Foster suspected that these roadblocks might be no accident. He had a hunch that they might be tied to Foley and the Russian Mafia, so he inquired, "Why has Commerce obstructed the flow of the Russian weapons-grade uranium to our enrichment plants?"

"I can't fathom it," snarled General Adair. "Congress passed a piss-poor bill two decades ago aimed at protecting the U.S. uranium mining industry. Powerful Western senators sponsored it on behalf of their constituents. The actual cause of the decline in American uranium mining was depletion of our richest ore bodies, due to decades of heavy mining. At the same time, around the world, very rich uranium ore deposits were discovered at a remarkable pace. It was ill-conceived legislation, which flew in the face of reality. Now Commerce's bastardized interpretation of this bill, has served to delay the Russian uranium flow to the U.S. That Department is frustrating the plans to get that dangerous weapons material out of our former enemy's hands. What a crock," spit out Adair.

An agitated Foster put down his coffee mug, rose and paced from wall to wall as he pondered what the hell was going on.

"Is this a deliberate slowdown? If so, why? What's Commerce's game?"

"I don't know. State and Defense are completely frustrated by Commerce's actions. Speaking for the military, we believe that those delays are counter to our national security interests."

Foster strongly agreed with that assessment. Shipment of the uranium to the U.S. would generate billions in revenue for Russia's ailing economy and place the nuclear material safely in U.S. hands. It had seemed to be a win-win arrangement for both countries. Foster was amazed at how the implementation of this uranium trade was being thwarted. Something smelled extremely rotten.

"General Adair, the President will inform Secretary of Defense Winston that you will be working directly for me on this matter. After I talk with the President, I suspect that one of your jobs will be to ensure the military's readiness for any action that becomes necessary. Also, we will undoubtedly ask for preliminary contingency planning to once again project power into central Asia and the Middle East. If we do find that the missing Soviet nuclear weapons are there in the wrong hands, time will be of the essence. The military must be ready for anything."

After General Adair left, North reported that a Tulsa FBI agent had delivered a secure phone to Mrs. Andrew. She was expecting a call. The agent had also warned her not to trust their own phone lines and certainly not Black Bear's. Thus Ben, who was still at work at Black Bear, knew nothing of the impending call.

"Don, ring Mrs. Andrew now."

A moment later North handed Foster the phone.

"Laura, I got your message that Ben is in trouble at Black Bear. What's going on there?"

"I'm scared to death for Ben, Mark. They have actually tried to kill him."

Since an avenue of release was finally open, Laura spilled out her concerns. Thoughts flowed out so rapidly they ran over each other. She told how a friend on the Highway Patrol had confirmed much of their suspicions.

Foster, trying to calm her, said, "Take your time, Laura. I want to hear the full story so relax. Take a few deep breaths. We will get to everything. First though, I want to know, how is your mother?"

This inadvertent blunder on Foster's part served only to remind Laura of how much she needed Ben. She couldn't stand Ben being in such danger.

"Mother died last year," Laura stated somberly. The reminder of the finality with which she was denied her mother's love still hurt terribly.

"I'm sorry, Laura. Shame on me for not knowing that. She was a grand lady who inspired everyone she met. She could always find the good in any situation or anyone. I'm embarrassed that you and Ben so thoughtfully remembered my loss of Elisabeth with flowers and a note, but..."

"Don't beat yourself up over that, Mark. We didn't tell you about it and Mom's death wasn't exactly national news."

Foster listened as Laura recounted the predicament Ben was in at Black Bear and her research confirming much of what he already had learned about NuEnergy being closely tied to the Russian Mob.

Recognizing the potential tie-in of the Andrews' problems to his investigation, he directed, "Use only the phone the FBI gave you. Have Ben call me as soon as he gets home. I will ask our Tulsa Agents to talk to the Oklahoma Patrol and to start a protective guard of you two. I want Ben back here to give me a first hand account of all that he knows and suspects. He has an insider's perspective that could be of great value to us."

"As long as you keep him safe, then it is okay. We aren't looking for anything but to live together in peace."

After hanging up, Laura had an uneasy feeling. Could her call to the vice president backfire and perversely mire Ben deeper in this mess?

CHAPTER
TEN

Day 3 6 P.M. Bandar-E-Abbas, Iran

The Chelyabinsk Shipping Company's container ship lay berthed in the giant Bandar-E Abbas port. The Russian vessel was delivering prized weapons to the Iranian military from Marseilles, France.

Despite wearing dark sunglasses, General Bakr Zarif squinted from the reflected brilliance of the harbor's thousand sparkling, setting suns. The seaport was one of the world's busiest. Much of Iran's international trade funneled through this bustling port, strategically situated on the Straits of Hormuz; the straits separated the Persian Gulf from the Gulf of Oman. Zarif counted no fewer than a dozen supertankers either loading crude or anchored awaiting their turn. The actual loading platforms for these behemoths of the sea were a half mile from the shore. Pipes fed the black gold under the water from the mammoth on-shore storage tanks to the deep-water loading docks and the glutinous ships.

General Zarif enjoyed each opportunity to leave his desert headquarters at Karaj for a journey to the coast. He relished the host of scents offered by the seaport. Whiffs of freshly caught fish mixed with the pungent smell of oil, and the stale stench of old dirty freighters. In the evening, though, the sea breeze cleansed the port with the cooler, cleaner air from the Gulf. The moist air soothed his desert-parched skin, as might an application of Aloe Vera lotion.

The gulls flew amidst the hectic activity around the dock, adding to the commotion with their antics and scolding. Occasionally one sharp-eyed bird's dive to the water's surface for a vulnerable fish would trigger a frenzy as the gull's many cousins horned in on the feast.

However, neither the supertankers, the gulls' antics, nor the welcome break from the desert had brought the general to the seaport

71

today. As chief of Iran's Special Weapons Division, he was here with his troops to oversee the unloading of a most valuable cargo. The mid-sized Russian-flagged container ship carried four fifty-foot-long containers, holding the capstone of his burgeoning arsenal.

Replete in his red and gold trimmed olive-green uniform, the general with his entourage watched as the onboard aft crane slowly lifted the last of his containers. Gaining sufficient height, the crane lazily swung the precious load over the dock, and after several minutes of lowering, it came to rest on the fourth and last military flatbed truck.

A Slavic man of average stature, with a day's growth of ebony beard darkening his already dark countenance, joined the interested spectator.

"That one does it. They are all safely in your hands now, General."

"Good."

"Boris Andropov sends his greetings to you."

"And mine to him."

"Our shipping company had no trouble whatsoever in purchasing these two cruises from the French. We told them the destination was Saudi Arabia but, frankly, the frogs didn't give a damn."

General Zarif motioned to the Russian to join him in his personal command car, which flew the Iranian flag and the general's personal flag, a flag born over two decades ago during an international crisis. It was the American flag upside down, which reminded him and all under his command of their mission to reverse the American domination of the region. His priority was to restore the Persian Empire to preeminence, while destroying the Great Satan. He now had a worthy ally in that endeavor, Comrade Andropov.

Once Zarif and his guest were inside, Zarif instructed the driver to follow the last truck. The driver surely knew to do that anyway, observed the Russian, but this was the military and generals were generals, even in Iran. He perceived that this General Zarif possessed a missionary zeal for his work. In his opinion, the man was dangerous. His goals were inimical to Russia's best interests, but this was Mafia business. The savvy Slav comprehended that Zarif's ambitions, Iran's money and the Mafia's far-flung criminal capabilities had merged, creating very strange bedfellows.

"So did the French firm demand an exorbitant price?"

"*Nyet.* Fifteen million U.S. dollars for each missile, and five million for each launch apparatus, just as we expected." Actually he had bargained for a lower price with the French, but Zarif didn't need to know that.

"So, I owe you twenty million plus shipping?"

"*Da.*"

"We did get the new Mach 3 ramjet with the stealth package, I assume?"

"*Da.*"

"Good. Very good." General Zarif opened a legal-sized briefcase containing bundles of large denomination U.S. bills. He closed it and opened a second.

"You will find the twenty million is all there. We will keep the second missile safe for the glorious day when Andropov will use it against the American devils."

Being only a deliveryman, the Slav didn't comprehend the implication of that statement except to reinforce his opinion that this Zarif was dangerous.

They continued the ride in silence. General Zarif's satisfaction was boundless. With this supersonic trump card the deck was stacked. His ambitious dreams would soon be fulfilled. What to many naysayers had seemed grandiose and out of reach twenty years ago, was now within his grasp.

Neither the Iranian President nor the commanding General of the Army were aware of all that Zarif was building and planning. Zarif's deceptiveness and his closeness to the Ayatollah had kept them in the dark.

In 1979 Zarif was a leader of the radical group that held the Americans hostage. They had brought the Carter administration to a standstill. Zarif still recalled the exhilarating sense of power when he had toyed with the helpless hostages. Telling them they were going to die, he placed a gun to the head of first one and then another blindfolded captive. Nefariously he would pull the trigger. They were infidels and deserved even worse. As these American devils fell apart under his torture, he gleefully told his compatriots, "You see how easy it is to defeat this decadent enemy." He had mocked those captives, who had prayed to their God, that it was he, Bakr Zarif, the true power, who held their lives in his hands. Their God was not worth praying to.

As he saw it, Iran had been used as a pawn in the American power struggle with the Soviets. How ineffectual Iran was back then. Well, both former cold war adversaries would feel the sting of a resurgent Persia before he was finished. A new order was coming to the world. His nuclear build-up was nearing completion.

Upon reaching the edge of the military base, the convoy of trucks turned into the army compound. Zarif's black limousine, with flags fluttering, followed the trucks. Clearing the gate with no observable check, the car and its occupants received only a properly stiff salute from the military guards policing the entrance. Zarif's guest assumed that the general's flag on the car was all the pass needed to gain entrance anywhere around here.

Once inside a warehouse on the base, Zarif showed where the two missiles were to be temporarily housed while being fitted with nuclear warheads.

"We shall keep both Andropov's missile and ours here."

After touring the warehouse, General Zarif instructed, "Follow me. I have a little surprise."

The heavy-set Russian panted as he trailed the fast-stepping general across the floor of the huge building. There were another two containers exactly like the four he had just delivered. Zarif shouted an order and a half dozen soldiers scurried to remove the top from one of those mysterious containers.

After climbing to a nearby balcony affording a view of the contents, the general instructed, "Come take a look."

After catching his breath, the amazed Russian remarked, "It's a cruise. Just like the two we brought you. Where did you get it?"

"It sure looks like one of the real things, comrade, but it's not. It's only an empty shell replica."

"What's the point?"

"The point is to thoroughly confuse the Great Satan. Undoubtedly the U.S., with their infernal space cameras, has photographed the arrival of the two missiles."

"How does this fake confuse them?"

"In about two weeks, after we fit our most destructive nuclear warheads on the two new arrivals, we will deploy. One of the new missiles with a real warhead and the phony missile and fake warhead will be taken to our northwestern frontier. Their cameras will tell them that both missiles have been deployed to the border."

"But what good is accomplished by taking the fake?"

Zarif gloated, "That leaves the one here in the clear for your big boss, Andropov."

"I still don't get it," admitted the confused Russian.

"That's fine, neither will the infidels until it is too late. Andropov and the rising Persian Empire have a little surprise in store for the Great Satan."

CHAPTER
ELEVEN

Day 3 6:30 p.m. North's Office White House

"You know it's been a challenging couple of days, Don. I have Russian Mafia, wealthy international corporations, missing nuclear weapons and all varieties of uranium filling this tired old brain of mine. How are you doing?"

"Actually, I'm enjoying this whole sordid business immensely. In backwards old Arizona the biggest crises we faced was how to keep all of California and Mexico from moving in, eh."

Foster just shook his head for there was no getting the best of North, "You aren't admitting in a left-handed way that some of us beltway folk actually do something of value, are you?"

"Well, there's a maverick in every herd," responded North.

The rejoinder forced a rare smile from Foster. "Touché, you ornery cowboy."

"I see that you pulled together one hell of a team in Adair, Stockton, Neiman and Garrison, so why on earth are you having some lost-in-space professor come here?"

"Don't forget, Don, that you are part of our team, too. On the professor question, I think that you especially should understand how I need insights into Russia that no one within the beltway can give me, eh."

"Touché yourself, Mr. witty Vice President. How clever. You shoved my own ideas back down my throat. That's my favorite trick."

Don had elicited still another hard-to-come-by grin from the stoic vice president.

Foster continued on a more serious note, "There is an aspect of this situation that, frankly, scares me shitless, and I don't scare easily."

"What's that?"

"You hit on it yesterday. You know that I'm an old cold-war warrior. The U.S. and Soviet armies faced each other for nearly fifty years with enough armaments to end life on earth, but it never developed into a shooting war. Do you know why?"

"Blind-assed luck?"

"Partially. It's also because both sides had a lot to lose and the leaders were at least rational enough to understand that truth. Today, despite our best efforts, we still face these Armageddon weapons in the hands of rogue countries led by maniacs. Just as scary, some of these deadly weapons may be held by mobsters. They have nothing to lose by using nuclear weapons. If the Russian Mafia hits us, how do we retaliate? Drop a bomb on R.M.'s Zurich headquarters?"

North laughed nervously at the problem, but offered, "We could send my roughest drilling crew over to teach them some goddamned manners. My boys would serve them their ugly, flea-bitten heads on a platter."

Foster couldn't help chuckling. He loved this Westerner's grit. "We may call on them before it's all over. Seriously though, I'm not so sure where the Russian leaders are coming from. That is why I want Dudaev's take. History is full of instances where our country has misread Russia's intentions, and I don't intend to make that same mistake. Oh, for the simple days of the Cold War. I understood Russia best when they were our sworn enemy."

North attempted to reassure Foster. "Well you and our crackerjack team must find a way to keep the worst from happening. You know that professor Dudaev is due here in twenty minutes."

"Yes. I am strangely nervous about his visit. He is such a perfectionist."

North laughed, "And you aren't? By the way, Garrison said to tell you that Dr. Andrew will be here tomorrow."

"Excellent. If we are lucky Ben will shed some light on why the Mafia is getting into the American nuclear power business."

Sending a signal that it was time to get back to work, Foster stood and abruptly brought the exchange to a close, "Okay, I must get ready for the professor."

Day 3 6:40 P.M. Vice President Foster's Office

North opened the door and ushered in the academician of Slavic and Jewish extraction, Professor Anatolii Dudaev. Foster immediately saw that the Professor retained the same sly twinkle in his eye. The bright glint almost seemed to say, "I have more secrets than you could ever guess."

Not waiting for formal introductions, the Professor taunted, "Who conquered Russia and most of the known world in the thirteenth century?"

Foster was astounded. This aging historian not only remembered him, but also recalled the one question he missed twenty years ago on his final exam. How did teachers acquire such an ability to recollect? "Well, sir, it sure wasn't just the Golden Horde. I know that."

"Correct. It was Genghis Khan's worldwide empire. The Golden Horde controlled only the western quarter of his kingdom. I see you learn from your mistakes. That is good."

The bemused North quickly concluded that, despite having work to do, this was one meeting he couldn't miss. Foster was obviously in for a rough time from this no-nonsense professor. North settled into a corner chair to enjoy the show.

"Professor, thank you for coming on such short notice. I know you keep very busy with your teaching and consulting, but I am in a predicament where mistakes are not allowed."

Dudaev, actually quite grateful to Stockton for this opportunity to talk with Foster, shrugged off the thanks, "No problem, Mr. Vice President."

"The President has delegated an urgent assignment to me. I desperately need insight into the present Russian leaders. What motivates these men, and how much can they be trusted?"

Professor Dudaev, most sought-after by the nation's most prestigious think tanks, pointedly replied, "Mr. Vice President, I know all of that. Director Stockton briefed me."

Dudaev was sending a not-so-subtle message that this session was to be all business, with no wasted time allowed. Foster sensed that Dudaev had adroitly seized control of the meeting. In North's vernacular, Dudaev had him by the balls.

"If you had been more attentive in class, Mark Foster," winked the slight Dudaev to North, "you might not be in such dire need of this refresher." With that trifling admonishment, he consolidated his authority over the get-together.

The professor carried a fishnet bag that formed a 1950's-style East European backpack. He plopped the well worn book, a treasured possession from an uncle long deceased, incongruously onto the vice president's dark cherry wood desk and withdrew a book.

Foster recalled that in one class session Dudaev had shared with them a little of his past. Dudaev's father, a Russian Slav, and his mother, a Jewish Pole, were imprisoned and presumably killed by the KGB for being suspected Nazi sympathizers. During the confusion of the German invasion at the outbreak of World War II, an uncle had taken the orphan and his sister to the Black Sea port of Odessa and paid their fare to the U.S. His uncle apparently did not have enough money to go himself. Dudaev never heard from him again and suspected one side or the other killed him during the war.

The waifs, ten-year-old Anatolii and his younger sister, Anna, had arrived quite alone in a strange land. Dudaev had told how he would follow the milk truck and steal freshly delivered milk from porches to keep his sister and himself from starving. He stressed the lasting debt he owed an uncle, who had literally given his life for him and his sister. Foster surmised that sense of indebtedness may be what drove Dudaev to become such a renowned Russian expert.

Sliding the book on Russian history toward the vice president, Dudaev demanded, "Let's get down to business. Turn to page one-fifty-six. What do you see there, Mr. Vice President?"

"A map."

"Don't waste my time. Showing what?"

"Showing the extent of a series of invasions of Russia over the period from the thirteenth to the twentieth century."

"Describe what the map shows in more detail."

The slender professor, whose white rumpled hair hung down over his brown forehead, nearly blocking his vision, reminded Foster of a disheveled Adm. Rickover, who was also a slight wisp of a man. Dudaev, like Rickover, seemed to radiate light through his genius and strength of character.

Foster replied, "The combined effect of those periodic invasions was that nearly all of Russian territory, except the extreme north-central, was conquered at least once and in many cases several times."

"By whom? From what directions?"

"Mongols, Germans, French, Poles, Austrians, Swedes and Anglo-Americans. From the east, south and west," he replied, not wishing to further raise Dudaev's ire.

The Professor amplified, "And the invasions of their homeland didn't start in the thirteenth century. Before that it was the Huns from 200 to 400 AD, the Avars from 560 to 600 and the Khazars from 650 to 700. The Ottoman, Persian and Byzantine Empires stressed and challenged Russia from the South at various times through the centuries.

"Points to be drawn from all of this are that the Russian people are damned tough, resourceful and yet extremely distrustful of their neighbors. The degree of their distrust, borders on paranoia, and is not well understood by Westerners. They have had a hostile climate to their north and aggressors on all other sides for, at least, the last two thousand years. Because of this extensive history of violent invasions they are and will always be wary of their neighbors.

"As a solution to these eternal challenges to their very survival, the Russian people have assented to a strong, powerful central government. They abdicated most claims to their personal freedoms in a Faustian bargain, which guaranteed their national survival. The Czars, and later the Communists, more than adequately filled the demand for that strong, authoritative government.

"Because of their tolerance of dictatorship, they don't appear to us to treasure personal freedoms as do citizens of the Western democracies. But to disabuse anyone of that notion, one must merely read the works of their greatest writers: Tolstoy, Pushkin, Sumurov, Pasternak, Solzhenitsyn, and Dostoevsky. These gifted men paint a portrait of the longings of a long-suffering people to whom history has dealt a continuous series of devastating blows. Despite the cruel twists of fate, the spiritual fire of the humble masses has never been quenched. Nor, unfortunately, has a collective vision of empire been entirely snuffed out. Now look at this."

Obviously relishing his assignment, Professor Dudaev bounded energetically around Foster's imposing desk. He unfolded a chart in front of the vice president, then returned to the far side of the desk.

The chart illustrated graphically the relative economic strength of Russia and its neighboring powers to the west, south and east. Standing on tiptoe while leaning forward with his arms braced on the desk, he got nose to nose with Foster, and loudly proclaimed, "This chart shows the gross domestic product of Russia, the European Union, China, Japan and the growing cadre of fundamentalist Islamic countries both ten years ago and now. This comparison shows that Russia is dramatically losing ground, economically speaking, relative to her neighbors.

"Now look at this map which shows the breakup of the Soviet Union and the progressive expansion of NATO and the European Union right to Russia's western doorstep. Even the Ukraine has expressed interest in joining NATO. Don't forget NATO's bombing of Serbia. In Russian eyes NATO beat up on her Slavic little brother in 1999. That tweaked their psyche nearly as much as the breakup of the Soviet Union. During the War on Terror, U.S. troops were stationed in the former Soviet Republics of Tajikistan, Uzbekistan and Georgia. You see, it begins to look a little like that first map I showed you. If you surmise that their fear of their neighbors is at a fever pitch, you are right.

"Now note this, Mr. Vice President. The Middle East and China, two of Russia's biggest border problems, are responsible for fifty percent of the military spending in the world. Much of that expenditure is by fundamentalist Islamic countries, such as Iran. That quite literally scares the 'hell' out of the Russians. They have rather unpleasant memories of wars in Islamic Afghanistan and Chechnia, and most recently, Dagestan. Did you know that the Azeris, based in Iran, are petitioning the World Court for the return to them of twenty-seven former Soviet cities in the Caucuses?

"So you see, this paints a picture of a country under siege, struggling with economically and militarily potent neighbors all around them. Russia could use a friend right now. Actually they could have used a friend for a long time, but were too proud and distrustful of everyone to acknowledge the fact. Despite recent apparent trends away from the West, they may have chosen the U.S. as that ally. They may trust you and President Arthur more than past administrations. Never, though, will they openly acknowledge that to you. Only their acts will make that evident. If you play your cards right at this opportune juncture, you may be able to count on Russia in ways you would never have dreamed possible."

"That is why I must assess Kruschev accurately," reminded Foster. "The CIA believes we can trust the Russian President but they aren't as sure about Kruschev. What can you tell me about him?"

The lithe professor lowered himself back into the chair directly across from Foster. He folded his legs under him in a manner reminding the kibitzing North of a little disheveled Buddhist monk. North found considerable humor in the incongruous analogy, but hid his amusement. He was impressed with this little guy. There was much more to this academician than met the eye. His uncommon authority had a basis that went deep, much deeper than North could comprehend.

Despite Dr. Anatolii Dudaev's seemingly irreverent behavior toward the vice president, the professor realized this briefing might be one of his most important assignments ever. Rather than shy from the tough task, Dudaev welcomed the challenge. Foster was going to learn more about Russia and its leaders in one sitting than he had bargained for.

"Patience! Forget Kruschev for now, Mark Foster. Pay close attention for a brief time and you will learn much about the great Russian Bear.

"I give my students a quiz at the beginning of each class. Here is one of the questions from that quiz. Which statement best describes Russia? One, Christianity has never been a living, vital force in Russia. Two, Christianity was brought to Russia in the eighteenth century by missionaries from Europe and the U.S. Three, Christianity has been an integral part of Russian life for over one thousand years. What's your answer to that question?"

"I am tempted to say number two," replied an unsure vice president.

Professor Dudaev's eyes rolled back in his head. "This may take longer than I thought! Sixty percent of my beginning students say number two, thirty-five percent say one, and only five percent give three as their answer. By the way, three is the correct response. I'm sure if you think back on it, you will remember that with the collapse of the Byzantine Empire a thousand years ago, Moscow became the eastern center of Christianity. Often Moscow in this role referred to itself as the Third Rome. That self-perception partially explains their belief that they are destined to rule an empire and it is a major factor dividing Russia from the Western World.

"In the last ten years the West has sent Christian missionaries to Russia and other CIS countries. Much good certainly comes from this, as I could relate if I had time. Suffice it to say, though, it is too often a further manifestation of our ignorance of and arrogance toward this complex country. Actually, the Christians in Russia have suffered a far more violent, frequent and prolonged repression of their faith than have most of those living in the West. Christianity was a strong force in Russia before the U.S. was a gleam in the Founding Fathers' eyes. Perhaps Russia should send missionaries here to tell us what it's like to defend one's faith to the death against one of the most concerted, sustained and grievous attacks against religion ever perpetrated.

"What is encouragingly different though about the Christian movement of today's Russia is that the Intelligentsia are increasingly embracing the faith. The past elitist attitude that religion was merely 'the opiate of the down-trodden masses' is changing. The newly elected Russian President stands as an example of this change. He is a professing, practicing Russian Orthodox.

"Despite being singled out for terrible persecution and especially vicious attacks, the Russian Orthodox Church is the only Soviet-wide institution to have survived in opposition to the seventy year rule by the Soviet Communist regime. However, great damage was done to the church and to Russia's claim as the Third Rome. I envision that a Fourth Rome will manifest itself, not as a city, a state or a country. Rather it will reside in the hearts of brave, freedom-loving, God-fearing people. The seed for the Fourth Rome was sown many years ago by a humble poet."

"Who?"

"Someone you probably never heard of, Viktor Sumurov."

"How did he do this?"

"It's a long story. Suffice it to say that Sumurov's writings helped inspire the dissident movement that began in the mid 1960's. One can see his influence in Solzhenitsyn's and Sakharov's beliefs. Each bravely advocated freedom of thought and diversity of political power, while severely criticizing the Soviet Communist Party."

Dudaev continued, "If you were briefed by Western Sovietologists and Kremlinologists, they almost universally oversimplify Russian history by focusing on the historical, political, economic and cultural background of the Slavs. They erroneously zero in on Moscow and St. Petersburg exclusively. Russia, despite the recent loss of empire, is still an amalgam of literally dozens of ethnic groups, languages and religions covering an incredibly large expanse of the European and Asian continents. Don't make the mistake of dismissing them lightly. There is still some bite left in the hassled, old Russian Bear."

"Another question that the students answer incorrectly is, have the secret police powers been greatly reduced within Russia today? Ninety-eight percent say yes, two percent say no. I suspect you'll get this question right if the CIA has done an adequate job in briefing you."

Foster nodded his head, signifying the answer was no. Thanks to Liz, he knew the answer. He marveled at what a job she had done earlier. Accepting his status as a student, he listened raptly as Dudaev fed him the insights he needed.

"Don't believe for a minute that the old KGB police powers are gone. They are still intact," instructed Dudaev. "So your Mr. Kruschev, as head of the FSB with its hundreds of thousands of agents, is a most important leader. He is feared by politicians, criminals and business tycoons alike. You need him. You know that. What you don't know is whether you can trust him."

Foster shrugged and admitted, "You are definitely right about that. I don't know."

"If the Russians called the U.S., and not vice versa over this 'urgent matter,' then chances are good that they want U.S. cooperation and help. That much we can surmise."

"Well, that figures. But still, what about Kruschev?"

Dudaev leaned in toward Foster and, seemingly to punctuate the importance of his next message, lowered his voice to a whisper, "Now listen very closely. I'm getting to him, Mark! Give it a rest!

"Atheist not Christian. He loves Mother Russia and will be against anything, and I mean anything, that in his perception hurts or threatens his beloved homeland. He will never relinquish power willingly. As long as he is alive and maybe even longer, he will be a force to be reckoned with in Russia. Whom or what do you suppose he sees as threats?"

"Economically and militarily powerful neighbors," speculated Foster, taking a cue from the professor's earlier presentation.

The twinkle in Dudaev's eyes brightened at the vice president's thoughtful answer. "Yes. You were one of my brighter students at that. What else?" His voice slowly rose.

Foster paused and pondered before hazarding a reply. "Their own weakened economy."

Professor Dudaev excitedly homed in on his next point. "And what is hurting their economy now more than anything?"

"Lack of free market know-how," Foster ventured, rather sure he was on a roll.

Professor Dudaev leapt from his chair like a Jack-in-the-Box shouting in three languages at once, "No! *Nein! Nyet!* Just when I was going to give you a gold star.

"They are plagued with pervasive corruption and ensconced organized criminals. These despicable mobsters have the Russian economy by the jugular vein and are sucking the lifeblood out of it. The crime wave in the U.S. in the twenties and thirties, during the days of prohibition, was a mere flicker of a candle compared to the firestorm of criminality consuming Russia today. This evil epidemic in Russia is more pervasive and debilitating by far than any crime wave in modern world history. It has tainted all, even former Russian Presidents."

Foster, trying to make a comeback from his latest mistake asked, "But doesn't a significant part of that criminal element reside in Kruschev's own FSB?"

"Yes! Yes! Now we can resolve your conundrum on whether to trust Kruschev. The monumental revolution of 1917 by the Bolsheviks, despite the awful upheavals and displacements of society wrought by that great struggle, succeeded only in replacing the Czarist form of totalitarianism exercised by the Romanov family with a new dictatorship. The substitute, the Leninist Communists, was a more devilish form of authoritarian government. At least under the Czars, cultural growth occurred occasionally. Under Communist dictatorship, Russian cultural and intellectual growth was stifled and, as a consequence, they fell further behind Western cultures in many areas.

"Now listen closely," Dudaev demanded, rapping a gnarled finger on Foster's fancy desk. "These may be the most momentous times in all of Russian history. The Russian people have a window of opportunity that comes their way only once or twice in a millennium. The true battle for the soul of Russia is now joined. This battle is far more significant to Russia and the world than the Bolshevik Revolution. Will the forces of civilization, humanity and religion triumph over the crushing corruption and criminal forces that grip Russia, threatening to engulf the country in a profoundly evil quagmire? The outcome of this great struggle could well hinge on how well you and Kruschev work together to face your quote, urgent crisis, unquote. So I'm going to equip you with the ability to deal with him."

North marveled at how cleverly this old professor was imparting vital Russian insights, and how apparently momentous were the implications of the struggle against the criminal element for Russia and the world. The stakes of this nuclear crisis, he gathered, had just risen.

"I am listening."

Dudaev advised, "Here is how you do it. If they called you first, as I said before, that is a positive sign. That means they probably already evaluated you and President Arthur and have determined you to be worthy and probably essential allies. When you talk with Kruschev, don't be arrogant. Listen to him carefully. Don't be devious, be forthright. Always remember Kruschev is your intellectual match. He is capable of discerning any deceit on your part."

North was astounded. It was almost as if Dudaev knew Kruschev personally.

"Tell him you are worried about the extent of corruption over there and, in particular, about the organized criminal element within his own FSB. If Kruschev claims that that's not a big problem, he probably doesn't trust you, or want you or the U.S. as a true ally and friend. With that answer, you should conclude that he has ulterior motives. He won't lie to a prospective friend or ally, and that would be an outright lie.

"If, on the other hand, he admits to the criminal infestation within his organization, you can be more certain that you two individuals and, more importantly, the U.S. and Russia, are going to wind up on the same side of this urgent crisis. But beware, he will still be tough to read. He won't tell you everything he knows. He may even attempt to manipulate you to a certain course of action that may or may not be what you would choose if you had all of the facts. So always turn over every stone, use all of your sources and evaluate them carefully. Kruschev will not lie to you if you are a friend, but I repeat, he won't necessarily tell you everything he knows either.

"So it's time for your final exam, Mark Foster. This time it won't be me grading you, it will be history. As you correctly stated earlier, you can't afford a wrong answer. Not this time. Remember, your crisis may be merely a manifestation of the titanic battle for the Russian soul which is engaged at this historical juncture. I pray that your country and Russia will unite and fly as joint eagles into a better future for our world."

Ending with that profound synopsis, the professor rose to his feet and embraced Foster with as big a Russian bear hug as he could muster. "I'm leaving you three books. They are on Russian history, culture and religion. You need to thoroughly understand each of these important aspects. If more of our leaders would take the time and effort to study the other nation's leaders, cultures and customs, the U.S. would be far more effective in its conduct of foreign affairs. Too often our country is a bumbling giant, who comes out okay only because of its overwhelming might. I am proud of you, my former student. Good luck and God's blessing be with you, Mark Foster."

"Thank you, Professor. You have been extremely helpful. Obviously you remembered when I took your class on Russian history. You know, I heard recently from the lady who tutored me so effectively back then."

North caught that Dudaev was apparently startled with that bit of news, but the professor recovered quickly and mumbled something that sounded like, it's a small world. This man puzzled North more than anyone he had ever met.

After the Professor left North turned to Foster and commented, "That little old guy is a handful, isn't he, Mr. Vice President? Strange as it sounds, he is the one man I wouldn't want to cross. If knowledge is power, then you were just face to face with the most powerful man in the world.

Foster shook his head in agreement. Yet, despite a few bruises to his ego, he had gotten what he needed. He now held new and important insights into Russia and its leaders that should enable him to deal more effectively with them.

Immersed in study, Foster looked at his watch. It was nearly 9 p.m. He had promised Dione that he would take her to dinner tonight to celebrate her passing the bar. Unfortunately, he still had hours of study ahead of him. He reluctantly decided to call her to see if he could put off the celebration for one more day.

He dialed Dione's number and waited nervously for her to answer. "Hello?"

"Hi, Honey. This is Dad. How are you doing? Have you come down out of the clouds yet?"

"Well, not really. I am starving and sure looking forward to dinner with you. It means a lot to me to know how much you care about my little achievements. Clinching the bar, hallelujah! On my first try, too. How about that?"

He gulped. This was going to be tough, torn once again between duty to country and love of family. "Dione, you bet I am one proud papa. What an achievement! Has Dedra heard the good news?"

"Yes. I called her right away. She says to say hi. Things are well with her. She wasn't surprised with the bar result. She said I always was the smart one."

"Now you are pulling my leg," Foster laughed. "She would never admit you were smarter."

"You're right, Dad," Dione giggled impishly. "I was just checking to see if your mind was here, or a thousand miles away on God knows what national crisis."

"Okay, okay, you are on to me. Which brings up something."

He paused to summon his courage. "Just as you playfully joked, there actually is a crisis. If I cancel out on dinner tonight, would you accept a substitute? Tomorrow you and I will dine at the restaurant of your choice. Georgetown has some great places. After that we can catch the new musical hit at Kennedy. They say 'The Third Millennium' is Andrew Lloyd Webber's best musical score yet."

Dione had grown accustomed to being stood up by her father. Many years ago she had come to terms with the reality of his devotion to his career. She realized it wasn't that he loved her less, but rather his all-consuming dedication to his country had always been paramount. All in the Foster family understood that fact of life. But knowing that still made it barely possible to accept tonight's disappointing cancellation. Recalling her mother's plea to always support him, she whispered to herself, "This one is for you, Mom."

Finally she answered, "Okay, Dad, I will let you off the hook this time. My law firm friends are throwing a celebration bash tomorrow night. It is in my honor. Why don't you come to that with me and we can do Kennedy some other night?"

"Well, I suppose I could. How many people will be there?"

"Fiftyish. My new best friend at work, Michelle, has made all of the arrangements."

"Who's she?"

"She's a beauty and real smart. You will like her."

"It would be a change of pace for my Secret Service agents. I will see if they think they can take care of you and me in that party scene. Will any other good looking ladies be there?" he asked, teasing Dione a little.

"Oh, yes. A couple of knockouts."

"I will use that to help convince our agents," he joked. "I will pick you up at seven tomorrow."

"You promise? No more excuses!"

"To the best of my ability."

"Love you, Dad."

He sighed and shook his head after hanging up. This crisis had strangely forced two reunions: today's with Professor Dudaev and tomorrow's with Ben Andrew. Turning to the mountains of paper on his desk, he settled in for a late night of study. He had to be fully prepared for tomorrow's call to Kruschev.

CHAPTER
TWELVE

Day 4 10 A.M. Black Bear Plant Manager's Office Near Tulsa, Oklahoma

Late last night in a long phone conversation with Vice President Foster, Ben was told that they wanted him in D.C. right away. A special plane would arrive at Tulsa's airfield this afternoon. It would ferry Ben to D.C. and back to Tulsa. Foster had cautioned that NuEnergy must not know of this trip.

Ben had been worried about how to handle Black Bear, but Plant Manager Zoglemann was unwittingly handing him his cover story on a silver platter.

He couldn't sound too eager about Zoglemann's proposal, so he played his cards carefully. Ben replied with feigned skepticism, "So, I am being sent to Munich."

"Yes, Dr. Andrew. That is right, you are to help with this year's fuel audit. You will be leaving early next week."

NuEnergy's new-found generosity was transparent. They were getting him out of their way so they could do as they wished with the new maintenance agreement. Ben factitiously told himself that they must have run out of ideas on how to kill him. Then he sobered up, maybe Munich was part of a new scheme to do him in. Whatever, he still had to handle this opportunity correctly.

"Then I won't be around for final negotiations on our maintenance contract. That is a problem!"

"Not really," smirked Zoglemann. "We are bringing in corporate maintenance planners. They will take over where you and your group left off. In fact, we are making a permanent shift of maintenance planning and scheduling responsibilities. From now on the corporate office will be in charge."

Ben was somewhat hurt, but far more worried, by that stripping away of his responsibilities. Over the past few months much of his group's work had been ripped away by the NuEnergy corporate office. Since they couldn't get him to agree to the unwise scaleback of Black Bear's sterling long-term maintenance program, they were just going around him.

He wasn't used to losing battles, but he sure wasn't winning many lately against NuEnergy. They seemed to hold all the cards and ruthlessly played them to their advantage.

"Well, I will go to Munich under two conditions. I need some personal time off between now and next week. Also, I will leave specific written conditions that must be incorporated in the maintenance contract."

Zoglemann looked in disbelief at Ben. "Perhaps you don't understand. You presuppose too much, Doctor. Your trip to Munich was intended as a reward for all of your past hard work. But, it's not optional. You will go. Also, you don't seem to grasp the fact that the Corporate Office is now in charge of the maintenance negotiations."

"Well you seem to have everything neatly arranged. I will go, since I obviously have no choice."

"We thought you would see it our way."

"I do need to take care of some personal business this afternoon and tomorrow, if I'm to leave for Europe that soon."

"Take all the time you need."

Ben left, cursing under his breath, "You SOB's think you won this round, but we shall see who wins the war."

Day 4 1:45 P.M. Laura's Bookstore Tulsa

Laura understood Ben's hyper state and his need to work off some of his frustrations; nevertheless she admonished him, "Stop. You have done enough on the store's inventory."

"Not done," Ben argued.

Laura stood her ground. "You and I can finish inventory when you get back from D.C."

"Okay."

Ben reluctantly put down the clipboard. He hated to break more bad news to Laura, but he saw no choice, "There's something else..."

Sensing something was wrong, Laura sat down.

"Laura, another complication's come up. NuEnergy ordered me to go to Germany next week."

"An order?"

"An order!"

"They really are SOB's."

"You are right about that."

"Why? What's their reason for this trip?"

"To audit the Munich Plant."

Laura shook her head, "No, Ben. No! It's too dangerous."

She looked at him questioningly. Didn't he remember about R.M. Holding. Through a subsidiary, they owned the Munich plant. Worse yet, NuEnergy operated it.

"It sounds like a setup to me. Don't go. Please quit."

Her moistened big blue eyes pleaded with him to listen to her and get away from the corrupt NuEnergy bunch.

Laura's reasoned, yet emotional, appeal momentarily trapped Ben. After some thought he offered a compromise solution. "I will talk to Mark about the Munich deal tonight. I will only go to Germany if he thinks it's safe or he provides protection."

Laura nodded in reluctant agreement, praying that their friend would not send Ben into more danger.

Laura understood that Ben's greatest strength was also his greatest weakness. Seemingly impervious to consequences, he took on battles that really weren't wise. She had seen him act this way many times during rock climbing outings. He would tackle a steep cliff without concern for the danger that lay ahead. He had mangled a hand that required reconstructive surgery as a result of one of those bold blunders. In her opinion he was again poised to take on a fight that wasn't his fight. The way she saw it this was the government's battle, not her Ben's. Hopefully Foster would see it that way and tell Ben to butt out.

CHAPTER THIRTEEN

Day 4 3:15 A.M. Vice President Foster's Office White House

Before placing the critical call to Russia's security chief, Vice President Foster had examined every available policy statement and newspaper article involving Kruschev. He had perused the books left by Professor Dudaev.

Pictures of the scowling Kruschev were foreboding. He was a sixty-year-old Russian who had relentlessly climbed to power during his long service in the former KGB, the KVD, and the FSB. Foster's curiosity was aroused, prompted by the man's close resemblance to the former Soviet Premier of the 60's, Nikita Kruschev.

"Is this guy related to Nikita? For some reason my briefings failed to answer that. Hell, maybe I'm not as prepared as I thought."

Liz, recognizing how apprehensive Foster was about this call, attempted to reassure the nervous vice president. "Our agency believes he's distantly related to the former Premier."

That speculative bit of information didn't ease Foster's anxiety. Everything he had read or heard only deepened the mystery surrounding Kruschev. The man was a walking set of contradictions.

Foster arose, stretched and circled around the office one last time. In his characteristic attempt to relax, he rolled his head from side to side like a boxer shedding punches. As much as he would like, he could no longer defer this conversation.

As Foster refilled his coffee mug he instructed, "Don, place the call. It's now or never, Liz. Let's hope you and Dudaev have managed to teach me enough."

"You are prepared and will do just fine, Mr. Vice President," reassured Neiman.

Cutting no slack for his nervous leader, Don yelled, "Pick up the phone, Mr. Vice President. It's final exam time, eh."

After a brief greeting and some stilted conversation on Moscow's and DC's weather, there was an awkward pause as Foster thought about his next move. He couldn't talk about the weather forever.

Vasilly Kruschev broke the uneasy hiatus, "You undoubtedly had a lot to learn in a short time."

"For sure, Director. Before we get started, though, permit me to ask one personal question."

"You are always free to ask…"

Foster chuckled at the unstated implication that Kruschev might or might not choose to answer. Perhaps he was talking to Russia's version of Don North, or even better, a mixture of Stockton and North. "Your name raised my curiosity. Would you, by any chance, be related to the late Soviet Premier, Nikita Kruschev?"

"Yes. My grandfather, Ivan Kruschev, was Nikita's cousin."

Foster nodded to Liz, who was listening so she could comment and advise, if necessary. Wisely resisting any jabs about the shoe-pounding Premier, Foster said instead, "I wondered if that wasn't the case."

"It wouldn't have been my portly appearance that gave you a clue, would it?" Kruschev knew full well that older Americans remembered Nikita as a fat, crude country bumpkin. Did the CIA think of him as cut from the same mold? If they did, he figured that was just fine. Let them think him a bumpkin. He preferred to be underestimated by friend and foe alike.

Kruschev continued to place Foster on the defensive. "My humor, you will find, is not quite as crass as that of my famous relative."

Foster, taken aback by the man's candor, was slowly grasping the truth that he had a tiger by the tail. He cautiously pressed ahead with the conversation.

"Director, appearance honestly might have been part of it, but the name itself is so well known here that the question is an obvious one."

"That makes sense."

"Thanks for speaking with me in English. I know that must make things more difficult for you. I'm afraid that like most Americans, I have not mastered your language."

"Not a problem."

"I never moved past that alphabet of yours, with the backward R's."

"No, yours are backwards," Kruschev sharply retorted. "We are well aware of the linguistically challenged Americans, so I am quite prepared to accommodate you. Actually I rather enjoy aspects of the English language. It affords such a plethora of venues with which to express a thought."

North, stifling his laughter, bent over holding his sides in the corner of the room. His boss had met his match again. Between Dudaev and Kruschev, the vice president was getting a double serving of humble pie.

Foster rolled his eyes and kicked himself for commenting on their alphabet. Boy had he been made to pay for that mistake. He took a deep breath, seeing that Professor Dudaev had not been kidding. This was one sharp cookie! Director Kruschev could more than match him quip for quip, even in English. His skills were the equal of James Stockton's linguistic talents. Never again would he underestimate the FSB Director.

This first stage of their conversation was a little like the first round of a boxing match between championship contenders. The boxers were feinting, jabbing and throwing just enough punches to feel out the opposition's defenses. After the first round Vasilly, with his brilliant counter punching, was clearly ahead on points.

Foster decided to tackle a central question of the crisis, but one that he felt should not further strain their shaky start. Slightly stretching the truth, he offered, "The CIA tells me that according to their estimates between twenty-five and fifty tactical nuclear warheads are missing from Kazakhstan. Also they believe that at least some of them have wound up in Iran. This seems to at least bracket your President's more precise statement that at least fifty tactical nuclear warheads have been smuggled out of Kazakhstan."

"We have an advantage or two over you," Kruschev explained. "After some persuasion, an informant at Semipalatinsk 'chose' to talk. As a result, we have obtained an accurate count on the missing warheads. Also we have acquired some ideas on who is responsible, but we should return to that later."

Foster took this to mean that Kruschev intended to be forthcoming and truthful with at least some information. That was encouraging.

"Great! And I can share our information as to where we believe some of those smuggled warheads are deployed."

Mentally making a note to return to that issue, Foster pressed forward. "Regarding the missing bomb-grade uranium. We have a huge problem coming up with an estimate even close to one hundred metric tons. My advisors tell me that record keeping of uranium quantities within the old Soviet Union was different from ours. They say that records were kept in rubles and not in kilograms. That complicates things." Foster had carefully chosen his words to avoid sounding critical of their sloppy record keeping.

Vasilly Kruschev, fully prepared for those questions, explained, "Reconstruction is the key. Our engineers went through the records at each enrichment plant and assayed the U-235 remaining in the old waste piles. I think you call that 'tails uranium,' for reasons that escape me."

Foster pushed the mute button and commented, "Just like ol' Munson said, Liz."

"From this research we concluded that the enrichment plant at Semipalatinsk clandestinely created an extra one hundred metric tons of bomb-grade uranium. This material was accumulated and carefully hidden over a long period of time. It was smuggled away from Semipalatinsk in the confusion of the early nineties. Most of those directly involved in the smuggling have either left or resisted our best and, I might add, our most persuasive efforts to find out where that material has gone. I wonder sometimes if those we have questioned even know of the uranium's ultimate destination."

Liz, taking notes as rapidly as possible, caught the use of the adjective "ultimate." On a notepad she rapidly wrote a question to alert the vice president. So, do they know of intermediate destinations? Foster nodded a thank you, for he intended to pursue that point if the opportunity arose.

Kruschev continued, "The other infuriating aspect of this situation is that it's too much bomb-grade material to be sold on the black market. No one rogue country needs such a large inventory."

"Director, that puzzles us, too. Have you ever heard of a Boris Andropov? He heads R.M. Holding Corporation?" Foster decided to steer the conversation, as Dudaev had suggested, toward the Mafia to test Kruschev's trustworthiness.

Kruschev replied, "I know a great deal about both Mr. Andropov and R.M. Holding Corporation, but rather than bore you, I suggest you tell me what you know first, then I will fill in."

"I would hate to play chess with this man," Foster whispered to Neiman and North. Yet he fully appreciated that the stakes of the game in which they were engaged were far greater than any chess match in history. He related most of what he knew about Andropov, but did not divulge that Andropov had been director of the Semipalatinsk Nuclear Complex in Kazakhstan. He wanted to see if Kruschev brought that up.

"I have Andropov's file here in front of me," Kruschev said. "You are right. He is head honcho, as you Americans say, of the Mafia. If you didn't bring him up, I was going to. Here is the low-down on Boris Yuriivich. He was born of Russian parents in Almaty, Kazakhstan, in 1948. His father, Yurii Andropov, a capable young engineer, immigrated in the thirties with tens of thousands of other Russians to Kazakhstan. The father settled in Almaty, the former capital, where he supervised the design and construction of many of the defense industry factories that were built there in the forties and fifties.

"Boris's mother, Katerina, was a gifted prima donna of the Bolshoi Ballet. Katerina followed in the tradition of other great ballerinas, such as Kshessinskaya and Anna Pavlova. Boris' father met her after attending a special, for Communist leaders only, Moscow performance of LaBayadere."

Liz, a ballet aficionado, was floored. This man even knew of the Bolshoi's greatest ballerinas. Maybe, though, it wasn't so unusual, she decided, because of the immense popularity of the Moscow troupe. She knew that Russians loved their ballet, their poets and their vodka.

"By that time Yurii was a high-ranking member of the Kazakhstan Communist Party and in charge of several weapons factories. Yurii and Katerina, despite, or maybe because of, their diverse backgrounds, fell in love, married and had one son, our Boris. Katerina, finding that she couldn't forego her beloved dancing, continued to star in the ballet and was mostly absent from home during Boris's formative years. Yurii was left with the job of rearing their young son.

"Boris Yuriivich became a child protégé of the father. He was a brilliant student. At age fifteen, the Soviet state sent him to Lebedev Institute of Physics, where he became the youngest physicist ever to graduate from there. He studied under Sakharov, but politically he was very different from the famous Sakharov."

Liz made another note. Was it her imagination or did Kruschev actually hint at admiration for, or at least, approval of the late Sakharov. That was a very strange attitude for the head of Russian security.

"Upon graduation Andropov was assigned to the Semipalatinsk Nuclear Complex in eastern Kazakhstan. He demonstrated management skills at Semipalatinsk that were highly unusual for one so gifted technically. He was promoted to director of the center in 1982. He was ruthlessly intolerant of those with average intelligence or mediocre performance. He also was a fanatic communist. During the latter years of the Cold War, it became his obsession to ensure that Soviet nuclear might was the equal to that of the U.S. The START agreements to him were the Soviet and Russian leaders ultimate ignominy in capitulating to the West. Nuclear arms were the one arena where, as he saw it, the Soviets could compete on an equal footing with your country. Boris had consistently emphasized the need for nuclear weapons testing. Hundreds of nuclear explosions at the test site near Semipalatinsk resulted from his drive for ever greater sophistication of our weapons."

Liz noted on her pad that Kruschev was deliberately giving them a tremendous dump on Boris. The why of that was not clear, unless Kruschev believed Andropov was involved in the heist. She had no way of knowing that every bit of this would be useful later.

"As I alluded to earlier, we discovered that Boris secretly altered the operation of the nuclear enrichment complex to produce more product than our flawed records indicated. We surmise that as a reaction to the perceived 'sellout' by his leaders, he turned criminal and plunged into the nuclear smuggling business. The officially non-existent one hundred metric tons of weapons-grade uranium, as well as fifty warheads, disappeared from Semipalatinsk. We are now quite sure that Andropov secretly set aside the fifty tactical warheads which were officially slated for testing. While claiming he had tested them underground, he actually had stockpiled them for some future purpose. As a consequence of the fall of the Communist Party, the Soviet Union's disintegration and the 'sellouts,' this embittered man embarked upon a criminal course of vengeance."

"Vengeance?"

"Yes, I will get to that, but continuing, perhaps the final straw sending Boris 'over the edge' was the famous Kazakh Poet, Olzhas Suleimenou. Olzhas organized the most popular political movement ever in the USSR. His protest against the continued testing of nuclear weapons in Kazakhstan gained popular support throughout the world. The poet cleverly courted Western antinuclear groups for financial and technical assistance. As Boris viewed it, even the public had turned against his sacred nuclear weapons program. After that final blow, we believe Boris's loyalty transferred to himself and his private ambitions. He detested the Soviet and Russian leaders, considering them *predatels,* and because of Suleimenou, he developed an even greater hatred for Russian writers. By far his greatest hatred, though, still is reserved for his old enemy, the U.S. So beware of the man and his organization. Vengeance may be on his agenda."

Liz scribbled another note. Maybe that was the reason for the detail on Andropov. It was a deliberate warning to watch out for him.

Foster's mind raced. This was an incredibly forthright, human and insightful account of Boris Andropov's life. Its frankness disarmed him. He had not expected this degree of candor from Vasilly. He saw that Liz was similarly struck by these revelations. What prompted such forthrightness? Obviously Kruschev wanted them to understand Boris Andropov. But, why? Just how dangerous was this Andropov? So far this conversation was extremely promising, but he still remained cautious. The emergent policy of the U.S. in this crisis must be on solid ground. Kruschev still might be withholding crucial information.

He carefully explored, "Director, I thank you for that revealing profile of Boris Andropov. It is quite unnerving to think that someone that brilliant is ramroding the Mafia."

"We share your concern. I must admit, though, I can't keep up with all of your colloquial expressions. Ramrod?" Kruschev prided himself on being familiar with most American idioms, but every once in a while a new one emerged to frustrate him.

"Ramrod just means to be aggressively in charge."

"Well, he is certainly that."

"You know, Director Kruschev, this discussion of criminals reminds me of a joke that I read recently in one of your Russian journals. Two killers were lying in ambush in Moscow with their guns loaded, waiting for a banker who was supposed to show up at 2:30 p.m. The banker didn't appear. Four o'clock arrived, but still no banker. Finally, at a quarter to seven, the one killer turned to the other and said, 'Listen, I'm worried that something may have happened to our banker.'"

Vasilly Kruschev laughed. "You are going to become corrupt reading Russian journals, Mr. Vice President. That allegory, though, is almost too true to be funny. Over thirty Russian bankers a year are murdered by the mobsters. The ones that aren't murdered are either unimportant or already in the Mafia camp."

"So the Russian bankers are either dead, insignificant, or mafiosos?"

"*Da*! That about sums it up."

"All kidding aside, criminal elements over there do worry us. My agents tell me that criminal activities exist even within the FSB itself. I am very concerned about that."

"Your concern is understandable. The Mob is pervasive in our society. It hurts me deeply to admit that our security agency, which was always motivated by the love of Russia, is now one of the entities infiltrated by the gangsters. That, however, is more our problem than yours."

Foster didn't quite agree that the FSB, or its predecessors, had always been motivated by the love for Russia, but Kruschev openly admitted that the mob influence on the FSB was a problem. That was the best answer possible. He gave a relieved thumbs-up sign to Liz.

Neiman noted the "love of Russia" comment from a different point of view. To her it may shed light on Kruschev's true motivation and it confirmed Dudaev's uncannily accurate assessment of him.

Vasilly Kruschev, realizing that he had been tested, was not to be outdone. He quickly and deftly turned the tables while sending an important warning. "From what my agents tell me, your government, over the last few years, has welcomed certain criminal elements right into your country and into your own governmental agencies. Commerce, Energy and law enforcement are areas you should watch closely. Also, from what I read in your papers, the Chinese have pretty well had their way with you and your nuclear secrets."

Recognizing the deft switch to the offensive accomplished by Kruschev, Foster countered, "Can you give me details?"

Again Liz had a different take. The warnings, she believed, may have been intended to be helpful.

"Read your own newspapers and magazines. That will give you a start. Let's not go there now."

As the vice president had promised, he briefly relayed what he knew about missile and bomb deployment in Iran and then reviewed where things stood. He had his answer. Apparently Russian President Strahkov and Director Kruschev wanted the U.S. as an ally, but why? Was the nuclear weapons crisis just a manifestation of their larger struggle against organized crime? What, if anything, was Kruschev holding back? Those were all questions for another day.

"Director, thank you for this exchange. We will talk again soon."

The conversation ended on a cordial note, with the agreement to talk two days hence.

The vice president turned to Liz, "What are your impressions?"

"I think my vice president has met his match." She smiled, hoping Foster wouldn't take her remark too personally. He didn't.

"Dudaev's test of Kruschev, which you skillfully applied, reveals that he wants our assistance. However, I think he was fully aware that he was under your scrutiny on that matter, and probably chose his answer accordingly."

"So what is it they want from us?"

"Two things. First, it appears to me that they have decided to take on the Mob. They know they can't win that battle without the help of the Western world. Secondly, they are terrified of nuclear-tipped missiles deployed by Iran on their southern border. Kruschev didn't say much about it, but I read him as plenty worried about that possibility. That is probably why he cooperated with Strahkov in uncovering the smuggling."

"So where does that leave us, Liz?"

"Here's my wild hypothesis, Mr. Vice President. Politically and militarily they can't handle the Iranian threat. Short of a first strike with nuclear arms, their military can't neutralize that problem. If they initiated a nuclear first strike, they would be committing national suicide. They are stymied. They want us to do the job for them."

CHAPTER
FOURTEEN

Day 4 6:30 P.M. CIA Headquarters Langley, Virginia

Two Secret Service men escorted Ben through a labyrinth of hallways to an inner office, which Stockton had provided. There Vice President Foster awaited him. Ben seldom was nervous, but today was different. Why was the vice president so anxious to meet him personally? Was it the NuEnergy-Mafia tie, which Laura had hit upon? Well, he would find out soon enough.

As the two stern men led him deeper into the vast facility, a flood of recollections, prompted by the imminent reunion, rushed through Ben's mind. He hadn't seen Mark Foster for fifteen years, yet the memories of their Navy days vividly returned. He and Foster had served together as officers in the nuclear submarine service. Ben had enlisted for five years of service and reported to the Naval Officer Candidate School in Newport, Rhode Island. There he first met Foster, a very conspicuous candidate at the school. He was older and one of very few blacks in the Naval Officer program. More striking and memorable, though, was the aura of charismatic leadership that the man had exuded. Foster became the battalion commander of their class of Naval officer candidates. In those days Ben developed deep respect for Foster, which later turned into a fast friendship.

Foster had been a sailor and, because of his talents, was one of the few enlisteds selected by the Navy to go through a special officer prep program. He was sent to college by the Navy, where he whizzed through the Nuclear Physics program at the University of Kansas, graduating magna cum laude. From there he went to the Naval Officer Candidate School where his and Ben's paths first crossed. Their diverse paths to the school meant that Foster was several years older than Ben.

100

The two were among a group of a half dozen officers from their class who were chosen to enter the nuclear submarine program. They were both assigned to New London, Connecticut, where nuclear subs were being constructed and tested.

After serving together Foster's and Ben's paths separated. Though Ben left the service, the families stayed in touch through the exchange of letters at Christmas. Ben recalled that in those early Navy days the gifts of intelligence and leadership that Foster possessed were quite evident. Laura and he were both sure that Foster would make admiral one day. As it turned out, they had underestimated his potential.

At last the moment was at hand. Here he was in the heart of CIA headquarters about to renew acquaintance with the vice president. Perhaps he should be in awe, but he wasn't. He was curious, damn curious about Black Bear, NuEnergy, the vice president, the Mafia, and if any of his misadventures at Black Bear made any sense. Would the vice president agree with Laura that Ben should get out of the Oklahoma plant and not go to Munich?

The escorting agents swung open the door and Ben saw him. It was as though the years melted away. Before him wasn't the vice president, but his old Navy companion. At the instant their eyes met they both recognized that though much had transpired in the intervening years, their friendship endured.

The two old friends shook hands and embraced.

"Mark, how are you?"

"Keeping damned busy."

"I believe that. Keeping busy was never a problem for you. I'm amazed you were actually advised of Laura's phone call. What on earth is going on?"

"A hell of a lot. We will get to all of that in due time. Damn, it's good to see you again."

"If NuEnergy had its way, I wouldn't be here or even breathing," joked Ben.

"I definitely want to hear about that bunch. They are a big-time problem."

Ben sized up Foster. To remain so obviously fit, his friend must still be practicing his martial arts. When Ben knew him, he was a seventh degree Black Belt, and competed successfully against the nation's best in full-contact contests.

Foster, too, was sizing up the situation. He was amazed at how strangely comforting it was to have his friend with him once again.

His wife was gone, but one of their best friends was back.

"Ben, I do believe you could still go a couple of downs on the football field."

"Only a couple?"

"Well—maybe more. Do you recall the time during practice you tackled our best running back so hard it sprung his thigh pad, actually reversing the damn thing? That poor guy had a thigh bruise so deep it didn't heal the rest of the season. When I tell that story, even coaches won't believe me."

"Those were great times. I had forgotten all about that incident. I must have hit him just right. I do remember, though, that Lis and Laura had their hands full keeping us out of trouble. The nightclubs full of Jar Heads are where I always had to bail your black ass out of trouble."

Foster playfully objected. "Bull shit! It was the other way around!"

Ben replied, "Whatever you say, Mr. Vice President."

Foster chuckled at Ben's feigned humility. That was the Ben he remembered. He wasn't cowered by anyone or anything. Apparently that hadn't changed.

"How's Laura?"

Ben welcomed the opportunity to tell about her. "She is fine. Her literary interests have found a new outlet. We recently opened a bookstore specializing in European literature. She manages the little store, writes occasional articles for magazines, and composes editorials for papers."

"What a talented lady. Laura pulled me through a couple of those Russian classes with her brilliant tutoring. Do you remember that? She had such an infectious joy for the subject that I wound up enjoying the classes immensely and learning a great deal. As you will discover soon, that training is turning out to be very important with what we are facing today."

"We? What do you mean we, Kemosabi?"

"It will become clear that you have happened into the path of some very bad people."

"Laura and I figured that out already."

After the two had a chance to catch up on the other's family, Foster started to explain why he had summoned Ben to D.C., "Your knowledge of NuEnergy's involvement in Black Bear is vital. We must hear everything."

The concern, evident in Foster's voice, reinforced the urgent plea for help.

Ben, though, needed little encouragement to express his opinion of NuEnergy. He spit out, "NuEnergy's the damnedest bastards I ever saw."

Foster laughed. He recalled that Ben's normally quiet demeanor would transform if the occasion required. The switch had occasionally helped him accomplish a goal. If their Navy football team was behind at half time, Ben would react hotly. He would fire up the team by challenging each member to dig deeper and fight harder. In that way he would turn a potential loss into a victory. Apparently those leadership traits remained intact.

"What is the problem with NuEnergy, Ben?"

"It's easier to say what is not!"

"Just pick the big issues for now."

"Well first, I believe that they sabotage power plants..."

Foster interrupted, "How? When? Which ones? How do you know this?"

"It's all engineering judgment and conjecture on my part. I have no proof, only suspicions. But I did some checking. In the last few years at least a dozen nuclear plants experienced strange shutdowns or outright accidents. Black Bear is the latest. I talked with the engineering managers at some of the other plants. Several are suspicious of sabotage.

"Here is the clincher. Following the accidents, each of these plants' operations were taken over by NuEnergy." Ben handed Foster the list.

Foster looked over the names and recognized them. All were mentioned in Garrison's earlier briefing.

Foster asked, "Why wouldn't the NRC suspect foul play?"

"A number of reasons. Complacency, naiveté, bureaucracy, and political expediency."

"Political expediency?"

"Yes, sabotage is not an explanation which they relish. Investigations of sabotage can involve other federal agencies. Often one of those becomes the lead investigator, forcing the NRC into a subservient role."

Foster noted the politically astute answer, which Ben gave. He probed deeper, "Why do you and some of your cohorts suspect sabotage?"

"The nature of each accident. There is a pattern. In each event an insider at the plant could have deliberately and rather simply changed a valve position or tampered with an instrument. The engineering fixes, which the NRC ordered in each event, were a band-aid fix and off the mark in my opinion."

"Why do you suspect NuEnergy Involvement?"

"In each case they moved in so swiftly that it would almost seem that they expected the event. They took over operations at each plant shortly after the incidents occurred. They are the beneficiaries."

"How convenient, but they could just be opportunists," said Foster, playing devil's advocate.

Ben strongly doubted that theory. "Could be, but they have benefited from the plants' misfortunes to the tune of hundreds of millions. Hold your opinion until after I give you all of my observations."

"Of course. Go ahead, Ben."

"What is happening at Black Bear is my second reason."

Ben went on to explain the strange plant accident, the nearly fatal brake failure of his blazer, the personal threats, and the emphasis upon short-term profits at the expense of long-term plant health. He described his attempt, at a NuEnergy Board meeting, to express his concerns for plant safety. Andropov, who was at the meeting, shut him down swiftly and surely with a fairly transparent threat that his career would not benefit from his harboring such belligerent attitudes toward NuEnergy policies.

That was enough for Foster. He volunteered, "Your suspicions of them are on target, Ben. I have just been probing to see how sure you were that NuEnergy is a problem. We even checked your phones. They are bugged, probably by NuEnergy. That is why it was important for the FBI to give you and Laura secure cell phones, but I interrupted again. What is your other reason to suspect NuEnergy deliberately harmed the plants?"

"Laura's research. She did an intensive Internet news search and constructed this chart of NuEnergy's ownership."

With a brief explanation of Laura's investigation Ben handed Foster the chart.

Despite the seriousness of the subject, Foster laughed, "Maybe I should hire Laura and fire the FBI. We could save the government a lot of money."

Puzzled, Ben asked, "What is so funny?"

"The FBI presented almost the same chart to me yesterday."

"Is that right? I will tell Laura. She will be pleased to know that her work was confirmed. Laura also found a couple of editorials in British papers, suggesting that the R.M. Holding Company has extensive Russian Mafia connections."

"Bingo! Laura goes to the head of the class."

Foster, seeing that the Andrews represented a surprising well-spring of information, probed further, "Have you ever heard of an enrichment plant in Munich?"

"You bet! That is unfortunately where we get our fuel for Black Bear. When NuEnergy took over, they forced us to cancel our favorable fuel contracts with U.S. and Canadian suppliers, and insisted that we procure our fuel from the Munich plant. I am being sent there next week to audit the place. Actually I am being forced to go because NuEnergy wants me out of town so they can sign a completely inadequate maintenance contract for Black Bear."

Foster couldn't believe his good fortune. Garrison and the rest of the team had, so far, drawn a blank on the Munich plant. They found information on the place nearly impossible to come by.

"Hold on a minute, Ben. This may be just the break we need."

Foster instructed one of his Secret Service escorts to call Garrison. While waiting for the call to go through, Foster partially explained to Ben why he was so interested in the enrichment plant. He told Ben, "After we finish here, we will get you back to Tulsa so you will be home before your friends at Black Bear miss you."

Ben watched as the Secret Service agent alerted Foster that he had Garrison on the line. With growing curiosity, Ben listened to the vice president's side of the conversation.

Foster asked Garrison, "Do you have anything more on the Munich Enrichment Plant?"

After listening intently to the answer Foster summed up, "So you are finding next to nothing. They have really bottled that place up, haven't they. Well, guess what? We may be in luck. My Navy friend and nuclear expert, Dr. Ben Andrew, has been invited to audit the blasted place. How in the hell is that for coincidence? Do you think that could be useful to us?"

Foster laughed and turned to Ben, "He says 'hell yes', except he's worried that you are a civilian without a thorough FBI background check."

Ben bristled at any suggestion that he was anything less than a patriot. "Tell him I held a Top Secret clearance in the Nuclear Navy and had my entire pedigree checked before going to work for Black Bear."

Foster replied, "Garrison knows all of that. He already ran an expedited check on you. He is just being cautious."

Foster turned his attention back to the phone, "I trust him. We will escort him over to you immediately. You brief him on all you know and want to know about that mystery plant. Also arrange for his protection while he is over there in Germany. Give him some ways to get in touch with us if emergencies arise."

Foster gave the phone back to the Secret Service man. After pausing for an extended moment, Foster moved forward decisively, taking Ben completely into his confidence. "Ben, you are going to be busy in Munich. Here is the entire deal. For almost a week now we have been investigating a nuclear weapons smuggling scheme. The conspiracy seems to have tentacles everywhere. We suspect that NuEnergy's Munich plant could tie into this whole mess, but we aren't sure how. We know so little about it. You can help us. Find out everything you can about the place."

Foster directed the security men, "Take Dr. Andrew to Garrison's office and then accompany him to the plane. Stick with him until he is safely back in Tulsa.

"Ben, tell Laura that we will get together as soon as all of this blows over. Tell her how sorry I am for her losses of son and mother."

"Mark, should I resign from Black Bear? Laura believes I should. She doesn't think I'm safe there."

"Tell her we will protect you. She shouldn't worry. You mustn't quit yet. It might raise suspicions."

"That's fine with me."

Ben doubted, however, that it would be fine with Laura. Not only was he not quitting Black Bear, but he was being asked to investigate NuEnergy's operations at Munich. No. Laura would definitely not appreciate this turn of events, but with Foster's assurance of protection she would have to accept it.

Strangely, he wasn't fearful of what he was being asked to do. As he saw it, the playing field between him and NuEnergy had just been leveled. For that he was thankful.

FIFTEEN

Day 4 7:45 P.M. Rockville, Maryland

With the Suburban sandwiched in the middle of a small convoy of Secret Service vehicles, the motorcade turned into the lengthy driveway lined with century-old white oaks. Beneath the oaks' protective canopy flourished extensive groves of dogwoods.

While Vice President Foster's troupe wound its way toward the nineteenth century Colonial home, Foster told Dione, "This would be a great show in the spring. Maybe we could catch it then."

Dione, still smarting from last night's cancellation, responded, "Surely you will be too busy for any spring sightseeing."

Foster sheepishly grinned, realizing that he deserved that shot.

Once the parade of vehicles stopped, the proud father and his daughter strolled arm-in-arm from the vice president's limo toward the Colonial home. Foster admired the setting of the grand old home owned by Walter Stranahan, the principal partner of the Stranahan, et al. legal firm.

Strategically resting on high ground, the magnificent home dominated a portion of Rockville, a fashionable suburb north of D.C., and offered an unobstructed view of the estate's gently rolling woodlands. Last season's abundant fallen leaves were coated by a light dusting of snow. The frosted carpet of faded browns, tinged by the fresh white, crunched under the troupe's feet. A full moon and the city shine from the suburbs illuminated the snowy woodland scene. The invigorating panorama momentarily swept away the cares of his secret investigation.

Thus refreshed he escorted his daughter, the guest of honor, up the front veranda stairs where the hosts, Walter and Ethel Stranahan, greeted them. Walter, a distinguished looking, slightly graying man, possessed an air of self-assuredness befitting a leader of one of Washington's most prestigious law firms. His wife was a slender, dark-haired, elegantly attractive woman, clearly fifteen years his junior.

While squarely meeting Foster's steely gaze, Walter Stranahan welcomed the pair with a confident handshake. "I appreciate your taking time to be here, Mr. Vice President. Welcome."

Foster replied, "It is my pleasure. Dione and I thank you for your kind hospitality."

Stranahan added, "I hope you enjoy the evening. We are proud of Dione's achievement."

"And so am I."

After those greetings a sizeable contingent of ever-vigilant FBI and Secret Service agents, as discreetly as possible, followed father and daughter into the home.

The Fosters had no more than left their coats with the butler when an extremely attractive woman rushed forward to hug Dione.

"Hi, Dione! Say that is quite a caravan of handsome men you arrived with. How lucky you are to be the vice president's daughter."

"Michelle, those men are Secret Service and are quite untouchable."

"Oh, I wouldn't bet on that," Michelle rejoined somewhat jokingly, but with a confident tone of one quite sure of her own allure.

The vice president was taken aback by her remark and her aggressive manner. She struck him as someone a little too forward and self-serving. Perhaps, not an appropriate friend for Dione.

Sensing the effect her remark had on him, Michelle Michote promptly turned on the charm. "What a great night. I am so happy for you, Dione. Oh, you will just love the group that's playing."

"Who are they?"

"A jazz ensemble from GW. They are sooo good. The vocalist is superb. I slipped them your list of favorites."

Dione, realizing that she hadn't introduced Michelle to her dad, belatedly announced, "Michelle, this is my dad."

With growing apprehension, Foster had observed the exchange between Dione and Michelle. Michelle was strikingly beautiful and she certainly didn't dress to minimize her abundant physical assets. He would guess Michelle's age to be about thirty, five years older than his daughter. Despite her beauty, he found Dione's new friend annoying. He decided though, for Dione's sake, to stow his apprehensions, at least for tonight, and warmly greeted her.

"Glad to meet you, Michelle. Dione tells me that you are a close friend. I am grateful she has someone at work to care about her."

Yes, Michelle thought, I shall take very good care of Dione. That is for sure.

Her good fortune at having the vice president's daughter as a close friend was not lost on her shady associates. Goldstein, to whom she reported, was most pleased with the development. Dione's work area and phone were already bugged by Goldstein's henchmen. It had been a year since Michelle's last big assignment from Goldstein. Getting rid of undesirable men had proven a piece of cake. She was ready for bigger fish to fry.

Demurely, Michelle employed a polite facade, responding, "I am most honored to meet you, sir." She coyly blushed, as if to imply that meeting such an important man made her shy. "You have a wonderful daughter. I am the one who is fortunate to have her as a friend."

Dione tugged at her dad's arm and caught Michelle by the hand. "Come on, dad. You must meet the rest of the partners. You come too, Michelle, in case I forget names."

After the introductory formalities, a familiar voice boomed from halfway across the room, "Mr. Vice President, I am surprised you have time to be away from the office."

Foster turned to spot Garrison, who stood half-a-head above the crowd. Wearing his characteristic broad grin, and with a pretty young woman in tow, he weaved his way purposefully through the crowd toward them.

Garrison had known that the vice president would be here tonight, but he had decided to surprise him. Once he saw the dazzling Michelle with the Fosters, he had headed their way. His intentions were to reach the vice president in time to meet the lovely creature.

Even from a distance Garrison had thoroughly checked her out. Her blond hair was arranged on her head in a manner that paid tribute to her height and yet suggested a saucy, almost mystical, quality that was at once compelling and intriguing. Her penetrating green eyes enlivened a tanned, high-cheekboned face, framed perfectly by long, dangling pearl white earrings. An elegant red silk dress of a deep rich texture adorned her lithe body.

Propriety dictated, though, that he not show undue interest in the lady since he was here with the host's daughter, Carol. His sense of what was right instructed him to cool it a bit.

"Mr. Vice President, I would like you to meet Carol Stranahan. She was kind enough to invite me to this auspicious occasion."

"I am pleased to meet you, Carol. Perhaps you already know my daughter, Dione, and her friend, Michelle."

"Yes, of course I do!"

"Ladies, this is a government coworker of mine, Brad Garrison."

As the four young people exchanged comments and small talk, the unexpected occurred. Brad and Michelle formed an instant and visceral dislike for each other. Foster surmised that perhaps similar characteristics caused the conflict. Each was very attractive to the opposite sex and quite accustomed to the adulation upon which they thrived. Strangely, they were almost competitors. He had no way of knowing that a deadly future would confirm that observation.

Foster relaxed a little from his frantic pace of the last few days. For once he felt that he didn't have to be on maximum alert. The live music emanating from the dance floor in the next room penetrated his tense body and helped him relax. The combo's music beckoned him. He watched the dancers.

Neither Dione nor her stunningly attractive friend, Michelle, suffered a shortage of eager dance partners. One of Michelle's more persistent pursuers was a man he found familiar but couldn't place. That bothered him. Typically he had no difficulty in recalling a name or a face. Was he getting old, like Stockton intimated?

Foster's attempt to recollect was interrupted by a tug on his arm. Dione insisted upon drawing her dad to the dance floor. "Come on, Dad. You are not too old to dance just once with your daughter."

Foster acceded to her pleadings and stepped onto the floor. Allowing the music to penetrate their collective consciousness, father and daughter skillfully blended with the swaying bodies on the floor.

As the song ended, Foster and Dione found themselves next to Michelle and her latest partner. As the dance combo and the excellent vocalist began a show-stopping arrangement of "Memories," Michelle enticingly invited, "Your dad's quite a dancer, Dione. May I have the honor of a dance with the most handsome vice president?"

"It's fine with me if you can convince Dad." Dione diplomatically sidestepped a decision that was properly her father's.

"I used up my quota of coordination and energy for the night," Foster artfully declined. He quickly turned away for unwillingly tears came to his eyes. This beautiful tune was his and Lis's favorite love song.

Despite his desire to relax and to give his daughter's friend the benefit of the doubt, something alerted him to be cautious. Being the first black man, and a widower, to serve as vice president of the

United States, he must always avoid any appearance of impropriety. Luckily for him, the persistent suitor of Michelle's could stand it no longer and whisked her away.

"Dione, who is that love-sick young man? I am sure I have seen him somewhere before."

"You probably have. He works in the Commerce Department at a fairly high level. Something about imports. He's totally nuts over Michelle. Sometimes they seem to be discussing D.O.C. business, which seems a bit strange to me."

It struck him like a thunderbolt. Foster kicked himself for not placing Foley earlier. He was the one caught by the security camera. Suddenly the euphoria over his daughter's celebration vanished. The cold chill of reality returned. He would call Brad later. The young agent had better get home early tonight, as he would be receiving more homework. Foster would have Michelle's and Foley's relationship investigated. He would not let his guard down again until this crisis was history.

CHAPTER
SIXTEEN

Day 8 1 P.M. Trans-Steppe Railroad Kazakhstan

The train rumbled relentlessly across the vast central Asian expanse of Kazakhstan. For three days the dingy compartment aboard the last swaying passenger car had served as Commander Hamad Barak's cramped headquarters. His trip had started far to the east in the fertile foothills of the towering, snow-clad Altai Mountains along the Kazakh-Russian border. The train had first hauled him and his cargo along the Turk-Siberian railroad route, southwest from Semipalatinsk to Almaty, the City of Apples and the former capital of Kazakhstan. After leaving Almaty, Commander Barak's train veered westerly and then northwesterly, as it struck out across the vast steppes, the treeless plains of Asia, toward a distant Moscow.

The cargo of newly mined uranium, which originated not far from Semipalatinsk, in the Altai Mountains was shepherded by Barak's Kazakh Border Guard. The Guard's role was to provide security for the uranium shipment.

Throughout the long day the old double-diesel locomotive labored along the endless tracks ever north and west. Towing the passenger cars and the boxcars, it traversed the featureless steppe, dropping only occasionally from the vast plain into the Syr Dar'ya River valley.

Commander Barak disgustedly noted that the Syr Dar'ya struggled vainly to deliver any liquid to the shriveling Aral Sea. For decades the rice and cotton farmers had irrigated this area intensely. Their ever-increasing demands, however, swallowed the river's water, preventing replenishment of the dying lake. As a result, what once was the large, flourishing sea of Hamad's boyhood was drying up into a contaminated dust flat. Industrial wastes and farm pesticides, con-

112

centrated in the dying sea furthered the agony. The winds blew the pollutants lying in the newly exposed sand flats into billowing poisonous dust clouds.

Hamad Barak deftly sharpened his dagger. He loathed what was happening to the sea that he had played in as a boy. The Aral of his youth was the largest body of water in the vast Asian space between the Caspian Sea and the Pacific Ocean. Its destruction, while certainly one of the world's major environmental disasters, was a personal tragedy to him. No more could his uncles earn their livelihood from this once abundant fishery. The sea had shrunk by more than half its surface area and by two thirds of its volume since 1960. If nothing changed, experts predicted, it would disappear altogether by 2020.

The cause of this disaster posed no mystery to Hamad. Long ago the damned Kremlin leaders pronounced the death sentence on the Aral. The *duraks* decided that the Empire should become self sufficient in cotton production. With their insatiable appetites, they repeatedly ordered the farmers to increase cotton production. As a result, ever-thirstier irrigation systems robbed the Amu Dar'ya and the Syr Dar'ya rivers, the main replenishment sources for the doomed sea. In frustration, Hamad drove his dagger deep into the wooden bench.

The diesel and the trailing cars, laden with their indifferent passengers and high-energy cargo, rolled mechanically onward past the nearby ecological disgrace.

Hamad, a tall, lean Kazakhstani, proudly traced his ancestry back to Ablai, who was the preeminent Kazakh of the middle horde in the 1770's. Ablai, an able politician, had adroitly balanced competing powers of Russians, Kalmyks and Manchus to maintain Kazakh control of the expansive steppe homeland of these proud, pastoral and nomadic people. The Kazakhs of Ablai's generation traced their ancestry back several more centuries to Genghis Khan's warrior hordes.

Commander Barak's facial features of high cheekbones, wide-set slanted eyes and leathery skin betrayed his Kazakh heritage. Like many of his Kazakh brothers, as a young man he had joined the Communist Party for purposes of expediency only. He insincerely espoused its tenets. No different from most Kazakhs, he had resented the steadily growing Russian dominance of his homeland. Hamad, through his leadership talents, advanced from a simple KGB agent to chief of the Southwestern branch of the Soviet Border Guard, which at that time was still part of the KGB.

After the demise of the Soviet Union, Barak had scrambled to secure a position of importance. Nursultan Nazarbaev, the President of the newly independent republic of Kazakhstan, and a politician of great cunning, appointed principally Kazakhs to his government. That practice bode well for Barak. He became chief of the newly formed Kazakh Border Guard. As chief of the Guard, he was now in a fairly autonomous position of providing security for three important areas: the Balkonur Cosmodrome, where Russian space vehicles were still launched; the Semipalatinsk Nuclear Complex, a sprawling amalgam of factories; and the border along the Caspian Sea.

Retrieving his dagger from its embedding, he tested the blade with his thumb before sheathing the weapon. He was satisfied that it remained sharp and ready for duty. Lighting another in his continuous string of Marlboros, the Guard Commander inhaled deeply, letting the smoke seep from his lungs ever so slowly.

During the early nineties, his responsibilities at Semipalatinsk had led him into a close association with the director of the Semipalatinsk Nuclear Complex, Boris Andropov. Their relationship developed contemporaneously with the cruel financial realities, which often left his border guard without pay for months at a time. Driven by these intolerable conditions, many of the Guard quit, joining local criminal gangs involved in extortion, racketeering and assassinations.

Desperate to prevent further attrition of his Guard, Hamad had proved vulnerable to unsavory solutions. Just such a deal was tendered. If he would help Andropov, generous amounts of money would flow to the Guard. Secretly moving nuclear weapons and nuclear weapons' ingredients from Semipalatinsk to a remote location along the desolate southern Kazakh Caspian coastline, protecting the hidden cache, and arranging periodic special shipments was Barak's part of the bargain. In return, Andropov underwrote generous salaries for Barak's guard.

There was one catch. Andropov demanded that Barak maintain absolute secrecy. That stipulation meant he must frustrate all attempts by the Russian FSB or others to uncover the whereabouts of the missing nuclear arms. So far he had kept the lid on the theft, and Andropov had rewarded him handsomely with healthy bonuses each year. As a result, he could afford all of the expensive cigarettes he desired and still have millions of Kazakh *tenge* left for other luxuries. Other luxuries, such as fancy clothes, expensive homes, or fast women, though, didn't interest Hamad. Any extra cash generally benefited those with a greater need.

Rationalizing that he was doing the right thing to take care of his

Kazakh guards, he had agreed to Andropov's deal. Also the opportunity to tweak the Russian Bear was irresistible. Getting the weapons out of here and away from Russia and its colonial tendencies seemed the best thing for Kazakhstan.

A tentative knock on Barak's door was followed by a shaky voice from the hall, "C-C-Commander Barak, this is Lt. Hani. W-W-We must talk."

"Come in. Why do you interrupt me?"

The border guard soldier, dressed in the guard's dark-green uniform, entered in obvious awe of his commander. He stuttered his message, "C-C-Commander, a warning signal flashed from wagon four. Sh-Sh-Shall one of us check it out?"

"Absolutely!" Hamad guessed that this was just another in the series of false alarms set off by this rough stretch of track, but he would abide no slacking of vigilance. "Take another soldier with you. Inspect thoroughly. We must be sure that all is well."

Backing out of the room as quickly as possible, the soldier responded, "Y-Y-Yes, sir, C-C-Commander!"

Moments later, a bold banging on Hamad's compartment door was followed by the familiar booming voice of the train's provodnik, Pavel Zivgenov. "Commander Barak, would you care for some kumiss?"

"Come in, Pavel, you big pest. What an ignorant question!" Hamad responded with a dry wit, while not visually betraying his playfulness. Like most natives, he relished the concoction of fermented mare's milk.

Pavel Zivgenov, a bear of a man, had been the *provodnik* serving on Hamad's train the last three trips. The two men had struck up a fast friendship. The sinewy Kazakh and the massive Russian enjoyed jawing at each other about everything, especially the relative merits of their respective cultures. A Western kibitzer would assume that they neither liked nor respected each other, but the exact opposite was true.

"Here is your stinking kumiss. I don't know how you Kazakhs get past the smell of the foul stuff," Pavel chided while slipping his huge bulk farther into Hamad's cramped compartment. "Whew, that explains it. The smoke has killed your ability to smell. Are you chain smoking those weeds?"

"So what if I am, Pavel? Smoking is one of the few pleasures you damned Russians didn't steal from us."

Provodnik Pavel, ignoring that zinger, persisted instead with his line of needling questions, "Do you really like this kumiss stuff, or do you just pretend? You know, honoring tradition and all that rot."

"It's not stuff, you ignoramus. It's a delicacy. Something that's missing from the Russian lexicon."

"Okay! Okay! You are the customer, so whatever you say. Heh, what are you reading there, Hamad?" He pointed at the open book lying on Hamad's table.

"Poems by one of our famous authors."

"Who?"

"A fourteenth century writer, Asan Kangi. He wrote at a time in your Russian culture, and I use the term loosely, Pavel, when there wasn't even a Russian who could spell culture, or poet, for that matter." Hamad loved bantering with the Russian giant and he knew this subject would ignite a spirited exchange.

"Your poet must have been very talented to write those verses from the back of a horse," Pavel countered. "Unlike your semi-gifted penman, several of our authors received worldwide acclaim, including Pulitzer Prizes."

Barak challenged, "How many of your authors were allowed out of your lovely country to receive their honors? In case you have forgotten, nil is the correct answer." After smashing his cigarette in mock disgust, he reached for another.

"Here, let me light that thing for you. Is this Marlboro country now? With that mustache of yours, you could pass as Asia's version of the Marlboro man."

Pavel bought himself a little time for thinking. "Let's call a truce." He purposefully moved to more neutral territory. "By the way, have you heard the latest joke on Communism?"

Commander Barak shrugged, "You *durak*! How do I know until you tell it?"

Unfazed Pavel began, "Two men are debating many things when one asks, 'Is Communism a science?' The other thinks for a long time before answering, 'No, if Communism were a science they would have tested it on dogs first.'"

"That's a good one!" Hamad laughed until tears came to his eyes and rolled down his leathery face. After recovering he offered, "Let me tell you about the Communist, the Socialist, and the Capitalist who arranged a meeting."

"Let's hear it."

"A Capitalist and a Communist waited for the Socialist, who finally showed up late to the meeting. He apologized. 'Sorry I'm late,' he said. 'I was standing in line for sausage.' The Capitalist asked the Socialist, 'What's a line?' The poor, befuddled Communist, though, inquired, 'What's a sausage?'"

The Russian roared and shook until the compartment walls creaked from the strain. His genuine love of humor was quite contagious. Finally, as his laughter subsided, he noted that it was good therapy to mock that disastrous system that drove both of their countries into poverty.

Pavel purposefully returned to the subject of the lyricists. "But seriously, knowing of your love of good literature, I brought you a gift. Here is Pushkin's *Eugene Onegin* and *The Captain's Daughter* written in Russian. You Kazakhs are indeed fortunate that we Russians came down here to the steppes and taught you our language. Now you may have the unparalleled delight of experiencing the best of Pushkin's masterpieces."

Revealing a depth of appreciation for the gifted poet that somewhat surprised Barak, the giant Slav elaborated, "Pushkin composed the most lilting lines. You must read them in Russian."

Barak knew this to be true. He remembered being told that it was impossible to translate the full magic of Pushkin's works into other languages. Perhaps other languages' morphemes were sufficiently different, frustrating all translation attempts.

Barak was genuinely touched with the gesture, "Thank you, my dear friend. This is indeed a most generous gift." He was fully aware of how loved Pushkin was by the Russian masses. Upon the poet's untimely death, literally hundreds of thousands of mourners had lined up to pay their respects.

Hamad though, couldn't resist a final jab at Pavel. "I thought maybe you were bringing me Sumurov's works. I particularly enjoyed his uncannily prophetic work, *A Corrupt Empire - When Will It Implode*."

Pavel for the first time winced. Sumurov was loved by the Russian populace, but not by the FSB or the Communists. In an attempt to hide his deep devotion to Sumurov, Pavel mouthed the party-line, "Fortunately most of his slanderous works aren't in print."

"That's no problem. I can get a copy from any Western country."

Pavel shrugged and moved to the door. "I must move on to the other passengers. I will be along later to see how you are doing. I must harass you again, my poor, uncivilized Kazakh friend."

Barak grabbed the nearest magazine and slung it at the retreating giant, "Be gone with you and your arrogant Slavness. Why don't you see if we could have a little heat on this train? You crooked Slavs are no doubt hoarding all the coal to sell on the Moscow black market. You and your corrupt countrymen couldn't go straight if your dwindling empire depended on it."

Chuckling to himself over the repartee, the Guard Commander settled back as best he could on his hard makeshift seat and opened to the middle of the book. "The country place where Eugene moped was a charming nook..."

After enjoying several pages, he glanced out his cubicle window. He had seen to it that his compartment had an intact window. Since railroad maintenance funds were limited, many windows were not repaired. Rather, they were simply boarded up. He hoped maintenance would start improving once the Kazakh economy was infused with more petroleum money from the West. Maybe then they could conduct repairs and, at least, afford enough coal to heat the damned train.

Guardsman Hani returned to Hamad's compartment to report, "C-C-Commander, there were no signs of trouble. The guards in each wagon report no problem. The rough track must have set off the alarm."

"Stay vigilant, Sergeant. We will tolerate no messing with our uranium."

With darkness approaching, Hamad reached up to turn on the reading light when the brilliantly lit Balkonur Cosmodrome launch gantries caught his eye. The train was passing a few miles south of the bustling Russian space launch facility. Hamad had been there often overseeing security arrangements. He knew that the giant Soyuz rocket, bathed by the floodlights, was poised to launch another section of the international space station. Eventually the lights from the space launch facility faded, leaving the lonely train enveloped in darkness and rolling onward across the bleak Kazakh plains.

Hours later, as promised, Pavel returned to check on his favorite passenger. He had found that the tight-lipped Barak would not talk much about the business that placed each of them on this train. Pavel had been able to learn only that Hamad always accompanied the uranium shipments from Semipalatinsk to the rail juncture at Kandagach, which was only two hours away to the northwest. Why this uranium transportation took the highest ranking Kazakh Border Guard's attention seemed curious to Pavel and his Moscow boss.

Despite their developing friendship, he had found it wasn't wise to press Hamad too hard about the uranium. For important reasons, however, he must try once more before they reached Kandagach.

"So, my friend, where are you headed next?" The *provodnik* hoped that Hamad would reveal something about his true mission.

"Oh, I will eventually go down to the Caspian to see how my border guard is doing at guarding our precious Kazakh territory from your expansionist Muslim buddies." Barak had artfully fashioned his answer, knowing it would get a rise out of Pavel and turn him off any more questions in the uranium area.

"They are not my buddies," Pavel bellowed in protest. "You Kazakhs and your fellow Muslims are like brothers. Some of those brothers of yours have big ideas though. You better watch out. What is the term those zealots to the south use? *Uma*! Isn't that the concept whereby all Islamic peoples will be united under one government? You Kazakhs better pray that the one government doesn't turn out to be Tehran's."

"If you Russians hadn't armed them to the teeth, they wouldn't be such a worry."

Pavel winced. "That's sadly true, Hamad. We are nearing Kandagach so I must get about my business." Pavel, his broad shoulders barely fitting through the narrow doorway, said with sincerity, "See you again, my friend." Despite his FSB assignment, Pavel respected the savvy Barak. He knew of the man's outstanding reputation, earned back in the Soviet era when they both served in the KGB.

"You take care, my Russian comrade," Commander Barak saluted a fond farewell to the mammoth Slav.

As Pavel Zivgenov circulated from compartment to compartment, he composed what he would tell Vasilly Kruschev about this trip. Not much to tell so far, he concluded, but maybe tonight his luck would improve. Hamad's Caspian Sea comment gave him a measure of hope. As one of the FSB's most valued agents, Pavel had been personally chosen by Kruschev for this mission. His sleuthing talents were exceptional and his anti-Chekist politics were confirmed by those Kruschev most trusted.

Pavel puzzled over how strange these times were. The difference between cultures, Russian and Kazakh, morality, good and evil, legal ities, criminal and law-abiding, had blurred. He truly liked Hamad, yet he was quite aware that he was a key player in the heist of the nuclear weapons.

Day 8 10:10 P.M. Kandagach

Despite Kandagach being a small town in the middle of the vast Kazakh plains, it was a major rail juncture. The rail line to the northwest stretched toward Moscow. To the southwest lay Atyrau, the Caspian Sea and Grozny. The line to the northeast served various Asian destinations in Russia east of the Ural Mountain and, of course, the rails from the southeast covered the lengthy course just traveled by Commander Barak and his uranium, uranium ostensibly destined through Moscow to the Munich Enrichment Facility.

Commander Barak's train pulled into the switchyard at Kandagach, where its trailing, uranium-bearing cargo wagons were immediately lopped off from the rest of the train. The well-worn locomotive with its dozen passenger cars pulled forward from the switchyard to the passenger depot. There the truncated train shut down, forcing the passengers, including Hamad, to depart. Throughout the night the railroad workers serviced, refueled, re-supplied and reconfigured the train, readying it for the long run on to Moscow.

Hamad, with his sheepskin satchel, which now held the Pushkin prose, strode directly to the Kandagach Restaurant in the center of town. The main street was paved, but it was in dire need of repair. Huge chunks of asphalt were torn away from many years of neglect. As he passed an intersection he was greeted by a gust of raw north wind. The dust from the dirt side road stung his leathery face. Tonight the bleakness of the gray windswept town somehow disturbed him. What was wrong? He arrived at the cafe without finding a satisfactory answer to that question.

The frontier-like restaurant offered Russian and Kazakh cuisines. Despite the late hour, the small cafe served several customers. Hamad scrutinized the patrons before selecting an isolated back-corner table. Mostly they were passengers, he surmised, waiting for their train to renew its journey. He dropped his bag on one of the wooden slat-backed chairs and settled into a companion chair, which afforded him a full, unobstructed view of the interior. He tugged at his shirt pocket for a new pack of Marlboros.

The waitress, an old friend, Galena Svyatskaya, her youth lost in her hard-spent years in this harsh part of the world, recognized him immediately, despite the dim light in the corner. She rushed to his table and playfully slipped onto his lap. Pulling the cigarette from Hamad's lips, she crushed it into the cigarette tray. "Still smoking those vile weeds, I see."

"I was until you did that."

Unfazed by the stern Hamad, Galena continued, "Do you want the usual? The kibuska is the best ever. I guarantee it. We grew some fine cabbage and mushrooms this year."

"Kibuska it is then."

As Galena left to turn in the order, Hamad requested, "When you get some of your customers satisfied, Galena, come back and tell me what is up around here. Something feels oddly out of place this trip."

"It's the damned weather, Hamad. Up 'til last week it was downright balmy, but then the cold winds hit with a vengeance. It's got everybody a little spooked. It never stayed warm so late."

"Maybe that's it," Hamad mumbled, not fully convinced.

'How's your mother?" he asked.

"She died last month." Deep sadness emanated from Galena's eyes, "Her last words were, 'You tell Hamad, *Dosvidanya*.' She was eternally grateful for your help in our hour of need. She kept all newspaper clippings about you. She was especially proud of the one telling about your becoming head of the Kazakh Border Guard. She worshipped you."

"And I her! Her death hurts. She was the bravest soul I ever met. She literally gave everything to protect you."

"Yes, I know." Fighting back tears, Galena turned away, "I better tend to some of these folk. I will be back later."

Hamad watched her serving the customers. Her proud bearing reminded him of her stalwart mother.

A dozen years ago he had surprised a pack of renegade Russian Border Guards torturing and raping Galena's mother for not divulging the youthful Galena's whereabouts. Accidentally stumbling onto the tragic scene, he had flown into a lethal rage. He slit the throats of all four of the animals. Afterwards he took a traumatized Galena and her badly wounded mother to the *bolnitza* at Kandagach. Since that horrible episode, he had provided for all of their material needs. Maybe someday, when his work slacked off, he could spend more time with the winsome Galena.

Day 8 11:35 P.M. Kandagach Switchyard

The switch engine busily juggled cargo cars around in preparation for their next destinations. The rearranging would go on most of the night. As part of the switching, the four wagons carrying the uranium from Semipalatinsk were shifted to a remote rail spur on the western outskirts of town. There they were left isolated and undisturbed, except for the border guards who remained locked inside each rail car.

Day 9 12:55 A.M. Kandagach Rail Spur

Emerging out of the gloom of the midnight hour, a convoy of gray Kazakh Border Guard trucks drew near. Low-hanging clouds blocked all light from the moon. The line of large Afghan war-vintage military trucks was accompanied by a contingent of two dozen border guard troops, part of Hamad's elite unit. The trucks parked near the four box cars.

The troops maneuvered two front-end loaders toward the isolated train cars. The soldiers unlocked the cars and greeted the guards inside with some good-natured joshing and roughhousing. After the horseplay the highly trained team settled down and began a systematic exchange of the silver-gray uranium bearing cylinders.

The loaders painstakingly moved the several ton, eight-foot-high canisters one at a time from the four rail cars to the waiting trucks. Identical cylinders were in turn carefully transferred from the trucks to the just-emptied spots in each wagon.

Lieutenant Turar Ryskulov, in command of this exchange, orchestrated the entire evolution. He supervised the positioning of each replacement cylinder to ensure that its location was exactly that of its just-removed counterpart. After two hours of steady work, this exacting late-night swap was completed. The train cars and their contents looked exactly the same as they had before, even down to the IAEA labels on each cylinder. However, the original natural uranium cylinders, brought to Kandagach by Barak's train, were now safely in the border guard trucks. Lieutenant Ryskulov personally examined everything one last time. Then he signaled for the trucks to pull out. Lumbering through the western outskirts of Kandagach, they set a course for the Caspian Sea, six hundred rough and dusty miles to the southwest.

Lt. Ryskulov watched them disappear into the murky night before signaling to two waiting autos that it was time for the final exchange. Eight Russian Mafia gunmen, wearing camouflage gear and with AK-47's slung over their backs, swaggered to the wagons. They took over the guarding of this replacement uranium cargo. After minimal correspondence with Ryskulov, the arrogant mobsters took their places in the uranium rail cars. He locked them in, where they would remain until they reached Munich. As his last duty, he activated the security system in each car.

Satisfied with the swap, Lt. Ryskulov turned his truck toward town and Commander Barak's favorite hangout. Parking in front of the restaurant and waiting for the dust from the nearby side road to blow on to the south, he scanned Kandagach's small business area. There wasn't much action at this time of night, except far down the street he saw a huge man walking east through the dark dusty night. A nasty night to be out thought Ryskulov.

Upon entering the cafe, he squinted in the dim light until he spotted Barak in the far corner. He pulled up a chair at his Commander's table and reported, "The switch is accomplished."

Barak nodded his approval. "Good. It was conveniently dark tonight."

"Yes, that always helps. You are going with me, aren't you?" inquired Ryskulov.

"If that old boat will hold together in this rough weather," challenged Barak.

"It should, but it will be an exciting ride."

"That relic has seen better days."

"Sailing up here from Iran with our precious cylinders was an experience. The wind was whipping up some heavy seas. I was afraid our uranium cargo would get water logged."

"Then you could have had your own nuclear meltdown," kidded Barak.

"I hadn't thought of that. Is that possible?" Ryskulov puzzled.

"I don't know. I suppose it depends on just what enrichment the Iranians have placed in those things."

Hamad leisurely finished his last helping of kibuska and squashed another cigarette butt into the overflowing tray of Marlboro remnants. "Let's go, Lieutenant."

Galena, seeing them about to leave, flew to Hamad. With her arms wrapped around his neck and her feet dangling in the air, she pleaded, "You come back soon, my dear Hamad. May Allah always protect you."

Stuffing a fistful of *tenge* into her apron pocket, he promised, "I will always be around to see that you are fit."

Hamad turned away, unsure why life was so brutal to the weak. Maybe that was life? Shaking off that uncomfortable answer, he followed Ryskulov out into the cold night.

Day 9 6:15 A.M. Kandagach Train Station

Pavel, tired from the hike back from the edge of town, hustled about his *provodnik* duties as his mind whirled over his good fortune. From an old abandoned rail car the FSB agent had watched and photographed the entire uranium switch. The car had been planted there for him by other FSB operatives. His night-vision binoculars had adequately illuminated the scene. The sensitive Sony camcorder had captured the entire exchange. Getting his huge bulk in and out of the rail car and the cold trek back to town had presented the greatest challenges. His imminent report to Kruschev at KGB headquarters would be most welcome.

CHAPTER
SEVENTEEN

Day 9 11 A.M. Munich Enrichment Plant

Ben Andrew stood toe to toe with the Munich manager. He had his fill of the stonewalling. The manager had steadfastly refused all of his requests to audit a key portion of the plant.

"Try to understand this. I expect to see the third section. That is where our uranium is delivered and where it's enriched, so that is what I shall audit."

The manager stubbornly stood his ground. "*Doktor* Andrew, I have explained that our most advanced centrifuges operate in that unit. We don't allow outsiders in there. You are not cleared for that area. The rest of the plant is open to you."

Ben didn't buy that excuse. These rebuffs rang hollow. He decided that he would try a threat.

"Look! I represent half of your customers. Upon their behalf, I am presenting a reasonable request that I be allowed to inspect the section where our Kazakh uranium is delivered and enriched. If I am denied that right, I will return home to report that you are in violation of our fuel contract. Furthermore, as a result of your refusal, you will be declared in default. We will immediately pursue other sources for our future fuel supply. Tell your Plant Manager that I expect a favorable reply. If you return with a *nein*, then all hell will break loose."

Why were they so dead set against his seeing that section? His stance was a calculated bluff, for he had no real authority in fuel procurement after the unfortunate NuEnergy takeover of Black Bear. The management here undoubtedly understood that as well, but they probably would not welcome the disturbance he threatened. He could shine a spotlight on their precious mystery unit and he could put them and NuEnergy in a tight spot with his unfavorable findings. He was betting that they did not want that.

After watching the manager leave in a huff, Ben turned to Hans, his ever-present, armed-guard escort and suggested that they head to the cafeteria for lunch. As they walked, Ben reflected upon what he had seen and accomplished this morning. He was pressing hard, very hard, and undoubtedly they would become curious about his persistence. It was a risk, however, he believed was worth taking. That third unit must hold some answers as to what was really going on here. To be of any help to Foster he must get into that section of the plant.

His initial impression of the Munich facility was that it was efficient at uranium purification, but it resembled an armed encampment. Never had he seen a civilian facility so intensely guarded. Certainly his armed-guard escort contributed to that image. The elaborate razor wire-topped security fence and the ominous guard towers surrounding the plant complex evinced a sinister intent. It seemed more a gulag than an enrichment plant. Why was this extreme security necessary?

His companion auditor, a NuEnergy exec, had taken suddenly quite ill. Ben could only guess at Foster's means of causing that illness, but the man's inability to make the audit trip had created a golden opportunity for him. The stooge's absence gave him unparalleled room to maneuver and he eagerly seized the opportunity. He guessed that the meeting which must be going on now between the plant manager and the manager he had just chewed out was a doozey.

Day 9 4 P.M. Munich Enrichment Plant

Ben and the gun-toting Hans removed their protective white coats and boots. Ben had spent most of the afternoon watching the discharge of the Kazakhstan cylinders and Hans had spent the time watching him.

Nothing at first appeared out of the ordinary, except that the Kazakh cylinders were always unloaded at this station and their uranium contents directed into the secret section. The discharge of the uranium from these cylinders, ostensibly Kazakh natural uranium in the chemical form of uranium hexafluoride, went about as he had seen at other enrichment plants. The unloading crew attached the big cylinders to a stainless steel pipe header and then heated the uranium. Upon heating the uranium compound transformed from a dense, heavy powder into a gas, which flowed from the cylinder into the pipe header.

Yet, he had caught one difference that made him curious. The unit three discharge times were much longer than those in the other units. The only thing accomplished by the increased time was a more complete mixing of the cylinder's contents. Why was mixing desirable? Mixing of what? Wasn't it all the same, natural uranium?

Could the Kazakh cylinders possibly contain something different? Otherwise, why on earth did they always come to this unit. He was told when he questioned this oddity that it was just for bookkeeping simplicity. That explanation made absolutely no sense to him. In every other enrichment plant he had seen, the incoming natural uranium was fungible, that is, it was interchangeable.

So why wasn't the Kazakh uranium fungible? Damn. He was stymied, piling up more questions than answers. Refusing to become frustrated, though, Ben reasoned that enough of these questions stacking up should start pointing to some answers.

While Ben washed up after his day in the plant, the sullen manager in charge of audits returned. "Dr. Andrew, the plant manager is quite disturbed with your uncompromising attitude. He wants to know if you would reconsider your request to see the commercially-sensitive unit."

"Absolutely not!"

"We were afraid that would be your answer, so we will allow you to inspect it briefly tomorrow afternoon, under stringent conditions. No cameras or other recording devices are allowed. You may take no notes while you are inspecting. Any summary of your audit report dealing with unit three must be cleared by us."

"That's fine. I agree to all of that," Ben lied.

If they were so scared of scrutiny, then he intended to scrutinize the hell out of the unit, somehow.

As Ben and Hans strode down the hall, nearing the plant exit, Ben's thoughts were suddenly cut short. One side of an apparently heated German conversation filtered through a partially open door. He gathered that the person, apparently the plant manager, must be on the phone. Ben understood German well enough to converse slowly and simply, but he had deliberately not divulged that fact. That subterfuge was paying off.

He translated the conversation as, "The *dummkopf* American demanded to see the third unit. Threatened all sorts of trouble."

There was a momentary silence, then the man resumed talking, "Yes, I know. It's too expensive. Yes, we shouldn't be starting it up for just one damned auditor, but I had no choice."

Wow! If he translated that correctly then he had really stirred up a hornet's nest and was once again crossways with NuEnergy's top management. By pushing so hard to see the third unit he was probably in renewed danger. Foster's promised protection better be close by and alert.

Day 9 10:15 P.M. Munich Biergarten

A Bavarian bier stein whizzed past Ben's face. Startled, he turned to spy a trail of spilt Weissbier leading to a nearby table, where rowdy, colorfully-dressed Germans were bellowing Bavarian ballads. Before he could react, two men from his table attired in slacks, red suspenders and white shirts with intricate border designs grabbed their chairs.

Spilling more Weissbier, they leaped to the top of Ben's massive oak-huen table. Brandishing their chairs menacingly over their heads, they hurled a string of German vindictives at the nearby table of bier stein-launching ruffians. Four of the dozen wildly gesturing Bavarians at the offending table, some with chairs in hand, fired back insults at the two standing on Ben's table.

Ben's face burned from a sudden rush of adrenaline. Expecting chairs to start flying at any moment, he searched around for cover. Surely the fighting was about to commence in earnest, as the angry men rapidly became more bellicose.

Suddenly, as if on cue, they all broke into boisterous laughter and while slapping each other on the back clambered back to the worn oak-planked floor. They ordered more brew brought to both tables.

Ben marveled at the strength of the stout maids, who easily carried eight of the giant mugs. He laughed, thinking, if the boys get out of hand again, these brawny women could put a stop to the mischief.

One of the pranksters at Ben's table turned to his friend, "*Ja. Es ist der Fohn.*"

Ben's curiosity got the best of him, "*Was ist der Fohn?*"

Sizing him up as American, they responded in English. "When the *Fohn's* blowing, people just get grumpy and crazy. They do all manner of stupid things, like those *dummkopfs* at the other table."

"But what is it?"

In mock seriousness the man consulted his partner, "Can we trust an American with one of our national secrets?"

"Sure, Sepp, why not! He looks harmless."

"It's a hot, dry wind. It starts as a cool, wet breeze flowing from the Mediterranean up the Italian side of the Alps. During that rise, all of the moisture is rung out of the air. After reaching the summit, it rushes down the north slope, picking up a lot of static electricity and

heat along the way. By the time it blows into town it has a thoroughly maddening effect on one's state of mind."

"Thanks. The *Fohn* may explain my two strange days here. What
were you saying to those gents at the other table?"

"We told them to throw only empty steins. That one still had perfectly good Weissbier in it."

The other Bavarian was grinning mightily for his partner, Sepp,
was once again toying with Ben.

Ben drank deeply from the mug brought by one of the lusty maids.
If he had interpreted correctly, she had told the Bavarian gents to
calm down or she would lay a mug or two upside their heads. He suspected the entire episode was a farce perpetrated to elicit a reaction
from the few foreigners in the crowd. He wondered if even the story
about the *Fohn* was a fabrication.

Ben's thoughts drifted back to the Munich plant. Would his plan
work? Could he keep the miniature tape recorder, which he had
bought this evening, hidden? Would it pick up the sounds of the
secret unit accurately enough to be useful to Foster's team? He shook
his head in disbelief. What was happening to him? Was he taking this
espionage business too seriously?

He finally emptied his last bier stein. Thanks to these chaps, he
had actually had some fun, but it was time to get back to the hotel.
He needed rest to be sharp tomorrow.

As he walked through the tavern doors, the din in the vast hall
faded, replaced by the cool quiet of the Munich night. Good beer, but
strong. He shivered. It felt far colder outside now than when he had
arrived. Assuming the FBI was close by, he wondered what they
thought of the rowdy Bavarians. He laughed. Maybe crusty ol' Sepp
was actually an undercover agent.

Day 10 8 A.M. Munich Enrichment Plant

On this last day of his inspection, Ben, by now quite familiar with
his rented pelican-blue Cabriolet, handily maneuvered it from the
crowded Autobahn into the Munich plant's parking lot. He found that the
sensitive response of the vehicle made it a pleasure to drive. Wow, the
sky was bright blue again this morning. That's probably thanks to the
Fohn, he chuckled recalling last night's meteorological lesson from Sepp.

Before leaving the driver's seat, he carefully checked to make sure
everything was in place. The tiny tape recorder was right where it

should be, taped to his waist. It certainly wasn't visible and he hoped the primarily plastic device wouldn't set off any alarms. His first-ever attempt at spying made him sense that he was being watched and scrutinized at all times. Even his thoughts might be transparent. He took a deep breath and stepped out of the car.

As he locked up the rental, he noticed that there was more vapor rising from the cooling pond this morning. Since the temperature and humidity were about the same as yesterday, the extra vapor could only mean that the plant was consuming more power today. That was strange, particularly since the plant had supposedly been operating at full capacity every day he was here.

Damn, he was barely out of the car and already a new puzzle had appeared. He must bring the vice president more than just questions.

He questioned himself. Was there really danger or was he exaggerating things? Nobody here had directly threatened him. Maybe he was just borrowing trouble based on what he had run into at Black Bear. Yet the Mafia and NuEnergy were tied to this plant, so caution was wise. He definitely needed to be careful. He laughed for his idea of being careful was about one hundred eighty out from Laura's.

As he negotiated the plant's security checks, his mind raced over the apparent increase in power consumption. He found no easy answer to the discrepancy, except that it squared with the German conversation he had overheard as he left yesterday that they were forced to start up the third unit.

Once again, he was greeted by Hans, his armed escort.

"*Guten Morgen, Herr Doktor.*"

"Good morning, Hans. So you are speaking German today. If so, it will be a monologue. That's about the only gimmick you people haven't attempted to frustrate my work here."

Hans laughed, "Lighten up, *Herr Doktor*. This is just my way of giving you a little flavor of the country you are in."

Ben shrugged and sarcastically replied, "Thanks for the consideration."

He followed Hans through the maze of corridors to the cafeteria. Today, thank God, he would see that elusive secret enclave.

While waiting for his breakfast of brauts, diced potatoes, heavily peppered eggs and thick coffee, Ben saw some German scribbling on a piece of paper passed to Hans by another guard. Catching a brief glimpse at the paper, he swore that it contained the name of the store where he bought the tape recorder.

Hans nodded to the guard with a "*ja.*"

Did they know about his tape recorder? How could they? Was that a subtle signal for him to drop his big idea of spying before it was too late? Well, no matter what, he wasn't backing down now.

After a long and boring morning it was finally time for the long-denied look at the third enclave. The tape he had wrapped around his waist to hold the miniature recorder in place was beginning to itch. His mind wandered. Laura would not be happy with him if she knew what was going on. She had been very disappointed that Foster had asked Ben to take on the Munich assignment. She made it clear to Ben that she had called Foster to secure protection for him, not to drag him deeper into this quagmire.

Ben and his grim entourage of guides and guards donned white lab coats over their street clothes. Protective glasses, radiation-monitoring devices and white cloth coverings for their shoes completed their outfits. With their protective gear in place, they padded in their cloth booties down the access corridor past units one and two to the mysterious third enclave.

Ben already noticed something peculiar. He could hear the high-pitched whine of the centrifuges emanating from behind the walls of units one and two, but no such sound came from three. The reason for this became evident when they passed through the unit's soundproofed door. The first two sections were not soundproofed but the third was. Why? Was it so that no one outside could tell if it was operating or not?

He and his bevy of escorts, once inside, were greeted by an imposing forest of tall metallic cylinders. It looked a little like he had walked into the base section of a gigantic pipe organ factory. These machines stretched to almost twice Ben's six-foot-one height. The spinning portions were invisible, closed securely inside the stationary exterior cylinder walls. As they spun they emitted a high-pitched sound, created by the precision parts rotating at tremendous speed. All of these machines were presumably at work separating the light uranium gas molecules from the heavy ones.

Just as in the other two units, there were the interconnecting, stainless-steel pipes between all the centrifuges. Everything seemed identical to the other units, so he was confused. How could this unit possibly be more efficient? As inconspicuously as possible he pressed his shirt to start the recorder.

Either the rotational speed of the centrifuges had to be greater, their mountings had to be more frictionless, or they had to be taller. They weren't taller. He could tell that at a glance. He could not discern visually if the mountings and bearings were the same as those in the other sections, but he suspected one couldn't improve much on the magnetic suspension design of the other units. Since the rotating components were hidden from view, he could not discern visually if they rotated faster or not. Each spinning cylinder, however, created a signature high-pitched whine. The frequency of that sound was a function of its speed of rotation. To Ben's untrained ear, this third section had a sound very similar in pitch to sections one and two. But of course, this wasn't hard proof of anything.

He figured that expert audio analysis of the noise, though, could yield a wealth of information. That is why he had taken what could prove to be a foolish risk. The tape recorder hidden under his shirt should be recording the sound of the whirling machines. Ben reasoned that Vice President Foster would have access to experts, who could analyze the sound and deduce a great deal about the third unit's operational mode.

He walked from one cascade to another, noting aloud where he was. This conversation with himself was, of course, for the subsequent analysis of his tape. His escorts, forewarned by security to watch for any suspicious acts and especially any indication of the presence of a tape recorder, became quite curious about his behavior.

Ben alibied that talking aloud was just his memory-enhancement technique.

He counted the same number of centrifuge housings as existed in each of the other two sections. However, the sound level was several decibels less in here than in the other sections. Maybe the reduced noise was caused by the soundproofed walls around this enclave, absorbing rather than reflecting and transmitting the sound, but he could not be sure of that.

He stole a glimpse at the inspection records of a valve in one of the cascades. The frequency of maintenance inspection was annually, whereas in sections one and two, it was monthly. Wow, that was odd for a unit that supposedly operated continuously. He placed his hand near one of the connecting stainless steel pipes. It was cool. How could that be since hot uranium gas supposedly flowed through it?

His exasperated escorts, totally fed up with his deliberate and thorough examination, snapped, "Do you plan to build one of these in Oklahoma? The detail of your inspection is entirely inappropriate. You are only an auditor, whose job is to confirm the quality of your product. The inspection is terminated. We leave now."

Since he had garnered all that he could from this foray into the forbidden, Ben didn't argue. With the wind-up of the climactic third enclave tour, he could write his report and get the hell out of here. He wasn't sure what caused all of his uneasiness, but the place made his skin crawl.

After Ben collected his papers from his temporary office, Hans, as impassive as ever, escorted him to the security building. Ben started through the exit for the last time. During the process, one was required to deposit his plant badge in a box and then walk past the last scanner, which operated on a similar premise to a department store shoplifting detector. The scanner verified that those leaving were not carrying their badges outside. He wanted to get one last read on the aggressive security forces in this place, so he paused, gulped and then deliberately kept his badge.

Emergency warning lights and sirens shattered the evening's calm. The shrill wailing of the sirens startled him. They were so loud that he did not hear the armed contingent rushing him from behind. Brandishing automatic weapons, a half dozen guards pounced on him before he could go any distance. They must have burst out of a nearby room that was especially equipped to secretly observe those leaving. These fellows apparently spoke no English, but weren't asking questions anyway. He was rudely thrust face down on the pavement with two submachine guns pressed against his head. His briefcases were scattered about on the asphalt. While one guard looked through the briefcases, another guard yanked him to his feet, braced him spread eagle against the wall and began a pat-down search.

Sweating profusely, he silently cursed, damn it all! He hadn't expected this severe a reaction. Had he outsmarted himself? This guard surely would discover his recorder. Did they suspect that thing was on him? They must know he bought one and stupidly he had just given them the chance they needed to find it.

Rudely patting Ben's sides, the guard felt right where the tape circled his waist.

Shit! Any moment he would find the damned thing, fretted Ben.

Upon a cue from the searching guard, a familiar voice shouted, "*Halt! Halt! Aufhoren!*"

The guards immediately ended their probing search.

Hans, reaching the scene on the run, demanded, "*Was gibt es hier? Doktor, did you forget to leave your badge?*"

Scrambling to his feet and gathering his strewn belongings, Ben admitted, "Yes, I must have been day dreaming about my trip back home. For once, I am actually glad to see you."

"I'm sorry for the rough stuff, *Doktor*. Give me the badge and you are free to go. *Sehr* sorry. Our guards overdid it."

Ben dusted off his clothes and straightened his coat and tie. He gathered up his violated briefcases and headed for his car. That was too close for comfort.

Automatic weapons to the head for a minor infraction seemed a bit of an over-reaction. At lease he now knew that the forces here were obviously on a hair-trigger alert, heavily armed and quite geared for a fight.

Retreating from the unsettling encounter to the relative safety of his Audi, he failed to see Hans conversing vigorously with the officer involved in the pat down. What Ben didn't know was that Hans was given confirmation that the tape recorder was on him. Hans reported the news to his supervisor. The plant manager would soon get orders from Andropov's inner-circle to secure the return of the tape and the recorder by any means necessary.

Ben wished to put space between himself and the damned plant as rapidly as possible. The Autobahn was the route that best served that purpose. Despite his best efforts to relax and forget the three tension-packed days of inspecting, his heart wouldn't stop racing. Apparently automatic weapons to the head had that effect.

He desperately searched for a theory to explain all that he had witnessed. The unique features of that mysterious third section perplexed him. Why was only that enclave soundproofed? What did the lower sound level signify? Why were there at least some cool pipes? Why were equipment inspections so infrequent? Why did the Kazakhstan shipments of natural uranium always go to the third unit? Why wasn't the Kazakh uranium treated as fungible? Was the third unit started up today just because of his inspection? If that section was normally shut down, how did the plant create enough enrichment?

A sixth sense warned him of danger, and sure enough, he spotted a black sedan following him. Whether he sped up or slowed down, it stayed a set distance behind him. As he entered Munich's outskirts, the sedan inched closer and turned when he turned.

Maybe it was Foster's promised FBI protection, but he doubted it. He was in no mood to take chances. He decided to lose them. The rush hour traffic could be used to his advantage. Stalled in the heavy traffic, he observed the traffic light ahead figuring out its timing. He purposely left room between his Cabriolet and the car ahead.

Now was his chance. He turned the wheel hard to the left and sped around the cars in front of him. Just as he planned, the light turned from yellow to red as he blazed through the intersection. He turned right at the next two intersections and swung into a parking spot.

He grabbed his brief cases and ran for the nearby department store. As he ran he glanced back. Damn. The black car had pulled up next to his car. Not waiting to see who followed, he ran through the huge store to a far door which opened onto another street.

Using the same evasive maneuver in two more stores he finally slowed down. It should be safe now to go back to his hotel room, get his things and clear out.

Once inside his room, he saw that the place had been thoroughly searched. What few clothes he had were all slightly out of place. His books, papers and notes were askew. Everything had been examined. A less than professional attempt to put things back as found had been made, yet these were no amateurs. He concluded that they had deliberately left items out of place, perhaps as a warning to him. A rare wave of fear washed over him.

Fortunately, none of the material in his room gave any indication of the mission he was on for the vice president, except... The tape recorder box and receipt had been in the wastebasket under other trash, yet now they lay on top. He concluded that was how they found out about his tape recorder. He chastised himself. Dumb, Ben. The guard during the pat-down search almost certainly confirmed that the tape recorder was on him, and the thugs who followed him were probably after it.

Was he in physical danger? Without doubt the answer was yes, especially when he recalled the vice president's warning and his own first-hand knowledge of how rough NuEnergy played. He figured Hans had stopped things at the plant only after allowing time to confirm that the tape recorder was on him. They intended to get it back, but they didn't want the act linked to the plant.

Hurriedly, he collected his belongings and scurried down the back stairs. He didn't bother to check out at the desk. He must avoid being followed. He wouldn't return to his rental car. Avis could pick it up later. He called Hertz from a pay phone and ordered a new car delivered to a hotel three blocks away. He followed an evasive route over to that hotel and took possession of the BMW 7 - Series Sedan.

As he drove toward Munich Airport, Ben struggled against a rising panic. This wasn't like him. His head-long rush to get out of Germany was contrary to his normally analytic approach to problems. He had been roughed up, chased by bad guys, had his room broken into, and secured a tape recording of potentially great national importance. Undoubtedly the plant's security forces wanted his tape badly enough to do anything. Was he being stupid by predictably heading straight for the airport?

Ben cautiously pulled into the Airport's parking garage. As anxious as he was to put space between himself and the plant thugs, he had settled down and alertly took in everything. Something struck him. Just ahead that parked car looked familiar. Wasn't that the same one that had chased him earlier? He was sure of it! With wheels screeching, he turned sharply toward the garage's exit ramp.

He figured that the thugs must be inside the airport monitoring all departures for the U.S. He couldn't fly out of here. An evasive course of action was necessary. He would drive through the Alps and across Germany's southern border to the Austrian town of Innsbruck. It was a far more circuitous way home, but hopefully safer.

Once on the Autobahn, which wound south through the foothills of the Alps, Ben floored it. He made a serious attempt to relax but couldn't. His heart raced as he envisioned every car as possibly following him. The steady barrage of hazards were affecting him mentally, as well as physically.

He forced his thoughts ahead. When he got to Innsbruck, he would call the vice president's secure phone number. He would explain the tape's significance to Foster and suggest that an emissary meet him in D.C. to pick it up.

Day 10 11:30 P.M. Flight out of Innsbruck

As the Austrian Airlines Airbus accelerated for the short hop to Paris, an exhausted Ben sank back into his seat. Finally he could relax, but his head was spinning. Events were nearly overwhelming him. Too much had happened in too short a time to make sense of it all. Yet so far he had not only survived but perhaps contributed something to Foster's investigation. Ben had told Foster that the third unit could be a front and was probably not functional.

Based upon what Foster had said over the phone, Ben suspected that his new role in life would be to help his old friend. Laura wouldn't be at all happy with this turn of events.

CHAPTER
EIGHTEEN

Day 13 2 A.M. Atyrau, Kazakhstan

A gray line of copiously laden Kazakh Border Guard trucks rolled through Atyrau's nearly deserted streets. The late hour was dictated by a wary Commander Hamad Barak since he was leery of this leg of the journey. With the FSB circling in ever closer, it was becoming more difficult for the shipments of uranium to pass unnoticed through this bustling business center. The early morning hours provided an advantage, in that it was easier for Barak to spot anything unusual.

Lieutenant Turar Ryskulov and Hamad Barak had caught up with and then trailed the truck procession from Kandagach through Atyrau. Ryskulov's Afghan-war vintage truck, with its defunct heater, had treated the pair to a cold two days of bumpy, dusty riding.

"Our roads are awful. The oil boom money hasn't filtered down to road repairs yet," fussed Ryskulov.

"This oil boom will never lead to real improvements. Our country is being raped once again. This time not by the Soviets, but by the oil-hungry Westerners," lamented Barak.

In the past the commerce around the Caspian Sea was limited to fishing, mining, manufacturing and shipping. On the populous western shore, former Soviet cities such as Baku, Azerbaijan, with a population of over one million, produced steel, chemicals, synthetic rubber and textiles. In contrast the eastern shore was relatively uninhabited. A few nomads eked out an existence in the space where the arid steppes collided with the sea. Some minerals had been extracted from the sparsely populated east side, but a change was coming. An oil boom relentlessly displaced the quiet along the eastern coast. Experts predicted that in terms of petroleum exports, the Caspian Sea region could eventually exceed the Persian Gulf in importance.

During the last decade, international oil consortiums invested billions of dollars, and equally valuable Western technology, in the development of the Caspian region's petroleum industry. Evolving from this huge enterprise were vast discoveries of rich reserves of oil. The largest of the fields, the mammoth Tengi oil field, possessed twice the estimated petroleum reserves of Alaska's north slope. These discoveries guaranteed that Kazakhstan soon would become one of the world's major oil exporters.

Spectacular reshaping of the Caspian's shoreline was also transpiring. Like the Aral Sea, this largest inland body of water in the world was significantly shrinking. As a result Atyrau, which once lay directly on the coast, now stood stranded miles from the retreating shoreline.

Before arriving seaside, Barak ordered, "Stop. I shall walk from here. You go on with the trucks."

Although the move struck Ryskulov as odd, he did not question Barak. He had learned that his cunning Commander always had a sound reason for his actions. While Ryskulov was stopped, the line of uranium-bearing trucks rolled on the final mile to the coast and the awaiting boat.

After agilely alighting from the truck, Hamad turned his back to the roaring wind. He struggled to light a fresh cigarette, then vanished into the blustery winter night.

Ryskulov, leaving his commander to the harsh elements, pushed on to catch up with the trucks before they arrived at the wind-swept Caspian Sea dock.

Just as Galena had explained to Hamad, the curse of central Asian winters, the frigid north wind, was blowing belatedly this year. Moderating in temperature and velocity only slightly as it swept over the Kazakh steppes, it fiercely attacked the northern Caspian coastline. Loose boards in the weathered dock slapped about, while the gusts forced the worn patrol boat to tear at its moorings. Groans and sighs emanated, seemingly from the sea, as the border guard boat, assaulted by the wind and sea, strained to break free of its shackles.

A freakish scene awaited Ryskulov. The sea was capped by two levels of ice; close in a high shelf, farther out lay a lower sheet of ice.

In normal winters the prevailing bitter wind commenced in December. The December blast of northern cold would cool the water and, at the same time, lower the level of the sea. This sea, which had no noticeable tides, did have a winter water-level shift. At the northern extremities of the Caspian, the water level during a routine winter gradually fell four to six feet during the sea's southern shift. Simultaneously the water temperature approached freezing. The ice would then form and thicken along this coastal area after the lower sea level was reached.

This winter season though was different for the Siberian winds failed to show up until late. Thus upon the bitter winds' retarded appearance, the water, already approaching freezing, formed ice quickly, several inches thick before the sea could shift south. As a consequence, large ice sheets near the dock and shore were left suspended several feet in the air, well above the sea's present level. Farther out from the dock and shore, of course, the ice sheets, supported only by the sea followed the sea level down.

"If you live long enough you will see everything," marveled Ryskulov.

Under the cover of night and the winter windstorm, the trucks rattled onto the dilapidated dock. The Kazakh troops initiated the transfer of the bulky uranium cylinders from the trucks to the patrol boat. Employing the front-end loaders, they moved the cylinders first onto the dock. The boat's hoist then lifted the heavy containers into the hold amidships. Ryskulov meticulously supervised each step.

Meanwhile, Barak silently approached the dock. Carefully scanning the waterfront as he crept closer, he inhaled deeply, defying the wind's attempt to tear the cigarette smoke away. Reaching a little-used entry to the dock, his pace became more deliberate. Watching his team at work, he noted with satisfaction that Ryskulov was carefully monitoring the uranium transfer to the boat.

Hamad scoured the dimly lit dock area for anything out of the ordinary. Suddenly, a slight motion caught his eye. He froze. As he squinted, the hazy image of a solitary man wearing a long fur coat came into focus. He wasn't a bum. Bums wouldn't be out here in this weather. Who would? What was his game? Hamad strongly suspected the Russian FSB was once again prowling too close.

Catlike, he melted into the moonlight's shadows. Watching the man's every action, he concluded that the interloper's purpose could not be legitimate. Soon enough, he saw what he suspected. Using a camera equipped with a large telephoto lens, the man was photographing the guard's operation. Hamad silently cursed. He ground the unfinished cigarette into the rough plank under his boot.

Patting his boot to assure the dagger was in place, he accepted what must be. Moving as a panther stalking its prey, Hamad slipped among the cargo boxes scattered about the dock. Methodically, he closed in.

Hamad saw that the agent remained unaware of the approaching judgment. The spy aimed his camera once again at Ryskulov's busy contingent of troops. Before he could snap the picture Hamad yanked him bodily into the air. The tall, lean man of great strength, held his victim suspended in the air by the throat with one callused hand while the other hand snatched away the camera. The Leica with its 110 mm telephoto lens clattered to the dock.

What light there was illuminated the shocked young man's eyes. They radiated a momentary plea for help. Desperation and panic contorted the face of the doomed agent. Hamad's hand flashed with steel. The dagger, with a twisting action, plunged deep into the man's gut. The light left his eyes and he sagged limply, still suspended in Hamad's iron grip.

Effortlessly the Guard Commander carried his victim over to the dock's edge and tossed the unconscious body down toward the ice sheets below. It crashed through the ice and fell through the intervening air space before splashing into the frigid water of the sea.

Satisfied that the FSB agent was history, Hamad cleaned his dagger and replaced it in his boot sheaf. Reaching for his cigarettes, he found them missing. Swearing under his breath about the loss, he crossed the springy planks toward his busy border guard contingent.

With the spy's confiscated camera slung over his shoulder, Hamad nodded to Ryskulov as he boarded the patrol craft. He was convinced that the FSB would not stop. They were surely closing in on his uranium enterprise. If so, this uranium switch would be even more difficult next time. Hamad rationalized with a touch of irony that at least he and his Guard were earning the big money Comrade Andropov paid. After kicking off his boots he admired the quality German-made Leica with its powerful lens. He hoped that the fall to the dock hadn't damaged the camera.

The cold saltwater shocked the severely wounded Russian back to consciousness. Deeply submerged in the icy waters, he desperately, yet instinctively, caught hold of a pier piling. Laboriously he pulled himself up toward the hidden layer of air.

His head protruded barely above the water, as he coughed up mouthfuls of seawater and blood. Gasping for air, he took inventory. Somehow he was still alive, but faced an extreme fight to remain so.

Fortunately, the thick plate of ice, which remained suspended, shrouded his grim struggle for life. The noise from the gale whipping the dock above overwhelmed the sound of his muffled coughs and gasps. Cold and bleeding, he clung desperately to the piling.

With an inherent will to live, he fought through the haze clouding his thoughts. Had the knife miraculously missed his vital organs? He knew he must get to warmth within minutes or hypothermia would finish what the blade had begun. An improbable strength returned to his torn body. The desperate spy, shielded by the icy roof, ripped off his shoes and coat and swam from piling to piling. Finally, with total exhaustion closing in upon him, he crawled to the relative safety of the shore, wet, cold and mortally wounded. Using some of the ice sheets as protection from the gales, he lay half dead on the wind-swept beach.

Pathetically curled up in a mixture of sand, blood and ice he was found by his FSB comrade. With his dying gasps the spy whispered a description of his assailant and what he had seen. After relaying his costly intelligence, he vomited blood, convulsed and died there on the frozen beach.

Pavel would soon receive a call from this gritty agent's companion.

Later, under Pavel's direction, FSB agents scoured the dock, finding only a pack of Marlboros, a trail of blood to the dock's edge and a hole in the ice. That find, though, coupled with the dying agent's story, confirmed Pavel's hunch as to who had murdered his fellow agent. He reported to Kruschev that Hamad Barak was the killer.

Day 14 5 P.M. Near the Kazakhstan Border Guard Base

Commander Barak climbed to the pilot's cabin to observe the final approach to the base. The rendezvous with Iran's General Zarif, a man he despised and feared, would soon take place. Yet, this breath-taking sight of his homeland made the journey a pleasure, despite his pending confrontation with Zarif.

After rounding the jutting, arid piece of land named Point Kyrzyk, the boat veered sharply east. In the lee of the mainland, the resilient patrol craft finally cruised into calmer waters. Rough waters or calm, Hamad thoroughly enjoyed the stark scenery surrounding the remote Kazakh outpost. This forlorn stretch of coastline near the Turkmenistan border awarded an appealing solitude. The vast blue sea mirrored the azure hue of the sky, the antithesis of the barren, colorless cliffs guarding the shore. The escarpment thrust hundreds of feet above the sea like a score of prehistoric mastodons frozen in time and space. Behind the silent gray sentinels extended the vast sweeping steppes, which dominated the central Asia landscape.

Startled, Barak saw something he had not seen before. A huge oil-drilling rig, with blazing nightlights outlining its huge silhouette, perched brazenly on the shoulders of the mastodonian bluffs.

"Damn," he lamented to Lt. Ryskulov. "We picked this spot for its remoteness. Now look. The mother of all petroleum reservoirs will probably be discovered right under our base."

As a low tendril of land appeared to the south, the boat veered to a more southeasterly course. The main coastline pressed in from the port side and the expanding spit of land crowded in from starboard. The land, like giant pincers, gradually closed in upon the water channel. The bay serving the base nestled where the two arms of land joined in pinching off any further intrusion of the sea.

In the last vestiges of twilight, Hamad easily distinguished the sleek Iranian vessel, replete with its bold navigational and convenience lights. His humble old patrol boat maneuvered into its berth behind the flashy frigate. Once the boat was secured, Hamad Barak hastened ashore. The frigate, flying the Iranian colors and Zarif's personal flag, signaled that the zealot General was here.

The lieutenant in charge of the base greeted the guard commander, "Welcome, Commander Barak. I trust your trip was satisfactory."

"The trip was uneventful, except for an encounter with one unfortunate spy."

"FSB?"

"That's my guess."

"They are relentless these days."

"You need to be alert here too."

"We are."

"You better be."

Taking that admonishment as the order it was intended to be, the officer reminded Barak, "Of course, your soldiers can't wait to hear from you, Commander. You must address them while you are here."

"After the General and I complete our inspection, I will chat with the troops. Rest assured, they are priority."

Hamad abruptly turned to Lieutenant Ryskulov, "Stay here this time. You must investigate that oilrig. See if any of those oil workers have ventured into this area. I wouldn't put it past the FSB to plant spies in the crew of that rig."

After assigning that task to Ryskulov, Hamad spotted General Bakr Zarif marching his way. He loathed the aggressive Iranian General. The man was dangerous. They had crossed swords every time they had met. The disdain they felt for each other grew more intense with each meeting. Even though Hamad sensed Zarif to be a vile man, this was business, so he grudgingly dealt with him.

"Commander Barak, it is good to see you again. The Caspian was a little angry this trip."

"It wasn't bad, especially once we rounded Point Kyzyk." Hamad abruptly cut off the feeble attempt at civility, suggesting instead, "General, let's get to the inventory." The less time spent with this radical the better.

"Very well."

Seizing the initiative, Barak barked, "Lieutenant, we are ready. Show us to the weapons."

The two leaders, accompanied by a bevy of Iranian nuclear experts, were escorted by Barak's troops a few hundred yards up the steep graveled road to the entrance of the deep underground storage complex.

General Zarif, ever alert, commented as they walked, "I see our assets are better defended this year. You have updated the SAMs. That is very good. This bleak hole houses weapons most valuable to my country. You better take good care of them."

Steaming at the deliberate insult, Barak carefully measured his reply. "Quite observant, General, but that isn't all. In addition to the latest Chinese SAMs, we recently acquired a dozen American-made Stingers. If there is ever an attack here, we will inflict a heavy toll on the aggressor."

"Yes, I suppose that is true."

"Of course, you know we already have SSM sites and machine gun emplacements, as well as the missile-armed patrol boat on duty nearby at all times. So as you correctly observe, the defenses are sound. I believe we could repel nearly any attack."

Barak intended this bravado for Zarif's consumption. Wisely Barak didn't turn his back even on his supposed partners.

Having made his point on the defenses, Commander Barak dealt with the insult, "By the way, if this is a bleak hole, then most of your country ranks as a stinking dung heap."

General Zarif grinned at Commander Barak's sharp retort. The response confirmed that he had drawn blood.

On the march up the hill, Barak reviewed his choice of sites. Except for the interloping oil drilling operation ten miles to the north, this remained the perfect location. Vegetation was so scarce that even the occasional nomadic shepherd rarely ventured near. How ironic that this forlorn corner of Kazakhstan, which now housed merchandise vital to the Iranians and the Mafia, might soon become a thriving oil field.

Almost as if Zarif read Barak's mind, he volunteered as they climbed toward the storage, "Our geologists say that there are some very promising formations under this area, so the drilling is probably here to stay. They estimate that in another five years, you Kazakhs will be producing and exporting more oil than we do. What are you going to do with all of your oil money, Commander?"

"Well, we are not going to waste it all as you do on military armaments!" taunted Barak.

General Zarif eagerly took up the challenge. "Well, you watch our domination of the Middle East and then see if you think our money was wasted."

Hamad knew this to be no idle threat. The tone of it within the context of recent Iranian ventures worried him plenty. As the two officers approached the weapons complex, Hamad drew deeply on his cigarette before replying. "You won't win any great prize in your mastery of the Middle East once the oil is gone. In that sandy morass of miserable humanity, everybody hates somebody. You will need all of your precious weapons just to keep the peace."

"Oh, but my dear Commander, don't you see. You miss the point," snorted Zarif disparagingly. "The oil revenues of all of the Middle East will pay for our military expenditures ten times over. It's merely a highly leveraged investment. Plus it is time to reinstate the Persian Empire to its rightful prominence in the world. It is destiny, you might say."

Barak was more than a little worried about "destiny" in the form of the expansionist tendencies of this power to their south. It did not seem just, but what did. Kazakhstan had not completely thrown off the yoke of Russian dominance before another threat emerged. That this was a Muslim power did not give Barak or his countrymen any comfort. Iran's fanatical Islamic government appeared to them to be extreme, almost a perversion of the religion that fit so well with the Kazakh's pastoral tendencies.

"I hope you aren't casting your greedy eyes this way. If we must, my border guard can reduce any invaders of yours to the status of fermenting camel droppings."

Zarif, feigning statesmanship, said, "Let us proceed with the business at hand. We will leave for another day grappling with these weighty subjects. This armpit in the desert contains the nuclear warheads we want and the bomb-grade uranium that the Mafia wants us to process for them. So let's confirm status and inventory without further delay."

Barak agreed to the momentary truce which Zarif had called and simultaneously violated. Fuming at that deliberate contradiction, he ordered the attending border guards to lead the way. He wanted this show over with.

General Zarif and Commander Barak, once within the reinforced underground storage facility, inspected the nuclear materials. They verified that fifteen tactical nuclear warheads remained. Each was carefully stored in a separate room with its own redundant climate control system. The two-foot-diameter plutonium warheads rested on pristine stainless-steel platforms, located four feet above the floor in each room. The elevated platforms eliminated any remote chance of flooding.

The remaining thirty metric tons of uranium were also stored in a controlled atmosphere. The configuration of the many widely separated small containers, about the size of a five-gallon dairy milk can, ensured a non-explosive arrangement and minimized deterioration over time.

The nuclear pact between the Iranians and Boris Andropov's Mafia benefited both parties. Both, however, put into practice President Ronald Reagan's famous admonition, "Trust, but verify." Hamad didn't miss the irony, in that the Mafia and Iran, both bitter enemies of the U.S., adopted the former American President's wisdom.

The general's experts found that all was in order. Commander Barak, therefore, gave his troops the go-ahead to load the frigate with this year's shipment of five warheads, as well as fifteen metric tons of bomb-grade uranium.

Barak didn't comprehend all of the details of the processing of the uranium that occurred in Karaj. He was aware, though, that this annual delivery of weapons-grade uranium was linked to the periodic cylinder exchanges at Kandagach. The Iranians took the diverted natural uranium cylinders into their nuclear complex at Karaj, where they altered the contents, then returned them to his border guard for the next Kandagach exchange. During a tour of Karaj he had spotted several Russian nuclear scientists who had worked years ago at the Semipalatinsk Nuclear Complex. After talking to them he had come close to understanding the nature of the Iranian-Mafia deal, close enough for him.

Finally, it was time for his soldiers. "Lieutenant, call the troops together. We will have our visit and then we will ship this stuff to Iran." Zarif could wait, he figured.

Day 14 11 P.M. South Caspian Sea

Barak settled in for the next leg of his journey south to Rashte. The old workhorse patrol boat, trailing in the wake of the elegant frigate, labored to keep up. At Rashte they would deliver the natural uranium cylinders, the bomb-grade uranium and the tactical nuclear warheads into the hands of Zarif's military.

His worries about these two powers, Russia to the north and Iran to the south, were escalating. He sensed that those two might be on a collision course. Could his game of pitting them against each other backfire, with his Kazakh guard caught in the middle of an approaching showdown? He devoutly prayed not.

He would be relieved when his role in the nuclear smuggling enterprise was history. It was a headache he didn't need anymore. Kruschev's FSB was hard on their trail. Kruschev, he appreciated from years of association with him in the old KGB, was not one to tangle with lightly.

He lit a cigarette and leaned back in his chair. He understood the Russian people as well as anyone, yet their national character baffled him. Great and brave Russians in the past had championed the rights of the peasants against the ruling tyrants at great personal peril. There was a strength in the Orthodox religious faith of the masses that he admired. Yet today there was a criminal element running rampant in Russia that seemingly would stop at nothing. The Mafia routinely stole life's essentials from Russia's long-suffering poor.

What was it about their national character that tolerated a criminal element that preyed so mercilessly on its own humble poor? He doubted if even their most insightful thinkers understood this enigma. Perhaps it was this flaw that prevented them from becoming a truly great people.

Certainly what he was doing was wrong, he admitted. He should not be working for the Mafia kingpin, Andropov. Yet there was a difference. His pact with the Mafia devils was designed to help his countrymen financially and to balance opposing forces surrounding Kazakhstan. Or was that merely a lame rationalization on his part?

Enough! He would ponder these matters no more. Instead he would enjoy Pushkin's prose for the duration of his Caspian cruise.

CHAPTER
NINETEEN

Day 15 7:15 P.M. Laura's Bookstore Tulsa

Ben was concerned about Laura. Since her mother's death last year she had occasional moments when tears came without warning or she would react to some happening in an almost paranoid manner. Yet, for the most part she had seemed to be fighting through those moody moments with a courage and determination that he admired.

Since his return from Munich, however, she had regressed and he mistakenly believed he knew why. He assumed that the rough events at Munich and the vice president's request for help caused her to worry for his safety.

Ben agonized over the situation. If he accepted Foster's call for assistance, then he would cause Laura more anguish. If he didn't…what then? Could he face himself knowing what he knew and refusing to help? The strangest analogy came to mind. He thought of the passenger heroes on United flight 93 on that fateful day, September 11, 2001. Several of the passengers aboard that hijacked flight, upon discerning the terrorists intentions to crash into one of D.C.'s edifices, rushed the hijackers, knowing that by doing so thousands of lives would be saved. The analogy came to mind that his Black Bear Plant had been hijacked by the NuEnergy mob and he could choose to wimp out and do nothing or fight the slow but sure destruction of the plant. However melodramatic the analogy, the answer was obvious to him. He would fight NuEnergy and do what he could to assist Foster. He would have to help Laura understand his decision.

As he watched Laura's reaction to the news of his intention to accept Foster's call, he reflected upon a simpler and happier time full of promise. A driving California rainstorm brought them together. That fortuitous soaker bestowed upon him life's greatest gift. His submarine had been temporarily based at Vallejo shipyard in the San Francisco Bay area. One late-fall Saturday, Ben attended the Navy-Stanford football game. After the game he had been caught by a surprise rainsquall. Running across the hilly campus, drenched by the storm, he bumped into a girl, a coed with an umbrella. She was the most beautiful girl he had ever seen. He was hopelessly smitten by the raven-haired beauty with the big sparkling blue eyes and a ready smile who offered to share her cover with him.

From that moment theirs had been an intense infatuation that matured over the years into a deep, refined love. Gradually he grew in appreciation of this person, who had agreed to share his future. Laura's love for literature and poetry, nourished by her mother, had obviously developed at an early age. While enrolled in graduate school at Stanford, she had even written and published a book of poetry, and another book on the History of Russian Writers. He was hopelessly in love with Laura, forever.

As Laura busied nervously about placing newly arrived books in their proper place on the shelves, Ben summed up, "Laura, I believe we are at a crossroads. What we decide today will show what we are made of. Foster wants my help for a couple of weeks to figure out the Munich plant and share all I know about NuEnergy. I believe that I should do that, but I don't want to leave you alone and afraid."

"I am afraid," Laura admitted as she fought back tears. "I don't want you to go. All I have is you and this store."

"You could temporarily close the store and come back to D.C. with me."

"And what would I do, sit in a hotel room all day? No thanks. I would rather stay here," Laura reluctantly concluded.

"You could write," Ben argued.

Laura silently went over to the coffee pot and absently filled Ben's cup with more French Roast. She debated how much more she should say. She decided not to make this more difficult than necessary for Ben. She somewhat understood that his sense of duty was rekindled by his ongoing battle with NuEnergy and through his reunion with his old Navy friend. She needed to make the best of the inevitable.

"Ben, how are you going to keep NuEnergy from becoming suspicious about your going to D.C.?"

"Foster and I created a great cover story."

Laura almost laughed for Ben actually seemed to be enjoying this sleuthing business.

"What is this grand cover story?"

"Ol' plant manager Zogelmann is going to be asked, probably today, by NEI to loan me to them to head up a safety committee. He will jump at the chance to get me out of Black Bear. Voila—the perfect cover."

Laura's face clouded over. She was thinking, "Just like Fred Bumgardner," but she said nothing.

Ben noticed that her face had turned white. "What's wrong, Laura?"

"Nothing," she lied.

Ben refused to accept her denial. "There is something, Laura. What is it?"

Thinking quickly, Laura decided she couldn't mention the similarity to Fred Bumgardner's situation. Instead she would bring up something else that was bothering her. She needed to talk about it anyway before Ben left for D.C.

"After mom died, I boxed up a lot of her papers until I had time to go through them."

Ben nodded.

"Well, while you were over in Munich getting in more trouble, I found a very strange letter."

"Yes, go on."

"Ben, the letter writer called Mom, Marina."

"That's weird. Marina doesn't sound at all like Ellena. Was this writer confusing her for someone else?"

"No. I don't think so. I know mother changed her name when she came to this country. But she never said what her real name was. Based on this letter I now suspect that it was Marina. She told me that she fled the Soviet Union when I was a baby and that she was still afraid of the Soviets and their security agencies. She never told me why but she warned me never to tell anyone that we had escaped. Until this letter showed up, I honored that. I accepted not knowing anything else about my past. Now I'm terribly curious."

"I would guess so."

Ben was somewhat offended for Laura had never told him that she and her mother had escaped the Soviets.

"I think you should have told me about that. Don't you trust me?"

"That's not it at all, Ben. It's just that until mother's death and all of this, I had repressed the whole thing, not even admitting to myself the mystery surrounding my past. Please don't be mad at me. I can't stand that."

"I'm not mad just surprised and hurt. But what you say makes sense. You had repressed the past and gone on with your life. I might have done the same thing. It's okay."

Ben knew that with all that was going on they could not afford a big tiff over this. He gave Laura a hug and a kiss and told her, "I want to hear everything. What else about the letter?"

"The letter writer is apparently a man. He must have communicated over the years with mother. He knew her real name. How could he know that, Ben?"

"What makes you think it was a man?"

"The style of writing. He told Marina that he had read my journal articles and said my essays were brilliant. Here is where it gets very strange. He said my literary ability and courageous themes were reminiscent of my grandfather's. Ben, I have no idea who my grandfather is. Mother always told me that she didn't know who her father was."

Ben was staggered and could find little to say, "How bizarre!"

"From the letter it's apparent that the writer and my mother corresponded frequently. Yet, I found no other letters in Mother's belongings. She must have destroyed them, perhaps in fear they would be discovered. This one arrived only a week before her death, so she wasn't able to dispose of it."

Ben shook his head. Events were encompassing them which he couldn't comprehend. They really didn't need any more challenges, but they just kept coming.

"There is something else, Ben. The writer understands much about Russia. He even closed the letter with a Russian term of endearment."

"As soon as I get back from D.C., we will get after this and see what we can figure out."

"Ben, maybe I have already discovered something. After reading the letter, I searched the Internet news libraries, using the name Marina, for any news story about Russia during the year 1970. That is supposedly the year of our escape."

Becoming quite caught up in this new mystery, Ben demanded, "Tell me already, what did you find?"

"A Marina Tarasova, a great equestrian on the Soviet team, dramatically escaped with her baby. Mother and baby disappeared from the face of the earth."

"Your mother was an expert equestrian. She taught you to ride. It fits. You are that baby!"

"Yes, I believe it is possible. Mother was a gifted horsewoman. The best I ever saw but she would never compete in shows. She stayed away from them like the plague. Now it is apparent why. She could afford no notoriety. The letter writer may be the only one who knows for sure who my mother and grandfather really were and for that matter, who I am."

Ben was stunned and for a long time silently hugged Laura as she cried softly.

"Can I do anything to help?"

"Just hold me forever."

As Laura regained her composure, she told Ben, "I believe that the writer is the key. If I'm ever to uncover my past, I must find him. It's apparent he knows more about me than I know about myself."

Knowing Laura's restless mind, Ben asked, "What else have you figured out?"

"Well, I only have speculations. As I said, the style and substance of the letter make me think that the writer is a man. He is an expert on Russia. He's old enough to have known my mother when she was Marina, and based on the letter's postmark, he may be from the Hartford, Connecticut area. Also his critique of my work demonstrates considerable writing expertise."

"You mean because he said you were good that makes him an expert?" Ben joked.

Laura elbowed him, "You know better than that."

"I don't know. You are pretty egotistical."

Ben was forcing Laura to lighten up. She possessed such a literary talent that sometimes her intensity and dedication worked against her. He figured that with all they were facing, they couldn't afford any self-inflicted handicaps.

Laura struck back, "Okay, Ben, maybe you don't want to hear where this leads."

"I am hooked. Don't you dare stop now."

"I researched all authors of Russian articles who were at least sixty-years old and lived in Connecticut."

"And?"

"And one name came up.

"Who?"

"Someone we met long ago."

Ben looked inquisitively at her, as if demanding, "Tell me who it is, you rascal."

"Dr. Dudaev!"

"Mark's and my professor?" Ben gasped.

"Yep! It's really a small world, isn't it?"

"So, what now?"

"Would it be ridiculous for me to write him asking for his help? I could tell him about my mother's letter, my desire to find its author and my need to learn who my Grandfather really is?"

Ben saw the great importance this quest had assumed to Laura. She needed something besides Ben to cling to. Her mysterious past was that something. "Absolutely! Write him!"

"Do you really think I should?"

"Yes. Do it. See what happens."

A jumble of emotions beset Laura. Her mother and her only child were gone. Now Ben was under siege by NuEnergy and the Mafia. A mystery man, maybe Dr. Dudaev, knew about her mother's and perhaps her grandfather's true identity. Ben was being called to Washington. She would be alone. With tears again welling in her eyes, she averted Ben's gaze. His strong, yet gentle, hand reached across the table and turned her face toward him. His smiling eyes offered her reassurance. He slid his chair closer and tenderly kissed away each tear.

"We have each other. We will get through this together. Remember, your mother left you so much. She gave you a strength that is still with you. It is you. I see it."

"Thanks, Ben. You are right. I need to shape up. But I don't want you to go. I'm afraid for you."

"I have the government protecting me now so you shouldn't worry."

"Ben, you call me every morning and every night."

"Of course. Remember, the phone works both ways. You call, too."

"We have been apart before, but this is different. Our lives are never going to be the same."

"Don't borrow trouble, Laura."

"Yes, you are right again. I must stay positive. Last night I wrote a little something for you. It's not quite complete, but I tried to capture how totally you are my hero. For some reason I couldn't come up with the last line, but the time will come when that ending is obvious. Promise to keep it with you. Don't laugh at my humble attempt to express what is in my heart."

Laura softly pressed the envelope, holding her composition, into Ben's hand. She whispered, "Open it after you are back in D.C."

CHAPTER
TWENTY

Day 18 3 P.M. NuEnergy Corporate Offices Houston, Texas

Boris Andropov hurtled upward in the glass-enclosed elevator, which exclusively served NuEnergy's executive suites. After penetrating the lower roof, the elevator afforded a spectacular view of downtown Houston. NuEnergy's building was one of the towering gold-tinted, glass-sided structures in the heart of town. These giants reflected the images of the surrounding skyscrapers of the plains and the ribbons of interstates weaving around their feet. The bright winter sun at its low angle cast sporadic glares from the golden behemoths.

From a rapidly changing perspective Andropov took in the scene as he and his two personal guards ascended to the building's top floor. Even though much of the country was in winter's icy grip, Houston was enjoying one of its frequent warm midwinter days. This moderate climate seemed surreal to him. He had survived the better part of two-dozen frigid winters in the dreary Semipalatinsk region. Yet, those severe winters were easier to survive than the economic malaise, which had choked the former Soviet empire like a poisonous fog.

Few of these coddled Texans, he opined, could survive for very long in the central Asian winters, and moreover what would happen here if government workers went unpaid for months on end? Revealing a hostile intent, he scoffed that he would love to find out. He held utter contempt for Americans who, in his opinion, were soft and spoiled.

Moreover, their government's cowboy mentality of ride in, fix it, ride out was reflective of these people's shallowness, arrogance and ignorance. These superficial people had never known severe hardship. Instant gratification was their God. Their attention span was no

153

more than a ten-second TV sound bite. He was astonished at how few understood other cultures, or spoke other languages. Many of these dunces were not even literate in English. What did these people do with their brains?

Andropov had understood that to achieve his global ambitions he would have to become proficient in the languages of the world's powers, as well as to acquaint himself with their customs and cultures. He had mastered six languages and had readily picked up U.S. business tactics. He honed his skills to the point where only rarely could an American executive effectively challenge him in contract negotiations. That particular prowess gave him great satisfaction. It was a thrill to beat the cocky capitalists at their own game. He generally kept well hidden the ruthlessly competitive undercurrent to his nature, except at times of frustration when its emergence would shake even the most hardened CEO.

In the last five years Boris, through a series of brilliant acquisitions and investments, had transformed his nuclear smuggling enterprise into a vast empire. The mammoth R.M. Holding Corporation served both as a conglomerate of legitimate enterprises and as a means to launder tens of billions of dollars from the various illegal Mafia operations. He had ruthlessly consolidated his authority over the Russian Mafia in North America, Central and Eastern Europe, Russia and the other CIS countries. He dominated his wholly owned subsidiaries, including NuEnergy, as absolutely as a puppeteer manipulated his marionettes.

The elevator abruptly stopped on the thirty-fifth floor and Boris, with his two Thieves-in-Law guards respectfully following him, stepped into the elaborately furnished NuEnergy corporate offices. A pleasantly plump, middle-aged receptionist greeted him, "How was your flight, Mr. Andropov?"

"It got me here."

Slightly taken aback by the abrupt reply, the receptionist informed him, "Mr. Parris is expecting you."

Andropov arrogantly paid her no heed. Instead he examined the surroundings.

Despite spending minimal time at the NuEnergy offices, he felt right at home. Decorated according to his wishes, plush hunter green carpets and oversized desks of burl oak filled the premises, which evinced his wealth and power.

The receptionist, unnerved by Andropov's demeanor, meekly offered, "I'll show you to Mr. Parris's office if you would like, Mr. Andropov."

"That won't be necessary. I trust you have more to do than usher me around my own premises."

With that curt admonishment, he left his two guards with the bewildered receptionist and proceeded toward Parris's suite at the end of the main hall. To his left was a series of executive offices for the vice presidents of NuEnergy, while a conference room wall formed the right side of the hall.

Andropov detoured into his favorite conference room. The upper portion of the partitions were entirely of glass. Playing with the switches on the control panel, he automatically moved drapes and blinds across the glass. Finally he converted it into a one-way mirror. Other controls operated an assortment of video conferencing and digital video equipment. Two magnificent Italian-crystal chandeliers illuminated the massive conference table. The outer windows provided a spectacular view of the surrounding skyscrapers. To his delight, two Renoir original masterpieces smuggled from the Hermitage by his St. Petersburg's gang now hung on the walls here.

Leaving the conference room and heading farther down the hall, he counted the NuEnergy nuclear plant pictures, which spanned the entire length of the left wall. At the end of the hall the picture of Black Bear, the last NuEnergy acquisition, had taken its place in the gallery. How prophetic that the line of plant pictures now filled the wall.

Despite takeover initiatives underway, he knew that NuEnergy would never operate more than the present thirty. Maintaining the takeover efforts was Andropov's ruse to avoid signaling how near fruition were his secret plans of devastation. Thirty were demanded to secure his scheme and thirty there were.

His cleverly conceived plan inexorably approached an explosive finale. Now that payoff was so close, he was intolerant of even a hint of a roadblock. Indeed, a couple of potential hurdles had appeared.

Andropov found the tall Ralph Parris, NuEnergy's president, awaiting him at his office door. Andropov and Parris greeted each other, not with personal warmth, but with deference and grudging respect for the other's abilities. Together they had captured the operational control of the U.S. nuclear plants, which garnered nearly three billion dollars income each year. Those returns placed NuEnergy high on the Fortune 500 list. NuEnergy's parent, R.M. Holding, to Andropov's great satisfaction, was at the top, far ahead of number two.

"Dr. Andropov, good to see you again."

Andropov nodded in reply. Parris's towering frame dwarfed Andropov's average stature, however, the body language exhibited by the two clearly indicated that Andropov held the upper hand in the relationship. Parris, sensitive to his boss's ego, used a specially adjusted chair whenever they met, which brought his head below Andropov's.

Both men sat down at the burl-oak table in Parris's office, with Andropov promptly setting the docket. "First, we will finalize our list of takeover targets. Then we shall discuss problems in maintaining control at the plants you now operate."

Andropov and his North American Chief, Ray Goldstein, were the only ones privy to the full extent of NuEnergy's intricately interwoven business and mob intrigues. NuEnergy executives were apprised only of their individual pieces of the puzzle. Parris, knowing more than the other executives, did suspect that Andropov's ultimate purpose for the plants ventured beyond his cognizance. Mob-controlled technicians and engineers in each plant had their roles to play, and Ralph Parris knew he was not the one setting their agenda. Goldstein communicated separately with each of the workers and Parris had incomplete knowledge of the nature of the mobster's dealings with those special employees.

Andropov asked, "Are all plants up and operating?"

"Yes."

"Good. Keep it that way. I want no outages for the next month. Is that clear?"

Although this arbitrary directive puzzled him, Parris dutifully replied, "Certainly."

In 1991 Andropov had first arrived in the U.S. as part of a joint Russian-Kazakh uranium marketing team. Their mission was to sell commercially enriched uranium fuel to U.S. nuclear power companies. At that time, Ralph Parris was the vice president in charge of one nuclear power plant in Rhode Island. Parris's utility purchased a moderate portion of enrichment from the foreign team. It was only the second such U.S. purchase of uranium enrichment from any former Iron Curtain country.

The delicate negotiations on the purchase contract had supplied the venue for the two men to become acquainted. Parris quickly grasped the extent of Andropov's genius, revealed by his strategic cunning and bargaining skills. Rarely had he been pitted against such a clever opponent. Because Andropov was equally impressed with Parris, he decided to take a major risk.

He offered Parris huge amounts of commercial uranium fuel at a fraction of market cost. Even though Parris suspected illegalities, or at least irregularities, he was interested. Parris' motive for becoming involved with Andropov's scheme was not totally recognized, even by him. New England Power, the utility he had worked for passed him over for CEO. Dismissing him as an engineer devoid of the requisite management skills, they had stung him deeply. His success as NuEnergy CEO was proving them wrong.

Parris and Andropov devised a means to bring Andropov's product clandestinely into the fuel stream of American nuclear power plants, without raising suspicions. First, the scheme called for total control of an enrichment plant. The Munich plant was constructed to fill that need. Secondly, they would have to acquire a large number of nuclear power plants. Andropov had mysteriously insisted that they must be American plants. Therein lay the real reason that Andropov needed Parris.

Most American utility executives of the nineties had no love affair with nuclear power. Wall Street analysts still evaluated the technology as risky. That negative assessment caused dividends to stockholders to suffer. Also, the typical utility executive's expertise was financial or legal, not technical. The executives' discomfort with nuclear technology was the underpinning on which the two built their empire. Their plan leveraged Andropov's supply of low cost fuel with Parris's superior technical capabilities of running nuclear plants. Their new company, NuEnergy, deceitfully appealed to the targeted utility CEOs by apparently assuming the operating risk and liability of the complex plants.

At first, the plan unfolded like clockwork. Many small and unsophisticated utilities, saddled with these burdensome plants, gladly turned over their operations to NuEnergy in return for a guaranteed income. In that manner NuEnergy promptly picked up fifteen nuclear plants from those vulnerable companies. Through Parris's expert management, they established excellent operating records. Despite that superior performance, Parris and Andropov were forced to resort to more malevolent techniques to gain the next fifteen. Even though Parris didn't know why, Andropov absolutely insisted upon NuEnergy acquiring thirty plants.

To pick up the last plants, Goldstein furnished technically qualified Mafia members, whom Parris helped finesse into jobs at the targeted utilities. After the engineers or technicians were securely employed at the plants, they sabotaged the units. The plants experienced either severe shut downs, or minor accidents followed by extensive investigations before operations could resume.

The contrived outages were very costly. Not coincidentally, this was when NuEnergy would step up and offer an opportune takeover. The great financial stress, which a lengthy outage caused, would usually drive the utility to make a decision in NuEnergy's favor. This method brought the required plants into Andropov's fold. With the recent addition of Oklahoma's Black Bear, Andropov had reached his goal.

Parris reported on his latest targets for takeover. "Our latest surveys show that two utilities with nuclear plants in the states of Minnesota and Iowa are most vulnerable. These utilities with their five nuclear plants are experiencing increasing competition from coal plants. Coal plants as far away as Wyoming and Montana are winning customers from within these utilities' districts. Also our studies indicate that these utilities are below the critical size essential for survival under the revitalized competition created by their states' deregulation initiatives. Consequently, these are our next prime takeover possibilities."

"Good. Let's go after them."

"They have requirements right now for experienced electrical engineers. We have some excellent electrical engineers with mob ties at several of our plants. I already suggested that some of them apply for those jobs. Of course, we will give them sterling recommendations. Those recommendations should land them the jobs."

"Good work. The sooner they get hired, the better. You also need to resubmit our takeover offers. Those bids must be on the table before our engineers arrange the outages that send the dupes our way."

Parris was getting tired of being scrunched down in his chair and would be relieved when Andropov left. He readily jumped into the next subject. "As you well know, Dr. Andropov, the main problem we face after a plant takeover is an occasional ethical manager who fights us on our maintenance priorities. Sensing a fraudulent nature in our process, they resist our changes. We have resorted to various schemes to remove those obstacles with good success to date."

"Is that so? A Dr. Ben Andrew presented quite a problem at Munich, as well as at Black Bear. Removal of this headache should be a top priority of yours, Mr. Parris. I find his continued disruptions unacceptable!"

Sensing Andropov's flaring anger, Parris was thankful that he had an answer to this challenge. "You hit the nail squarely on the head. He represents a stubborn problem that needs to be neutralized and we have."

"How?"

"A few days ago a most fortuitous request came into my office from the president of NEI. He wanted us to loan Dr. Andrew to them to lead a national committee on nuclear safety standards. I immediately said yes. Mr. Andrew left for D.C. yesterday."

"That is almost too convenient," Andropov snapped suspiciously. "Further, it's not enough! Something more permanent is in order."

"That's your department. You have the organization to deal with that. I don't want to know any more about it."

Andropov nodded, indicating that he would take care of it.

The dark side of Boris Andropov was unnerving, even to the steely Parris. Parris was comfortable with bullying, scheming and undercutting competitors to get to the top of the management chain. But Andropov was something else, brilliant, driven, but also brutal. He would stop at nothing to complete his agenda.

Parris had gotten into this partnership with Andropov nearly a decade ago and it had proven to be amazingly successful. But he knew that Andropov's agenda was beyond his comprehension, probably sinister, and most likely dangerous to everyone involved. He was trapped. He could never escape without a deadly response from Andropov's enforcement wing. Moreover, getting out would be tantamount to an admission that his success as NuEnergy CEO was fraudulent.

Parris was relieved when Andropov finally left. He let his huge frame sink back into his executive chair and closed his eyes. What was about to happen to Dr. Ben Andrew bothered him. But he told himself that it was out of his hands. He hadn't dictated the man's fate, and he certainly couldn't do anything about it. Worrying about it wouldn't help. So he deleted the thoughts of Ben Andrew from his mind. He knew it would work, he had done it before.

Returning to his car, Andropov called Brent Lepke, one of his chief North American lieutenants. Lepke took care of all the tough, dirty aspects of the business of the Russian Mob in North America.

"I want Dr. Ben Andrew of Black Bear eliminated. You will find him in D.C. working for NEI. You be the judge of how it's done, but it must appear accidental."

Lepke accepted the assignment willingly. He had even heard that Dr. Ben Andrew's wife had called the vice president to complain about NuEnergy. He knew Goldstein was already investigating the matter. Goldstein suspected Andrew's antics at Munich could be somehow tied to that call. Completion of his hit on Andrew would end the need for further inquiry into the Ben Andrew case.

TWENTY-ONE

Day 22 5 P.M. Sheraton Washington Hotel Washington, D.C.

The sprawling Sheraton Washington Hotel, Ben Andrew's home away from home, was near the Woodley Park Zoo metro exit. The venerable old building, resting prominently in northwest D.C., revealed decades of wear and tear. The formerly dark-red bricks that walled the older section had faded to a dull, dirty red. However, the newer, taller section, called the Towers, housed his room and boasted bricks of a fresher light-brown.

Evergreens, eastern white pines and magnolias, surrounded the hotel, providing green relief to the otherwise drab midwinter scene. An advantage of this location was its proximity to Rock Creek Park. Ben intended to squeeze in an occasional run along the park's winding, wooded paths. Despite being in the heart of the D.C. metropolis, the trail following Rock Creek offered several miles of quiet, forested respite. The park seemed removed, if only psychologically, from the frantic pace of the nation's Capitol.

Another attraction, a smorgasbord of excellent restaurants specializing in various international cuisines, lay just around the corner on Connecticut Avenue. He had already sampled Napoleon's, the Indian Curry House, and Arabian Nights, which specialized in French, Indian and Mideast cuisines. Many more fine establishments beckoned to him with their varied culinary temptations, but he wasn't sure whether his digestive system could handle a steady diet of such exotic foods.

Since the Nuclear Energy Institute (NEI) committee's work was ostensibly his reason for being in D.C., he had invested all of his time and energy at NEI. This cover for his true purpose demanded enough of his attention to make sure that no suspicions were aroused.

160

He had become a familiar sight in his committee office at the NEI headquarters building at 18th and L Streets. In the dark of early morning he would walk the few hundred feet from his hotel to the metro entrance. In a matter of minutes he would catch the commuter-packed southbound redline for a quick ride to the Farragut North exit. The trip's last leg involved a short climb up out of the tunnel and a brisk walk of less than a block to the NEI offices.

The nuclear industry funded NEI's work on tasks of mutual interest. Ben's committee assignment was to develop standards and companion interpretations that would hopefully curtail individual inspectors' discretionary abuse of the standards.

While pulling on his warm-ups, he stared out his window at the congested rush-hour traffic on Connecticut Avenue. His thoughts drifted. His routine was about to change, but that wasn't what worried him. The meeting tonight with Foster's entire crisis team concerned him. Would they accept him, a civilian, or would he be treated as an outsider? Because of the meeting tonight, he decided to call Laura now, earlier than normal.

Ben picked up the special phone given to him by Foster and hit speed-dial-one. He kicked off his Florsheims and sank into the motley-brown sofa in his hotel room as the phone automatically dialed Laura's secure phone.

"Hello, Ben. Why are you calling so early? Is something wrong?"

"No, nothing is wrong. There is a meeting tonight so thought I better call now."

"Just a minute, Ben. Hang on. I have to finish up with a customer. I will be right back."

As Ben waited his thoughts drifted to that bookstore which Laura loved so much. He was grateful that the hobby-turned-business served to somewhat take her mind off his being gone and mired in this Mafia mess.

Finally Laura returned to the phone. "Good news, I just sold four books. Business is getting a little better each week. Word-of-mouth is doing more than all of our advertising. What is happening back there?"

"Oh, my schedule is finally changing. No more NEI all day, only half days. I start working for Mark. Guess I will find out more about that tonight."

"That's right, you are going to the White House tonight for the first time, aren't you? That should be really interesting. Are you nervous?"

"A little."

Laura laughed, "I know you. You wouldn't admit it if you were scared to death."

"Actually, I am worried whether that bunch of high-powered government officials will accept me or just tolerate me because of my friendship with Mark."

"That is a good question. I almost hope they don't want you around so you can come back to me sooner. But I have to think that if these are folk Mark picked, they will be open-minded and quickly see that you have a valuable perspective. So don't worry about it. Just stand your ground like you always do."

Laura was surprised with her answer. She hadn't even wanted him to become part of this because of the danger, yet ... He was in it up to his neck and her only role left was not to whine about it but to help him through it. She asked, "What else is going on? Anything worthwhile at NEI today?"

"It was all pretty routine," Ben hedged.

He didn't want to worry her. He had asked NEI CEO, Bryan Williams, if he could see lists of past committees' support staffs. The staff assignments of Fred Bumgardner's group had seemed to jump off the page at him. Two on Fred's committee were long-time NEI staff personnel, but the third was a Michelle Michote, a lawyer from a D.C. law firm, Stranahan *et al*. He had made a mental note not to use any of those three people in his committee's work. Probably just silly superstition, but he wasn't about to take any unnecessary chances. He intended to ask Brad for all police files on Fred's death. He had always smelled a rat in Fred's demise, probably a Mafia rat. Instead of mentioning any of this to Laura he tried to change the subject.

"So have you received a reply from your letter to Dudaev?"

"No. Isn't that a little strange? It should be easy to answer, 'no go away it wasn't I who wrote the letter.' So maybe the answer isn't no."

"Logically you are right, Laura. Except he is a very busy man. Maybe he has been out of town or ill."

"That is possible, but my intuition tells me that he wrote the letter. The nature of his and mother's relationship is quite a mystery."

"You will get an answer. After this is over, if I have to, I will take you to confront him. You deserve an answer."

"Thanks, Ben. Have you read my poem?"

"Yes, every day. It is beautiful."

"Then you have an idea of how much you mean to me."

"Yes and that makes me the luckiest guy in the world. I have been thinking about when this is over and I get back to Tulsa. Why don't I work fulltime at the store? That would give you a little more time to write."

"That would be super. I started writing something."

"What about?"

"About how the Russian mob murdered Galina Starovoitova."

"Who on earth is Galina Starovoitova?"

"She was one of Russia's most courageous politicians. She boldly challenged the Mafia and was shot in the bargain."

Both Laura and Ben paused for the inherent message jumped out at them. Taking on the Mafia can get you killed. Neither acknowledged it though.

After the pause Ben spoke up, "I will call you tomorrow. Think about my idea on the bookstore."

"I will. I love you, Ben. Please be careful."

With a moment to spare, he pulled out his billfold and unfolded the paper which Laura had given him.

He sank deeper into the sofa and re-read her gift of love.

Laura's Prayer
My precious love, my joy, my soul's delight,
We met by God's design. Our ballad sang
In perfect harmony. Now Black Bear's gang
Corrupts the nation with its evil might;
And all my days are lived in constant fright
For you, around whom awesome dangers sprang.
As vicious men and governments harangue
Your service has been called to set things right.

My fondest dreams and fervent prayers entreat
That you should share the world's intrigues no more.
You risk your life to serve the earth's elite.
Be with us, God. Embrace us I implore.
In Your exalted Eden, pure, complete, - - -

Once again allowing the words to flow over him, he bathed in the warmth of Laura's caring message. His mind lingered on each thought, relishing its beauty, love and intricacy. The hope in Laura's poem touched his heart. He would have to get through this one last crisis and maybe then they could be together more, just as Laura prayed. He certainly shared Laura's desire for that future. He had always wondered what God's plan was for them. Maybe Laura had captured His promise in her poem, except why was the last line missing? Why couldn't Laura finish the sonnet? Maybe God hadn't revealed all to either of them yet. He wondered when that revelation would happen.

Clad in his running gear, he left the hotel for a brief jog in the Park. How did the FBI cover him on these runs without ever being seen?

TWENTY-TWO

Day 22 6:30 P.M. Washington Metro

Once again Ben rode the metro to the Farragut North station. Rather than follow his normal path to the NEI offices, he hesitantly turned south down 17th toward the White House. Upon reaching Pennsylvania Avenue, he noticed that to the east Pennsylvania was bereft of any automobile traffic. An army of three-foot-high concrete stumps ringed that section of the avenue, guarding the White House, he presumed, from the potential of terrorist car bombs. Sentries in automobiles stationed at the intersections guarded against any unauthorized vehicle's attempt to penetrate this once heavily traveled section of the avenue.

He noticed a ragtag bunch of young men playing street hockey. With in-line roller blades strapped to their feet, pads on their knees and ice hockey sticks brandished, they raced up and down the blocked off portion of Pennsylvania Avenue. Despite the cold, they were apparently competing in a contest similar to ice hockey. A couple of the concrete stumps served as goals. The scene made him smile. Not everyone in this town was a hot shot politician or a bureaucrat. That realization gave him comfort.

Looking at his watch, he saw that he had time to go south on 17th where the imposing Old Executive Office Building stood. After passing the historic structure, he turned east on State Place. Circling the most photographed portion of the White House grounds, he arrived at the east appointment gate. Some grand old magnolias, which he guessed must be nearly two hundred years old, graced the lawn. Sometime he would take a picture of them for Laura.

Unable to procrastinate any longer, Ben walked into the guard shack.

He shivered partially from the biting chill of the February evening, but probably more from nervous anticipation. This was his first visit to the White House and his first meeting with the vice president's team.

He handed his driver's license to the guard, who sternly asked, "Who are you here to see?"

"Vice President Foster."

"Hmmm, Foster. What's your hometown?"

"Tulsa, Oklahoma."

The guard appeared dubious, "Let me see a credit card with a picture."

Ben fumbled nervously. Finally, he located the requested card and handed it over.

Somewhat reluctantly, it seemed to Ben, the guard passed him on to the next guard. Under the close scrutiny of the second officer, his right palm was analyzed by the security computer. The guard checked a list and fortunately Ben's name appeared as an approved vice presidential visitor, so he was allowed to continue.

After a brief walk across the grounds, he and his escort headed down the hall in the west wing past further security desks. After passing the Oval Office he arrived at the vice president's office. He marveled at the unbelievable circumstances. Here he was, citizen Ben, dropping in on his old friend, the vice president.

Don North, situated in the office outside of Foster's, greeted Ben warmly upon his arrival. "Dr. Ben Andrew, we have been expecting you. Damn, it is good to see someone from outside the Beltway. If you need anything at all, just let me know. Otherwise you are welcome to go on in. Vice President Foster is expecting you."

"Thanks."

Ben took a deep breath and walked in. He spotted Foster bending over charts scattered across his table. He saw that Foster's old Navy mugs were serving as weights to keep the charts from rolling up.

"You are working too hard, Mr. Vice President," he chided tongue-in-cheek as he entered the room. His boldness surprised him, yet, he had always kidded Mark that he was too intense and worked too hard, so he had just naturally resumed the same banter he had always employed.

Foster, with his coat and tie discarded and sleeves rolled up, stood with his arms braced on the desktop. He looked up. "Hey there, Ben, glad you are here. We have been in need of your experience around here for a couple of days. How are you doing over at NEI?"

"The committee is falling into place. But I am more than ready to get after this uranium mystery." He wasn't kidding. He had thought constantly about how the uranium smuggling might relate to Black Bear and the Munich enrichment plant. The mystery bugged him and would until it was solved.

Foster invited, "Let's take a moment before the rest of the team arrives, I want to brief you on who the key players are.

"Don North, whom you just met, is my right-hand man. He is White House Chief-of-Staff. Fortunately, the President assigned him to me for the duration of this project."

"Yes, I just met him. He certainly made me feel welcome."

"He is the one that caught the significance of Laura's phone message. Despite his rough language, he is sharp and the kind of no-nonsense winner we need.

"General Adair is chairman of the Joint Chiefs of Staff. He is a four-star general who has commanded our policing forces in Korea and served as commander of an armored division in the Gulf War. He is brilliant, articulate and politically astute, a real asset.

"James Stockton is Director of Central Intelligence. James is a portly, vociferous, fifty-two-year-old former Senate chairman of the Armed Services Committee. As Director of Central Intelligence, he is perhaps the best appointment George W. ever made. His selection, not surprisingly, was ratified by the Senate in record time. He is a flamboyant red-haired fellow of Scottish extraction. He prefers to be called James. Doesn't like being referred to as director. He knows something about everything. James will be, I predict, one of the best Central Intelligence directors ever. I do have to reign in his unbridled enthusiasm occasionally. His speaking ability is almost hypnotic. Like everybody else in this town, he owns an over-sized ego."

"Does that include vice presidents?"

Foster laughed, "Certainly. Brad Garrison, FBI agent. This lanky thirty-eight-year-old is a bright, hard-working FBI agent. He has earned my respect and trust through his excellent performance. Garrison has another advantage. Before this task he served as chief of the Criminal Investigations branch, which has responsibility for tracking the ethnic Mobs. He is the one team member with whom you will work most closely.

"Elizabeth Neiman is the CIA's Russian and CIS analyst. She is a walking encyclopedia on the former Soviet states and is extremely insightful and articulate. In her intelligence and confidence she reminds me of your Laura. I double-checked Liz's 'take' on the

Russians against the renowned professor and consultant, Dudaev. It turns out that she was right on target."

Ben was stunned. That was the very man whom Laura suspected wrote her mother. He wasn't about to bring that up now. "Dudaev? He was the one who gave you an A minus in Russian History, right?"

"Shit! Does everyone remember that? How come you all recall my failings?"

"An A minus was only failing to you. That is what makes it so memorable."

Both men smiled as long-dormant memories flooded back. Each felt comfortable with the other. They knew how to dig without offending.

"Well, back to Liz. I instructed her to consult with Dudaev whenever she believes she should. She has already had two conferences with him. She listens to each dialogue that I have with Kruschev and that President Arthur has with Strahkov. She assists us in analyzing where the Russian leaders are coming from. Her help is vital since we can't afford to misread those two."

It was apparent to Ben that this talented bunch had Foster's complete trust and confidence. It was equally apparent that much was expected. He questioned more than ever whether he fit into this group. If he got a chance, however, he would quiz Liz about Dudaev. Maybe this was his opportunity to help Laura.

"It sounds like a brilliant collection of talents. Are you sure I belong?"

The vice president replied, "Don't worry, and don't turn bashful on me. That is not like you. You are needed. Listen to each of their reports. You will see rather quickly, I believe, where you fit into this investigation. Jump in whenever you can contribute. The team has begun putting together some very intriguing bits about the movement of this smuggled nuclear material."

Foster did not reveal to Ben that the President had questioned a civilian's presence at this meeting. Only Ben's former Navy clearance, a current expedited background check, and his friendship with Foster allayed Arthur's concerns. This meeting was to be a trial run for Ben's future involvement with the team. If Foster's team agreed that Ben's contribution was vital, then President Arthur would accept his involvement; otherwise Ben would be shunted aside. Foster though, had little doubt that Ben would pass the team's scrutiny.

"I couldn't bear to wait any longer to hear the reports on the uranium," Ben admitted.

"You will get an earful!"

"Before I forget it. Here are three books on the Mafia which Laura recommends."

"Thanks. All I need is more reading assignments, but I trust Laura. If she says they are worthwhile then Liz, Brad, James and I will read them."

North interrupted the two men, "It's 7:35. The team is here and they are chomping at the bit, Mr. Vice President."

He had deliberately stalled them, giving Foster and Ben a chance for their brief chat. North appreciated what Ben was up against and wished to give him every break.

Foster introduced each member to Ben making sure that the group was reminded of Ben's experience in the nuclear submarine service, his work at nuclear power plants, his knowledge of NuEnergy takeovers, as well as his recent adventure at the Munich facility. Ben squirmed uneasily, for he sensed that the vice president was selling him.

Each member gave him a polite but somewhat reserved welcome, obviously skeptical of his value to the team. Ben didn't blame them. At this moment, he wasn't so sure he should be here either.

"First let's review what we found out about Ben's favorite, the Munich Enrichment Plant. Oh yes, I should have told you all that Ben met the notorious Andropov at a NuEnergy Board meeting shortly after their takeover at Black Bear. An immediate hostility developed between the two."

"What were your impressions of the man?" Stockton seized upon this early opportunity to learn more about the Mafia chieftain, and to size up Ben.

"He is sinister, but brilliant. There is a vicious side to his personality that he can't hide. I think he wouldn't hesitate to remove anyone standing in his way. In fact, I suspect that may have happened to some of my comrades in the nuclear utilities. But I am the new one here, I should be listening."

"Thanks, Ben, for that brief insight. Liz and Brad will want to hear everything you can tell them about our Mafioso nemesis. After this meeting they will get together with you to glean all you know about Andropov.

"Getting back to the Munich business, here is what happened with the raw sound data that you brought back from Munich. A sound analysis expert and a centrifuge expert from the U.S. National Laboratories in Oak Ridge have analyzed the tape you brought back,

Ben. They found a few surprises. They estimate, based on the sound and your verbal labeling, that only a fourth of the centrifuges were actually operating in that suspect section. They also deduced that these centrifuges are no faster, nor more advanced in design, than the other centrifuges at Munich. In fact, they appear to be identical."

"Whoa!" Ben enthused. "That confirms some of my suspicions. They can't possibly be producing the amount of enrichment that they claim. There must be another source. Were you able to get the power usage history of that plant?"

"Yes, we have that for you."

Foster was very pleased to see Ben eagerly jumping into the fray. His friend indeed hadn't changed from the Ben he knew.

"You are looking at your first assignment. Take all of this new information and figure out exactly what that plant is doing.

"But hold on. There is more. Stockton's people have brand new pictures of a most interesting voyage of a Kazak Border Guard boat on the Caspian. Upon a heads-up from Kruschev, we sent our Aurora over the area. It fed us a wealth of intelligence."

Ben whistled in amazement. "Fascinating! So the Aurora's real, despite all of the official denials."

Stockton, with mock sternness, sent a reminder to Ben and the vice president that Ben wasn't yet an accepted part of the team. "Since you don't have Top Secret military clearance, Ben, I guess we will have to shoot you."

Everyone, including Ben, laughed at that crack. "I really hope you are just kidding, Director," Ben nervously probed. A little reassurance would help.

"Oh, sure I am," Stockton playfully replied, leaving Ben hanging.

Foster resumed, "As I said, Vasilly Kruschev tipped us off about this boat and its cargo. His FSB agents have uncovered a most suspicious exchange of nuclear materials. Go ahead, James. Give us the latest."

James eagerly assumed center stage. Powering up his portable DVD he began the show. "This first set of photos is along the Caspian Sea coast, south of Atyrau, where we see this docked Kazakh Border Guard boat. As I increase the magnification, you will be able to see a convoy of Afghan-war vintage trucks bearing Kazakhstan Border Guard markings parked along the dock. According to Kruschev's agents, the trucks brought the cargo of natural uranium from a train at Kandagach.

"This next set was taken a little over a day later. They show our same border guard patrol boat, but now it's moored at a remote

Caspian seashore location on the southern tip of Kazakhstan. Notice that just ahead of the Kazakhstan Border Guard craft lies an Iranian-flagged frigate. General, does that flag look familiar?"

"Affirmative. That is General Bakr Zarif's obscene flag. We, in this country, have wasted our time obsessing over Saddam and Bin Laden when our truly dangerous enemy in the Persian Gulf region is Iran's General Zarif, the cowardly torturer of unarmed civilians."

"You are absolutely right, General. The cargo being loaded onto the Iranian boat may be familiar to you as well. Let's look at the enhancements."

Ben caught that Zarif's personal flag looked exactly like an upside down U.S. flag, but wisely stifled any more comments or questions. His unwise comment on the top-secret Aurora had gotten him into enough trouble for the night.

After studying the pictures for a moment, General Adair responded with confidence and authority, "Quite familiar, indeed. Those are five Soviet tactical nuclear warheads! Kiev-class. Plutonium for compactness. We dismantled hundreds of those in cooperation with the Russians. They are a warhead designed for short to intermediate range, surface-to-surface missiles. Each warhead packs a punch of about twenty-thousand kilotons."

"Exactly right," James confirmed.

After showing those warheads being loaded aboard the Iranian boat, Stockton added, "General, I'll leave copies of this next set of the site area with you for your assessment of their defenses."

"When you complete that analysis, we may send copies to Kruschev. Ultimately that facility will be Russia's problem," Foster directed.

As Ben observed the efficient interactions among the team members, he adjudged them to be extremely capable and deadly serious individuals who worked well together. He could not help being impressed by Stockton's enthusiasm, especially when it was his turn to show-and-tell. He had an infectious fervor for his job.

"There is more," Stockton added. "Some containers, apparently stainless steel vessels about the size of 5 gallon milk cans were brought out of storage and loaded into the frigate."

"That looks like something I saw a few years ago in the Navy," Ben volunteered. "Those sure look like highly enriched uranium canisters."

"That's what we thought," Stockton confirmed. He saw a chance to test Ben by asking a question for which he already knew the answer. "How much bomb-grade uranium would you say might be in all of those containers?"

"Just based on what little I recall from past criticality calcs, I would say at least fifteen metric tons."

"My God," gasped Adair. "That's enough to blow up a small country. This must be some of Strahkov's missing one hundred metric tons."

Surprised, yet impressed with Ben's accurate answer, Stockton forged ahead, "Where do you all guess the next stop is for our border guard boat and the Iranian frigate?"

"Move on, James," the vice president warned, "or I'll let the team ring your neck."

"Yes, sir. Here we see the two ships at Rashte, Iran. This time they are unloading their nuclear cargo. These pictures give us a good view of this evolution."

As Stockton flashed a series of a dozen overhead photos onto the wall screen, he described the activities. "There go the five warheads and there's the bomb-grade uranium. But there's more. Uranium hexafluoride cylinders from the Kazakh boat. Have you seen those before, Ben?"

"Obviously not exactly those, but they look identical to the natural uranium cylinders that are shipped to any enrichment plant," Ben answered, not entirely sure where Stockton was driving. Ben was becoming annoyed with the continued testing. Did they think only those who lived in this town knew anything?

"Okay. Now for our very best resolution as we hone in on the label on one of those cylinders." Stockton flashed a photo of the cylinder's label.

Ben gasped, "That's an IAEA inspection label indicating it's natural uranium originating in Kazakhstan and heading for Munich. The label certifies that it left the Kazakh uranium mill ten days ago."

"It's going to Munich in a roundabout way, wouldn't you say?" James Stockton noted rather triumphantly, basking in the limelight of the moment. "Mr. Vice President, it appears that Kruschev gave us straight scoop on the Kazakh uranium switch."

"Finish your presentation, James," Vice President Foster ordered more emphatically this time. His patience with the testing of Ben was also nearing an end.

Stockton got the message, no more side trips and anyway, he had made up his mind that Ben would prove useful. "All of this nuclear cargo was loaded onto a fleet of specialized military trucks and taken inland about eighty miles to Iran's major nuclear weapons complex near Karaj. You see, the satellite photos even picked up the trucks and Zarif's personal limousine being driven through the entrance into their vast underground factory. Our radar satellites show that it's deeply buried and fortified.

"Here are the photos of the surroundings. Two SAM batteries and a multitude of armed guards surround the complex. The perimeter is fenced and mined. Also an armored division is encamped only a few miles north." Stockton illustrated the Karaj complex's extensive defenses through a series of photos, each of which revealed key defensive installations. His high-resolution shots allowed the team to see the area as if they were right there.

"How is our informant coming along, James?" Foster inquired. "We must find out what is going on inside."

"Mr. Vice President, as soon as our man gets his money, he will talk to us. It's one of the Russian scientists that immigrated to Iran years ago with the encouragement of Andropov. He became dissatisfied with his treatment at the hands of the Iranians. Last time he was in Tehran, he made overtures to us through the Canadian Embassy."

Foster commanded emphatically, "Damn it! Get him his money yesterday! I want his inside scoop!"

"Yes, sir. Will do, Mr. Vice President.

"Also we parked two of NSA's stealth geo-stationary satellites over there, and trained their cameras on the Karaj complex. We will scrutinize anything or anyone going in or out."

"James, leave a disk of this last set of photos for Adair's use."

"I brought an extra. I knew he would need it."

"Thank you, James. Garrison, you are up."

Garrison knew that was one hell of a tough act to follow. Yet, he focused on his report, giving it matter-of-factly.

"Bureau researchers have dug back through the immigration records of former Soviet citizens entering the U.S. in the nineties. Kruschev has been extremely helpful in identifying those migrants, who had criminal records or Mafia connections. There are literally several thousand ex-Soviets in the U.S. with extensive criminal pasts. We tracked the whereabouts of most of them. Many have gravitated to the larger East and West Coast cities and wound up in the North American Division of the Russian Mafia. They report to either Brent Lepke or Ray Goldstein, who themselves came here in 1995. Goldstein directs the white-collar criminal elements of the Russian Mob, and Lepke directs the thugs' activities. Lepke and Goldstein take their orders directly from Andropov. You all, and especially Ben, already know about him."

"Comrade Andropov is one busy bloke. He controls everything," Stockton enunciated what everyone else was thinking.

Ben gulped. So it was definitely the Mafia he was up against, just like Laura had said. Now, however, it was official.

"It is extremely important to find out more about Lepke and Goldstein," Foster snapped. "Put a twenty-four hour tail on them. Go to court for approval of wiretaps. Requisition records of any of their past cell-phone calls and any other records, including Internet usage, that you can lay your hands on. Spare no effort."

"Yes, sir. But there is more. Based on Ben's suspicions, which you passed on to me earlier, we investigated NuEnergy further and discovered an unsettling development. NuEnergy has employed about a hundred technicians and engineers that have close connections to the Russian Mob. They have spread around at least a couple of these mobsters to each NuEnergy plant. Apparently the background checks administered in those plants don't go back past the date the individual immigrated."

"How convenient," observed Foster.

"Isn't it? Apparently, NuEnergy has deliberately placed these skilled mobsters in key technical positions at each plant."

"Is one of them Helmut Nagy? He is a Bulgarian who was shoved down our throats by NuEnergy when they took over at Black Bear," Ben queried.

Searching through his files, Garrison looked at Ben with surprise and then nodded affirmatively, "Yes! How did you know that, Ben?"

"A suspicious streak runs through me." After a pause Ben explained, "Actually a highway patrolman friend checked into the guy's background for me."

Foster worriedly asked, "Any idea of their purpose? Why are Mafia thugs infiltrating the plants' operating organizations?"

"We have only conjecture at this point, Mr. Vice President."

Rapidly shedding any remaining insecurities, Ben spoke up again. "Brad, I would like to see all the records of these people and when they moved into each plant's organization. Together we might be able to figure out their purpose."

Remembering what Ben had told him in their earlier meeting about his suspicions of convenient sabotage enabling NuEnergy takeovers, Foster suspected their investigation might confirm Ben's ideas. Having read the team as accepting Ben, Foster instructed, "You work with Garrison on that, Ben. That is your second assignment. Figure out the reason for this infiltration and how threatening it is to the plants. But if you find out it's a sidetrack to our primary efforts, then drop it."

"May I have some NRC folk to help us?" Ben asked. "They have valuable databases on events and activities at these plants. Through them we can obtain the plants' operational histories without alerting any of NuEnergy's corrupt management."

Foster cautioned, "Yes, if the FBI clears the NRC officials you need."

"So far we believe the NRC is relatively untouched by any Mob influence," volunteered Garrison. "We will certainly check out whoever Ben wants to use."

"Then go ahead, you two. Use the NRC and the FBI. Ben, you and Garrison will obviously be working closely together on your assignments. Garrison will arrange an office for you at FBI headquarters. It's a little less obvious than walking in here everyday."

Foster then handed out specific assignments. "Liz, I want you to use CIA resources to develop a complete psychological profile of this Andropov character. Also avail yourself of Ben, Dudaev and anything further that Kruschev will share with us. Can you get that done in the next few days?"

"Yes, sir."

"James, I want a history lesson on Iran, including political, cultural and economic aspects from one of your analysts. Iran is obviously a big player in all of this. I want to understand them inside out.

"Garrison, in addition to working with Ben, you continue investigating our troublesome Undersecretary Foley. That NuEnergy flunky is far too interested in what we're doing in here, plus according to what Ben tells me, he is in the middle of fouling up the Russian-U.S. uranium deal." Mark's mind seemed to be racing in a thousand directions at once. The depth and breadth of what the team was facing was nearly overwhelming.

"General, what long-lead actions are necessary to be ready for any eventuality?"

"I think you, President Arthur, Secretary of Defense Winston and I should meet. Some relocation of our carrier battle groups, submarines and air wings would be prudent."

"We will have that meeting tomorrow," Foster assured the general. The politically astute Adair prompted, "Shouldn't we also research the War Powers Act and evaluate how and when to involve Congress? If this gets any hotter, that will become an issue. Involving that bunch of big mouths, while still maintaining secrecy, is nearly an impossibility."

Foster understood the military's frustration with Congress. He had often felt that way himself. He had been on both sides, the civilian control side and the military mission side. "You are right about that, but cut Congress some slack. They have a different role to play than we do. I will talk over with the President how best to involve them."

Foster abruptly called an end to the meeting. "Each of you has much to do. Get on it at flank speed." He laughed at his own choice of phrases and winked at Ben. "That's an old Navy term, eh Ben. It means move your butts."

The vice president asked Ben and Garrison to remain for a minute.

General Adair, quite impressed with Ben's display of knowledge and his hanging tough while obviously under the gun, made a special effort on his way out of saying, "I am glad you are with us. Your expertise is valuable. Let me know if you need anything."

Ben was relieved and yet awed with that obvious vote of approval. This was the Chairman of the Joint Chiefs of Staff telling him that he was accepted, "Thank you, General. I will do everything I can."

Somehow he would have to break the news to Laura that his involvement would last at least a couple more weeks.

James Stockton snapped his suspenders to announce that he was about to speak, "You are okay, Dr. Andrew. I second General Adair's observations. You are going to have your hands full though, working with this FBI firecracker. See if you can keep him from going off the deep end on us."

"Thank you, Director, but it's the other way around. I am depending on Agent Garrison to look after me."

After the two senior members of the team had confirmed that Ben was one of them, Liz Nieman asked, "When can I talk with you about Andropov?"

"Is tomorrow afternoon okay?"

"Fine. I'll call you then, Dr. Andrew."

"Just call me Ben, Liz."

Foster realized that Ben might be slightly overwhelmed with all of his assignments. As the new kid on the block, he might not want to admit it, so he asked, "Ben, can you keep up both the cover effort at NEI and support this at full strength?"

"Yes, although my NEI committee work won't get any A minuses from here on."

Foster laughed. Ben had always known how to keep him from winding up too tight. He turned to Garrison. "You show Ben the ropes and see that he gets anything he needs. Also keep a protective tail on him and Laura and continue to provide them secure phones."

Day 22 11:45 P.M. White House

Ben and Garrison took a corner of Foster's outer office to discuss logistics for tomorrow.

Garrison felt sympathy for Ben. Ben's uneasy sense of intrusion at tonight's meeting had been obvious. Yet the guy hadn't backed down. He had plenty of grit and he obviously had much to contribute. His background dictated that the two of them would be working together.

"Ben, when you come over to FBI Headquarters, just go to the reception desk and ask for me."

"I have some ideas about who in the NRC could help us the most. Here is a list I just scribbled together. It's prioritized top to bottom. If you start background checks right away we could move ahead quicker. Also, here are the names of my nuclear counterparts who died shortly after NuEnergy takeovers at their plants. One of them, a Fred Bumgardner, was a close friend. I am very suspicious about his death. Could you get the police reports on him?"

"Will do," Garrison promised, shaking his head as he took Ben's lists. This guy was wasting no time.

CHAPTER
TWENTY-THREE

Day 24 7:25 P.M. Hartford, Connecticut

The spry, albeit aging, Professor Dudaev, wearing a threadbare blue sweater, greeted Director Stockton at the door of his unpretentious white frame split-level home. He anticipated this to be his most significant meeting since his encounter in Germany with Solzhenitsyn thirty-five years ago.

"Come in, Director. Thanks for visiting on such short notice."

Stockton was curious and more than a little impatient with Dudaev. The nuclear smuggling crisis was demanding most of his time, yet Dudaev insisted upon a meeting at his home. Why? What could be so important?

Stockton replied with a forced politeness to Dudaev's greeting, "Curiosity alone dictates my trip. Your call has me mystified."

"I wish I could have been more forthcoming, but it wasn't wise to converse on this subject over the phone. What I have to say must be face to face. Did you review the CIA file?"

"Yes. Like I said, it served to tease."

Professor Dudaev, after a few failed attempts, lit a beaten-up pipe and motioned for Stockton to have a seat across from him at a table near the center of his expansive library.

Stockton had briefly surveyed the room and gathered that it contained the volume of some public libraries.

"I never saw such an elaborate private library. And, not surprisingly, I see that you have specialized in Russian materials."

"Yes and this collection is only the tip of the iceberg."

"What do you mean?"

"You will see at an appropriate time," replied Dudaev. "Suffice it to say I hold a tremendous wealth of private and public papers."

Stockton shook his head in amazement and frustration. Time was short, yet he loved who-done-its. That's why he was here, but this was too much. Was this old guy for real or had he gone a little daffy in his senior years? Stockton accepted this invitation from the professor with no idea that a letter from Laura Andrew to Dudaev was the catalyst forcing this meeting.

Also international events were reaching an opportune juncture, which Dudaev had long awaited. One development was that there was a CIA Director whom he trusted.

Slipping comfortably into his professorial role, Dudaev directed the conversation with a question. "So Director, tell me what you gleaned from the old CIA file."

"Not too much. It's a top-secret file classified 'For Director's Eyes Only.' It tells about the escape of Marina Tarasova and her baby from the Soviets. At the time it was judged so sensitive a rescue that the CIA director agreed to know only that you arranged the rescue and that you alone would create Marina's new identity. It doesn't tell why such an unusual arrangement was struck between you and our CIA. Can you explain that deal?"

"It's a long story starting nearly forty years ago. My closest Soviet comrades and former associates of Viktor Sumurov were fairly sure that Marina Tarasova was his daughter."

"So? That doesn't explain the screwy arrangement," prodded an impatient Stockton.

Unconcerned with Stockton's impatience, Dudaev continued at his methodical pace. "At the time, I alerted the CIA director that the Communists and the Chekists were on the verge of discovering who Marina was and would undoubtedly kill her when they confirmed her identity."

"They wouldn't have killed their champion equestrian, would they?"

"Oh, yes. Most certainly. It would have been an arranged accident that could never be hung on them."

Stockton was as puzzled as ever, "So why did you and the director make such an unusual deal?"

"The Soviets had spies in your organization but not in mine. We could better protect Marina than could the CIA."

Stockton caught the implication of a Dudaev organization. The CIA knew about Dudaev's involvement decades ago in supporting the dissident movement. But "my?" Was it his organization? And he talked about it in the present tense. Was it still active?

"Holy shit," Stockton thought. Puzzled and with fascination winning out over impatience, he listened intently as the Professor continued.

"The safety of Marina and her baby depended on us hiding them, yet I needed the help of the CIA and a British commando unit to pull off the escape. I think the old director agreed to the whole deal just to stick it to the Soviets."

"What was your motivation?"

"All dissidents owe a debt to Viktor Sumurov, one which can never be repaid. Saving his daughter and granddaughter was the least we could do."

"I didn't realize Sumurov was that important to the Soviet dissidents."

Out of neglect, Dudaev's pipe had gone out. He leaned forward and tapped the ashes into a tray. Finally after several attempts, he succeeded in relighting the worn artifact.

After the maddening hiatus the old man spoke, "He is more important than even the dissidents of that time knew.

"Relax, Director. Help yourself to some coffee and I will tell you what no one else in this world knows."

Stockton, though still not fully convinced that all of this was worth his time, did as told. He tried to recall all he knew about Viktor Sumurov. Stockton was spared having to recall Sumurov's story for Dudaev recounted the man's legacy.

"The poet Sumurov is the forerunner and the inspiration for the Soviet dissident movement of the '60's, '70's, and '80's. His martyrdom, his writings, his unshakeable love of Russia and his faith in God laid a foundation for future dissent. Brave and talented men, such as Solzhenitsyn and Sakharov, followed in his footsteps."

Stockton recalled that the Soviets, frustrated with failed torture attempts to coerce silence or cooperation from Sumurov, had killed him.

Stockton asked, "Professor, tell me how his daughter managed to survive."

"When Sumurov first became a problem to the Soviets, they banished his pregnant mistress to Borz'a, a small Soviet outpost near Mongolia and China. She lived in poverty and obscurity there and she apparently died giving birth to Viktor's daughter. The Borz'a church came upon what we believe was her child and arranged for a well-placed family to adopt the baby girl. They are the ones who nurtured and trained her to become a champion rider. Around 1970 the crackdown on dissidents became more severe. My compatriots in Russia believed she was in mortal danger, hence Marina's escape was arranged."

"So you did all of this out of a sense of gratitude to the martyred Sumurov?"

"Yes, but there was a bonus," added Dudaev.

"Why doesn't that surprise me?"

"Along with Sumurov's daughter, Marina, we smuggled out a full set of Sumurov's secret writings. These papers have never been seen by anyone but me, Solzhenitsyn and the one Soviet dissident cell that kept them safe until 1970."

"What's their importance?" Stockton queried.

Tamping his once again unlit pipe on the ashtray, Dudaev warned, "Here it gets complicated. Are you up to a brief lesson on the Soviet dissident movement?"

"Yep," Stockton said, while thinking that was a little condescending, but since this guy was a professor he cut him a little slack in the authoritative department.

"Have you read Solzhenitsyn's and Sakharov's writings?"

"Yes. So?"

"So, then you know that the two giants agreed about many things but departed company on some crucial matters, especially about how to build an acceptable successor government to the Communist Soviet Union."

"Yes, go on," encouraged Stockton.

"Solzhenitsyn's philosophy on moral passive resistance leading to transformation of the corrupt Soviet State is summarized in this book by Ronald Entz. Turn to page 75 and read aloud."

He read the pages thrust at him by Dudaev.

First, Solzhenitsyn's "From Under the Rubble" appeared. In it Solzhenitsyn "envisioned this rebirth: by traveling a path of repentance, self-limitation, and inner development."

In reading further, Stockton learned that Solzhenitsyn believed in a moral renaissance in which individual Russians, by liberating their own souls from the government's lies, would lead a transformation of Russia without shots being fired or blood being shed. Passive resistance by mere tens or hundreds of thousands, not even millions, was his panacea.

Solzhenitzyn's simple, but forceful, stance of moral, passive resistance was described effectively through humor by the dissident. In jest, he told of an incident involving a drunken worker. The inebriated man, who was in a crowd waiting for a bus in Moscow, turned to the others and said, "Solzhenitsyn tells us only not to applaud."

The courage and brilliance of Solzhenitsyn and Sakharov, demonstrated by their resistance of the Soviet system, came flooding back to Stockton as he read aloud the accounts of the famous dissidents' public statements.

The Professor took the book back from a confused Stockton, who felt, very much, like the student he had become.

"How does all of this pertain to Sumurov?"

"Stick with me a moment and you will see."

Dudaev explained, "Sakharov and Solzhenitsyn basically agreed that the Communist Soviet Union was corrupt, built on a lie, and wrongly denied basic human rights and liberties. Yet they totally disagreed about how to change it and what form the change would take. As you just read, Solzhenitsyn believed in a moral renaissance rooted in the best of Russian traditions. He discounted and yes, even distrusted, the West to play a constructive role in the process.

"On the other hand, Sakharov, the Soviet Physicist, believed that the West and technology could help in the reform process. Neither was clear upon the mechanics of the reformation or the end product, only per Solzhenitsyn, that the government be moral and honor Russian traditions and per Sakharov, that it be accepting of a diversity of beliefs, ideas, and faiths."

"Why this divergence on how to achieve reformation."

"Their backgrounds were different and they didn't have the benefit of Sumurov's works on the subject."

"What works? Nothing in his writings that I have ever seen covers these subjects."

Dudaev paused and puffed on his pipe to add emphasis to his next words.

"Believe me, there are such works. I have them. They came out of the Soviet Union with Marina Tarasova's escape. That was the only way we could save them. You will see his papers later tonight."

"Oh." For once, words failed Stockton.

"Sumurov, unlike Solzhenitsyn and Sakharov, laid out a comprehensive plan for the transformation of the Russian government after the predicted fall of Communism. It departed so extensively from Solzhenitsyn's thoughts that once Solzhenitsyn was banished from the Soviet Union, I traveled to Germany to discuss the Sumurov writings with him. After days of dialogue and a thorough examination of Sumurov's concepts, he finally agreed with me that Sumurov's ideas might work. Sumurov's concepts were philosophically somewhere between the two well-known dissidents. He put emphasis upon Russia solving its own problems, but anticipated that help from a trustworthy Western power would be needed. He advocated a Russian move toward democracy aided by a Western country just as America's independence was aided by an outside power, namely France. He also identified the chief stumbling blocks."

"Which were?"

"Chekists entrenched in the security apparatus, and a future criminal element."

"Wow! That guy has one hell of a crystal ball. Do you think Russia would ever trust the West to as great an extent as Sumurov deemed necessary?"

"Only with the right leadership in place on both sides. That is a goal which consumes my organization."

Stockton was amazed. There was the "my" again and that was a bold statement. Could Dudaev and his mystery group actually influence things to that great an extent?

Dudaev continued, "If Russia doesn't get outside help, they will never be much better off than they are today."

Dudaev went on to tell of a letter he had received from Marina's daughter. "Marina died last year. I secretly corresponded with her over the years. After Marina's death her daughter found one of my letters and deduced it might be from me."

"Does she know about any of this?"

"No."

"Why not tell her everything? The Soviets are history. What's the problem?" challenged Stockton.

"It's not that simple. She would still be in danger."

"From whom?"

"Chekists! Mafia! Both have reason to fear an heir, who reminds Russian citizens of Viktor Sumurov. His ideals becoming popular again could threaten their strangle hold on Russia."

"What do you propose?"

"First, we should take advantage of technology to make sure that this young woman is Viktor's granddaughter."

"Are you referring to DNA?" asked Stockton.

"Yes. My organization can secure a sample of Viktor's remains. If you could get a sample from Marina's daughter, then run the tests and see if there is a match?"

"I could if I knew who she was."

"Here's her letter."

Stockton read and reread the letter. He was flabbergasted. It couldn't be.

Unable to cover up his shock, Stockton exclaimed, "My God! It's Ben's Laura!"

Dudaev was confused by that exclamation. "How do you know her husband?"

"He is on our team, working for the vice president!"

Dudaev hadn't been aware of that development, but promptly discerned that it might change everything. He had watched both Ben and Laura over the years and foresaw an important role for them. Ben's involvement with the vice president could change things.

Revealing none of these thoughts, Dudaev offered, "If it proves out that Laura is Viktor's heir, then I can tell her exactly who she is and warn her of the enduring danger, a danger that prevented her mother from informing her of her heritage."

Stockton agreed, "Let's see what the DNA tests tell us."

Stockton had a million questions but he saved them for another day. It was apparent that Dudaev was far more of a force than he would ever have guessed. He wondered what motivated this man. Was he inspired by Viktor Sumurov's life and treatises, or something more? Just how influential was "his" group?

For the next few hours he scanned Sumurov's clandestine works. Dudaev was right, they were potent expressions of what must be. He had no way of knowing that the most poignant of Sumurov's secret works was not in the stack he was given to read.

CHAPTER
TWENTY-FOUR

Day 25 1 P.M. FBI Building

The monstrosity of a building again loomed in front of Ben. The skewed tetrahedron-shaped FBI headquarters, which fronted onto Pennsylvania Avenue between 9th and 10th streets, consisted of an exterior of daunting concrete slabs. For the first time he noticed that the slabs were punctuated by an array of small regular perforations resembling bullet holes. How fitting, Ben chuckled upon spying the holes, "Perhaps the agents use this ugly creation for target practice."

With a forced nonchalance, he sauntered into the foyer.

As he waited for Garrison to appear, he eyed the traffic through the busy foyer. It wasn't difficult to imagine a sidearm tucked under the coat of each person he saw in here. This was one of the few places lately where he felt completely safe. That sense of security had become a rarity since his Black Bear brakes incident and the confrontation and chase in Munich.

Garrison promptly appeared and upon taking a close look at Ben, asked, "How is my civilian friend doing today?"

"Okay."

"You look preoccupied."

Ben laughed nervously, "I guess I am. You know, I found out a few more things about Bumgardner."

"Tell me about it."

While listening to Ben's brief account, Garrison led his partner to the second floor, where the super-secure Strategic Information Operations Center (SIOC) was situated. A large portion of the SIOC now served as their command center, where their team worked in maximum security.

186

As they walked, Ben relayed, "This morning I asked NEI's CEO about Bumgardner's committee. Apparently, the staffing was dictated to him by Parris, the NuEnergy president. He had thought it somewhat odd at the time to receive such strict orders, but since NEI served the nuclear industry, he simply accepted Parris' dictates. Now get this. Fred was rumored to have had an affair with one of his staffers, a beautiful attorney named Michelle Michote. Brad, I am almost certain that something isn't right about his death."

Garrison stopped in midstride, "Michelle Michote. That is interesting." Maybe his impression of that stuck-on-herself dame was accurate.

Trying not to betray any concern, Garrison dialed a combination of numbers on a special lock on the vault door. Redundant video cameras monitored their entrance. Palm prints were verified. Finally, after all of these precautions, there was an ordinary padlock. Garrison inserted his key and took the open lock with him. Once inside he snapped the padlock shut, securing the door. No one could follow them in without his permission.

This was Ben's third time in here, yet he and the other civilians on the team were still being escorted. He guessed that FBI security rules demanded such escorting in this super secret complex.

The cubicled area where their team worked was equipped with video equipment that projected maps, charts and satellite photo images. Every team member had an advanced computer terminal, which allowed prompt access to the many classified databases maintained by the FBI, as well as those of the Nuclear Regulatory Commission (NRC) and the Institute of Nuclear Power Operations (INPO).

Ben and Garrison had assembled an unlikely assortment of talent consisting of NRC personnel, FBI agents and U.S. lab experts. Ben had specifically recommended NRC Region III administrator, Hazel Meyer, who had a reputation within the nuclear utility industry as the most capable of the NRC administrators. After receiving FBI clearances, Meyer and two NRC specialists had joined the team. Breakthroughs came rapidly after they arrived. Comparing NRC and FBI information, the regulators and the agents had made some significant discoveries on NuEnergy's apparent modus operandi.

Once in the SIOC, Ben took charge, suggesting, "Brad, since we are meeting with the vice president tonight, time is precious. If it's okay with you, let's split up. I will go over the Munich plant business with the lab techs and you continue to look into the NuEnergy takeover method."

"That is just fine, Dad."

Ben had started the bantering by jokingly labeling Garrison a child prodigy. Since Ben had worked him over more than once about his "youth and inexperience," Garrison had retaliated by teasing Ben about his "advanced" age.

Ben laughed, "If I were your dad, I wouldn't have said, 'If it's okay with you,' now would I?"

"Civilians," harrumphed Garrison.

"Talk to you in a couple of hours. Let's see where we stand then. Again I must insist that one of your agents bring me all of the D.C. police records on Fred Bumgardner's death."

"Okay, okay."

Garrison was starting to believe that Ben might have something on the Bumgardner death. Ben's mentioning Michelle Michote reinforced the wisdom of investigating far more than Ben realized. Garrison would explain Michelle Michote to Ben later. They were too pressed for time right now.

Day 25 3:15 P.M. FBI Building Fourth Floor

"I tracked Garrison's SIOC computers through the main server. His team has accessed NRC historical data on thirty nuclear plants."

"Which ones?"

"Here's the list."

Karpenko scanned the paper and easily recognized that it comprised all of the NuEnergy plants.

"Very interesting. Good work! Continue monitoring that bunch and keep me informed. The director himself authorized this scrutiny."

With that encouragement, the computer supervisor left Karpenko's office with orders to continue tracking Garrison's team.

Karpenko's intelligence on the vice president continued to grow, when the agent on White House cleaning detail reported that the vice president's meeting attendees included a civilian by the name of Dr. Ben Andrew. Andrew's name was gleaned from the confidential White House visitor's list. He also reported that all of the vice president's information was either stored on his computer or in his locked office file.

Karpenko could not resist gloating. What a great day this was. His contact, the Michote dame, would certainly be pleased with his work. The organization should be pleased enough to give him a big bonus. Maybe he could retire soon. Karpenko thrilled at the prospect.

Day 25 3.20 P.M. Strategic Information Operations Center (SIOC)

"Something about this police report on Bumgardner bothers me."

Ben couldn't put his finger on just what it was, so he read the report again. Bouncing each thought off the nearby Agent, he read, "Fred's body was found in the park still clutching his gun in his right hand. How's that sound to you? How did he get to the park?"

"The report doesn't say."

"Why not? Shouldn't the police have tried to find out?"

The agent just shrugged, for in reality the police should have tried to develop that fact.

"Would a man who killed himself still hold the gun, or would it drop?"

"It's possible that he would still grip it in death."

"Why didn't they find any traces of powder burns on his hand."

"That's strange all right, but it happens sometimes. Sloppy forensics at the crime scene often accounts for that."

"But why would the coroner still be so sure it was suicide? Wasn't there any suspicion of foul play?"

"I guess there might have been, but the preponderance of evidence supported the suicide theory. The weapon, the 357 magnum, was registered to Bumgardner and his fingerprints were all over it. Several people reported that he was despondent, which provides motive."

"I see it differently. I think someone wanted him permanently out of the Texas plants and set him up. Probably our Mafia buddies."

The frustrated agent just shrugged again while thinking, we have better things to do than chase this closed case. This guy is taking the spy business too seriously.

Ben based his assumption that it was the Mafia upon what he and Laura had heard from Fred's wife about his NuEnergy experience. He knew how out of character Fred's suicide was and how it had devastated his wife.

"That will be tough to prove. There is nothing pointing that way except your hunch," advised the agent.

Not dissuaded in the least, Ben doggedly hung on, "Of course it will be tough. They aren't amateurs. We must dig deep. Could we check cab records to see if one of the cabbies took Fred to the Island."

"We will do all of that, Ben, but the trail is cold," replied the exasperated agent.

"Wait a minute!" Finally, it hit Ben. That is what was wrong with the police report.

"The gun was in Fred's right hand. Fred's a lefty. I sat beside him in a conference where our writing arms were always bumping. He's a lefty all the way, so why is the gun in his right hand?"

For the first time the agent gave some credence to Ben's doubts.

"Well, if someone made this look like a suicide, you would certainly have your explanation for the missing powder residue and the wrong hand. Let me see if we can't reopen the investigation."

Ben was excited. He felt a small measure of satisfaction from the fact that maybe, just maybe, he could redeem his friend's reputation. He hoped Fred's wife would finally stop berating herself as if she were at fault for his suicide.

Day 25 3:45 P.M. SIOC

Ben updated Garrison on his team's findings on the Munich Enrichment plant. "Here's the deal. The third unit doesn't enrich uranium. The enrichment was accomplished years ago in a land far away."

"Listen, Dr. Seuss, if you cast this story in terms of *Green Eggs and Ham*, then we will have our first dead civilian ever in here."

"Just trying to relate to my under-aged audience, I am," Ben contended.

Garrison just shook his head and mumbled, trying very hard to avoid a broad grin. "Whatever. Go ahead."

"From our calcs, we conclude that they must be smuggling enrichment into Munich, probably as blended uranium. It's almost certainly hidden in the center of each Kazakh cylinder. Remember that the cylinders were diverted to Karaj, Iran, and others from Karaj replaced them? We believe that the Iranians reconfigure each cylinder by inserting blended uranium in the center. The perimeter of natural uranium is cover, hiding the valuable blended uranium. Billions of dollars worth of smuggled ex-Soviet enrichment is being clandestinely sold to the U.S. utilities under this ruse."

Garrison was impressed with Ben's development of such a complete analysis but he intended to test his friend thoroughly. He couldn't let him walk into tonight's meeting without every loose end being tied up.

"So, Ben, how does this blended uranium tie into the smuggled Kazakh bomb-grade uranium?"

"The smuggled stuff is undoubtedly converted to blended uranium at Karaj."

"But why can't the IAEA detect that it's not all natural uranium? They inspect at Munich, don't they?"

"That had me puzzled too for quite a while. The reason turns out to be fairly simple. The natural uranium surrounding the blended uranium shields it from detection."

"Okay, Ben, if you are so cock sure of that, why did they bother to build the third section at Munich?"

"It's a facade, a cover for what is really going on."

"Ah ha. Now I have one you can't answer. Don't they defeat their own purposes economically by having those costly centrifuges just sitting there idle in that third section?"

"Good try, Brad, but there's an answer for that, too. Recall that the audio analysis revealed only a fourth of the centrifuges were actually running when I was in there. Well, the others are undoubtedly fake. They have just enough real ones to fool anyone who might get in."

"Okay, Ben, but what happens in the plant once the cylinders are dumped into the header."

"Mixing happens. Lots of mixing. The Kazakh cylinders' contents of blended uranium and natural uranium mix at the unloading stage. Therefore, presto, once mixed it is commercial-grade uranium and is pumped right past the phony third unit."

Continuing his grilling of Ben, Garrison challenged, "But if that unit is normally idle, why don't the IAEA inspectors discover that fact?"

"Remember what I went through to get in there. NuEnergy pretends that it has uniquely efficient centrifuges. That trumped-up commercial sensitivity is the excuse they use to keep out even the IAEA folk. If on the rare occasion that someone does gain entry they start it up, just like they did for me. And only if you are very suspicious can you notice that anything is wrong. If I hadn't recorded the sound, we would never have figured out what was really going on in there."

"Okay, Ben. I'm beginning to believe you. How sure are you of all of this?"

"Very sure! Ninety-five percent. There is just no other way they can be coming up with that amount of enrichment."

"How could we be absolutely certain?" Garrison asked.

Ben responded, "Only one way. Inspect one of the incoming Kazakh cylinders."

"That's easier said than done."

"I have thought about how to do it. We would need to intercept a shipment before it arrived at Munich. Remember Stockton's briefing? He mentioned that a Kazakh uranium shipment is en route. His CIA agents reported that a train from Russia, carrying the uranium, is crossing Poland right now. Perhaps a Special Forces team could intercept the shipment and inspect one of those containers. But that wouldn't be easy either. I checked with Liz for anything she had heard about it. She recalled Kruschev telling Foster that those shipments are tightly guarded by the Mafia."

"Special Forces! Raids! Armed guards! You are really getting into the swing of this, Ben. But back in your day it was the Foreign Legion, wasn't it? Seriously, though, I think you have that Munich deal wired. Great job! We will see tonight if Foster thinks we need a sample. My bet is he will demand one."

Ben gathered that the third-degree from Garrison was both a test and a preparation for the vice president's meeting. He was quite eager to return the favor.

"Now, my friend, what have you and Hazel figured out? Don't keep me in suspense. Spill it. Please!"

"As you know, Hazel and the other NRC analysts accessed all the operating and performance records of the NuEnergy plants. My agents identified the nuclear plant technicians and engineers with Mafia ties. After an intensive cross comparison, a disturbing pattern emerged. Each of the last fifteen NuEnergy plants experienced a major, unplanned shutdown, or an accident, sometime in the months before they turned over operations to NuEnergy. The events were always after the Mafia techs had been hired."

Ben nodded. Just as he thought all along. His suspicions were on target, but finally the FBI and the NRC were convinced. Ben shook his head for it seemed a day late and a dollar short, since all the plants were now in NuEnergy's grip. The federal bureaucracy was lumbering, at best.

"I have one question, Brad. Why do they go after American plants? Why not foreign plants? CIA's developing profile shows that old Boris Andropov hates the U.S., so why is he doing business here in such a big way?"

Garrison just shrugged, "You got me there. I don't know. That's a very troubling question."

Ben didn't let the point drop. "Liz tells me that Andropov hates the U.S. with a burning passion. The Mafia's worldwide take is great compared to the amount of revenue that the U.S. venture produces. They could have funneled the stolen uranium, using the Munich Enrichment Plant, into foreign power plants just as easily as the ones over here. So what's his motive for operating in the U.S.?"

It bothered Garrison greatly that he didn't have an answer to that question.

"Damn you, Ben, with just one question, you got even big-time for the quizzing I dished out."

CHAPTER
TWENTY-FIVE

Day 25 5 P.M. Rock Creek Park Trail Washington, D. C.

Ben renewed his favorite activity, the run in Rock Creek Park. The excursion magically drained away the pent-up tensions of the day. This exercise also provided an interlude for his mind to roam freely over the many perplexities of the day.

Ben jogged at a warm-up pace down the hill, past the bustling shops and restaurants, toward the Rock Creek valley floor. The cold that still clung to the D.C. area stung, but in a few minutes when the blood flow increased, he would no longer feel the chill.

He found that the park trail was not without risk, for an occasional patch of ice, difficult to spot in the dusk, could easily send him sprawling. If he wasn't alert to that possibility, then this enjoyable tonic could be brought to a screeching halt with a twisted knee or ankle. He had never spotted the FBI tailing him on his previous runs and hadn't asked Garrison how they handled that phase of guarding him. He was perfectly happy ignoring their presence.

By choosing to head north for the first time into the more remote stretches beyond the Zoo grounds, he unknowingly fouled up the FBI's efforts to protect him. Striking out along the park trail for what was to be two and a half miles before turning back and retracing his steps to the Sheraton, he simply presumed he was adequately protected.

The setting sun's last rays, fragmented by the bare tree branches, filtered onto the creek valley floor, creating a crazy quilt pattern of shadows on the winding asphalt path. The fading sunlight, though, would be gone by the time he reached the turnaround.

193

He was moving at about his usual pace and was out a mile. This section through the zoo grounds led to the most solitary part of the park. He suddenly felt an unwelcome return of nervousness. Had those shadows off the trail moved or had recent events stirred his paranoia? Were his senses possibly warning him once again of danger? He looked around but saw no one. He told himself to forget it and shape up.

Finally he reached the portion of the path where he turned around to start back toward the old hotel. Most of the evening sunlight had faded away and the glow of the distant city lights gradually predominated as a dim source of illumination. What little visibility remained was provided by that reflected light. He could just barely make out the path as he began to retrace his steps. There had been only one other runner out here in this secluded section in the last several minutes. Despite his earlier case of nerves he was actually enjoying the remoteness of this route and made a mental note to come this way again.

Suddenly he caught the sound of shoes rhythmically, yet heavily, clomping along the path just ahead of him. His heart skipped a beat. Two runners burst out of the gathering dusk straight toward him. Their outlines grew clearer. Two stocky men in dark sweat suits and black stocking hats were panting hard. It was difficult to make out much else about them. They passed him, obviously laboring as they ran. They certainly did not appear to be accomplished runners, but he would sure hate to meet those boys in a dark alley. The irony of that thought struck him hard, for basically that is where he was.

With a newfound vigor in his stride, Ben progressed no more than a few yards past them when the two wheeled around and came at him at full speed. Recognizing the threat, he accelerated to a flat-out sprint. The two giving chase were losing ground. Maybe he could run his way out of trouble.

Suddenly without warning just ahead of him, a figure leapt from the side of the trail directly into his path. A flush of burning heat seared his entire body, yet strangely the passage of time slowed. His adrenaline glands released their entire inventory into his blood system. He reacted instinctively, placing a vicious kick into the attacking man's groin. All of the momentum of his sprint transferred destructively into the most vulnerable part of the man's body. The attacker, obviously in great pain, doubled over and crumbled onto the trail.

Ben tripped while trying to hurdle the fallen victim. Scrambling desperately he regained his footing. The delay, though, was just enough for the fastest of the two pursuers to catch and tackle him. They hit the frozen ground hard. The fall jarred Ben as might a fall on concrete. He struggled with the attacker as they rolled over and over across the frozen wooded grounds. The two combatants tumbled all the way down to the creek bank.

Ben fought free of the attacker's grip and scrambled to get away. The assailant, though, was able to grab one of his feet. Again he forced Ben to the ground.

The second mugger finally caught up and planted his stocky bulk squarely on Ben's chest. He began choking him. As Ben weakened from the loss of oxygen, the first thug released his feet and moved forward. He pulled out what appeared to be a syringe and grabbed for Ben's arm.

For a split second Ben felt absolute terror. Then desperate determination took over. He was not going to die this way.

Gasping for precious air, Ben mustered his waning strength for a last desperate move. He thrust his forearms first up between the choker's arms and then in a burst jerked his elbows outward, knocking loose the assailant's chokehold. The surprised thug's upper body, absent the support of his arms on Ben's neck, fell rapidly forward toward his prone victim.

At that same instant, Ben, with lightning quickness brought his own hands together. His left palm supported his right as it flashed upward, striking the falling face with great force. The impact of the blow upon the point of the nose was magnified by the upper body momentum of the falling attacker. His accelerating face met Ben's perfectly positioned flashing hands. At the moment of impact, Ben flexed his entire upper body as he might have when making a ferocious tackle. His body braced against the ground made the move even more effective. This multiplying of forces converged on the tip of the mugger's nose and resulted in instant devastation. The cartilage constituting the bridge of the nose shot inward and upward about three inches into the attacker's brain. The man fell limply, dead by the time he collapsed on top of Ben.

Still the last attacker maneuvered into position, growling and swearing unintelligibly. He wielded what Ben was now sure was a syringe. Ben was helplessly pinned by the dead thug's weight on his chest.

At this desperate instant, the last attacker went suddenly limp as the top half of his head disappeared into the dark of the night. Ben, summoning help from a hidden reservoir of strength, rolled the first dead attacker's body off him and into the path of the falling dead man.

The plunging needle, still held by the now lifeless body of the head-less assailant, punctured the discarded thug's chest.

In the melee, Ben had failed to hear the gunshot that ended the attack.

With renewed energy born of terror, he sprang to his feet and without looking back raced at full speed in the direction of the hotel. If he had looked, he would have seen two federal agents rushing onto the fight scene, weapons drawn. They had belatedly discovered Ben's altered jogging path.

Day 25 6:15 P.M. Ben's Hotel Room

Ben sank into the sofa too exhausted and frightened to think or analyze much of anything. He was just thankful to be alive. These attacks on him weren't easing up at all now that he was out of Black Bear and working with Foster. He had no idea, though, what that sig-nified. Gradually he became aware of pain. A throbbing in his right big toe and a burning sensation in his right palm announced that he had not escaped unscathed.

His secure phone rang. It was Garrison.

"Are you okay?"

"I don't know if I am or not."

"My guys almost didn't reach you in time. I am sorry, Ben."

Ben definitely had new questions as to whether he was in over his head, but... He had felt like that at half time of a football game where the other team was handing them their butts. He had almost always been able to rally himself and his team for a comeback in the second half, but this wasn't a game, so where did he stand?

"Ben, medics are on the way. They will check you over. You just stay there and rest. I can cover the meeting for you tonight."

Ben found himself answering in a manner that surprised him, "No! I intend to be there."

"We will see about that after the medics have a look. Again, I am sorry as hell about this, Ben."

After Garrison hung up, Ben dialed Laura's number just as he always did at this time of day. He couldn't have her worrying.

"Laura, how are things at the store?"

"Okay. Business is pretty good, but I still miss you. Will you be home soon?"

Ben assured her, "Soon. This mystery is nearly solved."

"I will believe it when I see you."

"Laura, I talked to Liz about Dudaev. He is a very trusted reference around here whenever the subject of Russia comes up."

By bringing up Dudaev, Ben was attempting to avoid telling Laura about tonight's incident. To his great relief it worked.

"Thanks, Ben. He is still the one I suspect was writing mother. I am determined to get his help in finding out what was really behind mother's flight from the Soviets. Also I must find out who my grandfather was."

As Ben waited for the medics to arrive, reality gradually sank in. He had probably just killed a man and seriously injured another. My God, what was he doing? What was happening to him? He was in a fight he couldn't fathom. He was hated in a way that he couldn't begin to comprehend. Was he a help or a liability to Foster?

"Settle down, Ben," he told himself. "Mark will tell you if you are not needed."

He hadn't told Laura about the attack. That wasn't like him. Could this crisis wind up driving a wedge between them? Maybe he should put as much thought and effort into preserving their relationship as in solving the world's problems.

TWENTY-SIX

Day 25 8 P.M. Vice President Foster's Office White House

As he walked into the vice president's office, Ben heard Foster explaining some of the nuances of the Presidential War Powers Act to General Adair.

As soon as Foster saw Ben, he stopped the discussion and asked, "Are you all right?"

Betraying deep concern, Foster took a worried inventory of his old friend.

Sensing a host of curious eyes checking him out, Ben responded, "Yes. The medics say I am fine. Just bruises, abrasions, and contusions. I feel, though, like I just survived the first day of contact football."

"Garrison called. He will be late. He told me what happened. His men are still cleaning up. You left quite a mess out there."

Immediately after his talk with Laura, Ben had decided to see this meeting through, but with the Munich mystery solved he figured that his services were no longer required. At that point he was ready to go home, yet, as the evening wore on he found that the attack affected him strangely. It hardened his resolve to see this conflict through to the bitter end. He was mad as hell and if he could possibly be useful he would stay.

The others had scrutinized Ben and astutely picked up on the swelling of his right hand, his puffy left eye, and a slight favoring of his right foot. North concluded that the man had been in one hell of a brawl. He was plenty proud of Ben. He was the kind of American who gave no quarter to the bad guys.

Foster turned his attention to the others and asked, "By the way, James, would you call those suspenders fire-engine red? My old American-flyer wagon was painted about that same shade of red."

"Deal with it, Mr. Vice President. I'm just infusing a little class in the habiliment department around here."

"Liz, do you think he's accomplished that?"

"I plead the fifth."

Stockton retorted, "If bland was in, you two would be fashion plates."

Ben had seen Foster employ this tactic of teasing years ago, when the stress levels were becoming extreme. It worked then to release tension and it seemed to work now. All had a good laugh about James's loud suspenders.

"If you are done Mr. Vice President, can I return to important matters?"

"By all means."

"Central Intelligence, in conjunction with the Space Imaging and Mapping Agency, has pored through literally tons of data from our spy satellites and planes. I won't explain how we reconstructed events in detail. Rather I shall focus on conclusions and results."

"Good!" nodded Foster.

In his resonant voice, James spun his tale. "One hundred metric tons of weapons-grade uranium, fifty tactical nuclear weapons and two strategic warheads were clandestinely removed from Semipalatinsk in the early nineties under Boris Andropov's direction."

"Strategic? Two? Are you sure?"

"Yes."

"Damn!"

Foster rose and began his pacing far earlier than in past meetings.

"Just verified it this evening. The Kazakh Border Guard took the loot to two locations. The first was the old Soviet defensive installation on the eastern Caspian shore. The place was modernized by the Mafia into a well-fortified nuclear weapons storage facility. You already saw pictures of it."

Ben gulped with the bad news. This crisis was escalating rapidly. My God, what had he gotten into?

"How big are they?"

"The strategic...?"

"You."

"Two hundred kiloton. Each has the power of twenty Hiroshimas."

"Where are they now?" Foster demanded.

"Years ago the two were shipped directly to Rashte and from there to Karaj."

"Maybe you didn't understand my question, James! Where are they now?"

"I understood it. I don't know. They may be deployed on advanced missiles or still in Karaj. They are definitely in the hands of General Zarif and that is not good."

Frustrated, Vice President Foster snapped, "Go on."

"Tactical nuclear warheads and weapons-grade uranium are transferred annually onto Iranian vessels. The stuff always winds up at the Karaj Nuclear Complex. From there the trail gets murkier. We don't know where the weapons-grade uranium goes. The nuclear warheads though are a different story. Some have been deployed on Iran's best missiles. As I just mentioned, we are not sure yet whether the strategic warheads have been deployed. A carefully shielded shipment going to Bandar-E-Abbas was photographed recently. It could have contained one or both of the big bombs. If so they deliberately kept them well shielded so unfortunately we can't be sure."

The vice president shook his head, not at all happy with the news coming from Stockton.

Despite the seriousness of his message, Ben truly enjoyed listening to the Scotsman. His deep voice and his flair for transforming his report into a suspense novel were captivating. He was Prairie Home Companion's Garrison Keillor of the security agency. Ben grasped the emerging picture of cooperation between Iran and the Mafia. He knew that in the past Russia hadn't exhibited any restraint in selling arms to Iran. They and the Chinese had armed Iran to the teeth. The Mafia though, it appeared, had supplied the frosting on the cake. Stockton's next words reinforced Ben's surmises.

"Iran originally acquired rocket engines from North Korea. To further upgrade their delivery systems, Russian technicians visited Zarif's Karaj facilities. After those visits, Iran began receiving assistance from Russia's state-run missile plants and technical universities. Technicians at Karaj with the help of engineers from NPO Trud, a prestigious Russian rocket-motor plant, developed the same missiles, which targeted Europe during the Cold War. Iran's newest missiles are based on the old Soviet SS-4 strategic rockets."

"Those longer-range rockets and Zarif's damned big bombs raise the ante dramatically," whistled Foster, whose pacing quickened as Stockton's revelations fell fast and furious.

"Yes. It certainly does. No enemy of Iran is safe. With the help of ex-Soviet technology and new Chinese guidance systems, given away by us in the nineties, Iran has completed development of a new family of missiles, capable of delivering these missing big bombs up to three-thousand miles."

"Stop, James!" The vice president had known about most of this past complicity of the Russians in helping Iran develop missiles, but the degree of their aid was alarming him, as it was the others. Despite Liz's and Dudaev's assurances, Foster still wasn't completely comfortable in trusting these new Russian leaders.

"So with friends like Russia, who the hell needs enemies? Liz, are we completely misreading this present bunch of Russian leaders?"

"No!"

Liz understood that Foster's inherent doubts of Russia's leaders had been reinforced by Stockton's briefing. She firmly believed, though, in the accuracy of her assessment of Strahkov and Kruschev and intended to defend her position. She believed that the U.S. wouldn't be well served in this crisis if its leaders reverted to hard-line thinking toward Russia. The interests of the U.S. and Russia were uniquely aligned in this crisis. Both would benefit by cooperating.

"I believe our readings of Strahkov and Kruschev are accurate. Russia is an enigma, even to itself at times. In the nineties there existed a fundamentally chaotic situation in the ex-Soviet Empire regarding weapons exports. Basically, Russia's hunger for cash and their paranoia of the West overruled their long-term security interests."

"And that's not the case today?" challenged Foster.

"Yes and no. The government at the top in the persons of Strahkov and Kruschev apparently want the hemorrhage of arms to potential adversaries, such as Iran and China, to stop. But there are various competing agencies and ministries, autonomous companies and whole defense industry-based cities that still want to sell their products on their own. Strahkov and Kruschev are aware that strategically the most serious threat to their country doesn't come from us. Rather, Iran, the aggressive theocracy on their exposed southern flank, represents a huge challenge. China to the south and east is also a growing concern for them."

"Liz, I pray that you are right."

Stockton spoke up in support of Liz. "Mr. Vice President, I had further, in depth conversations with Dudaev and he has completely convinced me that Liz's analysis is correct. From what he told me I firmly believe we can trust those two."

Listening to this fascinating exchange, Ben wondered just what Stockton had heard from Dudaev, which carried so much weight at this level of government policy setting. This Dudaev, his and Foster's former professor, had a uniquely vast knowledge and equally amazing influence.

Foster didn't follow up on James allusion to Dudaev. That strange omission surprised Ben. Foster instead seemed to accept the statement at face value. Ben wondered what Foster knew about Dudaev beyond his being their old professor.

"James, it would seem that while our country has been preoccupied with Iraq over the last decade, Iran has been quietly building into the true Middle-Eastern problem power."

"Yes, that's absolutely correct. Their theocracy's thirst for empire is a real problem."

Ben was growing uneasy for he could tell that despite the gravity of what had been revealed so far, James wasn't finished. Another shoe was about to drop. He had something else.

Don moved to the door, allowing Garrison to enter. "Sorry for the interruption, Mr. Vice President. Please go on, James."

Just arriving, Garrison, quite unaware of the building tension around Stockton's presentation, looked Ben over closely to see if he was okay. He then pulled up a chair beside him and rather admiringly whispered, "You scared the hell out of us tonight."

Stockton challenged, "General, how would you like to face those missing strategic bombs coming at you via the latest, low-flying, supersonic French cruise missile?"

"Why? Do they have them?"

"Yes. New analysis of our pictures reveals that a couple of weeks ago, two French cruises were delivered to Iran, thanks to their Mafia buddies. They wound up at Bandar-E-Abbas, the same place as the mysterious shielded shipment from Karaj."

"I will never malign your damned suspenders again, James. Now I know you are on a vendetta."

"Nope, like I said before, I wish to hell I were making all of this up."

"Why didn't the Russians tell us about all of this? Surely they are aware of these developments!" Foster addressed the question to no one in particular.

"That would be a good question for Kruschev," suggested Liz. "This may be the rest of the story, so to speak, as to why the Russian leaders so desperately want our help. My guess is the Russians hoped we would discover these facts for ourselves. They didn't want to admit to us how terrified they really are of the nuclear build-up and how desperately they are needing our help to neutralize Karaj. I believe that the Russians are probably scared to death of Iran's burgeoning arsenal, and are praying like hell that we will do something about it."

"Holy torpedoes, James, have you any more happy news for us?"

"Yes. They have an operation there that our new informant has heard about from his fellow Russian scientists. I caution, though, that he hasn't seen the evolution firsthand. The Iranian officials keep the scientists segregated, working on only their sectors of the complex within Karaj. Anyway, he says the weapons-grade uranium, which is originally in a metallic form, is transformed to a powdery uranium hexafluoride. After that chemical alteration, they mix the smuggled weapons-grade uranium with a large quantity of natural uranium powder, reducing its enrichment in the process to about twelve percent. He doesn't know beyond that where this oddly blended uranium product goes. He doesn't think any of the Russian scientists know. Only Iranians handle the finished product."

Ben could not contain himself. This was unexpected and precise confirmation of his team's theory. Momentarily forgetting his aching foot and thrilled to have this validation of Munich's operation, he jumped out of his chair, interrupting James.

"We know where the stuff goes. Both the amount and enrichment fit perfectly with our theory of what's going on at Munich. We will explain when it's our turn."

"Good! It's important to get independent verification of this type of intelligence." James, slightly amused at Ben's enthusiasm, took a deep breath and sat down.

Ben could tell that the team was extremely worried about Stockton's disclosures.

"What a mess! General, I am not suggesting we need to or should do anything yet, but let me ask you, if the President finds that diplomatic solutions aren't feasible and we find our security is threatened, do we have the resources to go into Iran and retrieve the stolen nuclear arsenal?"

"We have run contingency studies for this sort of a mission. They show we are on the ragged edge, since Presidential policy restricts us to only conventional arms."

"General, specifically what do your studies show?"

"There are several viable military approaches to neutralize the Iranian nuclear threat. First, we could use a B1B to deliver a burrowing nuclear bomb, which certainly would eliminate the underground complex at Karaj. One of our latest hypersonic cruise missiles bearing a strategic nuclear warhead could also do the job. But, a nuclear first strike is a step President Arthur is unwilling to take. He has made it abundantly clear that under his presidency, the U.S. will not be the first to use nuclear weapons. A conventional air attack can't completely destroy the Karaj complex. It's too well fortified and too far underground. Also, it's too heavily guarded for our Special Forces to do the job through sabotage alone. Thus, we have concluded that the landing of our Rangers and the Armored Cavalry is the only operative choice."

"That would take one hell of an airlift."

"For sure. Air dominance would have to be secured before our ground forces could land. A surprise, and I underline surprise, strike to disable their defenses would be a mandatory first step. Several hundred cruise missiles and dozens of stealth bomber sorties are required. After gaining air superiority, a battalion of Apache Longbows would be dispatched to the Karaj area to facilitate the troop landing and to fight alongside the Rangers and the Armored Cavalry. This would be a difficult operation involving considerable risk since Karaj is located in the interior of one of the world's most heavily militarized countries. The city of Tehran, with over ten million people and several crack divisions, is just fifty miles over the eastern horizon from the target."

"What's the earliest you could launch such an attack?"

"With the preliminary staging actions we have already taken, twenty days."

"Of course, we know that we will start to get the attention of the world with some of those military movements."

"Yes, that's true, Mr. Vice President. We could use the old War on Terror as cover or we could raise a ruckus in the U.N. Security Council about Syria's aggressive actions toward their neighbors. That could serve as cover for the real reason for our buildup."

"I will suggest to President Arthur that he and Secretary Kohlmeier consider that."

Listening to all of this, Ben still held out some hope that war could be avoided. He knew that the State Department must be advocating diplomacy. His job though, was just to figure out NuEnergy's game and where the missing uranium went, so he deliberately stayed out of the war part of the problem. Little did he know that the issues would blur together soon.

General Adair continued, "I think we also need another story covering the movement of our forces to Russian bases. The Russia-NATO Friendship Pact exercises would be convenient cover for that."

"Good suggestion. You should be a politician."

"In many ways I am, Mr. Vice President.

"Let me explain one proposed major deployment and its purpose. By positioning our SL-7 roll-on-roll-off ships loaded with our European division's equipment and troops in the northern Indian Ocean at the time of our Karaj attack, we achieve three objectives. It's a little like moving one's queen into an aggressive position on the chessboard and in the process, threatening and tying up several of the opposition's pieces. With that division strategically and boldly positioned in the Indian Ocean, they are only days away from Korea if events should require them there. Also, they are poised on Iran's southern flank only twenty-four hours away, which serves to tie up Iran's southern divisions worrying about that force. As a bonus, they may deter Pakistan or India from getting too 'trigger-happy' while we are dealing with Karaj. If we use the media cleverly enough, we can send just the right message, advertising the division's position and thus accomplish all three objectives."

"Excellent strategy, General! It's similar to the first Gulf War when our feigned attack from the Gulf served to tie up several Iraqi divisions facing the sea. It prevented the reinforcement of their other divisions when the real attack came over land. My congratulations. I'll work with the President on that one, too.

"What is your opinion? Should we involve the Chairman of the Senate Armed Services Committee?" questioned Foster.

General Adair replied, "I think it would be helpful."

"Not every Senator on that committee is to be trusted to keep his or her mouth shut, so we should wait as long as possible to involve anyone else. Some members of that Senate committee are political stooges for NuEnergy," Stockton cautioned.

Garrison nodded in agreement with Stockton's NuEnergy warning.

After a lengthy discussion of logistics, Foster suggested, "Let's take a five-minute break before we hear reports from Ben and Brad."

As Ben, favoring his throbbing right foot, limped down the hall toward the nearest bathroom, Garrison followed. "My men say that was a really close shave out there tonight. I am terribly sorry that happened, Ben. I asked them to analyze what went wrong and to develop an improved plan for your protection. Are you sure you are all right."

"I am okay, Brad, and don't be hard on your agents. After all, they did save my life. I probably screwed them up by running to the north tonight. I am most grateful to you and them. I have to admit, though, my body is a mass of aches and pains."

Garrison grimaced at that admission.

"What was the chemical in the syringe?" Ben asked.

"I'll tell you about it after the meeting."

The avoidance of an answer made Ben uneasy. Why wouldn't Garrison tell him about the syringe? Was Foster jumping on the war option too soon? Were things being kept from him? Maybe he wasn't an equal member of this team after all and maybe he should have known that all along. Right now he would bet that this was about the end of his involvement, a bet he would lose big-time.

TWENTY-SEVEN

Day 25 9:30 P.M. Vice President Foster's Office White House

Ben reported, "My conclusions on the Munich plant are the results of the collective efforts of Garrison's and my team. The bottom line is that the Munich Enrichment Plant is uniquely designed and operated to accept blended uranium. We are convinced that they receive the twelve percent stuff being produced at Karaj, the very uranium James told us about. The highly enriched uranium stolen from Kazakhstan is converted to blended uranium at Karaj. Then, in a devilishly clever way, it is introduced into the commercial nuclear fuel stream, using the Munich Enrichment Plant as cover. This secret insertion of the stolen uranium into the commercial arena creates a bonanza of billions of dollars for the Russian Mafia."

Ben concluded, "I was prepared before this meeting to say that we had a ninety-five percent confidence in this theory. However, after hearing Director Stockton's intelligence report, I must say our confidence is up to ninety-nine."

"Great work, Ben. The mystery of the missing uranium is solved! But I do have one question for you. How can we get to one hundred percent?"

Ben cast a knowing glance in Garrison's direction. Just as they had predicted, Foster wanted absolute proof.

"Inspect at least one of the Kazakh cylinders. Our team believes a Special Forces squad could be dispatched to board the train carrying the latest Kazakh shipment, open a cylinder and extract a sample of the uranium. Of course, they need to sample very precisely. We know it wouldn't be easy, since there are Mafia guards accompanying the uranium."

"I want that done. I must have absolute proof that your theory is correct. Ben, work with General Adair to get that operation arranged.

Do whatever must be done to confirm that blended uranium is being smuggled into Munich. Now let's hear your findings, Garrison."

Ben happily sat down as his throbbing hand and foot were proving to be major distractions. Apparently he wasn't quite finished with this mess. He had to see that a uranium sample was obtained so Foster could get his one hundred percent.

Garrison stood to address the group. "At least I don't have to follow one of James's phenomenal picture shows this time. However, sir James dropped so many bombs this evening that I thought we were under attack," quipped Garrison.

"Amen to that. I still suspect the suspenders comment brought all of that on," vainly quipped Foster.

After explaining how NuEnergy had gained control of the power plants, Garrison continued, "Just as Ben suspected all along, at least a dozen of the nuclear plant executives from the NuEnergy controlled plants have met various forms of Mafia-induced disasters. Ben nearly became their latest victim tonight. These utility managers all had one thing in common, an ethical standard that NuEnergy could not corrupt. Nor could they be coerced into leaving their jobs voluntarily to make space for the pliant handpicked puppets NuEnergy wished to install. The Mafia ingeniously created incidents to look natural so that the suspicions of law enforcement authorities weren't raised."

"Do you have enough evidence to make arrests?"

"In some cases, yes, and in others just strong leads. As a bonus, we hold the damaged remnant of Ben's attackers in custody. Eventually he will talk."

"Then still another aspect to deal with. They wanted control of those plants badly didn't they," said Foster, shaking his head at the growing complexity of this whole mess.

Garrison cautioned, "The plants, in addition to corrupt NuEnergy management, still have two or three Mafia techs employed at each, for unknown purposes."

"Are you ready to hazard a guess?"

"No. We aren't sure of their mission, but we do have some far-out theories that concern us."

Brad refrained from advancing the theory Ben and Liz were seriously considering. The psychological profile on Andropov, being developed within the CIA, was very disturbing. However, they were not sure enough of their idea to suggest anything tonight.

Foster, though, sensed that the three were far more worried about the plants than they were willing to say right now, so he pressed the issue. "Garrison, any sort of a Mafia threat to our nuclear power plants should be taken very seriously. You, Ben and Liz look into that more and prepare a proposal on how to ensure the plants' safety.

"General, you work with military strategists and planners. Use James and Central Intelligence information as needed. Develop contingency plans for an attack on Karaj. The mission's limited purpose would be to bring out the nuclear weapons, the weapons-grade and blended uranium and the scientists, while preventing the launch of any of Iran's nuclear weapons. Of course only the President can authorize an actual attack and he hasn't, but be prepared. This meeting is adjourned.

"Garrison, you, North and I need to talk. The rest of you are dismissed."

Without hesitation General Adair arose, explaining that he was late to his next engagement, but added, "Garrison, you take care of Ben. We need him healthy and kicking. Ben, I will call you later. We will plan a little uranium raid."

Day 25 10:30 P.M. White House

Stockton remained seated. "Frankly, my curiosity has gotten the best of me. Liz and I will stay, if that meets with your approval, Mr. Vice President."

Ben likewise added, "Me, too. I wish to hear this. If nothing else I want to know what the hell was in the syringe."

"There are several things," Garrison began. "The inquisitive Department of Commerce undersecretary, Vince Foley, is definitely on the Mafia payroll. He restricts the flow of legitimate Russian uranium. We have that from wire taps, e-mail, and phone records."

"Why? What's their game?"

"As to why, our conjecture is to drive up the world price of enrichment services, making the Mafia controlled uranium even more valuable. Also, the longer the bulk of the weapons-grade uranium stays in Russia, the more opportunity the Mafia has to grab hold of it. This uranium scam cuts deeply across government agencies and international business. It has been artfully orchestrated."

"Damned right. The plot runs deep and for what purpose? Money only or something else?"

Ben spoke up, "That's the question we are wrestling with right now, Mark."

Foster turned back to Garrison, "Do you have any more on Foley?"

"As to exactly how Foley's being paid, we are still not sure. We are watching him and his close associates to see how the money is being transferred. One of his suspicious associates is Michelle Michote."

Ben gulped. He was shocked by that new tidbit. This Michelle must be the same one who was involved with Fred Bumgardner. For now he opted to say nothing. He wasn't going to butt in again, but why hadn't Garrison told him about her when Ben had mentioned her earlier today. Again he wondered if he was out of the loop. He would talk with Garrison about that later. If it had been an oversight okay, but if it wasn't...

Garrison, unaware of Ben's consternation, continued his report, "In three days the R.M. Holding Corporation is holding its annual meeting in Switzerland. Our agents are attempting to bug their meeting places. Andropov holds two series of meetings, one for the semi-legitimate CEO's of each of R.M.'s wholly owned subsidiaries. The second set of meetings is for the Mafia leaders. If we can tap into those meetings, we could learn a lot about their operations."

"If James can help you with that, use him."

"I will."

"I want to hear immediately of any results."

"Yes, sir.

"Mr. Vice President, as you know, Ben had a close call this evening. Three assailants attacked him during his run in the park. It was a carefully devised scheme to kill him and make it look like he suffered a heart attack while jogging. It's a similar modus operandi to that of a couple of the deaths of other unfortunate executives, whom I mentioned earlier. The Mafia, though, ran into more than they bargained for in Ben.

"The planned method of death was most heinous. The chemical in the syringe was used in the past by the Thieves-in-Law. With it, they would eliminate a problem prison guard without leaving any trace of their handiwork, other than a needle puncture. The Soviets years ago developed this poison, Ricin, which induces clotting, forcing heart failure. Soviet KGB defectors admitted they had used Ricin on Bulgarian dissidents. By the time an autopsy's done, all trace of the chemical has dissipated."

Ben shuddered. He had come within an inch of that gruesome fate.

Garrison continued with a brief description of the attack on Ben. "Two are dead. We have the third assailant in custody. He suffered some injuries, compliments of Ben, that have permanently raised his voice an octave."

Stockton chuckled at that bit of extraneous news.

"You and James really thrive on this kind of stuff, don't you? So it ended reasonably well, but why didn't your men warn Ben of the danger? This was too close a call. It's unacceptable."

"We are reviewing that. I don't have all the answers yet."

"Well, get answers! Take no more chances with this man's life. If they will go to these lengths with what they know now about him, just think what danger he would be in if they get a clue that he is working for me and directly against them."

Foster paused, "Or have they possibly figured that out already? Be on guard. Upgrade the protection for Laura.

"Ben, I am sorry for the trouble I seem to be bringing you. You can call it quits anytime. You know that don't you?"

"I do. Thanks, but if you want me here I will stay."

"We need you but I hate what just happened. I feel responsible."

"Look, I was in serious trouble from the moment NuEnergy took over Black Bear and I chose to oppose their rotten crap. Before I got into this with you, Laura and I didn't have FBI protection and now we do, so I see it as a net gain in our safety. Without Brad's men riding to the rescue, I would be pushing up roses at a Tulsa cemetery. Now that I know Andropov is definitely responsible for the deaths of many of my colleagues, I would be damned if I didn't help bring him down."

Stockton, Foster, Garrison, and even Ben himself had not grasped, until now, the depth of the personal animosity he harbored for Andropov. They and he better understood his urgent need to even the score on behalf of his nuclear compatriots.

"Mr. Vice President, Ben's persistence uncovered that the supposed suicide of a Fred Bumgardner may have been murder. Ben discovered that the man apparently got involved in an affair. Get this! It was with Michelle Michote."

Ben, who was still upset with Garrison for not telling him what he knew about Michelle, observed a rare flash of fear on Foster's face.

The vice president fell back in his chair. For several moments he said nothing. Finally he asked Garrison, "Is Dione safe working that closely with Michelle?"

"I believe so. Secret Service and my agents are protecting her."

"Believe so? Damn it, that's not good enough. I want Ron in here right away.

"Find him, Don. He is to hustle his butt in here now."

Don rushed out to find the head of the White House Secret Service Detail.

"Ben, you go on and get some rest. I am more grateful to you than

I can ever express. Your digging into the Bumgardner affair may have warned us of Michelle Michote's devilish role in time to protect Dione."

Ben surmised that the potential threat to the vice president's daughter was why Garrison hadn't told him before what he knew about this Michelle dame, but he intended to confront Garrison about it anyway. He wouldn't operate with one hand tied behind his back.

After dismissing the team, Foster collapsed in his chair. With his face in his hands he questioned his own judgment. Was his damned call to duty placing his daughter at undue risk? Had he also callously used his good friend, Ben. Was he being selfish? Was anything more important than their safety? How would Lis advise him?

The sleet pounded against the window, but Foster, deep in reflection, failed to notice.

Day 25 11:55 P.M. Stockton's Car Washington, D.C.

"James," Liz began thoughtfully, "after listening to President Strahkov and President Arthur's recent conversations, I came up with what might be a crazy idea."

"What is it?"

After Liz's top-notch performance on this job, Stockton doubted if she ever had a crazy idea. Listening intently he drove his black BMW across the Theodore Roosevelt Bridge and then turned onto the George Washington Memorial Parkway. The windshield wipers struggled to remove the rapidly falling sleet.

"It's apparent that Strahkov idolizes his father. He believes that his father's resistance and that of others like him dealt the fatal blow to the Soviet Communists. His mother told him that his father's courage was nourished by a martyred Russian poet. Those early dissidents revered this lyricist as the inspirational heart and soul of their entire movement. His forbidden writings evoked strong emotions, while advancing the cause of human rights. The man apparently never wavered. He steadfastly exposed the truth about Soviet Communist oppression. This unconquerable writer stood firm in the face of persecution by the State and, by so doing, captured the imagination and admiration of those who later comprised the dissidents."

Knowing the answer, Stockton played dumb, "Who is this man who inspired the dissidents so?"

"Viktor Sumurov."

He hoped that Liz would drop this subject soon. Stockton disinterestedly asked, "So, what else?"

"He had a mistress. Supposedly, she was a beautiful and devoutly supportive woman whom Viktor never married for fear of bringing the Soviet's wrath down on her. For a time, despite the state's attempts to ruin them both, their love somehow blossomed. He might as well have married her, for they exiled her to a remote town on the Manchurian border. Legend has it that she died giving birth to Viktor's daughter. The child, it's rumored, grew up in that remote outpost of the Soviet Empire. There the trail dims. Strahkov has given the FSB two priority assignments. One, which you are aware of, was to give him a complete report on the status of nuclear armaments. What do you think the second task was?"

"Just go ahead and tell me, Liz," Stockton snapped as he pulled past the night guard into the CIA parking garage at Langley, Virginia. He was frustrated with this conversation, but relieved that at least the miserable sleet no longer bombarded his car. He definitely didn't like where Liz was headed. Should he share Dudaev's secrets with Liz or not?

Liz, unaware of Stockton's predicament, continued with her tale, "He wants the family of Viktor Sumurov traced. If any have survived, he wants them found and given a hero's welcome in Moscow. Further, he wants them to be provided with their every need for the rest of their lives."

"Why? Gratitude?"

"That's what it seems to be on the surface, but perhaps he also wishes to remind Russia of what Sumurov stood for: freedom, faith, courage, honesty!"

"So where do we enter into the picture?"

"With your permission, we could have Foster volunteer CIA's help in that search."

"Do we have anything that would help?"

"Actually, quite a bit. Lots of old records on the Soviet dissident groups. All of that could be of great help in tracking down any heirs of Viktor Sumurov."

This was one time that Liz was too smart for her own good. Stockton must either coax her out of this arena or take her into his confidence. Reluctantly, he chose the latter. He told her that he and Dudaev suspected Laura Andrew was Sumurov's granddaughter.

"Liz, I want you to go to Tulsa. Meet Laura and get a DNA sample. We will coordinate with Garrison. The apparent purpose of your trip will be to improve security around her and to check into some of her amazing articles on Russia. Dudaev told me of her keen, hard-hitting stories on Russian current events. This lady is apparently quite a thinker and a literary talent."

TWENTY-EIGHT

Day 27 11 P.M. Polish-German Border

The Comanche war machine hovered silently in the night sky above a remote stretch of the German-Polish border. With only minutes to spare, the two-man flight crew had reached their destination above the rail line connecting southern Germany with Moscow.

Their innovative Comanche was configured to maximize stealth and maneuverability. On this mission the power to attack was secondary, and so gone were the stub wings bearing Hellfire missiles. The payload this time was human. With Captain O'Banyon's veteran four-man team of Army Special Forces and one civilian nuclear expert onboard, the bird was poised to pounce on its prey.

Stressed with frustrating time constraints, O'Banyon fumed, "Horseshit! Two days isn't enough! Screw the Joint Chiefs Chairman! He better get his act together. How dare they order a civilian to be part of this. I don't care what he knows. How damned stupid are these armchair generals?"

Ben, quite aware that Captain Dan O'Banyon wasn't wild about his being on this mission, listened to this pointed tirade for the third time. That was enough. He didn't care if Captain O'Banyon's team was legend.

"Captain, you need to shape the hell up fast. Circumstances didn't allow more time. I am here because I know best what we are after. You need to concentrate on the mission and quit your damned bitching."

Ben had been in the Armed Services long enough to know that some griping was the norm and even healthy, but he couldn't let a direct challenge to him and General Adair go unchecked.

The verbal reprimand worked. While hanging above the attack locale, O'Banyon accepted the admonishment and put aside his frustrations. After all he was a soldier and mission success was paramount. He fastidiously demanded that each commando, as well as Dr. Andrew, recite his responsibilities one last time. Upon that final review of their plans, he was satisfied that they were as well prepared as time allowed.

O'Banyon's boys had performed the impossible more than once. Ben had learned from Adair that the list of their accomplishments was impressive. Working with the Israeli Secret Service during the War on Terrorism, they had stolen deep into Iraq and pinpointed Saddam Hussein's location. To this day, the tactics they used to accomplish that feat remained classified.

Ben marveled that here he hung in a copter with a bunch of rough, tough commandos. Not the company he had in mind even two days ago. What had happened to his once peaceful life? Risking his health and possibly his life day after day after day, wasn't his idea of fun. But this raid must bring back crucial evidence and he was here to make sure that it did.

The Comanche copilot alerted the team that the target train, advancing from the east, was now three minutes from its turn onto the stretch of siding paralleling the main track. Its detour to the siding would allow an eastbound express to pass at full speed on the mainline, while the westbound slowed its pace on the sidetrack. The team's operational plan relied heavily upon the train slowing considerably while on the siding. The targets precise speed depended upon the location and speed of the eastbound express. The range of possibilities meant that they could count on no more than thirty minutes to achieve their mission.

O'Banyon verified one last time with the pilot that his objective was to land on the third train car from the rear. That car trailed just behind the four boxcars loaded so carefully many days ago by Lt. Turar Ryskulov. O'Banyon's team would concentrate their attack on the last of those four boxcars.

Stockton had briefed Ben and O'Banyon that Kruschev's intelligence revealed that two Mafia guards protected each uranium-bearing car. Kruschev was unsure whether more guards were stationed elsewhere on the train, but advised that it would be wise to assume that there were more.

"The Mafia bad boys are in for a little surprise. They would piss their pants if they knew what was about to hit them," O'Banyon chortled with genuine confidence.

The copter abruptly broke out of its holding pattern and swooped down behind the slowing train. It dropped so rapidly Ben's stomach turned and his ears popped.

Closing swiftly and silently, the pilot maneuvered directly over the car trailing the last uranium-bearing boxcar. With the aid of the helicopter's computerized controls, the crew maintained a fixed height over the car as a lone black-clad figure, O'Banyon, rappelled to the roof.

Once he had unsnapped his harness, the Comanche pulled up and away into a following pattern. It hovered about one-thousand feet above and an eighth of a mile behind the westbound target.

Ben apprehensively checked his watch. This first stealthy evolution had taken about two minutes. Twenty-eight minutes left.

Ben and the rest of the Special Forces personnel, wearing blackened faces and black-night combat suits, waited aboard the copter. They were each fitted with advanced night-vision gear and communication headgear. The soldiers carried fully automatic weapons.

Captain O'Banyon's weapon, which had been strapped tightly to his side until he landed on the swaying train car roof, was now gripped in a ready position. Crouching to maintain his balance, O'Banyon scanned the car tops for anyone lurking there. Through his night-vision goggles, the soldier's cold gray eyes pierced the darkness. Nothing unexpected appeared. He checked his gear bag, all was in place and the way appeared clear.

The poorly maintained siding magnified the swaying motion of the cars. The muscular commando was forced to brace his feet against any deformity in the roof to avoid being pitched over the side.

Finally, as the train slowed, the swaying subsided somewhat, allowing him to regain his balance. He advanced along the top of the car until faced with the gap between cars. Beyond the eight-foot space, the uranium-filled boxcar rocked and rattled directly ahead of him.

O'Banyon easily hurdled the receding emptiness and landed cat-like with his legs slightly flexed. Still he was upright with weapon ready and eyes searching. His high-friction footgear gave him the traction he desperately needed.

After carefully scanning the scene, he determined that he was still alone. He dropped his gear bag to the rocking roof. From the satchel he pulled a laser drill, which he adroitly applied to the next task. The red light sliced through the blackness of the night and silently bored through the rail car roof, creating a half-inch-diameter hole.

He pulled a special mask from his gear bag and fit it over his head and helmet. It provided filtered air protecting him from stray vapors of the powerful knockout agent which he was about to discharge into the boxcar. He forced a tube, connected to a pressurized gas cylinder, into the newly drilled hole.

With the push of a button the high-pressure gas, a sleep-inducing drug mixed with a disorientation chemical, began diffusing into the boxcar. This super-concentrated toxin would quickly knock out the unsuspecting guards. Upon their awakening, they would be confused and unaware that time had passed. Through his headset, O'Banyon instructed the hovering Comanche to return to the train.

Hearing O'Banyon's order, Ben nervously glanced again at his watch. Six minutes had elapsed. Twenty-four minutes left. So far they were on schedule, but the tough part lay ahead of them.

As the Comanche again quietly maneuvered into position, this time directly above the last boxcar, the remaining commandos and Ben rappelled onto the roof. First came the black-clad soldiers. They took up their defensive positions on the rail car roof, immediately adapting themselves to the train's rocking motion. Lastly, Ben, weighted down with specialized gear for the job ahead, dropped onto the roof. His extensive rock climbing experience kept him from becoming totally petrified; however, hanging from a helicopter above a moving train full of gun-toting guards was not his idea of a good time.

In an attempt to hide his nervousness from these battle-hardened commandos, Ben willed his hands not to shake. The hard landing on the roof reminded him that his right foot was still tender from the skirmish in Rock Creek Park. He could have fallen and ruined the mission. Betraying his skittishness, he fumbled clumsily with his bulky gear.

Having dispatched its payload, the stealthy bird again withdrew into a holding pattern above and behind the slowed train. To watch for any surprise intervention, the copilot trained infrared cameras on the passenger cars.

Ben and the four commandos had just recovered from the wash of the withdrawing copter when the wake of the on-rushing express whipped them again. As the violent currents hit, Ben feared that he was going to be swept over the side. Only the abatement of the wind saved him.

While Ben was fighting to stay upright, O'Banyon rappelled over the side of the boxcar. Once again he employed the portable laser-cutting torch. He cut a hairline fissure through the lock on the boxcar door. Simultaneously, two of the team attached a pulley rig from the rear of the car to the now unlocked side door. With the mechanical advantage of the rig, the two forced the bulky door open. Their team-mate, Staff Sgt. Paul Schwatka, remained alertly on watch with weapon ready.

O'Banyon beckoned for Ben to lower himself and his weighty gear over the side. Ben's refresher rappelling training just the day before proved sufficient.

The soldiers were unaware that opening the boxcar door triggered an alarm in the rear passenger car. The flashing signal, announcing that car *vier's* door was ajar, was received by the Mafia guards with minimal concern since the unreliable system had falsely alarmed several times. Only one gunman was sent to the roof on what the guards assumed was a routine check.

Before entering the uranium car's toxic atmosphere, O'Banyon and Ben replaced their night vision equipment with gear similar to a miner's hat. This headgear was familiar to O'Banyon as a specialized adaptation of the Afghan cave outfits. With weapon ready, O'Banyon swung into the boxcar with Ben right behind. Protected from the gas by their M40 masks, the pair surveyed the room. Their carbide lamps, a part of their headgear, flashed bright yellow beams that cut through the haze in the musty, dimly lit boxcar.

A rapid, yet thorough perusal of the boxcar suggested to O'Banyon that with the guards sprawled unconscious on the floor all was apparently secure. He stepped over several empty Vodka bottles on his way to the prone guards. Upon checking each man's pulse, O'Banyon was reassured that the mercenaries were out for the count and silently mused at the amount of liquor consumed by the two. He believed that he could safely continue his job, but the undetected, tiny wire leading away from the doorframe signaled otherwise.

Ben picked out one of the uranium cylinders in the car for sampling. The hulking container, about eight feet tall and five feet in diameter weighed several tons and was much too massive for the two of them to budge. The uranium in these cylinders was a white powdery substance, much like a pasty flour except far heavier.

Ben checked the time. Twelve minutes down. Eighteen to go. They were now behind schedule by two minutes. He realized that if they didn't complete their mission before the train regained speed, their chances of getting off safely diminished greatly.

Dismissing that concern, Ben busily assembled his specialized sampling equipment as O'Banyon returned from checking the guards.

Just then they heard a sharp warning from the Comanche pilots, followed immediately by a faint burst of automatic weapons fire.

Through his headset, O'Banyon hissed, "What the hell is going on up there?"

Sgt. Schwatka calmly replied, "Bad guy number one, now dead guy number one. He showed up looking for trouble. He found it."

This did nothing for O'Banyon's confidence, and even less for Ben's. Now they had another issue. Were there other guards in those last cars? Had they heard the shots? Was this car wired for security? How long until the other guards missed their dead companion. O'Banyon realized that time was shorter than ever. He warned, "Be alert for more damned guards."

He motioned for Ben to ignore the gunfire and keep working.

Using one of the guard's chairs, Captain O'Banyon scrambled to the top of the chosen cylinder and again employed his laser-torch to slice a half-inch diameter hole in the top of the oversized barrel.

Ben, struggling with his heavy gear, clambered up after him. He attached a device, which appeared like a portable drill press, over the hole. He configured it to bore diagonally through the cylinder contents, and to extract a core sample of the white-powdery uranium hexafluoride. This process was similar to test drilling in a promising mining district where core samples were taken, but this of course, was on a much smaller scale. This miniature drilling employed ultrasound combined with hollow-tube boring to penetrate the cylinder and extract the sample.

After five minutes of drilling, extracting and storing, Ben, with a heavy load of uranium safely tucked in canisters in his backpack, yelled to O'Banyon, "I got the sample. Let's put things back together!"

"Right on, Ben. We are okay on time. Do the job right."

Ben had explained to O'Banyon that both IAEA and plant personnel would inspect the cylinders upon their arrival in Munich. Ben, as well as O'Banyon's superiors, had stressed the absolute necessity of leaving no evidence behind. Ben inserted segment after segment of natural uranium, which he had brought with him, into the hole he had just created. This extra effort to cover-up their intrusion pressed the thirty-minute window to the limit. Ben's watch revealed that twenty-four minutes had now elapsed. Three minutes behind schedule.

O'Banyon heard two more muffled bursts of gunfire. "Shit. More trouble up there?"

"Two more very dead bad guys, boss. It's okay. Things are under control," Schwatka assured O'Banyon.

Captain O'Banyon knew that with the early passage of the east-bound express that their train would soon be gathering speed. They had to keep moving. O'Banyon employed his laser to weld the circular piece of metal, which he had earlier removed, back into place.

Ben repacked his tools and secured the confiscated uranium in his bags. He then used a portable vac to pick up all of the very dense traces of uranium powder that had spilled. Next he scanned the box-car with a radiation detector to assure that all was clean.

Ben felt the train accelerating as it gathered speed. He swung out of the boxcar door on the ropes still strung from the roof. The heavy bag of stolen uranium dangled over his shoulder.

Staff Sgt. Schwatka grabbed the tense civilian's hand as he scrambled to the car top. The copter was back in position directly overhead with its lines dangling. Breathing heavily, Ben snapped onto one of the Comanche's lines and fastened his bag of uranium and tools to the other.

While Ben and his precious samples were retrieved by the Comanche crew, two commandos pulled the boxcar door closed. Schwatka tensely crouched on the roof, poised to take out any more hostile interference.

As the boxcar door slid into position, O'Banyon, still hanging over the side of the car, noticed the electrical contact. "Damn! I should have spotted that on the way in. That is what had the guards coming at us." Shaking off his disgust, he performed one last job. While two more of the squad ascended into the copter, he welded the cut lock back together.

Seeing that the Comanche still maintained its close overhead recovery position, O'Banyon clambered up the rope toward the roof. The wind from the copter blades and the accelerating train tore at him as he inched upward.

Once he regained the roof, he motioned to Schwatka to board the copter. The Sergeant promptly shouldered his weapon and snapped onto the Comanche's line.

Leaning against the buffeting gusts, O'Banyon gathered his gear and scanned for anything that might have been inadvertently left behind. He coiled up the remaining ropes and flung them over his shoulder. He fought to stand against the stiff wind stirred by the gathering speed of the train. A more rapid and willful swaying developed as the accelerating train curved back onto the mainline.

The car roof lurched and O'Banyon found himself sliding helpless-ly. Slipping over the edge, he frantically grabbed for a handrail. The ropes, which he had just gathered, slipped from his shoulder to the track bed below. Desperately clutching the handrail, he hung precariously over the side. The swaying train repeatedly banged him like a rag doll against the car's metal side.

The copter maneuvered lower, dangling a lifeline near the suspended soldier.

With a bold lunge he caught the whipping line. Holding on with one hand he snapped his extraction harness to the retrieval cable. He pushed away from the train and relaxed, letting the Comanche and its winch do the work. The copter pulled up and away from the train with the black-clad O'Banyon dangling by his harness from the end of the line.

From above Ben watched O'Banyon's escape. The man was tougher than anyone he had ever run into, that was for sure. Akin to a nighthawk with a fresh catch of small game in its talons, the Comanche rose away from the now vacant siding, vacant except for three strewn corpses and a few coils of rope. The whining onboard winch lifted O'Banyon safely into the mother ship's personnel hatch. Ben looked at his watch. Elapsed time for the mission was thirty-three minutes.

"Well, Dr. Andrew, we did it," O'Banyon celebrated. "It was a little messy, but you have your precious uranium." In his estimation, this civilian had performed well.

"Yep! Just another day at the office, eh," Ben cracked with a far more authentic nonchalance than he had felt a half-hour ago.

Schwatka briefed O'Banyon on the shootings, "My guess is that a signal from the boxcar alerted the Mafia guards."

O'Banyon disgustedly spat, "That is it exactly. I saw the damn contact on the way out. I must be slipping. I sure as hell missed it going in."

Sgt. Schwatka observed, "If this great Comanche crew hadn't warned us, it might be one of us ripening down there."

The thought forced O'Banyon to grimace. Despite his many dangerous missions, he took great pleasure in his record of losing very few men.

He ordered the copilot, "Call in the backup team. They are to commence recovery of the lost rope and the bodies. All evidence must permanently disappear."

Ben reviewed where things stood. Later in Munich three guards would be discovered missing. That unfortunately would create a real stir and many questions, especially if Andropov took an active interest in the incident. The guards in the three forward boxcars, though, probably hadn't heard the gunfire of the guards, nor the Special Forces suppressed response. The two-drugged guards, once they recovered, would be too confused to remember their names. So only three shreds of evidence remained—the weakened top of one cylinder, which undoubtedly would blow when heated, a tiny hole in the boxcar roof and three permanently AWOL guards.

At the sprawling Ramstein Air Force Base, Ben and the cored sample of uranium were hurriedly transferred to an awaiting Aurora. The secret supersonic jet would fly them directly to Langley Air Force Base in Virginia. From there the uranium would be coptered to the FBI Radiation Laboratories, and Ben would be coptered back to the FBI building in D.C. Ben estimated that in about four hours the FBI would be performing their analysis on the sample. Foster would soon have his one hundred percent.

TWENTY-NINE

Day 28 7 A.M. Zermatt, Switzerland

"Boris, I don't bring good news. Your trusted head of the Russian Division is a *predatel.*"

Boris Andropov listened in disbelief to the scar-faced Bupkov, who told of a traitor in their midst. Bupkov reigned as czar of the Thieves-in-Law, originally a collection of predominately white-collar thieves. Andropov and Bupkov had transformed the Thieves-in-Law into the brains, as well as, the muscle behind Andropov's criminal machine. This tightly knit gang of former Soviet prisoners, hardened by years of brutal treatment, had emerged as the formidable oversight and enforcement arm of the Mafia Empire. These clever, but ruthless men served as personal guards, carried out occasional high priority hits and conducted independent financial exams of Andropov's far-flung organization. With their essential help, Andropov garnered an independent scrutiny of his top Mafia chieftains.

"What has Kostenko done? Is it the plutonium?"

Years ago, Andropov had picked Alexi Kostenko to head the Mafia's Russian Division. But lately, Andropov had grown curious about Kostenko's lack of results in diverting plutonium. Yet his performance, otherwise, was exemplary.

"Alexi reports lies. He stole ten kilos of weapons-grade plut. His men have it for sale on the black market for ninety million dollars."

"I see," came the stolid response, although anger flashed from Andropov's eyes.

As the governor of Chelyabinsk, Kostenko was an influential leader in the Russian *Duma*. In addition, he ran an extensive network of trading companies that were Mafia-related business enterprises headquartered in the southern Ural Mountains. He also owned a large fleet of container ships and the largest chain of "Sports Centers" in Russia. Once truly sports centers, they now were actually training centers for Mafia thugs.

Bupkov, who had been mulling over Kostenko's apparent double-cross for a while, posed a solution. "I recommend we set up a counter-sting. My agents pose as terrorists, buy the plutonium, then kill Alexi and his henchmen."

Andropov, although enraged by the apparent traitorous behavior of Kostenko, cautioned Bupkov, "Wait. Let's not implement that plan yet. We will give Alexi a chance to amend his story. If he continues to hold out on us..."

Bupkov's scowl darkened. "We will wait as you say, but he isn't altering his lies. We must retire him forever."

"We shall see tonight."

"Next problem is also in the Russian region. It is equally unsettling. Vasilly Kruschev, FSB Chief, is falling in line with the politics of the Russian President. Both of the traitorous leaders are endeavoring to fight what they perceive as our organization's drain on the country's economy. Kruschev is systematically isolating and winnowing out our most useful FSB agents. He is a strange animal. We are not even sure he is truly a Chekist. No one knows what he is."

Andropov, upon receiving this additional negative news from Bupkov, reacted more forcefully. "Maybe Strahkov and Kruschev should depart this earth just as did Starovoitova. Doing in Starovoitova shaped up the spineless politicians for a few years. Perhaps they need a refresher as to who really runs the country."

"Don't forget, Boris, we operate in Russia only as long as the public tolerates us. Executing those two popular leaders could arouse the masses."

Bupkov understood that a judicious application of violence created the desired intimidation, whereas too much could have the opposite effect creating more resistance against Mafia dealings.

"The public's tolerance of us is showing signs of weakening," Bupkov continued. "Many conclude that we are robbing the country's wealth. Not even fear of murder cowers them as it once did. They sense they have nothing to lose. If we were facing a politically active Sumurov or Solzhenitsyn right now we would be in deep trouble."

"Fortunately they are dead! What is the solution to our public relations problem?" questioned a disturbed Andropov. This was almost too much bad news. At times he wondered if there was some hidden force aligned against his Mafia?

"Do nothing to upset the masses! There is still much blame to go around; the Communists for creating the pitiful mess, the present government for not fixing anything, and the Americans for being so fickle. It's best to leave blame at these culprits' feet, and do little to force the Mafia higher on that list."

"Agreed. We will not take out the traitors, Strahkov and Kruschev, yet," asserted Andropov. He wasn't in total agreement with this position, but felt it expedient to agree with his trusted associate for the moment, just to allow the conversation to continue.

"Another troublesome matter. Our Munich people suspect monkey business on the latest Kazakh uranium shipment. More investigation is required. Your European branch chief should report on that matter tonight."

"Move on!" ordered an exasperated Andropov, now almost certain someone was working against them. He had better figure out who and figure it out quickly.

Bupkov complied by reporting, "General Zarif says that the cruise and the big nuke are ready to be deployed against your 'sworn enemy' just as you and he agreed."

"Very good! Finally some good news." Andropov felt pressured. He couldn't afford to waste a minute to exact his retribution against America.

Bupkov did not totally understand the Zarif message, but he had a bad feeling about what it might mean.

Day 28 10:30 A.M. Room Below Andropov's Suite

The two FBI agents, posing as young lovers on a ski weekend, dismantled and packed up their recording devices. With their ultra-sensitive eavesdropping gear, they had just recorded the entire discussion between Bupkov and Andropov. Now they must slip safely past Bupkov's guards. They were prepared to make a dash for Paris and then transmit the entire recording to D.C. Garrison should have their "mother load" of scoop soon.

Day 28 2:30 P.M. Zermatt

The bright red Pratt and Whitney-powered EC-135 Eurocopter, piloted by two employees of R.M. Holding Corporation, rose from the alpine valley floor with Andropov and his contingent of guards on board. The throbbing noise, sudden motion and localized snowstorm created by the rotor wash of the ascending copter caused a sleigh-pulling horse to rear with fright. The equine bolted down the valley with its driver struggling to regain control.

Pointing down at the chaotic scene, Andropov contemptuously snorted to one of Bupkov's men, "That is undisciplined capitalist horse! A Soviet communist horse would never bolt like that."

Because Andropov was every bit a dictator, the guard, despite thinking the comment represented a simplistic and out-dated view of the world, nodded in apparent agreement.

As the helicopter, red in honor of Andropov's beloved party, soared higher, the semicircle of peaks to the south and the peaceful Alpine valley and quaint village below unfolded into a breath-taking panorama. The route to the next meeting was straight north through some of Switzerland's most rugged and scenic landscapes. The stunning vistas, however, could not distract Andropov from his mounting headaches.

Bupkov, normally a pillar of strength, had never before delivered so much bad news. Andropov struggled to make sense of it all: Kostenko's cheating on the plutonium, Kruschev's trying to remove Mafia influence from the FSB, and the public's increasing resistance against the Mafia. He didn't believe in chance or fate. Instead some unknown force must have intervened behind the scenes. These burgeoning difficulties, he believed, were a manifestation of that clandestine intervention.

Day 28 3:50 P.M. Swiss Alps

While the copter flew north at a constant elevation, the Zermatt valley floor fell away. Later the red bird turned into the Lotscheptal valley which led farther north, into the heart of Switzerland's mountain grandeur. The Lotscheptal valley gradually rose to meet the speeding copter, forcing the bird to climb steadily until reaching a lofty ten thousand feet. The craft, dwarfed by the surrounding spires, slipped through the pass between Breithorn and Grosshorn Mountains and then skirted alongside the escarpment, comprising the spectacular mountain range dominated by the bold Jungfrau.

Rousing from his troubled thoughts, Andropov spotted a team of climbers, with a great deal of equipment, encamped on the Jungfrau's steep sides. That struck him as odd, since the usual high risk of such midwinter climbs was worsened by recent heavy snows.

"Those climbers are nuts. Even the noise and rotor wash from our copter could trigger a slide there," observed the pilot.

For that reason he maneuvered farther away and turned west for the journey's final miles. They closed in on one of the world's most formidable structures.

Perched high atop Schilthorn Mountain, with its sheer cliffs diving several thousand feet on all sides, was an imposing stone building. Only two approaches were feasible to reach the Schilthorn summit, aerial tram or high-performance copter. The Pratt & Whitney engines, near their design limits, labored in the rarefied atmosphere to lift the Mafia contingent onto the gray-stone roof of the mountaintop resort.

Andropov anticipated that this gathering of his chief mobster lieutenants would most likely run through the night. Only his Mafia kingpins, most trusted guards and a few carefully screened employees of the facility inhabited the remote mountaintop location during this annual gathering. The remoteness made it simpler to accomplish total security.

CHAPTER
THIRTY

Day 28 5:10 P.M. Schilthorn Mountain Switzerland

Stepping from the copter into the rarefied air, Andropov, as was his habit, headed straight for the lookout platform on the northeast corner. From past meetings here, he was familiar with the unparalleled mountain vistas from this elevated terrace. Telescopes were located at the four corners of the roof, providing close-ups of the remarkable panorama of surrounding Alpine grandeur. To his disgust, his favorite view was not available. The telescope facing the Jungfrau was not functioning and a sign hanging on the out-of-order scope read *"detraque."* A flaw like this was intolerable. Greatly frustrated, he snarled to the nearest guard, "Find a mechanic and get this damned thing fixed."

He went below, not in the best of moods. Upon entering the conference hall he met his Mafia leaders. All were in attendance, except one. Filling in for the CIS Division head, was Hamad Barak, the Kazakh Border Guard Commander. Andropov warmly greeted Barak, one of his earliest associates. He then moved on to shake hands with the brilliant, but pudgy, Ray Goldstein. Andropov mysteriously whispered to the head of the Mafia's North American white-collar criminal enterprise, "Are you ready for the grand finale?"

Goldstein responded, "Nearly."

Andropov greeted his fellow Russian, Alexi Kostenko, with a hug followed by a peck on each cheek. He followed the obligatory greeting with a long piercing look straight into the man's soul. Kostenko's bearing, however, betrayed nothing.

He confronted a nervous and fidgety Brent Lepke, head of the mobster element of North America. Lepke was uncharacteristically ill-at-ease and avoided direct eye contact.

228

The stern, stone-faced Helmut Meyer, head of the European Branch of the Mafia and Ivan Bupkov, chief of the Thieves-in-Law, received brief acknowledgments. Standing near the door were three expressionless guards who worked for Bupkov.

After the generally brusque greetings to each leader, Andropov took command. "I presume you have all had dinner, so let's begin. Herr Meyer, we will hear from you first."

The gruff German mobster wasted no time with preamble. "Mysteriously, three guards from the last uranium shipment to Munich turned up missing. Speculation abounds that they fell from the train while reacting to a false alarm signal, but their bodies have not turned up. The Munich security officers investigating this incident believe that they may have been shot by unknown assailants. Their theory relies heavily upon reports of passengers who swear they heard shots. All possibilities are being considered, but so far there appears to be nothing missing and we found no evidence of tampering with the uranium. The guards in each boxcar swear no intrusion occurred and they heard nothing."

Bupkov suggested, "Our sources at the German military bases could help. If NATO's military was somehow involved, we will learn of it."

"Check that possibility out, Bupkov. Helmut, continue to investigate. There must be more to this. Leave nothing to chance," ordered Andropov.

A detailed discussion of the European operations extended for an additional hour. Andropov, quite satisfied with Meyer's report, suggested no major changes in direction. It squared closely with Bupkov's previous independent account. His European "criminal take" had been laundered through R.M. Holding Corporation. It showed up within R.M. as about five billion dollars of additional profits in Deutsche Erstes Bank and R.M.'s investment holdings.

Andropov dismissed Meyer, "Excellent! Please accept this gift for a job well done." One of the guards escorted the European leader with his million Euro check to the tram.

Commander Hamad Barak, chain-smoking his Marlboros, was next. Barak's presence at this summit was rare, which was fine with him. He had intently sized-up each of the mobsters. He disliked them and respected, perhaps feared, only one, Bupkov. The man was clever and tough. What Hamad had done, he had done for the guard and for Kazakhstan. He did not consider himself truly a part of the Mafia team. If the head of the Mafia in the non-Russian CIS republics wasn't absorbed with oil deals in the Caspian, Barak wouldn't have to be here.

Of great curiosity to Andropov was Barak's account of the suspected FSB spy, whom Barak had caught observing the loading of uranium at the Caspian Seaport. Barak curtly reported, "I summarily disposed of the irritant. More and more FSB agents are snooping around our uranium operations. My most trusted lieutenant suspects their spies are using the nearby oil-drilling operations to reconnoiter. I have ordered him to stop them. There will be a fire at that oil rig very soon."

Barak, admired by Andropov despite his irritating smoking addiction, was enthusiastically congratulated. "Your keeping the lid on the nuclear smuggling over the years has been a remarkable achievement. That feat is more important than you will ever know." He made a big show of providing Barak with a bonus check for two million U.S. dollars, saying, "Such superior performance by you deserves the largest bonus."

Barak was excused from the meeting and escorted to the tram. He had a strange sense that Andropov had become less stable. It was subtle but it was there. Something big was brewing in that guy's brilliant but misguided mind. He suspected that all of them would be profoundly impacted by whatever Andropov had in the works. Lighting a Marlboro, he pondered why he felt that way. Perhaps it was the body language. Andropov exhibited an unusual impatience, yet an almost euphoric arrogance of accomplishment. He had seen great athletes behave that way before a major competition. A competition for which they had trained and prepared long and hard, but feared that the unexpected would upset their big moment.

As the hour approached midnight, Andropov ordered coffee and torts served. At this pace the meeting would definitely continue throughout the night. The German menu wasn't difficult to decipher, but something about the language unsettled him. The sign on the telescope flew through his consciousness, but the image was fleeting. Maybe his angst was prompted by Bupkov's earlier gluttony of bad news. The looming showdown with Kostenko, yet to unfold tonight, surely contributed to his apprehensions.

Next on the agenda was the nervous Brent Lepke. Lepke's notes trembled slightly in his hands and his wavering voice lacked its usual force. Most of Lepke's report was positive, showing results on various enforcement and bribery efforts. He didn't, however, mention anything about the hit on Dr. Andrew.

Toward the end of Lepke's report, Andropov finally inquired, "How did it go with the Dr. Andrew job?" Seeing Lepke's face drain of color, he knew he had hit pay dirt. So this was why Lepke was so nervous.

Lepke reluctantly admitted, "We attempted the Bulgarian dissident treatment, but failed. Two of our men are dead and one is severely wounded and in FBI custody."

"Incredible!" Andropov thundered. "You incompetent ass! You dare to tell me that three of your hit men couldn't handle one worthless executive. Your men have lost it. You could not have screwed up worse."

Facing down Lepke, he demanded, "Tell me. How big a problem do we have with the idiot they captured? How much does he know?"

"He won't talk. He will tell them nothing."

"You fool! You don't know that."

"His loyalty to the Organization is beyond reproach. He knows the code." Of course, Lepke referred to the well-known truth that any Mafia member who cooperated with the police forfeited his life.

Andropov didn't buy Lepke's assurance. He could not tolerate the risk that the man would succumb to police coercions. Things could unravel. Too much was at stake. "Lepke, your foul-up has ramifications far beyond letting the damned Andrew worm squirm off the hook. We eliminated over a dozen NuEnergy execs without raising any suspicions. Now the FBI captures one of your rubes in the act. They might accidentally put two and two together."

The calculating Goldstein bit his tongue. He could add considerable fuel to the fire with what he had recently learned was going on at the FBI building and at the White House, but he wanted to see how this played out first. Andropov's wrath could turn on him if he wasn't careful.

The squirming Lepke dug still a deeper hole. "About the only safe thing left to do is to have Dr. Andrew and his damned misguided sense of ethics permanently reassigned to NEI. Parris could arrange that. That would get him out of Black Bear."

A deep frown etched on Andropov's face, alerting all that he was displeased. "You cowardly weasel. I don't like it! Something is wrong here! Three of our men go down. That's inconceivable! Incompetence alone can't explain it. That Andrew fellow isn't Superman in disguise, is he?"

Turning to his most trusted enforcer, he ordered, "Ivan, investigate this. Use all of our resources. Pick your moment, but terminate the prisoner's employment with us."

Lepke nervously tried to counter, "But that will hurt my organization's morale."

Andropov exploded, "Piss on morale! I demand performance! Your little losers failed miserably in this simple exercise. Your demotion is inevitable."

He then motioned to one of the guards and wheeled back squarely into Lepke's face, "Lepke, you have one year to turn your performance around. You will receive nothing. It is time for you to leave." With a sense of finality he shoved Lepke toward the door and the approaching guard.

For added emphasis, he tore Lepke's check into pieces in front of the dwindling group.

As soon as Lepke was out, Andropov sternly ordered, "Ivan, start a search for a replacement. We can't wait a year for that incompetent's demotion."

Only Alexi Kostenko and Ray Goldstein remained to be dealt with by Andropov.

Goldstein had plenty of dynamite information pertinent to the Andrew problem, but he had wisely let the previous scene play out and Lepke take all of the fire before revealing his new intelligence.

"Boris, there is more on the Andrew subject. Our sources have found that he is working with the FBI, the NRC and the vice president on something involving NuEnergy. They are onto something about the plants."

"For God's sake, is this a week for shitty news or what? What do you think the meddling doctor and his Washington comrades are up to, Goldstein?"

"Maybe it's the sabotage of the last fifteen plants that's got their suspicions up. At least that is what I surmise based on our insider's report on their FBI computer usage."

Andropov discerned that several seemingly independent events might tie together.

"This Andrew character was a complete asshole at the Munich plant. The security force there is convinced he smuggled out a tape recording of our fake section. Now that scene starts to make sense. He could have been put up to it by the vice president. After Dr. Pain-in-the-Butt was there, the vice president asked the German government for the plant's power history. All of that says they are getting close to uncovering our uranium smuggling scheme."

"Yes and maybe the three disappearing guards are somehow related to Andrew's antics," surmised Goldstein.

Andropov's thoughts flew far ahead of the conversation. His revenge timetable must be advanced. The vice president and his damned helper were getting too close for comfort. Promptness and surprise were the only aces he retained if his planned retribution was to succeed. A hit on Andrew wasn't optional anymore.

He whirled around to Bupkov, "Eliminate that festering sore from Black Bear. You pick how and when, but do it. No more mistakes."

After that ordered execution Andropov moved on to the next topic. "Alexi, let's review developments in your purview."

It was nearly three in the morning as Kostenko began his report. Andropov studied his mannerisms. They were not discernibly abnormal. He conceded that Kostenko was one cool customer, who was not about to reveal his reported plutonium theft.

Launching into a detailed rundown of the year's activities, Kostenko painted a mixed picture. He somewhat defensively reminded Andropov, "Much of our Division's operations has been 'legitimized.' The American and European international corporations have chosen to form joint ventures with R.M., rather than play a losing game of payoffs, kickbacks and murder."

Andropov knew full well that these new arrangements helped the American executives circumvent the U.S. Corrupt Practices Act. That act made it a crime for U.S. executives to offer payoffs with the intention of securing protection or favored treatment for their enterprises. In Russia alone, these joint ventures now produced $8 billion in net income annually for R.M. But this was none of Kostenko's business.

Andropov's annoyance with Kostenko was growing. The *Merzavetz* had strayed into areas that were not in his domain. He was sure that Kostenko was laying a foundation of excuses. For what? The plutonium caper? Well, he would find out soon enough. The cheating SOB would be permitted to sign his own death warrant.

"Alexi, you haven't mentioned any progress on plutonium. How is that project going?"

Kostenko's voice cracked ever so slightly, "We are a year behind our original plans. The workers at the MOX plant are now being paid on schedule. That makes bribery not so easy. German and French partners have installed oversights difficult for us to circumvent. We now plan to strike at the front end of the fuel fabrication process while weapons plutonium is still in the hands of the Russian military. Bribery still works well with those underpaid officers."

"So no success yet?"

"Nyet, but we remain optimistic."

Kostenko, with that very apparent and willful lie on the record, had unknowingly sealed his fate.

Andropov calmly changed the subject. "How are your efforts going to thwart the U.S.-Russian Uranium agreement?" He wanted to hear about this before Kostenko fell permanently silent.

"I have good news there. Our influence on the Russian negotiating team forced them to hold out for more advance payments, higher prices, and more rights to sell Russian natural uranium. The arrogant U.S. negotiators will never agree to all of that, so the deal is stalled."

"Part of your report is good. Your report in total, particularly in regards to plutonium, is deficient. You are dismissed without bonus."

As a grumbling Kostenko was escorted from the room by one of Bupkov's guards, he fumed to himself, "Fine, you arrogant son of a bitch. I will take care of my own bonus." The black market plutonium he figured would provide rewards far in excess of Andropov's lousy bonus.

After the traitor had left, Andropov calmly turned toward Bupkov, "Implement your sting. The jackal is no longer of value to us. He must pay for his lies."

Day 29 4:30 A.M. Schilthorn Mountain

As daylight approached, Boris Andropov was left with only Goldstein, Bupkov and one bodyguard. Boris told the guard to get some breakfast menus from the staff. As he looked over the Germanic menus, the earlier annoyance returned, the source of which eluded him. Oh well, he had much to cover with Goldstein.

Tackling the hearty breakfast of eggs, bratwurst and spicy potatoes, he gulped a mouthful of strong coffee, "First, how are we doing on the American end in stopping the Russian-U.S. uranium deal?"

"Good. Several years ago, I would have said excellent. Now, though, it's a little dicey."

"Clarify."

"Access to high governmental offices has become more difficult than it was in the nineties. We have only one reliable mole left inside the White House. Infiltrating this administration has proven difficult. On the positive side, though, Parris' old buddy, Vince Foley, has helped slow the legitimate uranium flow from Russia to the U.S."

"How?"

"Through a deliberately narrow interpretation of U.S. anti-dumping regulations."

"You weren't implying that our Uranium is not legitimate?" challenged Andropov.

Catching the tongue-in-cheek question, the wily Goldstein laughed, "Well, that is tough to answer."

"How locked in is Foley?"

"Completely. Besides money he receives our lovely Michelle's friendship," Goldstein replied.

"She is proving more valuable every day."

"For sure! That lady is a real talent. Tell Bupkov how you found her, Boris," suggested Goldstein. "It is an interesting story."

Andropov downed more of the tasty bratwursts and cleared his throat with another gulp of steaming coffee. He welcomed a brief break from the lengthy meeting.

"Ralph Parris knew her family. In fact, her father was a close friend of his. Mr. Michote was a devout Communist and a Soviet sympathizer who despised the U.S. He was a major leader in the Green-Peace protests and he steeped his stunningly beautiful daughter in his anti-U.S. philosophy. At the time I met the family, she had just won the Miss New Hampshire beauty contest. She advanced to the final round in the Miss America contest, but her talent as a dancer wasn't sufficient to edge out a piano-playing opponent. So even though she was undoubtedly the most beautiful girl in the contest, she didn't win. The runner-up scholarship, though, enabled her to attend Georgetown's law school. I kept in touch with her. Little by little I coaxed her into the Organization. She is a radical new-age environmentalist, who believes that the U.S., through its obscene wealth and disregard for the environment, perpetrates terrible harm upon mother earth. I played upon those beliefs, while gradually bringing her into our employ."

"Fortunately she is not as focused on all of the harm that was done to the environment by the Soviets, " snickered Bupkov.

After Bupkov's irreverent comment, the discerning Goldstein offered a possible explanation for Michelle's complete absorption in her role with the Mafia.

"She has a need to punish powerful men. Fortunately she doesn't see us as falling into that category. Conveniently, she sees U.S. officials and top Western business execs as the enemy. Perhaps she was a victim of childhood molestation by someone in authority? Who knows? Something is a little wacky with her, but it works for us.

"As you know, her close friend now is Dione Foster, the vice president's daughter."

"Yes. No doubt that can prove useful. You figure out a way to exploit that situation. Perhaps if nothing else, plant some ideas in the girl's head that she will carry back to her idiot father. Make sure Michelle is provided bonus pay this year. Can we get her in bed with the vice president? He is a widower, isn't he? Blackmailing him would be most satisfying."

"I already explored that with her. Poutingly, and with her ego quite crushed, she told me she was doubtful if that could be done. She says that he is totally consumed with his work. It quite upset her actually, because at a recent party given in honor of the vice president's daughter, she couldn't get to first base with him. She gets her kicks out of manipulating men. Running into the one in a million she can't twist around her little finger really deflates her."

"Wasn't she the one who set up Bumgardner?" asked Andropov.

Goldstein responded, "Yes and we probably should have used her to get rid of this Andrew problem instead of those three Lepke donkey dungs! One bit of trouble I haven't mentioned yet. The buffoon captured during the miserable Andrew hit is the one who polished off Bumgardner after he chickened out."

"Then it is more important than ever that he be eliminated," Andropov affirmed.

Bupkov nodded, indicating that he would take care of it.

After reinforcing his order to kill the captured thug, Andropov, with his curiosity aroused, turned his attention in another direction. "What are you doing to follow up on the Andrew-vice president connection?"

"So far, Michelle has been unable to pry anything useful out of Dione. Her wiles apparently don't work quite as well on women. We know that Vice President Foster quite suddenly was given an office in the West Wing. Our mole reports that General Adair, Central Intelligence Director Stockton, a CIA agent, and a young FBI bureau chief, visit the vice president's office frequently. Dr. Andrew has attended the last couple of those meetings."

"Could this activity of the vice president be tied to the Syria crisis? We hear the U.S. is stirring that up again, or is it tied to the NATO-Russia Friendship exercises? Or is it us they are after?"

"It could be any of those, or something just related to NuEnergy, like I mentioned earlier. It's conservative to assume, though, that it is us they are after. We will stay on it until we find out," assured Goldstein.

"Keep me closely advised," Andropov ordered. He wondered if this group collected by Foster was the hidden force responsible for all of the recent bad news. Yet, the U.S. government just wasn't that effective. It couldn't be them alone.

"Yes, sir. How times have changed. You know, in the nineties, at the cost of a mere fifty thousand dollar campaign contribution, I stayed at the White House and had coffee with the President. So far, though, we haven't been able to get close, let alone influence this President."

"Didn't our corporations contribute enough money to his party's campaigns? All it takes to own a U.S. politician, or a party for that matter, is money."

"Yes," replied Goldstein. "Several hundred thousand dollars. And I do have some slight progress to report. You have been invited to a White House dinner. The dinner, sixteen days from now, is for the biggest campaign contributors. You and several other major players are to be the honored guests of President Arthur."

"Good, maybe the new President can be seduced after all. I would take Princess Kristina, except that she is too much class for that citadel of capitalistic decadence."

"No, take her anyway," encouraged Goldstein. "She's a trump card. You know how the world went ga ga over the British princess, Diana. Kristina is starting to have that same effect on the world. Use her."

"Maybe now is the time, Ray, to share our little secret with Ivan," suggested Andropov.

Turning to Bupkov, with a rising crescendo, he revealed, "Ivan, I have one very special goal, which until now was known only by Ray and me. Revenge! Sweet revenge! Just and total hell will consume the U.S. imperialists. The Soviet infamy of the Cold War capitulation will be avenged. Retribution for the shamed Russian nation is only weeks away. Goldstein, you do have your sabotage of the nuclear plants arranged, don't you? It's time to send the world's only superpower into a tailspin leading straight to hell."

Bupkov was stunned. Had his boss gone mad? This had the ear-marks of an act of self-destruction. The Mafia wasn't powerful enough to take on the U.S. He maintained a shrewd, but skeptical, silence. In disbelief, he listened as the two discussed the destruction of the U.S. as though it were just another business deal. Then he recalled the message he had brought from Iran about the cruises and the bomb deployment. My God, was that part of this?

Meanwhile Goldstein was also reflecting for he knew that he had definitely reached a point of no return. He could no longer serve two masters. The decision was clear. He chose the mob over his former allegiance, an allegiance to a misguided Soviet martyr. He had his own reasons for supporting the attack on the U. S. and they were quite different from Andropov's. The day was coming when he would lead the Mafia. For the Mafia to strengthen he must weaken the one country powerful enough to stand up to it.

Andropov continued to lay out his strategy, a strategy that had Bupkov's head reeling with growing doubts about his boss.

"We have sold most of our smuggled uranium to the U.S. NuEnergy plants. We have enough left for only one or two more years. We will soon have new enrichment contracts with utilities in other countries. They will become the recipients of our remaining contra-band. Our poor long-term maintenance of the U.S. plants will start catching up with us anyway. In the years ahead, our profits from those plants would dwindle, if not totally evaporate. We must concentrate our future activities in the more lucrative and corruptible world markets of Europe and Asia. So the time is ripe to destroy the NuEnergy plants. In a few weeks, we will bring them all down."

Ivan Bupkov was about to ask why Boris would destroy his own plants, but then he remembered Boris and the Mafia didn't own them, the American utilities did. Goldstein, after evaluating Boris's ready-in-weeks edict, offered, "We can be ready in about one month."

Andropov, who fully intended a more rapid action, didn't want to pressure Goldstein any further this morning. He was about to ask Goldstein if he could also sabotage the five plants NuEnergy was attempting to take over. Before he could utter that thought, his eyes locked onto the sign above the door to the kitchen, which read *Kuche*. Suddenly his previous angst returned, rising to outright alarm. He emitted a roar, "Damn! That's it! Everything's in German up here except one thing."

He signaled for silence. He grabbed the remaining guard and Bupkov, and raced toward the observation deck. He motioned for the guard to tear the telescope, with the French "Out-of-Order" sign on it, from its mounting.

After a short struggle the guard succeeded. A miniature receiver/directional transmitter fell onto the deck.

Boris crushed the gear under his heal. In a fit of rage he kicked the offending pieces and the French-worded sign over the edge. The fragments rained down upon the rocks thousands of feet below. Now everything made sense, including the unlikely climbing party on the Jungfrau.

"Damn it! Someone was listening. Remember the climbers we saw on our flight here? They are fakes. Get the pilots and your guard and take care of the jackals."

Day 29 5:30 A.M. Jungfrau

The two FBI agents from the Paris branch office, posing as mountain climbers, had bivouacked halfway up the steep eastern face. They had climbed up to their perch two days ago and set up a mobile uplink station that encrypted and then relayed the Schilthorn-transmitter signal into space.

Earlier an agent, masquerading as the maintenance man, had planted the miniature spy gear in the telescope. He had trained the tiny transmitter onto the FBI's Jungfrau relay station. Not counting on Andropov's special interest in the scope, he had hung the French-worded sign declaring it *"detraque."*

The Jungfrau signal had been relayed to a secure U.S. communications satellite, which transmitted the information to the FBI offices where Liz and government interpreters had been intently listening for hours.

The agents operating the Jungfrau relay station had heard Andropov's exclamation of frustration, and then through their binoculars watched as the transmitter was discovered, destroyed and kicked over the cliff. Recognizing their immediate danger, they had hastily gathered their uplink gear together into their large backpacks and started scrambling down the treacherous snow-covered trail. The light snow, starting to fall, offered no refuge. It only made their footing on the precipitous mountainside more difficult. The extreme exertion at the high altitude caused the rapid beating of their hearts to boom louder and louder in their ears. Gradually, though, that internal pounding was drowned out by the rhythmic beating of the approaching red copter's propeller.

One agent hurried on while the other stopped and drew his pistol. The snow near the trapped agents spit up in powdery geysers of white as the automatic fire from the approaching helicopter barely missed its mark. The agent returned fire, wounding the guard doing the shooting. Suddenly a deafening roar, emanating from high above, drowned out all other sounds. The vibrations, induced by the copter and the gunfire, had tipped the precarious balance. Gravity at last won the tug-of-war. The mountains of white broke free and raced down the steep cliffs, straight toward the two doomed agents. Engulfing them and their equipment, the white fury swept the helpless men to the lower reaches of the mountain where tons of fine powdery snow settled, packed and piled over and around their bruised and broken bodies. A slow, cold suffocation cruelly and maddeningly snuffed out their lives.

The red angel of death turned back to Schilthorn. Bupkov, with his superficially wounded guard, picked up Goldstein and Andropov.

Andropov was fuming. Through clenched teeth he demanded, "Ray, have the plants ready in sixteen days!"

"Yes, sir."

Goldstein knew that the moment was at hand. If he played his cards correctly, he would soon be in charge of the Russian Mafia and, as a bonus, face a weakened U.S.A.

THIRTY-ONE

Day 28 One Hour Earlier FBI Building

This was the most eventful day by far for Ben's team. He thanked God for Liz. She and an FBI agent, both fluent in Russian and German, had been listening intently for hours, almost hypnotized by the drama of the Schilthorn meeting. She frequently made notes and occasionally alerted Ben or Garrison whenever the meeting demanded their full attention.

An FBI lab expert rushed into the SIOC with the report on the Kazakh uranium sample. Ben listened with tremendous satisfaction.

"Your theory that blended uranium is in the center of the Kazakh cylinders is right on target. Just like you predicted, it's exactly twelve percent."

"So the stolen uranium was right under our noses all along. It is the fuel for Black Bear and the other NuEnergy plants," mused Ben.

Ben sighed. In addition to this welcome confirmation of his theory about the stolen uranium, other, not so welcome, confirmations were coming fast and furious throughout the meeting of the Mafia kingpins. Andropov's plot to destroy the nuclear plants in one month, his hatred for and orders to kill Ben, Mafia intelligence on the vice president's team, the admission of their role in Fred Bumgardner's death, and Michelle Michote's key Mafia role were each, on their own, staggering revelations. A White House mole threatened the team's security and the mission's success. Ben wondered how near the vice president's inner circle the mole had penetrated.

Suddenly Liz jumped from her chair. "Listen! Something has gone wrong. Andropov just uttered a Russian 'Damn,' and something about everything is in German here, then there was silence."

A moment later they gasped as the signal from the Jungfrau relay station went dead.

An apprehensive Garrison jumped into action ordering Nieman, "Go to the White House, now. Tell the vice president what we learned here and that Ben and I will be ready to support a meeting by midnight. We will boil the tape of the Schilthorn meeting down to the highlights and dub over English translations. Tell him Ben's uranium sample verified his theory on Munich. Let him know that there have been security breaches and that I will cover that with him later. Don't forget to mention that the SOB Andropov is after the destruction of our nuclear plants.

"Ben, I must find out what has happened at Schilthorn. Can you and the others prepare a summary tape for the meeting? Cut it down to less than an hour of highlights."

"Sure. No problem as long as your multilingual agent helps me."

"He is yours along with anything else you need. I must call Paris."

"I pray your men over there are safe."

"I am afraid they need more than prayers."

Liz collected her notes and hurriedly left for the White House.

Garrison, now terribly concerned about his men, linked up to the FBI office in Paris. Also, extremely worried about security breaches, he put his most trusted assistant in charge of tracking down that aspect of the problem. Garrison warned the man, "Trust no one in FBI Computer Services. Rather, bring in a special security-cleared consultant on the pretense of auditing the Bureau's Computer Services. Find out how our group's computer activities are being monitored. If Director Lang sticks his nose in it, tell him that you are operating under my orders. If he wants to know anything, he can talk to me and I will tell him to take a hike."

While developing the tape, Ben brooded over the newly revealed plan to sabotage the plants. Wouldn't simultaneous sabotage of all of NuEnergy's plants result in a massive countrywide blackout? Worse it would trigger a major economic recession. He suspected that was Andropov's ultimate intention.

Day 29 12:20 A.M. White House

Ben entered the White House with his arms full of materials. The first two of Mark Foster's team meetings had been momentous enough. But Ben grasped that this gathering today was undoubtedly a point of no return. The course of world history would be impacted by decisions made by his country's leaders tonight. Underscoring the significance of the situation, he spotted President Arthur and the Secretaries of Defense and State already in Mark's office for the hastily convened late-night meeting. He easily recognized Secretaries Winston and Kohlmeier since he had often seen them on TV. He thought that they looked as nervous as cats cornered by a dog pack. Come to think of it, he was nervous too, except he was too busy to give in to emotions.

North saw Ben's bulky load and offered, "Let me take some of that, Ben. Go on in. The vice president wants you shown in immediately."

Ben observed that the usually flamboyant Stockton was even more hyper than normal, yet General Adair's demeanor was not detectably different. Ben's respect for both men continued to grow. He had no doubt that the general had the capabilities to formulate a successful strike, especially when there were tough solders like Sgt. Schwatka and Capt. O'Banyon around to do the heavy lifting.

Garrison had already informed Vice President Foster and the others of the tragic consequences of the drama on Jungfrau. First reports out of Switzerland were that two unidentified climbers, actually his agents, were presumed dead, buried hopelessly under mountains of snow. As the President and the nervous secretaries listened, a grieving Garrison finished recounting the Swiss disaster. Garrison had worked with both men closely in past assignments and was obviously greatly distressed over their loss. Their ultimate sacrifice, though, had revealed the Russian Mafia as never before.

Briefed earlier by Liz on the dramatic Schilthorn meeting, President Arthur recognized that he was in the proverbial hot seat. If he maintained too tight a security he would be criticized later; too little and he would blow any chances of surprise, and surprise was essential. If he acted too boldly he would be labeled a warmonger; too timidly and he would be branded weak. Was the security of the U.S. sufficiently threatened to justify the Joint Eagles military action or had the smoking gun not yet been discovered?

Foster began, "Let me express my deep appreciation for the great job each of you is doing. I couldn't have a more capable and dedicated group. Events are unfolding at a terrific pace. I believe that this meeting has such significance that I asked President Arthur, Secretary of Defense Winston and Secretary of State Kohlmeier to be here. They should enter into the decision process as we select a course of action. Not incidentally, we do have a quorum of the National Security Council."

President Arthur immediately clarified his role, "Even though I am here, I wish to make it clear that the vice president is in charge of this meeting. I, of course, retain final authority for any decision regarding military action."

"Thank you, Mr. President. So much is happening that I hardly know where to begin," admitted Foster.

"Maybe introductions are an appropriate start," suggested President Arthur.

"Good point. Dr. Ben Andrew, a utility executive and friend of mine from my Navy days, and FBI Agent Garrison have performed key roles in unraveling the mysterious conspiracy that now confronts us. The information they gleaned just today is, to put it mildly, staggering. Liz Neiman, CIA analyst on Russia, has proven invaluable. With expert CIA help, she's focused us on the Mafia leader's true intentions. A profile of Boris Andropov which bodes ill for the U.S. has emerged. That vile profile is about to be on full display."

The effervescent Secretary of State interrupted, "Oh come on, Mr. Vice President. You must be putting us on. Aren't you being somewhat melodramatic? Things can't be as serious as you let on."

"Secretary Kohlmeier, I assure you this is a deadly serious matter."

"Maybe, if it's that scary, I should have something to steady my nerves," said Secretary Kohlmeier somewhat sarcastically. She was suspicious of Foster's characterization of matters, since she had found him somewhat too hawkish for her liking.

Undeterred by Kohlmeier's comments, Foster resumed his stage-setting remarks, "First we will hear highlights, with an English translation dubbed in, from a recording our FBI just obtained. I am told that this is a revealing glimpse into the inner workings of the international Russian Mafia as their leaders gathered in a remote Swiss retreat to review their yearly progress and set new goals. Ben, roll the tape."

As Ben played the recording, the extent of the mob's criminal activities fell blow upon blow, battering all in Foster's office.

After the tape ended, Kohlmeier cracked the eerie silence, "Mr. Vice President, I never heard anything so damnable or threatening. We have a hell of a lot of work to do here tonight."

Foster acknowledged the accuracy of Kohlmeier's observations, and continued, "Thanks Ben for that summary. Now, back to the big picture."

Before Foster could finish his remarks, North, who had just left the room, burst in with one of Garrison's special agents. "Sorry to interrupt, Mr. Vice President, but more reports have just come out of Switzerland. Two FBI agents were able to record Bupkov and Andropov early yesterday morning. The transcripts just arrived. This agent will explain."

Garrison's assistant told how the recording had come about and summarized the new information. "Gleaned down to the essence, Andropov and Bupkov were discussing whether to do away with Kruschev and Strahkov. They also gloated over their murder of Starovoitova."

With that news Secretary Kohlmeier exploded, "So the SOBs actually admit killing that courageous lady. My God! They have no shame."

After Kohlmeier's emotional outburst, Garrison's assistant continued, "Bupkov also said something else that may or may not be important. Zarif sent a message through Bupkov that one of the biggest nukes and a cruise were being deployed against their sworn enemy."

Stockton frowned, "That doesn't square with our intelligence, but it does fit with their comments at Schilthorn. Something's dangerously amiss. The risk to our country is worsening."

From the profile of Andropov, Ben understood that his sworn enemy was the U.S. How could he deploy against the U.S.? Things were rapidly deteriorating. Coupling the bomb threat with the threat to the country's electrical system, the U.S. could be facing the worst terrorist strike in its history. Ben also sensed from the earlier conversation that the vice president would have his hands full with the feisty Secretary Kohlmeier if military solutions were proposed.

"Stockton, spare nothing. Find out what that deployment means. It must be one of the two strategic nuclear weapons you couldn't locate. Our military and police must be placed on full alert, but we can't raise our homeland security threat higher without blowing our secrecy."

President Arthur agreed, "Nothing would be gained and much would be lost by raising the level."

Foster was perplexed. Could he keep things focused? To his relief, President Arthur again came to the rescue.

The President effectively forced things back on track and dismissed Garrison's assistant. "Thanks for that update. I believe we must move forward with a coordinated plan to protect our nuclear plants, beef up security here and abroad, and prepare for military action to eliminate the nuclear threat posed by the Iranian and Mafia coalition. Those three objectives, Mr. Vice President, require prompt, covert, coordinated and decisive action. As we move forward, I have no doubt that we will have the full support of Strahkov and Kruschev, especially if they hear what we just heard."

"Thank you, Mr. President. Does anyone see our objectives differently?" questioned Foster. Grateful for the help, he paused, inviting other comments.

Secretary Kohlmeier boldly spoke up, "I protest what I perceive as a rush to a military solution. I just don't believe that diplomacy has been exhausted. Is covert military action the only solution still on the table? Our department suspects that General Zarif is a maverick, who doesn't fully represent the Iranian government."

As only he could, Stockton answered the challenge. "Madam Secretary, that government in Iran allows him to function freely. This threat presents an insidious danger to our country, far worse than the WTC attack and worse than even the Cuban missile crisis. At least in the Cuban crisis we had some idea where the missiles were.

"The information we heard tonight suggests that Boris Andropov, the Mafia head, could be after nothing less than the utter destruction of our country. Ben told us earlier what taking out thirty plants will do to this country. Any previous recession or even the Great Depression would be a picnic by comparison. I believe the course being laid out by the President and the vice president is the only one that adequately protects America. These enemies are depending upon us resorting to diplomacy and talk, Secretary Kohlmeier. Our society's openness and slowness to anger is what they so cleverly use against us."

Secretary Kohlmeier and Director Stockton had, in a few words, summed up both sides of the dilemma that the country faced. Openness played into the hands of the enemy. Yet secret military action stressed the very foundations of the American system of government.

Vice President Foster led into another matter, the role of Russia's leaders. "These new tapes give us confirmation on just how much the two men, Strahkov and Kruschev, can be trusted. They are quite literally locked in mortal combat with these criminals. Those two leaders have embarked on a most noble and, yet, personally dangerous crusade to break the Mafia's stranglehold on Russia. It's an understatement to say that their success is of great importance to us. We must not let the Mafia defeat them.

"Portions of this tape dealing with Andropov's intentions to rub out Kostenko offer us a unique opportunity to help Strahkov and

Kruschev in their battle. I propose that James fly to Russia with these tapes. If I were Kruschev, after hearing these, I would yank Alexi Kostenko in so he could hear how his Mafia boss has ordered him killed. Kruschev could tell him that if the Thieves-in-Law don't get him, his FSB security apparatus most assuredly will. Then Kruschev could point out that Kostenko's only chance of survival is to help. Kruschev could assure him that the FSB would do everything possible to protect him if he cooperates fully with Kruschev and Strahkov. Does anyone see that in a different light?"

"That's ingenious," Liz enthused. "I believe Kruschev would react just as you assume."

Ben interjected, "It is also important to get hold of that smuggled plutonium. We must get it off the black market before it winds up in more bombs aimed at us. Also, a new U.S. and Russian look at security at the Mixed-Oxide facility is mandatory. We can't allow a plutonium hemorrhage from that fouled-up place."

North smiled slyly. Ol' Ben was talking more and more like a Roustabout. He was gritty all right.

"Damned good points, Ben. Why don't you, Mr. Vice President, with Nieman listening, call Kruschev immediately after this meeting," the President suggested. "Tell him you are sending James with vital information for him and that as a quid pro quo, we want improvements in the security of their weapons-grade plutonium. James can state our position on the plutonium-safeguard points, just as we heard Ben do here."

Foster replied, "Yes sir, Mr. President. James, it looks like you are going to Moscow."

Enthusiastically, Stockton answered, "Mission accepted, sir."

General Adair cautioned, "Even with the element of surprise, we face an extremely complex military mission in Iran. Taking apart their nuclear facilities won't be easy. The extensive military buildup of that country over the last decade poses a grave challenge. This will be no picnic, no repeat of the Iraq wars or the War on Terror. We don't have the overwhelming strength advantage that we enjoyed then. Neither will we have the support of most other nations. The need for secrecy precludes even the attempt to gain such international support. It's only Russia, to a limited extent, and the U.S. in this one. There will certainly be far more casualties in this mission than in any U.S. military venture since Vietnam."

Ben spoke up, "Of course, the sooner we can place the nuclear plants under federal protection, the better. You all heard their plans to sabotage those plants and wreck our economy. If the Mafia were some-how alerted, we would run the risk of Andropov initiating the sabotage sooner, before we could act. That would spell disaster! So secrecy and promptness are vital in protecting the nuclear plants."

"Promptness and surprise are absolutely essential," agreed Vice President Foster.

Foster turned to General Adair, "One final time, when can you be ready?"

"The same date I gave you before, sixteen days from today."

"So the General's time frame governs here, is that correct?"

A silence, indicating agreement, followed.

"Then sixteen days from this evening, we will attack the Iranian nuclear base and simultaneously seize the NuEnergy plants in a coor-dinated action. Do you agree, Mr. President?"

"Yes. Take all steps to prepare for the attack and the plant takeover, but I will not give a final go ahead yet."

Ben figured that there was little chance of turning back. War had moved a step closer. He had a huge job ahead of him in planning a safe and stealthy takeover of the nuclear plants. He had only sixteen days to accomplish a minor miracle. The cold reality of what he faced sent a shiver down his spine.

Day 29 4:15 A.M. White House Oval Office

Secretary Kohlmeier was worried. War under her watch caused her to sense failure. Diplomacy was her preferred answer. Also, polit-ical astuteness prompted concern for her President's legacy.

Following Arthur back to the Oval Office, she lectured him, "Mr. President, I tell you this, you are running a serious political gamble that could cut short your career. It is easy to get in a war, but it is far tougher to avoid one or get out once things start. Congress will be furious with you."

"I know that, Madam Secretary. I have pondered the personal negatives, but it's better to gamble with my political career than the security of the nation. If there was a viable alternative I would take it, but I don't see one. Anything else exposes our country and our friends to unacceptable risk. My job is to protect our people."

Day 29 4:30 A.M. White House

After the others had left, each challenged with their respective tasks, Foster began a new subject with Garrison. "You heard what I heard, Brad. Do you still believe that Dione is safe at Stranahan near the poisonous Michelle? Should I pull her out of there?"

"I still would not advise that, Mr. Vice President. It might tip off the Mafia as to just how much we are on to them. My men are coordinating closely with the Secret Service. Your daughter will be kept safe. You can count on that. By keeping her there we reduce Mafia suspicion that we were the ones listening."

"It's your damn neck if anything happens to her. You do understand that, don't you?"

"Yes, sir!"

Garrison fully understood that his career would be history if anything happened to Dione, but he had confidence in her protection. Also he reasoned that a direct act by the Mafia against Dione would bring a spotlight on them that they didn't want right now.

"Can we do anything to throw them off track as to who was eavesdropping on them at Schilthorn," questioned Foster.

"We can try. I have a story, which we could float. It would state that Swiss officials have found two Russian thugs buried in the Jungfrau snow slide with some communications gear. That should create a little more dissension in the Mafia's hierarchy and take suspicion off of us."

"They are smart, Garrison. They will test other sources to confirm that account and try to find out for themselves the truth of the matter, so be careful. Don't outsmart yourself."

"That's where you could help, Mr. Vice President. We can use the fact that they are listening to your conversations with Dione. You could indicate in one of your talks with her that your job as vice president is turning out to be busy as hell with the Syrian situation heating up. She could say that she read this article on the discovery of Mafia bodies in Switzerland and you could say, oh, really, what are Italians doing there? Andropov believes that Americans are idiots anyway, so that might help verify his perception."

"So you want me to pose as an idiot? Do you think I can pull that off?"

A disconcerted expression came over Garrison's face. "I-I don't know how to answer that, Mr. Vice President," he stammered, realizing how thoroughly that he had trapped himself.

Foster enjoyed a rare laugh at Garrison's expense. Then he directed, "Let's move on." He intended to talk with Dione and let her know of the potential danger she was in. It would be her choice if she stayed with the firm, not his or Garrison's.

"Mr. Vice President, about the informant that Goldstein and Andropov talked about. Remember, they stated that there is a mole with access to the White House."

"Does that mean what I think it means?"

"I believe so. It means a security officer in or with access to the White House is on their payroll."

"What do we do about that?"

"I have a plan, but we need one person in the White House whom we know we can absolutely trust. He can't be a security officer. Who would you say fits that bill?"

Without hesitation Foster responded, "North!"

"Then invite him in. I have a truck-load for him to do."

Day 29 4:35 A.M. West Wing Hall White House

A dozen thoughts vied for priority in Liz's head. She should remind Garrison of the peril to their Mafia prisoner, and his value as a witness in the Bumgardner murder. Maybe the tape in which Andropov orders him killed could be used to convince the thug to cooperate with them. Perhaps he would talk more freely after hearing what his bosses have in store for him, but that strategy could also backfire by exposing the fact that they were the ones eavesdropping on Schilthorn. She shook her head. Things were getting dicey.

THIRTY-TWO

Day 31 7 A.M. Laura's Bookstore Tulsa

Laura was excited, because Ben had told her that today Liz was coming to visit her. Also, Laura had just heard some welcome news; Ben forecast that he should be home in a couple of weeks.

"Ben, I miss you. You have been gone too long. If you are not back here in two weeks, I am closing down this store and coming after you."

Ben laughed. "With all the people protecting you I should be able to spot the crowd coming from a mile away."

Laura laughed, "That is sadly true. Why can't things be like they were?"

"In a couple of weeks we will be back to normal, except I will be working at your store instead of Black Bear."

"That sounds delightful. But, is it too good to be true?"

"You will see soon enough. By the way, how's your latest article coming along?"

"The one on Starovoitova is interesting. I did tons of research on her. Everything points to a Mafia assassination of that poor woman, so I am writing an emotionally charged expose of her life, her fight against corruption, and her murder. In it I draw parallels to other martyrs in Soviet history."

"That sounds awesome, Laura."

"Awesome, except... am I right? My conclusion that she was murdered by the Mafia is based entirely on circumstantial information. What if I am wrong?"

After hearing Andropov's and Bupkov's admissions on the FBI's tapes, Ben knew she was absolutely correct. Without providing specifics he assured her, "You are right."

"How do you know that?" Laura asked.

"Just accept it, Laura. I can't tell you how I know."

"Accept, accept, accept. I must accept everything these days. Why not that, too?"

Even though half a continent away, Ben knew Laura was near tears. He seemed to have a knack these days for saying the wrong thing at the wrong time. Maybe he could change the subject without making matters worse.

Ben hazarded, "Have you heard from Dudaev, yet?"

"No-o... It's just more accept. Accept that I don't know who my grandfather is. Accept that Dudaev may never reply."

"Laura, stop it! I am sorry. I didn't mean to set you off again."

"It's okay. I cry easily these days. It's not your fault."

"Maybe, while Liz is there today, you can ask her about Dudaev. She sees him often."

"Actually I took matters into my own hands. I researched this Dudaev character backwards and forwards. He is much more than the professor of Soviet studies that we knew back in your Navy postgraduate days. What a mysterious and strangely influential character this man is and has been for a long, long time."

"What did you find that makes you think that?" asked Ben, who had come to the same conclusion from what he had heard about the professor.

"Way back in the early seventies there was an obscure news article in a Munich paper that tells of a meeting shortly after Solzhenitsyn was banished from the Soviet Union. It was a meeting between Dudaev and Solzhenitsyn. Nothing of substance was reported about the meeting. I believe the two men wished to keep the meeting secret, but some aggressive reporter happened onto their encounter."

"So? That doesn't shed much light on Dudaev or your past."

"Maybe yes. Maybe no."

"Go on."

"Well, there are several coincidences. For one thing, that meeting occurred only a year after Marina escaped the Soviet Union. Is that somehow connected to Dudaev meeting Solzhenitsyn? Or am I grasping at straws?"

"Maybe you are, but it's something to ponder. What other coincidences did you find?"

"After that meeting both men changed. Solzhenitsyn toned down his distrust of the West and his previous position that Russia could reform on its own through a moral renaissance."

"And?"

"And Dudaev became prominent, but in a subtle way. He is careful not to call undue attention to himself. Yet, he always pops up as a major shaper of America's perceptions of Russia. Sometimes I feel he doesn't so much write about history, as he creates it."

Ben could just imagine Laura's big blue eyes widening as she gave her fascinating spin on Dudaev. At least Ben had avoided any more tears.

"That's an interesting take on things. You know he influences Joint Eagles mightily. Everyone from President Arthur to Liz Nieman trusts him."

"Joint Eagles?"

"Yes, that is what I call the entire mission dealing with this crisis."

"Well done, Ben. There is a poetic bone hidden somewhere in that body of yours after all."

"Perhaps, but I haven't had the opportunity yet to suggest that label to Mark. Maybe it should just remain our code."

"No. You tell Mark. It's an appropriate acknowledgement of the unique cooperation between the two former cold-war enemies."

"Well, Liz is going to be at your place soon. And I must make my show at NEI so we had better cut this off."

"Remember, Ben. Two weeks or else!"

"I will."

"You be careful."

Laura lingered for some moments with the phone still in her hand. She knew Ben and Ben wasn't telling her everything. He didn't want her to worry. He was in more danger than he was admitting. But what could she do?

Day 30 8:15 A.M. Laura's Bookstore

Liz and an accompanying FBI agent entered the small specialty bookstore in the Urica Square Shopping Center. Liz cordially offered her hand to the attractive proprietor of the store.

"Mrs. Andrew, I am Liz Neiman from the CIA and this is FBI agent, Sherrill Stewart. Thank you for agreeing to meet with us."

"Sure. Welcome to Tulsa, and call me Laura. Mrs. Andrew makes me sound ancient. Would you like some coffee?"

"Yes. Thank you."

After sipping the coffee for a few minutes, Liz asked, "Is it okay if Agent Stewart looks around the store and the surroundings while we talk? We want to improve our protection of you and her review of the premises will help us do that."

"Yes, of course. Ben said your visit was for that purpose."

"It is, but don't worry too much. Ben and the vice president just want to take no chances on your safety."

"I hope Mark Foster is working as hard to protect Ben."

Liz was thrown off-stride with that comment. She didn't know how much Laura knew about Ben's close shave. After a pause which Laura noted, Liz answered, "They are the closest of friends. Vice President Foster would do anything to see that Ben is safe."

Laura nodded for that answer she believed was true, but perhaps not the whole story.

Liz changed the subject by asking, "You know, I am most intrigued with your past. Ben told me about your Russian heritage. I am a Russian specialist and am always trying to learn."

Liz had read several of Laura's articles. One published treatise on the insidious role of the Chekists in thwarting freedom for the Russian people was, in her opinion, brilliant. If it gained enough circulation it could conceivably help turn the spotlight on the Chekists. Liz believed that the bunch of cutthroats couldn't withstand the bright light of public scrutiny. Some at CIA headquarters wanted to take an active part in circulating Laura's article. Liz, though, had nixed that idea. She did not want the potential Sumurov heir further endangered by being directly pitted against the Chekists.

Laura wondered why Liz, a CIA specialist, was here if this was just about her protection. Couldn't the FBI handle the matter or did Liz's visit have another purpose? Was she just here because of her friendship with Ben and the need for more security? Laura decided to probe a little in an attempt to discover if something else was afoot.

"Ben tells me that you know Dudaev."

"Yes, I have met with him several times relative to the project Ben and I are on."

"Is he very helpful?"

"Very. He has tremendous insight into Russia."

"Certainly the CIA has plenty of their own Russian insight. Why do they need this tottering old professor?"

Laura's eyes, wide with curiosity, watched for the slightest reaction from Liz.

Liz punted. She realized that Laura was cleverly pumping her for info and scrutinizing her every reaction. She tried one stock answer that hopefully wouldn't tip off Laura as to how much they were dependent upon him and that she knew about Laura's pleading letter to him. "We need all valid viewpoints to avoid any mistakes."

Laura gathered Liz was being obscure on purpose, but acceptingly replied, "Well, I suppose that makes sense.

"Liz, would you do me a favor? Maybe a CIA analyst could help me. Would you look at this letter?"

Laura went on to explain the mysterious letter to her mother and her suspicion that Dudaev had written it.

Liz's mind flashed over a myriad possibilities. She tried to hide her discomfort as she read the letter. Laura was sharp and determined. She liked Laura, admired her intellect, and found that she desperately wished to help her. In a sense she was by getting a DNA sample.

Liz, with Laura eyeing her expression closely, read the letter while unsuccessfully attempting to betray nothing but the usual curiosity.

After Liz laid the note down, Laura asked, "What do you think? Who was Marina? Did Dudaev write the letter?"

"I don't know. It's possible," Liz replied.

"Then why haven't I heard from him? If he didn't write the letter, a 'no' would be easy. If the answer is yes, wouldn't it be the honorable and humane thing to tell me?"

Liz was touched. Her heart went out to this troubled lady. She didn't know what to say. "You are full of good logical questions. I wish I had good logical answers. Just don't give up. You will figure it out."

Attempting to change the subject, Liz volunteered, "I collect cups, Laura. These cups with your store's logo are so quaint. Could I have one?"

"Sure. I'll get you a clean one."

Liz couldn't argue with that logic, but when Laura was called away to wait on a customer, she switched the clean cup for Laura's used one. In case Agent Stewart hadn't gotten a DNA sample, Liz had.

After Liz and FBI agent Stewart left, Laura picked up the cups. She noticed that her cup was gone and the clean one was in its place. What was going on? Was this a clue to the real purpose of the visit? Did they come here to get a saliva sample from her? Laura thought, give me a little time and I will figure this out, Ms. Liz Niemann.

Day 30 6 P.M. Professor Dudaev's Home Hartford, Connecticut

Carrying an old beat-up briefcase, Dudaev crossed the Oriental rug in his perfectly-kept cherry wood library. He paused when he neared the bookcases on the far wall. Simultaneously he grabbed

Tolstoy's *War and Peace* and Sumurov's published collection of essays and pulled them each out about one inch. Quickly he returned them to their former resting place.

The big bookcase swung outward and the professor slipped through to a secret passage which led down a steep flights of stairs. The academician entered a room twice as big as his spacious upstairs library. In addition to a host of bookshelves, this underground space contained row upon row of files, full of Soviet and Russian government documents, original writings of Soviet and Russian authors and letters to him from many famous and not-so-famous dissidents.

He placed his weathered briefcase on a desk in the middle of the huge clandestine library. Opening it he pulled out a folder of published articles by Laura Andrew. Then he went to one of the vast array of files. He brought forth a collection of yellowed tattered pages covered with Russian handwriting. These disintegrating papers were the original Sumurov works that had accompanied Marina and Laura Tarasova out of Russia over thirty years ago and had remained in his care ever since. Until now he had believed that they were too contentious to release or publish. Russia, or previously the Soviet Union, would have seen them as seditionist and, if published by the U.S., almost an act of war. Since the right people were now in power in Russia and in the U.S., the time was nearing when they should be released.

From the dusty file Dudaev retrieved Sumurov's treatise on "The Future Russia." He took it to his desk, where he laid it beside Laura's articles. For hours he pored through Sumurov's forty-year-old works. It was indeed as he had remembered. The opportunity for Russia, which Sumurov had envisioned, would be manifest only after the fall of Communism, the disintegration of the Soviet regime, and the elimination of the Chekists. The latter was not yet accomplished.

Laura's and Viktor's essays were hauntingly similar in form. Dudaev was absolutely sure that the CIA's tests would verify Laura's birthright. Then he would be able to answer her letter in the affirmative. He was torn. Laura could be of some help in the looming battle with the Chekists and the Mafia, yet could he place Marina's daughter in harm's way? As he placed Laura's articles back in the file marked 'Ben and Laura Andrew, he decided that the future didn't need to be settled today. The qualities he and Marina had seen in Ben were fortuitously being put to the acid test by Ben's involvement with the vice president. He would wait a little longer.

Dudaev removed a letter from his briefcase. He scrutinized the message from Kruschev. Finally he was ready to compose a complicated and far reaching reply to the FSB leader.

Dear Vassily Ivanovich,

Thank you for your recent letter. Despite our different perceptions on the role religion plays in Russia's brighter future, we share many common goals for improvement in the lot of the Russian people. I would like to offer you some here-to-for-secret thoughts by the Russian martyr, Sumurov, on how this future could be obtained. It is a most remarkable treatise, written over forty years ago, yet it remains uncannily prophetic. In the seventies I discussed this work with Solzhenitsyn. He was swayed by it to such an extent that his distrust of the West's importance in a future assisting role diminished.

You will see that one key element of Sumurov's formulation for that brighter future is the defeat of the Chekist movement. The Chekists are a chain around your country's neck. They are drowning Russia. You are in the best position of any of us to deal the Chekists a fatal blow.

As you develop your precise plans for battle against them depend upon help from me and my people, as well as, the present U.S. administration.

Also, tell Strahkov that the CIA, with my help, is close to finding Viktor Sumurov's heir. I should be able to reveal who it is very soon.

I understand that Director Stockton is visiting you in the next few days. You can trust him. He and the vice president are two worthy allies. As I have outlined, you should structure your plans, fully relying upon their help.

The Mafia and the Chekists will come after you. I hope this isn't too morbid, but we must be prepared with your successor if that should become a necessity. My first choice is someone you might never have expected, Hamad Barak. What do you think?

Your course is to be lauded. At long last, through your courage and wisdom, a free Russia will start to emerge.

My best to you.

Your friend,

Professor Dudaev

THIRTY-THREE

Day 31 10:45 A.M. Oval Office White House

"So, Don, have you and Garrison narrowed the list of possible moles?" inquired President Arthur.

"Yes. The rat is one of these." North gestured to a list of a dozen names.

"You are absolutely sure it is not one of the agents covering this morning's meeting?"

"I am damned sure. Those two are as clean as hounds' teeth."

"Good. I just wanted to hear it directly from you. We can afford no mistakes."

President Arthur hesitated before asking, "What do you think of the vice president's team?"

"The best damned bunch of Americans ever assembled. I want that Ben Andrew with me in any future battle. He really pulled things together. This bunch could be better than my top oil field crew."

President Arthur laughed at that admission, "I agree with you that they are an extremely talented bunch. However, you are just partial to Ben because he is an outsider."

"Not really! Initially I liked him for that reason, now after seeing him in action, that is an honest assessment."

After disputing the President's good-natured accusation, North added, "Don't worry about the outcome of Joint Eagles. These terrorist assholes have no chance against us. We will win this thing even if I have to kick Andronov's face in myself."

"Joint Eagles, eh?"

"Yes, that is what Ben and I call the mission."

"Joint Eagles! Good. Quite appropriate. I think I will make that official."

As the time neared for his congressional visitors President Arthur turned pensive, "Give me five minutes alone, Don. Then send in Secretaries Kohlmeier and Winston."

After dismissing North, a preoccupied President Arthur gazed out through the patio doors onto the dormant rose garden. He held no illusions that this morning's encounter with the congressional leaders would be easy. History taught otherwise. When the opposition political party controlled either or both houses of Congress during emergencies requiring military action, explosive confrontations were probable. The President anticipated that the Joint Eagles venture would spark such a fight this morning.

He fully comprehended the intentions of the Constitutional framers. Weary of rule by absolute power of monarchy, they feared more than anything too much authority residing in the hands of one individual. Thus, they had ingeniously separated federal power into the three arms of government. That separation, though, made Joint Eagles all the more difficult for him.

Over a decade ago when the first President Bush assembled a worldwide coalition to deal with the Iraqi invasion of Kuwait, the U.S. Congress, controlled by the opposition party, had been the very last entity in the world to sign on in support of Desert Storm. Reluctantly the lawmakers finally relented, while still covering all of their bases. The second President Bush experienced only a slightly easier time of it with Congress.

This wasn't like the WTC event either. That overt act of terror forged an alliance in America and the world. Today, though, he faced a far more tenuous situation. He was trying to prevent an attack, one far worse than the WTC, but there was no overt act of terror to bring a nation together, let alone a worldwide coalition. Because of the pervasive nature of this current criminal nuclear threat, secrecy was paramount for Joint Eagles to have any chance. Thus, there would be no international coalition, no UN mandate, nor any public debate by Congress.

Fearing leaks, he was revealing his proposed action at this last possible moment to only the key leaders of Congress. Since mobilization was imminent, he must not only inform, but also educate and persuade them to support his solution to the crisis. They must help keep the veil of secrecy in place. The climax of today's meeting,

President Arthur anticipated, would occur when he locked horns with the Speaker of the House, the titular head of the opposition party.

Ignoring his severely aching back, the tall man walked across his office to the fireplace. Still deep in thought, he stared into the roaring flames. The Constitution, despite the complexities of this crisis, must be honored. After diligently researching the legal and constitutional aspects of his pending actions, how he must proceed with Congress had become apparent. It would not be an easy path or one without risk, but it was sound constitutionally.

Day 31 11:15 A.M. Oval Office White House

Once Secretary Winston and Secretary Kohlmeier arrived, President Arthur laid out the ground rules for the meeting. "The lawyers, the vice president's team, and you have prepared me well. I should be able to handle most questions from the Congressmen. If I need help, I'll turn to one of you. Otherwise just remain silent and let me struggle through this on my own."

The President's personal secretary interrupted, "Mr. President, the congressional leaders have arrived. Shall I show them in?"

"Yes."

President Arthur rose from behind his desk in the Oval Office, and with his long strides, quickly covered the distance to the door. He shook his head, "What a gaudy rug. Don is right about this place in more ways than one."

As the curious Congressional leaders arrived, President Arthur graciously welcomed them, offering each a warm handshake and a personal greeting. He inquired about their families and congratulated each on recent appointments or elections to leadership positions in Congress.

After the greetings he motioned them toward the sofas and chairs arranged near the fireplace. He asked one of the two Secret Service agents to close the door. Sizing them up, he prayed that North had chosen correctly.

President Arthur gingerly eased his lanky frame into the chair next to the fireplace. Not by accident, he faced the Speaker. In that way he could watch the congressman's reactions during the discussions.

Only two hours ago the Secretaries of State and Defense, at the President's direction, had hand delivered to each of the congressional leaders, under a "Top Secret - For Your Eyes Only" seal, a brief outline of the crisis and the purpose for this morning's meeting.

"I have asked you to join me, Secretary Winston, and Secretary Kohlmeier this morning to discuss a most insidious threat to our nation. At my direction, Vice President Foster has led an effort to solve a baffling disappearance of former Soviet nuclear weapons. In carrying out that task he uncovered a savage scheme of shadowy criminals and rogue countries that pose an imminent danger to America. He is, as each of you appreciates, uniquely qualified to marshal the nation's resources in this matter. Since he's fully consumed with this crisis as it races toward a climax, I excused him from being here today. I don't wish to divert him, even for this most important meeting. Vice President Foster, though, sends his warmest regards to each of you and his thanks in advance for your support."

Shifting forward in his chair, the President experienced a stabbing pain in his lower back. He eyed Speaker Buchanan. So far, except for a raised eyebrow at the, "thanks in advance for your support," phrase, he had detected no reaction other than polite attention.

President Arthur relayed how the crisis had unfolded, starting with the call from Alexander Strahkov thirty days ago. The congressional leaders' studied indifference evaporated as the unfolding saga held them spellbound. They peppered the President with constitutional, political and tactical questions, which President Arthur handled confidently. He never once turned to Secretary Kohlmeier or Secretary Winston for help.

President Arthur still suspected, though, that Speaker Buchanan was going to be trouble. The discussions were heating up. The congressman was his chief political antagonist. He came across outwardly as a good-ole country boy lawyer, but he was a capable and worthy foe.

"How long has this diversion or smuggling scheme gone on?" questioned Senator Collins.

"Since the nineties."

"Surely Russia didn't just now discover all of this?"

"That's a very astute question, Senator. It doesn't lend itself to a simple answer. The leadership situation in Russia changed dramatically after the last special election. The present leaders' resolve to deal with the Mafia's influence in general and the nuclear smuggling in particular has grown. Also their alarm with the rising military strength of the radical Islamic theocracies on their vulnerable southern border is a factor forcing them to ask us for help. Their new President, Alexander Strahkov, spearheaded the investigations which uncovered many details of the smuggling. But continuing..."

"So the damned Russians helped create the Frankenstein to their south and now they are sorry and want our help to subdue it!" Senator Donohue rather bitterly observed.

"Yes, Senator. Ironic and sad, isn't it? In the past, the short-term expediency of gaining cash from weapons sales won out over their own long-term strategic interests. The new leadership is appalled at just how dangerous a situation was created by their past policies, or more properly, non-policies."

"It sounds like this Andropov character is a cold-war-warrior holdout who is carrying on his own private war against us," astutely summarized Senate Majority Leader Collins.

"Are you sure we haven't got a few cold-war-warrior holdouts of our own that make this stuff up?" challenged Representative Dowell.

President Arthur heatedly responded to Dowell's insinuation, "I would stake my career on the accuracy of the CIA's analysis."

That triggered the first reaction from the Speaker. Under his breath but still loud enough for all to hear, he mumbled, "Ah would say that's exactly what yoh awh doing."

"Wow!" Kohlmeier whispered to Winston, "This is going to get bloody before it's over."

"Back to the armaments for a moment. We have known for some-time that Iran has been obtaining missiles from China and missile technology from Russia..."

Speaker Buchanan interrupted Senator Donohue in mid-sentence, "With friends like the Russians, yawl in the White House really don't need enemies." That remark brought snickers from the opposition party legislators.

Not letting another belligerent remark slide, an undaunted Donohue fired back, "I believe I made a similar observation earlier, Mr. Speaker. Try to be original, please. I hope you understood the astute and learned answer given by our President on the trustworthiness of the present Russian President."

Senator Donohue expected that the Speaker would be the President's chief protagonist today. He would slow him down a little if he could. "Before the Speaker interrupted, I was going to ask about the cruise missiles?" Obviously the Senate Armed Services Committee chairman was not in the least intimidated by the bullying tactics of the Speaker. "Would our ABLs be effective in guarding against these?" queried Donohue.

"Yes and no. The beauty of the ABL as a defensive weapon is its mobility and that it can bring a nuclear-armed ballistic missile down on the country which launched it. That is an extremely effective deterrent against even radical enemy launches of nuclear ballistics. The low-flying cruises, however, present a much tougher, but not impossible, target for the ABL."

Kohlmeier and Winston were amazed at how astutely the well-informed President led the sometimes-balky congressional leaders through the complexities of the crisis.

President Arthur, sensing that the time was right, summarized the situation. "So you see the threats are multiple and yet insidiously inter-woven. The Mafia criminal element has infiltrated several of our government agencies, which makes our attempts to deal effectively with the crisis even more delicate. To assure tight security, each person involved in the crisis has been thoroughly investigated by the FBI."

"Who's investigating the FBI?" questioned Speaker Buchanan sarcastically.

"That's really not a bad question," acknowledged the President diplomatically. "The vice president has been very selective about the agents he uses. We are now quite sure that the Mafia has sources within our federal law enforcement agencies. For that reason, we kept the number of personnel involved in our strategic planning to an absolute minimum. Even under this stringent security, information has leaked to the Mafia. You must trust no one. The Mafia undoubtedly has informants on your staffs."

"So, how and when do you plan to act?" prompted Senator Collins.

"We and the Russians will militarily remove the nuclear weapons and nuclear-technical capability from Iranian and Mafia control. Also, we will simultaneously move to protect our nuclear plants and our electrical supply from destruction. All of this will happen in exactly thirteen days under the tightest possible secrecy. Also, we have increased surveillance patrols along our borders."

Secretary Kohlmeier watched knowingly as Speaker Buchanan lit his trademark cigar, tensed and leaned forward in anticipation of what was coming next.

Kohlmeier nudged Winston, "Here is where the shit hits the fan."

The President elaborated, "This is what must be done. A surgical strike will be conducted by our military forces against Iran's nuclear weapon's locations and the Karaj nuclear facility. We will mount a massive airlift of Ranger and armored cavalry units. They will land, engage the enemy, capture the weapons and the Russian scientists at Karaj, and then destroy the offending facilities. Simultaneously,

German police in close cooperation with our FBI will seize the Munich Enrichment Plant. Russian troops will attack the Kazakh Border Guard and seize the nuclear weapons and bomb material presently hidden there. Meanwhile, federal teams will secure our nuclear plants. Several hundred suspected criminals in this country and overseas will be arrested. All of these activities must occur coincidentally, so that no portion of this conspiracy is alerted and allowed to react..."

No longer able to contain himself, Speaker Buchanan rose. With the cigar clenched in his teeth, he interrupted Arthur with a growl. "Mr. President, have yoh given yoh final go ahead for this attack?"

"Not yet. I am waiting until the last possible moment and I continue searching for any alternative."

"If yoh move ahead, are yoh going to do awl of this without asking congressional pahmission?"

"Yes. The need for secrecy is paramount. An open debate in Congress is impossible. It would lead to disaster. Our country's security would be unacceptably compromised."

The Speaker deliberately moved toward the closed door of the Oval Office as if he were about to leave. Just before reaching one of the expressionless Secret Service guards, he spun around and angrily fired at President Arthur, "Is yoh memory so pooh, Mr. President, that yoh don't recall yoh oath of office?"

A flash of anger roared through Arthur's being. Struggling not to yield to his instinctive anger, he took a deep breath before responding to the combative Speaker.

"I can quote that oath to you verbatim, Mr. Speaker. What part do you believe I forgot?"

"The part about 'preserve, protect and defend the Constitution of the United States' seems to be forgotten heah. Mah constituents in mah home state would not cotton to this behavior. It's moh fitting foh a powtentate than a duly elected servant of thuh people."

Calling upon every ounce of his will power, the President resisted a strong urge to thrash the pugnacious Speaker. Fortunately he was well prepared for this onslaught, for instead of a retaliatory strike, he slowly but surely set the trap. "I might remind you, Jack, that Article II, Section 2 of the Constitution states that 'The President shall be Commander in Chief of the Army and Navy of the U.S.' I am proposing to exercise my responsibilities as Commander in Chief to assure the security of the U.S. If I didn't do so, I would be derelict in my duties and, as you charge, unfaithful to my oath."

Speaker Buchanan, a constitutional lawyer himself, was more sure than ever that this showdown was going his way. He took a big puff on his cigar and stuck out his corpulent middle as he spoke. "Ah, but Mistah President, theah is also Article I, Section 8 which states 'Congress shall have powah to declare wah!' It is wah weah talking about heah, isn't it?"

Speaker Buchanan's posture and expression were similar to a pugilist about to declare victory.

President Arthur rose slowly to his full height and walked purposefully toward the Speaker until he stood toe to toe with him. He advanced his next argument while staring down into the cloud of smoke, encircling his opponent's fat face.

"During 1973, Jack, er, Mr. Speaker, the 81st Congress passed the War Powers Act. In it Congress attempted to clarify the power it possesses to 'declare war' versus the President's power as 'Commander in Chief.' It is most appropriate that we examine that act."

Speaker Buchanan, unfazed, peered upward to meet the President's steely gaze and irreverently belched cigar smoke into Arthur's face. He had not expected the President to bring up the 1973 War Powers Act. It was to be his trump card. Undeterred, though, he charged ahead. "Mr. President, Ahm glad you brought up the Wah Powahs Act for then yoh must know what event prompted Congress to pass that bill. That act was designed to nevah again allow a messed-up President to get us into a Vietnam-type debacle. Awh legislative body made moh specific Congress's right to be consulted priah to the President committing awh fowces in anothah country."

Still positioned only inches from Congressman Buchanan's face, President Arthur countered with a heightened, almost triumphant, aggressiveness. "You are only partially correct, Congressman. Yes, it was prompted by the most disastrous war in U.S. history. A war, by the way, which was conducted while Congress twiddled their thumbs and did little about it except to pass spending measures each year to cover the ever-escalating costs of that ill-conceived conflict.

"I pored over the language and the hearing record of the 'War Powers' bill closely with the best constitutional lawyers in the land. They point out the exception deliberately placed in that legislation by Congress, which states that the President is not required to consult with Congress if the military action required for the security of our country will last less than ninety days. This action I propose will last less than a week. There is no doubt that our security is threatened. So, according to the letter of the law, I propose to act within my constitutional and legal authority.

"Equally as important, though, as the letter of the law is the intent. Being a distinguished lawyer, you surely appreciate that principle. The preponderance of testimony during the congressional hearings on that bill makes one thing very clear. All understood that there undoubtedly could be future emergencies, which require the prompt, unilateral action of the President to provide for the 'common defense.' We face precisely that situation today. One that Congress long ago intelligently anticipated and provided for in its legislation. You would find the testimony most interesting and informative reading, Mr. Speaker." Arthur bit off the trenchant words signaling finality. Reinforcing that enough had been said on the subject, he turned back toward his chair.

Sec. Kohlmeier fought an overwhelming urge to stand and cheer her President.

President Arthur correctly perceived that Speaker Buchanan had not expected such a spirited and informed defense of his presidential prerogatives. The Speaker, despite his legal expertise, was not prepared to go to the depth to which the President had taken the argument. The President knew that he must now allow the proud congressional leader room to "save face." The old boy would undoubtedly welcome a chance to maneuver to a secure political posture. Arthur intended to allow him that luxury.

Fortunately, a perceptive Senate Majority Leader Collins correctly sized up where things stood. He reckoned that he could provide an assist to President Arthur at this crucial juncture in the meeting. Speaker Buchanan needed an escape from his verbal thrashing with, at least, a token appearance of victory.

"Gentlemen, gentlemen!" With all the authority he could muster, Senate Majority Leader Collins slowly and majestically rose to his feet. Moving to the space halfway between the two verbal combatants, he took over. "You both have provided a most excellent recounting of the constitutional powers of the Congress and the Presidency relative to military actions. I am sure, Mr. President, that you appreciate the congressional sensitivity in granting more authority to the President than our constitution allows?"

"Yes, and I certainly seek no such power."

Speaker Buchanan harrumphed at that remark as he slowly retreated to his chair. This wasn't going at all as he had expected. His mind was racing, searching for any means to snatch victory from the jaws of defeat.

Senator Collins, having successfully inserted himself into the discussion, waited for the President and the Speaker to be seated. "It seems our President has just laid at our feet one of the most extreme threats that our country has ever faced. To debate publicly the constitutionality or wisdom of the President's proposed actions would not be in the nation's best interests, nor ours as its elected leaders. We must act first and foremost as defenders of this great country at such perilous moments. If we in Congress doomed our President to failure in dealing with this national security threat, the American people would not be able to kick our butts out of office fast enough. Perhaps they would even find a way to recall us or place us on trial for treason."

Sec. Kohlmeier uttered a silent amen to that observation.

"It seems to me that your party, Mr. Speaker, has nothing to lose and everything to gain by letting the President proceed along a path which is obviously fraught with peril. If he fails, then your party will be able to ride that fact to victory after victory in future elections. Perhaps you could even force the President's resignation or proceed with his impeachment.

"On the other hand, if his plan is successful, then you have all done your patriotic duty and the right thing for the civilized world. It would surely be perceived in that light by the American people. It would appear to me that the military undertaking may result in considerable loss of life and equipment. Even in victory the public will hold that loss against the President. So Mr. Speaker, you and your party seem to be in a win-win political posture by letting President Arthur hang out there, totally vulnerable. In addition, and not by any means a trivial consideration, you are doing the right thing for the security of your country."

President Arthur could have hugged Sen. Collins, as those were exactly the arguments he had intended to advance. It was, however, far more effective coming from the majority leader.

Seeing the opportunity offered by Collins to seize the high ground of statesman, Speaker Buchanan acted. "Yawl do make good sense, Senatah Collins. It is fortunate indeed that we have yoh heah to bring us both to awh senses. The leadahs of awh loyal opposition pawty most assuredly will assume a bipartisan posture during this national crisis. Ah wish awh President and awh fowces God's speed in this coming battle. What can we do, Mr. President, to aid the cause?"

"I am deeply grateful for your statesmanship on this matter, Mr. Speaker. There are some areas where we do need help. We have already started troop and equipment movements, too numerous to address this morning, in preparation for the Joint Eagles battle.

"We developed two cover stories that we will use to deflect suspicions away from the real purpose of those deployments. If you are asked by the media or others about these buildups, we would appreciate it if you would say little. Act nonchalant. Refer questions to the Departments of Defense or State, but at the same time tacitly support the cover stories. I have briefing packets for each of you that give details on each of these stories. Secretaries Kohlmeier and Winston are prepared to go over these materials in detail with you at your earliest convenience."

The House Majority Leader had considered arguing about the use of force versus embargoes and diplomacy. After the verbal fireworks and the restored peace between the Speaker and the President, he wisely concluded that he should stay silent on the subject. Even he could see that diplomacy risked making a bad situation worse.

Senate Majority Leader Collins again took over, reminding all present that the congressional leaders' role was to help with the cover stories designed to ensure the complete surprise necessary for this venture.

"Please keep the vice president, his team and our soldiers in your prayers. Thank you's are not adequate to express my gratitude for your support."

Grant Arthur heaved a sigh of relief. The last big hurdle was cleared. Only his final decision to attack remained.

Sec. Kohlmeier left thankful that, after some judicious coaxing, the congressional leaders had risen above narrow self-interest to face the challenge squarely.

North, who had returned to the area, watched as the two carefully selected Secret Service agents left the room with the President. No agents had been allowed in any of the vice president's team meetings. These were the first, other than the Detail Commander, to learn about Joint Eagles. North prayed he had selected wisely. Even more fervently, he prayed that the loquacious congressional leaders could keep their damned yaps shut.

Day 31 4 P.M. Don North's Office

"Mr. North, an FBI agent gave us the third degree regarding the President's meeting."

"Who?"

"Karpenko."

"You told him nothing?"

"We told him we couldn't stand the FBI so why was he harassing us."

"Good work."

After the Secret Service men left, Don increased his suspects list by one.

CHAPTER
THIRTY-FOUR

Day 33 7 A.M. KGB Headquarters Moscow

Yesterday Kruschev had listened transfixed to the Schilthorn and the Zermatt tapes. After the Mafia activities had been revealed to the Russian leader as never before, Stockton relayed the American plutonium proliferation concerns. Kruschev accepted the U.S. requests for security improvements in the handling of plutonium as logical and reasonable, and he assured Stockton that they would work with U.S. experts to tighten security. Also, he would make every effort to recover the stolen plutonium. The scope of the newly revealed Mafia plutonium thefts alarmed him. The hemorrhage of nuclear materials continued in an even more dangerous form.

After lengthy dialogues on the threats posed by the Mafia, Kruschev quite favorably impressed with Stockton, suggested that he remain in Moscow one more night. Kruschev promised to give the American intelligence chief something very important for his safekeeping.

As the cold Moscow morning finally dawned, Stockton made his way to Kruschev's office. Kruschev's bleary eyes and yesterday's clothes told Stockton that the FSB Chief had spent the entire night working.

"Good morning, Director Stockton. We have much to cover."

"Good morning. Let's get to it."

Kruschev began, "I will not mince words. I am convinced that I can trust you. You and your vice president have earned my respect and confidence." Stockton was unaware that Dr. Dudaev's secret word on his behalf carried more weight than all other factors.

268

"Thank you, Chairman. I am honored to be considered a trusted friend of yours."

"Our friendship entails responsibility and action far more than honor."

Kruschev paused for a second to emphasize the next thought, "I realize that unless I draw back on all of my FSB reform initiatives or hide far underground, either the Mafia or the Chekists will kill me. I am not drawing back or hiding, so the future is set. I will most likely be assassinated. You, my replacement, President Strahkov, your President and Vice President Foster will be left behind to wage the next battle against these thugs."

Stockton was stunned. Kruschev's disarming honesty and dire prediction left him without suitable words. Stockton merely waited for Kruschev to continue. This was a meeting like no other. Its nature rattled him. Events were moving at an unbelievable pace.

"Real reform of the FSB must go forward with or without me. Russia must throw off the restraining shackles of the Chekists. I have begun the reformation process, which is still in its infancy. Like I said, I don't know how long I will be permitted to continue. The removal of the Chekists must happen, with or without me, or Russia will sink further into the quagmire of criminality. Here. You must guard this with your life."

With that admonition Kruschev handed over a thick notebook to Stockton.

Puzzled Stockton asked, "What is this?"

"It is the equivalent of your Declaration of Independence along with the blueprints and battle plans necessary to achieve that independence, an independence from our own corrupt institutions. As your Pogo once said, 'we have met the enemy, and he is us.'"

Stockton managed a nervous laugh, thinking, so at this tense moment you manage to quote our cartoon characters. Amazing!

Methodically, the two men spent the morning going through the document. Amazed Stockton deemed Kruschev to have thought of everything. His campaign against the Chekists was all encompassing and extremely clever. Stockton drew a parallel to the old west. The plan's strategy paralleled the way the cagey cowboy hunted buffalo, keep shooting the straggler so the herd wouldn't stampede. Kruschev was going after the lesser Chekists in his organization first so as not to alarm the big boys. He had already demoted or transferred several minor functionaries to frontier outposts.

The scheme called for a second phase of public denunciation of some of the mid-level Chekists. They would be accused, among other things, of allowing military secrets to flow to Russia's enemies. In essence they would be tried and thrown into prison for past sins.

The dislodgement of the Chekist Kingpins was the final piece of the puzzle and far trickier to accomplish. Public opinion would have to be mobilized, and the Mafia would have to be distracted during this final push. The Mafia full well understood their dependence on the Chekists for control of Russia, so they must be kept from riding to the rescue of these most influential Chekists. The distraction Kruschev contemplated was a well-timed full-scale assault upon the Mafia by the European, Russian, and American police. That aggressive policing would throw them off-stride so they couldn't effectively bail out the Chekists. The push on the top Chekists would be a public disclosure and denunciation of the Chekists crimes over the past century. It would require the coordinated support of the media and Russia's best writers. They would win this battle by molding public opinion, once and for all, against the Chekists. The last of the big-shots would be exposed, humiliated, and imprisoned.

After going through all of this, Kruschev told Stockton to turn to the first appendix.

Stockton observed, "This is a list of Russian names."

"Yes. It's all of the staunch Chekists in my organization. It begins with the most important and continues toward the least. Now turn to the next attachment."

Stockton did as directed, but was puzzled with the short list of names, beginning with Hamad Barak. "Isn't he the Kazakh involved in the Mafia's nuclear smuggling conspiracy? So is this a list of Mafia bad guys that need to be arrested?"

For the first time Kruschev laughed, "No. Just the opposite. Hamad Barak, Commander of the Kazak Border Guard, is first choice as my replacement."

"You are kidding!"

"No. Let me explain."

With growing fascination Stockton listened to Kruschev's logic on the matter. He had to admit that if events turned out as Kruschev predicted, Barak, if he wasn't killed during the Joint Eagles attack, might be a formidable FSB head.

Stockton listened as Kruschev placed a stunning caveat on the Barak choice. Professor Dudaev should be consulted and his agreement obtained at the time it became necessary to enlist Barak as FSB leader. Also the professor must advise Stockton and President Strahkov on how best to solicit Barak's services.

A flabbergasted Stockton looked at the weary Kruschev, "Dudaev? You are kidding! You know the professor?"

"Oh, yes. I certainly do." Then Kruschev dropped his mega-ton bomb, "I am a long-time member of his organization."

"Oh, my God!"

Without Kruschev explaining, Stockton understood why he was being given these papers. They would be safer with him than any-where in Russia plus his country's buy-in on the plan was vital. Kruschev wanted to obtain Stockton's and America's support now while he was still alive.

So Dudaev's organization reached to the highest levels in Russia. Just what was the nature of this group? How great was its influence? Why wasn't the CIA aware of it before now?

Day 35 6 P.M. CIA Headquarters

Deep within the CIA's most secure confines, Director Stockton nervously snapped his infamous red suspenders. They slapped against his ample mid-rift with a resounding echo, heard only by him. Just back from his Russian trip, he carried the most important set of papers he had ever possessed. Before closing the vault door he paused and contemplated the import captured on these pages. A battle plan of global dimensions envisioned a Russia finally free of the Chekists. He believed that the battle called for in these papers would initiate the second Joint Eagles war.

James shivered. He loved the spy business and mysteries, but this was eerie. A profound intellect and unfathomable dedication was at play here. He was caught up in something he certainly didn't control and only partially understood.

THIRTY-FIVE

Day 35 6 P.M. Ambrosia Lake, New Mexico

With tires and motor whining, the midnight-blue Subaru sped down the desolate road. Colonel Paul LaFrentz was fond of this lonely stretch of old blacktop, a road inviting speed. The true charm of this short route across the high-altitude desert floor, though, was that it led from the known to the unknown, from the worldly to the out-of-this-world. Starting at his home in Grants, LaFrentz plunged into a world that officially didn't exist.

This bewitching desert road also harbored ghosts of a past mining boom. Appearing like a giant's swing set, an occasional abandoned mine head frame still stood on the desert floor. The rusting towers, silhouetted by the moon, served as haunting reminders that once vast quantities of uranium ore worth billions were extracted from this desert. LaFrentz envisioned the apparitions of the ore-hauling trucks barreling down on him, radioactive dust and rocks flying. Those big rigs once carried uranium from the rich mines of the Grants Mineral Belt to the nearby mills.

This desolate area had experienced many boom-and-bust cycles, as the demand and price for the heavy yellow ore would rise only to dive precipitously. The ore bodies finally played out, so no longer did the tractor-trailers speed along the narrow highway. No such hazards existed now; even grazing cattle were not a problem. For the duration of the winter the livestock had all been shipped from this sparsely vegetated, open rangeland to feed lots in eastern New Mexico or to meat packers in the Texas Panhandle.

Because of tonight's space flight, Col. LaFrentz was eager to reach the base. It struck him as ironic that this once rich uranium district served as home for the two planes that would fire the first shots in this burgeoning nuclear crisis. This desert, which had yielded the ingredients for the first U.S. nuclear bombs, now cradled the planes that would help halt the terrorist use of nuclear weapons.

LaFrentz thrived upon these exciting missions and readily accepted the complete anonymity demanded by the Military Space Administration's Black Star project. No accolades were necessary. Piloting the world's ultimate plane, Black Star, was honor enough.

A decade ago, CIA operatives in conjunction with a wealthy U.S. business tycoon fashioned Southwestern Satellite Communications as part of an elaborate ruse. Southwest SatCom bought this remote section of desert purportedly for satellite uplink operations. Its real purpose, however, was to team with the Military Space Administration in secretly building Black Star and its hidden base. The tycoon used "special federal tax deductions" from his other enterprises to finance the Military Space Administration's covert development of the space plane. Through this elaborate dodge, the billions earmarked for the program appeared in no federal budgets. The money wasn't even in the Defense Department's "black" budget. Thus, any year-to-year Congressional budget battles were avoided, facilitating continuity of the project and absolute secrecy.

The Military Space Administration had selected its team of elite scientists and engineers from the ranks of the Navy, Air Force, NASA and the large aerospace contractors. The crack design team was initially assembled at Groom Lake, California. When it came time for absolute isolation during construction and flight-testing, the entire operation was transferred to the obscure and uniquely designed Ambrosia Lake base.

LaFrentz had graduated top in his class at the Air Force Academy just in time to serve in Desert Storm. As a pilot in the Air Force's 35th Fighter Wing, he had distinguished himself mission after mission with his unequaled piloting ability. He and his F-16 Strike Eagle, equipped with the HARM targeting system, had deftly baited and destroyed several Soviet-built Iraqi SA-8 surface-to-air missile batteries. He perfected techniques which were still taught in advanced Navy and Air Force combat flight schools. After the war, he flew exhibitions as the team leader of the Thunderbirds.

Six years ago, he was one of four gleaned from the cream of the military pilot pool for a top secret "astronaut" assignment. Joining him were two superior Top Guns from the Navy and one extremely talented Air Force comrade. The foursome were the only pilots ever to fly Black Star.

LaFrentz marveled that fiction lagged reality when it came to his plane, for there weren't even rumors of its existence. Its stealth, hypersonic speed, maneuverability in atmosphere or space and lethal weapons capabilities were without peer. Its remarkable technical capabilities explained some of his love for the plane, but it was more than that. The phenomenal missions jazzed him.

Reaching the end of the lonely blacktopped speedway, LaFrentz pulled up to the guard station where he and his car were extensively checked before he was allowed onto the Base. Normally the painstaking security checks didn't bother him, but tonight's delay irritated him.

He snapped at the Marine guard, "You know who I am. Get on with it."

After the rebuke, the guard deliberately slowed his inspection. He really didn't like these cocky, smartass pilots.

LaFrentz knew that he was cocky and that the Marine guards hated the pilots' guts. It was a mutual disdain, which each entity relished. Who couldn't guard a gate in the middle of the American Desert, he wondered.

Day 35 7:30 P.M. Black Star Hangar

A bevy of ground crew personnel scurried about as Col. LaFrentz strode across the subterranean hangar floor toward his unique plane. Dressed in his flexible, lightweight space suit, LaFrentz was dwarfed by Black Star, which perched high above him, piggybacked on the dark blue 747 mother ship. It looked as if a black rain cloud had settled directly over the modified 747. A several story-tall gantry stood beside the two linked planes. LaFrentz, still carrying his helmet, noted how all sound reverberated through the huge sarcophagus-like hangar. The sound and the sights created an eerie almost surreal sensation. Shaking off the feeling, he stepped into the gantry's elevator, musing that this was the first, shortest and slowest of his upward journeys tonight. The elevator lifted him and his accompanying support team fifty feet above the underground tarmac, where the technicians helped him slip into Black Star I's windowless cockpit.

Shortly after he was strapped in, the 747 engines roared to life and the vertically linked planes were pulled into takeoff position. The mother ship, with the black space plane hanging on as might an over-grown baby loon to its mother's back, accelerated along the under-ground runway. They remained out of sight until the climb to the earth's surface just prior to takeoff.

Day 35 8:20 P.M. Skies over Northeastern New Mexico

Far above eastern New Mexico and similar in appearance to the space shuttle being transported to its Florida launch site, Black Star passively rode atop the Boeing 747.

LaFrentz had been briefed that the sister ship, Black Star II, with Lt. Cmdr. Townsly at the controls, was already aloft heading for a spot in the heavens twenty-two thousand miles above him.

Thus far, LaFrentz's Black Star I, with its engines silent, had depleted none of its precious fuel. However, the ramjet/scramjet/rock-et propulsion system, fueled by liquid hydrogen, would soon spring to life, assuming the job of propelling Black Star.

In appearance, Black Star somewhat resembled spotter drawings of its officially "non-existent" cousin, the Aurora. A manned ramjet spy plane, the Aurora's existence had never been officially acknowl-edged. Both the Aurora and Black Star were shaped like a thin isosce-les triangle, with the trademark Delta-wing swept-back design and twin stabilizers. Black Star, as its name implied, was black in the default status. It was eighty feet long, longer by thirty feet than Aurora. The increased size was mandated by its weapons, big fuel tanks and its engines.

Strapped into the pilot's seat, Colonel LaFrentz worked through his last-minute pre-launch checklist. Upon confirmation that all sys-tems were fully functional, he was eager to cut loose from the slow, lumbering 747.

"Mother Ship ready for launch sequence. Can you confirm status, Little Brother?"

"Roger, Mother Ship. Little Brother's raring to soar."

"We are steady on course zero nine nine, 39,000 feet and 560 knots. Have a pleasant flight, Colonel."

As he watched the digital indicator counting down the final sec-onds until release, LaFrentz steeled himself for a jolt.

Five-four-three-two-one-Release.

As the first of a rapid succession of actions, the 747 latches sprang forward, thrusting Black Star ahead. The slightly slowed 747, now free of its burden, immediately circled hard to starboard.

LaFrentz promptly placed his plane in a steep dive, bearing to port. The still dormant black plane gained speed rapidly during the precipitous but powerless dive. Upon reaching Mach 2, Black Star's ramjet engine ignited, pressing LaFrentz back into his seat once again. He nosed the space plane upward. Black Star climbed for the first time under its own power. The acceleration forced his blood to pool in his extremities, causing a momentary light-headedness.

After those rapid-fire evolutions a fully fueled Black Star was on course five miles high and climbing. At a ground speed of over two thousand mph the accelerating plane continued to flatten LaFrentz into his seat. The lumbering jumbo jet had saved the space voyager thousands of pounds of fuel as well as the need for a bulky turbojet engine.

In another minute and a half of ramjet burn, Black Star roared to forty-five thousand feet and reached a blazing Mach 6.5. High above the Oklahoma prairies, the plane's engine reconfigured automatically, converting to the scramjet propulsion regime.

LaFrentz 's body was assaulted still another time as the scramjet burst to life, thrusting the plane and pilot upward. His anti-G gear and his own control of his body were both necessary to avoid blacking out under the smothering force. In mere minutes the scramjet accelerated the plane to Mach 12 at an altitude of sixty miles.

During this air-breathing portion of Black Star's flight the trailing infrared signature was eliminated by mixing a thin stream of the precious cryogenic fuel into the exhaust of the engines. The fuel resided in innovative tanks that were designed to withstand cryogenic temperatures from within, as well as an assault from without of the blistering heat of reentry.

With all but wispy vestiges of atmosphere left below, the derivative of the efficient Russian NK-44 rocket engine took over and thrust Black Star into space. In less than a half-hour after being set free by the 747 crew, the craft soared to eight thousand miles above the shrinking earth. LaFrentz settled his plane into orbit over the Middle East.

He didn't worry whether he was over friendly or enemy territory. His craft was nearly invisible. It absorbed rather than reflected radiant light waves. Black Star's electromagnetic skin, like a chameleon's, could if the situation required modify the plane's appearance so that it blended into whatever background existed. An elaborate set of computer-controlled sensors estimated what would be seen if the plane were not there. This information was transmitted to the counter-shading system of thin sheets of light-emitting polymers that glowed and changed color when properly charged.

The astounding sight of the colorful earth suspended against the infinite black heavens; the calm of floating weightless; and the peace of absolute quiet manifest a surreal sensation. LaFrentz found it as relaxing as floating on an air mattress in his swimming pool on a lazy summer day. It was strange how such an aggressive mission felt so tranquil.

Day 36 1 A.M. Geostationary Earth Orbit

LaFrentz's intricate maneuvering of his plane was about to bear fruit. He fine-tuned his path, coaxing the stealthy, black bird into a trailing position about twenty miles behind and below the first Iranian spy satellite. This initial rendezvous was nearing a climax.

"That's it. Come to Little Brother," LaFrentz crooned.

"So far so good. Number one is in my sites," exclaimed the charged-up pilot.

The Iranian trio of spy satellites, stalked by LaFrentz and Black Star I, had been thrust aloft over the past three years. They were in complementary geostationary elliptical orbits, and were timed to circle the earth once a day. Thus, all three remained over the Iranian time zone. They changed only in how close to earth they flew. Each satellite in a tilted elliptical orbit, once a day, approached within 180 miles of earth. Through proper sequencing, one of the three was always relatively close and usefully relaying intelligence to Iran.

LaFrentz reluctantly turned over the final approach to his craft's onboard Position and Fire Weapons computer (POF). POF systematically brought the attack craft into lethal firing position only one mile from the Iranian satellite.

The Black Star pilot struggled with a further sense of detachment, brought about by this abdication of final-approach navigating and piloting duties.

The laser weapon was a low-powered copy of the Army's much-publicized Mid-Infrared Advanced Chemical Laser, MIRACL. The Army's powerful version of this weapon was advertised as capable of destroying orbiting satellites from an earth base. He was not a scientist, but he doubted the official story put out by the Army. Too much atmospheric attenuation, he figured, for that claim to be believable. He suspected that the Army's public program served as cover for the development of the weapon he was about to use.

The laser, dubbed ZAP, would soon destroy the electronic nerve center of the Iranian satellite. Its light ray, while not harming the mechanical structure of the satellite, would turn its vital onboard electronic circuitry into electrical mush. Thus the enemy satellite would simply fail most mysteriously.

The POF computer notified LaFrentz that ZAP was primed for firing. He checked everything one last time. Satisfied that all was in order, he signaled a "go." A potent ray of purplish-red light belched forth from the nose of Black Star and promptly melted the orbiter's circuit boards.

LaFrentz's monitoring equipment immediately confirmed that the target was dead. "Persian bird number one, MIA, two to go," LaFrentz chortled, allowing himself a moment of celebration.

Black Star's Base Command in New Mexico, monitoring his sporadic broadcasts, responded, "Dead bird confirmed, Little Brother. Nice shot. How are you holding up?"

LaFrentz reported, "Fantastic. This is the best job in the universe."

He knew that the voice transmissions from Black Star were entirely secure. They were encoded, then directionally sent in brief electromagnetic bursts, which sporadically changed carrier frequency to frustrate any chance of an enemy intercepting the signals.

He fired the main rocket engine and maneuvered into a climb of several thousand miles, where he would intercept the next satellite diving toward him from the south. That second rendezvous would occur in a few hours.

With a little time before the next encounter, he took in the synthetic views of the earth from this unique perspective. Out of curiosity, he trained one of the array of remotely controlled cameras onto Iranian territory. He zoomed in with the high-resolution cameras on the Karaj Nuclear Complex far below. He focused on its perimeter, and then followed the security fence to one of the corner guard towers where the Iranian green, white and red flag flapped in the desert wind. Were his eyes deceiving him? Below the Iranian flag flew an upside down American flag. Shaking his head, he worried, "Maybe I have been in orbit too long. I can't tell up from down anymore."

Day 36 4:30 P.M. Geostationary Earth Orbit

For the third and last time the purplish-red beam of light spurted from Black Star I's nose. All of the energy in that beam burst upon the electronic nerve center of the final satellite, scrambling its circuits and its ability to function.

"Status of Persian bird number three is defunct. Can you confirm?"

"Roger Little Brother. Number three has fallen from the nest."

LaFrentz was relieved. He and Townsley, the pilot of Black Star II, who had downed problem communication satellites, had cleared the way for several Joint Eagles military buildups. Together they had made sure that neither private nor public satellites would be able to warn Iran or the Mafia of what the U.S. was about to do. Some of these operations, he understood, would be commencing even before he returned from space. In fact, if he was lucky, he would catch a couple of those rare events.

The darkness that had crept across the beautiful globe below him was relinquishing its grip. With the retreat of night and the appearance of the first sliver of dawn's light, he felt surprisingly renewed.

He maneuvered Black Star in preparation for the return to earth. A series of retro firings of the main rocket engine slowed the plane. As a consequence the plane swept downward into a lower orbit. By a combination of main rocket burns and firings of the lateral thrusters, he also shifted to a nearly polar sub-orbital circling of the earth. The phantom space plane coasted to about one hundred miles above the earth. Instead of sitting over the Middle East, the plane now raced north across Eastern Europe.

Day 36 6:30 P.M. Polar Orbit

LaFrentz recalled from General Adair's briefing that an unprecedented flight of twenty giant Russian Condors from Russia to Ramstein Air Base in Germany should be underway. His present pass over Russian territory should take him over that amazing action.

He understood that the Condor, once the largest plane in the world, was capable of carrying fifty percent more payload than the largest U.S. transport, the C-5 Lockheed Galaxy. Massed at Ramstein were forty of America's most advanced Abrams, the MIA3s. The monstrous Russian Condors would transport the formidable American tanks to the Baku Air Base in Azerbaijan, the southern most Russian base. Without approaching its record lift of 377,000 pounds, each Condor would easily carry two of the seventy-ton Abrams.

The Russian designator for the plane was the Antonov AN-124. However, LaFrentz felt its NATO name, the Condor, was more apropos. He had studied the history of this plane when he was at the Air Force Academy. Being a literature buff, he had been amazed to read that the second AN-124 prototype had been christened "The Ruslan," named after the giant hero of Russian folklore, immortalized by Russia's beloved poet, Pushkin. That recognition attested to the hero status still accorded the great Russian writers. He laughed, thinking no American submarine had ever been named the Mark Twain, nor an aircraft carrier christened the Tom Clancy. A carrier named the Michael Jordan, though, was a definite possibility. The two societies' values were very different, that was for sure.

As his plane crossed directly above Molensk Air Base in east central Russia, he trained the telescopic zoom cameras on the base, which was bathed in the dawn's early light. Sure enough, there they were.

He watched entranced as one after another the huge Condors majestically soared from the Base, commencing their history-making flight to Germany. The significance of the moment was breathtaking.

LaFrentz tore himself away from the hypnotic sight. Returning to business was unfortunately necessary. He did a quick reckoning of his track, figuring it would take about two and a half hours to complete the next two polar circles of the earth. His last passage should yield another spectacular sight as the American naval fleet made history. He would pass directly over the Strait of the Dardanelles, the water channel connecting the Mediterranean with the Black Sea.

Day 36 9 P.M. Final Polar Orbit

LaFrentz fidgeted anxiously in his cockpit and checked the time. His growing anticipation served only to slow this last trip around the earth to a crawl. It was taking forever. Tantalizingly, Black Star I ever so gradually brought him up across first the equator, then northeastern Africa. Finally the northern Egyptian coastline emerged from hiding. The sun had risen on a portion of the earth and ocean beneath him. The Mediterranean spread out sparkling blue to the east and progressively darker to the west where night lingered. The bifurcated globe of blue sea, brown earth and white swirls varied from impenetrable darkness to a kaleidoscope of color.

With his powerful cameras, he zoomed in on the entire Seventh Fleet group in constricted battle formation. The warships steamed toward their first ever Black Sea tour. Despite the tighter-than-normal formation, the ships were still spread over a vast area. The reflection of the rising sun clearly illuminated the wake of each ship. What an overwhelming sight!

No less than sixty of the U.S. Navy's warships, one mighty arm of the military-strike force being assembled for Joint Eagles, sailed toward the strait. The leading escort craft, destroyers and patrol boats, were already entering the mouth of the strait. Their destination, the Black Sea, was a body of water, which had formally been off limits to the U.S. Navy for most of the previous century.

The largest and most lethal craft in the fleet, the nuclear powered carrier, Kitty Hawk with its contingent of eighty aircraft dominated the scene. The mammoth floating airstrip, steaming toward the strait with twenty Super Hornets poised on its deck, was in the center of the formation. Several dozen escorting destroyers, cruisers and frigates were strategically positioned around the giant ship, on course as well for the Strait. LaFrentz was overwhelmed with his immense good fortune. Never had anyone had such a ringside seat at a more historic military mobilization.

By virtue of Russia and the Ukraine granting the American military access to the Black Sea, this potent strike force would be several hundred miles closer to its targets than if it had been forced to operate from the Mediterranean. The fleet, therefore, would be in a far better position to support the looming Joint Eagles air campaign.

Perversely LaFrentz's plane now seemed to speed up, carrying him too quickly away from the mesmerizing sight. Back at work, he maneuvered to a sub-orbital flight path, descending to the top of the troposphere as he crossed northern Europe for the last time. His sightseeing was definitely over as he hustled to properly prepare Black Star I for its fiery reentry. He checked the air-breathing engine's readiness to fire and initiated the thin ceramic skin deployment.

The aeronautical engineers had found that a pilot could conduct the reentry evolution far better than any pilotless craft. Despite phenomenal computer advances, human judgment still couldn't completely be replaced. This was one of the principal reasons that Black Star had developed as a manned program.

LaFrentz continued reconfiguring the protective covering by coaxing the expendable ceramic shields into place. This aeronautical miracle of stealth had required major innovations. Saving the polymer camouflage skin from damage during the fiery reentry had presented one of the knottier technical problems. Paul's deployment of the protective ceramic skin over the camouflaging surfaces allowed the expensive polymer sheets to survive, shielded from the intense heat of reentry. After reentry the spent ceramic would be jettisoned, restoring Black Star's stealth.

More than any other phase of the flight, the reentry maneuvers required his total concentration. These next moments were the only times Black Star was vulnerable to detection. Strange fiery streaks in the sky were occasionally seen by earth-bound observers. They had unknowingly witnessed Black Star's reentry. It was always explained away, however, by "official sources" as space debris falling out of orbit, or a meteor burning up upon entering earth's atmosphere.

THIRTY-SIX

Day 37 12:15 A.M. Central Asian Jet Stream

Once Black Stars' missions were achieved, CENTCOM accelerated the marshaling of its forces for the coming attack. As LaFrentz raced through the firestorm of reentry, a small band of U.S. Special Forces soldiers embarked upon a cold, dangerous and lonely night's ride high above the Caspian Sea. Captain Dan O'Banyon's commando team was sailing toward an excursion in the desert near the Karaj nuclear facility. O'Banyon's clandestine mission was no less significant than that of the Seventh Fleet in the Black Sea.

Suspended high above the Caspian Sea, ten Special Forces soldiers, wearing high-altitude flight suits, sailed silently south, propelled by the strong central Asian jet stream. At twenty-five thousand feet, the oversized paragliders captured the swift currents of the bitterly cold, rarefied ribbon of air, propelling the commandos inexorably toward the Iranian coast and their rendezvous with Karaj.

At this altitude the temperature fell to a bone-chilling thirty below, and the atmospheric oxygen was only a fraction of that necessary for the commando's survival. Their flight suits prevented freezing, but still the cold stung O'Banyon's squad. Each soldier carried a two-hour supply of oxygen in his backpack.

Despite the debilitating chill, O'Banyon's mind raced over the recent intelligence briefings on the Karaj fortress. CIA and National Security Agency (NSA) operatives had provided various shreds of data on the weapons factory at Karaj. The Iranians had attempted to frustrate Western Intelligence by deliberately employing many companies from different countries to design and supply the nuclear complex's systems. To some extent the obfuscation had worked, O'Banyon judged, or else he wouldn't be freezing his cajones off while floating into enemy territory.

The big problem was that nothing had been uncovered about how the underground fortress would be defended during an attack. O'Banyon's team had the formidable task of ascertaining the defensive strategies.

Trimming the specialized chutes to maximize lift, the commandos sacrificed speed for the crucial maintenance of altitude. Employing their high-altitude chutes and the advanced techniques taught at the Army's Special Forces schools, the soldiers floated ever closer to the enemy coastline. Drifting in the thin upper reaches of the clear starlit sky, O'Banyon watched the lights of the cities along the populous Iranian seaboard grow brighter and closer.

Still undetected the ten chutes slipped over the brightly lit enemy coastline as O'Banyon checked his altimeter. They had navigated thirty frigid miles above the Caspian Sea, losing a little over a mile of altitude. Since a formidable range of tall mountains still lay directly in their path, O'Banyon's greatest concern was maintaining sufficient elevation. If they descended too quickly, they wouldn't reach Karaj, rather they would fall far short of their target, lost in the rugged Alborz Mountains.

Sinking below the swift river of air, the squad of soldiers floated farther inland, but at a slower pace. The lights of the fertile coastal area gradually faded away behind them. The looming wall of darkness, the Alborz Mountain chain, rose menacingly in their path.

O'Banyon broke radio silence and ordered each soldier to jettison one full oxygen bottle. The bottles dropped unseen onto the remote foothills. Each commando now had only one nearly empty bottle.

While continuously consulting his military wrist computer and his GPS receiver for precise navigational guidance, O'Banyon directed his paraglider toward Ayatollah Pass. The dim directional light on the rear of his chute served as a beacon for his team, which stretched out behind him like a "V" formation of wild geese.

He reckoned that they would clear the pass with a mere fifty feet to spare. He cursed, "This is too damned close! Drop your last oxygen bottle now."

With labored breathing in the rarefied air, the floating commandos skimmed through the uninhabited pass barely above the rock-strewn highland. The silhouette of Mount Demavend, an extinct volcano, loomed high above them, a muted witness to their narrowly successful passage through the Alborz Mountains into Iran's interior.

"Whew," sighed O'Banyon. "Those damned mountains nearly screwed this deal."

Leaving the mountain range behind, they drifted southward still farther inland. The light down-sloping wind drove them relentlessly deeper into the heart of Iran. The vast arid interior plateau stretched out below them. The not so distant lights of Tehran glowed on the eastern horizon, reminding O'Banyon of the extreme danger accompanying this mission. Discovery would spell a terrible death as well as the betrayal of the entire Joint Eagles mission. For this reason each of his men voluntarily carried a deadly pill, which would be swallowed if the situation warranted.

After another twenty miles of floating across seemingly endless desolation, Dan's team found themselves above a modern oasis, the bustling Highway Four. There was no avoiding the busy highway. The main transportation artery west from Tehran had to be crossed. Even in the early morning hours the traffic was fairly heavy. O'Banyon knew that in a few days a section of that highway far below them was destined to become one busy mother of an airstrip. There would be one hell of a traffic jam when the Longbows explosively erected their roadblocks.

At least the below zero ordeal was over for the commandos. Each warrior breathed deeply, relishing the warmer, oxygen-rich desert air.

To avoid detection, the fliers circled west giving a wide berth to the Karaj Division's headquarters and the town of Karaj. Once clearing the division and the town, they turned east and glided low over their sandy, rock-strewn target only two miles south of the Karaj nuclear weapons complex.

After several hours in the foreign night sky, the Special Forces soldiers trimmed their glide chutes. The resulting dive dropped them south of the hill that was to become their temporary home.

Upon landing they stumbled awkwardly, stiff from the cold and the forced inactivity. Their feet stung from the impact of the earth and their leg muscles initially refused the hard work suddenly thrust upon them. Quickly regaining their coordination, though, the commandos buried their paragliders and other flight gear deep in the sand and changed into their desert camouflage.

Armed and ready for trouble, they scaled the hill south of the Karaj complex. Employing his wrist computer and maps to avoid land mines, O'Banyon and his commando squad scrambled to the summit where they burrowed into the sand. They pulled desert camouflage tarps over their strategically located new home, holes in the sand. Despite their presence and their great view of the Karaj Complex, there still appeared to be only sand, rocks and lizards residing on the hilltop.

Day 38 - 40 Karaj Hilltop

For three nights and days, with the aid of powerful binoculars, the American soldiers spied upon and catalogued every nuance of the exterior-guard activities at the weapons factory. Based upon those observations, they created a comprehensive timetable.

The dug-in commandos diligently studied the maps Intelligence had made of the grounds surrounding the complex. Time-lapse satellite pictures, disclosing where the guards walked and drove, coupled with computer analyses of their paths, had enabled Military Intelligence to map the mine-free corridors. Those safe lanes were used by O'Banyon's soldiers as they moved about.

The motion detector system installed inside the perimeter fence would be easily dealt with by the Special Forces intruders. The experienced O'Banyon was not without solutions. He held a couple of aces up his sleeve, one provided by nature and the other by Intelligence. The late afternoon windstorms often kicked up enough sand and dust to render the system useless. Also, a British agent, who had infiltrated the factory providing the Iranians with the motion-detection system, deliberately preset the focus of the machines on narrow beam. The commandos, therefore, could squirm under the motion-sensing rays with relative ease, even if the winds subsided.

At O'Banyon's request, a radar mapping satellite scanned the ground along the perimeter fence. A Milcom satellite relayed to his wrist receiver where the ground under the fence was of the correct texture to allow tunneling. Armed with that knowledge, the team working in shifts excavated a small tunnel just large enough for one solider at a time to snake through the secret passage to the interior yard. By sprinkling sand and rocks on top of their desert camouflage tarps, Sgt. Paul Schwatka hid the tunnel's entrance so completely that the eye alone could not discern its existence.

Day 41 11:30 P.M. Karaj Complex

The fifth night in enemy territory was to be the most eventful. Two of the commandos, who were familiar with the design of the ventilation system, entered the grounds inside the complex by snaking through the tunnel. Avoiding guards, dogs, mines, sensors and searchlights, the two, known affectionately as the Gophers, bolted across the final open space on their way from the tunnel to the ventilation intake.

After a tortuous crawl of a hundred meters through the one meter-diameter ventilation pipe, they took precise measurements which would confirm that it was built almost exactly as the CIA had described. Their purpose for exploring the piping was to evaluate its use as a possible entrance into the underground complex.

After an exhaustive night of crawling through the pipes measuring key sections, they cautiously and laboriously retreated. Returning to their base on the southern hilltop, they found all but one of their team gone.

Day 42 3 A.M. South of the Karaj Complex

Military Intelligence had briefed O'Banyon that the Karaj guards ranked major or above would be cognizant of the facility's defensive strategies. O'Banyon's squad had observed that the guards always worked in pairs, even when they left Karaj, so they would have to capture not one but two of the rag heads.

Interrogator, the nickname of O'Banyon's most savage soldier, had told him, "No problem. Two will yield more."

Tonight they staked out the lightly traveled secondary road running south from the complex. O'Banyon split his team into three groups. A forward lookout was dispatched, near the facility's south exit, to watch for guards leaving the base. Down the road a few miles, four of O'Banyon's commandos set up an ambush on the road directly below O'Banyon and one sharpshooter who covered the ambush scene from a nearby ridge.

After watching for hours, the forward lookout finally radioed, "Desert Fox Six, two pigeons are fleeing the coop. Their berets indicate that the ragheads are majors. ETA is five minutes."

Through his headset O'Banyon relayed, "This is Desert Fox Six. Guests are coming to our party. Prepare to welcome."

At a narrow spot in the winding, dusty desert road, a small group of camels milled aimlessly around. It had been no minor achievement to spirit the animals away from the nearby herd, but Prudhoe Paul had done it. In coaxing the animals to follow him, Paul had done the impossible once again.

Paul Schwatka, a Native American, had grown up in a small northern Alaska village near Prudhoe Bay. His heritage and his experience in the Arctic wilderness had equipped him with invaluable skills. He could stalk an enemy, even where there apparently was no cover whatsoever, and he possessed an uncanny ability to communicate with animals. Creatures great and small loved Prudhoe Paul.

Schwatka and his three companions lay in wait beneath the sand beside the road where the guards would soon pass. From the nearby rise, O'Banyon and a sharpshooter covered the four.

Watching the approaching jeep, O'Banyon reminded the soldier, "Remember, we want these two alive. Don't get trigger happy."

Then as if on cue, the camels wandered right onto the narrow road, blocking the path of the jeep. "How in the hell do you do it, Paul?" O'Banyon wondered aloud. In reality he understood "how" as well as anyone, since he had been regaled with endless stories of Prudhoe Paul's youthful exploits in the Arctic wilderness.

The beasts stymied the jeep. The guards swore and shook their fists at the dromedaries. Suddenly without warning, the sand relinquished the four camouflaged commandos. Before the shocked Iranian officers could react, the pair was restrained and swept away by the enigmatic men of war.

The commandos crashed the jeep into a nearby ravine. As a final sanitation of the scene, Paul coaxed the animals into a milling pattern that wiped out most signs of the Special Forces' presence. Finally, to obliterate any remaining trace, he rode the last camel around and then away from the crash site.

Day 42 8 A.M. Karaj Hilltop

The Special Forces soldier, Interrogator, whom his comrades respected yet feared, separated the captured majors. O'Banyon held ambivalent feelings toward Interrogator. The soldier possessed a vicious streak convenient for these circumstances. Fortunately, the ugly side of the man seemed to be controlled and never emerged unless the mission required it.

In fluent Farsi, Interrogator informed each captive that the one who talked first would be spared. The other would die a slow and excruciating death. For emphasis he described the death process in all of its gory detail. They would meet their insides up close and personal.

O'Banyon, who understood Farsi, shuddered, for under most circumstances that was no idle threat. The lethal Interrogator excelled at extracting intelligence. His inventory of methods, however, was limited under the present circumstances. These guards must be returned soon to the crash site, visibly unharmed, or a massive search would be mounted for them; a search O'Banyon's Special Forces team could not survive. For this reason, he ordered Interrogator to employ chemicals.

A somewhat disappointed Interrogator complied. He forcefully administered a combination of psychotomimetic inhalants to his separated victims. Allowing time for the drugs to take effect, he completely shifted gears. Gone was the animalistic Interrogator. In his place was Interrogator, the con man. Searching their papers he discovered their names and ranks. Putting on an Iranian general's hat and coat, carried in for just this occasion, he proceeded with the first drugged and disoriented soldier as though he were an Iranian general.

"Major Sumad, I am General Utel from General Bakr Zarif's staff. We are reviewing your understanding of the defense of Karaj. If your comprehension is sufficiently excellent, your promotion to major general is assured."

Playing out that charade with each of the chemically weakened enemy, Interrogator extracted the essence of their defensive plans. Vulnerable to the power of suggestion, they responded as he wished.

Satisfied with their stories, O'Banyon ordered Interrogator and Sgt. Schwatka to return the two captive officers to the scene of the crashed jeep.

Once back at the roadside site, Interrogator administered disorientation drugs. The prisoners' memories would be a blur. They and their superiors would hopefully conclude that the jeep crash had knocked them out, causing their fuzzy memory. Prudhoe Paul again cleansed the site of all vestiges of the commandos' presence. In the Iranian's subsequent inspection of the accident scene, the investigators would find evidence that the guards had swerved to avoid some stray camels and had suffered concussions when they crashed into the ravine.

The next night, O'Banyon ordered the Gophers back into the complex to check out aspects of the prisoners' stories. While the Gophers were about their assignment, a squad, led by O'Banyon, stealthily approached the Karaj complex and placed homing devices near the exterior guard towers of the complex. These devices would be remotely activated several days hence during the U.S. attack, guiding the Apache's miniature guided missiles to precise hits.

After all of the commandos returned to their hilltop base, O'Banyon's squad mulled over all that they had garnered. There in their grimy hole, a shrewd strategy to defeat Karaj's defenses sprang to life.

THIRTY-SEVEN

Day 38 7:30 P.M. Professor Dudaev's Home Hartford, Connecticut

Stockton's call earlier that the lab had completed Laura Andrew's DNA tests had served to tease. Stockton wouldn't relay the results over the phone, but insisted on a meeting. Dudaev tensely lit his pipe. He was about to learn if he had been right over the years about the birthrights of Marina and Laura. He was apprehensive. What if he had been wrong?

Liz Nieman was coming with Stockton. That was good because he had questions for her as well as for Stockton.

Pipe smoke billowed about him as he contemplated how his organization may have recently suffered one of its biggest setbacks ever. His reliable insiders within the Mafia, he reluctantly conceded, had been reduced by a disappointing one. The threat to him and his organization from the Mafia had greatly escalated.

He recalled better times when his organization mounted a massive maneuver to infiltrate the Mafia. His close associate, Goldstein, was the one who had succeeded in achieving a leadership role within the gang. Now with Goldstein no longer to be trusted, his guards were challenged as never before to keep Dudaev safe and to hide the full scope of his endeavors from the Mafia turncoat.

With a little time before Stockton and Nieman arrived, Dudaev tried unsuccessfully to put aside his mounting anxieties. As a last resort he retired to his secret library. There he read and re-read the collection of letters from Marina, specifically concentrating on those which told of Laura's husband, Ben.

Day 38 8:45 P.M. Professor Dudaev's Home

After a short greeting the boisterous Stockton broke the news to Dudaev, "I won't keep you waiting any longer. Laura definitely is the

290

granddaughter of your hero, Viktor Sumurov."

There it was, confirmation of what he had always believed. Dudaev took a deep breath before reacting. The ramifications of Laura's identity were many. Several things must be done including providing for Laura's protection and determining when it would be best to make public her identity.

"Under present circumstances, I believe that Laura would be in danger from the Russian Mafia and the Chekists if they learned that she is Sumurov's granddaughter."

That position disappointed Stockton, for he wished to exploit her heritage. Liz, disagreeing with Stockton's view, deliberately spoke up before Stockton could give his reasons for publicizing her identity. She told the Professor, who was relighting his pipe, "What I heard on the Shilthorn tapes tells me that you are probably right. We brought those tapes for you. We want your opinion on them."

For the next two hours the three listened to the excerpts from the Shilthorn tapes. Liz noted that Dudaev seemed to concentrate most intently whenever Goldstein spoke. She suspected that she knew why. At the completion of the tapes, she asked, "What do you know about this Goldstein?"

Dudaev debated whether he should tell Liz and Stockton what he knew about the mobster. For the moment he decided to dodge the question by returning to the earlier issue, "Liz, those tapes confirm that they would consider Laura a threat, especially since she has already proved to be a capable and courageous writer. Her identity can't be made public quite yet."

"Yet? When then?" questioned an impatient Stockton.

"That is the question. A time will come, if she and Ben assent, when it would be appropriate, but I may not live to see that day. I am old and history marches on, with or without any of us."

Neither Liz nor Stockton knew quite what to say to that resigned comment so they just waited for a detached Dudaev to continue. Liz noticed that at times his eyes had a far away look. Was he deliberately avoiding the question about Goldstein? Dudaev obviously felt pain relative to Goldstern.

Dudaev continued, "Laura, though, must be informed of her heritage."

Placing his unlit pipe down, he pulled an envelope from his worn briefcase.

He explained, "In the event that the tests turned out this way, I took the liberty to draft a reply to Laura's letter. My letter explains all

I know about her mother and her grandfather. Also I want Sumurov's secret, unpublished works to accompany the letter. She must have these."

Liz broke in, "You are going to give these to her yourself, aren't you?"

"Oh, how I wish I could. But that is impossible. Will you two deliver these for me?"

Liz protested, "You should be the one to tell her all of this?"

Dudaev determinedly stood his ground, "Normally, yes. Now, no."

"Explain," pleaded Liz.

"Goldstein," muttered Dudaev.

Liz had an inkling of what he meant, "Goldstein was your man, wasn't he?"

A pained look of one betrayed clouded Dudaev's face, "Yes. He was one of my most trusted lieutenants."

Dudaev explained who Goldstein was and how the man was a brilliant strategist. With his leadership the Mafia could become far more of a force than it was now.

"And he has turned on you and your cause."

"Yes, it seems so. It puts me and anyone I associate with in grave danger. That is why I am not going to see Laura. If circumstances were different I would love nothing more than to see Marina's daughter."

Liz thought she detected a tear in the crusty little man's eye. Dudaev, with an obvious effort to change the subject, asked, "How are preparations going for Joint Eagles?"

Stockton summed up Joint Eagles status realizing, especially since his Kruschev visit, that the cooperative aspect between Russia and the United States had special meaning to Dudaev.

After Stockton's briefing Dudaev asked, "So how is Laura's husband Ben handling himself?"

"Like a champ!" responded Stockton.

Dudaev continued the quizzing. "He is in the middle of something much bigger than civilians are accustomed to. The Mafia really hate him and want him gone."

"Yes, they are after him, but we intend to keep anything from happening to him. The country owes him protection for his faithful service."

"I would agree with that. Does he have good leadership qualities?"

"Superior! He is capable of taking on about anything."

"Do you see it that way, too, Liz?" queried Dudaev.

"Yes. He is very capable and fearless to a fault."

"Is he capable of handling complex and mysterious problems where there are no obvious road maps?"

"Absolutely," stated Stockton.

Dudaev pried further to find out what specific observations backed up their opinions. He found that they closely matched what Marina had observed in Ben over the years.

"How close are Ben and Laura, Liz? Are they deeply in love?"

"Very close. They talk on the phone all the time. Yet they are a unique couple. Their talents are so different. Each is a very capable individual in his or her own right, but if they tackle a problem together they are dynamite. What they figured out about NuEnergy and about you still amazes me.

"Ben is the outgoing fearless leader type, who analyzes everything from a technical point of view and then boldly charges forward once he reaches a conclusion. Laura is a lot like you. She is a scholar of history, especially Russian history. She is a literary talent. Her articles on Starovoitova and the Chekists are brilliant. They reveal a depth that is rare. Her bravery emerges in her writing. I am sure you know that.

"Despite, or maybe because of, their differences their love endures. One can see the depth of feeling they have for each other. Their eyes and their faces light up whenever they talk about the other person."

Dudaev nodded, "That is just how Marina described their relationship. She said together they were a most formidable team."

That line of questions by Dudaev puzzled Liz. Why was he so interested in Ben?

"Back to Goldstein. What more can you tell us about him?" asked Stockton.

"He was been an important lieutenant of mine for years. When it became apparent how grievously the Mafia was hurting Russia, he and I strategized on how to infiltrate their ranks. He succeeded in becoming head of the North American branch and thus wound up close to Andropov. For years his position yielded great dividends to my organization in our attempts to counter the Mafia's influence. However in the last year I have come to suspect that my former comrade could no longer be trusted. What he didn't know was that I had other sources in the mob as well. I always crosscheck information. He no longer provides reliable reports, and sometimes he is actually misleading. He has turned into my enemy. The tapes we just heard confirm that unhappy conclusion."

Stockton and Liz left with Dudaev's letter and papers for Laura and the task of telling her all. As they walked from the house Stockton observed, "Figuring out who Dudaev is, is like peeling an onion. You remove one layer of mystery and another mystery is waiting there more confounding than before. I think we will never grasp the full extent of this man's dominion."

Liz settled into the rental car's passenger seat and thought before answering. "Good analogy except that the fruits of his labors are far sweeter than the onion."

THIRTY-EIGHT

Day 40 6 A.M. Andrew's Home Tulsa Outskirts

An overwhelming force pulled Laura closer to the sheer face of the cliff. The jagged rocks tore at her bruised and bleeding arms as the inevitable slide brought her nearer the edge of doom. Her arms slipped over the rim and stretched down. She peered down after her extended limbs into a swirling cauldron of fog. With the exertion becoming nearly unbearable something struck her as strange. She grasped the force. It wasn't gripping her. She could just let go, get up and walk safely away, but she didn't. Why?

As the fog thinned briefly, obscurely at first the apparition of the dangling man, whose arms she held, appeared. She strained to see who it was. At first the face appeared to be Ben. Yes, it was her dear Ben, but his image transfigured. Ben faded away and a slight old man materialized. Was it Dudaev? Before she could be sure it too was gone and only a familiar faraway, yet reassuring, voice called to her. The voice sang in Russian verse about a vision, a vision of a brighter future. As she listened the fog evaporated and the force was gone, replaced by a pleasant light.

Terrified and sweating, Laura moaned and rolled over. Her arm draped across Ben's chest and her hand grasped his arm. Thank God he was here. She hadn't lost him. But it was a dream within a dream; he wasn't really here. She awoke, finding that she merely grasped a pillow. Ben was still in D.C. dealing with Joint Eagles.

Was the dream a warning or a premonition of a terrible future? Was she to lose Ben, too? She couldn't stand that possibility. The dream could be interpreted in so many ways. Halfway between sleep and consciousness, she lay in bed with her eyes closed pondering the meaning of the illusory vision. Whose was the singing voice, which

295

awakened a long dormant memory of a Russian lullaby she had heard as a child?

Coming up with few answers, she dismissed it. After all it was only a dream, which perhaps reflected her fear of losing Ben. Everyone else close to her was gone. Ben, though, would be home soon, thank God. Her Ben would be right next to her, where he must stay forever. No more Joint Eagles crusades for him.

She cried, not sure whether the fears were inspired by the stress of Ben's recent absence or something else. Maybe it was everything, she didn't know.

She wiped away more tears. She was glad Ben wasn't here to see her crying. That wouldn't be good. He didn't need any more worries.

The dream seemed so vivid, so real, that she just couldn't let it drop. Was the second face that of Dudaev? Today's much anticipated visit may have triggered that part of the dream, a dream full of irresistible transitions. She didn't want change. She just wanted Ben to stay by her side forever. Oh well, she chastised herself, "Settle down, Laura. It was only a dream."

Laura missed Ben. He was a strong, handsome principled man, yet so vulnerable. His very strength was his vulnerability. He wouldn't back down when he perceived that something wasn't right, no matter the forces arrayed against him.

During their last phone conversation, Ben hadn't wanted to tell her about his close shave in D.C., but she had divined that something was being left untold, so she had quizzed him until she got the truth. Tears and terror came again. She didn't believe that the Mafia would ever leave him alone.

I'm an emotional mess she told herself. This isn't like me. Is it still grief from my mother's death that has thrown me so off stride? Or is it the danger stalking Ben? I should try to think of only good things, except that isn't so easy these days.

Ben and she had talked of their future. Ben had suggested that when he got home he should take over the business management of the bookstore. That would free her to concentrate on her writing. He had read her Starovoitova exposé and assured her that it was very good. He insisted that she should author more articles like it. His idea had merit. Writing about Russia, made her feel alive. Their plan for the future excited her.

Finally Laura's thoughts turned toward today. This afternoon Liz Nieman was coming to visit her.

Liz had told her that she brought news from Dudaev. So, indeed, maybe the second face in her dream was that of Dudaev. She chastised herself. Forget the dumb dream. Company is coming and there is much to do before Liz arrives.

Excited about the meeting, she rolled out of bed.

Day 40 4:30 P.M. Laura's Bookstore Tulsa

Long after Liz had left, Laura clutched the Dudaev letter tightly and read it yet again.

Dear Laura,

Events sadly forbid my coming to see you in person and telling you all I know about your mother, Marina, and your grandfather, Viktor Sumurov. Yes, the gifted Viktor Sumurov was your grandfather.

Liz either has or will tell you how we know that for a fact, but I always believed Marina was his daughter and of course you his granddaughter. That is one reason that my compatriots and I, so many years ago, arranged for your and your mother's escape. The Communists and the Chekists were about to discover who you two were. Your lives were in grave danger.

That menace persists to this day. The Chekists fear even a dead Sumurov and the moral principles his works espouse. Once the Chekists and the Mafia are defeated the danger to you should subside. Until then you must be careful and not acknowledge publicly who you are.

The other reason for your and your mother's escape was to smuggle out Viktor Sumurov's final works. By now, Liz should have given you the originals. They are potent and quite explosive in the way that they challenge Russians to resist the evil of the Chekist system of fear and repression. Further you will see that he laid out an ingenious blueprint for a freer Russia. Many influential Russians, close friends of mine, have and are aligning themselves with that promise.

I revealed and discussed these writings of your grandfather with Solzhenitsyn over thirty years ago. They were so persuasive that the great dissident gave my followers and me his blessing to attempt to enact Sumurov's ideas.

Laura was perplexed. Just who was this man and his organization? He was much more than a mere tottering old professor.

Laura returned to the letter.

Your mother was a friend, and oh, much more. Yet, I saw her only once, immediately after you two arrived in America. It was not because I wished it that way, but because your and her safety demanded it. We wrote to each other weekly over the years. She described your development as a child and a young adult, so from afar I watched you grow up, marry and develop into a gifted writer.

Your mother represented all that is good and noble in Russia. She was a champion rider, maybe the best Russia ever produced. She had a strong faith in God and in the country she fled. I believe you inherited many of the virtues and talents of your mother and your grandfather.

Laura wiped away a tear before continuing.

I loved your mother and would have given nearly anything to have intimately shared her life, not from a maddening distance...

Laura could read no more. Her sadness was suffocating. Nearly choking she gasped for breath. Her mother and grandfather had endured so much. Was that her heritage as well? She must call Ben and talk to him about all of this.

THIRTY-NINE

Day 42 9 A.M. NRC Headquarters Bethesda, Maryland

"I am Dr. Ben Andrew from the Black Bear Plant in Oklahoma. You are here because Vice President Foster has called us to serve with him. Listen carefully. Our nation is in grave danger! A conspiracy led by organized crime has been uncovered. At the heart of this scheme is the destruction of our nation's nuclear plants. Your presence here today is a direct result of that threat." Ben spoke gravely and intensely, exhibiting none of the dubiety he felt moments ago when he first stepped in front of the assembled throng. By George, he was in this mess up to his ears and he would fight on with every ounce of strength God granted him.

He hastened to clarify how this matter involved them. "Your country needs your help to thwart this plot, a plot which would disable every NuEnergy power plant. Each of you has been assigned to a team. Each team's goal is to prevent the sabotage of one of those plants. If we all do our job well, we can defeat this devilish attempt to wreck our country."

He paused to let the impact of his words sink in on the nearly two hundred carefully chosen men and women. He definitely had their attention. Never had he addressed a more attentive audience.

Bethesda, bordering upon northwest D.C., was the setting for this unusual gathering. The Nuclear Regulatory Commission (NRC) periodically summoned nuclear plant operators to meetings here in precisely this hearing room. With this in mind, Ben had chosen Bethesda's NRC headquarters for this gathering. Luxuriously furnished in comparison with the rest of the headquarters, the room served the five commissioners, who normally presided far above the nuclear power commoners. It reminded Ben of a senate hearing room, where the senators held court, elevated far above the witnesses and spectators. Avoiding that affectation, Ben spoke from a stage below and in front of the commissioners' elevated bench. Also sitting near him were Garrison, Regional Administrator Friesen and the CEO of the Institute of Nuclear Power Operations (INPO), Admiral Yeager.

This room had never hosted such a diverse assortment of talent as was gathered here today. Ninety FBI agents, sixty nuclear plant technical experts from around the country, none, of course, from NuEnergy plants, and thirty NRC regulators comprised the crowd.

Ben's team had handpicked the utility and NRC personnel. The Bureau subjected those choices to an expedited, yet comprehensive, background scrutiny before they were cleared to participate here today. Upon their arrival this morning, they were informed that they had been picked for a dangerous assignment involving national security. Only a handful had said, "No, thanks."

Ben looked around the room before continuing and noted that several of Garrison's agents had secured the meeting room. The civilians in the audience, many of whom had been here before but under far different circumstances, had various expressions on their faces. Those looks ranged from disbelief or nervous concern to outright shock at the gravity of Ben's opening remarks. They had all labored in the nuclear vineyard where moments of high drama were rare, to say the least.

Ben, concerned about their well-being, was carefully watching the reactions of the civilians as he amplified upon what they faced.

"Let me be more specific. International criminals, known as the Russian Mafia, have developed a diabolical plan to shut down the U.S. by forcing a nearly nationwide blackout. At the heart of the scheme is the simultaneous sabotage of the NuEnergy nuclear plants, a feat that would trigger a widespread and prolonged power disruption. Much study and preparation must be done by each of you in the next few days to prevent this."

At the mention of the Mafia, a couple of the nuclear experts' faces drained of all color.

Ben paused and reminded them, "If any of you would like a drink, we have whatever you want in the back of the room. So feel free to get up and help yourself. I know this is unnerving news. I sympathize with you for all you must absorb and accomplish in such a short time. Anything to make the job easier and you more comfortable, we will gladly do."

One of his discerning industry acquaintances in the audience piped up, "Hey, Ben, are all of these agents in here to protect us? I never saw so many plain-clothes officers since the old days at the Nebraska rad-waste disposal meetings."

Ben laughed, "Those were some tense times up there in the Sand Hills, weren't they? You are partially correct, Roger. There are a large number of FBI agents here today. They will be working with you, and in a sense, provide you protection as well. They are an integral part of each team.

"It's my understanding that you utility and NRC personnel have been told that personal risk accompanies this assignment. We offer our profound gratitude for your courage and willingness to serve your country in the face of such danger. Vice President Foster asked me to convey his deepest appreciation to each of you.

"I must sternly remind you, though, that from the moment you walked into this room, all information shared with you is absolutely top secret."

Another civilian in the audience challenged, "Can't I even tell my wife what goes?"

Ben vehemently responded, "No!"

"I will name you as a witness in my divorce proceedings then."

"Tell her only that you are at an NRC workshop. Nothing more. After this is over, we will have a dinner for you and your families. Then they will learn what all of this was about and the vital service each of you gave your country.

"The NRC is promulgating a cover story for this meeting. They will report that a special workshop was convened to review declining security performance at many nuclear plants. New terrorist threats are given as the reason for closing today's meeting. In a sense that isn't far from the truth. It gives a plausible reason to the NuEnergy hierarchy, the Mafia and the rest of the world for the secrecy surrounding this 'NRC' meeting."

One of the engineers piped up, "So how long is this whole deal lasting?"

"You will be sequestered with your team until this mission is complete. Bear with me a few moments and you will learn the schedule.

"All NuEnergy plants are Mafia controlled through corrupt NuEnergy management. Mafia technicians and engineers at each plant possess the requisite technical capability and the necessary access to the plant's interior to sabotage all of the units almost simultaneously. We believe that their goal is to do such severe damage to the turbine generators that the plants won't return to power production for years. Some might never operate again.

"In addition, because of the loss of many large power plants all at once, the entire eastern and central U.S. electrical grid will go down faster than a Lennox Lewis sparring partner. The loss would cause huge secondary damage to our country's industry and economy, and, on a more personal level, the deaths of large numbers of our most vulnerable citizens. This extended blackout would likely trigger a severe recession, probably even a depression. The stakes are extremely high. Your success is a must!"

Ben deliberately avoided any mention of the military threat and the imminent U.S. response. These people had enough to deal with. Also the security of Joint Eagles was served by the omission.

"You will be here for the next two days as you assimilate the reams of material we assembled. You will see that quick action might be necessary. Your intimate and thorough knowledge of the design and layout of your assigned plant, its operational characteristics, its personnel and its procedures, are essential. Each plant team is composed of three FBI agents, one NRC inspector and two utility experts.

"Two days from now your team will travel to a location only a short distance from your assigned plant. Then upon a signal from us on the following evening, you will proceed to gain entry to each plant as promptly as possible."

One excitable engineer from Oregon questioned, "Is the FBI going to shoot their way in?"

"You have watched too many James Bond movies. Unless things go terribly wrong, it will be a subtle, orderly and non-violent entry.

"Simultaneously with your team's arrival at the plant, a resident NRC inspector will go to the control room and announce to the supervising operator that a National Emergency has been declared. He will inform them that the NRC is assuming operating control of the plant. The resident inspector will also instruct the operating supervisor that each plant's security force will be under the direct command of the Agent-in-Charge, who is the leader of your team. Over the next two days we will go into detail on each team's plans and objectives."

Pointing to those on the stage with him, Ben added, "My associates, their assistants, and I are prepared to take each team through the detailed info you must master over the next two days. From the moment your team was formed this morning, the Agent-in-Charge has become your boss, as well as your protector, so give him your full support.

"I am sure that many of you know NRC Administrator Friesen and Admiral Yeager, head of INPO. They and Agent Garrison have a few things to say before we break into smaller groups formed around the different plant designs."

Ben saw that those in the audience, some of whom had paled at the first mention of Mafia involvement, seemed okay and alert now. They all appeared ready for the challenges being placed upon them.

Friesen provided the group an overview of the plant entry technique under a declared National Emergency and then introduced Admiral Yeager.

The retired Admiral, an impressive figure with his polished bald-head, spoke confidently with a booming voice. "We will concentrate upon protecting the huge turbine generator in particular and the secondary side of the power plant in general. The public and the press always assume that the primary system is what terrorists would go after, but we believe that the electrical switchyards are the prime target of the Mafia techs. As Ben said, we think their goal is to do as much damage to the massive turbine generators as possible. This bunch of criminals is smart. They will almost certainly go after the more vulnerable secondary side of the plants. If the turbine speeds up, out of control, it can lead to catastrophic damage. Large chunks of metal from the turbine rotor blades start flying through anything in their way, and I do mean anything. You may have read about the one or two accidents of this type. If so then you know of the extensive damage that results."

"Read about it, hell! Admiral, I was there," spoke up one of the older engineers in the audience. "You aren't kidding. It's an ugly scene. Several hundred-pound pieces of metal, just like giant shrapnel, flew through the metal turbine casing and the turbine building walls as if they were paper. One of the damned missiles landed in a farmer's cornfield in the next county. After that accident the plant was decommissioned. It never produced another megawatt."

"Thanks for that first-hand account. Thirty of those destructive accidents and the resulting dire consequences to our nation are what you will be preventing, ladies and gentlemen."

Ben was anxious to finish this job for Laura had told him yesterday about Dudaev's revelation that she was Sumurov's granddaughter. Her range of emotions was extreme but, because of Joint Eagles, he couldn't be with her, yet. Eventually he would go home, hold her, and together they would try to make sense out of all of this.

CHAPTER
FORTY

Boris Andropov was furious. His face portrayed profound frustration. Had even comrade Bupkov failed him? Ivan Bupkov, the single most important cog in Andropov's Mafia machine, brought bad news for the second straight time.

"So Kostenko and his smuggled plutonium got away from you. This is completely intolerable. You have been with me for years and never have you performed so miserably. Have all of my people gone soft? Maybe you and your jokers need a refresher in a Siberian prison."

Bupkov was calculating even in the face of Andropov's boiling wrath. He understood that his leader's rage was triggered by frustration with the recent string of highly unusual failures. Bupkov's face flushed with heat from Andropov's verbal onslaught. The torture-inflicted scar from his right ear to the corner of his mouth itched from the heat.

The scar bore witness to one of his most difficult accomplishments. His head had been restrained by prison guards in a vice-like contraption as the wound was sliced incrementally and painfully each hour. All prisoners undergoing that torture had gone mad within a few hours. Yet, Ivan Bupkov, through his uncanny mind control abilities, had survived the ordeal, while remarkably retaining his sanity.

Bupkov carefully chose his rejoinder to Andropov's outburst. "The disappearance of Kostenko and the plutonium could have been orchestrated by only one person."

Andropov moved around until he gazed upon Bupkov's left profile. He didn't like peering at the ugly scar. The other side, though, wasn't much better. Bupkov's face bore a permanent scowl and his dark eyebrows scrunched down over his eyes, at times seemingly blocking his vision. The forward hunch of his shoulders forced a lurching, monster-like motion when he walked.

"And who is that?" asked Andropov impatiently.

"Kruschev. As you know, he is methodically weeding our people out of his security apparatus. That hurts. It's vital that we have a strong presence in the FSB. Get this. He has seemingly embarked on a traitorous path of reforming the FSB. He attempts to exorcise the Chekists from the ranks. Worship of Dzerzhinsky is at the heart of that organization's hold on Russia and our grip on the country as well. We depend upon the Chekists to help intimidate the masses."

Andropov heartily agreed, "Yes, Comrade Dzerzhinsky was a great communist patriot. He had more backbone than all of Russia's recent leaders combined. So you believe it is Kruschev who saved Kostenko?"

"Yes, Comrade Andropov, but there is more."

"What the hell else?"

"Strahkov has ordered Kruschev to search for heirs of Viktor Sumurov."

Andropov's temper flared again. He hated Russia's authors, especially that one. "That traitor, Sumurov, did more than anyone to destroy the Soviet Union."

Bupkov knew that the next revelation was going to upset Boris even more. It almost seemed to him that recently some hidden force was spitefully kicking sand in their faces.

"Boris, you better sit down. You really will not enjoy what comes next."

"Just get on with it."

"In response to Strahkov's direction, Kruschev secretly ordered a fragment of Viktor Sumurov's remains recovered and sent to the FBI for DNA matching."

"How do you know this?"

"An FSB agent, loyal to us, told me."

"Matching to whom?"

"Possible heirs."

Bupkov explained that his FSB insiders had reviewed old KGB files and found that back around 1970 a Marina and Laura Turusova were suspected by the Soviets of being the daughter and granddaughter of Viktor Sumurov. Before they could be killed they dramatically escaped. After their escape, as far as the KGB could discover, they disappeared from the face of the earth.

Bupkov continued, "The CIA or the FBI must have some idea about where the pair is hidden. With DNA they could identify them."

"So, the corruption by Kruschev of the FSB continues. Even more reason to kill him."

Bupkov was close to agreeing, but was more than a little uneasy about attempting an assassination of Kruschev. Kruschev was a different "kettle of borscht." A hit on him would have to be conducted within the Kremlin walls. The Mafia's best FSB and military resources would have to be employed. This was one of the few times he felt it necessary to question Andropov's judgment.

"The public in Russia could react negatively to a Kruschev assassination. We depend on the proletariat's general indifference. An act of violence of this magnitude could coalesce public opinion against us."

"We have no choice. He and Strahkov challenge us at every turn. Doing nothing means we eventually will lose. Killing Strahkov would certainly turn the public against us. Killing the less popular Kruschev is the only viable option. Anyway, it appears that he is the true brains and guts behind the Russian government's attempts to shut us down."

Bupkov, still composed, ruminated on this logic. Andropov was right. He might as well face it. Killing Kruschev was the only way. Everything pointed to Kruschev being the source of many of their problems, but he couldn't bring himself to assign such a superior intellect and dedication to Kruschev alone. Kruschev must have hidden help and very talented help at that.

Andropov asked, "If the FBI confirms the heirs of Sumurov, can you find out about it?"

"Yes."

"At that time we'll have another little going-away-party."

Andropov turned to another issue. "Kostenko's gone. We need a new head of the Russian region. It should be a highly placed government official from one of the wealthier *oblasts*."

"Kosov, the Governor of Novgorod has recently become leader of the Russian *Duma*. He would be our most influential choice," suggested Bupkov.

"Perhaps."

"He is a bitter political enemy of President Strahkov and is already an effective regional leader of the Mob in Novgorod. He could even become the next Russian President, if something should happen to Strahkov."

"That would be a shame if something bad befell Strahkov. But I agree, Kosov is the leading candidate. Have him meet me here in ten days."

Andropov's empire seemed to be under unusual pressure. The mysterious failure of one of their satellites together with the bugging of his meeting at Schilthorn concerned him. He was convinced that the U.S.

was behind both events, despite the story in the New York Times reporting that two Russian thugs were found in the Swiss snowslide. He just didn't believe that anyone in his own ranks would dare spy on him. Their fear of Bupkov's wrath was too great. The only possibility other than the U.S. was Kruschev and soon Kruschev would be history.

Bupkov departed with orders that would revamp the Mafia leadership in Russia and create an opening at the top in the FSB.

The next visitor, General Bakr Zarif, fully understood why he had been summoned. It was time for him to complete a special payment to Andropov. Iran owed the Mafia leader for both the nuclear weapons and the scientists. This, though, was not to be a cash payment, but rather it was a gift which the general relished giving. Only one person hated the Americans as much as he, and that was his ally, Andropov. That shared scorn melded them together in their march to power, wealth, and vengeance.

One of Bupkov's trusted lieutenants ushered General Zarif into another of Andropov's meeting rooms. Andropov, as an added precaution, changed rooms after each meeting to allow the Thieves-in-Law technicians an opportunity to sweep the room before and after its use to clear it of any bugs. Since Schilthorn, he was taking no chances.

"General Zarif, welcome. Thank you for visiting on such short notice. The travel is an inconvenience, but I am afraid it is necessary since we lost our secure satellite."

Standing tall, straight and proud in his dress olive green uniform, the general responded, "Dr. Andropov, my government is indebted to you. We welcome the opportunity to meet with you. We wish to provide what you require. We also experienced disturbing satellite failures. It would seem to be a strange coincidence, all of a sudden so many breakdowns."

Andropov concurred that the run of failures was not mere coincidence, but he lasered in on his overwhelming interest, "So what's the status of the weapon? Is it on the tanker?"

He was alluding to a Lebanese-flagged supertanker that had been loading the Iranian "black gold" at the Bandar e Abbas oil pipeline terminal.

"The tanker left port last week. Our hand-picked crew replaced the detained Lebanese crew. It's fully loaded. The oil is destined for a refinery in New Jersey," reported the general.

"I know all of that! What about the cruise?"

"It's onboard."

"With the strategic nuclear warhead?"

"Yes! All two hundred-kilos of mayhem. It is one of the two you brought us. My best launch crew is on the job."

"The tanker is to arrive directly off shore, due east of D.C. and south of New York City, in exactly three days."

"We understand. The speed will be appropriately adjusted."

"The missile is programmed properly for the target I gave you?"

"Yes. From launch it will take the missile only seven minutes to reach the heart of New York City."

"Good! Now timing is crucial. It must be launched at exactly 8:30 p.m. Eastern Standard Time. You adjusted the altitude of the explosion as I directed?"

"Yes, it will have maximum effect."

He knew that Andropov was maximizing the effect of the explosion. The precursor wind would flatten Manhattan and beyond.

"Excellent. The world will soon see what an amateur Usama was."

Andropov then asked in a contrived show of concern, "Your launch crew members are able to get away?"

"Yes. Our sub trails the tanker."

By running on batteries and closely shadowing the tanker, Iran's newest sub escaped the Gulf without detection. It trailed the tanker so that the missile crew could be returned home after the launch. The launcher would be thrown overboard and the tanker would innocently travel the remaining distance to the refinery.

Knowing all of this Zarif gloated, "The heathens will never know what hit them or from whence came their Armageddon."

Andropov asked, "Did you carry out the deception so that there is no hint of a missile on the ship?"

"Yes. It looks like we deployed both of our advanced cruises in our northwest region."

As the Iranian General departed, Andropov muttered to himself, "Your launch team will have company soon. A few of my Thieves-in-Law will join the party for insurance."

His plan, if he did say so himself, was a brilliantly conceived stroke to dismantle the U.S. The pompous Americans, complacent in their numbing affluence and self-assumed greatness, would have no clue that Armageddon was near. Once they woke up it would be too late. The U.S. would no longer be the world power after his forces were unleashed. Instead it would be reduced to a mere "has-been" in a devastating economic tailspin. The WTC attack was a picnic for the weak-kneed Americans by comparison to what was in store for the devils this time.

FORTY-ONE

Day 43 11:15 P.M. West Wing White House

The White House computer supervisor elatedly proclaimed, "North, they took the bait. Our phony files were just busted into by someone on a Department of Commerce computer. Before long we will be able to pin-point the computer used to accomplish the break-in."

Don North high-fived his companion. "Damn! That was close. We slipped all the real files off just in time."

North cut short the celebration and dialed Garrison's pager. As he waited for the agent to call back, he mentally scored his two big assignments, one down and one to go. He had probably just succeeded in protecting the vice president's files while throwing Foley and the Mafia temporarily off track, but he had not completed the big job. The Mafia mole, whose existence had been confirmed by the Shilthorn bugging, was proving elusive. North's suspects list was still quite long.

As his phone rang, North checked the caller I.D. before answering to make sure it was Garrison.

"Hello, Garrison. I thought you might want to hear some interesting news, but if I'm interfering with a steamy date..."

"Up yours, you lecherous old cowboy. This isn't steamy-date night. Ben's got me busy training the plant teams. What's your scoop?"

"Someone took our computer file bait, hook, line, and sinker."

"Who?"

"For sure it's someone from Commerce. My guess is that it is none other than our buddy, rotten old Foley. Give your tail on him a heads-up. If it is him, he will be making a beeline to Michelle with his stolen garbage."

"We are watching him. Listen, you ornery old man, I have a breakthrough on our search for the mole."

"Good. This SOB, whoever he is, has been a real careful dude."

"Here is what we got. My tail on Michote says she met a man last night in the parking garage at Tyson Corner Shopping Center. With a hat pulled low over his eyes, he seemed to appear from nowhere and after a brief conversation with our Mafia chick, he disappeared just as mysteriously."

"So, big deal, Garrison. How in the hell does that help anything?"

"Our agent had sensitive eavesdropping gear with him. He record-ed the conversation. The mystery man was passing confidential White House security details to Michelle. So he must be our mole. After some digital enhancement of the recording, our lab can compare his voiceprint to every security officer still on your suspects list. It may take a couple of days, but we will get him."

"Great work. I better reduce the list to just those whose where-abouts were unaccounted for at that hour last night. We will voice-test that shortened list first. We need to put a stop to this treacherous bas-tard fast."

"Good idea, Don. You know, I need to talk to you about that list of yours. How dare you have FBI agents on it," challenged Garrison with mock seriousness.

Garrison already knew that one of the FBI Computer Services supervisors had spied on his group's computer activities. He had placed him under surveillance, attempting to learn to whom he was reporting. That surveillance could reveal the mole. He sadly accepted the fact that the mole might be someone within his agency.

"Now, Garrison. Don't get defensive. You must remain objective. By the way, where were you last night?"

"You really are an SOB. I was out here at Bethesda with scads of Ben's civilian buddies."

North chuckled, "Well okay. That alibi should hold up."

North, with renewed hope of finding the mole, hung up. He des-perately wanted to uncover the traitor before tomorrow's Joint Eagles attack. The spy posed an unacceptable danger to his friends, President Arthur and Vice President Foster, as well as to the Joint Eagles mission.

Day 44 1 A.M. Michelle's Apartment

"So, my dear Vince, I hear you have some great news for the cause," cooed Michelle, while parading seductively about her luxurious townhouse in a sheer black nightgown, which generously revealed her classic beauty. She was driving Vince crazy with desire. Enjoying the tease, she poured two goblets of wine as she listened to the excited Vince.

"Yes, we broke through the White House computer security. I picked up copies of the vice president's meeting minutes. I also latched onto who was attending."

"Let me see those," Michelle implored, setting aside the goblets. Reaching for the papers she brushed a firm breast teasingly against Vince's arm. As she read through the pages slowly, her demeanor perceptibly cooled.

Upon reaching the end of the stack, she flung them in his face. "You idiot. They either set you up or you are a fraud who makes this crap up. These are fakes. Overnight privileges are suspended. No, canceled! Go home little boy!" Using both hands she firmly shoved the confused Vince toward the door.

"I don't get it."

"You are right, you don't and you won't, not ever again." Facing him she taunted, "You will miss this plenty, won't you?"

Since Agent Kostenko had already given Michelle insight into the activities of the vice president's team, she had recognized immediately that Vince Foley had been had. She quickly concluded that the elaborate ruse rendered Vince a liability.

After evicting Foley, Michelle called Goldstein via a Mafia-secured phone line. In coded conversation, she told of the liability which Vince now presented.

Michelle continued, "Our White House source reports that there is a covert venture called Joint Eagles that involves both Russia and the U.S. He doesn't know much about it, but suggests we pressure the most blackmailable Congressman, who attended the President's recent secret meeting. He could tell us what is going on. Thanks to stolen FBI files, we have enough goods on the congressman and his extramarital affairs so that he will have to cooperate with us or be ruined."

"The White House has made a fool of dumb old Vince."

"Worse yet, they must suspect his Mafia role since he broke into their fucking fake files. Undoubtedly they are tracing his every move. They probably followed him here. Hopefully they just think I am his girlfriend."

"Hopefully, but he's become a handicap to all of us. I will talk to Lepke about an immediate termination of Vince's employment."

"After I scorned him tonight, that sad little boy may take care of that for us," a self-congratulatory Michelle boasted.

Later the FBI agent, after listening through the tap on Goldstein's phone, reported on the conversation. Garrison realized that he would have to alert the targeted congressman that trouble was headed his way. He would warn him that if he disclosed anything to the Mafia the government would place him on trial for treason. He knew that the only way to insure the congressman's silence was to pose a bigger threat than the Mafia.

Day 44 2 A.M. Ben's Apartment

Ben couldn't sleep. Had he trained his teams well enough? What if's kept popping into his mind. He was one day away from the show-down of his life. He would send the teams out to each site today. What else should he tell them? Would any be killed? Sleep was an impossibility tonight.

He and Laura had talked earlier. Without giving details he had warned Laura that the next two days promised to be so hectic that he would not call. She was not to worry, though, for things would wrap up very soon.

Laura's mind never rested. She kept proving that fact. She had told Ben about the Viktor Sumurov papers. One point in particular bugged her. With Sumurov's pension for detail, he had advocated that a secret organization, a successor to the brave dissidents whom he believed would emerge after he was killed, must be formed and must influence events for decades to come. Laura had told Ben that she was beginning to suspect that such an organization existed and Dudaev led it. Why had Dudaev allowed her to have these papers when he undoubtedly knew that she would figure that out? Did he want to disclose the organization's existence to her, and if so, why?

Ben admitted that Laura was, once again, on to something. He smiled. He bet Laura wasn't sleeping tonight either, not until she figured out what was going on with Dudaev.

FORTY-TWO

Day 44 4 A.M. Stockton's Home Arlington, Virginia

Stockton's phone shattered the silence of the night. Struggling to awaken, James rolled over groping for the offending phone, "Hello! What is it?"

"Director, this is Professor Dudaev. Sorry to bother you at this hour, but we have a problem."

Hearing Dudaev on the line, Stockton roused quickly from his torpor. Dudaev wouldn't call, let alone at this hour, without a very good reason.

"Professor, what is it?"

"Urgent news. There is a major change in Andropov's plot. The Mafia's about to sabotage the NuEnergy plants and create a nation-wide blackout."

"We know that," replied Stockton.

"Do you know when?"

"In a couple of weeks."

"No! The sabotage will be tomorrow night!"

"Tomorrow? Are you sure? We didn't hear that in the Schilthorn meeting."

Dudaev went on to explain, "Andropov changed the timing because he suspects you Washington boys bugged his meeting."

"So Andropov advanced the timing to screw us up. Shit!"

Remembering his last conversation with Dudaev about Christian being a traitor, Stockton asked, "How reliable is your source?"

"Very reliable. She is one of several in my organization who has infiltrated the Mafia."

Stockton wasn't satisfied, "On a scale from one to ten where do you rank her reliability?"

"Eight."

"Why not a ten?"

"I never rank any double-agent a ten. I have seen too many sell out for money or power, or in some way succumb to seduction by the other side."

"A very wise answer, Professor. If you said ten I would say you are a fool."

Dudaev expanded upon his source. "Each previous report from this source has checked out. That positive track record is my best indication of reliability."

"No chance of a recent switch?"

Dudaev hesitated, "No indication of that."

Accepting that Dudaev's informant could be right, Stockton thanked Dudaev. He hurriedly pulled on his clothes. He must report this to Foster.

Day 44 5:15 A.M. Vice President's Office

The entire vice president's team, along with the President and Secretaries Winston and Kohlmeier, were in attendance as James Stockton arrived.

Foster greeted him, "Well, you sure stirred things up again, Director."

"Yes, I guess I have."

"How sure of all of this are you?"

"Not absolute, since I don't have independent confirmation. But everything fits the pattern of the Mafia as run by Andropov. I believe it is conservative to take the Dudaev information at face value."

Vice President Foster stated, "I want to hear the thoughts of each of you. General, you first."

"We are prepared to attack Iran tomorrow night. No sooner. We must do nothing to alert them of the pending strike or our soldiers will be placed at unacceptable risk."

Ben countered, "Right now our country's nuclear plants and our electrical grid are at unacceptable risk. The plant teams complete their training today and travel to the proximity of each plant tonight. I strongly urge they be allowed to move in and secure each plant, today before they are sabotaged."

General Adair challenged, "Doesn't part of your plan involve a declaration of national emergency by the President?"

"Yes."

"Presto. There goes our secrecy."

Ben had no good answer to that. He already suspected that the balancing of risks would dictate that he would not be allowed to send in his teams a day before the scheduled strike on Iran. But, he intended to try.

Trying to pacify Ben, Foster said, "I understand your concern, Ben, but we can't risk a military debacle to avoid plant damage and a blackout, no matter how debilitating that power outage could be. Plus there is a chance that Dudaev's intelligence is bogus."

Ben countered with his last argument, "What happens to our nation's defenses under an extended nationwide blackout situation?"

General Adair had to hand it to Ben. That was a clever point. "Nothing good happens, Ben, especially if it's widespread and prolonged." Adair privately questioned whether Pentagon contingency studies had adequately addressed that possibility.

President Arthur listened intently to the rest of the discussions before commanding, "Until notified otherwise by me, General, you have a go-ahead for the Joint Eagles strike tomorrow night. Ben, hold your teams out of the plants until the Joint Eagles strike commences. Stockton, keep checking the reliability of your source. Otherwise, each of you continue with your various tasks and report to Vice President Foster just as you have been."

Ben disappointedly headed back to Bethesda for further team training. He was frustrated. The risk to the plants was high and he had one arm tied behind his back. At least he could emphasize the sabotage in progress scenario in today's training.

Day 44 10 A.M. Stockton's Office CIA Headquarters

Nieman arrived to brief Stockton. Stockton was tired and irritable this morning. He dispensed with the usual niceties.

"So, Liz, what have you found out about our friend Goldstein?"

"I scoured the Schillhorn tape again, specifically to catch everything Goldstein contributed to the meeting."

"And?"

"He is cagey. As you know, he is one of Andropov's most trusted lieutenants. Andropov relies upon him and Bupkov more than anyone else. Goldstein cleverly let Lepke destroy himself and then put the final nail in the coffin with his Ben Andrew information. That could have been motivated by his ties to Dudaev, or it could have been one mobster doing-in a rival. Also it could have been a clever playing of his hand to enhance his own rise in power within the Mafia."

"Go on."

"He plays games. He used his Ben Andrew intelligence to tweak Andropov's loathing of the man. It was almost a deliberate attempt to prompt irrational behavior. Yet he has been a very good Mafia soldier, he is the one who has organized and masterminded the plant sabotage for Andropov, and he never disclosed any of this to his supposed boss, Dudaev. Very strange."

"Very strange, indeed. I know you. You must have a theory," challenged Stockton.

"I do."

Stockton, regaining for a moment a semblance of his old humor, joked, "Here's a nickel. Let's have it."

"Could it be that he is after Andropov's job?"

"Maybe. And then what?"

"I don't know for sure. Maybe he has subtly encouraged Andropov to go after the U.S., knowing that we will come after Andropov. That would leave Goldstein in great position to take over the Mafia. And he knows about Dudaev and could eventually neutralize him."

"But we are coming after Goldstein too."

"Yes, but... He may think he can give us the slip."

"Anything else, Liz?"

"One thing. I listened carefully to the Zermatt tape and to General Zarif's message to Andropov."

"You mean the message delivered by Bupkov?"

"Yes, of course I do."

"Then why didn't you say so?"

"I thought you knew that."

Stockton paused, looked at Liz's face and then grinned, "You are as tired and cross as I am aren't you. Truce?"

"Truce, but he definitely said the cruise and one of the big nukes were ready to be deployed against Andropov's and Zarif's sworn enemy."

"So. Our intelligence says they were both taken to northwestern Iran."

"You better check that intelligence again. The range of those missiles is six hundred miles, yet the sworn enemy is the U.S. A slight inconsistency."

Stockton was frustrated. He had a million things to do. The world was dumping on him today. He would delegate the missile and bomb whereabouts question to the NSA head.

FORTY-THREE

Day 45 1 A.M. SSN-712 Atlanta North Atlantic

The beads of perspiration on Sonarman Al Templin's forehead testified that this was no routine patrol. The spectrum of sound from the boat's array of hydrophones and passive sonar detectors was extremely difficult for him to decipher. The last four days had proven very taxing. His nerves were frayed. His stand on watch was only one hour old and he was already exhausted.

The only thing keeping him and the boat's other sonarmen sane was the availability of the advanced TB-23 towed array of sensors. This array of hydrophones trailed almost a thousand feet, over three football fields in length, behind the Atlanta. On routine patrols he wasn't forced to such complete reliance on these sensors.

Petty Officer Second Class Templin was unaware that the buildup for the Joint Eagles attack was the reason he and his companions were left in this difficult fix. A week ago fifteen of the Flight II, Los Angeles-class fast-attack submarines, with their formidable firepower, had been ordered away from their patrols along the U.S. coasts to new stations. The fifteen submarines had raced from either the Atlantic or Pacific coast to the Middle East.

After the departure of those boats, each sub remaining on patrol off the U.S. coast had to cover a much greater area. This forced the Atlanta and the others on defensive patrol, to travel at a far noisier twenty knots, instead of their normal, quiet twelve-knot pace. That increase in speed created much more noise. This heightened background interference had Templin and the other sonarmen climbing the bulkheads as they struggled to pick up targets before the targets spotted them.

As he scanned his BSY-1 screens, which displayed the frequency and amplitude of detected sound, and listened through his headset, he picked up a contact. The signal was very strong, even though they were still some fifteen miles astern and starboard of the target. The Atlanta was closing rapidly on the slow moving object.

Templin yelled to the Sonar Watch Officer, "Target bearing ten o'clock. Request OOD to reduce speed to ten knots."

"Roger," replied the Sonar Watch Officer. Picking up the boat's intercom, he relayed, "We're I.D.ing a target. Request speed reduction to ten knots."

As soon as the boat reduced speed, the background disturbance faded and listening became much easier. Templin's earphones indicated rather quickly that it was a large surface ship. The frequency spectrum displayed on the BSY-1 screen confirmed that it had all the characteristics of a fully loaded supertanker. He was ready to complete his assessment of the ho-hum contact and have his superior relay the final classification to the Officer of the Deck (OOD), when something faintly familiar on the BSY-1 screen caught his eye. It puzzled him.

"Lieutenant, come here and look at this. Take my earphones. Listen."

Grabbing the headset, the officer listened and stared at the screen for several minutes. He threw up his hands in frustration, "I just hear tanker wake noise."

Taking back the earphones, Petty Officer Templin contorted his face with a puzzled expression. He was positive that something faintly familiar was buried amidst all of the wake noise. The overpowering wake signal behind the tanker nearly hid a very weak indication. He was convinced that there was something else out there! But what?

He requested, "Ask the OOD to maneuver farther to starboard."

From that improved perspective, the signal along the length of the tanker's wake cleared up somewhat, but the clearer signal puzzled him even more. Damn it! What was lurking behind the tanker?

Operating on a hunch, or experience, or maybe a combination of both, he scrutinized the spectrum behind and below the tanker one last time. Sure enough, about two miles behind the tanker at a depth of one hundred feet, nearly camouflaged in the wake noise, was a submarine. The characteristic signature from the sub reminded Templin of a past I.D.

"I have seen this guy before. Yes! On duty station in the Persian Gulf, when we tracked the Iranian diesel boats. I would bet my next leave that this is one of those babies running quiet mode. The SOBs really don't want to be spotted. They know that we patrol these waters, so they are on their batteries."

During the nineties the Iranians had purchased a fleet of four diesel electric-powered, Kilo-class submarines from the Russians. That is where he had seen this signal before! What the hell was a Kilo-class doing over here? It was only one hundred miles off Cape Hatteras! He must get a double-check.

He called the other sonarman over for confirmation. The signal was extremely weak because of the target sub's slow speed and its use of batteries, but they both agreed that unmistakably it was a Russian-made Kilo-class boat. His comrade thumped him on the back. "Great work, Al! You literally pulled a needle out of a haystack this time."

The OOD summoned the Atlanta's Skipper, Captain Allen, to the control room. After the briefing by his OOD, Captain Allen assumed command. He ordered the Atlanta to stay submerged at a one-hundred-foot depth, and to assume a safe trailing position behind the foreign boat. He alerted all onboard to follow quiet-mode procedures until further notice. Captain Allen authorized Miller to prepare a message. "Inform COMSUBLANT of our interloper."

Lt. Miller did as directed.

"COMSUBLANT: SSN Atlanta at longitude 72° 31', latitude 35° 10'. Time 0130. Course 330°. We are trailing a Kilo-class, Russian-made diesel submarine. The boat is behind a supertanker, maintaining a constant two-mile distance. Atlanta will trail the sub until receiving further instructions."

Captain Allen chose the secure Submarine-Launched One-Way Transmitter (SLOT) method for communicating the message. While the Atlanta cruised submerged, hidden and quiet, the SLOT buoy containing the bombshell message was ejected from the Atlanta's forward three-inch-diameter signal ejector launcher. Buoyancy forces popped it to the surface, where it bobbed silent and small on the rough Atlantic.

Once the enemy target sailed safely out of radio range, the floating ball would spring to life and transmit its cryptic message to a U.S. military communications satellite. The satellite had a special channel reserved for just this manner of transmission. For now, though, there was nothing more for Captain Allen to do than to maintain the

Atlanta's present holding pattern, check all systems and wait for instructions from COMSUBLANT (Commander of Submarine Forces in the Atlantic).

When the fleet of subs had left for the Middle East, Captain Allen, despite being warned to be on heightened alert, had expected no excitement here. He had been rather disappointed that the Atlanta was not chosen for the Joint Eagles expeditionary forces, but rather was left behind to merely patrol the U.S. coastal waters.

"So much for routine," muttered Captain Allen.

He suspected that COMSUBLANT at Norfolk, Virginia would refer the disposition of the Kilo-class sighting to Joint Eagles Central Command (CENTCOM) at MacDill Air Force Base in Florida. CENTCOM would have to consult satellite and other intelligence resources to ascertain what was going on with this strange pair. Thus, he did not expect to receive additional instructions for several hours.

As Captain Allen maneuvered the Atlanta into a safe following position, the rough seas above, churned by the passage of a recent northeaster, tossed angry waves at the unyielding tanker and the still-silent SLOT buoy. The huge tanker, unfazed by the rough seas, plowed steadily toward the Northeast Coast and away from the tiny tossed-about buoy.

Finally the flotsam appearing, yet vital message-bearing orb sprang to life, alerting Military Command of the intruder.

Day 45 3 A.M. CENTCOM Tampa Bay

General Abraham Ribikoff, CENTCOM Commander, briefed Joint Chiefs of Staff Chairman General Adair via military phone of the strange message CENTCOM had received from the Atlanta.

"I asked for any collateral information on the supertanker and the Kilo-class boat from both CIA and Military Intelligence. So far we know very little, only that the tanker flies a Lebanese flag. It took on its load of oil at Bandar-E Abbas, Iran, and is bound for a refinery in New Jersey. Our satellites are programmed to extensively photograph any ship leaving Iran, so useful data are undoubtedly stored in our computers."

General Adair stated curtly, "I don't like it. No foreign sub has ventured this close to our coast since the Cold War ended. Never has a diesel boat come this near. It would have to refuel to make it this far, wouldn't it? What an odd coincidence, a tanker and a sub from Iran today of all days. I don't like it at all. Director Stockton will look into this personally for you. I'll contact him immediately. He will report directly to you, General. Stay in close touch with me until this situation is clarified."

Day 45 4:15 A.M. NSA (National Security Agency) Headquarters

Because of the earlier heads-up from Stockton, the NSA Chief was able to report, "Director Stockton, we are through about half of the stored satellite files on the tanker. There are a few satellite computers still being downloading. Here is what we have so far. The tanker took on oil at Bandar-E-Abbas, and a bit more."

"What's the 'bit more,' Jesse?" demanded Stockton.

Jesse Stull, the chief of the National Security Agency (NSA) satellite files, had his whole organization activated. They were looking into every shred of info on the tanker.

"The 'bit more' is bad news. The Iranians slipped an advanced cruise missile onto the tanker, as well as some soldiers attending the missile and what appears to be a launch apparatus."

"Exactly what missile?"

"Not sure, but appears to be one of France's newest."

Stockton was puzzled. Intelligence reported that the only two advanced cruises Iran possessed were deployed in northwestern Iran. What the hell was going on? Hell, Liz was right all along to be worried about the cruises.

Stockton had brought in branch chiefs of Military Intelligence as well as CIA's Iranian experts. He fired orders in ten directions at once.

He directed the CIA and Military Intelligence, "I want reports from Iran on anything we know on the whereabouts of their cruises. How many, where, what warheads? I was told that the only two advance cruises were deployed in the northwestern corner of Iran. Double check that.

"Naval Intelligence, we want the exact location of every Iranian sub, now!

"Have the Air Force get a Global Hawk over that tanker immediately. I want every possible view of the blasted ship by every detector in our arsenal."

After directing the initiatives, Stockton called Secretary Kohlmeier, "Check with the Lebanese. Ask them for detailed descriptions of every crewmember they have on this boat. Call me as soon as you learn anything."

Turning to his CIA weapons specialist, he ordered, "I want the complete specs on that cruise missile and its launch capabilities. Get me answers within the hour or heads will roll."

Day 45 6:05 A.M. CENTCOM Clearwater, Florida

"General Adair, Director Stockton has given us a fairly complete picture." General Ribikoff summed up, "The tanker has an Iranian missile-launch crew onboard. We specked out the missile. It's an advanced Mach 3 stealth bird, armed with a strategic nuclear warhead, probably one of the two smuggled out of Kazakhstan. Based on pictures of Iranian troop and equipment movements we suspect that the other big warhead is in northwest Iran.

"Yesterday an armed contingent of the Russian Mafia's enforcement wing boarded the tanker. They were dropped in by copter as the ship passed Bermuda. We traced the bird. It's owned by an R.M. subsidiary.

"The trailing sub is almost certainly an Iranian boat. For a week the Navy has been unable to locate one of the Iranian subs that normally prowls the Persian Gulf. This is undoubtedly it. Its mission is uncertain, but it could be to spirit the Iranian launch crew and the Mafia contingent to safety after the launch."

"So Director Stockton believes they intend to launch the missile at us," General Adair asked.

"Yes. Everything points to that. An advanced cruise this close to our shores poses extreme challenges. Our defenses are stressed to the limit. We are pursuing any and every means to neutralize the threat. We must prevent an attack while maintaining the integrity of the tanker and the secrecy around the pending Joint Eagles strike."

"That is a tall order."

"Yes, sir. EPA warns us that a major oil spill in this location would be devastating to the marine environment. That eliminates some of our options. I ordered the Sam Houston to the area."

"That's a converted sub, isn't it?"

"Yes, sir. It carries a SEAL squad. We will task them with boarding the tanker and eliminating the threat of a launch. We don't want to act overtly, though, before our initial Joint Eagles attack this evening. So we are faced with confounding constraints all over the place. Of course, if the slime balls start preparations to launch earlier, we will be forced to act."

Day 45 6:30 A.M. SSN Atlanta North Atlantic

The submerged Atlanta received a brief order from COMSUBLANT, via ultra low frequency (ULF) radio signal.

"Rise cautiously to periscope depth. Drop back another five miles. Further orders will follow in thirty minutes."

Day 45 7 A.M. SSN Atlanta North Atlantic

Thirty minutes later the substantive message arrived.

"Continue to track targets. Extremely dangerous situation. Sub is Iranian. Supertanker is Lebanese flag-bearing ship, ostensibly delivering oil from Iran to a refinery in New Jersey. Hidden on the tanker is a supersonic cruise missile with a nuclear warhead and an Iranian launch crew. You should stand by to launch torpedoes targeting Iranian sub. Instructions to fire could come at anytime. Exercise extreme caution to avoid detection. Do not, under any circumstances, damage the tanker."

Captain Allen relayed these orders to his officers and crew. All realized that the stalking mission could go on indefinitely or end at any moment in a burst of action.

Day 45 1 P.M. SSN Sam Houston North Atlantic

The Sam Houston raced southwestward at flank speed to deliver its specialty Navy SEAL unit to the vicinity of the supertanker. Meanwhile, the tanker with the nuclear armed missile pressed steadily north northwest, ever closer to the populous East Coast.

The Sam Houston, SSN-609, was one of eight former boomers, submarine-launched ballistic missile (SLBM) nuclear submarines, which were now assigned to special warfare duties. In the early 1980's, it was one of the first to be decommissioned from the SLBM fleet. After removal of the missile fire control and other missile control and support systems the sub was converted to its present modified configuration. Concrete ballast was placed in the bores of some of the empty missile silos to compensate for the weight of the absent Polaris missiles. Some of the tubes were completely removed and others were converted into equipment stowage, or modified to serve as compression locks for swimmers' exit. Accommodations onboard were enlarged to accept up to sixty additional troops, most often SEALs. These sea-going warriors added to the ship's normal complement of about one hundred thirty crewmembers.

Modifications to the sub's hatches and deck allowed two dry deck shelter (DDS) assemblies to be mounted topside. On this cruise, each

DDS assembly housed a Mark IX Swimmer Delivery Vehicle (SDV). The two DDS structures stood side by side, directly over former missile launch silos. Except for being under the sea, they resembled space-age garages, something the Jetsons might use.

The SEAL leader onboard the Sam Houston was Lt. Cmdr. Bart Ward, a thirty-three-year-old veteran of numerous campaigns. As the Sam Houston charged at flank speed toward its rendezvous with the tanker, Ward re-read the last paragraph of the latest briefing.

"To avoid detection, your team will proceed as follows. The Sam Houston's crew will facilitate your team's departure, but the sub must maintain a distance of fifteen miles from the tanker. Staying submerged and exercising maximum stealth, use the SDVs to approach the tanker. Assume covert-strike position onboard the ship. We will stay in contact with you, via the MILCOMs. You will be instructed when to attack."

Ward had to admit that this promised to be as tough as any mission he had ever seen. The margin for error was negligible and the consequences of a mistake devastating.

"These assholes really intend to blow up an East Coast city." Ward growled to his squad, "We won't be taking prisoners on this outing."

The only positive aspect of this mission that he could spot was that it should be over one way or the other today. Many SEAL missions lasted for many grueling days, although the actual fighting was normally brief, intense and decisive.

Lt. Cmdr. Ward's men inherited a proud SEAL heritage. During Vietnam and since, the SEALs proved themselves to be extremely effective fighting units. The physical and mental rigor of their training ensured none but the fittest became SEALs. More importantly though, the training developed the skills necessary for survival under grueling conditions, and it drove home the concept of teamwork. Individual heroics were subservient to the team's success. Perhaps for this reason they didn't seek or receive much recognition. Even during the Vietnam War, only three SEALs received the Congressional Medal of Honor.

The captain of the Sam Houston alerted Ward that the boat would soon be in the proximity of the tanker. The SEALs should prepare to disembark.

The Sam Houston, while maintaining periscope depth, slowed until it was barely crawling forward. Periscope depth meant that the

SEALs would leave the boat's protection at the sub's deck level, which was still sixty feet below the storm-tossed surface of the Atlantic.

At Ward's command, the twelve SEALs donned their diving suits. Then they entered the swimmer's pressure chamber through the entry hatch. After entry the hatch was shut and dogged secure, leaving the SEALs isolated in the modified chamber awaiting the shock of the cold Atlantic waters. The roomy chamber accommodated all twelve commandos, who nervously adjusted their masks one last time in anticipation of what would come next.

Ward barked out a series of commands to flood the swimmer's chamber. They unlatched the exit hatch, opened the vent valve, then the flood valve to allow the frigid seawater into the chamber. With the cold water swirling around them, each SEAL, despite his protective wet suit, felt the cold penetrate to the bone. The water level rose past their masks and over their heads to the top lip of the exit hatch. The SEALs then closed the vent valve and watched as still more water flowed in. Finally they closed the flood valve and just cracked the valve marked "blow." This increased the pressure inside the flooded chamber and cracked the seal on the exit hatch.

The lead swimmer pushed the hatch open and the others swam through it into the water-filled exit tunnel. The tube led upward where it branched to each of the overhead DDSs. Once the divers swam through the watery tunnel into the DDSs, Bart closed and secured the exit, reporting, "Divers out." The chamber operator then essentially reversed the process, purging the swimmer's exit chamber, readying it, if needed, for further use.

The four SEALs designated as the SDV pilots, swam through the two DDSs garages directly to their respective lashed-down miniature sub. They immediately started the onboard electric motors, then stowed their portable breathing gear and activated the Mark XV computerized mixed-gas underwater breathing apparatus in each SDV. This underwater breathing equipment eliminated exhaust bubbles, greatly enhancing stealth.

Meanwhile, the other eight SEALs, with no immediate need for stealth, used their conventional individual air supply packs as they busily went about their disembarking tasks. Two closed the hatches to the chamber tunnels from which they had just emerged. Two others operated the controls, which opened the doors. The huge, bulbous-nosed, hydraulically powered front of the DDSs swung majestically open. The SEALs maneuvered the sleds holding each SDV.

Each sled thrust out through the open door with its miniature submarine still strapped to it. In a coordinated effort, the subs were released from the sleds. Now free of their moorings, they sailed about under their own power. The eight SEALs that made up the attack contingent returned the sleds to the DDSs and stored their portable breathing apparatus in the waterlogged garages. All then boarded the awaiting subs where they hooked up to the Mark XV breathing system.

Throughout these maneuvers the Sam Houston lay nearly dead in the water, resembling a giant, resting whale with smaller scavenger fish, the SEALs and the SDVs, slithering about the huge host.

Ward checked with each pilot, "Are Fishes One and Two ready?"

Upon receiving a verbal thumbs up, he instructed, "Ascend to four fathoms."

Ward's orders echoed through the SEALs' headsets, "Set speed at four knots on course two-four-five."

With a special antenna, which reached to the surface from his SDV, he could use GPS navigation and receive updates on the movement of the enemy onboard the tanker.

Now alone in the vastness of the cold and hostile North Atlantic Ocean, the squad's two silent subs propelled the chilled warriors relentlessly closer to their violent appointment with the Mafia and the Iranians. The still, deep, and silent surroundings were in sharp contrast to the turbulent Atlantic just above them, and the violent rendezvous with the behemoth that lay ahead.

FORTY-FOUR

Day 45 Earlier 8:30 A.M. EST Minot AFB North Dakota

In the pre-dawn hours the venerable thirty-nine-year-old Prairie Warrior taxied onto the Minot AFB runway. Overnight a cold front, propelled by a fast-moving Alberta Clipper, roared through North Dakota, bringing a dusting of fresh snow. The gusty north winds, ushered in by the front, whipped up a ground blizzard, which rearranged the season's accumulation of snow. The Air Force ground crews had repeatedly cleared the snow from the runways, only to watch it perversely blow back.

As the taxiing bomber's lights played on the snow drifting down the north-to-south runway, the pavement appeared to the two pilots like a waving white stream washing toward them. The stream merged into a ubiquitous blanket of white, which enveloped the armed-to-the-hilt plane and the swirling runway.

The B-52H, the premier heavy bomber in the world, was largely unaffected by adverse climatic conditions like those found in Minot. The only concession made to the below zero temperatures and the blowing snow was that the crew had warmed up the BUFF (Big Ugly Fat Fucker) for an additional hour prior to takeoff. The five-man crew consisted of the two pilots, a navigator (NAV), a radar navigator (RN) and an electronic counter-measures (ECM) specialist.

Colonel Gene Bolt, in close coordination with his copilot, directed the Stratofortress with its deadly load down the snowy runway at ever-greater speed. In unison they thrust the throttles forward. The drooping wings appeared to levitate to a horizontal position as the mammoth heavily loaded bomber lifted off the snowy runway. Despite climbing, its nose still appeared to tilt down, an optical illusion unique to the BUFF.

"Commander to NAV, confirm heading and speed."

"Bear to course zero-five-zero."

"Zero-five-zero it is!"

The NAV, with an almost continual litany with the two pilots, directed, "Cleared for climb to twenty-five thousand. Increase speed to four fifty. Maintain heading zero-five-zero. Maintain relative position fifteen hundred feet starboard of Charlie bomber." Charlie bomber was the nearest of fifteen other B-52Hs accompanying Prairie Warrior on this mission to Central Asia.

The Prairie Warrior's emblem emblazoned on its nose was a large replica of the Lion King. The "circle of life" of the B-52H was considerably longer than its namesake, the Disney caricature, Mufasa. Military planning called for the Warrior and the entire B-52H fleet, built in 1961 and '62, to still be ruling the skies in the year 2030 and perhaps beyond. An aviation superlative without peer, the bomber's service life could span an unprecedented seven decades.

Now far above the blowing snow, the sixteen B-52s from the 5th Bombardment Wing at SAC's Minot base majestically climbed toward a cruising altitude of 35,000 feet. While still climbing, they maneuvered into formation and veered onto their great circle route. This shortest path would carry them far north, first over Manitoba, then Hudson Bay, Greenland and finally down across the Barents Sea to the northern coast of Russia. From there they would fly south across the heart of European Russia to the Caspian Sea.

Colonel Bolt advised his crew, "Next stop the Caspian. Get comfortable mates; we are in for one hell of a long day."

At a speed of 550 mph, the trip from Minot to the Caspian Sea would take nearly eleven hours. Thus, upon the fleet's return to Minot early tomorrow morning, the airtime would approach one full day.

Only the re-engined B-52 Stratofortresses were called upon for this job. The re-engined planes, with the more fuel-efficient RB-211 engines, four engines on each Stratofortress, required only one refueling for the entire round trip. The unmodified bombers, powered conventionally by eight TF-33 jet engines, would have required two refuelings. Since Joint Eagles was stretching the U.S. tanker refueling resources to the limit, CENTCOM specified that only re-engined B-52's be employed. Bolt figured that was how Minot got the job. CENTCOM needed their flock of re-engined BUFFs.

As a young B-52 pilot when President Bush, father of George W., ordered the stand-down of nuclear alert forces, Bolt had experienced that dramatic end to the Cold War's continual state of readiness. Prior to September 28, 1991, the Stratofortress crews had literally kept on the edge of their seats.

Bolt hadn't been involved, or yet born for that matter, in the earlier days of the Cold War. He marveled that this plane was older than he was. When he was a baby, this same B-52 flew Chrome Dome alert missions. It or other Stratofortresses stayed aloft continuously with high-yield nuclear weapons onboard ready to attack the Soviet Union upon an instant's notice.

How times had changed! Here they would be flying over the very heart of Russia in the bomber that was conceived for the sole purpose of destroying that country.

Bolt wasn't really philosophical enough to figure out what all of this meant. Was the world a safer place since the Cold War ended? The need for this mission signaled that the answer most likely was no. Perhaps the end of the Cold War only signified that alliances had shifted. The threats now were more transitory, irrational and diffuse.

Halfway across Manitoba, after reaching cruising altitude and speed, Bolt turned the piloting over to his younger copilot. During the takeoff and assent, both pilots had been extremely busy controlling the aircraft. With taxing moments still lying ahead, Bolt seized this relatively calm interlude to attempt to relax and enjoy the late winter sunrise.

Without warning, disturbing doubt attacked Colonel Bolt. To actually deliver such devastating power was at once exhilarating, yet troubling. Did anyone have the right to play God? Had he a right to kill? He thought he had put those questions behind him, but apparently until now they had remained merely academic.

After some uncomfortable moments, the demand for duty prevailed. He was responsible to his crew, his superiors and to the American people, whom he had sworn to defend. He could not expect to always be a peacetime soldier. He must do what he was trained and sworn to do.

Day 45 10:30 A.M. EST Above Hudson Bay

With his doubts vanquished, he watched the day brighten as the oblique rays from the struggling southern sun glanced off the frozen expanse below them. What a vast, empty, yet beautiful, land! In the summer he loved fishing for walleyes and lake trout in those northern lakes.

The grand perspective of the world available to the pilots, was denied to his navigator (NAV) and radar navigator (RN). Since no windows graced their quarters, they could view the sight only in "living" black and white through the steerable television. The NAV and RN were behind and below the cockpit in what the crewmen derogatorily referred to as the "black hole of Calcutta!" They sat in side-by-side downward ejection seats.

The NAV's chief duty was the self-evident job of guiding the Stratofortress from home to target, as well as providing time control. Another duty of the NAV, accomplishing missile programming, had consumed him. Since some of the bomber's birds were going after moving targets, including mobile radar and missile launch units on rail cars, the latest coordinates of the targets were needed. Military satellites constantly relayed the current location of these targets to the Prairie Warrior. He directed the latest coordinates to the appropriate missile's computer.

Prairie Warrior's twenty AGM-98Us, now being primed for action, were far more lethal than Desert Storm's 86C version. The AGM-98U's advanced stealth features easily defeated enemy radars. The radars would have better luck tracking a migrating wren ten miles away than locating an incoming 98U. The missile, powered by a turbofan/ramjet engine, could deliver its 1,500-pound conventional warhead up to 1,500 miles away from its release from the mother ship.

The Stratofortress carried twelve missiles externally under its wings and eight more internally. Even though the 98U had existed for several years, it had not been used since the Pentagon wished not to reveal its existence. Bolt understood that revelation time had arrived.

Meanwhile, under the direction of the NAV, the B-52's computer chose whether the 98U's Global Position System (GPS), or its Terrain Contour Matching Guidance System (TCMGS), or a combination of the two would best direct each missile to its target. Based upon that selection, it then downloaded the requisite data to each missile's computer. On this occasion the choice was simple. All twenty missiles would employ GPS guidance across the Caspian Sea and then TCMGS would take over for those missiles continuing inland.

Bolt shuddered, for if this had been a nuclear mission, the Prairie Warrior alone would literally be delivering Armageddon. Twenty AGM-98Ns, each minimally armed with a two-hundred-kiloton thermonuclear device, would have replaced the 98Us. Thus, one Stratofortress' nuclear payload would be, at least, four hundred times more powerful than that visited upon Hiroshima. Of great tactical significance, the B-52 itself need no longer penetrate enemy air space, that job had been transferred to the nearly invisible missiles. The implications of that nuclear scenario were too incredible to ponder.

Day 45 6:45 P.M. EST Prairie Warrior Over Barents Sea

The refueling tanker fleet was in the air awaiting the bombers' arrival. The Prairie Warrior, leading the first wave of eight B-52s, showed up precisely on schedule. This refueling was the most exacting maneuver of the entire flight. Bolt was pleased to see that the 190th Air Refueling Wing out of Forbes Field in Topeka, Kansas, were the ones called upon to service them today. He had often worked with them.

Bolt assumed control of the plane. Maneuvering very deliberately, he carefully approached their assigned KC-135R, while still remaining one thousand feet below and nearly one mile behind the tanker. Ahead of him he could see the tanker's lights shining brightly in the dark sky.

Once stabilized relative to the tanker, Gene coaxed his craft into a cautious climb. The ascent culminated in the Warrior's arrival at the pre-contact position, fifty feet below the tanker's boom "on the 30° line." He looked up at the tanker's boom operator, who in turn was intently watching them.

Despite his extensive refueling experience, Gene's body was covered with perspiration. His heart raced and his hands grew clammy. Overcoming his nervousness, the pilot settled the old bomber safely into the precontact position. The tanker's trailing air-refueling boom, set at a 30 degree incline, was not yet fully extended. Bolt signaled the tanker, "Prairie Warrior advancing to contact position."

He nudged the throttles of the Prairie Warrior forward about one-quarter knob width. As the plane slowly approached the tanker, he quickly adjusted power back to the same fuel flow setting as at pre-contact. The Prairie Warrior obediently slid into refueling position. With the bomber stabilized in relation to the tanker, the tanker's boom operator extended the telescoping portion of the boom into the bomber's fuel receptacle. The receptacle toggles automatically latched, indicating that a good contact was achieved.

With the two giants mated, the KC-135R opened the spigots wide and the precious JP-8 fuel gushed into the hungry BUFF. The copilot directed the 6,500 pounds-per-minute flow into one after another of the BUFF's twelve fuel tanks. This flow rate, roughly equivalent to filling one automobile gas tank every second, continued for twenty minutes. With the fuel flowing, the two planes remained locked together.

Even though Bolt had performed this operation a dozen times, it demanded his total concentration. Only once previously had the proximity alarms gone off on him, and once was enough. On that occasion some rare high-altitude turbulence had hit them in the middle of a refueling. Before he could disengage, he had come within mere feet of a collision.

After that incident, he had proposed new safety features, which were added. Now newly installed proximity sensors, if detecting a near collision, automatically increased the tanker power, while throttling back the bomber's engines. That innovation could open up space between the two planes far faster than could human reaction. Also, the flow of fuel would automatically cease and the receptacle toggles would release.

The re-engined Prairie Warrior, after taking on this replenishment fuel today, had sufficient supply to deliver its payload of cruises and return home.

Day 45 6:45 P.M. EST Prairie Warrior in Russian Airspace

Soon after completing the refueling, the formation of B-52s droned across Russia's frozen Arctic coastline. The icy landscape of northern Russia was shrouded by the Russian night.

Bolt grew unexplainably edgy. Suddenly, streaking at nearly three times the speed of the B-52s, the Sukhoi fighters materialized on his radar screen. He understood from briefings that the fighters were on their side this time, yet his instincts, honed by years of training, told him it was time to fight. Old habits were hard to break. Bolt's mind finally conquered his instincts and his years of training. At last he relaxed and soaked in the uniqueness of the moment.

The Russian SU-35 fighters were escorting the American bomber fleet, although Gene felt that was unnecessary since the B-52s would not be approaching the Iranian border. There must be another reason for the escort. He guessed that this perhaps was a face saving measure by the Russian military. On the other hand, the Russians might not completely trust the U.S and the fighters could be Russia's insurance policy, insurance that the B-52 fleet kept on its prearranged mission and nothing more.

The U.S. had an insurance policy as well. Five additional B-52's, carrying a maximum load of nuclear armaments, circled over Iceland. They would stay airborne until all sixteen Buffs returned safely from Russian airspace. This was an uneasy alliance, at best, between former cold-war foes. Joint Eagles perhaps, but eagles with talons poised to tear each other's heart out.

Despite the darkness, the SU-35 fighter pilots put on a spectacular aerial show of speed and maneuverability. The sliver of new moon rising over the vast Russian expanse added negligible light. Bolt's radar and the fighters' lights provided the only evidence of the Sukhois' antics. These jets were the latest and most maneuverable variant of the Sukhoi SU-27. Russian scientists had developed thrust-vectoring in all spatial directions, as well as a speed-reducing flap. No operational U.S. fighter had these features.

Bolt gasped as one of the fighters performed a maneuver he had never seen before. The SU-35 flying directly in front of the Warrior suddenly dropped from view. Bolt's radar tracked the fighter as it slowed and then slipped under him only to promptly climb up directly behind him. He shook his head in amazement for no U.S. fighter could duplicate that feat.

Establishing voice contact with the fighter pilot, Bolt remarked in awe, "After seeing that I'm glad that you are on our side. I never saw that trick before."

The Russian pilot replied in English, heavily laden with a Russian accent, "That vas little velcome to Mother Russia. Ve also very glad you here as friends. Ve accompany to Moscow. There flight of more ordinary SU-29's take over escort duty."

This was unbelievable. Times were changing in ways Bolt couldn't fathom.

CHAPTER
FORTY-FIVE

Day 45 Earlier 5:30 P.M. Director Stockton's Office

Since Dudaev's warning call of early yesterday morning, Director Stockton had been awake and working frantically. Even the high-strung director was starting to wear down. His efforts to uncover the mystery surrounding the tanker and the Iranian sub were complete. This morning he had reported his findings to CENTCOM. Now he was preparing to advise the President on whether Joint Eagles should go forward with the missile attack on Iran.

The President's final decision to attack or not was only two hours away. The B-52s and the submarine fleet would be in position to launch their missiles by 7:30 P.M. Unless the President stopped it, that launch would go forward.

As Stockton was pouring a cup of the strongest coffee he could brew, Liz arrived.

Immediately she saw in his eyes how tired he was. She apologized, "Director, I hate to bother you again, but..."

"Go ahead, Liz. I'm too high on caffeine to care anymore. Do to me what you will."

"There is something of a surprise that you should know about."

"Nothing can surprise me anymore."

"Do you want to bet?"

"Not with you."

"Our CIA Middle East experts have pieced together a fascinating glimpse of the politics in Iran. General Zarif is, and has been for some time, locked in a power struggle with the Iranian Commanding General. Much of Zarif's authority comes from his close ties with the radical Ayatollah, while Commanding General Hassan is allied with the moderate, reformist president."

"Liz, I am too tired to sort this out. Just tell me what it means."

"It means the missile off our East Coast is apparently a result of Zarif having won one round in that power struggle, or it is covert and their president knows nothing about it."

"And?"

"And we don't want our actions to help Zarif win another round or..."

"No one over there is winning anything if Joint Eagles succeeds," contended Stockton.

"Yes and no."

Stockton's tired eyes pleaded for Liz to explain.

"You are right. No one over there wins in the short term, however, they march to a different drummer in those ancient countries. Wars and hostilities go on for decades or centuries, whereas we in the U.S. believe decisive victory must occur in days, weeks, or at the most, months. Our public's inability to stay focused on a problem exacerbates this trait."

"So..."

"Sure we go ahead and we beat the shit out of them in Joint Eagles, but whose hand does it strengthen in the long run?"

Despite its significance, Stockton was impatient with this new slant on things. Still he mustered a questioned reply, "Is the answer the radical, extremist, U.S.-hating faction represented by Zarif and the Ayatollah?"

Liz chuckled for she had never seen Stockton this tired, short-fused, and punchy. She responded, "Almost certainly yes."

"So where does that leave us?"

"In my opinion, Joint Eagles should go forward, but not all the way."

"You mean we should wimp-out?"

"No. We should answer the East Coast missile threat with a punishing air attack so that Zarif's actions are not rewarded, but the ground soldier portion of the war could be going too far. It might rouse the Iranian people against us and force them into Zarif's camp."

Stockton observed with some irony, "You are starting to sound like Secretary Kohlmeier. I don't agree with you yet. I must think about it."

Liz, without the slightest hesitation, responded, "Thanks for the compliment. I consider it an honor that I sound like the distinguished Secretary."

"Okay, Liz. Call Secretary Kohlmeier. Make her aware of all of this and see, as if I don't already know, what her read on it is. I will inform the President of this perspective of yours. Making these ungodly tough decisions, that is why he gets paid the big bucks."

Stockton was honestly thankful he didn't have to make the ultimate, go or no-go decision on Joint Eagles.

Day 45 6:20 P.M. Vice President Foster's office

Garrison and Ben, desperate to send in the plant teams without further delay, decided that Ben, being Foster's close friend, stood the best chance of convincing Foster to act now.

Yesterday and today had been frustrating for both Ben and Garrison. They had, based on Dudaev's warning, modified the teams' training to concentrate on the strong possibility that they would arrive at the plants with little or no time to spare and under the very dangerous circumstance of sabotage in progress. They had given each civilian a new chance to back out. None, though, had taken the offer. Both the long hours and the possibility that some of them could be killed had frayed Ben's nerves. Yet, he was determined not to lose another argument. The military had won yesterday's debate as they insisted that the plant teams not go in the day before the first wave of missiles were launched. Now, with the missile launch only an hour away, Ben believed he could wait no longer.

Ben advanced the logic to Foster for no more delays, "Thousands of our most vulnerable civilians could be harmed by a massive extended power outage. They could freeze or those in hospitals could lose their life-support. Isn't it our government's primary job to protect the health and safety of its citizens?"

Foster stopped him short, "I agree with you, Ben. You and Brad get on with it. I will deal with any bitches from the military."

Ben didn't take time to thank Foster. That could be done later. He turned to Garrison, "Let's go. We haven't a minute to lose."

Day 45 6:30 P.M. Oval Office

Arriving with Director Stockton and Secretary of Defense Winston, Vice President Foster entered the Oval Office at a dire moment in the country's history. The SEALs, nuclear subs, and the newest ABL were all in position to defend the East Coast from the Iranian-Mafia nuclear attack. Foster had dispatched General Adair to CENTCOM headquarters to review and approve CENTCOM's handling of the nuclear threat. On top of all of that, the final decision to launch the Joint Eagles strike on Iran was at hand.

Foster, Stockton, Winston, and Kohlmeier were all summoned to offer their last-minute advice on the pending attack to their President.

President Arthur asked each of them to brief him on the latest developments. He listened intently as they complied with succinct summaries of the rapidly evolving situation.

After those briefings President Arthur spoke, "You have heard all opinions and information on the matter; now it is time to offer your advice on whether I should allow the attack on Iran to go forward."

Arthur paused, looking squarely at Stockton. "Director, you are first."

"In one word, attack!"

"Secretary Winston?"

"With the nuclear threat posed to our country by the tanker there can be no doubt. Attack with full force."

"Secretary Kohlmeier?"

Adjusting her sitting position uneasily the Secretary replied, "It pains me to say this, but go forward. Attack. However, allow me to call my Iranian counterpart just before you address the nation later tonight and see if their president understands the consequences of Zarif's terrorist actions."

"Yes. You may do that, Madame Secretary."

"Mr. Vice President, your recommendation, please."

"Attack with the missiles and our full air power, but... After Secretary Kohlmeier's diplomatic efforts we must review matters again before we send in our troops."

Receiving that unanimous advice, President Arthur did not hesitate further, "Call CENTCOM. Give them permission to unleash the missiles and the planes. God help us and our nation."

Day 45 7.30 P.M. EST Prairie Warrior Over Caspian Sea

After eleven airborne hours, Prairie Warrior and its companions reached their destination above the northern end of the Caspian Sea.

Lt. Cmdr. Bolt received coded confirmation that the President had just given the final go ahead for launch. Unknown to Bolt, a discovery of an Iranian launch crew and a nuclear tipped missile near the U.S. coast had provided the final impetus to the President to order the strike.

At precisely the appointed moment, Bolt's crew cut loose the first missile from its external pylon mooring under the left wing. Once it had dropped several hundred feet, its fuel-efficient turbofan engine ignited. The flight fins flipped out and locked into position. The cruise's onboard computer took over guidance.

Accelerating as it dove to within fifty feet of the Caspian Sea's surface, the bird struck a GPS-guided course due south. Behind it a flock of uncaged Prairie Warrior 98Us closely following.

Each B-52 in turn released its answer to Iran's treachery. Not far behind the Prairie Warrior's contingent, hundreds of stealthy birds-of-a-feather followed.

While still over the Caspian Sea, the lead missile and several of its cousins passed undetected only a few feet above the spinning radar masts of a Russian armada of Corvettes and fast-attack patrol craft sailing into battle on the eastern Kazakhstan coast. The Slavic fleet's objective was the storage complex where Barak's troops guarded the smuggled nuclear booty. Even though the Russian shipboard radars never detected any of the stealth missiles' passage, one or two shocked deck hands swore that they had heard something whiz past.

As the lead missile neared the Iranian coast, its guidance mode, as preordained, switched to the nose-mounted night-sensitive TV camera. The missile transitioned into a hovering mode while its camera searched, found and locked onto the target. Based on the camera images and the range to target, the missile's computer ordered the maneuvers that sent it toward the pre-selected spot on the radar installation. Switching to ramjet propulsion, the missile accelerated to a speed greater than Mach 2. At the heightened velocity it penetrated the target exactly as programmed. After knifing into the hemispherical cover of the radar dome for the preset fraction of a second, the fifteen-hundred-pound warhead exploded.

Fragments of the radar facility blew hundreds of feet into the air. Large chunks of plastics, metal and concrete rained down upon the surrounding shore. Smaller pieces continued to filter down for a time. Finally a suffocating dust cloud shrouded the site.

By the time the dust had settled from that first explosion, the Prairie Warrior and all but one of the old BUFFs were far away flying North over central Russia.

A lagging Stratofortress unleashed the last twenty missiles. They would fly to the Iranian coast and hover in assigned holding patterns. Once preliminary damage assessment was completed by CENTCOM staff, military satellites would relay instructions to these hovering missiles to hit any surviving targets.

CHAPTER
FORTY-SIX

Day 45 Earlier 6:35 P.M. Command Center White House

Garrison thundered to his assistants, "Order every plant team in now!"

With maps plastering the walls, phone banks ringing and computer terminals humming, hulking stacks of plant materials inundated Ben, Garrison and their bustling team. The intensified activity in their temporary command post in the West Wing basement had reached a fever pitch.

Just back from convincing Foster to allow the teams to act, Ben reckoned that the odds were stacked against them. His biggest fear, sabotage in progress, was almost a certainty. Though Garrison's FBI personnel were frantically calling each team, sending them in early on an emergency basis, it wasn't early enough.

Since the NRC resident inspectors at each plant had an important role to play, Ben snapped, "Hazel, notify your residents that the Federal Emergency is declared. We are moving in now. No more delays."

Despite all of the activity Ben was not heartened. It was now too close a race between the saboteurs and the plant teams. Was the permanent demise of many of the plants, a nationwide blackout, and a resulting economic depression inevitable? Had he overlooked any possibility? Again he reviewed the situation for anything they had missed. They suspected that the criminals intended to destroy the massive turbine generators at each plant. Was there something about the vulnerable turbine generator that offered a way to save it?

Ben fully understood why the intricate, multi-stage turbine generator was the Mafia target. It was the largest and most expensive piece of equipment in the plant. If it was destroyed, a utility might never be able to justify the huge replacement and repair costs. Those plants so destroyed might never run again. That loss, which would greatly prolong and worsen the economic impact on the nation, was exactly what Andropov so diabolically desired. Somehow Ben must prevent that enduring damage from happening.

The switchyard was where the power generated by a power plant merged into the massive national electrical grid system. That vast system of interconnecting high voltage lines tied together electrical power consumers and producers from Maine to Florida, from Virginia to Kansas and Louisiana to Minnesota. Could that interconnection possibly be helpful in his attempts to avoid plant damage and a subsequent nationwide blackout? Or was it only a liability?

He also remembered that if a nuclear plant were at or below eighty percent of full power, the turbine was far safer since the overspeed protection was not needed. If under eighty the fail-safe atmospheric reliefs could do the protection job by themselves. The damnable thing was that because of this extremely cold night, all of the huge NuEnergy nuclear plants as well as the rest of the nation's plants were running flat out at one hundred percent. Even the damned weather was against them.

He could not very well call up NuEnergy's Mafia management and say, "Hey this is ol' troublesome Ben, remember me? Could you please turn your plants down to eighty percent for a while?"

But if he could somehow coax the power down without alerting the Mafia management, could he avoid catastrophic damage? Probably the answer was yes, but the chances of a short-term nationwide blackout would increase. Could both plant damage and a blackout be avoided?

No. It appeared a catch-22. Every potential solution, other than the plant teams which were now rushing in, led to an increased risk of either a massive outage or plant damage. A twenty percent power reduction of thirty plants, even if it could be done, was equivalent to pulling six huge plants off the U.S. grid at once. The central dispatcher would kill him if he did that. Wait! That was it. The central dispatcher. He could hold the key to this dilemma. Why hadn't they thought of him before?

The central dispatcher, the "big honcho," of the entire grid operated from a central location at the huge Mid America Power Company, which was based in Louisville, Kentucky. It was his job to balance the power produced and the power consumed throughout the entire electrical system. He, and he alone, had the authority to call individual utility dispatchers, or in extreme circumstances the actual plant control room, to order more or less power. He was the only one with authority to bypass the plant management. Could that be the needed opening?

Ben grabbed Garrison by the shoulders and spun him around, "Get Foster here pronto."

Ben turned to the head of INPO, Admiral Yeager, "Call Edison Electric Institute. Ask them for the central dispatcher's phone number. Tell them who you are and that it's an emergency."

Then he questioned NRC Administrator Friesen, "Hazel, check my memory. Eighty percent is the threshold for turbine generator overspeed protection, isn't it?" Not waiting for an answer, Ben fired another question, "How long does it take to bring a plant safely down to that level?"

Friesen asked, "What do you have up your sleeve, Ben?"

"Maybe a way out of tonight's miserable mess, but answer my questions."

"Yes. Eighty percent is correct. In answer to your second question, you can bring a plant safely down to eighty percent power in about thirty minutes.

"Are you thinking about taking all thirty units down at once? Wouldn't the U.S. electrical grid fail if you did that?"

Ben suggested, "What if we just took the seventeen Eastern time zone plants down while bringing other power on-line? Due to time zone differences NuEnergy's eastern plants could be the ones in the most immediate danger."

Hazel admitted, "I really don't know. Why Eastern only?"

"Based upon Dudaev's information the Central time zones saboteurs should be about an hour behind the Eastern thugs. He said their sabotage would occur after regular quitting time."

Hazel said, "I see. Still you should talk to the central dispatcher. He is the one who knows how big a hit the grid can take."

Ben recalled that this super dispatcher, who controlled the nationwide electrical grid, maintained the system balance by keeping the frequency close to 60 Hertz (Hz). If the system became unbalanced, for example, power consumed exceeded power produced, then the frequency across the entire grid would fall below 60 Hz. If this happened, the dispatcher would discern which utility or utilities were under-producing, call their dispatchers and tell them to add more power to the grid. Once that was accomplished, the frequency would rise back to 60 Hz and all would be well.

Admiral Yeager interrupted Ben's thoughts, "We have the dispatcher's phone number. The EEI office took some persuading. I told them to call me back here at the White House. That did it."

"Good, when you get him, hold him on the line."

A moment later Yaeger announced, "He is holding, Ben. His name is David Morgan."

"Good! I will take it."

Ben began, "Mr. Morgan, I am Dr. Ben Andrew in the White House working with the vice president. We have a national emergency on our hands. I believe you can help us."

"How do I know this to be true?"

"We are sending you a fax of the Declaration of National Emergency signed by the President. It is coded to verify authenticity. Check your operating manual and you will readily confirm this. In a minute the vice president will brief you.

"Before he gets here though I have a question for you. How many big base load plants can you lose without the grid going down?"

"Six to eight in a short period of time will definitely do it."

"Four wouldn't?" Ben calculated that bringing the Eastern Time Zone's seventeen plants down to eighty percent was roughly equivalent to the complete loss of four.

"Four would rock us pretty good tonight, but we wouldn't go down. Our frequency would drop from 60 to about 59.7. 59.5 is where we go completely out of business. If the frequency ever drops to 59.5, power plants around the country would sense trouble and essentially 'abandon ship.' Each would separate from the grid and shutdown automatically to protect itself from damage. Then we have a blackout closing down everything east of the Rockies. Fortunately that has never happened."

Garrison's assistant returned to the hectic White House nerve center with Vice President Foster.

Ben immediately relayed, "Mark, the central dispatcher is on the line. He can help us. Introduce yourself, confirm that this is a national emergency and tell him that I have full authority."

"Anything else?"

"No! Just give me the phone back after you are through. Morgan and I are going to become fast friends before this night is over."

Nodding, the vice president took the phone from Ben, "Hello, Mr. Morgan. This is Vice President Foster. We are appealing for your help. Our country is facing an extreme emergency. I understand you control the national electrical grid from there in Louisville."

"Yes, sir, that is correct. Everything east of the Rockies comes under my jurisdiction."

"Your grid is under attack tonight. Saboteurs are bent upon creating an extended nationwide blackout and the permanent destruction of many plants. I ask for your cooperation by supporting Dr. Andrew. It's up to you and Dr. Andrew to save our electrical system. I will put him back on the line."

Ben grabbed the phone, "There is no time to lose. You must order seventeen plants down to eighty percent. Are you ready for the names?"

"Yes, sir."

Ben waved a thanks to the departing vice president and then started listing the plants, beginning with the NuEnergy plants in New England. He completed his list with the Gator River Plant in Florida.

"Since you are going to lose a huge amount of power, and it is very likely several NuEnergy plants will be completely lost tonight, you are going to see a large deficit."

"That's the understatement of the year, Dr. Andrew."

"Order every utility to increase power from anything that makes electrons flow. Economics be damned. Tell them if they don't cooperate fully, they will get an ass kicking from a very angry vice president. Also tell them to start shedding non-essential loads.

"Meanwhile, order the operating supervisors to ramp those seventeen plants down to eighty percent power as fast as their tech specs allow. Once you get those started down, we have thirteen more in the Central zone to worry about."

Ben had just gambled bigger than he could ever have imagined he would. He had deliberately increased the chances of a short-term blackout in order to better avoid the plants' ultimate devastation and a prolonged economic crisis.

Ben leaned back and caught a whiff of the stale air in the room. Nearly choking, he fussed, "Jez, it smells like a locker room in here. The ventilation system is totally inadequate. Someone see if we can at least get some fans brought in."

Catching the irony of ordering the use of more electricity, no matter how minute, he corrected himself, "Belay that. Forget it."

CHAPTER
FORTY-SEVEN

Day 45 7:03 P.M. EST Road to Black Bear Plant Tulsa

Minutes ago the crisis call from Garrison's assistant came to the Black Bear team with the curt order, "Get to Black Bear immediately! Timing is crucial. You must secure the plant now. Be cautious. Things could get damn sticky. Assume sabotage in progress."

As the speeding Taurus ate up the remaining miles to the plant, the massive hulk of the Black Bear cooling tower loomed before them. FBI Agent Paul Brown fumed at the traffic coming from Black Bear, "Damn hayseed drivers are going to kill us."

The awesome sight of the nuclear plant structures was lost on the team on this wild ride. Brown's dodging of the out-coming Kamikazes distracted them somewhat from the formidable challenges lying ahead.

Upon twilight's arrival the plant lights automatically switched on, bathing the cooling tower and the hemispherical dome of the reactor building in a yellowish brilliance.

Water vapor rose hundreds of feet above the dominating cooling tower before finally diffusing into the atmosphere. The southern plains sunset, enhanced by generous amounts of atmospheric dust, colored the rising vapor an ethereal pink. Below the vapor the elliptical top rim of the lofty cooling tower flashed with white aircraft warning lights.

Brown whizzed by an elaborate electronic sign at the entrance to the plant site, which flashed the message of the day in bright orange letters, "Welcome to Black Bear Plant, 350 Consecutive Days at Full Power." Everyone in the car doubted that the sign would proclaim 351 tomorrow.

344

Day 45 7:05 P.M. EST Black Bear Switchyard

Working efficiently, the criminal technician, Helmut Nagy, with a special pass to the switchyard from Plant Manager Zogelmann, attached the wires leading from the first package of explosives to the antenna. The bomb, located near a massive transformer, should bring the plant down, but he was taking no chances. He took extra time to wire the bomb in a manner to thwart disarmament. According to Goldstein's orders, he was to do the job right.

Admiring his handiwork he mumbled, "Only a fool would try to disarm this baby. This is just like the old days when we blew up dissidents' homes."

Helmut picked up the second bomb. As he worked on it, he recalled how, on one very foggy day over a month ago, these same explosives had sailed across the fence to him. Since then he had stored them in Plant Manager Zogelmann's personal locker. It had been a long wait, but today the explosives would blow Black Bear straight to hell.

He had no idea that his treachery was, under Goldstein's orders, multiplied many fold.

Day 45 7:06 EST Black Bear Parking Lot

Racing into the parking lot, Agent-in-Charge Brown weaved through the parked cars to the front row. Leaving lengthy tire skid marks, he screeched the Taurus to a stop in the spot marked "Reserved for the Plant Manager." It was good news that this particular spot was empty, since it suggested that Plant Manager Zogelmann, who was one of those linked closely to the Mafia, wasn't in. One less problem thought a slightly relieved Brown.

Led by Brown, the team burst purposefully into the visitor's lobby of the main security building. They felt as if they were swimming up stream as the last of the exiting plant employees rushed past them. That was good news as well, since it meant that most of the extraneous personnel would soon be safely out of harm's way.

Brown snorted, "Good riddance. Only the night-shift and a couple of shit-heads will be left to deal with."

The FBI had briefed the team that based upon criminal background checks there were two Mafia techs at Black Bear.

A double security fence and security equipment, which included motion detectors and closed circuit TV cameras, completely surrounded the Black Bear facility. The only viable way in for the team was through this controlled entrance in the security building. Only a properly authorized person could pass through the gates to the secure side of the building. To get inside one must negotiate metal and explosive detectors and secured gates requiring palm-print checks.

Without alerting NuEnergy's management, the NRC had cleverly taken care of some of the team's entry preliminaries. NRC Administrator, Hazel Friesen, had arranged for each team member's palm print to be entered into the NRC's central security computer. Routinely, the palm-print information of NRC inspectors was forwarded to the individual plant's security computer just before the inspectors were scheduled for a plant visit. As far as Black Bear's security force knew, the team's palm prints, which the computer had received today, were just routine personnel data for the next contingent of NRC inspectors.

Agent Brown, Inspector Smith and the two utility experts, Grow and Neitzel, cleared the metal detector, the explosive sniffer and finally the palm reader without a hitch. Four of the six were now safely through the security barriers. Now they must directly confront the plant security force, while the remaining two heavily armed federal agents, Templeton and Jones, waited with the team's weapons on the visitor side of the building. The entrance plan, of necessity, called for them to wait, since their equipment would set off the detectors and would cause the plant security force to scramble to the scene. Obviously that confrontation was something they wished to avoid.

NRC Inspector Smith flashed his I.D. and informed the nearest plant security guard, "I am NRC Inspector Smith. This is a federal emergency. We must speak with the security supervisor immediately."

The flustered guard told Smith and the others to wait where they were, while he retreated to an inner office. Shortly he returned with his supervisor.

Agent Brown showed his government credentials and, with bold authority, informed the supervisor, "President Arthur has declared a federal emergency at Black Bear. The NRC has assumed control of this plant."

"The hell you say."

"The NRC resident is now in the control room, serving the operating supervisor an official order signed by the NRC Chairman and President Arthur. Here is a copy of that order."

The supervisor, whose nametag revealed him to be Phil Miller, fumbled over the order, turning it sidewise and upside down while inspecting it. Agent Brown patiently, but firmly, suggested, "Call the control room now! Confirm what I just told you."

The stressed security supervisor, recovering a little of his lost composure, defiantly responded, "Wait here while I check your story. I must figure out what the hell is going down."

He disgustedly tromped back into his office to check Brown's story with the control room.

After what seemed an interminable delay to Brown, Supervisor Miller returned with three volumes of his security procedures under his arm. "Yep, you were right. The control room confirms what you said, but I jes don't get it at all. There has got to be a procedure governing this sit-sh-ation here somewhere."

Inspector Smith stepped forward to coach the confused Miller, "Supervisor, the correct procedure is in Volume II. Look at II-32. The second paragraph on the first page states that the plant security force will cooperate with Federal authorities when there is a federal emergency."

"Yep! I see that, but..." drawled the puzzled Miller, scratching his head.

"You are to support the Feds with all of your resources. Essentially you are now an FBI deputy."

Deputy was the magic word. It triggered the desired response. Supervisor Miller puffed up with that bit of news. He read the procedure ever so carefully, and finally said, "Okay, how ken I hep?"

Agent Brown, no longer to be denied, took command. "Deputy Miller, instruct your forces that my agents are coming in with their gear and weapons and will bypass your detectors."

Slamming a slip of paper bearing two names into the Supervisor's palm, Brown barked, "Look these up in your computer. I want their location pinpointed immediately. You have their names and badge numbers. Get a move on, Deputy! Inspector Smith and I will use your office as our command center for the duration.

"Smith, report our status to Washington immediately."

"Roger."

Moments later, federal deputy Phil Miller full of self-importance announced, "We located the two."

His attitude was evolving. He was now eager to help. The realization that this promised more excitement than he had ever experienced was hitting home. He had always dreamed of becoming an FBI agent, but had found the college degree just too big a stumbling block. So this was his big chance to operate with the agency. An FBI deputy!

Hell! He might even get a medal or a commendation. Maybe folk around here would finally forget about the damned dog "Neutron" episode and treat him with a little respect.

Now actually solicitous, Miller reported, "The tech you want is in the switchyard, and the operator is on the third level of the turbine building."

"Damn! We wasted too much f—- time," Brown bellowed.

Still determined to avoid disaster, he ordered, "Give me six of your best guards!"

Brown briefly explained the situation to the guards. Grow and Templeton were dispatched with three security guards to the electrical switchyard. Jones, Neitzel and three more plant security guards headed for the third level of the turbine building.

Based on the locations of the two suspected mafiosos, Brown guessed that the overspeed protection was already out and that a bomb was planted in the switchyard. Black Bear was teetering on the brink of disaster.

Once those two groups were on their way, Smith and Brown continued communications with D.C. and the Black Bear Control Room. The rest of the plant security force stood by, anxious for any piece of the action.

"Black Bear to White House. We are in the plant and proceeding per plan, but status is code red. Suspects are in position to carry out sabotage."

FORTY-EIGHT

Day 45 7:45 P.M. CENTCOM MacDill AFB Florida

General Adair's jet skimmed above the tranquil Tampa Bay to a smooth landing. A contingent of the Air Base's Special Police met and escorted the Joint Chiefs Chairman across the post to CENTCOM headquarters. The general, aware of the mobilization of the resident 91st Air Refueling Squadron to the Middle East, noted that the squadron's absence contributed to the apparent repose of the base. A casual observer could easily be deceived by the apparent lack of base activity and the serenity of the base's palms, which swayed gently in the warm ocean breezes.

However, intense action was hidden deep within the weathered, sprawling, three-story building. Because of its inauspicious gray exterior, the Air Force command structure's importance was masked. Only the nearby towers with the webs of antennae and clusters of microwave and satellite dishes hinted at the truth that Joint Eagles Central Command, CENTCOM, toiled inside. The military's high-tech tools of war funneled their wealth of intelligence on Joint Eagles through this labyrinth of towers and dishes, directly to General Ribikoff's CENTCOM staff.

General Adair was all too aware that little time remained before the nuclear-tipped missile on the tanker would be ready for launch. He was here to ratify CENTCOM's decision on how best to stop it. Not a second could be wasted.

Entering the old building, Adair noted that it was like switching from a black and white still photo to a surround-sound big-screen movie theatre. Real-time data on every aspect of the Joint Eagles battle was at the fingertips of the dozens of scurrying military specialists serving as CENTCOM staff. This instant access to battlefield status, including even the locations and types of every enemy and friendly vehicle, enabled Ribikoff's Staff at CENTCOM to make strategic command decisions involving the action half a world away.

Moving on, General Adair saw that electronically updated maps lit the walls of General Abraham Ribikoff's inner command nerve center. In a user-friendly manner, the colorful charts displayed the positions of vital satellites, air resources, attack submarines, carrier task forces and each cruise missile target.

General Adair hurried past three Army Colonels gathered around a table-top scale replica of the Karaj area. They were busily discussing strategy for the Apache Long Bow Helicopter Squadron.

One officer worried, "The issue is training. I am not convinced that the Long Bow crews are sufficiently trained."

The second Colonel took exception with the first, "The last few years have made a big difference. They couldn't have handled the job in the late nineties, but I believe now our pilots will excel."

Other officers from the Engineering Corp were discussing how much abuse a section of Highway Four, the main traffic artery running west from Tehran, would take under tomorrow's intense pounding. The heavy air transport traffic created by the landing of the Armored Calvary Regiment's men and machines would pulverize a highway section in about an hour, they concluded.

On one wall above a group of seated, but very alert, military specialists, a set of two-dozen TV monitors displayed live pictures from the Iranian theater of operations. The specialists watched as one brief picture segment after another, transmitted from the nose-cone camera of each cruise missile, depicted the final seconds of each enemy target's existence. These short sequences typically showed the target looming ever larger, seemingly rushing at the camera. Then suddenly each transmission ceased. These videos were providing instant witness to the cruise attacks' accuracy. The B-52 armada and the sub pack's missiles were having a devastating effect on key Iranian military installations.

Amidst the hubbub, the self-assured CENTCOM Commander greeted General Adair. General Ribikoff, in his early fifties, was a tall, lean, capable Air Force general with a distinguished career. During the Gulf War he served as an F-117 pilot. A masterful military strategist, he was also a most charismatic leader. This rare combination of qualities had propelled him up through the Air Force ranks to general in nearly record time.

General Ribikoff explained to General Adair, "After staff views those pictures which you see coming in live, only the extent of damage is left to conjecture. If a cruise misses a target, one of our loitering cruises is sent in to finish the job. Complete Battle Damage Assessment, though, is left to J-Staff. Based on their work, we will decide where F-117's are needed. They will mop up on any of these initial objectives."

On a wall a large, less sophisticated, obviously hastily added East Coast map, thumb-tacked to the wall, pinpointed the current locations of the Lebanese oil tanker and the Iranian sub. Also the positions of the submarines Atlanta, Sam Houston and Salt Lake City, and the circling ABL were shown. An advancing two hundred mile arc around the tanker encompassed those areas CENTCOM believed were most likely targeted. The quick-strike circle had relentlessly shifted north and now included New York City, Washington D.C. and most of the large metropolises in the Northeast.

"General, that captain over there," General Ribikoff nodded toward the desk and cubicle across from them, "is a SEAL. He is in constant communication with the SEAL Team Squad Leader. His TV screens are giving him live shots of the tanker. We are getting those valuable looks from various sources."

General Adair shook his head. The place was literally awash in data. Even he was staggered by the wealth of info pouring into the command staff. The military had struggled, just as had most civilian ventures, to stay abreast of the technology revolution. All of this high-tech in action drove home to General Adair how dramatically these radical changes, many of which had happened under his watch, had revolutionized warfare. Joint Eagles, in many respects, would bear only slight resemblance to past conflicts. One thing, though, hadn't changed. Ground troops were necessary to achieve the mission's objectives, which unfortunately meant American lives would be lost.

General Adair wasted no time, "The decision is at hand, General. Let's get to the East Coast business."

General Abraham Ribikoff stated his preference up front and without hesitation, "The SEALs are our best bet. They have the greatest chance of eliminating the threat without collateral damage. The SEAL squad is hidden in attack position on the tanker. They are ready to annihilate the aggressors.

"If the SEALs should fail to halt the launch, the Salt Lake City's interceptor missiles, one armed conventionally and one with the neutron bomb, or the ABL and its laser are our only viable alternatives. The neutron bomb is untested, but could theoretically disarm the enemy warhead in mid-flight. Methods, other than the neutron bomb, can stop the missile but not a nuclear explosion.

General Adair minced no words, "Any untested method concerns me, gentlemen."

"That's why the best answer is the SEALs," responded Ribikoff.

Having to replow this ground with Adair at this hectic moment was frustrating. Yet Ribikoff realized that with millions of American lives at stake, General Adair's demand for this final review was reasonable and prudent.

"Our pictures show that the launch apparatus is nearly ready. You can see that on this screen right here, General. We estimate that the crew will be able to launch in twenty minutes. We must give the SEALs a go-ahead within the next few minutes. If we don't we jeopardize their ability to halt the firing," warned Ribikoff.

"Yes, I understand that time has nearly run out. However, I want answers to a few final questions before we act. One of your staff here is a SEAL, I believe."

A Navy captain spoke up, "That's correct, General. I am, sir."

"Captain, what are the chances of the SEALs stopping the launch?"

"They can do it, sir. The element of surprise, their superior firepower and training, and especially their absolute dedication to their goal, gives them the upper hand. They will experience casualties though. It won't be pretty."

"Captain, I don't want words that tell me what I already know. What are the chances of their stopping the launch? Quantify it."

"Ninety percent, sir."

"So, General, even if we give the SEALs a go-ahead, there is still one chance in ten that the damned thing, still live-armed, launches toward one of our East Coast cities. We still don't know which city, do we?"

"No. Intelligence doesn't have an answer to that. That wall map over there shows that any of the East Coast cities from Boston to Richmond are well within its quick-strike range. Our hunch, though, is that the objective is New York City."

Ribikoff briefly explained to Adair how he had considered ordering the Salt Lake City's neutron bomb exploded above the tanker. It could kill the enemy onboard and halt a launch, but his staff concluded that the risk of collateral damage to the tanker was too great. His staff had also considered sending the Salt Lake intercept missile in close enough to the tanker so that the neutron bomb would disarm the missile, but again, an uncertain outcome and the potential for a devastating oil spill nixed that option.

He pointed out the obvious; the secrecy required for Joint Eagles had dictated that no action be taken against the tanker until after the first wave of B-52 and submarine missiles had been unleashed on Iran. That constraint had allowed the danger to slip closer to shore, making intercept more difficult. Turbulent weather conditions had rendered a poison-gas attack upon the ship impractical.

General Ribikoff continued, "Downwind is thankfully out to sea tonight. So a public radiation alert, which would certainly set off mass hysteria all along the coast killing many needlessly in a resulting stampede, is not necessary or prudent.

"If the weapon hits a metropolitan area, the destruction and death toll will be astronomical. If the Iranians are sophisticated enough to explode it at optimum altitude, it can flatten any city."

"What do we do if the SEALs can't stop the launch? Can disaster still be avoided?"

An Air Force Colonel on General Ribikoff's staff spoke. "The Airborne Laser, ABL, will stop the missile short of its target, but it can't prevent an explosion."

"Can the ABL shoot it down before it gets to land?"

"The chances are ninety-nine out of a hundred that we can prevent landfall. The damned Iranians somehow got hold of a missile with advanced ramjet technology, so it leaves us a very tiny time window for an ocean intercept."

"Thank you, Colonel. What are the chances of success with the mini-neutron bomb? Do you actually believe the bomb can disarm their weapon while it is in mid-flight?'

The weapons expert on the staff, seeing that General Adair wanted answers quantified, estimated, "I can only give it a fifty-fifty chance, sir. The latest Nuclear Test Ban Treaty makes it impossible to test this incredible defensive use of the weapon."

"General Ribikoff, without further delay, unleash the SEALs. God help us all if those warriors fail."

After giving his order, Adair turned to watch the SEAL assault on the screens in Ribikoff's office.

Day 45 8:20 P.M. SSN Salt Lake City North Atlantic

The SSN 716, Salt Lake City, neared the end of its flank speed sprint through the Atlantic depths. Earlier this afternoon the submarine had been summoned to Norfolk Naval Shipyard. There the special nuclear warhead accompanied by a team of weapons specialists came aboard. While the boat raced toward its battle station, the specialists had worked feverishly to ready the weapon.

The nuclear explosive device, type AA-44, was an advanced thermonuclear weapon, commonly referred to as the mini-neutron bomb. The fire-control crew had mounted the warhead on the Navy's advanced anti-missile missile, the AGI-2000, which was capable of speeds exceeding Mach 5. The interceptor missile, with its thermonuclear warhead in tube six of the VLS launch system now pointed skyward, primed for launch.

The bomb did not earn its strange name, mini neutron, from its use of exceptionally tiny neutrons. Rather the name signified that it was a low yield, thermonuclear device that upon exploding produced a lethal burst of neutron radiation.

As launch time approached, the team of specialists aboard the Salt Lake City monitored atmospheric conditions, including the humidity in the intercept area. The airborne water molecules would alter the weapon's neutron beam before it impinged upon the enemy's nuclear warhead. Accounting for the climatological conditions and the details of the enemy weapon's design supplied earlier today by Kruschev, the experts made their final estimate.

While the submarine strained for its last knot of speed, the lead scientist relayed the final calculation to the weapons control officer of the Salt Lake City.

"The blast window for disarmament is three hundred to five hundred feet from the target."

"You are kidding! That narrow!"

"Not kidding. Wish we were. A closer detonation and the enemy bomb goes off prematurely. Farther away and the armed weapon continues unaffected toward its target."

Shaking his head in disbelief the weapons officer swore, "Damn! You are asking for the moon. That means a window of a mere fraction of a second. You better say a prayer for our SEALs."

Finally, the Salt Lake City slowed as it approached launch station. The sub's interceptor missiles were ready if called upon. The worried fire-control officer knew that if the SEALs failed to stop the launch, his AA-44 weapon was the last remaining chance to prevent a hostile nuclear explosion.

Day 45 8:21 P.M. ABL Skies Above the Northeast Coastline

Earlier today, the newest addition to the American ABL fleet had been called home from the skies above the Turkish-Iranian border. After the five thousand mile flight, the flying laser weapon, with no time to spare, refueled in mid-air and immediately assumed a circling pattern at twenty thousand feet above the New Jersey coast. With its unique attack laser activated, it was prepared to shoot down the missile if all else failed.

The cruise missile faced by the ABL crew tonight presented a challenging target. This low-flying supersonic cruise missile could travel less than one hundred feet above the earth's surface. Hence this would be no easy, high-altitude shot far above all atmosphere. The light beam would have to traverse down through the dense lower reaches of the earth's atmosphere. That is why this unique ABL was summoned by CENTCOM.

This ABL was armed with a second laser system, one uniquely qualified for low altitude targets. With its improved atmospheric transmission, this laser used a set of chemicals producing a longer wavelength beam of 3.8 micron. It was the big brother of Black Star's laser weapon, but still basically a miniature version of the Army's Mid-Infrared Advanced Chemical Laser (MIRACL).

The chemicals were already activated and had reached critical state, primed to fire a powerful beam of light upon an instant's notice. If the SEALs and the AA-44 failed, the Air Force crew in the ABL would shoot down the missile, but they couldn't prevent an explosion.

Crews aboard the Salt Lake City and the ABL held their collective breath. The SEALs, the sub and the ABL were all that stood between millions of Americans and Andropov's nuclear bomb.

CHAPTER
FORTY-NINE

Day 45 8:22 P.M. Supertanker North Atlantic

Four pairs of strategically hidden, black-clad fighters, with weapons ready, crouched around the ship's perimeter. Behind the safety railing skirting the ship's deck, each SEAL, buffeted by the Atlantic's winter winds, prayed that the attack signal would come before they froze.

Ward's commandos were beyond impatient. The damn delay was the only thing working against them. The harsh wind drained precious energy from their already depleted reserves and threatened hypothermia. Before long, they would each be a block of ice. Why couldn't CENTCOM make a blasted decision?

Several hours ago, the eight chilled warriors, led by Lt. Cmdr. Ward, had left behind the minimal comforts of their submerged mini-subs. They swam under water directly into the tanker's path. Fighting the treacherous currents created by the behemoth's advance through the sea, the SEALs, while still remaining submerged, struggled to attach themselves to the tanker's hull. They latched onto the giant ship, as might a school of angrily attacking octopi. With suction cups on their feet, knees, elbows and hands they strained to hold on while the current viciously tore at them.

Slowly the uninvited guests ascended. Upon reaching the surface, the rough sea assailed them with its full fury. If not secured to the hull, the ocean's violent swells and waves would have dashed them as mere salt spray against the cold steel sides.

Once Ward's squad had cleared the surging waterline, things became only slightly easier. Having jettisoned their swim fins and goggles, they were left with their load of weapons and fifteen vertical feet to scale to reach the deck.

An hour ago, under orders from CENTCOM, the SEALs at the bow of the ship launched two miniature planes holding tiny cameras, which transmitted pictures to the circling Aurora. Captain Fisher at CENTCOM received the pictures and remotely controlled their flight. The SEALs concluded that attack time was approaching since the planes would run out of power in less than two hours.

Finally, Ward's MX 300 helmet and headset resonated with Captain Fisher's long-awaited order. "Sea Lion Six, execute now! God be with you."

Before commanding the attack, Ward checked the readiness of each SEAL. He found that all were eager for battle.

Ward ordered, "CENTCOM, watch for any unexpected movement of the rotten bastards. Let's crash their damned party. Execute! Execute! Execute!"

Ward and five SEALs sprang from hiding. At last there were no restraints. The time for action was now. The fate of their country rested in their hands. From three directions three pairs of dark figures bolted swiftly across the open deck. They converged upon the superstructure and launch area from both sides and the back. As their six comrades raced forward, the SEAL sharpshooters at the bow, employing their modified polymer and stainless-steel M-14 sniper rifles, picked off the two Mafia lookouts stationed on top of the superstructure. Their lifeless bodies pitched forward and fell into the blustery night.

Each corpse hit with a sickening thud against the unyielding, cold steel deck near the attacking Ward. Ward's partner, undaunted by the bodies landing nearby, shattered the lock on the superstructure's main door with a volley of slugs from his Remington 7188 C. Half of the metal door disintegrated. An instant later, Ward leaped through the demolished door and launched a stun grenade into the room where eight Mafia gunmen were loitering.

He quickly withdrew reloaded his CAR-15's M203 Grenade Launcher, whirled and fired a second stun grenade. It exploded near the six Mafia thugs guarding the launch area on the port side deck.

The gunfire near the launch area was intense. Bart's trained ear discerned that, so far, friendly fire predominated. That was a very good sign.

One miniature plane, guided by CENTCOM, flew through the fragmented front door.

Ward and Haden's lightning attack had taken the eight Thieves-in-Law inside completely by surprise. The flying minicam revealed that in a confused panic the mobsters grabbed for their AK-47's and fired blindly. Not yet sure of their targets, they managed to kill one of their own.

Advised of those developments, Ward and Haden, firing continuously, sprang through the door into the Mafia's quarters. The mafiosos retreated from the duo's withering fire. Four opted to flee through the rear door.

Bart warned the two SEALs at the rear, "Rear guard, rear guard, this is Sea Lion Six. Four shits are headed your way! Flush them!"

The four fleeing desperadoes met a murderous wall of SEAL buckshot and submachine-gun bullets. They dropped, their weapons silenced and their bodies shredded by the intense volley of the two SEALs at the rear of the structure.

"Your intelligence, CENTCOM Six, is super. Keep it up," Ward implored.

While the war was raging inside the superstructure, the bow SEAL snipers brought their deadly accurate fire on the six confused port-side Mafia around the launch crew. Two enemy gunmen, preparing to shoot at the attacking port-side SEALs, fell with small entrance bullet holes and gaping exit wounds.

Spooked by the massacre at the rear of the superstructure, two of the three remaining interior thugs made a break for the front door. They chose unwisely to take their chances against Ward and his partner, Carl Haden. Firing wildly, the two mafiosos ran straight to their termination. Ward and Haden, warned of their approach by Captain Fisher, met their frantic race for the front exit with ear-shattering CAR-15 and shotgun volleys. The two thugs died in mid-stride amidst a gory spray of flesh and blood.

Ward carefully slipped farther into the lower level. Checking the room he found the gruesome remnants of seven terrorists. Only one of the original eight, who had been on deck level, had escaped. According to Captain Fisher, the escapee was fleeing to the upper levels of the superstructure. The pursuing micro plane tracked his retreat.

Ward ordered both SEALs at the rear to reinforce the two SEALs in the firefight near the missile. He had heard the steady roar of weapons over there and gathered from the sounds that the fight there was still in doubt. Ward then motioned to Haden as he headed for the stairs, "Follow me."

Ward and Haden leapt up the stairs several at a time, closing in on the Mafia and the Iranian crewmen still high above them in the Captain's bridge area. For the moment they could forget about the four second-shift Iranian crewmen who had been sleeping. CENTCOM's Captain Fisher relayed that they were armed with pistols but were cowering in their second-deck quarters.

While climbing, Ward, acting upon new information from Fisher, instructed the sharpshooters at the bow to concentrate all of their support on the battle at the launch site. Less than a minute had elapsed since the SEALs had sprung into action. By Ward's count at least eleven of the eighteen Mafia thugs, as well as all five missile-launch crewmen, were no longer breathing.

Forty-Five Seconds Earlier Launch Area

Since the priority was to stop the launch, all of the launch team were cut down immediately by Petty Officers Anderson and Sandoval's ferocious attack. Charging from the port side railing with guns constantly blazing, the two SEALs eliminated any chance of a launch. This strategy of temporarily ignoring the nearby Mafia gunmen while killing the launch crew, involved high personal risk to Anderson and Sandoval. Bart's stun grenade had helped some. It had effectively, if only momentarily, incapacitated the nearby Mafia thugs.

Lance Anderson, the youngest on the team, had dreamed of being a SEAL as long as he could remember. An Army Brat who had moved around the world from school to school, he had retained two constants in his life, a desire to be a SEAL and a love of athletics. Since he had excelled in high school football and track, several junior colleges had recruited him. Despite their attractive offers, he opted for his dream, the Navy SEAL program.

Every second of this battle stretched into an eternity for Anderson. It was as if somebody had placed his life's VCR on a slow frame-by-frame play. Within seconds that seemed a lifetime, Sandoval and he had mowed down all of the Iranian launch crew.

"Those fuckers won't be killing any Americans tonight," Sandoval announced triumphantly.

The Mafia at the launch area, initially confused by Ward's grenade and the intense volleys from the two attacking SEALs, recovered enough to commence shooting in the direction of the attacking duo. Both SEALs dove for cover behind metal boxes of launch tools. Anderson, while in midair, still in a frame-by-frame mode, heard two shots from the bow and started a thought. "Good, our boys in front are hitting the bas..." Then excruciating pain shot through his body. One frame later another hail of AK-47 rounds tore into him. There were no more video frames of life or pain for Lance Anderson.

Only seconds after Anderson's death the two SEALs from the rear joined Sandoval in the fight around the missile. Aware that Anderson was hit, they charged with an awful ferocity. Unleashing a stream of withering salvos, they turned the tide of battle decisively in the SEALs' favor. Emotion, adrenaline and the need for mission achievement drove the murderous assault. Three more Mafia fell under a relentless crossfire.

The remaining mobster threw up his hands with his weapon overhead in a belated attempt at surrender. Simultaneously, bullets from two directions struck him. A short burst from an MP-5 sent 9 mm slugs through the Mafia gunman's head and throat as a .308 round from one of the SEAL sniper's modified M-14 sheered his spinal cord from the base of his skull, killing him instantly. The SEALs' job was not to take prisoners but to save American lives.

Sandoval ran to his downed partner, Anderson. He detected no pulse. The gruesome extent of the wounds told him there was no hope. He sadly passed his hand over his young friend's blankly staring eyes. They reflexively closed for the last time.

Top Deck of Superstructure

Meanwhile, the three remaining Mafia thugs had taken up defensive positions in the bridge high above the struggle near the missile. Two had been there all along, apparently to see to the proper behavior of the Iranian crew and to stay in radio contact with the Iranian sub, which had expectantly moved closer and risen to periscope depth.

Those two Mafiosos were joined by the refugee from the fighting below. He had raced up the stairs and bolted through the door. He slammed and locked it. Gasping for breath, he crouched behind the bulkhead, with AK-47 poised for the final assault, which he knew was coming.

Haden and Ward, breathing heavily, paused upon reaching the top level. Checking his watch, Ward saw that only two minutes had elapsed since the attack began. On the bow side of the hall was a door. Captain Fisher informed them that it led to the bridge. The miniature spy plane hovered at the end of the hall. The other miniature flew about outside in front of the pilot's window. It furnished a complete view of the bridge and its occupants to CENTCOM's Captain Fisher.

A large room containing all of the navigational and steerage equipment on the huge floating oilcan was revealed. The expansive glass windows on the bow side of the room afforded the crew an unobstructed view of the forward section of the boat and the dark, angry sea beyond.

Ward, upon hearing that the launch site battle had subsided, turned all of his attention to the bridge. "CENTCOM, do your pictures show where the last three jokers are?" His wildly pulsing heart, brought about by the extreme exertion of the climb and the battle-induced adrenaline coursing through his veins, actually interfered with his hearing.

Understanding this phenomenon, Captain Fisher shouted, "We show all three on the Captain's bridge."

"Give me their exact locations."

"One's hiding in a crouching position behind the bulkhead to the port side of the door to the bridge. One is near the man who appears to be the captain. The third has gone to the controls at the forward consoles. Who knows what his game is? He may be trying to start a dump of oil or something."

"Sea Lion Six to Bow team. Have you got a shot at any of those SOBs on the bridge?"

"Affirmative. The one nearest the window is ours."

"Good, but don't shoot until you hear Carl and me fire."

"Captain Fisher, the one by the door, I need his exact location."

"He's crouched down near the bulkhead. I would say about seven feet to the port side of the door."

"Okay. How far away from the door are the other two assholes?"

"The one, probably the leader is near the captain. He is poised, AK-47 at the ready, facing the door twenty feet away at twelve o'clock. The other is standing near the front equipment consoles at two o'clock, some thirty feet away with his gun slung over his shoulder."

"Roger. Once we blast open the door, send the plane straight at the Mafia leader?"

"Got you! Will do!"

"Bow men, do you still have a clean shot?"

"Affirmative. The one near the window is history."

"Carl, fill that Remington with slugs. The first shot's for the door. Then I want a pattern of those babies placed about two feet high where the crouched thug hides. I am going in once you start shooting."

As Haden raised his shotgun to fire, a desperate message crackled in Bart's headset. "Hold it! Hold it, Sea Lion Six! There is big trouble!

The head honcho by the Captain has a console giving him pictures of you and Carl. They are watching your every move. They will destroy you the minute you start your attack."

"What angle do they have on us?"

"The camera must be high on the stern bulkhead. Can you spot it?"

Ward frantically scanned the hall for the offending camera. Once he spotted it, he signaled Carl where to aim his first blast from the shotgun.

A slug from Haden's shotgun ended the monitor's functional existence.

"Now, " ordered Ward.

Haden's shotgun belched forth its next slugs and the door blew apart. He commenced spraying the remaining rounds through the wall in the pattern Ward had ordered. The munitions severed the crouched gunman's torso.

Bart delayed a split second, allowing the plane to do its thing. It buzzed in straight at the Mafia leader near the Captain, hitting him squarely in the face.

While the confused man swatted at the annoyance, Ward dived head first through the door with his CAR-15 blazing. Rolling over quickly, his weapon firing continuously, he cut down the distracted Mafia leader near the Captain. The Captain grabbed the submachine gun out of the dying man's hands and attempted to shoot the prone warrior.

By then Haden, who had reloaded with buckshot, burst into the room. He sprayed shot from his deadly Remington into the Captain. The stream of buckshot riddled the Captain like a sieve before he collapsed to the deck.

A single, well-placed .308 round had already penetrated the window and the last Mafia terrorist's brain. The remaining Iranian crewman was on his knees, wounded in the foot. With his hands high over his head he pleaded in a flood of his native Farsi for his life. Haden grabbed him roughly and handcuffed him to the console railing.

The SEALs' volleys had knocked several gaping holes in the front windows. The North Atlantic's cold, salt-saturated air whistled through the room as if to purge the growing stench of death.

While the fight on the bridge was still raging, Sandoval and the other two SEALs had captured the two engineering crewmembers, who were cowering in the engine spaces. They had put up no resistance.

Suddenly Bart heard four rapid M-14 reports.

"What's going on, Bow?"

One of the sharpshooters stationed at the front of the giant ship replied, "Four dead men just tore out of hiding with pistols drawn ready to fire on our team. We cut short their antics."

Ward proudly proclaimed to Fisher, "We got them all. Fight is over. There will be no missile launch tonight. Get an evac copter in here right away. We have a SEAL casualty, a wounded Iranian crewman, and two captured Iranians. The rest of the vermin need body bags."

"The chopper with a medic crew is on its way, Sea Lion Six. A U.S. crew to pilot the tanker will be dropped onboard shortly. They will turn this monster around and take it out to sea until we are sure everything is neutralized. Backup Marine forces will be landing momentarily. A group of nuclear specialists, who still must verify weapon disarmament, will be with the Marines. Terrific work. The terrorist shits got what they deserved. You SEALs have the gratitude of a nation. We will miss Lance."

"So will we. God rest his soul."

The timer on the bomb was down to four minutes, when the captured crew member started yelling frantically in broken English, "Ve all die. Ve all die soon."

One minute before the SEAL onslaught had commenced, the captain on the bridge had remotely activated the nuclear weapon's over-ride timer, setting the bomb to go off in no more than eleven minutes. With launch countdown then at T minus three minutes, that would allow time for the missile to arrive over New York. The SEALs, having stopped the launch, were now only four minutes away from being vaporized.

Bart guessed the meaning of the crewman's torrent of garbled words, "CENTCOM, the bomb's live-armed. Get those specialists here now or we are all toast."

Day 45 8:28 P.M. The SSN Atlanta North Atlantic

The SSN Atlanta had sustained its alert status for a "nerve-fraying" twelve hours. Fortunately, the crew was hardened to alerts from its many missions of searching and confronting the still formidable Russian Oscar-class cruise-missile submarines. In contrast to today's lengthy and tense stalk, those missions were often a sprint-and-drift operation, designed to locate any Russian sub that might be threatening a carrier task group. On those alerts, there were, at least, periodic bursts of activity. Today's alert had been quite different. Never had they experienced a more nerve-wracking day. It had stretched into an interminably tense wait. Throughout the eternal day the Atlanta had held its trailing position directly behind the Iranian sub, which shadowed the supertanker. Upon new orders from COMSUBLANT, the U.S. attack boat had crept to within eight thousand yards of the target.

The order to fire came at exactly 8:29 p.m., just as Captain Allan saw that the Iranian boat had begun what appeared to be an attempt to gain speed and maneuver away. Allan ordered two wire-guided MK-48 ADCAP torpedoes launched. The torpedoes from this firing angle would strike near the Iranian sub's propeller shafts.

Both torpedoes found their mark. The explosions popped the shaft seals, flooding the engine spaces. The Iranian sub resisted at first, but gradually and inevitably slipped into its final dive. It wallowed like a mortally wounded whale, on a helpless one-way trip to the floor of the North Atlantic. As Iran's Kilo-class submarine slipped ever deeper, the cold waters of the Atlantic relentlessly splintered one bulkhead after another, eventually flooding every compartment.

Day 45 8:29 P.M. CENTCOM MacDill AFB Florida

General Ribikoff pressed his staff, "How soon can the experts board the tanker?"

He referred to the bomb disarmament team, which was now in a copter enroute to the distressed tanker.

"Two minutes," replied a Naval Commander.

"That's too late. In three and a half minutes the thing explodes."

"Commander, contact the Salt Lake City. Tell them they have three minutes to get their missile with the magic neutron bomb to the ship. Set the range of explosion so that it'll disarm the enemy bomb."

"Yes, sir, but ..."

"But what?"

"Even if we can get it there that fast, it is lethal to all on board the tanker."

"Doesn't matter. Try it. Send in the missile. Have the lead copter pick up Ward's team. The other copters need to run like hell."

Day 45 8:31 P.M. Navy HC-3 Helicopter Atlantic Ocean

After Ward's commandos had scrambled aboard, the Navy's HC-3 copter lifted off the tanker's forward deck. It struck a course to the north at maximum speed.

Still in continuous communications with CENTCOM, Ward demanded, "Captain Fisher, what's the ETA of the Salt Lake City's missile?"

"Fifty seconds."

"That's too late. The damned bomb is set to blow in thirty seconds."

Ward informed the pilot, "We have one chance to survive. Ditch this thing."

"Not me. You SEALs can have the damned water if you love it so."

"Okay. It's your life. Drop down to twenty feet. We will jump and you and your passengers can take your chances in the air," said Ward.

Once the copter lowered, the seven SEALs dove into the stormy Atlantic. Captain Ward estimated that they were at least two miles from the tanker. As they bailed out, he shouted a final order, "Stay submerged as long as you can. Use earplugs if you ever want to hear anything again."

As the SEALs were swallowed by the angry sea, the doomed pilot full throttled the copter.

The shock wave swept across the sea toward the fleeing copter. Instantly its prop turned to spaghetti and its body twisted around the trapped crewmen and the disarmament specialists. The deformed copter fell to the water and at first skipped across the surface. The relentless waves, though, soon engulfed the downed machine. The trapped men were spared a slow, lingering radiation-induced death.

After several minutes underwater, Captain Ward surfaced. His microphone no longer worked. He couldn't yet tell if his men had survived. He waited to fire a flare since no one could see it anyway. Compared to the towering mushroom cloud to the south his flare was rendered insignificant.

CHAPTER
FIFTY

Day 45 Earlier 7:42 P.M. Command Center White House

An eternity seemed to have slipped past while Ben awaited word from Central Dispatcher Dave Morgan. Despite his impatience, he realized that Morgan had his hands full bringing the threatened nuclear plants down to the relatively secure eighty percent. Furthermore, Morgan's assistants were contacting every utility that might own any extra resources ordering them to bring on power of any kind.

Overhearing the frustrated swearing of Morgan's aids, Ben could tell that they were running into trouble. The Arctic air currently spreading across the Midwest and Eastern seaboard was the problem. The cold air mass seeping in behind the Northeaster, which had pounded the East Coast for the past two days, was creating record demands for electricity. There apparently wasn't much reserve power to be found.

Ben prayed that his strategy of bringing the plants down to a safe power level didn't backfire. What if his attempt to prevent catastrophic damage to the plants actually pushed the country into a blackout? Well, it was a calculated risk that he had taken. He couldn't dwell on that choice any longer. There was no turning back now.

One huge map of the U.S., equipped with colored lights pinpointing each of the NuEnergy plant locations, stood high in the front of the room, enabling all to see the latest status. Ben had just directed that the color scheme be changed. A red light indicated that the plant was in jeopardy, still above eighty percent power and terrorists not yet in custody. Yellow would signify power safely below eighty percent, but sabotage still possible. Green would indicate that the plant

366

was out of the woods with both a safe power achieved and the Mafia thwarted. Blinking red would announce that the plant had been sabotaged and its power production lost.

A quick glance over at the map told Ben that at this early stage of the struggle all lights were red, signifying that extreme danger lurked at every plant.

He checked on Garrison occasionally. Garrison's task of tracking each team's progress as they attempted plant entry was huge. Additionally, CENTCOM had become more and more worried about the ramifications of a power outage on defense installations, so they were demanding continuous updates from Admiral Yeager.

Ben saw that five yellow lights had just appeared at plant sites in Florida, North Carolina and New Jersey. The rest were still red. "Well, at least those five can't be destroyed." He allowed himself a slight measure of satisfaction for that small achievement.

Finally the beleaguered dispatcher returned to the line. "That was the hairiest half hour of my life. All thirty of those NuEnergy babies are headed down to eighty percent, just like you and the vice president wanted. Those in the Central Time Zone, though, are lagging the first bunch."

"That's okay, in fact, that's great, Dave," Ben responded. "Word here is that five have already reached the eighty percent level."

"Yes, I can confirm that. Several others are getting close. We have problems though. My dispatchers are having real trouble scrounging up any backup power. The cold wave has left damned little extra power out there. We contacted half the utilities already, but received very few promises of more power. Fortunately there are a few companies in the South Central states which have some available reserves. We told the bigger utilities that they should commence shedding all non-essential load, and consider starting rolling blackouts. Trouble is, all of that takes more time than we have."

Ben, trying to keep Morgan's spirits up, congratulated the dispatcher. "Good moves! It all helps. Because of your action, we will prevent permanent damage to many of the plants. That's an awesome accomplishment. That grid of yours would be pretty anemic, Dave, if you didn't have any of those big producers in the future."

"Speaking of anemic, the system is damned sickly right now. The frequency is down to 59.8 and it's dropping fast. The power reduction of the NuEnergy plants is rapidly unbalancing my system. The frequency has been this low only once. In '93 the floods along the Mississippi, Ohio and Missouri rivers wiped out dozens of our coal plants during the summer air-conditioning peak. That time it was the nuclear plants that saved our ass. Funny how history turns full circle. Now it is the coal and gas boys that must come through. If nothing else goes wrong and the Southwestern and South Central coal and gas plants come through, the frequency should bottom out at a little below 59.7 after all of these plants reach eighty percent. That's damn low, a modern record, and too close to 59.5 for comfort."

Ben knew that they were going to get far closer to the precipice of 59.5 than Morgan's estimate. He reminded Morgan of the danger that many NuEnergy plants faced from the Mafia. "Even with our best efforts we could lose several plants from Mafia sabotage."

Morgan groaned, "That will kill us."

"That is why you must, pardon the expression, light a fire under the utilities. Don't mince words with them. Tell them that they must fire up absolutely everything they have. We do mean everything. Economics or convenience be damned. If they don't, Vice President Foster is going to kick butt, and believe me, he knows how."

"That's all fine and good, Ben, but you can't squeeze blood from a turnip."

Morgan paused as Ben's message sank in. "Are you kidding about the Mafia?"

"No! They are out to wreck our country. Also be aware that there are five more plants that NuEnergy hasn't taken over yet, Dave. As a protective measure NRC resident inspectors have just ordered them down to eighty percent. We suspect that the Mafia has enough technicians and engineers already at those five plants to sabotage them."

"You guys aren't really taking more plants down in power," anguished Morgan.

"Yes, I am afraid so, Dave. They are all in Nebraska, Iowa and Minnesota. The plants are Slate Creek, Northern Lights, Lone Wolf, Sioux Nation and Corn Capitol. FBI agents are on their way to those plants now. At least, since they are not yet operated by NuEnergy, we were able to alert their security groups directly. They are working with us from the get go."

With that disclosure Morgan was very worried. He told Ben that the odds of avoiding a blackout had slipped below fifty-fifty.

Ben relayed the bad news to Yeager, "Inform CENTCOM that the chances of saving the grid are less than fifty-fifty."

Ben looked at his watch, "7:50 p.m. There must be some answers somewhere. Have we overlooked anything?"

In desperation he turned to Hazel Friesen and Admiral Yeager, imploring them for any ideas they might have.

"You know," the retired Admiral recalled while rubbing his hand thoughtfully over his depilated head, "Years ago in my submariner days, we faced a similar problem, but on a much smaller scale. After a hurricane, a tiny Caribbean Island had a serious power shortage. We hooked up our submarine plant's electrical generator to their grids and lit their lights for them. Too bad we can't do that here."

At first Ben scoffed, "All the nuclear subs in the fleet wouldn't make a dent in this problem. Plus they are all damned busy right now."

Suddenly it struck him. A light dawned. "God Bless you, Admiral. You just saved our hides. Hallelujah! I just hope it's not too late."

Ben gratefully saluted the confounded admiral and hastily returned to the phone and the dispatcher. He had a solution for Morgan, but it would challenge the dispatcher to the limit.

Day 45 8:02 P.M. Black Bear Plant Oklahoma

Before the two groups moved out, FBI Agent Brown briefed them, "The Black Bear power level is at ninety-two percent. The control room tells me that it will drop over the next thirty minutes to a safer eighty percent, but that may be too late."

"So we must do our job," observed civilian Rod Grow.

Brown agreed, "Damned right. It's up to us. Stop the traitorous trash. They won't get this plant if we can help it."

Both groups left Brown and the security building on the run.

While Agent Jones, civilian expert Neitzel, and three security guards scrambled to the third level of the turbine building, the other group, headed by Agent Templeton, raced for the switchyard. The three plant security officers, shotguns at the ready, along with Templeton and Grow, barreled through the administration building's cafeteria at a full gallop, knocking over chairs as they rushed past a handful of stunned workers.

Black Bear's night-shift mechanics, leisurely enjoying their coffee before taking on their maintenance tasks, were alarmed by the sight of the armed men rushing through their break area. They had watched the security forces drill for emergency events before, but this looked far more serious than any drill.

Plant Security Guard Bachelor, who was in better shape than his two coworkers, led the switchyard team out of the administration building and around the maintenance shops. They tore along the side of the six-story tall turbine building, which loomed large on their left.

Despite carrying the majority of the heavy bomb detection and protective gear, Agent Templeton was still right behind Bachelor when they rounded the corner of the turbine building. The switchyard, the assumed Mafia target, burst into full view only a hundred and fifty feet to the rear of the turbine building.

Templeton, whose home was Arizona, fleetingly marveled, "This switchyard looks a little like a dense stand of pipestone cactus."

Suddenly, he glimpsed a figure slipping away. Upon spying the team, the individual bolted. Dashing for the far side of the turbine building, the fugitive drew a pistol. While running for cover he fired. One of the bullets smashed into Rod Grow's protective vest, knocking him down.

Templeton dropped his gear, drew his pistol and fell to one knee, yelling, "FBI! Halt! Raise your hands over your head."

The man ignored the commands and kept running and firing at Templeton. The agent aimed carefully with both arms extended and squeezed the trigger. His gun bucked as flame stabbed into the Oklahoma night. The suspect spun around. Grabbing his leg, he limped toward the far corner of the turbine building.

Agent Templeton shouted to two of the security guards, "Go get the shit. He dropped his gun when I hit him, but be careful. He may have other arms."

The two security guards sprinted after the wounded fugitive as Templeton picked up his bomb detection gear and signaled Grow and Bachelor to follow him. The three approached the switchyard. The yard was enclosed by its own security fence.

Grow tested the gate to the inner sanctum of the switchyard, "Damn! It's locked."

Bachelor fumbled for the key to the lock.

Unwilling to waste more time, Templeton shouted, "Stand back." Pointing his pistol at the offending lock, he blasted it into useless shards of metal.

Once inside, the three found themselves dwarfed by the towering transformers, capacitors and huge relays. Even the transformers were bigger than he had perceived from a distance. Everything was huge. The 340,000-volt overhead wires and cables led away huge amounts of electricity to the main population centers of Oklahoma.

To Templeton, the place almost seemed alive. The crackling sound, similar to a large brush fire, resonated in his ears as the extreme voltage struggled to breakdown the surrounding air. A cool winter evening breeze, blowing into the switchyard, surprisingly forced warm air into their faces. Brian marveled that even in winter, the waste heat from this huge equipment created a mild microclimate. He sensed the hair standing up on the back of his neck, either from his growing tension or from the electrical fields. The excited hair, he guessed, was a consequence of both factors.

Grow showed the two officers where they could move safely through the maze of equipment. Templeton, with Bachelor's help, donned his heavy protective jacket and helmet. Before beginning his search for the bombs, he waved the men accompanying him out of the yard.

Bachelor, though, refused to leave, "I am staying. What can I do to help?"

"Look for anything like an antenna, wires or a package that doesn't appear to belong in here. Here put this stuff on."

Templeton quickly confirmed that his bomb detection gear would not work in these extreme electrical fields. The ozone, produced by the high voltage air breakdown, confounded the detection gear, which worked on the principle of sniffing explosive odors. Tonight the only option was visual.

After what seemed an eternity, but in truth was less than a minute, he spotted two small antennas, one on each side of the yard. They were each mounted on top of huge capacitors. So, the method of detonation was to be a radio signal! Probably the Mafia engineer in the turbine building would set off the bombs once he had disabled the turbine generator's over-speed protection. That signal, Templeton figured, could come at any moment.

He waved Bachelor out, "Go on! Get the hell out of here! Now! Hurry!"

Alone except for Agent-In-Charge Brown's voice in his earphone, the nervous agent inspected the Mafia's handiwork. Wires led from each of the antennas to packages that surely were plastic explosives. Each package was placed near a huge transformer. If the bombs were detonated before he could disarm them, he knew that the switchyard would turn into a massive high voltage inferno.

Continuing his nearly constant phone conversation with Brown, Templeton reported, "I found two bombs."

"Two? What's the detonation method?"

"They are wired for a radio signal. This is no amateur job. The SOB's wired them in the 'cops-coffin' technique."

Brown understood what that meant. Only one of the three wires could be safely cut.

"Please advise. Shall I proceed to disarm them?"

"Plant status is critical for the next twenty minutes. Power is still too high. Jones reports that the overspeed is disabled. She, Neitzel, and a plant operator are trying to repair it. Time may be too short for that, though. Their security guards are searching for the Mafia SOB. He's still at large and probably has the transmitter detonator with him. You should get the hell out of there. You are in extreme danger."

Templeton mulled over his options. No way could a backup bomb squad get out here in time. If he left, it was probably curtains for Black Bear. And that, he knew, could spell blackout and a major headache for the entire country. He thought briefly of his pregnant wife, Lori Sue, and the two and four year old youngsters at home. Forcing those visions from his mind he faced what he was trained to do.

"I am staying. These must be disarmed. I think I can do it."

"God's speed, Brian."

Templeton studied the wires running from the first antenna. He selected the yellow lead as the one he would cut. It exhibited more tension than the other two. From his training on bomb disarmament he remembered that could be a clue. If he were wrong, his life was over. His whole body was awash in sweat as he cut through the wire to the first bomb. Nothing happened. He had succeeded! One down and one to go.

With his heavy protective gear hampering his movements, he awkwardly crossed the switchyard. He felt as if he had been in here for a lifetime. Now which wire must be cut? Sweating so profusely that his thick gloves almost slipped off, he studied the layout and concluded that the taut red middle wire should be severed.

As his trembling gloved hand brought the cutters into position, a radio signal flashed from the turbine building. The high-frequency signal defied the electrical interference in the yard. The bomb exploded in Templeton's mask-covered face.

In a fraction of a second, his hand, glove, cutters and forearm vaporized. His mask perforated his face with a thousand lacerations. His distorted body, even before the wounds could commence bleeding, hurtled through the air, smashing up against a massive step-up transformer. Within milliseconds of the awful human ravages, the bomb blast destroyed the transformer and the other nearby equipment.

An amount of power capable of lighting and powering Oklahoma City detoured from its normal path. Instead of flowing into the overhead high voltage lines, the stream of electricity arced down through the equipment and Templeton's body into the ground around the switchyard. Huge high-energy arcs flashed blue, red and yellow from transformer to capacitor to relay. The agent's charred and smoking remains continued to serve as conduit for much of this energy, which sought the least resistant path to the earth.

Stunned and sickened, Grow and Bachelor shakily rose to their feet. Since Templeton was far beyond their help, they stumbled away from the burning and still flashing ruins of the switchyard toward the relative safety of the turbine building.

Suddenly, a huge boom knocked them off their feet. Grow glanced toward the far end of the turbine building where steam roared upward in billowing, towering plumes. The thunderous roar approximated that of a charging locomotive. Accompanying the deafening sound was a terrifying sight, similar to a venting volcano spewing steam and gases high into the atmosphere. The steam plume boiled upward hundreds of feet into the night sky. Grow knew this furious scene signaled that the steam atmospheric reliefs had blown open.

When all else failed, those giant vent valves helped protect the turbine generator. He realized that both, the atmospheric relief valves and the overspeed protection were required to avoid damage to the turbine if the plant was producing above eighty percent power. Since he hadn't heard or seen any flying metal projectiles from the turbine-generator, he narrowed things down to two possibilities. Either the power had dropped below eighty percent, or the other group had managed to restore the overspeed circuitry. He would find out which later.

The two dazed men limped back to the security building. Agent Brown was well aware of the fate of his comrade, Brian Templeton. Though severely shaken by the personal and plant losses, Brown continued to aggressively perform his command duties. He greeted the two men returning from the switchyard, "You two go get some rest. You look like hell. One of these guards will show you where you can clean up."

As they left Brown's temporary command center, Grow spotted a group of three entering the security building. The two security guards who had raced after the saboteur at the switchyard dragged a hand-cuffed man between them. The man's rumpled hair and clothes gave graphic evidence that there had been a one-sided struggle. He quite obviously had lost. His leg was wrapped in a makeshift compress bandage, the wound undoubtedly a result of Templeton's shot. Upon seeing the raw rage in Brown's eyes, Grow knew that the prisoner was not in for a happy welcome.

"Good work, men. Bring big tough Helmut here." Brown fought hard not to lose his cool. He sat the man in a chair then leaned forward, pinning both of his arms to the chair, while his face was only inches from the captured thug. "You worthless little shit-stain son-of-a-bitch. You are going to tell me everything you know or we will stake your sorry ass on top of the nearest rattlesnake den."

A look of defiance crossed Helmut's face. He had seen a few rattlers around when he had run the service road every noon hour. This cowboy didn't scare him.

The angry agent threw a pad of paper and a pen from the nearest desk at the captive. "Start writing or we will turn you over to your superiors. Goldstein and his friends know how to deal with failures like you. We will see that the word goes out ahead of you that you were fully cooperative. It's either that end for you or you cooperate with us now. Oh, by the way, you SOB, you have the following rights."

Brown spit out the Miranda Rights litany rapidly, almost as an allegation. "I am deadly serious, you write down all you know or you are going back to your bosses with a note of thanks from us for all of your generous cooperation. You will be lucky if they just kill you. You blew up my friend tonight. Don't even think about defying me."

Brown then directed the two guards, "Put him in a room with a table. Watch him. If he stops writing, call me."

Grow, returning from the washroom, asked, "How did the other group fare?"

"They managed to repair the damaged circuitry just seconds before the blast. The power hadn't dropped to eighty percent, so it was a damned good thing they got it fixed. All of you saved Black Bear from the scrap heap. It will produce power again," Brown summed up matter-of-factly.

The security guards called in to Brown that the other Mafia operator was in custody. Not realizing that he and his accomplice had achieved only half of their mission, the defiant man had taunted his captors that they were too late to stop his detonation of the bomb. He chortled that Black Bear was history. In actuality, Black Bear was damaged but not to the degree intended by the saboteurs.

Brown snapped, "Bring that worthless SOB to me, now!"

Brown turned to Smith, "Tell headquarters we caught the sons of bitches, but they may not survive the night. The plant wasn't destroyed, thanks to our team, but it's down. Tell Garrison that we lost Templeton."

Listening to all of this, Grow estimated that it would be several weeks before the switchyard could be rebuilt and Black Bear returned to power.

Day 45 Fifteen Minutes Earlier 8:15 P.M. Andrews' Home Tulsa, Oklahoma

After the lights dimmed and flickered in their home, Laura dropped her pen and ran out on their back deck. With a sinking sensation she peered in the direction of Black Bear. What an eerie sight. A vast billowing plume of steam, illuminated by brilliant multi-colored flashes of light, grew ever bigger. She felt sick to her stomach. Immediately she guessed that the Mafia had done in Black Bear.

Yesterday Ben had warned her that something could happen to the plants. He told her that he would be out of touch for a couple of days, but then he would call and very soon he was coming home.

He had better come home soon for she had much to tell him. Since learning of her heritage as a Sumurov, she found that her curiosity had not abated. She had carefully read her grandfather's works. The man had forecast precisely how Russia should move to freedom and democracy.

He envisioned a one-hundred year process of evolution, but not an evolution left to chance. An underground organization led by one of his disciples must point history in the right direction. Laura suspected that this individual existed, and more and more she was convinced it was Professor Dudaev. From this new perspective she had started researching this strangely influential little man and found out many interesting tidbits. But things didn't add up. In the letters given her by Dudaev, there were unexplained discussions back and forth between Dudaev and Marina. At times they showed an unusual interest in her husband, Ben.

She wanted Ben home. She had discovered that she needed him far more than she needed to learn about her heritage. Heritage was the past. Ben was the future.

CHAPTER
FIFTY-ONE

Day 45 Earlier 7:50 P.M. Andropov's Limousine Washington, D.C.

In sharp contrast to the hectic White House scene, Boris Andropov and Princess Kristina luxuriated in the rear seat as the black limousine wound south through heavy traffic along Connecticut Avenue. Princess Kristina puzzled over her escort's almost euphoric mood. It didn't quite add up. Going to the White House couldn't be this big a deal for old Comrade Boris. This definitely wasn't his favorite hangout.

What she didn't know was that Andropov believed this day would be a milestone, an object lesson on the virtue of perseverance for the weak-kneed Russian leadership, who had given up so readily on the great Soviet system.

Andropov received another in a string of calls. To thwart tracking by the Feds he switched cell phones after nearly every call. The phones had been stolen and then reprogrammed by Goldstein's communications geniuses.

Ivan Bupkov reported, "I talked with Kosov. He will meet you in Zurich the day after tomorrow. He understands that his promotion is pending and he is quite confident and optimistic about taking over from Kostenko."

"Good, he could be our most influential Russian division leader yet."

"We are on the trail of the traitor Kostenko. Some of our FSB friends informed us that he's on Tobago. Soon he will receive a deadly visit from us."

"Good riddance."

"Also we are watching Kruschev's pattern of movements. A rare window of opportunity is opening up. A hit is on."

376

Andropov listened, with a smile that was growing broader with each new piece of information. "Excellent report, Ivan. This is shaping up to be a fantastic day."

After finishing with Bupkov, Andropov called the Munich Enrichment Plant manager. "Have you signed new enrichment contracts?"

"Yes, sir, but haven't we oversold?"

"No!"

"But we can't serve all of these new customers and still honor the existing American contracts."

"Don't worry about it. Things will work out."

Kristina, quite familiar with this man's drifting off in his thoughts, caught the self-satisfied grin. This ebullient, grinning Boris was quite abnormal. Recently he had been tense, obviously nervous about something. Today, though, he seemed relieved, as if some great weight had been removed from his shoulders.

Attempting to uncover what was going on with him, she playfully teased, "I hope that smirk on your face is from last night's aerobics."

Not to be easily manipulated by the Princess, he retorted, "No, it's about something even more satisfying."

Pouting, and with a hand caressing and teasing Boris, Kristina cooed, "Impossible. You couldn't possibly find anyone better than I am, baby."

He silently allowed, that was true. But the night with the Swedish Princess was merely a pleasant prelude to this grand evening. The U.S. going down in flames was the main act. Damn it! The discussion with Munich reminded him of still one more thing that had gone wrong lately.

One of the Kazakh uranium cylinders, when heated, had blown its gaseous contents of smuggled, blended uranium all over the place. Once the cylinder was pressurized a strangely weakened spot had given way. A complete report would be delivered to him this week.

What if a pesky auditor like Dr. Andrew had seen that accident? Why did that man so get under his skin? Maybe he was getting closer to the truth of that puzzle.

Goldstein had reported that Dr. Andrew was working with the FBI and the vice president. Further the irritant had convened a secret meeting at NRC headquarters a few days ago. What was that all about? Anyway, he had been right all along to distrust that typical American do-gooder. His elimination was long overdue.

It's a good thing that he had advanced the nuclear plants' destruction and the missile attack to today. Those dumbshits, given enough time, might actually figure out a few things. While dessert was served at tonight's White House dinner, his nuclear dessert would be served upon New York City.

His attack was carefully coordinated to bring down the U.S. The WTC attack had fortuitously served as a gage as to what it took to stop the U.S. economic engine and demoralize the people. This attack would accomplish both objectives.

Andropov made one last call before he entered the lair of the enemy. Goldstein was to give him one final briefing before he would take a step into the White House. His plan must be working perfectly or he would forego the White House scene and disappear.

"Ray, give me the status on the missile and the plants."

"The sabotage at all thirty-five sites is underway. The plants will soon be dropping like flies. The missile will be launched within the hour. Your plan is on course. Enjoy your dinner. If anything goes wrong I will alert you through your pager. I wish I could be there to see all of the horror-struck faces."

Andropov had no way of knowing that Goldstein alluded to his face as well as those of his White House hosts. Goldstein believed that the U.S. could save some of the plants, but he didn't think they could stop the missile. The results would be mixed which was perfect. It opened wide the Mafia leadership possibilities for him and at a perfect time when the U.S. was crippled. Now he must shake the FBI and high-tail it to safety.

Andropov's limo wound its way through the security barriers and checks on Pennsylvania Avenue and past the straggly bunch of in-line roller bladders. It pulled into the drive at the north portico, where the vice president and Dione waited for the arriving dignitaries. Secure with Goldstein's assurance that his plan was on course, Andropov stepped out of the car.

He immediately sensed that the vice president disliked him. He really didn't care, for the feeling was mutual.

When Foster shook his hand, it seemed more a test than a greeting. Andropov responded to the force of Foster's grip with his own aggressive clasp. Their locked hands symbolized the greater struggle swirling about them.

Andropov almost laughed at Foster's discomfort in forcing a polite greeting.

"This should be a most enjoyable evening, Mr. Andropov. We are grateful you and your royal companion could join us."

"Yes, I certainly hope the evening lives up to my highest expectations," challenged Andropov, with a double entendre.

If not for the recent revelations and briefings about the tanker, the missile and the plant sabotage, Foster would not have grasped the full implication of Andropov's remark.

"Seldom do events fulfill unrealistic expectations," retorted Foster with his own subtle meaning.

That reply didn't set well with Andropov. Had Foster answered subtlety with subtlety? Was he that smart? Probably not.

In sharp contrast to the enmity between the men, the two women, one blond and fair skinned, the other ebony, liked each other immediately. Dione graciously greeted the glamorous Swedish Princess Kristina, resplendent in her long shimmering black gown and waist-length Siberian fox fur.

Dione, in a conservative, yet attractive dark red dress, smiled warmly as she grasped Kristina's hand. "Welcome. You are as gorgeous as I had imagined. I want to hear all about the life of a princess."

The two ominously silent men and the two pleasantly chatting women scaled the portico stairs, following the red carpet rolled out for the occasion. As they passed through the grand north entry of the White House, each harbored very different expectations for the evening.

Day 45 7:55 P.M. White House State Dining Room

President Arthur, accompanied by his First Lady, Gayle, suggested to the crowd that they should move on to the State Dining Room and find their seats. The Marine band played a medley of lively Broadway tunes as the guests drifted to their assigned tables.

The vice president's table guests included Boris Andropov and Sweden's Princess Kristina. Also included were Michelle Michote and her escort, Peter Sunborg, the popular playboy tennis sensation who had won Wimbledon for the last two years. Completing the guest list were a computer business tycoon, his attractive spouse, the Secretary of Energy, her preoccupied husband and finally, Mark's daughter, Dione.

Prior to taking his seat, Boris Andropov deliberately passed near Michelle and whispered, "Are you completely prepared?"

Michelle, who had already turned many heads, was stunningly attired in a form-fitting black satin gown. "Of course," she melodically replied while giving him a reassuring and flirtatious smile. She was quite ready for the remote possibility of trouble and was somewhat insulted that he felt it necessary to ask.

Andropov looked at his watch. It was nearly 8. He estimated that this gathering would never get to the main course. The lights were going to go out very soon. The world's only superpower, ha! Not for long. They couldn't be a superpower without power, he chuckled.

Andropov gloated that the lights were going out, big time, in New York City. He adjusted his pager, which was set on vibration mode. If it went off, that would be Goldstein alerting him that problems had developed. He believed that he had left nothing to chance.

The vice president sat to Andropov's left. Separating the two antagonists was Princess Kristina. Dione sat to the left of the vice president next to Michelle's latest conquest.

How cooperative of them, mused Andropov. On top of everything else, for my evening's amusement I get to rough up the cerebrally challenged American vice president.

Andropov turned toward Foster and spoke discourteously past the princess. "I understand that you served as Commander of the U.S. Pacific Submarine Fleet."

"Yes, that's correct. Times, though, have changed greatly since then. The Cold War was a very dangerous period."

Andropov pretended to ignore the vice president's observation, although it had succeeded in tweaking his pain that the Cold War had ended so ingloriously for the Soviets. Instead of acknowledging Foster's point, he replied, "I understand your submarines were quite an engineering feat of stealth, maneuverability and moderate speed."

"Moderate?"

Boris dug into the perceived weakness. "Yes, I read many Soviet captains' accounts on how they ran circles around your subs."

"You were reading propaganda, Mr. Andropov. Your boats didn't outrun any of our Los Angeles-class subs," retorted a furious Foster.

"I can't believe that."

"Well, believe it. The only speed advantage you ever gained resulted from the tons of shielding your designers deliberately left out. Your country willingly sacrificed your sailors' lives for the advantage of a few more knots. That reflects an intrinsic difference in the values of our two countries."

Unfazed outwardly, but actually quite surprised at the sharpness of the vice president's reply, Andropov retorted from a perspective born of a very different and a far harsher value system. "Yes, our people are willing to suffer, enabling the state's achievement of greater glory."

"Well, I will have to agree with your premise that your beloved empire ensured their suffering," countered Foster with a growing desire to thrash this arrogant relic from the cold war.

By now all at the table had grown silent and stared uncomfortably, while the heated dialogue raged. Dione, aware of her dad's rising irritation, lured him into a conversation about tennis involving her and Sunborg.

Kristina had never seen this unpleasant side of Boris so clearly exposed. Was he simply picking a fight with the vice president of the United States for no good reason? She was beginning to wonder if perhaps the paparazzi were preferable to this man's company and protection.

CHAPTER
FIFTY-TWO

Day 45 8:10 P.M. Command Center White House

Morgan returned to the phone to update Ben. "Those last five plants are on their way down to eighty percent. In a half hour they will be safe."

Ben had just looked at the map. Yellow, green, red and flashing red lit up the big board like it was Christmas; yet, it was no joyous Noel. Rather it was a time of rapid-fire developments leading to the brink of disaster. Four blinking red lights appeared on the map, one in Oklahoma, one in Missouri, and two in New Jersey, signifying that four plants, one being Black Bear, had been knocked off-line. The question of whether the majority of the plant teams would prevail against the Mob still hung in the balance.

Upon spotting the blinking red light in Oklahoma, which signaled that Black Bear was down, Ben felt a helpless sinking feeling. All of his work and he couldn't even save his own plant. "What happened to Black Bear? Was it catastrophic?"

"Not catastrophic. But one totally blown up switchyard," Garrison responded.

"Is the team okay?"

"No. One of our agents was killed."

"I am sorry, Brad."

Since Ben and Laura lived only a few miles from Black Bear, Ben suspected that Laura had witnessed the steam relief spectacle. He was thankful that he had warned her that something could happen today. "Brad, could you have someone call Laura and assure her that it's okay and tell her I will see her soon?"

After being assured by Garrison that he would take care of the call to Laura, Ben turned back to the phone to fill in Morgan on the

382

downed plants and his brainstorm for more power.

Morgan groaned, "The frequency is down to 59.65. We're now in a nationwide brownout situation. Another drop of .15 and we close up shop. There just aren't enough coal or gas turbine reserves available tonight to make up for what we are losing. Every plant east of the Rockies that can be fired up is already running. Non-essential power shedding can't happen quickly enough to save us."

Hearing the despair in Morgan's voice, Ben knew it was now or never. The Admiral Yeager-inspired brainstorm must work or else...

"You have done a superb job. The grid is not lost yet, Dave. What about Canada?"

After pausing to let the thought sink in, Ben added. "Several new high-voltage transmission lines span the border. Maybe we can bring in enough power from our northern neighbor to offset our losses. I checked with the weather bureau. The cold wave is not affecting them as severely as it is us. They should have power to spare."

Morgan's spirits brightened immediately. "Yes, that's a terrific idea. The only trouble is I don't deal directly with the Canadian utilities. That's why I hadn't thought of it myself. To get that power down here, my center would have to coordinate with the U.S. utilities on our northern border. They handle arrangements with the Canuks. Each utility up there has its own contractual agreement with the Canadians. Thus they actually control the flow of electricity from our northern neighbor."

"Just call the biggest utilities on the border first. While you are doing that, our President will call the Canadian Premier and stress the urgency of our plea. He will ask them to send us every megawatt they can."

"Okay. I'll call one in Minnesota and one in upstate New York immediately. My assistants will contact the smaller ones in Michigan, Maine and Vermont. If your weather scoop is right then Ontario and Quebec should have extra power."

"It's right. Don't worry."

"I am plenty worried. We are two plants away from shutting down the whole country."

"Go! Make those calls! Tell the utilities that it's orders from the President and that promptness is everything. If they don't act immediately, President Arthur himself will be up to see them tomorrow and heads will roll. Fax them copies of the Emergency Declaration. Get back to me as soon as you can.

Ben looked at his watch...8:20. Garrison yelled from across the room, "We have lost five plants altogether."

"I know. I saw the new one go up on the board." Ben knew that they were only two plants away from losing the battle unless the Canadian power kicked in fast.

Ten minutes later Morgan came back on the line. "The good news is the Canadian power may start flowing in a matter of minutes. The bad news is, it may be too little too late. We lost one more plant."

"What's the frequency now?"

"59.55 and still going down, although a little slower as some reserve power out of the Southwest is offsetting some of our losses. Also, the involuntary brownout has reduced demand somewhat. All of that helps, but not enough."

"Is the nonessential power shedding helping any?"

Dave replied. "Yes. Slowly. But it takes time. All of the utilities have declared local emergencies. They are in the process of shutting down all nonessential factories in their areas. But again it all takes time and we are in a minute-to-minute situation."

Garrison yelled at Ben again, "My agent in Iowa reports that the Des Moines plant is history."

"The turbine?"

"Yep. The damned thing disintegrated. Pieces flew everywhere, just like the admiral said. One huge chunk of shrapnel hurtled through the trunk of our agent's car. Get this, they were still a mile from the plant."

Ben shook his head as he listened to Morgan.

"Our frequency is down to 59.5. A plant in Iowa was lost," a depressed Morgan informed Ben. "We are teetering on the brink."

"I know."

"This is the worst nationwide electrical situation possible. If the Canadian power doesn't kick in big time we are lost."

After conferring with Ben, Admiral Yeager called CENTCOM. "Chances of a blackout are almost a certainty."

The admiral, understanding that their team desperately needed a morale boost, relayed, "CENTCOM reports that the SEALs on the tanker are kicking Iranian and Mafia ass."

Ben got up and paced nervously around the office, with his headphones askew and his FBI hat, cocked in an unlikely angle. The hat was given to him during a happier moment by the agents on his and Garrison's team. He felt totally helpless. There was nothing else he could do. He had gambled that he could avoid even a short-term blackout while saving the plants from destruction. The gamble was failing.

After a wait of minutes that seemed an eternity, Morgan came back on line, "The Canadian power is starting to roll in big time. Whatever your President told the Premier, it must have worked. We have a chance. Even though we just lost one more plant, one in Pennsylvania, the frequency shivered a little, but still held at just slightly above 59.5 cps. We are not dead yet!"

Garrison reported, "We lost still another one, Ben. But there is good news. Twenty-eight of the teams report complete control of the situation at their respective plants. Only two plants, one in Georgia and one in Virginia, still hang in the balance."

Ben confirmed status on the big map, which showed seven flashing red, twenty-one green and two yellow lights. The plant teams had done their job remarkably well under the worst of circumstances. Only the Des Moines plant, which wasn't one of the thirty receiving a plant team, had been permanently destroyed.

"Dave, hang in there. We control all but two of the plants," Ben consoled the harried dispatcher.

"Our site resident inspectors report from the five NuEnergy takeover targets that four of them are now safely operating at eighty percent and are under FBI and NRC control," relayed Hazel Friesen. "The site security forces at those four plants located the Mafia technicians and engineers in time. They are under arrest. You know about the fifth. The Des Moines plant will never operate again."

Ben, for the first time, allowed himself to believe that they just might escape a blackout by the barest of margins. He updated the Admiral, "Things have turned. There is a slight chance of avoiding a blackout."

Garrison signaled Ben with a thumbs up that the plant in Georgia had just gone green. One plant left.

Ben's phone line crackled as an ebullient Morgan returned, "Ben, good news! The frequency is actually going up. After the last plant was lost, it bottomed out at just under 59.5. It's now at 59.6 and rising steadily. The power is now surging across the border from Houlton, Maine, to International Falls. We are going to make it unless your mobsters take out a half dozen more plants."

"No chance of that, Dave. Garrison just signaled that the last plant is now secure. They are all safely under federal protection." Ben tossed his hat in the air and joyously shouted, "We did it! We won! No outage tonight! Only one plant destroyed!"

Ben was overwhelmed. It was over. His battle was won. The grid was safe. The remaining plants were safe. Seven had been damaged, but only one, the Des Moines plant, was destroyed.

"I am coming down to Kentucky next week, Dave. I will buy you and that wonderful crew of yours dinner and whatever you all like most to drink. I am more grateful to you than I can ..."

Overjoyed with tears of happiness and relief streaming down his face, Ben gave all of the team high fives as they crowded close to congratulate him. "What a bunch. I love you all."

Garrison brought Ben's hat back to him. "Don't lose this Ben. It's official FBI cover to remind you of who bails your sorry ass out of trouble all the time."

With that admonishment Garrison stuffed the hat on Ben's head while Ben was trying to listen to Morgan.

"Dr. Andrew, you certainly made my shift an exciting one. One thing I am sure of is that our emergency procedures will be modified extensively after tonight's panic."

"So something of value came out of this mess."

"Yes. Maybe so, Ben. By the way, my associates vote overwhelmingly for a few bottles of good ol' boy Kentucky Bourbon."

After setting the Louisville celebration for next week, Ben turned to Garrison. "Let's take a break. You and I need to get the hell out of here for a few minutes. The team can deal with the mop-up and the arrests." He knew that this was their best chance for a respite.

Garrison agreed and the two friends, each with a jumble of emotions ranging from elation and relief to grief and sorrow, headed for the door.

Ben ruminated on how surreal this moment was. They had just beaten a major portion of Andropov's plan for the U.S.'s destruction and Yeager had just relayed that the SEALs had won their battle. The U.S. was apparently safe, yet something troubled him. He sensed that things weren't as tidy as they appeared.

Since being summoned by Foster six weeks ago, he had been totally wrapped up in this international intrigue working twenty hours a day. Yet the victory was hollow. Was it the Oklahoma plant going down? Was it worrying about Laura or the Mafia's expressed determination to get him? Maybe it was the loss of Garrison's agent. He remembered meeting the young man at NRC Headquarters. Now he was dead. He knew that was bothering Garrison plenty right now.

Maybe his uneasiness was from the sense of so much still to be done. The FBI and Secret Service agents were preparing to arrest Boris Andropov and Michelle Michote upstairs after dinner. Several days of intense Joint Eagles fighting lay ahead. Yet, something other than all of these things bothered Ben. It was a sense of foreboding, which he just couldn't shake. Something was about to go horribly wrong. Had the vice president's team underestimated Andropov's cunning and resolve?

After Ben and Brad Garrison left, a stunned, pale-faced Admiral Yaeger reported, "CENTCOM says the bomb on the tanker just exploded. My God! We had a nuclear explosion only twenty miles off our coast."

FIFTY-THREE

Day 45 8:36 P.M. White House Security Center

A red-faced Karpenko yelled at his agent in charge of White House surveillance, "You idiot! Why are you monitoring the guest restroom? Switch to the south entrance where you can do some good."

With that vital alteration accomplished, Karpenko stormed out, free to resume his mission.

Day 45 8:37 P.M. White House Rest Room

"Closed Temporarily for Maintenance," proclaimed the yellow sign standing on the hall floor in front of the men's rest room near the State Dining Room. Inside FBI agent Karpenko was going through a routine security inspection of the room, except... A short time ago, he had removed two pistols from the White House weapons arsenal. He pulled them from his coat and wrapped them in a yellow towel. He hid the towel at the bottom of a deep basket of white courtesy hand towels.

Since he had been informed only an hour ago that the arrests of Andropov and Michote were imminent, he was forced to act in this last desperate manner. He had received too little warning for anything other than activation of the emergency escape plan. A call to the Thieves-in-Law, delivery of the guns and a coded message to Goldstein was all that he could do for now. He fully expected a huge bonus for his efforts. Retirement loomed large in his sights.

Why hadn't he heard of this arrest plan earlier? During the last few days he sensed that information, for some reason, was being withheld from him. Were they on to his role as Mafia-informant? If so wouldn't they have arrested him? Karpenko withdrew his own 9 mm pistol from its shoulder harness and checked that the chamber and clip were loaded. If Andropov and Michote needed his help, he was ready.

Day 45 8:38 P.M. Command Center

A call came into the command center, "This is FBI. Give me Garrison. It's urgent!"
"Can we take a message, he just stepped out."
"No. I will call North."

Day 45 8:39 P.M. North's Office

The phone rang in North's office.
"Hello, this is North."
"North, we got a voice match. Your man is one of our own, FBI Agent Ike Karpenko."
"Are you sure?"
"Absolutely. He is over there now, on duty at the White House."
"Shit!"
Hanging up, North grabbed the Secret Service agent nearest him, "It's an emergency, Higgins, come with me."
"I can't. I only take orders from the President or my superior."
"Look, you know how close the President and I are. It's just like getting an order from President Arthur. You come or else I will have your butt kicked so far out of here that you will have to learn a new language just to read the sign that tells you how to pull your head out of your ass."
North knew that the arrest of Andropov and Michote was scheduled after the dinner. He couldn't allow an armed supporter of Andropov to have the run of the White House. Shit, the man even knew of the pending arrest. This posed an unacceptable danger to the President and vice president.
Agent Higgins, trapped in a conundrum, quickly assessed the graphic urgings of North. His training taught him to take orders from only the President or the head of the Secret Service detail at the White House, yet, he thought the world of North. Never had he seen the White House Chief-of-Staff this insistent. His instincts told him to trust North on this one.
"Okay, North! Let's go!"
As North and Higgins raced toward Ben's command center, North breathlessly explained the situation to the uniformed officer.

Day 45 8:40 P.M. White House State Dining Room

Andropov was increasingly distraught. He checked his watch again, noting that it was now 8:40. The lights should be out, but there was no sign of a disruption. Also the missile should have hit New York by now. If anything had gone wrong Goldstein would have buzzed him, but he hadn't. Things didn't add up. A continuous string of couriers bringing notes to the vice president implied to him that something big was up. Vice President Foster was following some major development some-where. Foster had reacted to the last message, with an involuntary gasp. Had the bomb just hit New York? Maybe the lights were out over just part of the country, but that made no sense. When he had probed to find out, Vice President Foster had brushed aside his inquiries.

One thing for sure, he was an expert at spotting undercover agents. He had already picked out the phony waiter at their table as an agent. The unsure way the server handled some of the table eti-quette compared to the other *maitre d's* in the room gave him away. Chuckling at his own pun, he noted that the dumb waiter had even poured his coffee refill from the left, not even picking up the cup. He also spotted other agents watching his table. He was sure that even the supposed husband of the Secretary of Energy was a plant. His car-riage, aloofness and unrelenting alertness gave him away. Had he made an unforgivable mistake of underestimating his enemy?

He could sense his heart rate rising. Most uncharacteristically, his hands were clammy. He had always been in control of events. He ruled destiny. Destiny didn't rule him. His tie felt as if it were chok-ing him. The possibility that his decade-long fight for revenge might be in trouble was too much to bear. He would never accept failure.

Maybe Goldstein had just delayed the plant sabotage for some rea-son. Besides there was still the missile. He would still win. He must. His long anticipated moment of triumph couldn't be denied. He would not be reduced to a mere fugitive.

Day 45 8:43 P.M. Ambassador Hotel

After receiving the urgent summons from Karpenko, the helicopter commanded by the Thieves-in-Law landed on the heliport atop the Ambassador Hotel only two miles and two minutes from the White House. Armed with its hand-held stinger missiles, the crew was poised to fly to 1600 Pennsylvania Avenue to whisk their boss, Michelle, Karpenko, and the hostages away. They awaited only final word from Karpenko.

Day 45 8:45 P.M. White House State Dining Room

Whom could he trust here in the lair of this arrogant enemy? Only two, Michelle and his over-paid agent, Karpenko. Michelle had been briefed on how to follow his lead and to watch for a signal. If escape became necessary, her role would be crucial. He must find out if Karpenko was attempting to warn him of danger. Why hadn't Goldstein sent a warning? Very strange. He was unable to shake a rising sense of panic. He had experienced a similar feeling only once before, just before the Soviet Union collapsed. But he would not surrender, not then, not now, not ever!

It was during the bedlam wrought by the blackout and the bomb that he planned to exit triumphantly with his princess on his arm. If, however, escape became mandatory, the princess would have to find her own way home.

Could the vice president sense his alarm? The man was becoming bolder as the evening wore on. Hell, the SOB was asking him another question.

"Do you still follow weapons development, Dr. Andropov?"

"Yes, but of course," he answered, wondering where is this guy headed.

"What do you think the ultimate terrorist weapon would be against a superpower such as the U.S.?"

"I haven't given that a lot of thought," lied Andropov.

How arrogant! Superpower indeed! This nitwit vice president, though, had an answer for every challenge he hurled at him. The U.S. had almost always elected bozos for vice president. Why did he have to run into the one exception? His long held prejudice against the American Black made this series of debates with the vice president an especially bitter pill to swallow. He dabbed with his napkin at the rivulets of water running from his brow. That had never happened. He admonished himself, "Stay cool! You can't let this situation or this jerk rattle you."

"Oh come now, you must have an opinion," Foster burrowed in deeper "Undoubtedly you have an educated viewpoint on this matter. Let me make it easier for you. Let's take, say, a stealth supersonic cruise missile? Let's postulate an advanced one that could be launched at, say, the U.S. from close range. That would be tough for us to deal with, wouldn't it?"

My God! Where was this *Mergavets* headed? Boris could feel his heart pounding. Blood was rushing to his brain, causing a light-headed sensation. He had never experienced a moment like this. His own wits were always, if not superior, certainly sufficient. Did they know about the missile, or was it just a bluff or a dumb-assed accident?

He "gutted it up" for one last verbal battle with this uncanny opponent. "Yes, they are extremely difficult to detect and even more difficult to stop, but of course to have one close enough to your country to do any damage would be quite a trick."

"Yes, that's certainly true, quite a trick indeed. Let's take a cruise missile of advanced design. Let's say the latest French version. How big a nuclear warhead could such a missile carry?"

Hell, they must know! Boris thoughts raced, "Anywhere from a tactical twenty kiloton on up."

"On up to what, Mr. Andropov? Would you say two hundred kilos is possible?"

"Perhaps that's the limit for you Americans, but the Soviets could place a thermonuclear device of at least one megaton on such a missile."

"What Soviets? I thought that the evil empire had collapsed?"

Before the two protagonists completely came to blows, Dione elbowed her father and said loudly enough for the entire table to hear, "The main course looks scrumptious. Wow! What fabulous looking salmon and the Chicken Cordon Blue looks so tempting."

She succeeded once again in stopping the heated hostilities between the two enemies before it boiled completely out of control. She had never seen her dad like this. He really didn't like this guy at all.

Andropov's thoughts were racing. The power wasn't out. Something surely had gone wrong. The damned vice president actually must know about the missile. Did the FSB get Kostenko to talk? That couldn't be it, though, because Kostenko didn't know about these plans. At a minimum, the vice president was wise to some of NuEnergy's past deeds. He must be the reason for some of Ivan Bupkov's negative reports. Could it be that they would try to arrest him here? Had they caught on to his plant sabotage scheme? Damn! If so, where was Goldstein's warning? He had to get away from this table to think and check for a message from Karpenko.

"I must be excused. Where's the men's room?"

"Through the main doors, down the hall, then left." Foster nodded ever so slightly to an agent positioned at the door to follow Andropov. Believing that the restroom was monitored by security, Foster mistakenly assumed that the one agent was sufficient.

Once in the rest room, Andropov checked to see if the way was clear. It wasn't. A man had entered behind him. The jerk-off who had followed him in here was undoubtedly a security agent. So, he was under complete surveillance! His arrest must be planned. He perfunctorily washed his hands and grabbed a towel from the courtesy basket. Slyly searching through the basket of towels, he saw his contact's yellow-toweled message. He gulped, for that signaled that his arrest was imminent.

He nonchalantly covered up the cloth and the enclosed cache and moved to the urinal. The man followed to the one next to him. All of the frustrations of the evening welled up. The years of anticipation of this triumphant moment were in vain. This evening was turning into a nightmare. He whirled while still relieving himself, spraying the agent next to him.

"Hey, what the hell...," yelled the surprised man, jumping back and bending over to brush away the mess.

"Let's see what happened here." Andropov stepped toward the wetted agent, grabbing the confused man by the neck and forcing his head down to meet his rising knee. The man's body went limp and crumpled to the floor. He searched inside the fallen agent's coat, finding the shoulder harness and a badge. Sure enough he was FBI. Struggling, he dragged the fellow to one of the stalls. With a maximum effort, he lifted the limp body up on the stool and closed the stall door.

Brushing himself off, he straightened his coat and tie. He must act now. The unconscious agent would be found momentarily. He returned to the hand towel basket and grabbed the two guns wrapped in the yellow towel.

He and Michelle's arrests were planned, but that would never happen. Goldstein, strangely AWOL tonight, had previously briefed him on the defensive strategies employed by White House security. Armed with that vital knowledge, he, Michelle and their accomplice could still defeat this bunch of idiots.

Upon returning to the table, he nodded to Michelle then commenced eating his Chicken Cordon Blue in the European style. By holding the fork upside down in his left hand and the knife in his right, the intended message was sent to Michelle that things had gone wrong and he needed her help. Michelle switched to the same eating style, which was the prearranged sign that she understood and was ready to follow his lead. Once again he switched his eating style, alerting Michelle that the time for action was now.

In a flash the desperate Andropov tossed a pistol across the table to Michelle. In a continuous motion, he pulled out the other gun while jumping behind the vice president. He grasped Foster by the coat collar and shoved the pistol roughly against his temple.

He yelled at Michelle, "Jam that gun into the girl's back. Shoot anyone making a move."

As instructed, Michelle grabbed a handful of the stunned girl's hair and pressed the pistol into her ribs. Foster's muscles tensed at seeing his daughter in trouble. With a supreme exercise of self-control he restrained himself from an instinctive retaliation. The safety of his daughter and the safety of the guests in the room dictated no action yet.

He could see that the plain-clothes agents around the room were reacting as though they were thinking the same way. The nearby tables of big contributors and government officials were stunned and frozen in place by the unbelievable drama.

Andropov ordered, "Get to your feet slowly. Any false moves and your daughter is history."

"Everyone just stay put. We have a mad man on our hands," warned Foster.

"You really do have a death wish, don't you, Mr. Smart-ass Vice President. Tell all the agents, including that asshole waiter and this phony husband, to get over there to the wall and face it or you and your daughter are dead."

"Go ahead. It's all right. We don't want anyone hurt. Do as this buffoon says."

In response to that cut, Andropov forced the gun muzzle harder against the vice president's temple. "Don't get cute again, Mr. Vice President, I have had absolutely enough out of you. It would give me great pleasure to pull this trigger."

Yelling to the crowd, Andropov ordered, "All of you clear away from that door."

Once his orders were obeyed, he snapped at Michelle, "Follow me. That's it. Right here. Keep that gun in the bitch's back."

He shouted a warning, "One wrong move out of anyone and these two are on their way to hell. Don't get in our way!"

He and Michelle slowly retreated across the crowded dining room toward the hall door with their hostages as their shields. A plain-clothes officer near the last table unwisely started to draw his weapon from his shoulder holster.

Andropov screamed, "Don't!"

Foster yelled at the impetuous agent, "Do as he says."

He wanted to get out of the crowded room before he made any move. He believed an opportunity to turn the tables on Andropov would present itself. If nothing else the sharp shooters outside would stop this. No way would this maniac be allowed to escape.

Andropov shoved the taller vice president forward ahead of him and continued to use the man and his daughter as shields. The tightly bunched foursome made their way slowly down the hall toward the main north door.

Ready to spring into action, a dozen plain-clothes officers, including Karpenko, trailed the four at a safe distance.

Once he was outside the White House, Andropov planned to continue with his hostages to the incoming copter. He could hear the approaching bird. Good! It was arriving on time just as Karpenko must have ordered. At least he could count on him. He had been briefed that the White House outside defense forces didn't dare fire on the copter as long as he and Michelle held hostages.

At this desperate instant Garrison and Ben, who were enjoying their well-earned break after winning the battle for the electrical grid, climbed the stairs from the West Wing basement. Garrison's pager vibrated. It was North. North could wait a minute. Garrison intended to just gain a peek at the festivities in the State Dining Room. Then he and Ben would return to business.

As they reached the top of the stairs, both men caught the essence of the drama unfolding in the hallway. Garrison, reaching for his gun, stopped Ben with a push. He signaled for silence. "You head for cover. I am going to help stop this."

Garrison could see that Andropov had himself well shielded by the vice president, Dione and Michelle, so that Garrison or the trailing marksmen had no low-risk chance at picking off the pair. Once outside the White House, though, he figured the sharpshooters stationed in the nearby buildings would be able to place a shot in the exact spot of Andropov's and Michelle's brains, where even a reflexive pull of the trigger would be prevented. He whispered that bit of intelligence to Ben.

Then he moaned, "Oh shit."

Andropov had stopped at the door and was demanding helmets and flack vests for Michelle and himself.

Garrison groaned, "This guy is no idiot. He knows what's waiting for him outside. Only an insider could have told him that. Our hands are tied."

Hearing Garrison's despair Ben concluded that something must be done now. He reacted instinctively. "Brad, those are my friends.

I'm going to distract the two piss-ants. Be ready to shoot."

Ben broke free of Garrison's restraining attempts and cleared the last three steps in one bound. He raced as one possessed down the hall straight toward the four.

Upon seeing the racing Ben, the trailing agents were confused and unsure of what to do.

Garrison muttered a muffled string of profanities, but, guessing what Ben intended, he promptly resolved that he had better shoot Michelle first, then Andropov. Even though Andropov was armed, Foster had an even chance of taking care of himself.

The hostages and their captors were on hold at the north entrance, waiting for the protective gear which Andropov demanded, when they heard a screaming man approach. Turning they saw a crazed figure bolting straight toward them, hollering from only a few yards away.

With a calculated show of insanity designed to confuse and throw Andropov off his game, Ben gestured wildly at the four and shouted, "Hey Michelle, you commy bitch. Did you screw enough Bumgardners to get a promotion? Screw you both!"

With that, Ben ripped off his FBI hat, threw it at the two and then dived for what minimal cover the floor offered.

Both Andropov and Michelle, momentarily confused by the crazy antics of Ben, had frozen. However, both captors in a fatal reflexive action turned their pistols away from the hostages and toward the wild man and the incoming hat.

At that moment of opportunity, Garrison's semiautomatic barked, and in nearly the same instant, Foster whirled with a spinning karate kick that exploded with a devastating crack on Andropov's jaw.

As the Mafia Chieftain fell toward the floor, out cold from the punishing blow to his head, he still managed a reflex squeeze of the trigger. The bullet found a victim. Ben heard the sickening thud behind him as it struck Garrison.

Garrison grabbed his leg with one hand, but kept his eyes and gun trained on the scene. As an unconscious Andropov flopped to the floor, Michelle, seriously wounded by Garrison in one arm, slumped to her knees. Yet she determinedly took aim at the prone and unarmed Ben. Garrison had no choice. He fired again, this time with an intent to kill. He was unaware that fellow Agent Karpenko's pistol was aimed at his head. In a split second Karpenko would finish off Garrison.

As Garrison watched Michelle fall to the floor, he puzzled, "That shot of mine sounded like two shots. Is there an echo or am I delirious?" Then totally confused he saw his fellow FBI agent, one of the trailing contingent down the main hall, slump to the floor. Dazed and badly hurt, Garrison collapsed on the top step.

A companion drama had unfolded which prompted Garrison's confusion. Agent Karpenko's drawn gun, unlike those of the other agents, had been trained, not on the kidnappers, but on Garrison. Just as Karpenko squeezed the trigger, intending to kill Garrison, another shot rang out simultaneously with Garrison's final shot at Michelle. This blast came from the stairs behind Garrison where Secret Service Agent Higgins' gun bucked.

Higgins and North had rushed up the stairs onto the scene of the battle barely in time to spot Karpenko drawing a bead on Garrison. Higgins had performed the most gut-wrenching act of his life. He shot a fellow officer, a traitor, before the Judas could execute Garrison.

Michelle, her eyes staring upward into oblivion, lay sprawled on the floor just short of the north exit. Her lifeless hands clutched her chest where dark red blood oozed through a hole in the black satin dress. The gushing fluid covered her hands and streamed down onto the marble floor in an ever-expanding pool. Eventually the flowing crimson merged with the red welcome carpet leading outside to the hovering red copter.

Upon receiving the news that the hostage situation inside was resolved, the marksmen outside wasted no time. They shot the unsuspecting thugs and the crew of the hovering copter. The bird, now pilotless, spiraled out of control. A second later Stinger AA missiles launched by the White House Secret Service north side team blew the bird and all occupants apart. Flaming pieces rained down a red deluge on the secure section of Pennsylvania Avenue where the roller bladers had romped earlier.

Meanwhile, as the outside drama reached its explosive finale, agents inside ran to the battle scene from every direction to cover the vice president and Dione. Foster cradled his shaken daughter, easing her to the ground. Then, leaving her in the care of the medics, he pushed through his protective Secret Service detail and ran to the exhausted Ben, who was just regaining his feet, "God bless you, Ben. Are you okay?"

"I'm fine, but Brad isn't."

Both Ben and Foster elbowed past a multitude of plain-clothes and uniformed agents to the wounded Garrison. North was already administering first aid, pressing his shirt into the wound in an attempt to stem the bleeding.

North, looking up into the concerned faces explained, "Karpenko was our traitor. He nearly killed Brad."

Too worried to know what to say to his friend, a shaken Ben asked, "Are you okay?"

"No problem! That was a damn foolish move on your part, partner, but thank God you acted. That was a very bad scene. Old Boris just might have pulled off his escape. Then curtains, a dead vice president and daughter."

Garrison, obviously in great pain and growing faint from the loss of blood, confidently whispered, "I'm going to be all right, you old fart. It just hurts like hell.

"Ben, you are in charge of our team. My associates know what to do on the policing front. They can take care of the arrests and coordinate with the German police on the Munich Plant seizure.

"You know, Mr. Vice President, someone has to stay around here to look out for this crazy civilian. And, I ask you, what would the D.C. debutantes do without me?"

The smile faded, but the irrepressible gleam in his eyes endured. That indestructible spark gave Ben hope that Garrison would pull through.

Foster straightened up, instructing the lead Secret Service agent, "Keep the doors to the State Dining Room closed until all of this is cleaned up. I don't want the guests knowing who did what to whom out here. Tell them everything is okay and I will talk with them in a minute."

He ordered, "Throw Andropov into the deepest, darkest hole you can find. Our most secure cell will be his Highness's new home."

Andropov, handcuffed and still groggy was prone on the floor, covered by a host of officers. His jaw was fractured, compliments of his enemies. In shock, but slowly coming to grips with how completely his night of grand vengeance had turned into his ultimate ignominy, he resolved that if he did nothing else, he would even the score somehow. At a minimum he would get that SOB Andrew and the traitorous Goldstein.

Turning to the medics who tended Garrison, Foster demanded, "You take care of this man. Get him to Bethesda. You save him or, God help me..."

After giving more orders to the agents, and more thanks to Ben, the vice president returned to the dining hall to assure the guests that all was under control. The President left for the Oval Office to inform the American people of the unfolding crisis.

Ben tried to walk back to the command center, but found he couldn't. His legs wouldn't hold him. He sagged to the floor. While attempting to regaining control of his body, he thought things through. With Garrison out of commission he must pull himself together and return to the command center for there were still the Munich plant seizure, the arrests, and the nuclear plants' recovery to monitor.

Ben's mood confused him. Only some of the uneasiness he had felt earlier had gone away. Andropov's plot was defeated and the Mafioso chief was in handcuffs. He should be relieved, even elated, but he wasn't. He was worried. Was it the nuclear explosion so near the U.S. coast or the still potent Mafia which had new scores to settle? Some of those scores were with him.

PART II
War

FIFTY-FOUR

Day 45 9:02 P.M. The Vice President's Office White House

After helping calm the dinner guests, Vice President Foster returned to his office to receive the latest briefings on Joint Eagles.

General Adair, now airborne and bound for Washington, called in to matter-of-factly report, "Mr. Vice President, our cruise hits were superbly effective. We experienced only minimal losses in the Iranian theater so far. The battle for air dominance will continue through the balance of the night. If all continues to go well, the way will be clear for our troop landing.

"With the East Coast threat in the mop-up phase, CENTCOM can concentrate entirely on the war over there. I placed a Pentagon Admiral in charge of the East Coast aftermath. He will coordinate with all government agencies in securing the area of the blast and the sea lanes affected by the radioactive fallout."

"Did the SEALs survive the blast?"

"Yes, we pulled the exhausted men out of the water moments ago, but we lost three copters and many military personnel."

"How many?"

"At least twenty."

Foster grimaced but continued to quiz General Adair, "How much oil pollution is there?"

"Not too much. Most of the oil burned or evaporated in the blast. The biggest problem is airborne radiation."

"But that's headed out to sea, right?"

"Yes. Changing subjects, a welcome bit of news is that our commandos in Iran have uncovered a great deal about the Karaj defenses."

Foster replied, "Thank you, General. Your military team's performing superbly. Give all at CENTCOM a 'well done.'"

In lieu of the injured Garrison, Ben arrived in Foster's office to relay that the Munich plant seizure and the Mafia suspect arrests were still ongoing. Ben reported, "Goldstein somehow slipped through the FBI dragnet. Several German police were killed in the early stages of the Munich plant takeover. The German authorities obviously met very stiff resistance. Of course I am not surprised after what I ran into over there."

Foster nodded indicating that he understood.

Ben continued, "The FBI found Undersecretary Foley hanging in his office closet. It looks like suicide, but nothing is being ruled out. The FBI figures it could have been the Mafia's doing since he had become a liability to them."

"Yes. They are pretty good at fake suicides, aren't they?"

The stream of vice presidential briefings continued as Secretary Kohlmeier rushed past the departing Ben Andrew to share her important news with Foster. "I just talked with the Iranian Secretary of State. He acted as though he had no knowledge of the Iranian missile, the Iranian sub, the launch crew, and the nuclear bomb aboard the tanker. As soon as I told him about it, he cut short the conversation, saying that he must see his President immediately. I believe he is either the best actor in the world or he was truly shocked and uninformed. He told me that you or I should expect a message back very shortly. I told him that he and his President better listen very carefully to our President's address."

Foster observed, "So intelligence was probably correct. There are two opposing factions over there."

"It appears so. If the President's speech sets the right tone, and we hear the right words from my Iranian counterpart, we could still avoid having to send troops into Karaj."

Handing a set of papers to Kohlmeier, Foster said, "Here is a copy of Arthur's speech. Read it and give me any changes right away."

Day 15 9.07 P.M. Local Time

"Don, the damn television lights have to go off now. Don't allow them back on until I say. They are hot, bright and a damned bother. Make sure all the mikes are off, too. No security info is leaking out of here tonight.

"And keep the press away from me," snapped the President. " Press Secretary McClanahan can entertain the piranhas. Inform the flesh-eaters that there will be press feedings every hour, and that I will hold a news conference tomorrow at noon. They can pick my bones clean then.

"Have you sent a copy of my speech to all of the Senate and Congressional leaders?"

North calmly responded, "Yes," but privately he questioned how many more damned balls could he keep in the air.

With a signaling wink and nod to Foster, he suggested, "McClanahan and I took care of things, Mr. President. Why don't you just spend these last minutes going over current status with Vice President Foster? That way you will be sure you are up to date on everything."

Foster caught the cue from North to help calm President Arthur so that North could take care of last minute business. Negotiating a path around the TV lights and cameras to President Arthur's side, Foster reassured him, "You put together an excellent speech, Mr. President. You should just relax so you can project a calm, yet firm, demeanor to the world."

"That is exactly what I should do. But it's easier said than done," sighed Arthur, shrugging and rolling his shoulders in a vain attempt to relieve the tightness in his back.

"So much has happened today and there is still a war to be fought. It is hard to relax. Are you really holding up okay or is it just an act?"

"I am fine, Mr. President."

"I suppose you are. Ben's another one who seems to just gear up for whatever is dished out. I sometimes wonder if you ex-submariners are human."

"Sub service seems to have steeled these old bones well for the crisis we face, that's for sure. I think Ben and I almost thrive on it."

"Are Dione and Garrison okay?"

"Yes, sir. Don't worry about any of that. One more thing, Mr. President. Secretary Kohlmeier and I have modified your speech slightly. There is a slim chance the war can end if the Iranian President listens closely and acts appropriately. You must mobilize our nation for the possibility of a ground war, while giving the Iranian President a chance to avoid it."

"That's all, huh?"

Don called out, "Thirty seconds to air time, Mr. President."

"Then turn on the blasted lights! I don't want to be squinting when the cameras go live."

Foster gave the President a reassuring squeeze on the shoulder. Having done all he could he moved to the side of the Oval Office, away from President Arthur and the bright lights.

The President, now bathed in the glare of national and world attention, sat at his desk with the United States flag at his right and the presidential seal imprinted on the front of his desk. Despite the annoying lights and the tension of the day, the lanky President, with an able assist from his makeup artist, now appeared calm but appropriately stern and business-like. His demeanor matched the seriousness of the message he was about to deliver.

"Five, four, three, two, one! You are live, Mr. President."

"Good evening, my fellow Americans. Tonight we face a severe threat to our nation's security and to the security of our allies and friends around the world. A nuclear terrorist attack was blunted tonight near our shores; however, a nuclear explosion did occur at sea.

"The assault was part of an international conspiracy to cripple our country. The intent of these despicable terrorists was to kill millions of our citizens, but thanks to our most courageous soldiers they have failed. There is no longer any danger to our East Coast.

The radiation from the blast is at sea and drifting away. Immediately after I finish, FEMA Director Gonzales and Coast Guard Captain Jackson will discuss exactly where the evacuated sea lanes are."

The President briefly described the crisis, including the attack on the electrical supply system, the nuclear missile threat along the East Coast, and the nuclear weapons under Mafia and radical Iranian control. Then he explained:

"Because of the infiltration of our government by these criminals, I was forced to maintain the tightest possible secrecy during the planning and initial execution of our self defense. For that reason, only now, are we advising our allies of our actions. Regrettably, I could not openly obtain the advice and consent of Congress or seek a UN resolution supporting our action. Circumstances did not allow that preferred course of action. The extreme danger to the United States mandated that I act swiftly and surely to defend our country. Under our Constitution, as the Commander in Chief, I have so acted in our common defense."

The President paused, wondering if this was coming across to the American people properly, or would they be incensed at the secrecy this crisis required? It was too late to worry. The die was cast.

"Now let me address President Fatola directly. Forces within Iran collaborated with international criminals to threaten millions of American lives. Perhaps, Mr. President, you have been misled by rogue factions within your government. If so, you must act now to prevent further bloodshed. If you do, hostilities can be brought to a quick end. If you do nothing, rest assured that we will take necessary steps to blunt the threat to our security and the region's security.

Any further provocation by your country and we will most assuredly visit upon you a devastating response."

Foster hoped that President Fatola understood what Arthur was saying. Any more nukes launched by them and they were getting one shoved up their ass. Maybe he should have written the President's speech stating it that bluntly. He chuckled. It seemed North's no-non-sense approach to life was rubbing off on him. Even though having read the speech many times, Foster was impressed with the President's ability to summon support for the Joint Eagles crusade which lay ahead, while still offering an ultimatum and an olive branch to Iran.

"Also, any other nations in any theater around the world should be advised, we have the ability and the will to defend our friends. We will not hesitate to answer aggression any-where with great resistance and absolute retaliation.

"Joint Eagles, a coordinated policing action by the United States and Russia will eliminate the nuclear threat by these criminal aggressors. In the hours and days ahead, the Secretary of Defense will keep you informed on military progress.

"The only limitation on the press releases will be that, of course, we will not disclose any military information that will jeopardize our armed services' men and women or their mis-sion. I am sure you share my desire to protect them in their hour of perilous service to our country. I appeal to the press to exercise restraint, respecting our nation's desire to assure the safety of these young soldiers who serve our country so bravely.

"Let us not forget that our sons and daughters, the pilots of screaming fighters, the seamen aboard swift powerful warships and the brave soldiers fighting on the ground are our nation's true heroes. They risk everything so that we may remain safe and free, free from nuclear terrorism.

"Please join me with your wishes and prayers for their safe and swift return home. Theirs is a most noble enterprise. God bless America and goodnight."

James Stockton had slipped into the room during the climax of the President's address. Spotting Foster, he moved over to him as unobtrusively as he could. It wasn't in his normally boisterous nature to make a quiet entrance. Foster, noticing this unusual behavior, wondered if James was sick or more likely just dead tired from two days and two nights of non-stop action.

"Mr. Vice President, I need to speak with you. We have terrible news from Moscow."

Foster followed Stockton into the hall as the congratulatory White House staff flocked around the President.

"They assassinated Kruschev! He and his personal bodyguards were reportedly blown to bits."

"No. It can't be. How? Where?"

"He was in transit back to FSB headquarters after personally reporting to President Strahkov on Joint Eagles. A Russian army attack helicopter pulled off the hit. There apparently weren't pieces bigger than a postage stamp left."

"Shit! So the Mafia and the SOB Chekists will now have their way with Russia."

Foster's shoulders visibly sagged with that blow. "Are you sure of this, James? There must be no question. There is too much at stake. Russia is going to be in real trouble without him."

"Yes, on all counts. I am sorry to bring you this awful news. I know how much you grew to trust and respect that courageous man."

Foster turned and slowly headed alone back down the hallway to his office.

As Stockton watched his shaken friend walk away, he questioned whether the time was right to reveal all to Foster. Freed of his pledge to not tell anyone of Kruschev's plan as long as Kruschev lived, Stockton decided that the revelations could wait no longer.

He caught up with Foster, "There are several things you need to know, Mr. Vice President. Can we go to your office?"

It was then that Foster learned of Kruschev's plan, secretly inspired by Dudaev, for the Chekist's defeat. Stockton explained how the far-reaching scheme addressed even the contingency of Kruschev's assassination. That Dudaev led a super secret cabal of Russian dissidents was explained including the amazing fact that Kruschev had been a member of Dudaev's movement. He expounded upon the major role Dudaev played and was still playing in shaping Russia's future.

Stockton also told of Laura's heritage and Dudaev's involvement as her and her mother's savior. He explained just how mysterious Dudaev and his organization were and how Dudaev had quizzed both Liz and him about Ben. His unexplained interest in Ben simply added to the enigma surrounding this man.

Finally, he explained how Kruschev had predicted that he would be assassinated and despite facing that possibility, had bravely gone forward with the reforms designed to root out the Chekists. Both men sat for a moment in silent awe of the unequivocal commitment to country exhibited by the courageous Kruschev.

Foster recovered enough from the flood of disclosures by Stockton to pronounce, "Shame on us, James, if we don't do everything possible to see that Kruschev's plan is enacted."

FIFTY-FIVE

Day 45 10:23 P.M. FBI Detention Center

Boris Andropov's wrath centered on two individuals. One was the bedeviling Dr. Andrew. That worm must not get away with defying him. He could not be allowed to live. Damn Lepke for not finishing him off when he had the chance. Because of Lepke's failure, this creep still lived, and was responsible for his being in jail.

Goldstein was the other one in trouble with Andropov. Either Goldstein was captured or he had betrayed him. He would find out which it was. If the explanation was betrayal, then the scoundrel would pay dearly. He must establish communication with the outside and especially with Bupkov.

On the brighter side, dealing with these FBI scum was child's play. They were as transparent as glass; puffed up little policemen full of their own self-importance. No wonder that the KGB ran circles around these neophytes throughout the cold war. They had actually tried to interrogate him, forcing him to laugh in their faces. He had defiantly quoted the Communist Manifesto, which even though partially meant to enlighten, served to his delight to anger his guards. Angry police were ineffective police.

In addition to his own wits, Andropov was forced to rely upon his most trusted attorney. Cranston must extricate him from this legal morass and carry messages to his organization. Assessing his legal situation, he wasn't confident that Cranston could free him. He would probably have to resort to bribery of guards and judges. No problem since Americans would always sell out for a few dollars.

With his broken jaw, Andropov's one allowed call was a muffled and painful one. His whispered message was short, "Get over here now, Cranston."

"Where?"

"FBI Headquarters! I am under arrest!"

Day 45 10:30 P.M. Cranston's Virginia Mansion

Rodney Cranston, one of the country's preeminent criminal defense attorneys, clicked off his phone. He correctly concluded that the President's speech, which he watched earlier, and Andropov's arrest were somehow related.

After unlocking the wall safe in his expansive personal library, he pulled out the Mafia's secret-code manual. Since he would undoubtedly be given coded messages by Andropov, he reviewed the current encryptions.

While performing that review he received still another call. It was Goldstein. Goldstein explained that he was on a private plane heading for Guatemala. "The management of our organization has changed. Andropov is no longer in command. I am. For your continued value to us, I hope you adjust to the management changes and act accordingly. Freeing Andropov is not a high priority."

After that warning Cranston was unsure of what to do.

Should he go all out to free Andropov or do as Goldstein suggested and sabotage Andropov's defense. All he could be sure of was that one leader was arrested, and the other was fleeing the country. A struggle for control of the Mafia was quite apparently underway. Cranston knew that the outcome of that contest could be swayed either way by one man, Ivan Bupkov.

Until he could discern where Bupkov stood, Cranston would hedge his bets and encourage both Andropov and Goldstein to believe he was with them.

CHAPTER
FIFTY-SIX

Day 48 8 A.M. Middle East Time Karaj Weapons Complex Iran

General Zarif was frightened. Throughout the night he had grown steadily more alarmed. What the hell was going on? They had lost all communications with military headquarters and the rest of the world as well. The unnerving explosions had worsened as the night wore on.

Zarif reasoned that the air attack on Iran must be the doing of the Americans. No one else could mount such an intense assault. Was their objective his facility or even him? Was the assault retaliation for the bomb he sent to New York? The bomb should have obliterated the city and there should be no evidence linking him to the attack. Or had something gone wrong? Were they after him? Damn the lack of communications. Well, they weren't going to get him or his nuclear weapons factory.

Zarif concluded that it was suicide for him to remain here. If the Americans did come after him, he was a sitting duck in this hole. The Yankee Devils had wanted to get their hands on him for twenty-five years, but he was too smart for them.

Betraying none of the fear he felt, he ordered, "Colonel Seljuk, you assume command. I will try to break through to Military Headquarters. I must find out what is going on. Defend this site to the death of every last man if necessary. If it appears you will be attacked here, I will bring reinforcements. So hold on at all costs! Help will come!"

Barely acknowledging Colonel Seljuk's salute, Zarif scurried from the control room and ordered the driver of his personal car, "Military headquarters on the double. Take the south exit and the secondary road south."

He would take back roads all the way to Tehran.

Day 48 8:20 A.M. Near Karaj Weapons Complex

Prudhoe Paul on south road patrol watched as the limo flying an upside down American flag sped south. He sighted in the general. The butt was right in his crosshairs. He was sorely tempted to squeeze the trigger. He could execute the hated Zarif, but thought better of it. He mustn't tip off Iran that American Special Forces were this close.

"Shit! Just as we expected, the spineless wimp flees. Captain and Interrogator will be disappointed. Interrogator had special treats in store for that asshole."

CHAPTER
FIFTY-SEVEN

Day 48 9:15 A.M. Middle East Time Baku AFB Azerbaijan

The Longbow, ferrying Captain O'Banyon and Interrogator out of the war zone, dropped onto the crowded tarmac at the sprawling Russian air base in Baku. As the copter landed, a prodigious spectacle greeted O'Banyon. He paused before disembarking and attempted to take in the vast assemblage of aircraft and armaments.

Stretching to the horizon in all directions stood a colossal array of hundreds of American military transports. Huge C-5 Galaxies, gleaming new C-17 Globemasters and the older protruding-nosed Hercules were everywhere. The deafening roar of dozens of revving aircraft engines was punctuated every few seconds by the throbbing of a loaded-to-the-limit transport, lumbering down the runway toward takeoff.

He saw a host of the U.S. transports climbing in the southern sky. Those planes, he knew, were the first wave of the most intense airlift of troops into battle in history. Within two hours the Third Armored Calvary Regiment (ACR) would begin landing at the makeshift strip near Karaj, which was already controlled by the Rangers and a Longbow squadron. The Regiment's job was to decimate the Karaj Division. That, military planners calculated, would take a day or two. Then the way would be clear for the Rangers to finish business at the Karaj Nuclear Complex.

Gazing toward the far horizon, O'Banyon was surprised to spot a fleet of the old Russian condors. He marveled at how, even in the distance, the giants dwarfed the largest American transports. He had no idea that they had delivered the M1A3s from Ramstein.

Half of the soldiers and equipment of the Third ACR were unloaded awaiting the transports' return. The other half, he figured,

413

was already loaded on the hundreds of transports arrayed before him. Over the next seven-hour period each American plane would deliver two loads of ACR warriors and armaments into the war zone. He reasoned that Baku was a vital launching pad for the invasion, since it was close enough to Karaj to allow each plane to complete two round trips in a short time span. Otherwise the ambitious airlift would have been impossible as there simply weren't enough American transports to do this job if each could make only one trip.

Leaving his team behind in enemy territory bothered O'Banyon. He had never left them alone in the field before. However, his squad had collected such vital insight into the Karaj nuclear weapons fortress that Military Intelligence insisted upon talking directly with Interrogator and Special Forces Joint Command compelled O'Banyon's appearance before them. The commandos' help was mandatory in refining the Ranger's attack plans. O'Banyon believed that without his team's discoveries and insights the Second Ranger Battalion would unwittingly march into a bloody debacle at Karaj.

In the spidery shadow cast by the Longbow, Military officials met the two disembarking soldiers. A dirty and smelly Interrogator was whisked away by a contingent of Intelligence officers. He faced a thorough debriefing by Military Intelligence.

O'Banyon, equally unkempt, was escorted away from the crowded tarmac in an Army HMMWV to the building housing the temporary Joint Theater Command Headquarters. The command team of Second Ranger Battalion Commander, Lieutenant Colonel Potter, Joint Special Operations Commander (JSOC), Colonel Mays, and Joint Force Commander (JFC), General Griffith, anxiously awaited Captain O'Banyon's arrival.

Day 48 9:30 A.M. Joint Theater Command Headquarters Baku

A no-nonsense, General Griffith greeted the grimy soldier. "Welcome, Captain. We know you are damned tired but we must talk now. Every second is vital. The Tehran divisions worry me. If they advance on the Karaj battle zone, they can screw up everything. You know Colonels Potter and Mays, I believe."

"Yes, sir. Good to see both of you again."

"Your team has collected vital insight. That is why you are here."

"I am ready to help in any way I can, General."

Even though O'Banyon was dead tired, he was incredibly alert.

Adrenalin does that for an exhausted person, he reasoned. The less sleep he got, the more adrenalin seemed to kick in.

"If all goes as planned and the Third hands the Karaj Division their butts, then you and I will be going to Karaj day after tomorrow," the stocky poker-faced Ranger Commander announced brusquely.

"Good. The sooner I return to my unit, the better, sir."

"We understand that sentiment. It is highly unusual to call you back here, but your field intelligence is so vital that normal communication channels are not adequate. We could not risk compromising security. Let's get down to business," General Griffith directed. "Tell us, Captain, what you learned of Karaj's defenses."

"Sirs, a death trap awaits our troops. Once the fortress is directly under siege, two chemicals are injected into the main ventilation system. The first chemical is an iodine compound in aerosol form. It will saturate any of our ABC masks in a matter of minutes. Once that occurs, the other chemical, which is a new variant of VX nerve gas, will go right through our troops' saturated masks. None of the vaccinations given to the soldiers immunize them against this new strain. The whole Ranger Battalion would suffer horribly, and die soon after entering the compound. Meanwhile, the Iranian defenders' masks retain their effectiveness in that toxic environment. We don't believe they have developed a vaccine against that strain of nerve gas, so they are dependent on their masks."

"Aren't you sure?" questioned Gen. Griffith.

"Both captured soldiers told us they had no vaccine, but I can't be a hundred percent."

"Go on, Captain," growled Gen. Griffith.

"Once their defensive measures kick in, the control room is isolated. It's equipped with its own ventilation system. It's the nerve center of the entire complex, no pun intended. The control room inhabitants, including the guard commanders, can work unencumbered in their spaces without protective masks and suits because they have pristine air. General Bakr Zarif, himself, could be there."

General Griffith suffered, "Anyone who gets that demented coward will be promoted two ranks on the spot."

"If he sticks around, we will get him. He is such a coward though, that at the first sign of trouble he will hightail it to safety.

"But back to the Karaj defenses, a closed-circuit TV system allows the vermin in the control room to view all areas of the compound. Thus, the control room commanders can effectively direct their guards' activities while under attack.

"A guard force of four hundred troops is stationed outside on the perimeter of the compound. Another two hundred equally armed defenders, backed by the nerve gas, are located within the deep underground complex. They can withstand nearly any assault on the blasted place."

"It sounds like we would experience unacceptable casualties trying to capture the compound. We should just call in a B-1B with a burrowing nuke to finish off the place," Colonel Mays blustered.

"With all respect, Colonel, there is a way to take Karaj without experiencing heavy casualties," countered O'Banyon. He had observed that Colonel Mays was becoming increasingly agitated.

O'Banyon and the others understood that the Colonel was simply blowing hot air. In his election campaign President Arthur had vowed never to be the first to use nuclear weapons. And, despite the close call with the nuclear blast on the tanker, everyone assumed he would still honor his promise.

"You said nearly any assault, Captain. You must have some ideas," said General Griffith ignoring Colonel Mays' useless contribution.

"Sir, my men have been in the ventilation system. They know it literally inside out. We can turn the tables on the ragheads."

"How's that, Captain?" asked the general.

"First, we feign an attack on their perimeter defenses near their main gate. Meanwhile, my men will have secretly entered the complex's ventilation system. That phony attack must be just aggressive enough to force the defenders inside the complex to initiate their defensive strategies. The chemicals will be released into the ventilation system and the interior defensive forces will don their masks."

"Presto! Your men are dead," growled Colonel Mays.

"Wrong, Colonel! My men in the vent pipe don't do anything to the first non-toxic chemical. We allow the iodine aerosol to be distributed throughout the compound but we divert the nerve gas. Instead of it entering the main ventilation system, it will, with our help, flow into the isolated control room."

"Are you absolutely sure you can do that? How on God's earth can you?" questioned Colonel Mays.

"Yes, I am sure, Colonel. With careful timing we can divert the nerve gas to the control room commanders. We must manufacture two simple devices here at the base, which I will take back with me."

"That redirection of the gas helps some, but still we face a deadly interior fight," cautioned a dubious Colonel. "The exterior battle doesn't concern me since we can bring in the Longbows. With their cruises and Hellfires they will decimate the exterior defenses. That part of the battle won't lead to heavy casualties, but..."

Colonel Potter had been listening quietly with growing respect for Captain O'Banyon. The man's reputation preceded him. It was definitely time to interject an assist. "If I am not mistaken, Colonel, the captain has something else up his sleeve. Let's hear him out."

"Once we accomplish the diversion of the nerve gas, we have a tremendous advantage. The control-room boys fry. Their commanders are out of the picture rather quickly, so nobody is left to direct the interior guard forces."

"But that still leaves two hundred heavily armed guards to deal with on their home turf. It could disintegrate into bloody room-to-room, hand-to-hand combat," postulated Colonel Mays.

He rose and began to pace the floor, nervously banging a map casing against his palm. It had been years since he served on a Special Forces mission. He clearly felt upstaged and threatened by the present-day real McCoy, the living legend, Dan O'Banyon.

Patiently O'Banyon explained, "Here is how we neutralize their advantage. They will have their special ABC masks on, which means they won't also have the benefit of thermal or night vision goggles. They are dependent on lights. That is where we finish turning the tables on the ragheads. My men will disrupt the main power, as well as, the emergency power to the place. Once we know the nerve gas has been diverted and the power is off the Rangers can attack the darkened fortress with no ABC masks at all.

The enemy guards, though, don't know that they are not exposed to the nerve gas, so they must wear their ABC masks. With the aid of the Ranger's superb thermal and night vision gear, they will overpower the blinded and leaderless internal guard force."

Colonel Mays was left stunned and speechless by the unexpected brilliance of the plan. His arms dropped limply to his sides. He sank into a sullen silence, momentarily at a loss. The map case slipped out of his hand and loudly clattered to the floor. It rolled relentlessly all the way to the far corner of the room.

General Griffith leaned back in his chair, pondering the proposed assault. Slowly a broadening smile spread across his normally impassive face, as he comprehended the full extent of the plan's genius.

He spoke, unable to hide his absolute satisfaction with O'Banyon, "Captain, you work with my staff. Firm up the details for the attack I believe your strategy has merit. If Army Intelligence confirms Interrogator's work, then I will request General Ribikoff's approval of your attack plan. Also try to get a couple of hours of sleep. We will get you back to your men soon. Only a major setback today or tomorrow will stop your return to Zarif's damned nuclear weapons factory."

General Griffith was unaware of events unfolding in D.C. and Tehran. Secretary Kohlmeier was desperately attempting to fashion a last-minute negotiated settlement, which could negate the necessity of the land attack. As far as he knew the attack was on. The first contingent of the Third ACR was within thirty minutes of landing near Karaj. Time was short. The landing of the regiment was imminent.

CHAPTER
FIFTY-EIGHT

Day 48 9:45 A.M. Middle East Time General Zarif's Limo Outskirts of Tehran

General Zarif was within minutes of Military Command Headquarters. Magically his car's communication equipment began working again. He reasoned that the Americans must not be jamming communications near Tehran. He had no way of knowing how right he was. The Americans needed communication paths open to the Iranian President, so no interference of signals around Tehran was presently allowed.

As he approached the Command Center, General Zarif answered a call from Commanding General Hassan.

General Hassan said, "We wondered what happened to you, General. We have received no word out of Karaj."

"There is one hell of an air attack around there, but I am sure you know that. I have no idea what is to follow. Do you?"

"A few clues," General Hassan carefully couched his reply. "I just wanted to be sure you were safe. We will talk as soon as you reach Headquarters."

A half mile before Zarif's limo arrived at the Command Center gate, a man jumped directly into the car's path.

Recognizing the man's beret, Zarif ordered his driver, "Stop the car."

The raggedly clothed man was apparently a Zukan warrior. Since the Zukans were fierce allies, he opened the door and motioned to the man to get in.

"General Zarif, thank Allah, it is you. There is troubling word from Baku. The Americans are there big time. They have massed hundreds of transport planes, thousands of troops, and much armored equipment."

"So that is what comes next! An invasion! Probably aimed at my military complex. What is the news from America?"

"The U.S. President in a speech yesterday claimed that Iran and the Mafia were responsible for an abortive nuclear strike on America. The story is the missile was stopped at the last minute."

Zarif grimaced at that disappointing news, but attempted not to reveal his utter dismay. He stiffly said, "Thanks. I needed to know that."

Zarif worried that if President Fatola believed the American devils, he might put two and two together. Would he blame him? Well it could go either way. Fatola could possibly figure out a few things. Since that could be the case, he must act now.

Zarif gave the insurgent a medallion of special significance. Before handing it over, though, he marked four letters on its back—B-A-K-U. "Get this to our launch crew at the Medalia Mosque. What is the quickest you can do that?"

"One or two days."

"Go! Tell them this is the real thing. The target is the infested Baku base. Armageddon is at hand for Iran's enemies. How convenient of the American devils to array themselves within easy range of my last big nuke."

After sending the Zukan warrior on the destructive mission, Zarif, unsure of what manner of greeting awaited him, ordered his driver to proceed to the gate. He still had the Ayatollah on his side. Things would go his way eventually and best of all, the American army and a Russian base would be obliterated.

Day 48 9:51 A.M. Command Center Gate Tehran

The moment General Zarif's car arrived at the gate, a contingent of Iranian commandos materialized with their weapons trained upon the car, which flew the upside down American flag. They dragged the driver out of the car and forced him face down on the pavement with a host of semi-automatics trained on him. Others yanked open the rear doors and unceremoniously dumped out a yelling and cursing Zarif. The commandos removed his pistol and holster, handcuffed him and led him away.

CHAPTER
FIFTY-NINE

Day 47 10:30 P.M. EST Oval Office Washington, D.C.

President Arthur, Vice President Foster, Director Stockton, Secretaries Kohlmeier and Winston, and North listened as General Adair briefed them on the military situation in Iran. Adair laid out the urgency of the moment.

"The lead transports carrying the Third are only minutes from a Karaj landing. A decision of go or no-go on our troops must be made now," sternly admonished Adair.

Secretary Kohlmeier bluntly advocated, "I say we stop the attack. They arrested Zarif and President Fatola promises to dismantle the Karaj Complex. Also he assures us that they will commence a unilateral cease fire."

General Adair managed a rare laugh, "They don't have much left to cease fire with, now do they? What assurances have we that they won't renege on any promises and renew their nuclear buildup or release more nukes on their enemies in the future?"

Foster was undecided. Secretary Kohlmeier may be right. But the general was right, too, in that guarantees were a must.

Foster summarized, "General, we accomplished a great deal; the secret weapons storage site in Kazakhstan is under Russian control. That cuts off Iran's most important source of weapons. Ben reports that the Germans control the Munich Plant, stopping the Mafia's moneymaker. New York and our nuclear plants are safe and you took out nearly all of Iran's deployed missiles, both nuclear and conventional. Their Karaj weapons complex is not worth much without those supporting centers and materials."

Stockton disagreed, "Two problems with that assessment, Mr. Vice President. There is enriched uranium and a dozen bombs there and they are producing tritium at Isfahan. With the ex-Soviet scientists, they can turn the tritium into thermonuclear weapons. The more we delay the worse things get."

North, who seldom contributed at these meetings, spoke up. "You know, when my drilling company cut a deal with an oil company that we didn't trust, we demanded collateral. Wouldn't that work here? Have them place their bank assets in escrow in Switzerland, eh."

"Good for you, you old rascal," enthused President Arthur. "If they mean what they say, then they will agree to place their European and Asian bank accounts in escrow under mutually agreeable conditions."

North added, "You bet. And have them do it immediately, before you stop the attack. The banks can arrange those transactions in minutes by wire transfer. You will find out real fast if their president is serious about tearing down Karaj. My hunch is you may also find out that the Ayatollah is the real power and the President is merely a figurehead."

Adair didn't like where this was headed and questioned, "Why would they agree to turn over their money? They don't trust us anymore than we trust them."

"The why is to avoid the humiliation and the further pounding you are about to administer to them," stated a resolute North.

Foster spoke up, "North could be right. They are a proud people. His solution has merit. It has a chance. I think you should propose this to President Fatola along with a graphic description of what will happen if he doesn't cooperate."

President Arthur decided, "Let's try it. Call in Secretary of the Treasury Claussen. We need his help. We have only minutes to pull this deal together. I will call Fatola. Kohlmeier, have Claussen bring us the list of Iran's bank holdings. General, alert CENTCOM. If necessary, have the lead transports circle the landing site."

After the President's emergency meeting ended with the decision to attempt to halt the conflict, President Arthur, Secretary Kohlmeier and Secretary of the Treasury Claussen worked feverishly. Calls flew back and forth between Tehran, D.C., and the European and Asian banks.

A last-second phone call from President Fatola struck President Arthur hard. Ashen faced, he ordered the team, "Forget it. The Ayatollah has turned thumbs down on the deal. Their President intimates that the Ayatollah believes that Iranian public opinion will turn against us after this attack and the Ayatollah's control of the country will be consolidated. In time, Iran can rebuild and renew their weapon's programs. The Ayatollah figures that our assault will only buy us time, but they have plenty of time."

A dejected President Arthur told General Adair, "The attack on Karaj goes forward."

CHAPTER
SIXTY

Day 50 7:15 A.M. Middle East Time Near Karaj

What a welcome sight. As O'Banyon floated down toward the Karaj Desert, he spotted his men. Special Forces teammate, Sergeant Prudhoe Paul, rushed to help him control his chute.

"Welcome, Captain. Did you have a pleasant vacation?"

"Vacation was great. I actually slept in a bed."

"How nice. How was the caviar at the Savoy? Our main course was the usual crappy Iranian sand and a few raw lizards," Prudhoe Paul chided.

"My heart bleeds for you, so I lined up lots of work. Your rest in the sand is over. You are all in for one unbelievable day."

While O'Banyon was regaining his footing, Interrogator floated to a pinpoint landing. Out of cussed orneriness, he kicked over one of the homing beacons as he touched down. Several of the team tackled him and roughed him up before he could release the chute.

"You ugly bastards. You all are chicken-livered SOBs. If you didn't need my help, I would have stayed on leave," he stormed in mock anger.

The first of Colonel Potter's five hundred Rangers began landing nearby just south of the Special Forces' hilltop home.

They were touching down well within the circle of American-controlled territory, which, thanks to the Third ACR's aggressive action, had grown to approximately a ten-mile-diameter circle. It extended past the landing strip to the northwest, as well as to the northeast past the nuclear complex and the smoking ruins of the decimated Karaj Division. Only the completely encircled, but still heavily defended underground nuclear weapons factory remained to be captured. The Rangers and O'Banyon's squad had the job of taking the complex.

424

When they were no longer needed to help the first of the landing Rangers, O'Banyon called his soldiers together. He briefed them on their role in today's attack and divided them into three squads, the Gophers, the Persians and the Boomers. The Persians and Boomers each requisitioned a DPV that had been air-dropped earlier. They loaded up the armed dune buggies with provisions, explosives and weapons. In the Iranian dawn, they raced eagerly across the desert floor toward their final rendezvous with the complex.

Lt. Col. Potter's Rangers gathered their air-dropped supplies, including M202 rocket launchers, 60 mm M224 mortars, 90 mm recoilless rifles as well as the remaining DPVs and HMMWVs. Every Ranger officer and Special Forces squad leader had two vital tools. Strapped to one wrist was a miniature GPS receiver, giving their precise locations and strapped on the other wrist was a miniature computer, no bigger than a watch.

The tiny computer revealed the locations of all friendly and enemy forces in their immediate vicinity. Global Hawks and geo-stationary spy satellites collected the raw information and pictures. This intelligence was transmitted to the main processing computer in a circling E-8. It reduced and processed the data, sending it on to CENTCOM. It also relayed site-specific enemy locations back to the Global Hawks circling above the complex. In turn localized information was relayed to each officer's wrist computer giving him vital information on the location of nearby forces, both enemy and friendly.

Colonel Mays called from JSOC's Baku command center to alert Colonel Potter and Captain O'Banyon, "Warthogs from our bases in Turkey, the Superhornets from the Nimitz and our Apaches are engaging two advancing Iranian divisions on the southwestern outskirts of Tehran."

Colonel Mays continued, "The battle is still raging, but many of those two divisions' tanks and artillery are now in ruins. It appears that those divisions' advances will soon be blunted. A third division, however, is showing signs of mobilizing and, if it moves aggressively, it could arrive in your area in about ten hours, even with harassing attacks by our planes. The problem is that many of the Apaches have no more Hellfires, so they are being withdrawn. Only those armed Longbows guarding the area around the weapons complex and the airstrip remain. You have a 'go' for the attack, but don't waste time. Get in and get out fast!"

Potter and O'Banyon now knew timing was extremely critical. Their plans assumed that the capture of the complex and the evacuation of the weapons would take close to ten hours. And that was assuming that everything went smoothly, which never was the case.

Day 50 9 A.M. Military Command Center Tehran

At the Ayatollah's insistence, General Zarif was released. Zarif refused to be dissuaded as he adamantly argued with General Hassan. "We must save the Karaj Weapons Complex, no matter the cost. It's the cornerstone of our dominance of the region."

"We have already lost three divisions. The Karaj unit and two from Tehran are rubble. Without air support, even our Alpha Division is vulnerable."

"I don't agree. Our T-90's in Alpha Division can only be taken out by their best missiles. Their supply must be nearly exhausted. Alpha Division must attack full force or the American's will castrate us by removing all of our nukes. The Ayatollah will not respect our shrinking from our God-given responsibilities."

"Perhaps," General Hassan reluctantly bowed to General Zarif's aggressive logic and thinly veiled threat to invoke, once again, his close ties with the Ayatollah. He directed Military Command staff, "All out attack by Alpha Division."

That decision brought a satisfied smirk to General Zarif's strained face. That division would shut down the American invaders. His weapon's factory would be saved.

CHAPTER
SIXTY-ONE

Day 50 9:30 A.M. Karaj Nuclear Weapons Complex

The three-man, desert-camouflaged Gopher squad led by Sgt. Ken Davey, despite being laden with tools and weapons, squirmed through their narrow tunnel under the nuclear complex's perimeter fence. Without the luxury of darkness the squad needed help. The dash across the yard to the ventilation pipe was the problem. It would be suicide in the daylight, especially with the nervous guards on heightened alert.

For that reason, the Boomer squad deliberately set off a series of explosives a hundred meters to the southeast of the perimeter fence. That string of blasts, kicking sand plumes high into the air, startled the already edgy guards. The jumpy defenders knew full well that the Karaj Division had been wiped out, and that they were vulnerable to an attack at any time. Suspending their routine guard activities, the unnerved soldiers sent volleys of fire in the direction of the explosions.

That precisely orchestrated diversion provided the Gophers their opportunity. Careful to stay along a mine-free corridor, they bolted undetected past the preoccupied troops to the ventilation system entrance.

If the diversion was too ferocious the interior defenders would trigger their emergency defenses. Then the gas would flow in the vent pipes and the Gophers would die.

Despite that possibility the Gophers did not hesitate. Two of the Gophers watched with CAR-15s ready as Sgt. Davey sliced through the wire covering the vent intake. Not knowing for sure whether or not he and his companions faced the deadly nerve gas, he grabbed his satchel of specialized tools and dived into pipe hell, as he termed it,

427

for the third and last time. Right behind him the other two commandos crawled into the cramped darkness of the three-foot-diameter
ventilation pipe. Sergeant Davey had been here before, but not under
the imminent danger of death by nerve gas. He knew timing and performance were everything. Life or death for him and his comrades
hung in the balance. If things were working properly, the Gophers had
exactly twenty-five minutes to reach the poison chemical insertion
point and to rig the flow of gas to the advantage of the attackers.

The bright beams of their miner-type lights illuminated the way
as they snaked through the pipe. Pulling forward with their elbows
was an exhausting struggle. The pipe wasn't level. At times it rose
only to fall farther along. At one spot it dropped vertically twenty-five
feet. A grapple hook and ropes were employed to negotiate that
obstacle.

The protective masks covered their faces, but they knew that the
masks provided only limited protection should the gas start flowing
before they could divert its path. Ignoring aching elbows and knees,
they inched on toward their goal. There was no time for rest. If the
crucial valve to the control room closed before they got there, they
and with them many Rangers and Special Forces would die. That
nightmarish reality transcended the pain inflicted by the torturous
crawl.

At last they reached the key valve. "Thank God, it's still open. No
flow yet," a relieved Sgt. Davey exclaimed. "Let's get to work."

Each knew the valve would shut quickly once the control room
operators responded to the next impending attack.

"Hand me the O'Banyon crescent," Sgt. Davey ordered. O'Banyon
had brought back from Baku a strange looking, but precision-
machined, sheet metal plate. The crescent-shaped plate, looking like
a cookie with a huge bite taken out of it, was nearly a foot in diameter and a quarter-inch thick. It was pierced with a steel two-inch-
diameter tube, which was welded perpendicular to the surface of the
plate and protruded about a half foot on each side of the plate. The
tube, if all went well, would soon be passing some very noxious gas to
some extremely surprised control room inhabitants.

Attempting to force the O'Banyon crescent into the open valve
seat, Sgt. Davey surprisingly ran into trouble. "The damned thing
doesn't fit!"

"Let me have a look," said Jim, squirming into position. He had
hung out in his Dad's auto repair garage in Allentown, PA since he was
old enough to walk. There wasn't a mechanical problem that he hadn't

seen. The problem was immediately apparent. Spalling had occurred in the valve seat, probably from previous test closings of the valve.

Day 50 9:55 A.M. South Entrance of Karaj Complex

Suddenly all hell broke loose. Both south guard towers took direct hits from the nearby Longbow. As bodies and tower fragments fell toward the sand, a platoon of Rangers riding HMMWVs and DPVs raced up to the perimeter to rake the remaining south defenders with deadly fire.

The response from the Iranian soldiers was intense. Several Rangers were killed or wounded. After the brief firefight, upon a command from Col. Potter, the Ranger platoon retreated. Potter believed they had surely forced the interior defenders into their emergency procedures. He would know for sure only when he heard from the Gophers. If he didn't hear... He didn't want to think of that possibility.

Meantime the main body of Rangers circled to the north. The true attack would come later from that direction.

Day 50 9:59 A.M. Karaj Ventilation System

After several unsuccessful tries to force the plate into place, Jim frantically scraped and carved at the bulging metal around the valve seat with his combat knife. With a final feverish effort to clear the area of the extraneous metal, he was able to jam the crescent into place.

Only seconds later the valve, on a remote signal from the Karaj control room, slammed into the O'Banyon crescent. The slamming triggered a signal in the control room announcing that the isolation valve had shut and seated properly. The Iranian operators believed that their control room was now safely isolated from the rest of the complex. They had no idea that they were fatally wrong.

"Great work, Jim, but get your mask back on pronto," ordered Sgt. Davey. He knew the next step in the fortress's defensive strategy would be to release the lethal combination of gases into the ventilation system.

Sweating profusely from the extra exertion, the confined space, and the hot protective suits, each man found his face drenched. The masks steamed over, making it even more difficult to work in this tubular Hades. Suddenly they heard the hiss as the iodine aerosol flow commenced.

A muffled order emanated from behind Sgt. Davey's mask, "Hurry! The fucking nerve gas will follow any second. Finish the caulking."

To complete the diversion of the VX nerve gas into the O'Banyon crescent tube, a ten foot length of two-inch-diameter steel-braided flex hose with metal fittings and clamps at each end had to be installed. The commandos forced the ends of the hose into place on the VX injection pipe and the protrusion on the O'Banyon crescent. Even as they hurriedly tightened the clamps, the nerve gas commenced flowing. Now, with the two O'Banyon devices in place, the stream of deadly gas was diverted past the exhausted Gophers, straight into the control room, where the unsuspecting operators and guard commanders would soon be inhaling a lethal dose of their own medicine.

"Whew!" wheezed Sgt. Davey. "That was way too close for comfort."

The victorious Gophers were not finished. Their remaining task was to pull their tired butts out of the elongated tomb and signal Col. Potter and Capt. O'Banyon that things were a "go."

Day 50 10:05 A.M. Perimeter of Karaj Nuclear Weapons Complex

Meanwhile, above ground and just outside the complex, O'Banyon's Persians waited nervously in their DPV. They were poised to move in once they got an all clear from the Gopher squad. A short time ago they watched as the platoon of Rangers, backed by the Longbow, faked an all-out assault on the main south entrance of the Karaj complex. The Boomer squad had activated some of the previously planted homing devices, enabling the Apache Longbow's miniguided missiles to annihilate the two south guard towers and the south perimeter fence. Then they had watched as the Ranger decoys allowed themselves to be driven back by the defenders' mortars.

O'Banyon anxiously awaited word from the Gophers. Finally the welcome message from Sgt. Davey resounded in O'Banyon's headset, "Sand Rat Six, the Gophers hit a homerun."

That's what the Ranger's main force and the Persians had been waiting to hear.

O'Banyon, his juices flowing, radioed Col. Potter, "Chicken Little, this is Sand Rat Six. We are a go for the full-scale assault. The Persians are going in now!"

He then turned to his squad, "Let's go! Hang on and be ready for anything."

The Persian squad's DPV roared, largely uncontested, through a gaping hole where the perimeter fence had earlier stood. With their mounted machine gun firing upon anything that moved, they raced around the southwest corner of the main building.

Unexpectedly they ran straight into six Iranian guards. With submachine guns at the ready, the enemy soldiers were rushing from the rear to reinforce the depleted ranks defending the southern side of the complex. The Iranians immediately spread out and fell to the ground, raking the Persians with point-blank fire.

"Damn it!" O'Banyon's enemy positioning computer had not warned him of their presence. "So much for this worthless piece of crap," he cursed as he opened up with his CAR-15.

Prudhoe Paul aimed their DPV straight at the center of the prone enemy. Operating the M2 heavy machine gun, Sgt. Bill Eagleton cut loose a withering barrage into the prone soldiers. The scattered Iranian guards shot at the charging DPV until silenced by the Persian's assault.

The Persian's vehicle swerved wildly as its driver, Prudhoe Paul, pitched mortally wounded to the sand. Captain O'Banyon leaped over into the drivers seat and upon regaining control of the runaway vehicle, turned back for his fallen comrade. He picked up Paul's riddled body and laid him, as gently as he could, on a pile of ammo in the back.

It was as though he had just lost a brother, but he couldn't let up. Many lives still depended on his attention to duty.

With the brief firefight over, the three remaining Persians drove around the building without further incident until they reached the emergency diesel fuel storage tank.

"The retards located this tank out here in the open. A major goof," Sgt. Eagleton chortled.

The tank stored the diesel fuel for the generator that provided emergency electrical power to the complex. If the facility lost their main power source, the tank's loss meant no power and no lights. Today there was no "if" about it.

Day 50 10:10 A.M. 2 Miles East of Karaj Nuclear Weapons Complex

After creating the earlier explosive disturbance that allowed the Gophers to sneak into the ventilation system, the Boomer squad had raced south across the sand and rocks. Their armed racer followed the weapons complex's power supply lines. They had already visited two towers, attaching satchel charges to the tower legs. The high-voltage lines, held aloft by the towers, delivered electricity to the nuclear complex from the, still intact, Tehran power plants.

Interrogator carried the last forty-pound M-138 satchel charge in a canvas shoulder bag. He deftly positioned it, lashed it to one of the tower's supporting legs, and then primed it with a non-electric blasting cap on the end of a section of time fuse.

Pausing a moment to admire his handiwork, Interrogator, grinning with great satisfaction, congratulated himself, "Beautiful! A masterpiece, if I do say so myself."

After savoring his handiwork for almost too long, Interrogator, with his companions yelling at him, ran back to the militarized dune buggy. The moment Interrogator jumped in, the driver gunned the four-wheeled rocket chair. Clearing about fifty yards, with the sand still swirling from the spinning tires, the Boomers' last charge and the others on the adjacent towers ignited.

The towers, separated from their supports, hung stubbornly in place while clouds of sand and dust billowed upward enveloping their bases. Finally the structures gradually disappeared, slowly melting into the localized sand storms. As they fell, the towers pulled down the high-voltage lines. Massive electrical currents arced from the lines to anything close.

"The sandstorms are alive with color. Wow!" thrilled an ecstatic Interrogator.

A relay somewhere eventually tripped off the power, ending the spectacular light show. With their first demolition job done, the Boomer squad raced back to the staging area to pick up the rest of their explosives. They had just begun their work for the day.

Day 50 10:30 A.M. Karaj Nuclear Weapons Complex

O'Banyon's Persian squad heard the explosions to the east. The subsequent flickering of the exterior lighting told them that the Boomer squad had successfully completed their mission. The message from a hyped Interrogator confirmed that assumption. "Sand Rat Six, the Boomers have pulled the plug."

The flickering lights indicated to O'Banyon that indeed the emergency power had kicked on. He checked the emergency tank's flow meter and confirmed that the emergency diesel generator had automatically started. By his estimate, those in the control room knew none of this for they most likely had already taken their last tortured breath of noxious air, replete with their own poison.

This last source of electricity to the trapped Iranian defenders was soon to be denied. After O'Banyon cut the line, diesel fuel gushed everywhere. Bill Eagleton and Sgt. Jay Nichols, a muscular black Kansan nicknamed Jay Hawk, hurriedly fit a hose and clamp valve in place of the cutaway section of pipe and closed off the flow. The remaining diesel fuel was for their later use.

"Chicken Little Six, the sky has fallen. Let's go finish off this nest of blinded terrorists. We will give you light in exactly fifteen minutes."

Lt. Col. Potter, alias Chicken Little Six, radioed the attack order to the two nearby Longbows. The copters simultaneously let fly their Hellfires. One smashed the heavily fortified back entrance of the compound, and the second missile blew apart the main front entrance. Several more followed, eliminating all but fragments of the exterior guard force. Now it was up to the Rangers.

The main contingent of the interior guard force had been lured toward the southern entrance of the complex by the earlier bluffed attack and the newest explosion. Their advanced ABC masks, which they had donned to protect them from what they believed to be nerve gas, did nothing but inhibit their ability to see. The diverted nerve gas though had cut them off from their strangely silent Command Center. The Iranian soldiers were unaware that the facility operators as well as the guard commander, Colonel Seljuk, sprawled dead inside the locked control room.

Blinded and leaderless, the interior guard force began their defense of the complex in disarray. The disarray soon became chaos and escalated to absolute panic as the main Ranger contingent charged through the demolished rear entrance. The first waves of attacking Rangers raced their DPVs at full speed right through the smoldering outer back entrance with their M2 machine guns ablaze. The overwhelmed guards at the entrance fell quickly under the lightening onslaught.

The lead DPV, with an AT-4 anti-armor rocket launcher, charged down the long, ten-percent grade of the rear entrance tunnel. After the descent, the way was found to be barricaded by a heavily fortified door. The AT-4 rockets blew away that final restraint.

Now Colonel Potter's Rangers were in the main facility, nearly two hundred feet below the surface. The underground cavern echoed deafeningly as the Rangers spread out, pressing the attack on all three levels.

The fortified complex was large with driveways and ramps between levels that allowed the DPVs access to most areas. With their thermal vision gear, the Rangers easily located and attacked the disorganized enemy. The battle rapidly turned into a major rout.

The fighting dispersed throughout the complex as small, terrified bands of guards ran blindly for any cover they could find. They shot wildly at sounds and gun flashes as they retreated. The guards couldn't hide from the Rangers who uncannily pressed their attack. The invaders seemed to be everywhere and saw everything.

As the interior fighting raged, O'Banyon and Eagleton slipped into the back entrance. They raced down into the complex. O'Banyon had stationed Sgt. Jay Hawk at the emergency fuel supply tank with their DPV and Paul's body. Jay's specific orders were to renew the flow in exactly fifteen minutes. In the meantime, he was to guard the fuel supply and make sure Paul's body was evacuated with the first Ranger contingent that headed west for the landing strip.

Wearing their night-vision goggles, O'Banyon and Eagleton continued their sprint past riddled enemy bodies which lay where they had fallen only moments before. The two commandos reached the first level of the complex where the fragmented battle still raged. Their destination was the control room, two levels below. To guard against being killed by friendly fire, they each wore special thermal medallions identifying them as part of the American force. Down and down into the bowels of the complex they raced.

Nearing the polluted control room they grabbed enemy ABC masks and suits from two dead Iranian troopers. "You won't be needing these, but we sure as hell will," O'Banyon explained to the unhearing enemy.

Upon reaching the control room, they donned their newly requisitioned masks and suits. Using portable halogen lights to see, O'Banyon planted a tiny C-4 charge, which blew the control room lock away. Kicking aside two bodies, he pushed into the control center, then closed and promptly barricaded the door behind them to keep the nerve gas contained and away from their troops.

A horrible sight, eerily lit in a crimson hue by the battery-powered emergency lights, greeted them. It was a house of death. The obscene truth, that death by nerve gas was hideous, was sickeningly apparent. The enemy operators and commanders lay lifeless and contorted on the control room floor, eyes burned, yet wide with shock. They had suffered what was intended for the Rangers. The VX nerve gas left their exposed skin blistered, chemically burned and blackened. Their innards obviously had suffered even worse, as the poison liquefied their guts. Gory jell oozed from their body openings. The masks worn by the two Americans, mercifully, diffused the sickening stench that permeated the room.

O'Banyon, even though a hardened veteran, was caught off guard. He fought a nearly overpowering urge to vomit. Never had he witnessed firsthand the appalling effects of biological warfare. He identified one of the debauched bodies as Colonel Seljuk.

"Damn, General piss-ant Zarif isn't here. Paul was right. The cringing coward ran for it," lamented O'Banyon.

Despite the horrible sight, they had to hustle to restore the power, dilute the poison, and evacuate the nuclear weapons before the charging Tehran Division overran them. The Rangers expected the lights to be coming back on in exactly six minutes, so they had to activate the control room fast.

CHAPTER
SIXTY-TWO

Day 50 11:10 A.M. Ranger Controlled Landing Strip

The First Ranger Battalion and the Air Combat Control Team had been operating the landing strip at a frantic and unrelenting pace for three days. Now they were the busiest yet. They were in a race against the clock to get the victorious Third Armored Calvary Regiment evacuated before they were overrun by the charging enemy division.

The line of triumphant fighters, who had thrashed the surprised and out-gunned Karaj Division, stretched with their armor from the makeshift airstrip to the eastern horizon. Air Combat directed the landing, loading and clearing for takeoff of four cargo planes every minute in a maximum effort to lift the Third out of harm's way. The bullfrog-like Globemasters now taking off were ferrying the last of the seventy-ton Abrams away from the Iranian desert strip.

Incongruent with the massive exodus, three C-5 Galaxies had just landed, bringing equipment to the temporary base. Six specialized trucks, designed to carry nuclear weapons and bomb-grade uranium, were expeditiously driven down the ramps of the huge transports. Picking up an escort of two-dozen Second Ranger Battalion troops in DPVs and HMMWVs, the trucks promptly headed east past the interminable queue of evacuating ACR troops and equipment.

Each Ranger knew how precious time was. They had all heard about the advance of the crack Iranian division from the Tehran area. They knew that even as they pressed the specialized trucks rapidly east, the Tehran Division was closing in on them from the east.

Day 50 11:40 A.M. Military Command Center Tehran

General Zarif explained to General Hassan what he had heard

436

about the activities at Baku.

General Hassan listened with rapt attention. "Is this believable, and if so, what do we do about it?"

Zarif was ready for those questions, "Yes, it is true. It is the only way the Americans could have airlifted so many resources in so fast. They must have staged the lift from no more than three hundred miles away. That is why all of our contingency studies showed they could never mount such an attack. The damned traitorous Russians have allowed this to happen by making the Baku base available to the Americans. In fact, they must have encouraged it."

"So what do you recommend?"

"We make both the Americans and the Russians pay for destroying our country. We air express our big nuke to Baku and one of our smaller ones to the Carrier Nimitz."

"Even if our President agrees with those actions, what will the Americans and Russians do in response? You should have heard the American President's warning."

General Zarif knew that it really didn't matter what the Iranian President decided. His medallion in the Zukan Warrior's hands ordained that the missile would be launched. He wished, however, to drag the general and the President to his point of view. His enemies must pay and he must consolidate his power.

"What have they already done to us? Bombed us into the Stone Age with a sneak attack while invading our country, all without provocation. If we have any pride left, we must retaliate with everything we have. Damn the repercussions."

"You make sense, General Zarif. I will request permission from our President."

Day 50 3:40 P.M. Northwest Iran

After receiving General Zarif's medallion, an unusual flurry of activity was transpiring in a most unlikely venue. Near Tabriz an Iranian launch crew rolled the truck carrying the ramjet cruise and its launcher out from under the Mosque. They had avoided attack by the Americans, who were reluctant to strike a holy place. Moreover the Yankees had been tricked into believing a nearby phony cruise was the real thing. The fake had been deployed where American satellites could easily spot it. Sure enough the first wave of American cruise attacks had destroyed the impostor, leaving the real missile and its strategic nuclear warhead untouched. The launch crew worked feverishly under Zarif's attack orders. Soon the Baku Air Base and all of its troops, planes and arms would be vaporized.

Day 50 3:44 A.M. Oval Office Washington, D.C.

President Arthur listened in disbelief to Vice President Foster.

"CIA has finally answered my question, 'where are the two strategic bombs.'"

"Big deal. We know about the one on the tanker. Once the mushroom cloud appeared it didn't take a genius to say there it is, or was."

Foster realized that the just awakened President Arthur had had enough, so he ignored his cross comment. "The other bomb just came out of hiding. It is being readied now. CENTCOM thinks they intend to strike our forces at Baku. The ABL is in position to shoot it down."

"Shoot it down where?"

"On the Iranians."

"Try to bring it down in a remote portion of that country."

"We will try."

CHAPTER
SIXTY-THREE

Day 50 4:45 P.M. Karaj Landing Strip

Col. Potter, with a battle-weary but triumphant band of Rangers, retreated west across the desert toward the landing strip. They clung to anything and everything that moved. Even captured enemy jeeps had been commandeered. They brought with them their wounded and dead, as well as, the captured Russian engineers and technicians. With them also were the six specialized trucks, filled to capacity with the captured nuclear weapons and nuclear weapons ingredients. Potter shuddered as he felt the distant rumbles from the T-90's big guns.

JSOC alerted the colonel, "Chicken Little Six, the Iranian division is charging toward you nearly unchallenged. The Nimitz fighters can only harass them. Those flyboys have used up all of their tank-busting missiles. Better move it out!"

"No shit! What the hell does Command think we are doing, sightseeing?" muttered an irritable Potter.

Only a half dozen Longbows, with a mere dozen Hellfire missiles among them, remained to defend the Rangers' final evacuation from the beat-up air strip. Colonel Potter had left ten of his Ranger explosives experts behind in the Karaj Weapons Complex to work with the Boomer and Persian squads. They were wiring the complex with enough explosives to erase the place permanently. Potter was apprehensive. "They better blow it soon and get the hell out of there. The damned Iranians will overrun them any second."

As if in answer to his desperate prayer, Potter witnessed a massive eruption of earth to the east followed many seconds later by a thunderous rolling boom. The nuclear weapons complex was, at last, history.

Almost as a reflection of that explosion an intense flash of light, many times brighter than the noonday sun, appeared in the north-western sky, lighting up Potter's besieged convoy even though it was midday. The white light quickly turned to an expanding and glowing bright red incandescent cloud of gases. Even before the telltale cloud mushroomed toward the stratosphere, Colonel Potter recognized that the explosion was nuclear, and a big one at that. What the hell was going on?

In an immediate answer to his wondering, JSOC's message crack-led in Potter's earphone. The additional static he presumed was caused by interference created by the nuclear explosion. "Chicken Little Six, keep moving to the airstrip ASAP. Don't worry about the explosion you just saw. Iran's own nuclear weapon was sent down on them, compliments of our ABL."

Potter's grimy ragtag convoy of vehicles finally approached the airstrip. Potter counted four Globemasters and seven Hercules wait-ing for them with their engines revved. He directed the nuclear weapons-bearing trucks to three of the Globemasters. Two trucks lumbered up the rear loading ramps of each of the mammoth trans-ports. The Globemasters, once loaded, were given immediate clear-ance for takeoff by the remaining skeleton crew of the Ranger First. Within minutes they were airborne.

"Whew," Potter sighed in relief, "at least the nuclear weapons are out of here. Now it's our turn."

Similar in sound to an approaching thunderstorm, the rumbling war sounds of the advancing enemy tanks and the pesky U.S. fighters were much closer now. Under the limited protective umbrella of the Longbows, Potter's convoy of troops hurried to the waiting armada of Hercules and the one remaining Globemaster. Potter felt the earth violently shake from the explosions. They were definitely on the busi-ness end of the enemy's 115 mm guns.

The tanks had apparently shifted into a sprint toward the airstrip. Shaking his head in utter admiration for those gritty Nimitz pilots, he watched the weary air wing pilots' last futile attempts to slow the advancing enemy.

Potter surmised that the Iranians had figured out that the Americans didn't have the weapons to stop them anymore and had shifted into high gear. At least the ACR was out of danger and the cap-tured weapons were in the air.

Potter's lieutenants calculated that because of lack of space, they would be forced to leave dozens of vehicles behind. Potter ordered their one remaining Bradley to fire on their own vehicles. They wouldn't leave them for the Iranians.

Just then Potter saw three of the AH-64's launch the last of their Hellfires in the direction of the advancing tanks. The not-so-distant fireballs, followed by the sound of the explosions less than a half minute later, told Potter that the tank forces had just been reduced, but the advance elements were only five miles away. Their potent guns were nearly in range of the airstrip. The desperate, trapped American ground forces had only three defending copters left. No time for the Bradley to finish its job. Potter ordered it onto the remaining Globemaster.

"They are getting close enough to put some of those shells right on us."

"I want all my Rangers and the First Ranger troops on these Hercules! Save one plane for me and my directs. We will wait for O'Banyon's commandos and my demolition boys.

"Pilots get the hell out of here! Take off every ten seconds. Damn protocol! Just go!"

The sixth Hercules took off to the west, climbing rapidly away from the hostile desert with a full load of Rangers. Only one plane remained. Potter and a half dozen Ranger officers, the last transport and three defending Apaches were all that were left. They would wait a little longer for O'Banyon's boys.

After what seemed an eternity to Colonel Potter, a racing DPV appeared in the distance, zigzagging in an evasive pattern toward the nearly deserted airstrip. Then he saw three more closely following it.

"They have those dune buggies in overdrive for sure," exclaimed an elated Potter. "Come on O'Banyon. Move it!"

The shells from the closest enemy tanks were kicking up huge clouds of desert dust as they zeroed in their guns on the fleeing Boomers, Persians and demolition Rangers.

"Chicken Little Six to Longbows, fire whatever is left and evacuate."

The last three Apaches let fly their remaining Hellfires. In abject frustration their pilots pulled away to the northwest, leaving the last transport undefended. The huge explosions of T-90's blowing apart were now much closer. Potter estimated those last destroyed tanks were definitely within range of the abandoned strip. More tanks would roll in momentarily to replace those just knocked out. The big shells would descend on them soon.

O'Banyon's troops raced their speed buggies straight up the ramp into the lone remaining transport. The driver of the last smoking, dust-caked DPV to screech to a halt in the Hercules was Capt. O'Banyon. He hopped down, saluted an anxious Colonel Potter, and reported, "Mission accomplished, sir."

"Seat belt buckled and tray table up, men. We are getting the hell out of Dodge."

Just then a huge explosion blew a hole in the runway in front of the taxing Hercules. Another volley blew to bits some of the HMMWVs and other vehicles, which the Rangers had been riding a short time ago.

"The dumbshits blew those up and saved us the trouble," snickered Potter.

In a desperate quest for liftoff the Hercules taxied painfully slowly along the broken down highway and around the new crater. Another blast hit just a few feet to the side of the besieged transport, causing the right wing to vibrate dangerously. Flying sand from the explosion pitted Potter's window so badly he could no longer see out. He moved to the other side, convinced that the end was near. They weren't going to escape.

Suddenly out of nowhere, screeching low over the desert floor, a squadron of lethally armed F/A-18E Superhornets materialized. They screamed in from the north right over the besieged Hercules. They released sixty AGM-100s.

A huge series of blasts just three miles to the southeast rocked the transport as it gathered speed. Sixty tanks had just become instant piles of smoking scrap. The lone battered Hercules rolled roughly down the worn-out runway. Bouncing wildly, it strained for takeoff speed.

Potter and O'Banyon had no idea that their saviors were fighters from the Nuclear Carrier Kitty Hawk. CENTCOM had ordered them in from the Black Sea as a desperation eleventh-hour move to protect their evacuation.

Also, high above and miles to the north, unseen by the fleeing Americans in the last transport out of Karaj, two B-1B Bombers released tank-destroying sensor-fused weapons. Each of the sub munitions upon reaching the ground searched out a tank. The overhead satellite relayed to each sub-munition accurate position information on the one hundred closest tanks of the third Iranian Division. As the last battered and bruised Hercules finally lifted off the broken highway, the soldiers and their transport were hammered by a series of ear-shattering concussions as the pressure waves from the B-1B munitions buffeted them. A hundred separate explosions had rained down all hell upon the stalled Alpha Division.

PART III
Revenge

CHAPTER
SIXTY-FOUR

Day 60 8 P.M. Atyrau, Kazakhstan

A solitary figure anguished over his awful loss. With shoulders hunched forward as though suffering from a vicious blow to the gut, the tall man shuffled listlessly through the freshly dug mounds of earth. He had staggered slowly across the forlorn landscape for hours. Still the disturbed earth stretched across the Kazakhstan National Cemetery as far as he could see. He stopped at each grave marker and wept. These were his dearest friends and countrymen. Now they were gone.

The soul within Hamad's lean frame was tortured almost beyond endurance. Here lay his loyal soldiers who had trusted him to provide for them. God knows he had tried, but that wasn't good enough. Hundreds of his most courageous guardsmen were dead. His guilt was overwhelming. What had he done wrong? What must he do now? Why didn't Allah provide answers?

Haunting doubt had plagued him since Schilthorn. After that meeting he had seriously questioned whether he belonged with that bunch of Mafia cutthroats. With the likes of Andropov, Goldstein and Zarif maybe the nuclear weapons weren't in better hands after all. Had this war been his fault? He was desperately confused and haunted. No answers were forthcoming, only puzzlements, debilitating guilt and a terrible loneliness. Why had he been spared? Shouldn't he lie here with his men? Had Allah forsaken him?

The surprise Russian attack on the weapons storage complex had been devastating. Only a handful of defenders had survived. What cruel twist of fate had taken him to the Balkenour Cosmodrome on the day of the attack? Did he survive only to be tortured with unquenchable guilt? Was there nowhere to turn?

Tormented almost to madness, Hamad resolved to flee to Kandagach. Maybe the bedeviling questions and horrid realities wouldn't follow him there. Maybe Galena could nourish his wounded soul back to health.

He stomped a half-finished cigarette into the freshly turned earth. Even the damned cigarettes gagged him.

SIXTY-FIVE

Day 83 1 P.M. Oval Office White House Washington, D.C.

"President Arthur, I wish to thank you and Vice President Foster for meeting with me."

"You are our friend. We will always have time for you, President Strahkov," assured Arthur.

"The Joint Eagles aftermath has been far more favorable for your country than for mine," observed a weary Strahkov.

President Arthur knew that to be true. U.S. public opinion polls showed strong approval for his handling of the nuclear threat. Congress was the most upset body as they sensed that the Joint Eagles conflict had siphoned power and credibility away from them to the Presidency. But congressmen could read polls and they understood that there wasn't much they could do about it.

On the other hand, Russia's inability to extricate itself from the clutches of the Mob was becoming clearer daily.

Under a *Duma* ultimatum even the Dzerzhinsky Statue was reinstated at the Moscow FSB headquarters. The partners of the mob, the Chekists, had obviously staged a comeback from Kruschev's purge and were nearly as entrenched as before.

Realizing all of this, President Arthur probed, "We hear troubling reports out of Russia, but please give us your perspective."

"Our logistic support of the military strike against Iran has caused a severe backlash of public sentiment in the Caucus region and in many of our southern republics. Unrest is nearing the boiling point. We fear secessionist movements, if not outright civil war, may break out soon in some of our heavily Moslem *oblasts*. These internal pressures threaten to rip Russia apart."

446

With dark circles under his eyes, Alexander Strahkov looked years older than he had only months earlier. "With our government under siege, the Mafia has seized upon this opportunity to tighten its choke hold on our economy. Kosov, Kostenko's replacement, is extremely unscrupulous and bold. The *Duma* has essentially become his personal forum. Things are really quite desperate. I am becoming more isolated every day."

"Is there anything we can do?" asked a concerned President Arthur.

"Not much, right now. Russia needs strong moral leaders in every branch of government. More honest and courageous leaders must be elected to the *Duma*. Our poets, journalists, philosophers, and religious leaders must come to Russia's aid for they alone can appeal to our people's hearts. If they mount an aggressive campaign to expose the criminals for what they are, maybe our lost sense of morality can be restored.

"That is the only way the renewal, called for so many years ago by Solzhenitsyn, can be sparked. The people need to become indignant, disgusted and repulsed with the corruption and vice that permeates Russia today. The masses must be roused to once again be proud to be Russian. They must be inspired by the legacy of the martyred prophet, Sumurov, to live on a higher moral plain.

"One thing you could do that would help. Could you allow us to publicize that Mrs. Andrew is Viktor Sumurov's granddaughter? That might help remind the masses of him and encourage some of our writers to follow in his footsteps."

Foster bristled at that suggestion. Without hesitation he responded, "No. She and her husband would be placed in great danger. I owe it to them to guarantee their safety."

Sensing the personal depth of Foster's resolve, Strahkov let the issue drop without further argument for the moment. However he mumbled something about an opportunity lost.

As a test of Strahkov's sincerity in dealing with the worsening criminal problem, President Arthur queried, "Have you tried to bring Hamad Barak on as the leader of the FSB? I understand that the late Kruschev marked Barak as the one man who should replace him."

"Good question. That is next on my agenda. After I leave here, I am flying to Kazakhstan. It's reported that Barak is holed up in Kandagach. Apparently he still grieves deeply. His loss of so many guardsmen devastated him. Yet, Kruschev precisely predicted that reaction. A deep depression he said would set in, yet he believed that

Barak was resilient enough to pull through while harboring a deep hatred for the Mafia leadership. Let us hope that Kruschev's predictions remain accurate. I will try to convince Barak to consider the job of FSB head. Pray that our talks go well."

Changing subjects, Strahkov inquired, "Can you brief me on the Andropov legal situation over here. We have trouble understanding why his chances to go free aren't nil. What goes with your justice system?"

"President Strahkov, sometimes guilty people go free here since our society's inclination is to err on the side of protecting the citizens' rights against a strong central government. Those safeguards offer someone like Andropov, who has unlimited financial resources, the opportunity to manipulate those protections to avoid being brought to justice. This could be one of those times."

"Then extradite him to us. We can take care of business. We are not overrun by greedy lawyers yet. Anyway, he is not a citizen of your country."

Foster resisted jabbing Strahkov that if they could take care of business so damned well, why was the place overrun with criminals. Which was worse, he mused—being overrun with criminals or lawyers? Stifling his thoughts, he conceded, "Maybe we should consider extradition."

The Andropov team of attorneys had been surprisingly inept at defending Andropov. Foster was aware of the opinion of Garrison and Liz that the legal ineptness signified that Goldstein was winning control of the Mafia.

President Strahkov reiterated his position, "We will commence extradition proceedings. Russia can deal with the traitor swiftly and surely. The *Duma* has already passed a resolution recommending extradition."

Foster was confused about that *Duma* action. How strange. Why would a *Duma*, controlled by Kosov, want Andropov extradited? How did that square with Goldstein's ascendancy to Mafia chieftain? If Goldstein was winning why did Kosov want Andropov brought to Russia? Maybe it was a Goldstein scheme to tighten the noose around Andropov's neck. Maybe the Mafia machine, deeply entrenched in the Russian bureaucracies, could more easily murder, or free, Andropov if he was in Russia.

After mulling these possibilities over Vice President Foster observed, "You really need a favorable election result in the *Duma* this fall. You could use some allies in that legislative body."

"You are right about that. We are hopeful. A surprising and unexplainable surge of support for reform candidates has emerged."

CHAPTER
SIXTY-SIX

Day 113 8:30 A. M. Loon Lake Ontario, Canada

Cloaked in the early morning's calm, Ben's canoe slipped silently across the tranquil bay. Seemingly unbothered by his passing craft, the nearby loons took turns diving into the lake's depths where a feast of small fish awaited. Surfacing after nearly a minute of underwater gorging, one of the red-eyed, black-and-white-checked birds uttered a haunting call to its mate.

As the bird's song rolled across the still water, Ben puzzled about its meaning. Perhaps the ancient fowl bragged that the fishing was good, or fussed about Ben's interloping canoe. Maybe it was merely saying to its mate, "Your turn to feed." Since Laura had spotted their nest just above the waterline across the bay from their cabin, he figured that the fascinating birds would remain their neighbors for the season.

The loons' loud repertoire of cries consisted of four distinct calls, calls not necessarily restricted to daylight hours. Surprisingly, their noise occasionally increased at night. The sporadic nocturnal commotion led him to wonder if the two loons were hosting a party on the sprawling lake.

Each call presented a unique sound and meaning. One song resembled trills, another yodeling, but the loon's plaintive wail was the defining sound of the wild northern lake country. Ben found that the birds' presence and their serenades assuaged his anxieties. Their variety of antics provided a welcome tonic, helping him unwind from his part in the Joint Eagles episode. His lingering fear for Laura's and his safety magically subsided when their song filled the air.

His damn old football-damaged knees hurt from kneeling. The canoe demanded that agonizing posture to ensure the craft's stability.

Dumped once in the cold lake had been quite enough to drive that lesson home. With a deft rotation of his wrist, he stroked the oar through the water. Properly employed, the paddle served a dual purpose of propulsion and steerage, removing the necessity of switching the paddle from side to side. How many more tricks simplifying life's daily tasks in this rugged North Woods environment were there to master? Plenty, Ben suspected, answering his own question.

His canoe slipped to the side of the small six by thirty-foot plank dock, which served their isolated log cabin. The only other cabin, or cottage, to borrow the Canadians' terminology, was a half mile away. It housed a special occupant, an FBI Agent he knew simply as Ray.

Despite Ben's arrival at the shore, the dock and their moored red and silver boat were the only visible signs of civilization. All that faced him otherwise was green, with blue sparkling above and below. What a change! A month ago in late April, when they first arrived in their exile paradise, their cabin, surrounded by majestic pines, firs, and spruces, could still be seen from the lake. Now, however, the burgeoning foliage of paper birch, aspen and alder added to the enveloping green, which screened the cabin's existence. The aroma of burning birch logs drifted down to the lake, providing pleasant odoriferous proof of the cabin's proximity. The smoke from the crackling fire in the cabin's stove tickled his nose, making him sneeze.

Ben tossed his fishing rod, tackle box and landing net onto the tiny dock and retrieved the dripping string of four wiggling walleyes from the water. He had worked hard for his catch by tantalizing the fish with a variety of lures and bait.

The challenge derived from winter's reluctance to loosen its grip on these northern lakes. The last of the ice had melted only a few weeks ago. The cold water ordained that the walleyes remained in the deepest holes, sluggish and not yet ready to ascend into the shallow water for spawning. He was still learning where the best holes were in this lake; nevertheless, he and Laura had always caught enough to eat.

Anxious to show Laura his morning catch, he climbed up the moderately inclined trail to their forested retreat. Skirting a white pine, holding Laura's hummingbird feeder, he smiled at the flourishing garden of columbine, wild roses and violets beneath the lofty evergreen. She had found the plants in the surrounding woods and transplanted a sprinkling of her favorites to this spot, where they could be admired from the cabin's side window. For some varieties it was still too early to bloom, though the columbine and wild roses, Laura told him, would flower soon. From the table where she spent hours writing, she could watch the hovering and darting of the energetic ruby-throated hummingbirds as they fought turf wars above her wild-flower garden.

"It's cold out there, Ben. Come in," Laura invited, while throwing another log on the fire.

"You are right, honey. My fingers have lost their feeling," Ben exaggerated slightly while pouring a cup of freshly perked coffee.

"You couldn't survive without your fix of coffee, could you?"

"No," Ben admitted as his cold hands readily grasped the warm mug. The aroma and the taste of the coffee brew seemed to him as much a part of this place as the loon's plaintive wail.

Ben's thoughts involuntarily turned to Laura and their predicament. In many ways, she loved being here. After all that had intervened in their lives, she still rejoiced for this opportunity to live and write in a North Woods paradise. Except for one stumbling block, she seemed able to take the losses and disappointments and move forward. She feared she would lose him. She was terrified that the Mafia would come after him sooner or later. He thought it an exaggerated fear, yet, he too was worried.

"I see you had some luck. What did they bite on?"

"The yellow jig and minnows. I caught these in that same hole we fished yesterday. They haven't moved out of there yet, but they put up a little better fight today."

Ben had picked up on how Laura loved everything about these interwoven woods and lakes. She untiringly recorded the species of birds, trees, plants and forest animals. Her insatiable appetite to partake of every nuance of this environment, except for the mosquitoes and flies, amazed him. These natural surroundings and the quiet time had revitalized her writing. This wild northern landscape magically stimulated her creative impulses. The genesis of several poems, essays and short stories, as well as the developing biography on Sumurov, lay strewn about on the table.

Ben warmed up with his steaming coffee, but best of all, he downed several of Laura's delicacy, apple-slice pancakes. After breakfast, she handed him a couple of pans and unceremoniously put him to work. "The guy that catches them cleans them."

He couldn't argue with that logic, so he headed back down the trail to the water's edge to filet his catch. Unsheathing the buck knife, he ran his thumb testingly across the blade, eyeing the fish for a cut. He found that a keen blade made the job a breeze. Perhaps another North Woods secret discovered without a crisis being the teacher.

Ben and Laura had reluctantly accepted the FBI's offered protection. Ben remembered how surprised Foster and Garrison had been at Laura's insistence upon a remote northern locale for their new lives. She vigorously bargained with them that their exile must be a secluded North Woods setting. When the FBI found this cabin and showed them pictures and maps, they both reacted enthusiastically. It didn't matter when Garrison warned them that it might be too remote and lacking in modern conveniences. To the contrary, that very isolation provided the lure. If they must lose contact with their past, then they might as well pick a rustic setting where they could enjoy their solitude.

As Ben ran the filet knife along the cleaning board, separating skin from flesh, he recalled Garrison's proposed compromise. The Andrews could stay in the cabin in the late spring, summer and fall months, but would have to move into nearby Thunder Bay when the lakes began to freeze. Once the long Canadian winter closed in, the logistics for their protection at the cabin would be impossible.

Once all had been set for their switch in identities, they bade an emotional farewell to their friends and Ben's parents. Garrison had assured Ben that his parents would be well taken care of and protected.

Ben and Laura sold their house and Laura's beloved bookshop in Tulsa, and her outstanding equine jumper, Champion. She insisted, though, that she be allowed to save many of her treasured volumes, including all of Sumurov's works given her by Dudaev. They placed their limited estate, resulting from the sales, in a trust for safekeeping while they lived out their new identities, hidden from the Mob. The FBI Witness Protection and Relocation program developed their new profiles, a reclusive farm couple from northern Iowa, who moved to Canada and took up residency in western Ontario Province.

The trip to their new lives had been circuitous. With only a few suitcases holding their clothes and their few precious possessions, they first flew to London as Ben and Laura Andrew. Then with the use of interim identities, they were whisked via train through the Euro tunnel from England to Paris. Once in Paris, they met bureau agents who set them up with their new identities as the Iowa couple. They had at that moment become officially and legally George and Ethel Hensley. As he washed the filets in a pan of lake water, Ben recalled what an eerie sensation that had been. Legally Ben and Laura Andrew existed no more.

Flying from Paris to Montreal, under their aliases, the Hensleys, they had little except each other to remind them of their true identities. Yet both had kept a few mementos with which they would not part. Ben held on to his FBI hat, a picture of Black Bear, Laura's unfinished sonnet, and also a big bag of Starbuck's French Roast coffee beans. Laura retained a dozen of her favorite books, the historically significant Sumurov materials and Marina's letters sent to her by Dudaev, as well as pictures of her mother and son. It had been an uneasy juxtaposition into an unknown future for them both.

The knowledge that she was actually Viktor Sumurov's granddaughter and her project to write a Viktor Sumurov biography helped her deal with this separation from their previous world. She rationalized that maybe she wasn't giving up everything. With a chance to write about her martyred grandfather, she could, maybe someday, showcase some of his previously secret works and acquaint a new generation with the faith and courage of this man. This possibility, Ben saw, gave her renewed purpose.

Deep down inside, Ben, having been attacked and marked for extinction by the Mafia, felt no real sense of security despite the FBI's best efforts. However, he tried not to reveal his nervousness to Laura. She didn't need any handicaps as she labored over her compositions. Despite his best efforts to defeat the Mafia, he had struck only a small blow, but in the process he had stirred up a hornet's nest and brought danger to Laura. He felt guilt and sadness about her being in danger and uprooted. But when he expressed his regrets to Laura, she squelched that as silliness and needless guilt. In no uncertain terms, she told him that she was proud of him and everything he had done. She went on to say that being with him was what she desired most. Danger had forced its way into their lives and that was just how it was.

When Ben returned from his fish cleaning duties, Laura took the filets. "Some for lunch. The rest I'll freeze."

An old propane refrigerator, standing against the wall near the back door, had a freezer compartment, which allowed her the luxury of keeping any extra fish they had caught.

After hanging his navy-blue parka on the hook behind the front door, Ben lingered near the corner table. Staring out through the big front window and then the single side window, which framed Laura's flower garden, he fumbled curiously with the papers strewn on the rustic pine table.

The front picture window offered an expansive view, mystically penetrating beyond the dense stand of trees. Ben could see across the bay and beyond to the main body of Loon Lake. Ben and Laura had thrilled to a month of mesmerizing Canadian sunsets framed by that grand window.

This far north the sun did not really set. Rather, it descended slowly, sliding to the north as if buoyed by the distant treetops. From their cabin vantage point, they had watched as the late evening sun reluctantly vanished behind the wooded peninsula across the bay only to reappear beyond that spit of land as a blazing orange fireball. Finally, the stubborn sun would lose its battle with the lake. Then in apparent defiance of that defeat, the most dramatic colors of the evening blazed forth across the heavens and the lake. The water aggrandized the burst of beauty by mimicking the sky's sizzling red, violent orange and cool violet hues. Amazingly the kaleidoscope of colors endured far into the night, as even those last vestiges of light continued a northward drift.

"I see several new pages. What about?"

"Yes. I tried something new. I took a time out from Viktor's biography. Read it. Give me your comments. I labeled it 'Beginnings.' It's one of the more esoteric writings I ever attempted. I am thinking that maybe I should just stick to describing the flight of the humble hummingbird and leave the exploration of the deeper meanings of life to other, more erudite, authors."

Ben picked up the fresh pages and started to read, pausing to ask, "What prompted you to select the topic beginnings?"

"Maybe our banishment from our old lives and loved ones lost. Or maybe it was Dudaev's revelations that prompted the thoughts. In many ways I feel that we are at a new beginning. Perhaps that is life, a series of beginnings. Although, leaving so much and so many behind could be construed to be the opposite. Life could be negatively viewed as a series of endings. But if I thought of it that way, I would not find any hope or purpose for our continued existence."

Ben nodded and sat down at the table to read the fresh lines. He knew what she meant. They did not have the luxury to give in to fear or sadness. Rather, they had to search for God's purpose at each stage of their journey.

Laura's essay pondered whether Ben's and her recent traumas were ordained by a Creator in order to secure a greater good for His people. Ben had certainly blunted the Mafia's evil plans. Somehow she doubted that was merely accidental, but perhaps it was willed by a higher power. Was she spirited to this beautiful and quiet exile to capture the life of the martyred Sumurov in a manner that would inspire? Or was that presumptive, and merely a lame rationalization for their predicament? Could she, or anyone, possibly comprehend the Creator's ultimate purpose? Rather than strive to understand that purpose, should she instead humbly accept her entrusted role? Would that acquiescence to a higher authority supply meaning and fulfillment?

Ben dropped the unfinished papers reverently back on the table, "You do have a gift."

"Thanks, Ben. Maybe it will turn out okay. You know, my grandfather didn't go into self-imposed exile. He fought courageously with his last tortured breath for the country he loved. He didn't shrink from what God called him to do. Sometimes I feel that I should be out there, in public, writing for those who need hope. But instead here I hide.

"Marina's letters puzzle me. It's almost as though she and Dudaev were evaluating you and me. For what? Or is it just my over-active imagination?"

Laura sat down next to Ben and with tears in her eyes admitted, "But I don't know what I want and I don't understand God's will for us. I don't want to fight anymore and I don't want you to fight either. All I want is to be here with you forever. Nobody has the right to take our last bit of personal happiness away."

"No. Nobody does." Stroking her soft dark hair, Ben cradled Laura's head to his chest.

Sobbing deeply, Laura said, "I don't know, Ben. I have the rather helpless sense that even up here, we are still at the mercy of forces that won't allow us life, much less a shared and peaceful life."

"Your writings are beautiful, but you are worrying entirely too much, Laura. You must believe in what you wrote in *Beginnings*. Perhaps it is God's will that we are both here together in this woodland paradise. Let's live each day He grants us to the fullest. That is all we can do. I believe that good will come of all of this just as you wrote."

Laura blurted out her biggest worry, "I don't think the Mafia is ever going to let you be."

Ben lifted her teary-eyed face toward his and kissed her tenderly. "Laura, Laura! Stop it! The protection Brad arranged for us will work. You will see."

Ben desperately elaborated, trying to assure her, and himself, "Did you notice that the same two game wardens are at the marina every time we are there? The FBI has placed three guards up here with us, those two at the marina and our Boreal Peninsula neighbor, agent Ray."

Laura had named their home, Boreal Peninsula, in honor of the explosive variety of Boreal and Great Lakes plants and trees that grew around their new home.

"If we are so safe here with our new identities, why do they need to be guarding us?"

"I don't know," Ben admitted. "Maybe it's just Mark and Brad being extra cautious. Remember, they said if there was even a hint of trouble they would signal us either through the FBI guards up here, or through your favorite, the Thunder Bay radio."

"Yes, I know. I am forced to suffer CTOB's awful music every evening. After one or two twangy songs the message board finally comes on to relieve my pain."

"At least we hear occasional snippets of news about the aftermath of the war," replied Ben, desperately searching for anything to turn Laura from her worries. She still suffered spells of depression stemming, he assumed, from Marina's death and this was one of those times.

"Only bits since the Canadians could care less about Joint Eagles."

Acknowledging her own negativity, Laura proposed a cure, an adventure. "Let's take a couple of days and explore the string of lakes to the north."

"Great idea. I have wanted to investigate up there. They say several moose were spotted browsing in that stretch of lakes. Let's get everything ready and I will tell Agent Ray of our plans. We can start out early tomorrow morning. There are a couple of portages to negotiate so it's the canoe."

"Our knees should be mush after two days of paddling in that torture chamber."

Ben laughed, "Laura, that's the last negative thought you are allowed."

CHAPTER
SIXTY-SEVEN

Day 115 Early Morning Odessa, Ukraine

During an interlude between briefings by his various cell leaders, Dudaev evaluated the latest report. For security reasons, he kept cell leaders separate, so separate in fact that only one of them knew the identity of any of the others. His Moscow leader, charged with influencing the outcome of the upcoming *Duma* elections, had just reported with extreme optimism that many of their candidates were in position to win. The composition of the *Duma* could shift dramatically away from the hard-liners and communists.

Despite that optimistic assessment, it appeared that Kosov still presented a problem, since he would probably retain great influence in the legislative body. That Russian division leader of the Mafia, no matter whether he reported to Goldstein or Andropov, was hurting Russia terribly and presented an imposing challenge to President Strahkov. Through the *Duma* and the Mafia he thwarted nearly all of Strahkov's initiatives.

Until the *Duma* could be changed and Kosov dealt with, Dudaev had advised Strahkov not to bring Barak in to head the FSB. For Barak to have a fighting chance of ripping out the Chekist plague, a more favorable legislative environment must first be created. According to the predictions he had just heard, the next election would represent a significant step in moderating the *Duma*.

For the first time in his organization's history Dudaev was sorely tempted to authorize an assassination. Kosov must be removed for Russia to have a realistic chance of freedom from the Chekist tyranny and the Mafia's plundering. The Mafia had weathered Joint Eagles remarkably well

Since fleeing Hartford, Dudaev had gone underground. He surreptitiously moved from city to city and country to country to frustrate the Mafia's attempts to track him. How ironic that he was now here in Odessa where, sixty-five years ago, his uncle had placed him and his sister on a ship to America. Geographically he had come full circle. Was there a significance to that beyond the curious? Had his life's work also come full circle?

Before leaving for tonight's intelligence briefing, Dudaev, after studying the assessment of each *Duma* candidate's chances, assigned an appropriate sum of money for each campaign from his ample treasury. His treasurer would accomplish the distribution of monies.

Day 115 Two Hours Later Deserted Wharf on Odessa's Black Sea Coast

The late night breeze chilled Dudaev, but not as much as the alarming message.

Dudaev's intelligence chief reported, "The Thieves-in-Law top assassins entered Canada two weeks ago. Through forged identities and with stolen cars and boats they set up shop in Thunder Bay. They chartered a plane to tour the forests and lakes north and west of Thunder Bay. They are after somebody important. They have cased the area with a fine-tooth comb and thrown their best resources into what is shaping up as a big time hit."

Even though it was dark, the woman providing the report was sure she detected a tear in Dr. Dudaev's eye. She had never before witnessed a show of emotion by the Professor. Why would this news affect him so strongly?

Dudaev knew very well who the killers were after. Before Dudaev had disappeared, Liz assured him that Ben and Laura would be safe, since the FBI had placed them in the witness protection program and moved them to the vicinity of Thunder Bay.

After a long pause Dudaev asked, "Who do we have tracking them?"

"Leoneski."

"Can he kill them all?"

"Kill the killers? How intriguing! He is more a stalker than a killer, although he might be able to get one or two of them if they separate."

"Tell him to try. Track them wherever they go. He must do anything that he can."

A troubled Dudaev took stock. What was happening to him? He had ordered killings tonight and had thought about another. He had never resorted to these extremes before in the decades-long struggle for the future of Russia. Was he any better than the Mafia? Did the ends justify the means? He was old and didn't have long to live. Was he trying to force things along on his timetable rather than God's?

Dudaev grabbed his cell phone. He must warn Garrison. Through his organization's secure communication satellite, his call arrived at a phone in FBI headquarters.

"Hello, this is Garrison's office. May I help you?"

"Get me Garrison immediately. I must talk with him. This is Professor Dudaev."

After delivering the warning about the Andrews' eminent danger, Dudaev concentrated on his last big task. Despite his age he must assure the survival of his organization, for their goal of a free, democratic and moral Russia was not yet realized. His group must transcend his leadership. After much discussion he and each of his cell leaders had agreed upon who should succeed him. Yet the chosen pair were now in mortal danger.

He gave an envelope containing a letter for Ben and Laura to his security chief. If the couple somehow survived the pending attack, Dudaev's appeal to them must be delivered.

Once the security official left, Dudaev smiled and lit his stubborn pipe. The memory of Viktor Sumurov's daughter, Marina, was a special blessing to him. The image of that beautiful woman would never fade from his heart. Was his love for Marina influencing his choice of leaders? Yes and no, he admitted. Her opinion had carried great weight with him. Years ago she had written one very special letter to him which he had kept to this day. In it she expressed her respect for Laura's husband, Ben. She had elaborated on the leadership skills, strength and courage of her son-in-law. She had noted that her daughter's literary talents and historical perspective complimented Ben's strengths. Under certain circumstances they could be a most formidable force. When working together, they were as a pair of eagles ruling their domain from on high.

Ben's phenomenal performance in Joint Eagles and Laura's outstanding articles on Starovoitova and the Chekists confirmed the late Marina's opinion. The Joint Eagles leaders had strongly vouched for Ben's leadership qualities. The couple had, so far, not only survived the Mafia assault upon Ben, Black Dan, and Amerion, but they had contributed mightily to the mission. If God somehow spared Ben and Laura then there could be no doubt that their ascendancy to leadership was ordained. With the letter he enclosed Marina's letter of evaluation. He needed it no longer and it would help Ben and Laura better understand why they were chosen to lead. They were his and Marina's Joint Eagles. He prayed that they would survive and Sumurov's legacy to Russia would finally be consummated through their management of his organization.

CHAPTER
SIXTY-EIGHT

Day 115 3:30 P.M. Eagle Lake Marina Ontario, Canada

A dark-blue Chevy dually super cab, towing a boat-trailer, arrived at the Eagle Lake Marina dock. The three fishermen inelegantly backed the truck and trailer down the ramp. They obviously hadn't backed a trailer often. After several futile attempts where they came closer to launching the truck than the boat, the incompetents finally floated the twenty-foot fiberglass vessel, complete with cab and inboard motor.

The men towed it triumphantly across the water to the nearest dock tie-up point. Outfitted as fishermen out for the day, they roughly tossed their fishing poles, tackle and coolers from the truck into the waiting boat. Such little regard for one's expensive fishing gear was not the norm.

Just as they were ready to shove off, two uniformed officials, ostensibly Fish and Game wardens, strolled down the dock to the boat and asked to see their fishing licenses and identifications. The sportsmen's IDs attested that they were from Thunder Bay. The Fish and Game officials, actually the FBI agents Ben had spotted earlier, noted that all appeared in order, but questioned the fishermen, "Are you here for the day?"

The fisherman at the boat's controls responded with a slight hint of an East European accent, "Ve are fishing for Valleyes and Northerns in the lakes and the river."

After a cursory check, the Fish and Game officials wished them good luck and good fishing and watched as the high-powered boat sped away from the dock and out onto Eagle Lake. A half dozen groups of sportsmen had embarked from the dock today and up to

461

now none had triggered any suspicions.

Agent-in-Charge, Doug Christopher, asked, "What do you think, Keith?"

"Something is not right about them. Those guys don't strike me as the typical Canadian fishermen coming through here. Too many coolers, no landing net, too rough on the poles and no Canadian accent, eh!"

"Hell, they didn't even wave like Canadians."

"You mean, the reluctant stiff arm in the air like it's an imposition to acknowledge your presence?"

"Exactly. Plus, no one has fished the river yet. They are the first using an inboard rather than an outboard motor. They seemed phony to me."

"They sure couldn't back a trailer worth a damn. I thought for a while they would have to carry the boat to get it in the water."

"Keith, call the Mounties. Initiate a trace on their truck tag. Also follow up on their fishing licenses with the Ontario Provincials. Have the Canuks run through the standard NCIC check, as well as Interpol, just to be safe. While you are doing that, I will alert Ray. From his cabin lookout he could see their boat if it approaches the Andrews' cabin."

Agent Keith Brockhurst went about the business of calling the authorities.

After giving Ray a heads up, Agent-in-charge Christopher, with a growing uneasiness, watched through his binoculars until the speeding boat rounded a point of land and disappeared.

Day 115 3:45 P.M. Fishing Boat Eagle Lake

"Do you think they suspected us?"

"*Da.*"

"Good. The trap is vorking. They vill soon be fish bait."

Day 115 4:45 P.M. FBI Cabin on Boreal Peninsula

After the heads-up call from Christopher, Ray grabbed his rifle and radio and climbed the ladder to his lookout nest on top of his little cabin. He watched anxiously for the return of the Andrews and for the suspicious boat. From his perch high on Boreal Ridge, he intently scanned across Loon Lake toward the Dakota River. He saw no sign of the suspects' boat. Finally, though, to his great relief, he did spot the Andrews' canoe lazily drifting across Loon Lake from the north. He put his high-power scope on them and verified that they were okay.

Day 115 5 P.M. Loon Lake

It was late afternoon as Ben and Laura paddled their canoe across Loon Lake. Soon, they would be able to stretch their aching legs. Despite their sore limbs, it had been a delightful two-day trip. They proudly claimed a string of Walleyes.

As if offering a grand finale to their journey, a pair of eagles majestically circled higher and higher until they were mere dots in the blue sky. Laura watched as the dots merged.

Laura stopped paddling and exclaimed excitedly, "Ben! Ben! Look at those two. See! See how high they are. This is the eagles' rendition of sealing their marriage vows. With locked talons and eyes fixed on each other, they will free-fall faster and faster. Just seconds before they crash to earth they will break apart."

Ben watched transfixed. "Wow! You are right! That is exactly what they did."

"After that ceremony, they remain paired until one of them dies. Indian legend has it that their spirits will soar united forever.

"Maybe it's an omen, Ben. I hope it's a good one, but I just can't shake the feeling that we are in danger here. Something terrible is going to happen."

Ben, at a loss for soothing words, continued silently paddling. Even this grand excursion hadn't changed anything. Laura's apprehensions remained. If only he could somehow exorcise their fears. Reality, though, prevented either of them from believing that personal safety was achievable.

After the sight of the soaring eagles, a jumble of words fought for form in Laura's head. She silently rejoiced, "That's it! *Unite our souls. Like eagles, let us soar.* Tonight I will surprise Ben by finishing his poem." She knew that the old romantic still carried it in his wallet. For the moment her melancholy was abated.

Day 115 6 P.M. Eagle Lake Marina

Agent Christopher had remained extremely nervous since he and Brockhurst had watched the three suspicious yokels come through earlier this afternoon.

"Keith, there is radio gear in our boat. I say we go looking for that phony bunch. The Canadian authorities can still contact us once they run their checks. Ray says he hasn't seen their boat come out of the Dakota. I know the fishing ain't that good in the damn river. Something is amiss."

"Something is rotten and it's not fish."

"Give Ray a call, Keith. Alert him that we are coming his way. Ask him if he has seen anything recently."

With growing angst the agents roared away from the marina dock. Before Brockhurst could call Ray, a call came in from the Mounties.

Brockhurst grabbed the receiver, "Yes. What did you find out?"

After the message from the Mounties, Brockhurst, his face flushed with nervous energy and the biting wind, turned to Christopher, "There's a shit load of trouble! The truck and boat are stolen. The names don't check. They are frauds."

"They could be a Mafia hit squad. Call Ray. Place him on high alert. If this gets any worse, we better call Garrison. Also, alert the Mounties that we may need their help. It's full throttle for the river."

"This is too easy," puzzled Brockhurst.

"Yep! It's almost like they wanted us to figure them out."

Day 115 6:15 P.M. Nykratin Nation Land

Three men in camouflage gear arrived at the far east end of Loon Lake. They had remained unseen by taking a little used jeep trail through the densely wooded Nykratin Nation's land. Their dirty black four-wheel drive Bronco towed an old boat outfitted with a fifty-horse outboard and a smaller trolling motor. They promptly launched the aluminum-hulled, dark-brown vessel. Two of the thugs, armed with suppressed sniper rifles and MP-5 submachine guns, boarded the craft.

The third man backed the Bronco and boat trailer into some tall brush where it couldn't be seen from the air or land unless one stumbled right on it. He checked his weapons and settled in for a restless wait.

The two pros set the boat upon a course toward the Andrews' Boreal Peninsula some five miles to the west. The enlarged photos, which they carried, revealed the exact location of the two target cabins. They had flown over this area several times on reconnaissance missions. The leader studied the photos one last time, while the other thug guided the boat toward the Andrews' home. Throttled down, the fifty-horse motor propelled the boat at a leisurely pace that would place them near the peninsula in twenty minutes.

While still a mile away, they switched to the quieter trolling motor to avoid being heard on their approach. Finally they killed even the small motor and cautiously paddled the last hundred yards to the east shore of Boreal Peninsula. They knew from their cohort's radio messages that the agent at the cabin should be distracted, just as planned, looking to the west for their partners' boat. Since they approached from behind him, the agent was a sitting duck.

Day 115 6:20 P.M. Dakota River

"Our scanner just picked up a message. Something like ve're on schedule to arrive at peninsula at 6:40. The voice had a thick Eastern European accent. What the hell could that mean?"

"I don't know, Keith, and I sure as hell don't like any of this. Hand me my weapon. Be ready for anything."

The wind had kicked up out of the southwest and stung Doug's eyes. Low clouds menacingly rolled in, graying what had been a bright sunny day. The two lawmen had learned that the weather up here was full of sudden unpredictable turns. As they sped through the river, a call came in on their radio, "This is Garrison."

"What's up?"

"Big trouble is headed your way."

"It's already here," replied Brockhurst, as he rapid-fire recounted the day's events.

"Be careful. This is an elite team of assassins. It's not like them to be careless. Be damned cautious. I smell a trap."

"That possibility entered our heads, too."

"We are calling the Canadian authorities for backup. Tell Ray to get down to the Andrews' cabin, pronto. He must warn them."

As Brockhurst started to respond, their speeding boat rounded a tight bend in the river. A sudden spray of bullets riddled the craft. Agent Brockhurst let out an agonizing cry and pitched over the side before he could answer Garrison or fire a shot. The radio he had been using exploded into a thousand pieces.

Christopher felt a sting in his left shoulder. He recognized the warm flow of blood down his arm. The reserve fuel tank was hit and gas emptied onto the boat's floor. There was only one thing he could do that made any sense. He could at least even the odds.

Swinging the speeding boat around full circle, he headed, with a wide-open throttle, straight for the shoreline where the shots were originating. Still twenty yards away from the ambushers, he focused on the partially hidden boat lying behind two rotting Jack pines that had fallen from the riverbank into the water.

The three thugs fired automatic weapons at him and his boat. Several more bullets found their mark. Though near death he somehow still gripped the wheel, holding the boat on course. Another round of fire racked Christopher's body. Miraculously, though, for another fraction of a second, the boat, guided by a dead man, remained true to its course. Saturated with gas, it plowed over the nearest fallen pine and cut into the Mafia boat. The collision ignited a conflagration that consumed everyone in the two boats.

Day 115 6:40 P.M. Ray's Cabin

The gusty southwest wind masked all sounds from the lake. The lowering clouds rapidly reduced visibility. With his rifle in the lookout support ready to fire, Ray had to completely rely upon sight. From the vantage point above his cabin, he squinted as he scanned the area to the west. Warned by his two comrades that trouble could come from that direction, he ignored the eastern section of the lake. Since the warning call, he had heard nothing from them. The eerie silence was highly unusual. They were intending to sail through the Dakota River and across Loon Lake to his location. He should be able to spot them by now, but they were nowhere to be seen. A few minutes ago he thought he caught a flash of light from the vicinity of the river, but under these deteriorating weather conditions he couldn't be sure.

He tried his radio, "Keith. Keith. Come in. This is Ray."

An alarmed Ray received no reply.

Suddenly a call came across his radio. While still peering to the west he grabbed the receiver. It was Garrison.

Day 115 One Minute Earlier 6:39 P.M. Garrison's Office Washington, D.C.

After the transmission from Brockhurst went dead, Garrison went ballistic. He feared the worst. Just as today's tip from Dudaev had suggested, Bupkov's elite killers had learned of the Andrews' whereabouts and were moving in on the unsuspecting pair. How in the hell Dudaev had found out about this Mafia attack was a mystery to him, but that didn't matter now.

Garrison barked orders to his subordinates, "Call the Mounties. Tell them it's Code Red. They must move in force upon the Andrews' cabin. Call CTOB. Tell them to activate the emergency message to the Hensleys."

As Garrison rang Ray's number, he cursed himself, "Damn it! I should be there. There's no excuse..."

The phone rang. His berating of himself ended abruptly with Ray's welcome voice."

"Ray, something's gone terribly wrong there. Get to the Andrews' cabin immediately. Protect them at all costs."

"Yes..."

The second phone went dead on Garrison. Tears welled up in his eyes. Turning to his assistant he ordered, "Tell the Canuks to hurry. It's up to them. The SOBs have almost certainly taken out all of our men."

Brad buried his head in his arms and cursed, "Damn! Damn! Damn! I'm sorry Ben. I'm sorry Laura! Please, God, forgive me. Protect them. They are in Your hands now."

Garrison knew that the Mounties could not get there for an hour. He could only imagine what had happened.

The actual scene was as bad as he feared. As Ray had spun around to descend from his perch atop the cabin, a bullet penetrated his brain. The fatal attack had unexpectedly come from the east. He fell instantly dead.

Day 115 6:50 P.M. Boreal Peninsula

The two seasoned killers on Boreal Peninsula's ridge had concluded from the radio messages that their partners and the FBI forces in the Dakota River had eliminated each other. Good! Not perfect, but still O.K. Bupkov's plan was still workable.

The two stealthy stalkers, weapons ready, slipped away from Ray's cabin into the thick brush and timber. They forced their way relentlessly through the dense underbrush and down the steep western slope of Boreal Peninsula toward the Andrews' cabin. They were in no great hurry for no agents were left to defend the Andrews. Therefore they had at least an hour before help could arrive.

The assassins leisurely staked out the cabin and amusedly observed the couple's activities. They prepared carefully for the final execution of Bupkov's orders.

Day 115 7:10 P.M. Andrews' Cabin

Laura and Ben went about their evening tasks, tired but exuberant over their grand two-day adventure. Unaware of the nearby killers surveying their every move, they set about the chores of putting away supplies, fetching water and cleaning their new catch of fish. After finishing a supper of fresh fish, Ben concluded that the low clouds, which had moved in so suddenly, had scuttled any sunset watching tonight.

He pushed away from the dinner table, grabbed his coat, and headed out the back door, "It's going to be cool tonight and dark early. I better fetch some extra logs from the shed."

During his absence, Laura saw her opportunity. She opened Ben's billfold and unfolded the worn paper. Proudly she penciled in the last line of her poem, *Unite our souls. Like eagles, let us soar.* Knowing that he read it nearly every night, she smiled at how surprised he would be.

She flipped the radio switch and tuned to CTOB for the message board.

As Ben walked out to the shed, an uneasy sensation returned as he recalled Laura's earlier interpretation of the eagles' high-speed dive. He gathered an armful of logs. The chain saw he had used a little earlier in the evening was sitting there still warm. Remembering that while the saw was warm was a good time to adjust the tension on the cutting belt, he added it to the load of logs. He staggered awkwardly toward the cabin with the bulky burden.

Inside, Laura sighed, "Thank you, Lord." The end of the last nerve-grating song mercifully approached. The message board was next. The warning crackled, like a rifle shot, over the airwaves.

"We have a new urgent message for the Hensleys on Loon Lake. Bears have been spotted in the area."

Laura rushed to the back door screaming, "Ben! Ben! There's a warning message on the radio."

Ben dropped the logs. The fallen timbers rolled every which way. Holding the saw tightly, he grabbed for his pistol as he ran for the back door of the cabin. A hail of bullets, thrown off slightly by Laura's yell and his sudden bolt, still found flesh. Two of the slugs penetrated his right thigh. As he stumbled into the cabin, Laura grabbed a towel and wound it tightly around his wounded leg in an attempt to slow the blood flow.

Thinking through a rising panic, Ben still gripped the chain saw. "Damn, I dropped the pistol outside."

Grimacing as he strained to force the refrigerator out from the wall, he bit his tongue to avoid yelling out from the stabbing pain. Finally he succeeded in wedging himself between the icebox and the wall. He was where he wanted to be, within easy reach of the back door.

He motioned to Laura to douse the kerosene lantern and to get down behind the hot potbelly stove in the center of the cabin. The timing of the attack and the saw had given him an idea. Maybe they had a chance.

The towel Laura had tied over his wound was already soaked through with blood. He feared that he couldn't remain conscious very much longer. He willed that he would not pass out.

A voice with an unmistakable Russian accent shouted to the trapped couple, "Mister, you come out, ve just vant you. You give up, and ve not hurt your woman."

Laura yelled, "Don't believe the sonofabitch, Ben."

Then she unleashed a torrent of Russian expletives that described the butchers in the most vulgar of terms. She had been scared, but now she was mad. Really mad! She grabbed the stove poker and placed its business end in the roaring fire before crouching behind the potbelly stove. She also laid the filet knife nearby. If either assassin came near her she intended to slice off whatever she could.

Cornered in their cabin they waited for what seemed like hours, hiding as best they could. Laura was resigned to the hail of gunfire that would certainly come. Ben's last-minute scheme, though, depended on his hunch that the attackers would wait for dark to try to enter the cabin. He figured that they had timed their attack so they would have the advantage of night-vision gear. Also, he figured help would come soon. The radio message told him that Garrison knew about the danger. Where the hell was Ray? The thugs must have gotten him.

Outside, the two Mafiosos discussed their next move. On this low overcast night, the wily professionals strategized that with the FBI agents dead, they could afford to wait a little longer for darkness to envelope Boreal Peninsula. Ben had guessed correctly.

As the dark deepened, one attacker crept toward the back door. Tripping over one of the spilled logs, he sent it crashing into the near-by brush. The sound, piercing the deadly stillness of the approaching night, shook Ben momentarily out of his gathering delirium.

Meanwhile, the other assassin circled around to the front of the cabin, and cautiously approached the big front window. He closed in on the starkly forlorn cabin, confident that with his night-vision scope he would easily locate the two.

Upon reaching the front, he guardedly climbed onto the wooden deck. Employing his night scope, he scanned the interior. To his surprise he could spot neither of the trapped pair. As he looked in the stove's direction, its strong infrared signature momentarily stunned him. Seeing flashing stars and spiraling circles he jerked the machine gun aside, while swearing in Russian. After recovering from the sudden blinding, he ordered his partner in. He would cover him from the front window.

Inside, Laura whispered to Ben that one was coming in the rear door at any moment. Ben, fighting a nearly overwhelming urge to doze, crouched behind the refrigerator. Its cool temperatures had frustrated the assassin's attempts to spot him. His right fist was frozen around the handle of the saw, while his left hand gripped the pull-cord. He prayed that the old McCulloch was still warm enough to start with one tug. As his thumb pushed the prime bulb he held his breath, listening for any sound.

The back screen door groaned ever so slightly as it eased open. The dark, surreal image of the machine gun's shortened barrel pushing through the opening spooked Ben. Had he passed out? Was he dreaming? No, and the moment was now or never.

He pulled. The saw sputtered and then roared to life. The chain clattered and whined. The sudden noise reverberated throughout the cabin. The invading Mafioso, startled by the clattering chain and the loud engine, swung his gun toward the nearby racket. The refrigerator interrupted the motion of the weapon's barrel.

Ben leaped from his crouch, mustering all of his remaining strength to savagely swing the raging, full-throttled saw upward into the phantom-like outline of the gun handle. The spiraling belt of metal teeth engaged first the assassin's flesh and then the gun's steel, spraying blood and sparks everywhere.

There was a terrible scream as the saw screeched to a grinding halt against the metal. A severed hand and an abandoned MP-5 fell to the floor. The wounded killer, screaming in agony and clutching a bloody stump instead of a weapon, whirled and berserkly sprinted headlong up the ridge.

Now Ben was clearly visible in the second assassin's thermal scope. The gunman opened up with a point-blank volley. As Ben reached for the retreating man's fallen gun, he held the saw up in an attempt to fend off the bullets.

Two more missiles, however, found their way past the saw and into their victim. Tearing into Ben's chest the bullets terminated his thoughts. He fell unconscious to the floor as the retrieved gun clattered uselessly to the floor beside him.

His assailant took careful aim, preparing to pump a last murderous volley into the still body. He yelled, "Dr. Andrew, you shall die now. Andropov has repaid you in full."

Suddenly without warning, something hard smacked against the side of the killer's head. He was knocked off balance by the violent blow. Then he smelled an ugly odor, reminiscent of frying flesh. With his free hand he touched the spot where the poker had landed and immediately jerked his hand away from the heat emanating from the smoldering hole.

The skin and hair had evaporated from the red-hot poker, which Laura brandished with a desperate frenzy. Before the dazed man could react, another searing blow fell against his throat. Half his larynx instantly melted away with that blast.

At that same moment a seaplane, with searchlights playing across the peninsula, buzzed the cabin at the treetop level. The twice-burned thug fell in terrible agony to the deck. His MP-5 uselessly clattered to the weathered boards. The mortally wounded assassin's last tortured instinct signaled escape. He writhed about in a futile attempt to flee.

With both hands, a hysterical Laura raised the red-hot poker high over her head for one final thrust. Down came the glowing steel rod, driven with all of her strength, a strength born of panic and surging anger. The blazing-hot spear burned straight through the gaping mouth and upper neck before imbedding itself in the wooden deck. The killer died skewered to the platform.

The plane, equipped with pontoons, each bigger than Ben's empty canoe, circled and descended to a landing on the Andrews' bay. It rudely invaded the home of Ben's favorite loons. Pulled by the slowing prop, it noisily taxied to the small dock serving the Andrews' cabin.

Four Canadian Mounties leaped out and raced up the hill toward the cabin. Upon hearing a boat's departure from the other side of the

Peninsula, the Mounty in charge, Captain Pierre LaBrue, assumed it must be the attackers' boat. He ordered the Mounty with the radio set to stop and call the two fast-closing planes of troopers. "Dispatch one plane to chase the boat. Have the other search the river. Garrison suspects that something major went down in the Dakota."

LaBrue and the two remaining troopers continued at a full sprint toward the cabin. Leaping over the dead attacker pinioned to the smoking wood of the deck, they found a hysterical Laura. She was frantically tying bandages over Ben's bleeding wounds.

She screamed at the Mounties, "They shot my Ben! God help me!"

Then more subdued she moaned, "Oh! No! Don't die, Ben. You mustn't."

One of them sedated Laura while LaBrue and the other Mounty ministered to the severely wounded Ben. LaBrue found a faint pulse. It was readily apparent that the man had lost a great amount of blood from his leg wound. His left arm appeared shattered. The chest wound was hard to diagnose. Pierre yelled to the radio operator who had just reached the cabin, "Call Thunder Bay Life-Watch."

The Mounty shouted into his radio, "Thunder Bay! Thunder Bay Hospital! Send the air ambulance immediately! We have a badly wounded man here on Loon Lake, coordinates L-5, G-10. He needs transfusions. His I.D. indicates type O, negative. Bring a bunch of units."

While listening to occasional briefings by the Mounty with the radio, Pierre became more worried about the wounded man's sinking condition. He asked, "How soon till the rescue plane gets here?"

"Fifteen minutes."

"Damn! That is too late!" Pierre fumed, "I won't lose this man. Call the doctor on duty at the hospital. Ask if I can administer intravenous fluids."

The answer came back promptly, "Doc says yes."

With that go-ahead, LaBrue jabbed a needle into a vein in Ben's arm. He hung the jar high on one of the rough, knotty pine rafters, and watched as the sustaining fluid drained into the unconscious Ben. Precariously, the terribly wounded man clung to life.

While the fluids dripped into Ben, further updates came in. The boat with the one-handed gunman flew over the old dam and crashed into the rocks and rapids below. Also another fugitive was found dead by the Nykratin Nation Constables. His throat had been mysteriously slashed. There was no sign of who might have done it.

Later Garrison would guess that it must have been one of Dudaev's agents, who had done what little he could to even the odds for the Andrews.

As Ben's stretcher was loaded into the Life-Watch plane, a distressingly mournful wail, a belated warning by the bay's loons, rolled across the lake. Laura, under heavy sedation, failed to notice the cry.

CHAPTER
SIXTY-NINE

Day 116 8 P.M. Thunder Bay Hospital

An apologetic vice president, accompanied by Garrison, Nieman and hoards of federal agents, had arrived at Thunder Bay Hospital early this morning. It was obvious to Laura that Foster and Garrison blamed themselves. Foster for pulling Ben into this mess, and Garrison for not protecting him adequately. Despite her best attempts, Laura was unable to dissuade them from assuming guilt.

Vice President Foster had ordered Garrison, Nieman and an armed contingent of agents to stay with Laura and Ben. He would tolerate nothing less than the absolute protection of these two people. No more mistakes. Liz was to help Laura in any way she could.

Maintaining a constant vigil at Ben's bed in Thunder Bay Hospital, Laura slept little. She watched faithfully for any sign of improvement in his condition. He had not regained consciousness and seemed to be slipping ever nearer death. She hated all of the tubes violating his body. Despite their usefulness in feeding, medicating and supplying him oxygen, she felt they were a humiliation to him. With labored breathing, he struggled for life. His chest wounds were heavily bandaged and his left arm was splinted. His persistent pale countenance greatly unnerved her.

While watching Ben's life ebb, Laura fretted. Her thoughts were not coherent. Things that once seemed important no longer mattered. Her will for Ben to live, though, was focused like a laser.

Tears moistened her eyes. A strange despair suddenly plagued her. Ben may never see the finished sonnet. She had created the last line too late.

474

A sudden chill gripped the room. Laura shivered as though all heat had been siphoned from her and from her surroundings. The alarm signaling Ben's heart failure resonated in the cold vacuum enveloping her. She dropped her pen, pushed the emergency call button and, with time suspended, flew across space to Ben's side.

Determined to never let go, she embraced him and whispered, "Ben, please stay. Don't leave me alone."

For moments that stretched into an eternity she held him close while the nurses scrambled in a desperate attempt to revive him. Miraculously the heart monitor announced a renewed pulse. As Ben's heart resumed a steady beat, a tearful Laura thanked God.

Moments later the head nurse comforted her, "That man is awfully tough. I am not sure how he survived this crisis. Our treatment and chemicals alone can't explain it. I believe he returned to be with you. He heard your soul cry for him."

Despite the terror and tension of recent days, an unusual calm settled over Laura. Ben was going to live; she was sure of that. Strangely, she was no longer fearful. She and Ben had endured, even survived, the Mafia's best shot. She was not going into hiding again and was quite confident Ben would share that sentiment. She knew him. Hell, he would seek revenge and would sign up with anyone that helped him achieve it. She would not stand in his way, rather she would stand with him. Tomorrow she would tell Liz that they were no longer in the witness protection program.

On the hospital form in front of her, she crossed off the patient's phony name of Phil Hensley and replaced it with Ben Andrew.

Within the week the letter from Oddesa, a letter to Marina's and Dudaev's Joint Eagles containing a profound call to service, would arrive.